A Dance in Time Copy

Book 1 of The Gods of Time

J.C. Hidalgo & Michael M. Johnson

Contents

To my wife, Vashty, who spent countless hours enduring my crazy
dream—
always supporting it with love, yet always keeping it real.
This one's for you.
—J.C. Hidalgo

To my family—
Fifteen years, you watched me write, pushed through some insane
early mornings and late nights.
Cruz, your love and strength carried me past doubt and fears.
To my daughters and my mother, you all helped over the years.
You all were my anchors, held me down with love so true
I never drowned in the madness so I dedicate this to you.
— Michael M. Johnson

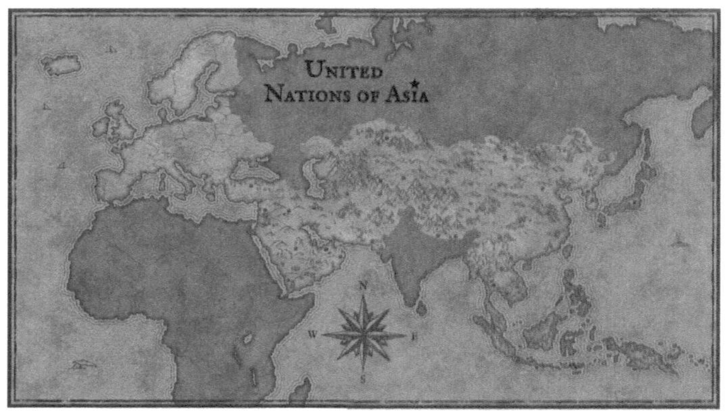
UNITED
NATIONS OF ASIA
N
W   E
S

PROLOGUE

Mazamitla, Mexico, 2072

S melling pillows was an addiction for Malaya, or at least that's what her mother said. She would always sleep on the edge of her bed, careful to preserve the scent. But after her father died, everything changed. Crying herself to sleep became a nightly routine, and she'd often wake up on the floor beside his bed, her face buried in his pillow, sometimes hearing his voice.

What does one do with a loved one's possessions?

For years, her mother preserved his things, but she wasn't spending much time at home lately. Neither was Malaya.

In the dim light of her rustic cabin, Malaya stood before the mirror, the reflection of her military dress laid out on the bed catching her eye. It was more than a uniform; it was a symbol of the path she'd chosen—a path her mother, Lilith Castillo-Grant, had neither understood nor supported.

Her fingers traced the fabric, each fold a reminder of the day she enlisted. That decision, made in the shadow of her father's tragic death, was her silent rebellion against the loss of Project Bungee and her attempt to escape the suffocating grief.

Her father, Dr. Jeffrey Grant, had been a pioneer, the first to brave time travel. His final, ill-fated journey to 3000 BC Puerto Rico haunted her. Objects passing through portals, the collapse of wormholes, the black holes... it was all too much. The memory lurked in her mind, an ever-present ghost.

Applying cream to her freckled skin, Malaya tried to focus on the present. Two years had passed since she cracked the quantum equation for time travel, only to have the government commandeer their project. Despite her mother's reassurances, Malaya felt the sting of betrayal.

Resolved not to let her hard work fall entirely into governmental hands, she enlisted. Even though Lilith used her influence to keep her stationed in New Seattle, Malaya found solace in staying busy, avoiding the painful memories of her father.

Her fingers hesitated over her phone, before she finally sent a text to the one man who never let her down: her grandfather. Despite being a former US president, he had a soft spot for his granddaughter's ambitions.

"Anything?" she typed, her heart racing.

His reply was simple and to the point. *"You're in...but let me tell your mother,"* it read.

A triumphant smile lit up her face, her heart skipping with excitement. I'm back on the project.

This was her chance not just to contribute to her family's legacy, but to infuse it with her own vision and identity. Her late father pioneered antimatter research, while her mother, Lilith Castillo-Grant, was hailed as the Elon Musk of her era. But Malaya was determined to carve her own path, to prove she was more than just a Castillo-Grant.

As she anticipated her return to the lab, a sense of purpose filled her. This wasn't just about following in her family's footsteps; it was about forging a path that was distinctly hers, proving that she could stand on her own in the world of science.

The next morning, Malaya was up before sunrise, a new habit of hers. Although enlisting gave her a sense of freedom, it wasn't without consequences. Lilith guilt-tripped Malaya and dragged her across the border to an isolated cabin in Mexico—it could have been worse. The private chef served them her favorite chilaquiles, totopos soaked in a green hot sauce, topped with shredded beef, chicken, and chorizo, topped with two sunny-side-up eggs.

Afterward, they toured the countryside, seeing a side of nature she hadn't seen since their last family vacation in Greece. The stroll through the city was the most jaw dropping, with lush green rolling hills and fields of golden corn stalks that swayed in the gentle breeze.

They came across a picturesque lake, its crystal-clear waters reflecting the sun, creating a shimmering display of light. The vibrant colors of wildflowers dotted the landscape, adding a pop of color to the otherwise grassy surroundings. But as they strolled through the nearby city, they saw a different side of Mexico.

The borderless alliance of Mexico, America, and Canada has hurt the city. The streets were filled with American coffee shops and American sushi, but none of Mexico's heart.

After dinner, the day concluded with them returning to the cabin, surrounded by warm, honey-hued logs and a fire.

"*Mija*, sit. We need to talk," Lilith said.

Malaya sat on the plush upholstered sofa across from the crackling fire, trying to relax as her mother talked crazy. Papi would know what to do, Malaya thought, not recognizing the woman in front of her. Sure, she wore her designer clothes and had the beauty mark near her left cheek, but... Mama has lost her mind.

"Ma, I know with Papi's passing—"

"I'm not crazy," her mother interrupted. "My visions are real. The Darviants are in danger. You are in danger. This world is in danger, and we have the power to stop it."

Darviants? she thought, a flicker of disbelief clouding her thoughts. To her, the word felt like a conjuration from a realm of fantasy, as if lifted straight from the extravagant tales of folklore or the colorful world of comic books.

The very notion seemed to dance on the edge of reality, bordering on the fantastic and the implausible. Darviants–beings or concepts that defied the very essence of human understanding–belonged more to the realm of myth and legend than to the empirical world she was anchored in.

"Mami," Malaya began, her voice tinged with incredulity, "humans don't have powers. Are you even hearing yourself? We're scientists." Her words reverberated through the rustic cabin, bouncing off the aged wooden walls. Malaya stood up, the creaking floorboards beneath her feet adding a sense of urgency to her movements. She paced back and forth, the flickering candlelight casting eerie shadows on the log walls.

"So are we supposed to ignore what happened to Papi, how he died?" Malaya continued, her frustration mounting with each step. "Time traveling again is not the answer. And some crack-pot dream isn't the answer either. Sages? Immortal beings?" She scoffed, her tone laced with a mixture of disbelief and skepticism.

"Listen, we need to go over all the math again, see what went wrong." Lilith placed her hands on her cheeks. "Do you trust me?"

Malaya nodded with a raised brow.

Lilith looked at the fireplace, and the flames intensified. She opened her hand, and a bottle of water slid to her like it was on an invisible rope. "It took me years to learn how to control my abilities. Now that we're testing the wormholes... my powers have increased. I believe they are linked, I don't know. What I do know is that no matter how strong I am, I still can't do this without you."

Malaya backed away from her. She started shaking her head. "No, no," she said to herself, flopping down on the couch. "This can't be happening. You can't be this delusional. I can't help you." Malaya looked up. "I won't. If what you said is true. And those monsters you plan to wake are real, then won't they kill thousands of people?"

"Unfortunately, yes," her mother sighed, taking a seat next to her—she grabbed her hand. "Look at their lives as historical data. We will simply reshape it, to prevent our world from crumbling. It can save millions. "

Malaya swallowed the lump forming in her throat, trying to fight back the sick feeling in her stomach, listening to her mother justify the egregious act she was about to commit. Is this a joke? A trick? Did she just display telekinesis?

Thousands of books flooded her mind. She remembered word-for-word... no, she relived reading them. Nothing made sense. None of the text had explanations. None of them could console her, especially not her father.

Lilith dropped to her knees. "I'm coming to you because I love you, because I don't want any secrets, because I want you by my side, but I will get the Sage, with or without your help."

Malaya's eyes widened. Her heart raced, wondering who this woman was sitting across from her. This wasn't the mother she knew. She was someone else—she was delusional.

Even if it were true, Lilith was willing and ready to risk everything because of a dream. She didn't value the lives of humans who set the foundation for the world they lived in, thinking of them as nothing more than historical pawns.

Mass murder?

Malaya snatched away and sprang to her feet, unable to fight back tears. She squeezed her fist so tight she thought her nails could puncture her skin.

A flare of heat rushed through her veins, igniting every nerve ending. The quivering within her intensified, becoming a turbulent storm within.

"Calm down," her mother pleaded. "You're losing control."

Malaya didn't know what she was doing or how to stop it. A white light forced her eyes closed.

She opened them to an all-white room, and sweet, strong perfume filled the air.

"Mama," she said with uncertainty, staring at the back of a woman with curly brown hair in a white gown.

There was something familiar about her. When she turned, Malaya's heart sank. "*Abuela,*" the words escaped her trembling lips.

She hadn't seen her grandmother before, other than in old pictures. Her mother barely spoke of her, but her grandfather raved about her every chance he got. Angie, *mi angel*, he called her always with a smile. She was dead, killed by extremists of the United Nations of Asia when her mother was a child, yet here she was, a journalist covering the superpower.

This has to be a dream, Malaya thought, frozen in place.

"My sweet angel, this is no dream," she said with a warm smile.

"You can hear my thoughts?" Malaya said.

"Yes. It was my gift, like you, I am—" she smiled. "I was a Darviant, a telepath like your mother, but you are something more, a caracaracol. It's why you can communicate with me. You are a conduit to other sides."

"A Darviant medium," Malaya repeated, tears rolling down her face. "No, I-I—"

"You want to be normal." She sighed, stepping closer to Malaya. "We are meant to be more. Your mother knows that more than anyone."

"My mother, she wants to—"

"I know, and you must help her, guide her onto the right path."

Malaya took a step back. "No. I won't. We can't know the future, the outcomes. There are too many variables. The world we live in, it's not perfect, but it's free of violence, war, pollution."

"It's a mask, *mi linda nieta*. There is something greater on the horizon. That's why your mother needs you, but you are still blind, young, and naïve."

"And you're dead," Malaya snapped, wanting to take back her words, but it was too late. "Sorry, if it's true, knowing the future. Why didn't you stop them from killing you?"

"We aren't the only Darviants. I wasn't strong enough, but your mother is. Unfortunately, you are not. You must get strong. A war is coming. It's time for you to go."

"Wait!"

She touched Malaya's cheek—white light flashed again. Malaya was back in the cabin, staring at her mother with fear in her eyes. "Mama," Malaya said, trying to move but couldn't. No matter how hard she tried, she couldn't move any part of her body.

"Try to keep calm," said a brown-skinned, middle-aged man with a fine ponytail.

He dressed casually, but blue and red ribbons wrapped around his wrist. The man held an ancient-looking brown clay pipe with a face carved into it. His thick brown brows furrowed as he put a large pipe in his mouth and inhaled.

If she didn't know any better, she swore his eyes glowed. She couldn't tell reality from a dream.

He exhaled a dark cloudy substance that resembled smoke, but it wasn't. Autofluorescence particles shone from the thick cloud that moved around Malaya as if they were alive.

The room spun—her eyes flickered as tension surging through her body was released.

"What is this, mama," Malaya slurred, feeling lightheaded. She must have blacked out for a second because she woke up with her head lying in her mother's lap. The smoke had cleared, and the man with the ribbons was gone.

"I saw *abuela*, mama."

"I know," her mother said, her voice shaky, tears in her eyes. "And I'm sorry. I know now you're not ready."

"Ready for what?"

"To save the world." Her mom opened the container of tongue patches and placed one in her mouth.

Malaya struggled to speak, unable to fight the sleepiness and intense fog clouding her mind. "We-we'll talk again tomorrow, okay?"

Her mom wiped the tears falling down her cheek. "No, baby. You won't remember a thing."

"Wha—" Malaya tried, but she couldn't fight the darkness from taking over.

LILITH

New Seattle, 2075

It's not stealing if it's yours, she reminded herself. Lilith pressed her designer handbag against her black pencil dress, sweat beading on her olive skin despite New Seattle's bitter cold.

Years of planning came down to this. Stealing from her own company. The Quantum Power Cell sat thousands of feet below MEV Inc—the world's leading nuclear fusion corporation. Her family's legacy, until the government seized it weeks ago. Without the QPC, time travel was impossible. Without time travel, she couldn't change the timeline.

She tilted her wide-brim hat at the unarmed guard, forcing a smile. *Unarmed*—even after decades, this world's transformation amazed her.

She remembered a time when guns coursed through old Seattle's streets as relentlessly as the flu during the pandemic. That was before the U.N.A. invasion, before her neighborhood's fragile peace was shattered. Even the untouchable had been touched.

Two blue laser-beams scanned her body. *That was forty years ago,* she reminded herself.

This wasn't about revenge. Yet the thought haunted her, even in this apparent utopia. Beyond the bright lights and clean energy, New Seattle harbored secrets. She was the keeper of the darkest one.

"Good evening, Mrs. Castillo-Grant. It's been quite some time," the guard greeted, his wide eyes and welcoming smile betraying a hint of recognition.

Lilith nodded, her expression composed. Her sunglasses projected holographic overlays, streams of data flickering across her vision. But when she glanced at the guard, his information field was blank.

Odd, she thought.

In a world stripped bare of privacy, his government-issued protections spoke louder than words.

"It's been too long," she replied smoothly, her voice steady, though her heartbeat quickened.

The guard stepped aside, waving her through. She kept her stride measured, her heels clicking against the polished floor of the lobby.

Ads buzzed at the edges of her display, reminders of MEV duties—meetings, phone calls, tasks queued for attention.

"System off," she muttered, her voice low but firm. The augmented reality dissolved. She had work to do.

The elevator slowed. She cursed herself as it stopped and opened to an SIA operative with oversized sunglasses and handcuffs dangling from his waist. She frantically pressed the door's close button.

"Good evening, Mrs. Castillo-Grant," he said, reaching out to stop the doors from closing.

She wondered if he could hear her heart thumping over the floor indicator. Her hands trembled at the thought of being caught. Or worse, what she'd have to do to make sure that didn't happen. Lilith needed to know if he was a threat.

Touching his hand wouldn't be enough, but his sunglasses made it impossible to look into his eyes—she didn't have another choice. She slowly removed her long black glove. At the right moment, she pretended to lose her balance. Their hands touched. She was pulled into his mind.

Bryce Bennett.

Like everyone, Bryce had his secrets, things she didn't care to see. It had taken her years to master how to block out the noise as she searched through their past, present, and future memories. Though, she was careful not to see their end, never wanting to burden herself with death or play god.

Got it, she thought, latching on to a future memory. One that saw him leading SIA operatives, briefing them on the stolen QPC.

"Are you okay?" Bryce asked, breaking the connection.

She was back, looking at her reflection in his sunglasses, gritting her teeth, though she was careful not to show how pissed she was for not taking them off. Then again, something that blatant could give credence to the rumors that she was a Darviant, a telepath, to be specific.

"These heels and that drop don't mix," she said in a fake, bashful tone.

Silence accompanied their ride. It was clear Bryce didn't know the extent of power—he didn't know what she was. Otherwise, he would have stopped her. Wouldn't he?

What if he knew? *What if this was him being careful*, she thought. Where was he leading them to? More importantly, when will they get there?

Touching him again wasn't an option. Once she disconnected, there was no going back, at least not for a while.

Anxiousness twisted her stomach as she struggled at the thought of being caught. *This was too important to let anyone stand in my way, but I can stop it.*

Thoughts of her vision about the death of the Darvinats allowed her hand to hover over her earring. She cautiously popped out the diamond. Motivated by the prophetic nightmare of horrid screams and the crimson pool where Darviants lay, she opened her palm, levitating the diamond behind Bryce's neck. Killing one man to save millions was the right thing to do.

Tightness gripped her body, making it difficult to control. *I can't do this*, she thought and closed her palm, understanding time was forever changing. She popped the stud back into place.

Killing him now didn't mean she wouldn't get caught. *I just need to be more careful. Don't make a scene.*

The elevator stopped, and its doors opened. Bryce stepped aside to let her lead. "After you."

Lilith showed Bryce her old, deep-level clearance badge. "Apologies."

He exited, and the doors closed, but her heart still pounded. She thought of her late husband. She couldn't imagine doing this without him, or at all. Though none of it would have been possible without his sacrifice. *Jeff, I need you now more than ever.*

Bryce was just one obstacle. Years of planning and preparation could come crashing down at any moment. She took a deep breath before removing her glove and opening the secondary panel.

Access Denied. The scanner rejected her palm print.

"Yurei, come in," Lilith said, pressing the earbud.

"Ms. C?" Yurei replied.

"What do I do?"

"The gum, Ms. C."

Lilith slapped her forehead. "Right."

With trembling hands, she opened a small container housing a gum-like substance that she placed on the panel.

Access Granted.

"Just remember it's temporary," said Yurei. "The system will reset itself. The light on your necklace is your indicator; there will be a continuous flash. If you're still inside when it turns red, the sensors will detect you, and game over."

"Understood."

"If it fails, you may have to resort to Plan B."

"I'm not whacking James."

"Understood. Oh, one more thing, Ms. C. Once you press the button, you will lose all communication with the outside world. So, don't forget your drops. The liquid contacts grant us access, enabling us to adjust on the fly."

The elevator dropped thousands of feet below New Seattle into MEV Energy's secret labs, a precaution ensuring the protection of the world's most dangerous discoveries. Only a select few had access. Unfortunately, those who gave the approval knew less about science and more about politics. Yet they had a hand in her company.

That boiling feeling in the pit of her stomach made its way atop her olive skin. The flashing light on the locket sped up. She smiled and entered the simple lobby.

"James," she called, looking through the top of her sunglasses. Her voice echoed off the sleek silver walls.

James stood up. "It's been a while, Ms. Castillo," he said, puffing out his chest to show his SIA patch. If not for his rich brown skin, he would have blushed.

"Just Lilith," she replied, handing him the badge.

The slot on the desk swallowed it. Her heart raced, watching James toggle through controls.

"Come in." She whispered, forgetting the communication was dead.

"Ma'am?" James questioned, startling Lilith.

"Uh, how's Orenthal?"

"He's been MIA," he said, turning his attention back to the panel. "It's been that way for a while."

"Give your father time. I'm sure he'll come around." Her words felt hollow, her own father's shadow looming in her thoughts. Timing his arrival was critical, but none of it would matter if they denied her access.

"How's Malaya?"

"Malaya... she's—"

"Approved, Lilith Castillo," the AI interrupted, its clinical tone cutting through her hesitation, silencing the lie before it could form about the fragile state of their relationship.

She sighed, her relief temporary as James swiped the surface of the desk. A small port opened, releasing a mechanical mosquito that hovered ominously.

"Is this necessary?" she asked, her voice carefully measured, though she already knew the answer. Still, a fragile hope lingered that he might grant her some leeway.

"DNA samples are required as part of the recent changes to the security protocol. It's excessive to subject the CEO of the company to such measures, if you ask me."

Silence filled the air. *Come on, James, let me through.*

"Unfortunately, it's out of my hands," he said, eyeing her long black gloves.

"Right," she said, slowly removing it. Part of her wanted to abort—it was too late.

Its sting trapped her. There was irony in the possibility of her blood causing her to go to jail. The insect descended into the port. James scanned the result—he silently walked from behind the desk.

Lilith caught herself biting her lip. Her watch flicked faster with every passing second. Maybe it wasn't too late to run. Maybe Yurei was right. She passed her hand over her earring, unsure she could do it, but she would have to.

"All clear," James said, shattering the tension, handing her a lab coat too big for her five-foot-five frame.

The sliding doors opened. She crossed into the short, well-lit corridor en route to the door at the end. She lifted her glasses and looked into the scanner, hoping they could override the program.

Retinal scan complete.

Insulators lined the lab's ceiling, connecting tubes to a glass cylinder containing the most powerful energy source in the world, the quantum power cell. Lilith placed a decoder chip onto the glass. After it detracted, she dug into her bag, removing a lump of clay. It morphed into a silver metallic orb, an exact copy of the QPC.

The warning light warmed her chest. She made the switch, but it wasn't over yet. Before boarding the elevator, she locked eyes with James. Lilith no longer looked into James's eyes; she looked through them—searching his mind.

Unlike her early victim, Lilith had more palpable access. It was as if she was James in a virtual reality game, except she had no control over the outcome—she could only watch. It took less time to find what she needed.

General Williams and his SIA operatives storming the lab—her father wasn't far behind. The monitor behind James gave her exactly what she was looking for. A date. *Perfect.*

She noticed his eyes stuck on the blinking light in the middle of her chest. *It's over.*

Part of her wondered if she could live with herself if she killed him until she realized James did not know.

He sized her up, unaware of the warning light blinking on his security tablet. Lilith cleared her throat, snapping James's eyes back to her. "I'm sorry, ma'am," he said, pointing his eyes at the floor.

"You're so cute," Lilith passed her hand over his cheek. "It's our secret, though you can make up for it by escorting me to the elevator."

She thanked James and watched him stroll to his desk. The doors couldn't close fast enough. Her stomach turned as the elevator ascended. "I've been compromised. Is there an escape route? Can you hear me?"

"Yes, we're here," said Yurei. "The timer has a thirty-six-second delay. You have just enough time to reach your car."

Lilith sighed. "Thank you. I will contact you soon."

She removed the earbuds before entering the busy lobby of MEV's main floor. The glass walls radiated an obnoxious amount of artificial sunlight. Despite the night sky, Lilith wished she could hide its shadows.

The walk to the garage took forever. She avoided hellos and eye contact, feeling the slightest look could give her away. In a world where parents feared their own children, she couldn't trust anyone. They threw around words like *brave* and *heroes* for those who shaped this new utopian society. However, they had no quarrels about crushing the life of anyone who went against the status quo.

The door hissed behind her, and she exhaled once more. Stealing humanity's greatest achievement was only the first obstacle—she needed a clean getaway. A car wasn't going to work.

The unmanned automated vehicle, or UAV, was her getaway vehicle. They were outlawed in the US. Emergency vehicles were the exception. She was told hiding in plain sight was her best option. Yet, there was nothing more obvious than an unmarked UAV. Convenience and style were more her thing. The sidewall slid up, and Lilith hurried inside. "Auto-drive."

Relief started to set in as she pulled away from MEV into the light snowfall. Christmas decor lit downtown Seattle's skyscrapers, along with halo ads plastered alongside the buildings.

"Red wine," she said, settling in the leather seats that faced one another before she placed a call on her burner phone to General Kakashi Sato. "Kakashi, it's Lilith. Do you have the Kojiki?" She paused, listening intently to the response from the other end. Her eyes narrowed as she processed the information. The Seattle lights and concern flickered across her features.

"And Maki? I hope so..." she trailed off. "We've come too far to back down now... I know from experience how difficult this will be for her. But it's necessary. We can't afford any mistakes."

Lilith's brows furrowed. "No, I'm about to make my move. I have the QPC."

After a brief, tense silence hung between them before Kakashi spoke. She clenched the phone, her hands shaking from the rush of adrenaline. "Understood. Stay alert, Kakashi. We're entering uncharted territory."

Ending the call, Lilith took a deep breath, the gravity of her actions sinking in. There was no turning back now. With a swift, decisive motion, she broke the phone in half, severing the last link to the conversation. She rolled down the window, allowing the pieces to fall to the ground.

She held her trembling hands until the adrenaline subsided, allowing her to lay her head back and sip her wine. The streets from this height always fascinated her. Every single person down there had their own life as vivid as hers, living in absolute peace.

At what cost?

Freedom scared people. So did the All-Father, a name Americans called the UNA. After all, the United Nations of Asia ruled the skies. They watched over the US with an all-seeing eye and subdued the idea of freedom with law. It was ironic how their last free city was lawless. Humanity had truly lost its way.

This once proud country preferred to hate her for being too rich while overlooking the advancements she and her family made for humanity—maybe they hated her for sharing her free energy. Fusion was no longer thirty years away. It was now, and she believed all humans deserved it, even the enemy.

That was why she couldn't fault her daughter for not wanting to uproot this world—a world she helped create. *Why break the utopia? Why wake to reality?* She often asked herself. Today, the questions seemed more prevalent than answers.

This was their perfect world. Yet, the wrong joke may get you killed. The perfect world, where popular belief wins over individual merit, and complete evil was always the enemy of the moment.

She called her daughter, wanting to tell her the truth about why she was missing her birthday, but upon hearing her voice, she froze.

No, Malaya can't know, not after what happened in Mexico. She needs to experience the truth. This world would never accept a Darviant—it needs to be saved from itself.

Blue light and a voice from the com interrupted her. "You are violating UNA law 012408. Air space is restitution. Land the aircraft immediately."

"Sorry, *mija*. I have to go." She hung up the phone.

"I have UNA clearance. Sending. Please advise." Lilith said, uploading the flash drive.

The rain fell as she waited in silence. Four drones circled the square UAV. They were larger than Lilith expected. She hadn't seen one up close. It was an odd saucer shape–the words United Nations of Asia etched on the panels.

"Confirmed."

I owe you, Abi.

The UAV started to lose altitude. The emergency landing warning blinked red.

"Wait, wait, what is going on?" Lilith stood up.

She rolled up her sleeve. A sun tattoo covered a screen she had embedded in her forearm. She read the text message that came across it.

President Ross issued a Code Red. All aircraft are grounding, and phone lines are dead. Get out.

Already? she thought.

"Manual drive activated," the AI said.

"I really, really owe you one," she said, inputting coordinates somewhere close for a safe landing, her old stomping grounds.

An explosion knocked her off her feet, slamming her hard enough to bite her tongue. Another soon followed. The drones were firing shots.

"What the heck? I have UNA access."

Pieces of the outer hull fell off. Lilith kicked off her heels and ripped the bottom of her dress, allowing her to gain her footing.

Over the years, she'd trained in private with the help of one man, the only man who could teach her to control her abilities. With Sensei's help, she discovered this new ability. However, controlling matter wasn't something she'd done other than objects in his kwoon. It was all about strength and control, like training for a sport. This was the main event.

With her eyes closed and deep breaths, she reached out her arm, feeling the invisible rope from her hand to the drone. It was lighter than expected. She yanked it, slamming it to the other—sending them on a free fall. But the velocity and air drag proved more difficult than she expected—it took the wind out of her.

After avoiding the skyscraper, a bloody Lilith grabbed both drones with one hand and the UAV with the other, decreasing her descent, but it wouldn't hold long.

Lilith watched the fast-approaching New Seattle shoreline. She calculated her speed and descent. *I'm not going to make it—I have no choice.* She once again slammed the drones onto one another—her free fall continued.

Her hands trembled as she reached for the suitcase underneath her chair. A golden dagger shone in the darkness. She sliced her finger, allowing the blood to drip onto the golden hilt—its green rune glowed.

Ten seconds was all she had, but a thought was all she needed. The ground was fast approaching.

Take me to my old office.

With that thought, she was swept away.

Lilith opened her eyes, finding herself seated at her dusky old desk in the Hanford building, a place entwined with memories of the love of her life. She was some two hundred miles away from MEV, in a nuclear site that was untraceable back to her, effectively serving as a hidden sanctuary for her family's covert operations. The desk, familiar and worn, anchored her in the dimly lit room that had once buzzed with activity but now lay shrouded in secrecy.

With a weary sigh, Lilith leaned back in her chair, allowing a momentary sense of relief to wash over her. She glanced around the room, its walls lined with remnants of past research and faded photographs, each telling a story of their own. Outside, the building presented itself as an abandoned laboratory, a façade that concealed the hive of activity now taking place behind its unassuming walls..

"Computer... I mean Kirby, code *Lee, Uncanny 9163.*"

The wall opened to the small staff of scientists working diligently to make sure this jump happened. All eyes turned to her, understandably so, given she looked like she'd been through hell. Though they dare not stop working.

So many have sacrificed for my vision...our vision. They've risked everything, which is more than I could have asked.

Meeting her halfway was her brother-in-law and lead physicist, Joseph. "Since the SIA hasn't followed you through the doors, I take it that everything was a success?" he asked. His voice was calmer than he had any right to be.

"You don't know the half of it. Ghost came through, and I took down a couple of UNA drones. Oh, and I have it," Lilith replied.

His jaw dropped, and his brows raised atop his glasses. "You took down drones? And they say youth is wasted on the young,"

"It's a story for another time."

Joseph nodded. "It always is. So... Where is it?"

She handed him the power cell.

Scientists gathered in admiration of the faint blue light within the ridges of the QPC. With one stern look at the crowd, the scientists dispersed.

She inched closer to Joseph. "It's a code red already, and I saw something... I don't think we have much time."

Joseph rubbed his hand through his salt and pepper comb-over. "With a majority of the staff aboard the Intrepid, it'll be difficult to keep the wormhole open long enough for you to make more than one jump. There's the antimatter problem. If it's exhausted, the Bungee will be severed—"

"Leaving me trapped between realms. I got it," Lilith replied. She could still see the worry on his face, but it wasn't about the jump.

"Did you see them?" asked Joseph. "Malaya and Shay."

"No, and I wasn't expecting to. I get why you're anxious, but our connection to Project Bungee makes it all believable. Shay has the gift to persuade, better than anyone I've ever met. She can handle anyone. And don't worry about your niece. I have her under control."

"She was expecting you. It's her birthday, after all."

"My daughter will have to forgive me. Lives are at risk," her snide tone echoed her expression.

Joseph's shoulder slumped in defeat.

They spent the next few minutes going over their strategy and how she was supposed to make it back before they left the lab for good. He still fought her tooth and nail about her jumping back, but it had to be her. She was the only one who had time-traveled before, but never this far. Jeff had, and it got him killed.

After they parted, she went around the lab, ensuring everything was okay. She walked up the winding staircase to her office. She could see Sheldon pacing with the tablet, light reflecting off his glasses. He stopped to acknowledge her. The bags under his eyes were a clear sign he hadn't rested.

His eyes were not their usual beady blue, but all black as he read algorithms. He was one of the best algorithmic technopaths she knew. Sheldon informed her of any last-minute changes to the timeline and where exactly she needed to jump.

"This is where he's located or expected to be," he said, displaying a map of ancient Laconia. "If the Sacred Text is correct, saving him now would solidify the changes needed to complete phase one."

"And Vasilis—"

A scientist burst into the room. Her rich brown skin flushed with worry.

"What's wrong?" Lilith demanded.

"SIA agents just landed on the roof."

"Security open feed," Sheldon pushed his glasses on his nose.

Part of the wall changed, displaying five armed soldiers. "*The Raging Bull* unit. We've been had."

The covert unit was comprised of highly skilled elite members operating outside of official regulations. Lilith realized the team must have been split, as evidenced by the individuals they had sent. She remembered Bryce Bennett as the fourth in command, a detail that came to her from reading his mind. As she gazed closer at the feed, she felt her throat tighten.

Sheldon tossed the scientist a phone. "Black Alert, we're moving up the extraction. Advise the others that we're moving through the tunnel tonight."

She nodded in agreement; her orange hair bounced as she rushed back to the lab.

Lilith turned to Sheldon. "Make sure Captain Bishop is ready. Once I'm gone, take the QPC and go!"

Lilith changed into the wardrobe necessary for her to blend in. She hurried toward the center of the Quantum Station, where a super-computer stretched around the center of the lab, encasing the ivory, oval-shaped pod. Joseph waited for her inside, near the Quantum Pod—with last-minute instructions. His words stumbled over one another before handing her the grainy silver relic.

The Medallion, they called it. Green light chased the crevasses of the device intentionally designed to fit the Mayan calendar. She tucked it inside her chiton dress.

Hurry, this has to work, she thought, waiting for the pod door to open.

She climbed inside the pod—the door sealed her inside. A purple glow engulfed the room, and so did the familiar whirring sound of an open wormhole. Intense purple light filled the pod, taking her away from her world into another.

VASILIS

Sparta, 428 BC

"You are still too weak, Vasilis," said the young woman. She held her dory close to her nearly nude body. "And you have a small cock."

Earth covered his sweaty face and filled his mouth, a familiar taste as of late. Vasilis spat out what dirt remained. "One day you will cry for it, girl," he said. He climbed to his feet and grabbed his spear.

"I doubt it, boy," Nefeli said, regaining her stance. Her spearhead dripped with his blood.

He searched for the rag wrapped around his waist. The clanking of fine armor broke his concentration. Three men emerge from the villa's pillars. Two of the soldiers stood by the door. The other removed his helmet and walked towards him, his eyebrows scrunched. It was an odd sight this early in the morning. The summer sun just broke the dry land, and his mother wasn't even up yet.

"Agis," Vasilis said, his voice filled with excitement. He knew two things. One, if Agis was there, his father wasn't far behind, and two, a battle would soon be underway.

Father once told him Agis was the most fearsome of the Eurypontids, and his son, Midas, was quite the warrior. His father once mentioned that though Midas was two winters older, he and Vasilis shared a bond unlike any other in Sparta. Like Vasilis, Midas's grandfather was a great man; some say the last great king of the old ways. Sparta once ruled with two kings, but that all changed when Vasilis's father, Vasilius, came to power.

Agis unsheathed his sword. Without a word, he yanked Vasilis by the arm onto the stone steps.

"What are you doing?" Nefeli said, holding her dory.

Agis ignored her. Vasilis thought for sure he would die, but dare not react. *Nefeli could take him and his crooked nose.*

Before Vasilis knew it, chunks of his light brown hair landed beside him, and its long strands stung the cut on his bleeding arm, leaving him with nothing more than a stubble with an awkward blend of white to his golden skin. "You'll be fine, boy," Agis said, sheathing his blade.

Nefeli wrapped his arm. "Stay strong. The king is here."

A platoon of men stormed in as she walked out. They circled the square courtyard, filing every stone wall. King Vasilius wore bronze armor and a red cloak. Vasilis stood up, waving away a servant that offered water. He did his best to wipe the emotion from his heart, ignoring everyone but his father.

Vasilius turned to Agis first. Their forearms met. "Thank you, friend," he said before Agis withdrew.

His father yanked by the arm, pulling him close. He stared up at him. His fair skin pinked as he grinned through his clipped beard. "Ah, son, your journey to becoming a true Spartan starts now," he said, rubbing his head. "You will not worry about doubters. Embrace being different and overcome the odds just like your father, my father before me, and your mother."

Vasilis nodded. Though he did not understand why he was different from the other kids.

Was it because he was the son of the king? Or was it because his mother was referred to as an outsider?

Vasilis heard the whispers that he was a foreigner from some island where he was raised by Helot slaves. Some thought him too young or stupid to hear what they said, but he wasn't.

When he was older, he would make them pay for the names they called his mother. *My sword will be mightier than my fist.*

"But it starts by defeating your enemies with your mind," he said, tapping the side of his head.

"What is going on here?"

Vasilis's heart sank. His mother's voice sent chills across his skin. Kara marched towards her husband, ignoring his men.

"Vasilis!" she said, grabbing his head. "What is the meaning of this? He was proud of his long hair."

"His hair will grow back."

King Vasilius dismissed his men. He looked at Vasilis and pointed at the small brown bear. "Go, practice your wrestling."

Vasilis followed orders but kept his ear on his parents. "Well?" Kara asked.

"I have made a decision," Vasilius said, barely bringing his voice to a whisper. "It's time for war."

"What, are you sure? If you do this, then…"

The bear tackled Vasilis to the ground. He looked up at his father, rubbing his hilt. "I will bury it in the same location the Helots found your mother, taking away what they desire most."

"Control," Kara said. She faced Vasilis—he jumped up, hoping she didn't catch him spying. "He's not ready," she said. "He is seven. Surely the Agoge can wait a year."

"We agreed."

"You agreed! They have not approved of me or my people. To them, our son is a half-breed… Helot scum."

"He will manage or die trying!"

Vasilis did his best to hold the bear down, wanting to stay within ear range. Vasilius pulled Kara closer. Placing his hand on her chin. "My lady, he has your fire, my strength, your cunning mind. I trust him more than I can say for everyone else."

"I don't trust *them*," she said, stroking his long, ash-brown hair. Her fingers twirled between a few strands of plaits and locks. "This will change everything."

"This is my will, the weapon, and the boy." Vasilius kissed her hand. "Agis now!"

"Mother." Vasilis ran to hug her. Agis and two guards tore him away from his shouting mother.

Guards held his mother back as they both reached out for one another. Like all Spartan kids, he would not see his mother again for some time, as the journey to become a true Spartan starts at seven.

The lump in Vasilis's throat soon passed, although it took weeks for the shock to fade and for reality to set in. The harsh ground rubbed against his bare feet. He wore nothing more than cloth, and for dinner, blood soup, a marriage of pig's blood, and vinegar.

For Vasilis, these obstacles weren't new, so he thrived in the barracks of the forest. One morning, the pack was tasked with racing up a steep hill. It was almost time for the pack leader's selection. Vasilis used it as motivation, knowing he had to shine now more than ever.

This is my chance. They will recognize me as one of them.

"Come here, boy," a senior Agoge member said, his voice in a slow growl. "Why have you stopped here? This is no place for a prince. You were moved up to age nine. Go on and climb the rest of the hill. You must not fail your test."

The faint smell of smoke filled the air. His burning legs carried him to the summit atop the grass hill, where a group already stacked wood on the fire.

"Are you Vasilis?" the instructor questioned.

Vasilis nodded.

"You are last. So, you'll sing for us. After you fetch more firewood."

Vasilis collected wood from the large area covered in patches of brown grass, unaware of the three large boys behind him. "What are you doing here? Go back to your golden villa and Helot slave mother," said the dark-haired boy.

"Peasant," Vasilis said, drawing first blood with a punch to the nose.

The others rushed to hold him back, allowing his attacker to recover and strike. "My name is Hecktor, remember it," the boy said. "You will find the most firewood down there."

A kick to the gut sent Vasilis tumbling through shards of rock to the bottom of a hill. The bruises on his scale paled to his pride as he lay until the darkness took over. "Traitors," he whispered as he faded to black.

When he woke, he was back at the camp, his wounds covered in rags.

"I'm Elias," said a boy, standing over him. "Let's be friends."

"My name is Midas," said another. His hair was blond, and he was much taller than any kid he'd ever seen. "You should gather more firewood."

Vasilis smiled.

Over the next few days, Vasilis learned he wasn't the only outsider. Each of them had their own story. Midas, the son of Agis, was everything his father once boasted, with formidable stature and strength beyond what any boy should have.

Elias, the son of a warrior Seth, who painted his legacy in so much blood the gods feared him—so Elias said. Still, that commonality forged an unbreakable bond between the three boys. Hector and his mates did their best to make their lives miserable, and the other Agoge members found it quite entertaining.

Any other time, his amazing plans wouldn't include anyone else. How could they? Most people didn't understand him. He was of Hercules's blood, a prince, but also scum and weird. *No, I can trust them. They are like me.*

"I have a plan," Vasilis said.

"Give up," Elias said, lying next to the small fire. "They will never recognize us."

"Everything we've been doing is wrong. We have to defeat the enemy with our mind," Vasilis said.

"What's the plan?" Midas questioned.

"We make Hecktor look like a coward in the eyes of the overseers."

Vasilis stood up. "Just make sure the instructor follows you to the Red Cave. Elias, you're the bait."

The boys went their separate ways. Vasilis snuck past the soldiers into his villas, retrieving what he thought would change his life. Before he left, he spotted his mother. The lump in his throat returned, but he knew this was not the time for emotions. It was deep into the night when he returned to the cave.

There was always something special about the Red Cave. He heard stories about the hound of Hades, who guarded the cave. *Death would come to those not worthy*, he remembered one of the children saying, but he didn't believe them. *Why would Hades send his hound to guard a cave? If there was something here—*

Something behind a pile of rocks tugged him, sending chills through his body. A low growl from outside the cave called his attention. A red-eyed, two-headed dog walked past the entrance. *Cerberus?* He stood up.

"Vasilis!" Elias said, running into the cave. "They're right behind me."

"You know what to do."

Elias fell to his knees and waited for the boys to arrive. Vasilis crunched into a dark corner, waiting for his prey. Hecktor was the first to walk in, armed and ready. "What a wonderful place to die?"

The other two surrounded Elias, holding small daggers. "My brothers will never turn their back on me," Elias said with a grin.

Vasilis's mind wandered. *Does this mean we are brothers? Brothers trust one another. They are not traitors. Wait... that's the signal.* He ran and tackled Hecktor, kicking him in the face. The other two boys grappled him, throwing him down. "Big mistake," he said, pointing behind them.

A bear suddenly burst out of the cave, its roar echoing menacingly. The startled kids scattered and ran out in a frantic cash. Midas and the instructor walked in as they ran out. Vasilis and Elias strutted behind them, holding the bear by a rope.

"I guess you need new pack leaders," Vasilis said, his actions not just a show of bravery but a display of strategic thinking and leadership.

In a society where resilience, judgment, strength and cunning were paramount, Vasilis, along with Midas and Elias, had demonstrated these Spartan virtues brilliantly. Their coordinated plan and its successful execution showcased their potential as leaders, impressing both peers and elders.

From then on, time at the Agoge became less complicated. Although they would always be targets themselves, they would not have it any other way.

Here, among the youth of Sparta, where the strong survived to become elite, leadership was not just claimed but earned through acts of courage and wit. That day marked a significant turn in their journey, as the three of them rose above the rest, forming a formidable group of their own, poised to lead and conquer.

Six years later, things changed quickly when the senior Spartans came to retrieve Vasilis. At age thirteen, he was forced to return home. People gathered in the streets of Sparta to honor the fallen and celebrate their victory, but this felt different.

Stillness filled the air and carried the sound of clanking metal of the returning warriors. Seth, their captain, was the first to appear. A bearded man next to Vasilis spat and grumbled something too low to understand as Seth and his men approached.

Perhaps he should not admire Seth, but after hearing tales at the Agoge, Vasilis did. Seth once slew an army of a hundred men. His reason? Farming land, he felt, was owed to him by the Ephors. There were no repercussions, not from anyone, not even the kings. The tales made him seem like a giant or a god. But he was a man, smaller than Vasilis had imagined.

The people parted, allowing the men to pass. Vasilis scanned the crowd, searching for his father. He found him dead on his shield.

"Here lies King Vasilius, who fought with honor," Seth's voice rang throughout the city with pride. "He did not cower, nor did he show fear, a great king who will forever be remembered as more than a king. He was my brother as he fought in the greatest war with the god. He will forever live in our hearts, for he... *we* are Sparta!"

The crowd erupted, and celebrations began. There was no time to mourn, nor was there a place for it in Sparta. Days went by, and Vasilis and the trainees were set to resume their training. He wanted to see his mother one more time. He searched, but she was nowhere to be found.

It was the dead of night, but like the days before, he could not sleep. He sat alone, sharpening his blade, humming the warriors' tune his father sang to him many nights. Part of him hurt, wondering how his father allowed himself to die by the sword of an army with inferior prowess.

He stopped. Hearing footsteps approach—he jumped up, swinging his kopis, the metal clanging as it deflected off the intruders' vanguard.

"Relax, boy," said the intruder.

"Lysander?" Vasilis said.

He removed the hood of his cloak. His beard was whiter than the last time he saw him and covered most of the scars on his face.

"What are you doing here?" Vasilis asked.

"Grab your things. We must go," Lysander said.

"No, I have to resume my training."

"You will not return to the Agoge," he said, grabbing Vasilis's scabbard—tossing it to him. "Let's go. Your mother will explain everything."

They rode miles through the night, reaching his mother at the peak of dawn. He jumped off his horse, leaving Lysander behind. "Mother, what is the meaning of this?" he said, storming the villa. "Do you understand how hard I've had to work to gain their trust?"

"I'm sorry, son, but you're in danger. Did Lysander not tell you," she said, looking over Vasilis's shoulder.

"No," said Lysander. "I figure it was best to hear it from you."

"Danger, how?"

"Your father," she said. "One of his own murdered him..."

Vasilis snatched his hand away. He knew she was telling the truth. She was always honest with him, as was his father, no matter the circumstance. His eyes burned, and a painful knot formed in the back of his throat. He could see his mother's mouth move, but his heart thumped so loud that it was hard to hear what she was saying. She placed her soft hand on his shoulder.

"I know it's troubling, but I have a way to save us," she said. "I've requested an audience with the Gerousia."

"If what you say is true, then you must not go alone," said Vasilis.

Traitors, he thought. *Everywhere I go, everyone speaks of honor, yet they have none. I will not forfeit my mother.* He clenched his fist.

"I'll have you," she said, touching his face. "There is one other person as well, but we must go."

"What about you?" Vasilis directed his question toward Lysander.

"I have to retrieve someone else," he replied, leaving the villa.

The council of elders waited inside the crowded villa. Ten elders dressed in their blood-red tunics and head garments. Some elders stared in disdain at Vasilis and his mother. He squeezed the hilt of his kopis. *I could slit each of their throats before they could cry for help.*

His mother shot him a stern look. He stood erect and loosened his grip. She cleared her throat. "I must beg you. Please do not void the current agreement between Sparta and the Helots."

The men began talking amongst themselves. It was difficult to make out the words, but their expressions said everything. One man stood up. "Who are you to ask such a thing? You were made queen for the people. King Vasilius is dead, and again the people will vote for a new king—that king will determine your fate."

Kara stepped forward. "What about that of the greatest threat to all of humanity, the latent beast you carefully guard?"

"What do you know?" The same man shouted.

"I and I alone possess the location of the weapon," she said, allowing the words to sink in. "And the only one who can properly wield it.

"We have Midas–" said Peter.

"Who lost his sword?" Kara said, interrupting him. "The blood of a Champion stands here before you. Keep me as your queen and Vasilis as the last Champion of Sparta."

The men erupted in shouts, "A Helot as queen, a half-breed as a successor, never again!"

"Quiet, all of you!" A woman said, quieting the room. Everyone turned their attention to the woman with flowing white hair gracefully entering the hall.

Gorgo, they whispered. She had not been seen since Nicomedes had her exiled. It was the first time Vasilis saw his great-grandmother, but no one was more surprised than her son Petros, who could not believe his eyes.

"We need not discuss matters of this magnitude in front of a child," he said.

Gorgo looked at Vasilis. "They will not harm your mother, child. Wait outside."

Kara nodded in agreement, and Vasilis waited close enough to hear what they were saying. "Mother, with all due respect, these matters do not concern you," said Pleistarchus.

"Sparta is my home," replied Gorgo. "I will not see her fall or divided again. Have you forgotten the last revolt? If she is cast aside and the Helots are forgotten, it will happen again. Is the Sage not a greater threat than a Helot among Spartan royals?"

A quietness fell over the room for a while until an elder spoke. "Of course, the Sage is a greater danger, but not all of Sparta will agree that this woman should be queen. Are you suggesting we conspire to make her queen?"

The mystical Sage? They believe? Vasilis thought.

"We all have done worse," Gorgo replied. "Kara has the answer to a problem far greater than a title. I ask, who among you can wield the Blade of the Champion?"

A hand on Vasilis's shoulder caused him to jump. "Dammit, Lysander, you have to stop sneaking up on me."

"If they caught you eavesdropping—"

"I would gut them like cattle," Vasilis interrupted.

Lysander smirked. "The fire in you reminds me of your father." He brought his voice to a whisper. "There is a woman at Apollo's temple. She is not of this world, but she possesses answers to questions you will soon have."

"What are you talking about?"

As the words left his mouth, a slight glow snuck from underneath Lysander's cloak. "What is that?"

"Vasilis," someone called, grabbing his attention. "You didn't answer my question." he looked back, but Lysander had vanished.

"Vasilis, did you not hear them?" questioned Kara.

"Sorry, mother," Vasilis said and followed his mother back inside.

"With great regret, we must inform you that your rank will be revoked," an elder said. "Your family is only royalty to the Spartan people by name. You will act as an understudy to Seth. Perhaps with time, you may earn your way back."

Their voices blended with the thumping of his heart. His stomach sank to his knees, which buckled. "Mother, please!"

Kara walked over to Vasilis. "You mustn't question the elders."

"Why is this happening?" he asked.

"We will discuss it during our travels. We must depart immediately."

They journeyed to a place he was familiar with, the Red Cave. He struggled with the thought of starting from nothing, working for a Spartan ostracized by his people. What would that mean for him? He wanted to ask, but dared not. Instead, they rode in silence.

Father, if only you were here. If only... I will avenge you one day. These traitors will pay.

His mind continued searching for answers. And the more he searched, the more his stomach turned. He wasn't sure what he wanted or what he should do, nor what was the secret the elders kept. Part of him wanted to scream in anger, while the other side wanted to cry into his mother's arms. But there wasn't any place for weakness, not in Sparta. *Father, I'm so lost.*

Kara moved a cluster of rocks, then dug with her bare hands. "Your father buried this here, hoping you'd someday wield it," she said, handing him a sword.

The Blade of the Champion. The words echoed in Vasilis's mind as his gaze lingered on the glowing Cerberus hilt. The faint red glow emanating from the eyes of the three-headed hound traced the blade's intricate metal creases, casting an eerie shadow in the dim light of the chamber.

His hand shook as he reached out to grasp the hilt of the weapon, his fingers wrapping around the solid tail that formed its pommel. The three snarling heads of the kopis encased the blade; their fangs bared in a menacing grin.

As his fingers traced the intricate patterns etched into the blade, he couldn't help but marvel at the impeccable craftsmanship. The hilt was adorned with precious gems, their fierce glint matching that of the weapon's powerful aura.

"I knew it," Kara said. "You are the one to wield Forsaken."

"What are you not telling me, Mother?" he said, sheathing Forsaken.

"There is no more to discuss. You know what you are permitted to know. Now, do you want to spend our last few moments together in debate, or do you want to test out Forsaken?" Vasilis did not wish to squabble with his mother, not now.

Two years passed since his father's death, and it still bothered him. No one else spoke of it, but there was something unsettling about how his father died. Lysander's words replayed in his head. Vasilis closed in on Apollo's temple–high up in Delphi's mountain. It was a small settlement, modest housing with the temple at its center, surrounded by a grand peristalsis, with six and fifteen columns along the side.

If anyone could answer my questions, the high priestess could. From what they claimed, it was she who helped to reshape Sparta, an oracle unlike any other.

His mind raced, staring at the clustered stars holding Forsaken, pondering the afterlife of his father. He dare not question the beliefs of Greece aloud. If a mere man would reap the benefits of the afterlife, surely a king would.

Sounds from a distance alerted the boy. He gathered himself, adjusting the rag around his waist — his only piece of attire. "Pythia," he called out, sitting up.

The winds picked up, blowing toward the caves where light broke through the darkness. So too did the woman. A slight gust brushed her light brown hair onto her shoulders. Vasilis's hands trembled. Before he knew it, he was standing in front of her, sinking into her brown eyes.

"Can you tell me for certain that my father was betrayed, or was Lysander wrong about you?"

There was a brief pause before the woman spoke. Her accent changed. Even with his years of studying other languages, he couldn't recognize it. "Lysander was right. My gift is not of this world, nor am I. Yes, I can see the future and perform acts you will not believe, but I am not a true high priestess."

"False god," he said, turning away.

"Stop!"

It felt as if stone walls closed in on him from all sides, creating unbreakable stillness. Though he still felt the wind at his back and saw the woman standing in front of him.

"The gods did not choose me, but my gifts are greater than a mere oracle," she said. "It's why the highest of the high kiss my feet and spend days yearning for my words..." her voice trailed, her eyes locked onto his hilt.

"Don't," Vasilis pleaded, struggling to move, but Forsaken left him and landed in her hand.

The look in her eyes was one he was familiar with when he first held Forsaken. "Vasilis, I want to help you, but you must allow your mother to deal with your father's death. You are destined for greatness. You must train hard and lead the world from destruction." She returned the sword to him and unsheathed a blade of her own.

Vasilis wanted to, but dared not beg for his life as he struggled to unbind himself from her magic.

"Give this to your mother. On it, there's a message in Samoan, her native tongue," she said, unbinding him—floating him the dagger.

"Who should I say gave this to her?"

"Lilith."

MALAYA

New Seattle, 2075

Ivory dice danced across the marble floor, tapping against Malaya's high heels as she retreated toward the entrance. With a nasty look cast towards the men, she continued her stride toward the hostess' greeting room, hopeful that the security pad's chiming signaled her guest's arrival.

As the metal door clanked open, the guard briefly peeked outside and discreetly tucked away his pistol before turning to greet a guest.

Where are you, Mom? She headed back, taking a deep breath before pulling back the curtain dampers.

Serene classical music hit her face as she opened the door. She walked into the dimly lit lounge. Its high, hand-painted ceiling wrapped around the oversized chandelier, and the endless bar stretched across most of the room.

Surrounded by luxury, her heart ached with an unfillable void. Her father's passing left a lingering black hole of grief, particularly palpable on days like this. Now, her mother's absence only deepened this feeling, casting a shadow of profound loneliness.

A memory surfaced. Malaya at a grand soirée four years prior, a high-society staple. The grand ballroom shimmered with golden light and crystal reflections. As the celebrated young scientist, Malaya Castillo-Grant navigated the elite crowd, her insights earning admiration.

Her father's words lingered, "You're not just a scientist. You're a symbol. Embrace it."

Shaking off the memory, Malaya smiled faintly, her gaze sweeping over the lounge. "It's been too long since I enjoyed a good party," she murmured to herself.

Lifting the hem of her forest gown, she navigated through the tables crowded with revelers lost in their own worlds of ecstasy, though they took the time to acknowledge her as she passed in route to the VIP section.

"May I offer you a drink, Ms. Castillo-Grant?" the waiter asked.

"Malta."

"As you wish."

Kat tilted her head. "Really?"

Malaya flicked her brown french braid off her shoulder. "Comfort drink."

"It's your birthday, loosen up," she urged, sliding the drink toward her.

"No, no. Things happen when I drink."

Kat smirked. "I almost forgot about that thing with David. In the closet, of all places—"

Malaya's cheeks flushed deeper. "Okay, okay," she muttered, eager to change the subject. "Let's not bring up my ex, especially not with my boyfriend about to get here."

The waiter turned to Kat, his gaze briefly dropping to the mesh-covered breasts of her black jumpsuit. "Anything else for you, Ms. Bennett?"

"Hennessy. And make sure you get those bionic eyes checked out; they appear to be malfunctioning."

"Certainly," the waiter replied, his robotic voice lower than normal.

Malaya turned to him. "Oh, and please inform me when my mother arrives. I don't want to get caught off guard."

"Of course," he said before leaving.

Malaya relentlessly tapped her phone until the light that illuminated her honey skin faded to black. Crap.

"The table will charge it."

Malaya looked into her friend's pale green eyes. "I'm sorry."

"It's your mother, isn't it?"

Malaya nodded. Kat smiled and pushed the foamed drink toward her. "Just take a drink of your nonalcoholic beverage to take the edge off."

"You know what bothers me? Freaking secrets."

"It's just—" Malaya rubbed her face. "Everyone has them... Different faces. I work with my mother, but ever since the turnover, I don't know her anymore. Of course, she pretends to be the same, but ugh. Then there's Aaron, a walking cliché of tall, dark, and mysterious."

"This isn't HOA. We opted for a lifestyle with secrets. Look around. My family is the royal family of secrets. You know what else?"

Kat leaned forward, grasping Malaya's hands. "Your father's death affected your mother more than she's letting on."

Malaya sighed. "Okay, maybe I am being inconsiderate, but she hasn't called. And I'm telling you, she's been off lately."

"It's still early, plus your boy toy isn't here yet. Speaking of which, you said he's mysterious. Can't you suck the secrets out of him?" Kat's cheeks reddened instantly. "That didn't come out right."

They both laughed.

"I doubt I can get anything out of him. He's CIA. Besides, I did my own digging, to no avail. I will not press, but it'll be refreshing to have a world with fewer secrets..."

Malaya stared at her friend. *Maybe I should be the one to break the cycle of lies and secrets.* She leaned over to her friend and whispered, "Project Bungee—"

Kat nearly spat out her drink. "I don't think—"

"It was me. I broke the code."

"Excuse me, ladies," a familiar voice said. "Should I come back? This conversation looks intense."

"Aaron," Malaya said.

"Happy birthday," he said before they kissed. "It's a pleasure to finally meet you, Katherine."

Kat brushed back the messy strands of her braided blond hair. "That's funny. From what I hear, we hardly know you."

Malaya wanted to do more than side-eye her big-mouthed friend.

"No foreplay, huh? Straight to the point." Aaron said, handing his tan long coat and hat to the waiter.

"Should I have worn all black, too?" Malaya said, pointing at his attire.

"Great minds think alike," said Kat.

"We already ordered," said Malaya. "Hope you don't mind."

"Not at all," said Aaron. "I had sushi on the plane, though I'll take what Kat's having."

He leaned back in his chair, sparking cannabis rolled in cigar paper. "Where's Mrs. Castillo-Grant?"

"Running late," said Kat. "So, did Malaya ever tell you how we met?"

"Vaguely."

"I'm crushed." Kat smiled, accepting the blunt Aaron offered. "I guess she wouldn't have, considering she lost the epic battle."

Malaya raised a brow. "That's not how I remember it."

"She's lucky we didn't get kicked out," Kat said. "But when your grandmother's name is on the building, you have a little leeway."

The House of Angela was a place of magic, a haven for the gifted. It was more than just bricks and mortar; it was a second home, infused with memories and a sense of belonging. Malaya couldn't help but feel a small yearning as she thought of its halls, the very embodiment of her past, encapsulated by the simple acronym, HOA.

Malaya's phone vibrated. *Mom*. Her heart pumped out of her chest. "I have to take this. You can tell Aaron how I wrecked your status as the House of Angela's it girl," she said before walking into the host room.

"Mami... *que*... Did you forget? So, what's keeping you? Oh, I see... Mom, wait..." Her words stumbled over each other, desperate for connection, but the line went dead.

Malaya stared at her phone in disbelief, her heart sinking like a stone in her chest. "Did she really just hang up on me?" She checked her signal, fingers trembling with frustration and disappointment.

"Ugh," she groaned, feeling the weight of her mother's absence like a heavy shackle dragging her back to the table. *She's really going to leave me stranded.*

Part of her hoped that she could eat her anger, but that was quickly doused by the sight before her. "What the freak!" she said, locking eyes with the massive head on her plate.

"What's wrong?" said Aaron

Kat leaned over. "It's the fish. It—"

"Has a freaking head!" Malaya interrupted. "Are the chefs mindless droids as well?"

The android opened its mouth. Malaya put her hand up. "It was rhetorical."

The chef came out to apologize for something that she knew was an honest mistake, but she couldn't let it go. She sat down without saying a word, unable to stop her leg from trembling.

"Do you want to talk?" Kat said, reaching for her hand.

"No." She took out a small pouch and placed a patch underneath her tongue.

"Malaya?" Kat said, with a wide-eyed expression shared by Aaron.

"I have a script, and it's something much stronger."

Aaron looked at his watch and leaned over to Malaya. "The internet... it's still working?"

"In here, curfew is nonexistent," said Kat

"Internet speakeasy," Aaron said. "I would have thought of an underground location, but a penthouse is... genius."

Kat took a sip. "Gotta love my family... they found their way around those UNA sanctions. They have way too much power."

Aaron grabbed the drink. "I'll drink to that."

They continued to talk politics, a subject she cared little about. Too often, people had something to say but never a solution, at least not a logical one. Her grandfather understood, despite how history tells it, his decision.

The Treaty of Democracy was the right decision. Yes, America adhered to strict laws handed down by the Alliance—at least there was no more fighting. Decades later, people still had something negative to say.

Not today.

"What was the alternative?" Malaya said. "The continuation of World War III, a supercontinent taking the lowly US by force. Or did you both forget Russia was close to joining if not for—"

The chef brought Malaya's food, stopping her from going deeper into her tangent. *It was perfect.* However, it was hard to enjoy, given the tense aura that clung to her. She looked at Kat and Aaron getting along, trying to help her enjoy the night.

It's not fair to the two of them. At least they showed. Why, Mom? Why, of all days, did you let work get in the way today?

"Sorry," Malaya said, breaking the awkward tension she had created.

She hoped a few forced laughs and smiles would hide the disappointment still sitting in the pit of her now full stomach.

Kat looked at her phone. "Time for me to swoop. We'll connect later, but you need the downtime."

She handed Malaya a key card. "Your suite is next door," she said with a suspicious grin.

They embraced, and Kat whispered. "I'm sorry about your mom. For her to miss today, her daughter's birthday... it had to be important. You know your mom."

"Yeah," Malaya said at Kat's feeble attempt, but she was right about her mother. She was always searching for a way to make the world a better place. Part of her felt a little guilty for thinking so selfishly.

"I love you," said Kat.

"Love you too."

Aaron tipped his cup to Kat. "Merry Christmas."

After dessert, Malaya and Aaron made their way to the penthouse suite. Candles illuminated the room decorated with flowers and balloons. Aaron grabbed her hand. "Something's bothering you. If you need some time alone—"

"No," said Malaya. "I'll be fine."

"I believe you," he said as they walked toward the bed. "Fine or not. I'm going to tell you something my mother always told me. When things aren't where you need them to be in here." He touched her heart. "Go back to your happy place and enjoy the simpler things."

"That's cute. She was a wise woman."

He nodded. A smile crossed his deep mahogany face. "She appreciated life. Never showed weakness, but she always had a smile on her face, like the way you smiled when Kat brought up HOA. You always talk about how great it was. That's your happy place, even if the teachers drove you crazy."

Malaya smiled. Aaron was right. She didn't realize it until now. Not being around HOA had created a void she missed. The adventure, the camaraderie. "I was supposed to send a car for Jordan anyway... maybe," Malaya paused. "I don't know. It's just been so long."

"Trust me," he said.

Malaya looked into his brown eyes. She brushed back the few dreadlocks that fell in his face. "You're right." She leaned in and kissed him. "You also make me happy."

"I'm glad to hear it," he said.

The radiant smile across his face was contagious. "Thanks to Kat, we can stream some banned anime, classics—"

"So, *Naruto* and chill?"

Morning sun rays peeked inside, but a kiss from Aaron woke her. "Wake up, sleeping beauty. I got called into work, but I ordered room service," he said, getting dressed. "Oh, and this was at the front door."

He handed Malaya a box with her mother's name on it. She started to open it, then stopped.

"What is it?" Aaron asked, tying his boots.

"I think I'll open it later."

After breakfast, Aaron left, and she went home and on the edge of her bed with her stomach in knots, staring at her mother's gift. *Fine.*

She slowly removed the top. The box encased her father's axe—tears streamed down her face.

It was a souvenir from his first-time jump. It was their family secret, though he kept it framed in his home office. She wiped her tears and started to put it back in the box—she stopped. There was something else underneath the layer of cardboard. She removed a wooden puzzle box.

What do we have here? she thought, analyzing the numbers and symbols.

Her mom knew her all too well, so she had to know it wouldn't take long for her to figure out the combination within seconds.

It opened to what looked like an expensive ruby. Her mother always did things big, but there was something special about it. It was almost as if visible energy flowed within it. *It must be a combo of light refraction and high chromium.* She clasped the chain around her neck.

This was amazing, but it didn't make up for her not being there. She took a deep breath as Aaron's advice came to mind.

Go to your happy place.

MALAYA

New Seattle, 2075

The pungent aroma of freshly burned hair and grease pulled Malaya away from the fantasy story she immersed herself in. For her, diving into the realm of fantasy had become increasingly challenging.

As a toddler, she easily delved into classics from Brando Sando, but now, her analytical mind left her dissecting every excerpt, memorizing every sentence, and storing every word as if they were mere data, rather than parts of a cohesive story. One has only so much bandwidth.

Malaya sighed.

Closing the novel, her curiosity piqued by the ever-present smell, growing stronger with each step down the black steel stairway, the reused wood creaking beneath her feet. Memories of her childhood flooded back—the mingling scents of Fabuloso and the rhythmic beats of classic salsa stirring her awake.

She recalled the groan she let out each time, knowing it signaled the start of cleaning chores, followed by moments of solace, watching Saturday morning cartoons. And sometimes her father would lament the changes in child ad laws by the senate afforded her things he didn't have as a child.

"Lucky you," he would always say.

Her fingers lightly traced the necklace her late father had gifted her, housing a red rune—a painful reminder of their family's loss. A knot tightened in her stomach, a familiar ache accompanying memories of the old mines.

In the vast, dimly lit expanse of a secret laboratory, Malaya uncovered the final piece of the puzzle—decoding the ancient mechanisms behind the quantum power cell, a relic of science far beyond their time. This enigmatic device, once a theoretical marvel, held the key to unlocking the impossible: time travel.

But the breakthrough was not without sacrifice. It was a discovery etched in tragedy, as her father gave his life to help Malaya understand the intricacies of the QPC, forever binding their legacy to the mysteries of time.

Jeff Grant sacrificed himself, becoming the first man to ever time travel. She shivered at the memory of his demise, the way his skin hung from his hands and face as he withered away. A memory that continues to haunt her to this day.

As she neared the bottom, cartoons mixed in with the sizzle of the hot comb, the smell came along with a yelp. There were only two people that would do their hair in a speakeasy. *Arya and Emma, of course.*

The twins sat in the VIP lounge that doubled as a mini suite, a Bennet family special. An adjustable partition separated the room from the bar area that, when activated, gave the guest a full view of the party. Plush furniture and lavish décor made up the private suite. Abstract art pieces adorned the red brick walls, the infamous trademark for the underground elite.

If these walls could talk. Malaya imagined they'd whisper some of the darkest secrets known to man.

"Ugh," she shook away the thought, noting that at least for today, the walls held elegant V-neck winter dresses.

Arya sat, her eyes squinting as her sister used a wet napkin to cool the comb; It sizzled as it landed. Both had amazing light brown skin with freckles to complement. They both usually had dark golden curls with perfect bounce, but today Ayra was straightening out her hair.

"What's going on here?" Malaya said, making her way to the espresso machine.

"We're going to church," Emma said, warming the comb on an electric stove.

"On a Saturday?"

Arya flinched when her sister grabbed her hair. "Oh. There was a search warrant issued on our house."

"And yours, by the way," Emma added.

"Wait what!"

Emma continued, "Grandpa said not to worry, something about a new SUV rule thingy."

Malaya stood in the kitchen, the rich scent of brewing Cuban coffee heavy in the air, mingling with the tension that surrounded her. She couldn't shake the feeling of unease in her gut—a familiar companion whenever thoughts of the SUV surfaced.

The Subterranean Underwater Vessel, a secretive government facility that no one knew existed, held within its walls the legacy of her family—Project Bungee, the quantum power cell and the Quantum Portal. These were not just projects. They were her father's life's work until his tragic death.

After his passing, control of the project shifted to the government, leaving Malaya to pick up the pieces of her shattered family legacy.

Determined to honor her father's sacrifices, Malaya devoted herself to maintaining the operational integrity of the Quantum Portal within the SUV. The memory of her father's demise drove her to prevent any recurrence of the mistakes that led to his downfall.

With two quantum power cells now in existence—one housed within MEV, her mother's company, and the other concealed within the SUV—rumors swirled of a potential consolidation. This move held the promise of bringing together the fractured halves of her family.

Despite her mother's absence, Malaya clung to hope that this could be a chance for reconciliation, a chance to mend the bonds strained by tragedy and time.

At least she had her cousins, Arya and Emma, with her when she worked on SUV. She wondered if her mother knew just how amazing these two prodigies from the House of Angela were.

The twins were part of the Youth Intelligence Division. Though Malaya wasn't exactly sure of their mission or purpose.

Still, their presence would offer some comfort in the midst of this uncertainty as it did now.

How did we get here? Malaya poured herself a cup of coffee, reflecting on the lessons she had learned about the state of affairs.

This shift in social structure stemmed from the aftermath of World War III. America's once-capitalistic society was forced to concede defeat. Consequently, compromises on personal freedoms became commonplace.

Yet invasive practices, such as home searches, remained unsettlingly frequent. Of course, someone who sparingly worked for the government was not exempt.

She took a sip of her unsweetened coffee. Malaya frowned, finding its bitterness reminiscent of politics.

"So, when are you going back to SUV?" Arya said.

Malaya glanced around, as if expecting spies to be listening in. "Don't speak of it so casually," she said, her tone serious. "SUV doesn't exist, and you're interns for the CIA, that's all."

"Alright, we get it," Arya replied.

"Why would they need to search our homes?" Malaya asked. "And why was I not informed?"

Her cousins merely shrugged in response.

A sick feeling turned Malaya's stomach as she thought that maybe this could this be the reason her mother didn't show up last night. Maybe they raided her too. *But to bail on my b-day?*

Malaya grappled with conflicting emotions. It wasn't the first time her mother had ignored her calls. As one of the most renowned figures globally, Lilith Castilo-Grant's schedule was always packed. However, the recent surge of missing scientists, all tied to physicists and time travel, didn't help.

She couldn't help but wonder if another government had learned of their project and developed their way to time travel.

Was that even possible? Would they really kidnap a scientist and my mom? Malaya scoffed at how ridiculous it sounded in her head. She dare not say out loud. She'd leave that to Reddit News and MSNBC.

She resolved to focus on her return to her happy place—HOA. She'd try her mother again later.

"Do you want to come?" one of the twins said, breaking Malaya from her stupor, her eyes coming away from the coffee.

"Come where?" said Malaya.

"Church, duh," Arya answered.

"She is an atheist, remember?" said Emma.

"She is actually agnostic," Arya replied. Malaya's mouth opened to jump in. Arya was technically right, but the two of them were in their own world, going back and forth, bickering, almost completing their sentence. It was cute and sometimes deadly; it was best to just leave them be.

With a resigned smile, she headed back upstairs to her suite, gathered her belongings, and set off in search of Kat. The least she could do was thank her for an amazing party and giving her the time alone with Aaron.

Of course, Kat was nowhere to be seen. Malaya used the VIP elevator to take the direct route to the parking lot, avoiding Kat's family in the process. It's not that she didn't like them. Uncle V was cool, and Bryce wasn't hard on the eyes, but he could be intense. However, their family business always made her uncomfortable.

After using the VIP elevator to bypass Kat's family, Malaya arrived at the expansive private garage. She had a clear plan in mind—head home, shower quickly, get ready, lower the convertible top of her car, and cruise through the cool morning to her home away from home, HOA.

With her mom being MIA, she longed for the comfort of friendly faces, especially Jordan's. It had been weeks since she'd last seen him. Maybe he'd forgive her once she saw the gift she got him.

As the door slid open, she gasped in disbelief, her eyes fixating on the glowing label affixed to her back window, *Violation Car Disabled*.

"I've been *stung*," she snapped, pacing around the car.

With a futile glance around the garage, she searched for the elusive Droid responsible for tagging her vehicle.

Of the things these hackers could do, you'd think they would find a way to disable those stupid androids. Or these stupid boxes. She tugged at the sleek metal device mounted on the hood of her car.

"Ugh," she growled in frustration.

Not only would she have to pay a fee, but her vehicle was now off-limits for a set amount of time. This time, it was four hours. It felt like the more peace they enjoyed, the less freedom they endured.

The price for peace after the war, after America couldn't stomach the chaos, the blood, the loss. Restrictions from the enemy, the United Nations of Asia, an empty name given they conquered most of Europe. Seattle took the brunt of the force.

Outside of Pearl Harbor and 9-11, where America was attacked through the air, July 4 marked the birth of America's first ground attack, tarnishing its day of independence and forcing America to embrace socialism, a double-edged sword of course, but the end of the western world as they knew it.

The ensuing battle left Seattle in ruins, which gave birth to New Seattle. A modern marvel thanks to the money her family poured into the city, but lacked the charm of the original.

Malaya's phone rang. *Mom,* she thought, checking the caller ID, sighing as she saw it was not her mother but her boss.

Why are you calling me on a Saturday, sir? She ignored it, but it rang again.

She wanted so badly to send him to voicemail, but he likely wouldn't stop calling.

Privately, Malaya worked on her family's project. Publicly she worked with Lance Corp, pushing the boundaries of theoretical physics. This was supposed to be the start of her vacation, but he wasn't the worst boss in the world.

Malaya sighed. "Accept."

Her contacts project an overlay of Mr. Schwartz, a tall middle age German refugee. The device also projected three feet in all directions, his classic nineteenth century home office.

"Malaya, my deepest, sincere apologies," he began. "I know you value your time off. Unfortunately, another of our peers has gone missing, and three of our interns quit. Scared to the bones, I tell you."

She rubbed her forehead, already shaking her head before he even asked her the question.

"Terribly sorry, but with the shortage, and my Ted Talk rapidly approaching, I need the manpower... *woman* power," he smartly corrected. "To complete my research."

"I already have a stack of papers on my desk, and I have plans..." She trailed off, frustration taking the best of her.

"Malaya please. You know what this means to the company, you'll have the entire facility to yourself. It'll be like working from a home office, with security, of course."

"You're asking me to do the task of three."

"I'll be working from my end, of course."

"So the task of two."

He gave her a ruthless grin. "Fair enough. I owe you one."

"You owe me a hundred, and an Uber. My car was stung."

"Done. I'll even pay for the fee. Oh, and extra bandwidth, in case you get inspired on the way."

She waved him off, ending the call.

Her Uber arrived on time, a boring silver automated vehicle. It made her yearn for her Rx7. The sporty classic Mazda was an elegant black gem among the stale gray hue of the contemporary city. She couldn't afford to drive it, anyway. The petrol fee was a backbreaker, even for her. Bandwidth was hard to come by for most. As for money. Well, her mother was one of the richest humans of all time, but as she loved reminding her, that was her money, not Malaya's.

The AI took control of the car, zipping out of the garage and attaching itself to the magnetic rail. A clank confirmed the roof's attachment to the manorial. The vehicle glided through the city. The cloth chairs faced one another, offering a three hundred and sixty-degree view of the city.

She could see the MEV and the protestors in the parking lot. The reignition of the age-old debate: Is clean energy for America and its allies only? Or is it a human right, enemy or not?

"Tint," Malaya commanded.

The glass darkened, and a soft orange light came on. She activated the center table, and a white light shone over it. Better she start on her own paper, *Bridging Realms: Exploring Quantum Portals in Interstellar Travel.*

It would be a pregame to his talk following his TED talk, a way to warm up the scientific community. She ensured not to outshine him, knowing men's egos are more fragile than they admit. He would receive all the glory, and that was okay with her.

She preferred the title of the underachieving prodigy with the mediocre job, the runt of her family's empire. It didn't matter; she could never do enough or accomplish enough for her mother.

Malaya took a brief break at home for some reprieve. After her shower, she changed into her favorite X-Men shirt, tights, and Chucks before hopping back into the Uber.

Heading to the office, she soon lost herself in her work, the detachment of the rail snapping her back to reality. The electromagnetic under magnets took over, guiding her to a stop at her office.

She published the paper before exiting. The facility was twenty stories tall, with a silver frame made up of glass. It was round, similar to the Leaning Tower of Pisa.

She searched her purse for her badge when a young voice grabbed her attention. "Excuse me ma'am, but are you Malaya Castillo-Grant?,"

The sweet voice of the young boy melted her heart. Despite his unassuming appearance with brown skin and silky hair, his eyes bore maturity beyond his years.

Malaya smiled. "Oh yes, would you like a selfie? Maybe an autograph?" She searched for a pen.

"I have one right here." The boy brushed a strand of his fine hair behind his ear before retrieving a pen from his fanny pack. "Here's your pen, bitch!"

"Wha..."

A black substance shot out of the pen-like device all over her shirt.

"You deserve more for what MEV is doing, supplying dictatorship! And the expansion," he choked.

Part of her wanted to explain that she wasn't part of MEV and her mother's decision to supply the world with nearly limitless clean energy was her decision, not Malaya's. But the other half wanted to strangle the kid. She loved her X-Men shirt. *Who knows if this comes off?*

Security tackled him to the ground before she could say or do anything.

"Are you alright, ma'am?" the security guard said, a short bald man.

Malaya sniffed the black substance. It seemed to be just ink, and not some black venom. "Yeah, I think so. Thanks."

She looked back at the boy as he was arrested. Their eyes met. "My father lost his business thanks to MEV! It's all your fault!"

Her heart ached for him, consumed by the urge to offer solace and heartfelt apologies. If only she could find the words to express her regret for their actions. But before she could even try, he was ushered out, leaving her feeling helpless, but she wasn't powerless.

She was then escorted all the way to her office, where a guard stood watch at her door. Malaya quickly retrieved her Meta-suite, feeling relieved that there were no prying eyes around today.

The bodysuit required to be skin-tight—loose clothing threw off the AI. Malaya had nothing to be ashamed of; she worked on her figure, and her athletic build was maintained long after her track and field days ended.

As she stepped onto the platform, what seemed like an empty white room exploded with halo light. The platinum-gray suit glowed like a Christmas tree with neon blues and soft whites. Several AIs activated, ready to assist her.

Malaya was the conductor in an orchestra of AI. She controlled the direction and depth of the research. AI errors were fixed and its flawed logic pointed out. Her bare feet walked along the cold metallic floor.

It was made of omnidirectional square tile that moved as she did, allowing freedom. She thought about the boy and the reach her family had. He was so young, but his eyes told the story of a child who did not walk in a child's shoes.

My family cost his father his job. He couldn't have been older than thirteen. There's no telling what else he had gone through.

The world had changed over the decades. Malaya had known that much.

The Third World War had prompted governments to harness the talents of their best young minds. Institutions like her family's House of Angela, named after her grandmother, had become renowned for nurturing such exceptional abilities. Earning good grades wasn't sufficient for admission to HOA. Applicants needed to showcase a unique gift or specialty to contribute to the cause.

Again, her mind drifted back to the boy, who saw her as a monster responsible for his current situation. Perhaps she was. It's not like she was in the know of anything outside of her job, Project Bunge... her mom.

Malaya sighed, desperately eager to finish her work and return to her second home, a place where she made unbreakable friendships: HOA. *My happy place.*

She spent most of the night researching, pushing the boundaries of knowledge and science.

By the time she showered and made it to the elevator, UNA drones roamed skies, and the sun was over the old Seattle needle, the last remembrance of a time past.

It was a simple job, just how her father started off. Despite her love for it, there was something that was always left empty.

The elevator door opened with a chime, and a little girl waited on the other side. She had strawberry-blond hair, with milk-white skin, and honey eyes. "Malaya! I mean, Ms. Castillo," Malaya flinched, as she held on to her purse. "Excuse me," Malaya slipped past her.

"I loved your paper on *Bridging Realms: Exploring Quantum Portals in Interstellar Travel,*" she said, her voice shifting slightly as she pronounced the title, an attempt to sound more mature. "I just published that a few hours ago." Her eyes brightened, twisting her purple scarf. "I received a notification." They rejoined, discussing the paper in detail, Malaya finding solace in her brilliance.

"How about a selfie?"

"Yes! Please!" They took the picture, and she saw her off.

She called for her car, expecting her time to have expired. The AI was supposed to bring it on its own. Glancing at her watch, she saw it glow, indicating the direction of her car as it approached. But then, to her dismay, the watch flashed red. "No!"

"How could the AI crash? Darn it! And how the heck am I getting to HOA?"

SETH

Sparta, 418 BC

Seth carefully cut into the poppy plant, releasing its potent aroma. The thick sap oozed onto his spoon, then onto his wife's. She tasted it, her expression softening into contentment as she cradled their daughter, Hera, in her arms. Seth felt a rush of warmth as he watched her. Their daughter nestled between them. With her legs propped on the armrest, he felt a sense of closeness, even entrapment, in the moment. Yet, it was a pleasant confinement, as they shared this fleeting escape into bliss together.

Seth dipped the spoon in wine, taking it in slowly, admiring his wife's elaborate tight brown coiffure, though he dared not touch it.

"Vashti," Seth whispered before kissing her forehead, a light attempt at waking her. He needed to know what she thought. This election was a result of a fallen king—one he'd stabbed in the back, a man he loved as a brother. The man his wife once called brother. "You were saying?"

"You are the one that is sleeping," she slurred. "We must do what needs to be done, regardless of our selfish ambitions. Take care of your end. I will take care of mine."

Vashti sat up and reignited a candle. Red wax dripped onto the large fine table. "The Gerousia will elect you. Once you are king, you must marry Kara. We will deal with the aftermath when it arrives."

His mouth pinched. She returned the look. "Can a woman not complete this task?"

"My lack of faith in you has less to do with you being a woman than it does with your presumptive nature... where do we draw the line?"

"There is no line when it comes to my children," Vashti said, carrying Hera to the room.

Later that night, two thuds on the door woke him. He looked at his blade, then remembered he was expecting his son. "Enter."

His son placed a torch on the wall fixture. The extra light highlighted his small home, a far cry from his former grand villa that was drenched in marble. Although the exterior was painted white with fine stone, internally, it needed work—three rooms and a cold stone floor was the sum of its parts. Despite his small victories, they were drowning politically and financially. The thought reignited his inner flame.

Elias removed his brown hooded cloak. "Why must your summons drag me out in the middle of the night?"

"Sit. We have matters to discuss."

"Hera?" said Elias, looking around the room.

"Sleeping." Seth stood and clasped his hand behind his back—facing the painting on the wall, feeling the effects of opioids, which helped clear his mind, but his soul still felt the weight of his actions.

Seth took a deep breath and poured himself some wine. "Attacking was stupid."

"I warned the commander, but he left me no choice."

"You warned him to bend the knee in front of his men. Vasilis and Midas will not always be here to clean up your mess." He took a sip. "Go ahead, say something clever."

Elias's brows furrowed. His sinister deep blue eyes stared at Seth. "Father, the men are yours... mission accomplished. No harm came from it."

"You not learning is harmful, Elias." Seth sighed. "It is time for you to become a man and take what is rightfully ours: power. Kara is getting more of it, and if we don't stop it in its infancy, we will stay in their shadow."

"Vasilis is my brother. I will not touch his mother."

"Not his mother, but an elder, Kyrios. There is no greater Kara supporter in Gerousia, and my strategy requires a vacant seat."

Seth could see Elias's relief. He handed him a scroll. "Place this in his room, and son—it has to be clean, a suicide."

"Is that all?"

"Ephialtes will require a visit as well," Seth said, handing his son a cup of wine. "He is the one who Sparta wants as king—have Midas pay him a visit."

Elias nodded and walked over to his sister, passing his hand over her head. "She just started to walk," Seth said, unable to hide his pride. This was a rare moment his family was together—his dreams aligned.

Elias kissed his sleeping mother before Seth led them away.

"You can't expect Vasilis's alliance with certainty," said Elias.

"This plot is not common knowledge. Upon his return from war, the deed will have been completed—he will have no option."

"Who will take Kyrois's seat?"

Seth dipped a sap latent spoon into his wine, staring at his son, wondering if he should tell him who. *Words tend to travel fast in Sparta. If I tell him I am to become king, who then would he tell? Will the elders then plot against me as I did to Vasilius? But he deserved it—*

"Don't shut me out," Elias said. "How will I learn to play the game if I have little knowledge of the participants?"

He is right, Seth thought, taking a sip of wine. "Lynceus."

"Lysanders's brother? He's aligned with Kara's cause."

"Yes. A perfect candidate for the seat. He'll elect me as a favor, and you will secure his family by marriage."

"Nafeli? Not bad," Elias smirked. "But she will protest."

"She will comply if she wants the rest of her family to survive."

"What do you mean by that?"

"You will eliminate Hecktor."

Elias exploded out of his chair. "You're not serious—I will not kill her brother!"

"You *will*. Everything has a price. I need reassurance. After the deed is done, you will transfer his two brothers into your pack—for close observation."

"It's time to become a man," Vashti said, emerging from the shadows, walking toward them. "Must our family forever live in the darkness of solitude?"

"Mother," the pain in Elias's voice was apparent.

"Thanks to Vasilius, your sister lives in the dirt. Now, what will you do about it?"

Elias kissed his mother's hand. "Whatever has to be done."

At camp the next morning, Seth strategized with his brigade. This was the invasion to change everything. Conquering the Athenians was no easy task. So, he called upon the power gifted to him by the gods.

Seth looked toward the clouds as nature took control. It was as if the winds carried him from his body into the animal of his choosing, an eagle.

Decades of practice made the transfer easier. He cut through the warm wind circling above the camp of his oblivious enemy—conjuring a strategy, relishing in the freedom that was soaring in the air.

Seth returned with instructions for his cavalry to march ahead. "We will join you shortly. Mother Sparta needs you. Do this, and you will get more than half the crop."

He watched Viktor take his men into the lion's den, knowing the results. "What is it?" he said, feeling Elias creeping behind him.

"Are you seriously going to hand them land?"

"There will not be many of them left. Now, ready your men for the hills." He turned to Midas. "Lead your men to the river. Vasilis and I will attack from the flank. They will be surrounded."

Less than half of Viktors' men returned. He was not among them. Seth took the body of an eagle once more. Blood of his enemies soaked the ground, and inside, he smiled.

From his bird's-eye view, he saw endless corpses scattered across the land and victorious, unassuming warriors marching their way—as he planned. He returned to his body, readying to end the life of those unlucky enough to survive.

So he did, leading the way, driving his spear through one enemy after another, fighting alongside Sparta's greatest warrior—the dead king's son.

Seth marveled at Vasilis's prowess as he cut down men with blinding speed, a speed that rivaled his sons and strength that nearly mirrored

Midas's. Their gifts rivaled any man he had faced, yet neither boy had reached their full potential.

Blood of the gods runs through our veins, aiding in our many victories. This will be the easiest one yet, Seth thought as the small army of one hundred men fell with ease.

Dull pain radiated through Seth's body. His vision soon blurred, and voices muffled. He looked down at the arrow piercing his side.

This wasn't his first time being shot by an arrow. He survived worse even as an infant—at least from the stories he was told, but this felt different. He looked up at the familiar man on his knees, holding a bow. Vasilis decapitated him as Seth blacked out.

"Seth, Seth," he heard someone call. He opened his eyes to Vasilis, helping him to his feet. "Elias is on his way," said Vasilis. "I'll take you to the healer."

"Make sure it's your mother," Seth said in a frail voice that mimicked the rest of his body. He struggled to keep his eyes open. He woke to the beautiful brown eyes of the woman his wife wanted him to marry. Her smooth, light brown skin glistened in the daylight.

"Kara," he said, seeing the surprised look on her face.

His vision came and went. Despite the threat of death fast approaching, it was still odd for him to see Spartiates laughing and drinking under the same tent with Helots and dwellers. This unification was the doing of the women he knew would soon save his life.

Kara, you are special, he thought as he lay at her mercy, watching her give orders.

"Midas, remove the chest plate and move him inside. Vasilis, fetch my tools. And you bite down on this," she said, placing a plank of wood inside his mouth.

As his vision blurred, Seth watched through a haze of agony as Kara took a tool to open the wound further. A gut-wrenching pain surged through him when she removed the poisonous metal, making him gag. She then stuffed the wound with a rag.

Seth eyed the plant fibers that she liked to use as threads. But to his horror, she reached for the fiery cauterizing rod instead. An unrelenting torrent of pain, akin to the fury of Hades, engulfed his body. He bit down on the wooden bite block with such force that it shattered, and the overwhelming pain soon ushered him into darkness.

Seth awoke moments later to the scent of Kara's herbs masking the smell of death and easing his pain. Midas stood next to his bed, signaling for Kara.

She stopped cleaning her tools and placed her hand on Midas's shoulder. "Go get Elias."

"Gratitude, my lady," Seth said, his voice barely a whisper.

"Don't thank me yet."

"Will he live?" Vasilis said from across the tent.

"This is unusual," Kara said, mixing her herbs. "I have to examine him further. That is not possible with an audience." His debilitating thought of failure made the pain in his ribs worse. Years of battles prepared him for this moment, death. Turning his head felt like moving a boulder with his neck. He looked at Vasilis, seeing the pain in his eyes.

"Sorry, kid, you should not have to go through this again."

"What are you talking about?" Vasilis said, his voice cracked. "She will heal you."

Seth felt his life slipping with each passing moment. Perhaps it was the poison playing tricks on his mind, but he knew the gods would favor Mother Sparta. He knew his battles, his sacrifices were worth the riches the gods would rain down on the greatest city in all of Greece. He searched Vasilis' eyes, seeing the man he watched grow into a fearsome warrior.

For a moment, Seth thought he was looking in the eyes of Vasilius. *His father did not deserve such a son,* he thought.

Seth grabbed Vasilis's chest plate, starring in the eyes of a true Spartan, no matter the blood that ran through his veins.

"Your mother can only comfort my transition, kid. This... this is life Vasilis, one the gods blessed me to have. I must ask you one thing. Look after your brothers and forgive them when you can. Now go."

Vasilis grabbed his helmet and exited.

Seth laid his head back and sighed, accepting his fate. He wasn't afraid. All he could think about was his son, and daughter—abandoning them. Death meant his daughter would wed without a father to guide her and forcing his son into the role of the head of the house. His wife, Vashti. Would she hate him? Would she bed another?

Seth breathed an agonizing sigh. He lived a warrior's life of both conquest, defense, and honor. Now, he would embrace a warrior's death. *May the gods open the gates,* he thought.

"It is the will of the gods," he said, his eyes closed. "My life is in their hands."

As Seth's words faded into the heavy air, he felt a subtle shift beside him. Turning slightly, he saw Kara leaning closer, her presence a silent yet forceful counterpoint to his resignation.

Kara leaned over and whispered to Seth. "No. It's in mine."

Seth looked at her. Her gaze, fierce with anger, fixed upon a green bottle.

"It's an odd feeling, I know, being trapped in your own body," said Kara. "Do you know how long I have waited for this moment?"

Seth's stomach turned. He tried but failed to lift his head.

"What... have you done?"

"Even after finding out what you did, the thought of killing you weighed on me."

How did she find out I killed him? Did she know he was a traitor?

"He was a brother to me," said Seth. "Understand... he forced my hand, Kara."

Goosebumps overtook his body. He coughed profusely until he tasted blood in his mouth.

"He trusted you, loved you with all his heart. He risked it all to protect you, to free you from the elders. And you could not show him the decency of killing him face to face. Instead, you shoved your blade into his back. For that, you are a coward."

Kara leaned in and whispered. "I was not a killer, Seth, but you pushed me."

"And now you can seize Sparta—" he coughed again. "I crowned my own killer... and I didn't see it coming... well played."

"The world turns around you, and still you play their games. Those shitty old elders placed Midas and Vasilis under your care for a reason; to undermine you—you are so ignorant."

"Well, they failed. They would never betray me..." The room spun, and his vision blurred, yet he saw things clearer than ever. "You've taken the power Sparta would have otherwise denied you. History never fails. One life must be lost for another to gain power, and you deserve it. You will fare well in the game for the throne. Kara, there's so much you don't know... I hope Vashti has mercy on you."

"What are you saying?"

"Next time I see you, I'll tell you. For now, know that I forgive you."

Kara paused—her eyes softened. "You looked after Vasilis. For this, I will have mercy." She cut his arm and wiped a purple herb into it. "You will regain enough strength to move your arm. Once the poison settles, the pain will be unbearable."

She placed a bottle of clear liquid next to him. "This will kill you almost instantly—without pain. It's up to you."

"Thank you for allowing me a warrior's death. At least in my men's eyes. For what it's worth… I've always loved you."

Kara froze for a moment. "None of that matters now, Seth," she said, exiting the tent.

Seth regained some of his motor functions. *I deserve a slow death, but I am a coward.* He grabbed the bottle and drank it.

The pain subsided, but his chest and throat tightened. He could hear commotion right outside the tent. "Vasilius, forgive me. Here I come."

His vision faded, but he saw bright, spiraling colors forcing his eyes closed. When he opened them, he was no longer in the tent—he wasn't in Sparta.

MALAYA

New Seattle, 2075

It was strange to think of HOA as her happy place. Like many who walked these halls as teens, she had grown up within its walls. Unlike some, she knew who her parents were. The school itself remained much the same—grand halls opening into sweeping staircases and expansive rooms that seemed frozen in time.

The walls were adorned with paintings and antique furniture. The air is thick with the scent of polish and old books. She always thought of it as a real X Mansion, without the X-Men. She wished she could be happier, but that stunt her mom pulled, missing her birthday, had her shaken.

If only Papi was here. She sighed just before arriving. *Sensei.*

"Concentrate," Sensei said. "You need to re-center. Don't fight the anger—channel it."

Malaya reacquainted herself with the wing-chung dummy. Her chest pounded through the black uniform with each rhythmic blow.

"You have not changed," he said. "You're trapped within the walls of your mind. Breathe. Allow the pain to drain from you through the tips of your fingers, releasing with each strike."

"Yes, Sensei," she said, absorbing his words like the dummy did her anger.

Convert anger into production.

Sensei lived by the code. His wife and daughter died in a fire.

A fire... tragic, she thought.

Though he never spoke of them, he often caressed their family picture. Sunlight from the glass ceiling bathed their memorial, a deliberate touch—Sensei's way. At eighty, he related to students effortlessly, his silver hair and beard the only hint of his age.

People called him Silver Wolf, and he was fond of the nickname, but not the idea of counting his age. He had a saying. "Nature determines my age, but I determine my own state of mind."

Of course, Sensei didn't know she knew his age, much like he didn't know she figured out one of the dummies held its combination to the safe room where he kept memories of former students.

"There you are," he said, closing his eyes, enjoying the rhythmic clunks.

With that, the wall in front of her opened, revealing a safe. The safe hissed open. Sensei and Malaya just stared at the contents inside, then at one another. She wondered if he would lie to her. If he would continue to hide things like her mother did, like Aaron did.

Sensei cleared his throat. "Oh... it's my personal safe." Her eyes moved to the energy rifle hanging on the wall. He continued. "That's

Jordan's. Would you believe he created it out of scrap parts? The boy is bright; yet at the same time, dumber than this... dummy."

She shook her head. "On school grounds."

"He reminds me of you."

"Hey, I wasn't *that* bad."

They shared a smile. "You did well," he said, tossing her a towel. "I remember the day your parents brought you here... to me. Your gifts—"

"I would not call severe HSAM a gift," Malaya said before wiping her face. Highly superior autobiographical memory was a gift for some, but for her, she did more than remember her life; she relived it.

His white brows softened like he wanted to say something, but his expression quickly changed. "Maybe you should come by more often."

"The lab keeps me busy, but I will do my best, I promise."

"I must clean," said Sensei. "If I see Jordan, I will tell him you are looking for him."

Malaya showered and put on her leggings and a flannel shirt, which she tied around her waist. She laced up her Chucks and grabbed her skateboard. Before she left, she took one last glance around and smiled, seeing the safe room sitting open with a broom next to the door and some boxes stacked on the outside.

Maybe I will come by more often, she thought to herself.

As Malaya stepped through the kwoon's back door into the HOA courtyard, the murmurs of a crowd filled the air. The courtyard, with its gardens, statues, and ponds, served both as decoration and a divider for the school's factions—a system of self-governance Headmistress Babcock endorsed. The stone-and-brick mansion, despite its age, boasted state-of-the-art technology, including high-tech security and an underground lab.

Scanning the crowd, she spotted Yuk Fat instead of Jordan. She slid onto the bench beside him, his hoodie pulsing with rap music. Without hesitation, she yanked it off, nearly dislodging his beanie.

"What the heck?" Jin said, brushing back the lone strand of black hair that brushed his sandy cheeks.

"Is that how you treat an old friend? Yuk."

"I'm not a kid anymore, and you know not to call me that..." He peeked over Malaya's shoulder and cursed to himself before pulling the hoodie back over his head. "It's Herman Burns and the Omega Princes."

"I see." Malaya leaned into Jin. "So, do the thing that you do, your *potential variance*."

Jin agreed. He couldn't help but show off. He hid behind his book and whispered as Herman approached. "Privileged, narcissist, aggressive, attention seeker who hid his loneliness behind his group affiliation. Traditionalist, a decisive planner, organized, true leader, as evidenced by his opting to walk beside his crew. He's very selective. Oh, he's going to stop here, but under no circumstances do you say anything!"

"Excuse me, Mr. Banana, did you say something?" Herman said, scratching his rust-colored hair.

"More like a bruised banana," a group member added. They erupted in laughter. "And look who he's with—"

"Shut up, this is Malaya Grant-Castillo," Herman said, his voice deepened. "Show some respect." He looked at Jin. "It appears you're lost. This is Omega Prince terrain, you UNA bitch."

Malaya got up. Jordan was one of his only few friends, and Kat was his senior mentor. Given his nationality, there weren't many volunteers. Jin shook his head. "I'm good," he said, sitting upright, snidely looking around. He leaned forward. "Looks like a recreational area to me."

Herman squinted his eyes and smirked. "This kid must not understand English." He narrowed his brows. "Let me say it in *Asian*," he said in a stereotypical Chinese accent. "Get out of here or get rocked—"

Jin tossed the book at Herman and jumped off the bench to kick another member.

Three OP members lunged at Jin. Malaya edged forward on the bench, torn between staying out of it or stepping in. She knew intervening could ruin him socially.

Jin met the first with a wild swing, clipping his shoulder more than landing a clean hit. The second came at him fast, throwing a sloppy right hook. Jin ducked too late, the punch grazing his temple, but he stumbled into a desperate kick that sent the attacker sprawling. A third rushed in, only to catch Jin's foot squarely in his chest—a strike more instinct than precision—that knocked him clean off his feet.

It was messy, chaotic, and anything but graceful. But Jin was still standing.

Malaya's jaw dropped. *There was no way he should have all that power. He's not the same kid.*

More OP members rushed to Herman's aid, readying to attack Jin. Jeers and cheers grew louder. Malaya jumped up. Her hands trembled. They were used to typing and texting, lifting an occasional box, but fighting... well, scientists didn't fight. She couldn't allow Jin to get jumped.

"Watch out!" Malaya warned, a bit too late. Jin was blindsided with a punch in the jaw.

"Help him," she whispered, doubt and anxiousness in her tone, watching Jin struggle. Even with his newfound strength, he couldn't win.

Malaya's clenched fist trembled, wanting to help. Though a large part of her knew she would do more harm than good.

Don't be a coward. With her jaws tightened—fueled by adrenaline, Malaya rushed to help her friend.

She grabbed a tall blond boy by the arm, stopping him from hitting Jin. "That was stupid," he said before his large fist slammed into her jaw. Distorted jeers accompanied pain as she stumbled backwards into the arms of an onlooker.

Fighting the dizziness, with the help of a stranger, she stood upright. She shook off the cobwebs seeing Herman on the ground. A few of his lackeys tried to help him up. Her distraction helped, Jin took the upper hand.

A smile threatened to cross her face, but her jaw hurt too much.

Herman's face reddened. He pressed buttons on his metallic wristband. A holographic file with Jin's bio appeared. "For violation of Code 372, you're getting tagged."

A red light scanned Jin. More of his lackey's flooded the courtyard. So many boys that Herman himself was washed into his crew of minions. Smartly, Jin tried to back away but stumbled on a garden structure falling on his back.

No one bothered to help. Most of them cared more about their social status and recording than lending a helping hand. He curled into the fetal position. Malaya fought through the crowd, and lay on top of him, absorbing the painful boots stomping her body. She held him nevertheless, crying in agony.

Suddenly, a voice, sweet as honey sliced through the chaos, capturing everyone's attention. "Malaya Grant?"

Omega Prince members let up, but the pain did not subside. Though Malaya struggled to rise off the ground. She rolled off of Jin, her hazy gaze lingered on the sky.

"Malaya!" Jin said, his voice fragile. His concern betrayed his youth.

"I'm okay."

I recognize that voice anywhere, Malaya thought.

Abigail Kenda.

Jin helped her up, whipping the dirt from her face. The guilt on his face was apparent. The crowd parted for the petite member of The Orthodox—one of the senior factions. This team consisted of ragtag tech runners and *outcasts*.

Legend has it, they were the only faction that dared challenge *the Few*, a supposed mythological faction that ran the school from the shadows. Abigail hadn't changed. She still wore heavy dark makeup around her eyes and red lipstick.

"Still finding your way into trouble," said Abigail.

"Just looking out for a friend," Malaya grinned.

"Are you alright? That was brutal."

"I'll be fine. It's not my first beat down."

"Stay out of this, Kenda," Herman pleaded. "I'm a senior prefect, too—besides, Jin is not part of your faction."

"As prefects, we keep order," said Abigail. "You're disrupting that, so you see, Herman, we have everything to do with this."

Her iris glowed iced green. It spiraled mechanically around her pupils, and blood oozed from her tear ducts. Herman's scanner malfunctioned, and his wristband short-circuited—he ripped it off. The crowd gasped, taking a step back as it hit the floor.

Malaya joined the crowd, watching with wide eyes. The Orthodox were the most elite hacking faction HOA, but this was next level even for them. "So, advance. When did this happen?"

"They upgraded," said Jin.

They? Malaya questioned, realizing Abigail's brothers were lurking within the crowd.

Herman fumed as he picked up his scanner. "We will finish this... Omega's out."

The crowd disbursed, and Abigail walked between Malaya and Jin. "You see Yuk Fat, no need to fight. There are more ways to skin an Omega. My offer still stands. Join us."

"It's Jin, and no, thanks." He walked over and picked up his book. "I'll tell Jordan you're here."

"Welcome back," said Abigail. They embraced. "How's Ms. C?"

Abigail's question forced her feelings to resurface. *Oh, she's distant, preoccupied, and unwilling to make things bette*r. "We're great."

"Jordan's here," Abigail said. She stopped before they parted. "Don't be a ghost, Malaya."

Malaya nodded and turned to see Headmistress Babcock escorting Jordan with her familiar firm grip on the sleeve of his hooded jacket.

"Malaya Castillo-Grant, are you responsible for this?" she released Jordan, pointing at the hoverboard, holding up a laser rifle in the other hand.

The board was a gift for his thirteenth birthday, or at least the assigned day of his birth given to him after being dropped on HOA's doorstep. The Headmistress rarely bent the rules, but today she allowed her to take Jordan off-campus. It was Christmas, after all.

"Headmistress, long time no see."

"Answer my question?" the Headmistress demanded.

"I didn't rat," said Jordan. "I tried to tell her I built it, but you see where it got me," Jordan shrugged. His lone dimple showed as he smiled.

"Yes and no. The rifle is for MEV's young engineer project. I have a safe code—"

"Of course," Babcock said in a harmonious tone that never changed. "You've been a constant in his life for as long as I can remember, and it is showing."

"Whatever he damaged, I'll cover it, I promise."

She straightened her blue lapel jacket and smiled. "Money will not suffice. Consider a return. Under your mentorship, the gifted students would thrive—Jordan sure has."

Malaya paused, taken aback by the offer. "I'll do my best to come by more often."

"Fair enough." The Headmistress smiled. "Don't forget about curfew. We have the gift exchange and Christmas pageant," she said before walking away.

"Yes, ma'am," Malaya replied before they exited HOA.

"Thanks for bailing me out, again," said Jordan.

"Please, your mischief pales in comparison to yours truly."

"Even after all these years, your reputation precedes you. Oh, speaking of mischief... I gave this bad boy an upgrade," he said, showing off the thrusters he added to the hoverboard.

He placed it on the ground and whipped out a controller. Plasma sputtered from the thrusters until it hovered with power.

"I'm impressed," Malaya said. "So, is that why you were MIA?"

"Yea, that and working on the photon rifle," he said, bringing the board down.

"Wow," Malaya said. "What's gotten into you? I knew you were smart, but you're—"

"One of *them*," he smirked.

Malaya rolled her eyes.

"Still don't believe, huh?" Jordan said, shaking his head.

"Nope. Evolution stops with us. There isn't some genetic mutation that makes anyone different, so these *Darviants* are nothing more than a myth. People like Lilly, Luke, and even Abigail are scientific marvels with explanatory abilities like a genetically superior athlete, predisposed to be sis foot eight."

"Wow, you really do have an explanation for everything."

"I don't limit myself to the divine. Neither should you." Malaya nudged him.

A black-tented suburban stopped in front of them. The doors opened to two masked men dressed in black.

"Jordan, run!" she yelled before the BolaWRAP gun fired a shot. It curved and wrapped around her legs. She crashed to the concrete, cursing as the men pulled a sack over her head and carried her into the black suburban.

JOSE CASTILLO

Coast of New Seattle, 2076

Stillness pinned Jose Castillo to his lone spot at the head of the table. He had spoken in front of millions, but this felt different—it *was* different. Decades of life experiences taught him that life could change in a blink of an eye, but this, this was...well, different. It was evident when he got the call from Bradley about how Malaya was dragged in. This wasn't the way he wanted to spend his granddaughter's birthday weekend, yet here they were.

Glowing haptic red gel colored the flustered faces of everyone in the room. The Cabinet flew from Washington to New Seattle at the behest of the news Jose dropped on them. His revelation about time travel silenced the room. Most eyes wandered away from him toward Malaya and Shay, who, unlike President Ross, sat composed. President

Ross rubbed between his blue eyes. "Continue," he said, placing his glasses back on his face.

"Nothing is flat, not even this surface," Malaya said, meticulously sliding her hand across the table. "If you look close enough, you'll find imperfections, holes, tiny crevasses on a scale smaller than atoms, otherwise referred to as the fourth dimension."

Malaya put on a glove that allowed her to control the red gel. "If you look deep enough, you'll see that wormholes are all around us. Antimatter gives us enough power to expand the wormhole, but any passing matter adds positive energy—destabilizing the wormhole. Negative radiation, however, dampens the positive energy.

"Thus, a wormhole makes time travel plausible, but instability makes it disastrous." She slammed her hands together, crushing the display. "However, with exotic matter and a healthy dose of negative radiation, singularity stabilization and human transportation became possible."

"I just have one simple question," Vice President Tara Potter said, raising her hand. "Why?"

"To introduce the world to a new form of military training," said Minister of Defense General Bradley Williams. His voice carried a smooth Southern drawl throughout the room, commanding their attention. He straightened his firmly pressed navy-blue jacket and removed his five-star insignia hat.

"We designed the Spartan Program as a means to protect our borders. Imagine each of the six sectors with its own private force. A group of Spartan-trained operatives."

Calling everyone's attention was Secretary of Energy Nawat Hodges. An older gentleman with a suit that was a little too big for him with an even bigger red bowtie. "Another private force? I'm sure there were less barbaric uses for it, like archaeology or anthropology perhaps."

"All of it," said Jose, seeing the insulted look on Bradley's face.

Nawat removed his glasses, cleaning them with his handkerchief. "While fascinating, there are serious consequences when playing god, time fluxes and paradoxes, paradigm shifts..."

"We've taken extreme precautionary measures with the recommencing of the Damage Control Center headed by Emily Benoist."

The room turned their attention to the twenty-two-year-old with hazel bangs, mindlessly thumbing through her tablet. Malaya cleared her throat. "Emily," she mumbled under her breath.

"Oh, sorry," said Emily. She pushed her glasses onto her rosy face and began her presentation. "The DCC was established before the first jump to monitor, minimize, and prevent paradoxes. However, time has its own rules. For example, a jumper cannot murder baby Hitler hoping to stop the Holocaust. We call it the Hitler Paradox.

"If you pull the trigger, that moment will repeat itself, creating an endless loop, or the firearm will not fire. Simply put, something would always happen. The *Mirror Paradox* is another self-established law which prohibits a jumper from traveling to a period where they currently exist."

"What about parallel dimensions?" questioned Hodges. "Wouldn't time branch off?"

"There's still no evidence," said Emily

As Emily continued, Jose's mind drifted to a resting notion of his daughter being in danger. *Lilith, kidnapped? Forced to work?*

The visceral thought made no sense. Neither did the idea that the UNA was involved. The precision, the risk level of an operation like this needed someone on the inside... Swaddling the worry, was the possibility of something far more sinister.

Could Lilith be involved? Only she could pull this off.

The mere thought sent a shock wave of dread through him. His parental side urged him to stay quiet, but he had a duty to these people, to this country—to the world. He had to say something.

Hodges's voice brought him back. "Could a jumper travel to the future?"

"Outside of Einstein's theory of relativity. No, only backward through time," said Emily. "The limits have not been tested until now. What this individual did was unprecedented, even for a *Ghost Jump*."

"Ghost Jump?" Hodge questioned.

"I'll take it from here, Emily. Thank you." Shay stood, her deep brown skin contrasting against the black of her lapel dress; its golden buttons glimmered like her eyes, reflecting the lights of the conference room.

"A Ghost Jump transports a jumper's physical body into the quantum realm. However, to those on the other side, they appear transparent despite them keeping their physical form, hence the term ghost. The benefit allows the jumper to move transversely on a quantum plane. The negative, at least from an explorer's perspective, is the inability to touch anything."

"Like an astral projection," Hodge said, leaning forward as if it were just him and Shay in the room. "Could you do more if you wanted to? Could you be there physically?"

"There was only one attempt at a physical jump," Shay continued. "My brother, Jeffery Grant. There were some complications, to say the least, but it worked."

Hodge and Shay continued as Jose drifted into thought, unable to shake the uneasy feeling he had about all of this. He's seen heists on the grandest scales—he was even part of a few. Stealing something of this magnitude was impressive, with dangers far greater than anyone could have imagined, even if it were in the hands of his own daughter, especially his daughter—he needed to find her.

What if she has nothing to do with this? But why would she have a fictitious company? Jose thought, recalling the report he received from the Raging Bull raid on the old nuclear site. *It had taken longer than expected to get a full report. After all, they did several sweeps. It was empty. You saw that for yourself.*

Speaker of the House, Arlen Reyes, was new on board. It showed in her pale face, wide-eyed expression, and loose tie, as if it weren't sixty-five degrees in the room. She raised her hand. "What does this mean for the leaders of the North and South American Alliance? Will they be informed?"

"No," said President Ross. "And the same goes for the governors of the sectors. This stays between the people in this room."

"Understood, sir, but the treaty requires transparency, especially to Canada and Mexico—"

"I'm well aware of the treaty, Arlen," President Ross interrupted. "But we can't risk the UNA finding out or cause an unnecessary uproar."

"If the UNA gets involved, we'd be up shit creek," Bradley said. His tone was condescending and laced with sarcasm—Jose knew why. "Who knows? Maybe they've taken Lilith and the others. But what can we do without disrupting diplomacy? God knows we don't want to pick a fight with the Alliance."

Bradley's eyes locked on him. Jose smirked before taking a drink of his cold coffee. It was a jab he'd heard for decades since the day he signed the treaty. Bradley never let it go. He would have never signed the treaty, not just because of Red, or the Alpha Kings, but because he hated the UNA—Jose did too.

Millions of lives were lost during the trying time, including his wife. If they had taken Lilith, there wasn't a line he wouldn't cross—Bradley knew that.

Jose's eyes wandered into the red gel. His mind flowed to a time when his skin was more elastic, where things were less complicated between them. A time when he wasn't as confident about where he was going after years of hiding in the shadows, but Bradley was. It was a day he'd never forget—the day he had to lose control to take what he needed in order to change the world.

***

The helicopter ruffled the thin tie of his tailored suit. A young man, Tom, sat next to him, admiring the bright oceanic view. "I must admit, an offshore platform is genius."

Tom pressed a button on the headset. "Mr. Williams, I thank you for hedging your bets with me. I'm sure I will make the Oval Office."

"Call me Bradley!" He shouted from the pilot's chair. "Jose and I are just Red's wingmen. That kid you met down there, Ammo, well, he's the real deal, with real potential, but not as much as you, Tom. I'm sure you will aid the private force sector."

Jose felt Bradley look at him. He knew what was about to happen before Bradley spoke the words. "It's now or never," said Bradley.

Tom looked at Jose; his heart raced, wondering if Tom could see his trembling hand. "Are you okay?" Tom questioned.

"The tail rotors actin' up," Bradley shouted.

The chopper wobbled; Jose's seat belt tightened. "Brad, stop playing. This is not the time!"

"Is everything alright?" Tom's voice trembled, fear evident on his face as he clutched the seat. Unbeknownst to him, his fear was more justified than he could imagine.

"Now, Jay!" Bradley shouted.

The helicopter spiraled, and everything went mute. There was no fear of the impending crash, but the death of who he was. Everything Angela had grown to love, what he stood for, the example he hoped Lilith could follow, was going to die, one way or another.

He stared at his watch for as long as he dared, but he knew not to call Bradley's bluff. Jose knew what had to happen, what he had to become. He pressed a button on his watch and activated a blade. He swung his arm, slicing Tom's throat.

"It's done!" he said, not caring to cover his face from the squirting blood.

The chopper leveled; Tom slumped over; this wasn't the first, but it was different. He was innocent, not an enemy. Jose stared at his bloody hands, the same hands he once tucked Lilith in with.

"Autopilot," Bradley said, walking over to Jose. "It's done. It's over."

Bradley grabbed Jose's hands, taking Tom's blood, wiping it on himself. "We're in this together now," he said with a faint smile. "You will become president one day. Together, we will fix this world."

***

A nudge from Bradley pulled him back. "Take this," he said, shaking a flask underneath the table. "It fights off old demons."

Jose took it. *I'm a father first, and I won't let her down again, at least not without a thorough investigation—it's the least I can do.*

"What now?" said Randal Mayor. "You have a world-renowned physicist who is also the head of the world's leading energy company, missing, along with dozens of scientists."

"Cell Agents were activated to track down Lilith and Joseph," Bradley said, directing his eyes to Malaya and Shay.

"What about the other missing scientists?" Mayor added. "I guess we're going to push them aside."

Malaya sprang to her feet. "Of course not. Their lives are no less important."

"Yet their names were glossed over." Mayor fired back.

"That's enough, you two!" President Ross shouted. "We have to work as a unit. While your concerns are valid, Lilith and Joseph are high-priority—it's that simple. Now, we must focus on what's next. Open the files in front of you."

Each member of the Cabinet placed their palm on the table, unsealing their digital files. It wasn't enough to know who the jumper was. They needed to know where and when. Tracking them was key. That was the job of the Damage Control Center.

"There's always a residue of radiation," said Emily. "With the help of the Lucy Program, the DCC narrowed the whereabouts of the jumper's last location."

Emily activated the program. The gel took the shape of a woman's face.

"Welcome," the AI said in her soft, robotic voice.

"Lucy's an interactive AI, designed to monitor a jumper and decipher time fluxes or changes made by an unnatural source," said Emily. "She can also transform into any three-dimensional topographical map in history. Lucy, show us fifth-century Sparta."

"As you wish," replied Lucy, transforming the entire table into a display of Laconia.

Jose cleared his throat. "The next step is to prepare a team of operatives for a reconnaissance mission."

"The medallions are laced with ghost radiation and serve multiple purposes," Malaya said. "One primary function is the opening and containing a wormhole large enough for multiple people to travel.

"Unfortunately, the further you jump, the more energy you use. Even with MEVs nuclear fusion, that amount of energy takes time and programming. It will take weeks to learn."

"We don't have weeks," said President Ross. "We need to apprehend the suspect immediately. General, is there an agent qualified for this mission?"

"Yes." Williams paused. "Ms. Castillo."

Jose stood up. "That's not happening."

"He's right," Malaya said. "Basic military training does not mean I'm capable of survival in a foreign land. I—"

"We are talking about the fate of humanity, sweetheart," said Bradley. "Mr. President, if I may?"

With the president's nod, he continued. "I assure you, we cannot afford to send my men. Need I remind you all that there are no scientists with Ms. Castillo-Grant's capabilities and knowledge? This is her family project, and she is, after all, a former track star and child physicist—this isn't a combat mission, people. It's taking notes, something she's done all her life.

Look, even with the neuro link, they'll be at an extraordinary disadvantage, and again—it requires time, Mr. President. Time is something we simply do not have—no pun intended, sir."

"For those reasons, I hate to risk it," said the president. "But..."

There was a pregnant pause as he swept his gaze across it, his eyes reflecting a blend of apprehension and resolve. They lingered on each family member before finally settling on Malaya. Jose knew, at that moment, he had his mind made up.

The president sighed. "Humanity is at risk. Who better than you to keep the timeline intact? A Special Intelligence Agent will accompany her. We will pair her with the SIA's finest, Agent Mamba. From what I hear, he's a chameleon capable of blending in like no other…"

Jose's eyes glanced at his old friend. *Williams knows more than he's letting on,* he thought. *I'm sure he's made moves in the shadows. Sending his guy—a real killer. I need to find out more information.*

He rubbed his face, unable to wipe away the frustration. His eyes found his granddaughter. She wanted him to disagree, but he couldn't.

"Okay," Jose said.

"We'll arrange a meeting between you two," said Bradley. "We can assign an agent to neuro link with for extensive environmental training."

"No," Malaya said. "I prefer good old-fashioned field training."

"I'll make sure you are trained by the elite," said Bradley. "Captain Austin Winters."

"I'll send for him immediately," said President Ross.

Mayor raised his hand. "Now that we have a plan in place, this *jumper* can be anywhere, doing anything to the timeline. How would we know what's changed?"

"Inside the white box, you'll find the Cowan Shield," said Emily. "It's a chip that uses special technology to remove our consciousness from the space-time continuum, thus making us immune to paradigm shifts. Simply put, we'll remember things as they were."

A warning from an agent trying to enter the meeting room forced Emily to shut down Lucy. The AI lowered in favor of a plain table before allowing their guests in.

"Mr. President, there was an attack on the UNA," the incoming agent said.

Ross frantically leaped to his feet. "Stan, display live news feed," he commanded the AI.

Smoke and flames covered the background of the reporter on TV. *"Jennifer King reporting live—"*

A hooded all-white faceless mask interrupted the news feed. The image fluttered back and forth, and the word Ghost appeared on the screen. A distorted voice stuttered as the signal faded. *"Your reign of terror will end. Release her!"*

The words changed to *Lilith Castillo.* *"Free her, or we will find you. We will never stop. We will never die. We are ideal. We are change. We are Ghost."*

The ghost face mask appeared once more before an advisory warning.

A second later, live footage of the UNA's Headquarters being leveled appeared. The room erupted with questions about Ghost and what it would mean for the US if what everyone feared was true. *Someone in the UNA forced Lilith to steal the device, and now their emperor was dead. Maybe I should reach out to Red unless Bradley already did—*

"Papa." Malaya shook him. "We have to find mom."

MALAYA

Coast of New Seattle, 2076

Malaya sprang to her feet. The panic of being late to her first day of training. There was no time for a shower, so she settled for brushing her teeth and rinsing with mouthwash and bolted out of her room, clad in her boots and tank top. Excitement and dread filled her simultaneously. She was one day closer to time traveling.

As she entered the chrome-lined corridor, the noise level increased dramatically. The sound of dozens of agents filled the air, their voices echoing off the reinforced steel walls. Displays, warning lights, and blinking screens dotted the walls, adding to the chaotic atmosphere. The scent of alcohol hung heavy in the air.

She huffed and rolled her eyes, swept her hair back behind her ears. *One more meeting, then training*, she thought, making a beeline for her grandfather's command center. She was running late to see him, which would push her training back. Despite how vague he was with his message, she couldn't shake the feeling of uncertainty over what he wanted to talk about.

The last two weeks had been hectic, to say the least. Meetings stacked atop one another with Malaya spending a lot of time with Emily and the Damage Control Center, strategizing preventative measures and potential paradoxes. With the collaborative efforts of Lucy, the sophisticated AI designed to monitor time, and so much more. She was a queen bee of AI, orchestrating a hive of subordinate worker bee AIs, each assigned to specific tasks.

Malaya indulged in discovering and learning new and vital information for safeguarding time. Yet, the stimulating process and critical nature of her work couldn't stop Malaya's mind from wandering about her grandfather. She had not seen him since the day the emperor died.

Even then, he was distant. Each passing day intensified the nagging feeling of wanting to know what her grandfather was up to.

As she walked, she passed by a group of SIA operatives arguing and caught a glimpse of Bryce Bennett. He turned his broad shoulders and quickly walked away, avoiding her eyes. Bennett was one of the last people to see her mother before she went missing, and Malaya wanted to stop him and find out what he knew. But she held back, knowing that interfering in the investigation could only make things worse.

Please be alright, Mom. Chills covered her back. A month had passed since the bombing, yet she still hadn't contacted anyone. And no one contacted them, not even for a ransom. Malaya shook her head, trying to wash away any negative thoughts.

Part of her longed for Aaron. Not just the comfort of his embrace, but his words of wisdom. It was because of him she reconnected with a place she once called home, HOA. He was always there for her, but there were times when he'd disappear, like now.

She had not heard from him in weeks, now that she was thousands of feet underground, they wouldn't have any contact for who knows how long. She pushed the thought to the back of her mind. Her mother was missing, and she was thinking about her boyfriend.

Maybe Ghost saved her after all. Ghost. Who are they, and what kind of name is that?

"Look, Commander Diya, it's your favorite Barbie," an agent shouted, elbowing James.

"Yeah, and I'm her Ken," James said, causing hysteria.

Ignore it. It's not worth it, not with everything else going on.

"How do you like your steak, sir?" another soldier shouted.

"Brandon, must you always be a chauvinistic bottom feeder?" Esther said, flicking her comrade in the ear. "Don't let him bait you," she warned Malaya.

James grabbed Jacob by the shoulder. "Relax, Lieutenant Commander Berkovich. Jacobs is just having a little fun. Isn't that right?"

"Yes, sir!" Jacobs said.

"Idiots," Esther said, rubbing her forehead. Her brown ponytail couldn't hide her pinked cheeks.

"To answer your question, Lieutenant Jacobs, I like my meat thick," James said, stalking Malaya, too close for comfort.

Enough is enough, Malaya thought. "It's a shame you're into *thick meat*, James. Here I am thinking you were a man's man."

James smirked. "Didn't you have your legs wrapped around my neck during training?"

With a confused expression, Esther places her hand on her jaw. "I remember you begging her to stop."

Malaya continued down the hall. "Oh, I almost forgot." She stopped and dug into her pocket, tossing two stress balls to James. "Here, I took these... your balls."

Laughter erupted.

"I can have you reprimanded for not saluting a commanding officer!"

"Oh yeah, that's right. Go cry to my grandfather—good luck with that."

Malaya boarded the lift, leaving behind the laughter for the electric hum and AI escort she commanded.

Lights from the passing floors brushed against her face. *What could he want that he needed to meet in secret?*

"Arrived, floor five. Have a great day," said the AI.

Her grandfather stood with Kat and her burly black pit bull, Sniper. Three teenagers stood with their hands clasped behind their backs—she recognized two of them, Arya and Emma, her cousins.

So they're training under Kat, she thought, observing the twins attempting to conceal their smiles. Malaya felt the urge to hug them and tell them how proud of them she was. *There would be time for that later.*

At times, it felt strange to have so many family members gathered in such a secretive location. However, Malaya's family was anything but ordinary; a blend of military and scientific backgrounds ran deep within their lineage. Despite her familiarity with their backgrounds, Malaya couldn't help but feel a sense of awe at what her grandfather had accomplished with the SUV and how it had transformed their family dynamic.

As Kat dismissed the group, Malaya's grandfather turned to Malaya and Kat. "I'll give you two some time."

Malaya kneeled next to Sniper. With the okay from Kat, Sniper barked, and his tail wagged as he rubbed against Malaya.

"I'm guessing those were the Elite Eight recruits?"

"Yup, the best HOA has to offer."

"How are Emma and Arya?"

"Kickass," said Kat. "Wouldn't be surprised if they're in the field soon, but the twins aren't the only ones. There are some other kids: Bryan, Aliyah Dean, Alice and Jayden. They're special."

"What about Yuk Fat and Jordan Snow? I imagine they were on the list."

"Yuk's parents wouldn't allow it, and Jordan, well, he simply declined."

"Wow, I can't believe Jordan turned down a chance to be next to you," Malaya teased.

Kat shrugged. "His loss."

Malaya raised a brow, and they both laughed.

Jose cleared his throat. "Agent Bennett. I need my granddaughter now."

Kat nodded. "We'll catch up later." She made her way to the lift.

Her grandfather paced in silence, uncharacteristically for him. *Given everything that's happened, he had a right to be nervous. C'mon Malaya.* She thought, walking over to a vending machine for a canned Malta. *His daughter was missing, someone was time traveling, the UNA emperor was dead, and the US was getting blamed.*

It was quiet enough to hear the faint droning from the hydro turbine, and the sound of her slurping was driving her crazy. She needed to ask. "Papa, what's going on?"

"We have to wait for your aunt."

"Well, you're making me nervous."

"Sorry, *mija*," he said, stopping his nervous pace.

"Where is Aunt Shay, anyway?"

"On her way. She seems rejuvenated since leaving the Cabinet and taking back command of the DCC."

"At least she has something to keep her distracted." Malaya sighed. "With Joseph and mom missing... I really hope they are okay."

"I'm sure they are."

"Have you heard something?" Malaya asked.

"Let's just wait for Shay."

Nothing about his expression said it was good news. Now she was pacing. The AI broke the silence. *"Arrived, floor five. Have a great day."*

Malaya sighed in relief as Shay walked in with a smile that reminded Malaya of her father. So did her large brown eyes and rich, deep brown skin. After her father died, Malaya couldn't stand to be around her aunt. She reminded her too much of him. Luckily, Shay spent much of her time in Washington, DC, until recent events.

"What did I walk in on?" Shay asked with an arched brow.

"Gramps has some news about the missing."

"Oh?"

Jose placed his hand on the scanner, opening the door to his room. "I think you two should sit."

"I'm jealous," Shay said as they sat down on the small concave sofa.

He walked to the minibar and poured himself Scotch. He took a drink before offering Shay a glass.

Shay shook her head no. "Jose, you're scaring us."

Jose took another drink. "Lilith, Joseph, Sheldon, and the dozens of other missing people, scientists, are all connected."

"Papa, please spare us the suspense," Malaya said.

"I think they may have orchestrated the entire thing."

"*They?*" Shay asked, not letting his words sink in. "As in my husband opting to leave his family and work with who... *Lilith?*" She laughed. "Have you met Joseph?"

Malaya sprang to her feet. "Are you serious? After what happened to my dad, you really think she'd risk her life, tarnish his legacy, *our* legacy?"

"Bradley wanted to jump-start the Spartan Training Program for some time," Shay added. "How do we know it isn't him?"

"C'mon, Shay," said Jose. "Bradley won't risk his political future. He's next up..."

Malaya's disdain was palpable. Her hands trembled, the telltale sign of an impending episode. "You're saying your daughter, a physicist, was responsible for a theft, kidnapping, and murder?"

The tremors worsened, and a vivid memory invaded her mind—her mother's fear-stricken face in a cabin, a young man with tribal tattoos chanting beside the roaring fireplace. Despite knowing it was only a dream, she felt powerless to shake it off. She heard her grandfather's frantic voice calling for her medicine, but she couldn't reach it.

Her aunt's steady hand placed a patch on her tongue, and her aunt's gentle touch on her cheek brought her back to reality. "There we go... relax."

Malaya let out a sigh of relief as the shaking subsided, and the dream became a distant memory. She knew that she would eventually pour it into her art diary, a cherished gift from her mother meant to soothe her mind. It had been a while since she experienced dream-induced convulsions, and even longer since she picked up a pen to create something that wasn't a complex equation. However, with everything going on, she realized she had neglected her medication, and she vowed to not let that happen again.

Jose took a seat. "I know it's hard to believe, but I know your mother, the power she has, and what destroying the UNA means to her. No, I can't explain why Joseph would keep this from you, but—"

"You're reaching," Shay said. "If this was revenge, why not shut down the reactors?"

"I'm not sure."

"How do you explain time traveling to Sparta?"

"I don't know."

"I'm working to get more answers, but Lilith is one of the world's most well-connected people. Rose and Nate Albright are known associates of Lilith's, who launched Bright Prosthetics in China just over a year ago. Even if Lilith isn't traveling, she is pulling some powerful strings, and with Kosimoto's death last month, who knows what's next?"

Shay raised an eyebrow. "How do you know all of this?"

"Forget that." Malaya jumped up. "How long have you been following her?"

"That's not important."

Malaya rubbed her forehead. "I can't believe you. You two haven't spoken in what? Two years yet, you do this."

Jose stood up. "I have to inform the Cabinet of my suspicion."

"You can't be serious."

"They'll crucify her," said Shay. "We would be implicated as well."

"I am, and they won't," Jose said. "Getting ahead of this will help her cause. They'll understand."

Malaya's wristband beeped. *Incoming message from President Ross.* Malaya answered the hologram. "Yes, Mr. President?"

"There's someone I'd like you to meet. Your grandfather will fill in on your way to the Command Bridge."

"Yes, Mr. President."

Malaya left her grandfather, feeling her blood boil and her stomach turning at his accusations. She waited inside the command room, staring out the large window overlooking the deep-sea life of the Pacific.

Mom, a criminal. Lilith was a lot of things to her, distant at times, secretive, workaholic, philanthropist, her hero. *Risking her company, her family's safety for what? More power?*

A nagging sensation tugged at the back of her mind, a whisper of doubt suggesting there was something she was missing, or perhaps misremembering, or forgetting?

Impossible, I don't forget? she mentally protested, her confidence in her own memory clashing with the unsettling possibility of its frailness.

Could her mind have been altered? The idea flickered like a conspiracy theory, tempting yet implausible. Malaya struggled to rationalize it, bringing on a migraine.

The door beeped open. President Ross walked in with the man who would train her these next few weeks. He was well-built for his age, though not surprising considering how her grandfather gushed over the former Navy seal.

"I'd like to officially introduce Captain Austin Winters," said President Ross.

Malaya shook Captain Winters's hand, which was rugged, like his weathered face and bald head. His piercing blue eyes and stern expression were intense but offset by a blond goatee. The door beeped again, and her grandfather walked in. She turned her back.

"The legendary Captain Austin Winters, the way you saved those children... I'm a fan," Jose said. "I also heard stories of your sea battles pale in comparison to your combat skills."

"Thank you, sir. Glad I could help train a young soldier."

"If you're ready, we can begin training now," Austin said. "Time is of the essence, Captain."

Malaya nodded, and the two left.

The aquatic scenery divided the long corridors, and made the awkward silence on the way less intense, her mind drifting back to her mother.

"Agent Castillo," Captain Winters broke the silence. "Whatever's distracting you, let it go or use it as motivation. I'm not sure where you're going, but I am sure that they won't give a shit. You can't afford distractions."

"Yes, sir," she said, though she couldn't help but think it was easy for him to say when he wasn't ignorant of the world around him, she was.

They soon arrived at the entrance to the *Chrono-Simulation* chamber. Captain Winters scanned his badge, and the door opened with a quiet beep. "Okay, Malaya, leave your distractions at the door," he said, motioning for her to follow him inside.

The door closed behind them, and Malaya gasped in amazement at what she saw. They stood atop a mountain. The sun blazed high overhead; its warm rays bathed the busy city below. Vendors filled the bustling street, and the ring of the blacksmith's hammer echoed through the air. Towering stone and marble buildings cast long shadows over the city, and the sea sparkled in the distance.

"Where are we?" Captain Winters questioned, sharing her amazement.

"Ancient Laconia," Malaya replied.

There was a brief moment of silence. Winters cleared his throat and turned to Malaya. "Let's get to work."

After training, she could barely walk. The floor vibrated slightly beneath her wobbly legs, the hum of the engines filling her ears and making her headache worse. Her throbbing muscles felt like the first day of track practice, maybe worse, like the first day she trained with Sensei. Training with a dummy was one thing. What Winters put her through was death, then survival and reconnaissance courses on her off days.

She couldn't land a hit on Winters, and he made sure she paid for it, slamming her to the ground over and over. She hoped he'd forgive her for vomiting on him, though part of her felt a bit of satisfaction since it ended training early.

Sending me instead of an agent. I'm going to wreck him the next time I see him.

"Ms. Castillo-Grant!" The sound of General Williams' shouting stopped Malaya before she boarded the lift.

Be respectful, she reminded herself, as if she'd ever disrespect the Secretary of Defense. She turned with a smile on her face. "General Williams, nice to see you," she said, trying to hide the pain.

"A head-butt isn't pleasant, but it'll get the job done," Captain Winters had told her.

She exhaled before turning around with a clenched-teeth smile. She was still annoyed that Williams volunteered her for this operation, though she understood the logic behind the decision.

"I hear your training with Winters is going well," he said. "I hope you aren't distracted."

"My focus is my mission, sir..." Malaya's eyes gravitated toward a soldier in a black combat uniform approaching. His dreadlocks sprung from the black metallic helmet. Though his identity was concealed, there was something familiar about him.

General Williams looked back. "This here is Agent Mamba," he said, meeting the agent halfway. "Agent Mamba, meet Malaya. You two will partner up on this recon mission."

Silence followed a queasy feeling. "Take it off."

"Excuse me?" questioned General Williams.

"Tell him to remove his helmet. Sir. I need to know who I'm working with."

She could hear the latches unbuckle, unable to tell if he was moving in slow motion or if it was the gravity of the moment.

Just like that, it was over.

Aaron, she thought, feeling a punch in the stomach of betrayal. Yet there was a sense of relief that she finally knew what his true occupation was.

"I'm sorry," he mouthed before extending his gloved hand.

"It's a pleasure to meet you, Agent Castillo-Grant." It took everything to keep the fire inside from spewing out of her mouth, accepting his gesture.

"Let's hurry up... We're late to the briefing," said General Williams, walking around her to board the lift.

"Quantum Room," said General Williams.

Malaya and Aaron stood behind General Williams. She did her best to ignore his pleading eyes. *How long was he working with them? Did he know mom was missing?*

Chills shot down her back as she entered the Quantum Room, feeling the deep hum of the turbine, and seeing the ring for the first time. Its spherical door hatch sat at the apex of a ramp—closed, waiting for her to be opened. Supercomputers formed an outer layer around the interactive topographic map, a more advanced version of Lucy.

Agents of the Damage Control Center gathered around Emily and Shay, briefing the Cabinet on the journey ahead. General Williams led them down the stairs, introducing Aaron to everyone. She avoided her grandfather, looking at her from the corner of his eye.

"Are you not looking forward to this historically marvelous adventure?" Natwat said, placing his hand on her shoulder. "Greece, home to some of the greatest minds, and it doesn't hurt you'll have some eye candy near your side.

"*Eye candy*," Malaya scoffed. "More like a lying piece of—"

"Woah," Natwat interrupted. "Did I miss something?"

Malaya brought her voice to a whisper. "Remember the *boyfriend* I was telling you about?"

"No!" Natwat peaked behind Malaya. "You and he are... When did you find out he was your traveling companion?"

"Today," Malaya sighed. "I wanted to wreck him, but his news wasn't the only punch in the gut."

Natwat pointed behind Malaya with his nose. Emily and Shay approached.

"I'm glad you could finally meet Agent Walker. He was my finest addition to the Raging Bull Program before my resignation," said Shay. "I know your interaction was brief, but what do you think?"

"I think she knows him pretty well," Natwat mumbled.

"I'm sorry?" Shay said.

Malaya rolled her eyes and pulled her aunt closer. "Emily didn't tell you—"

Shay dismissed the team and lowered her voice. "We'll talk about this later."

They both watched Jose, General Williams, and the president speaking.

Shay cursed. "He's telling them." She turned away.

As Malaya observed the unfolding scene, she saw President Ross' jaw drop in disbelief. The revelation that Lilith Castillo-Grant was at the heart of the crisis sent visible shockwaves through the room. Expressions morphed from worry to outright dismay, each face reflecting a unique blend of emotions. Bradley Williams stood out with his mouth twisted in a silent snarl of anger.

Amidst this din of reactions, Malaya's gaze lingered on her grandfather. The shame etching itself across his features was palpable, stirring a mix of empathy and sorrow within her.

"I've told you all of this in good faith," Jose said, though his words were latent, with a hidden agenda. "In return for our cooperation and this information, I ask you to provide us with immunity."

As Malaya continued to listen to him speak, and their responses—her blood boiled. *Immunity*, she scoffed at the thought as eyes slowly drifted in her direction.

Fury carried her over to her aunt, who truly distracted herself. Malaya relayed the information with the biased intensity of an innocent person trying to defend their honor. Shay tried, but failed to calm her down with some political talk about this being part of the process.

"We did nothing wrong," Malaya snapped, her voice carrying across the room and causing a ripple of uneasy silence and glances showing a mix of sympathy and confusion.

Deep down, Malaya knew her words didn't matter, and her aunt told her as much.

"Malaya, I get it," Shay said. "But what can we do right now?"

"Find my mother," her voice quivered as she fought the burning behind her eyes.

Malaya tightened her jaw, swallowing the lump in her throat, fighting the overwhelming urge to storm off, to completely abandon this mission in favor of her condo, a day at the spa to take her mind off of this day.

"A fruitless thought of a child," Malaya told herself, despite feeling very child-like shrinking under the disappointed stare of a parent. The difference was that this was the United States Government.

She found herself walking up the ramp, toward the spheric door that would soon open to a portal. She caressed the metal, wanting nothing more than to be away from the peering judgment of the very people who still expected her to help catch this criminal somehow. Her aunt was right. What could she do?

Whoever was behind this deserved whatever was coming to them, especially now, after dragging her family down with it. There was no realistic or logical sense to turning back. Where would she run anyway? At least time travel could take her away from all of this while giving her a chance to find who was responsible.

Feeling a hand on her shoulder, Malaya turned to see Aaron. The petty side of her wanted to avoid the dishonest SIA operative. Yet she needed the soft, caring wisdom of the man she loved.

"That was some pretty heavy stuff," Aaron said, rubbing his beard. "I know you're pissed at me, hurt by all of this, but... The thing I admire most about you is your resilience, your toughness. I remember when you held the production of Esquire for printing misinformation about that philanthropist.

Malaya raised a brow. She didn't know he knew about that, or anyone, for that matter.

"Paying the staff salary," Aaron added, "putting the pressure on the owner to not just recant, but devote an entire issue dedicated to their work. That was a boss move."

Boss move? She wanted to smile, finding his choice of outdated phrases funny.

"That willingness to go out on a limb," Aaron continued, "to help other people, is the reason why all this won't break you. Good things happen to people like you."

Malaya's cheeks flushed, but she did not dare let the smile creep on her face.

"Thank you," Malaya said. "But it's funny you know me so well Because I'm starting to feel like I don't know you at all."

"I deserve that, but what did you expect me to do? How could I tell you I worked for your family?"

"In those exact words."

"That's not fair."

"You were gone for months, was it you?" she said, inching closer. "Did my grandfather have you spying on my mother?"

As she asked the question, a part of her felt guilty for accusing him so directly. It was a low blow, fueled more by her own frustrations and fears than by logic or evidence. But she couldn't help it; the pain of betrayal and the confusion swirling inside her demanded an outlet, and Aaron, unfortunately, was the nearest target. Plus, he deserved it.

Aaron looked back at the others, still engaging in conversation. He grabbed her hand; she wanted to snatch it away, but the warm feeling of comfort she needed surged through her body, stopping her.

"You know my job requires that I keep secrets, but it wasn't spying on your mother. I'm sorry you're going through this. I'm here now. We're in this together. Incoming."

"The president?" she said through clenched teeth before putting on a fake yet nervous smile.

"Well, it's great to see you two getting along." President Ross patted Aaron's shoulders. "Malaya, I'm sorry your mother put you all through this. I hope Jose is wrong, but you know your grandfather."

"Put me through what, sir? She hasn't been found guilty of anything—" Malaya paused, catching her grandfather's eyes, telling her two things. He was sorry, and she should relax.

Malaya sighed. "I can't focus on that. My focus is on the mission."

"I like the way you think," said President Ross.

She looked past the president toward her grandfather, who intercepted Aaron. Wondering how many more secrets were being kept between the two of them—she walked toward them.

Jose tilted his head to the side. "There's something familiar about you, Agent Walker."

"I have one of those faces."

Malaya cleared her throat, stopping any further integration.

"Watch out for her," said Jose. "Not that she needs it."

"Yes, sir."

After one last briefing, they found themselves in front of the silver sphincter door hatch. They inserted the QPC, giving Malaya the okay to program their medallions—the hatch opened to intense blackness. They boarded the ramp and stopped at the threshold, looking at one another. She grabbed Aaron's hand, not caring what anyone thought before taking their final step into the Quantum Portal.

QUINTUS

Coast of Greece, 417 BC

Quintus observed quietly. Julius was confident that their plan would succeed this time. They had been in this situation for too long, and the shackles around his neck and wrist reminded Quintus of his captivity. He wondered if Julius had as much at stake as he did.

Although he never talked about it during training or their travels, the secrets between them didn't get in the way of their mission.

Julius, glancing over the merchant's shoulder, stroked his knotted beard—a habit Quintus noticed often occurred when things were going well. However, the merchant's flushed red face suggested a different story.

"I am risking my reputation here," the merchant said. "Wine and gold are not enough, even for the best in Magna Graecia."

"What more can I offer you?"

Brutus tugged on his beard. Their contact had warned them he was difficult and spoiled by his wealth, but he had one irresistible desire.

"We can get you one of those Laconia women from Sparta," Quintus shouted from where he was chained.

Julius's brown eyes pierced Quintus in protest.

"Deal," Brutus replied, flashing his gold tooth. "Your boat awaits. I'll get the slaves."

"I'm all for bargaining, but are you going to risk the mission?" Julius whispered as they were unloading barrels of wine from their cart.

"Of course not," said Quintus. "We go in, grab Elias and Midas, and into the portal we go. It should be easier than Corinth."

"Anything is easier than Corinth," Julius said, both of them laughing. Julius cleared his throat. "We can't afford any more delays," he said, pointing to the medallion around his neck. "Our secondary objective may have to wait. We'll gather as much information on the hilts as possible, and Lilith will understand."

"Sorry, friend, but I have different plans. Since we are not bringing Brutus the girl, we have a little more time."

"One more thing!" Brutus shouted, accompanied by two unkempt men, both of whom were larger than the merchant. "Should you encounter any problems, my little brothers, Nero and Titus, will make sure you return with my merchandise."

Behind the merchant's wide back, the two slaves that Julius had bought, Marcus and Koisis, were hidden. Nero instructed them to sit down, and Julius and Titus took their seats in the bow while Nero sat in the boat's stern, next to Quintus. The two boys took their place as the first rowers.

"Well, this changes things," Quintus whispered through his fake smile.

After several days of travel, the young men became ill, with Koisis having the worst symptoms and vomiting occasionally. They didn't belong on the boat any more than Quintus did, but unlike him, they didn't have nanotechnology or access to modern medicine. Unlike him, they were not playing a role.

"Easy, friend," Quintus said, helping Koisis.

"Row," Nero shouted, kicking Marcus in the back and onto Quintus. "He's not dead."

Quintus felt the weight of his past as a gladiator in the arena, bearing down on him as he locked eyes with Nero's piercing gaze. The memories of shackles and the constant threat of death always lingered. His years of battle had honed his skills, but he was more than that. He was a Champion gifted with abilities that set him apart, abilities that only added to his lethal capability.

I should end him.

Quintus caught Julius's eye as he helped Koisis back to his seat, reminding him of not just their mission, but what he had to lose. He thought of Lilith's promise.

I will reunite you with your family.

A calm washed over him, allowing him to reclaim his emotions. He couldn't let himself be consumed by violence. Quintus took a deep breath, reclaiming his role and focus. "To think I once had the world at my fingertips. Now a warm bed would suffice."

"You talk too much," said Nero. "It's no wonder why they've fallen ill. Trust me, no one here gives a shit about your dead wife or daughter or any other tale you've come up with."

"Fair enough, friend. After all, what am I but a slave?"

It was a connection he felt to this ancient land, a lineage shared with the souls of centuries past. Although his actual birth lay hundreds of years in the future, the pull of history and heritage was undeniable.

The excitement within him grew as they were only a few miles away from the storied city of Sparta, a place etched in legend and shrouded in the heroics of time. His mission was clear yet daunting: to find Elias, the valiant son of Seth the Conqueror, and his inseparable ally, Midas, the child of Agis.

The landscape around him bore the marks of history, with rugged hills rolling into the horizon, interspersed with olive groves that seemed to whisper tales of ancient warriors. The air was thick with the scent of the sea, mingling with the earthy aroma of the land, creating a heady mix that fueled his resolve.

Every step towards Sparta felt like a journey back through time, walking the path of legends, ready to etch his own story into the annals of this fabled land.

The road ahead was not one to be underestimated for Sparta's two Champions, Midas and Vasilis. They were always together, and Elias was never far behind. The thought of facing them was not an easy one. Yet, he couldn't deny the thrill of the challenge.

"*Champions*," he said to himself with a smile.

Not long ago, the notion of Champions, guardians tasked to vanquish a legendary mystical Sage, was but a fantastical childhood tale. Yet all that changed when he met a Champion in a Roman arena. A warrior of unparalleled athleticism, her abilities defied the limitations of mere mortals. It was only then his own powers began to manifest, his body straining to keep pace with her every move. In the end, it was his prowess that sealed the victory with effortless grace. *I owe you more than you will ever know, Tabiti.*

Elias and Midas won't come easy, he thought.

"There's a village just ahead," said Julius. "Quintus and I will return with the horse and carriage."

Nero stepped between them. "The slave stays," he said, shoving Quintus.

"I don't recall asking your permission," Julius said, removing the hood of his cloak. The coolness in his brown eyes disappeared.

"Easy, friend," Quintus said, stepping in front of Julius. "I'll stay to help unload. As you said, we can't afford any setbacks."

Julius looked past Quintus. He took a deep breath before pulling the cowl over his mouth and hood over his head. "It's difficult to tell which one of you is the slave," Nero said as Julius walked away.

They set up camp after unloading the barrels. Quintus waited up for Julius, who returned in the dead of night.

"Any word from Lysander?" Quintus asked.

"Yes. Well, through a messenger, we will meet with Kara as planned." Julius walked closer, "but this timeline was altered."

"How?"

They heard rustling from the men waking up. Quintus, Marcus, and Koisis sat in the cart with the barrels. Nero and Titus trailed them on their horses.

"Pssst," Marcus whispered.

"What is it, kid?"

"You and Julius... I know you're not who you say you are."

"Yes, I'm more complex than the average man."

"Sure... But it's more than that. You have island skin tan, like Koisis. You were a gladiator, yet you have no scars."

"I'm difficult to cut, boy."

"Julius's dark skin makes him of Havilah descent. Like me, his dialect is too perfect for a foreigner, and I overheard everything. I have what some may call a superior hearing."

"What do you want?"

"To help," he said. "In exchange for our freedom."

"*Our* freedom?" Koisis said with surprise.

The marketplace was more foreign to him than expected. After all, he once walked these same stone paths. "Move, slave," said Nero, shoving Quintus. "On your knees."

Quintus joined the sobbing boys on the unforgiving dirt, realizing just as Marcus and Koisis had, his fate was in the hands of a woman he did not know.

A young man of authority approached, looking over the product. "The boys are fragile, and this pretty man's hands are soft. He is best suited as a wife in the barrack."

The Spartans laughed, angering both Nero and Titus.

Fix this, Quintus thought, looking back at Julius.

Julius pulled Quintus up, slapping his toned stomach. "Don't let him fool you. He has won many Rudis. He is a Roman gladiator! Men from all over have fallen by these soft hands—some say even Spartans."

The laughter ceased.

A woman's voice parted the silent warriors. "He should prove it." Her sweet smell followed her as she examined Quintus.

"Julius? Is that you under there?" A hooded man pushed the Spartans aside. "It's me, Lysander. Kara, this is Julius, a famous merchant—we met overseas."

"He talks big," Kara replied.

"He's not the only one with a big ego," Quintus said, his eyes locked with Kara, flashing a grin at the short-haired, radiant woman. Her dark brown eyes were stern yet nurturing, soft, like that of her dusky skin.

Kara was everything Lilith described her to be, everything the history books said she would be. Kara, the Polynesian, raised a Helot, who would become queen and reshape Sparta's history. However, as he learned, she was more —the woman who killed Seth the Conqueror.

"Watch your tongue!" Nero shouted.

"It's fine," Kara said. "Let's see what he has, perhaps a demonstration."

Quintus lifted his dimpled chin in defiance, his dirty blond hair falling into his face. "There are three Spartans here. It wouldn't be fair to them."

"Leave the hand chains on." Kara directed Nero to loosen the shackles on his ankles. "Now the odds are even."

With a sly grin, Nero removed a piece of cloth from his waist. "In the arena, he fought men without sight," he said, addressing the crowd. "He shall demonstrate his prowess blindfolded."

The market's crowd murmured with excitement. The bustling agora was packed with spectators, all eager for a show. Dust hung in the late afternoon air, illuminated by the fading sunlight that cast an amber glow over the roughly hewn stone buildings.

Weathered wooden stalls bursting with bright fabrics, clay pots, bronze tools, and pyramids of fresh fruit and vegetables lined the circular paved clearing. Merchants yelled out deals over the din, while shoppers jostled to collect their purchases before the entertainment began. Children darted underfoot chasing dogs or each other. Old men lounged in any available scrap of shade, fanning themselves lazily and squinting at the impromptu arena taking shape.

The crowd tightened around Quintus and the Spartans, spectators shoving for the best view, their roar rising as Kara stepped forward to start the match. The hardscrabble peasants and tradesmen of Sparta could never dream of affording the prestigious spectacles at the amphitheater reserved for citizens. But here, for a fleeting moment, glory and bloodlust were theirs for the taking.

Kara held up her hand, silencing the crowd. "That is not necessary."

"I insist," Nero said, blindfolding Quintus. "You want to kill me," he whispered. "I saw the look in your eyes on the boat, but you won't get that chance. Fight!" He shoved Quintus in the back.

The rapid clanking of metal grew closer, sending a chill down Quintus's spine. He wondered how they could be so confident, given the circumstances. Quintus was blindfolded, yet he didn't show an ounce of fear. Shouldn't that have been a warning sign of who they were facing?

He wasn't going to play their games. With a swift move, he wrapped the chain around the incoming blade, impelling it into the attacker, hearing his jaw crush. Another one approached.

The tall one. He used his shoulders to springboard into another attacker.

Jeers and boos erupted from the crowd. His heart pumped, fueling him with the feeling he only got in the arena. Quintus's heart raced with the thrill of battle, but he was also aware of the deadly consequences if he failed.

"Behind you!" Marcus shouted.

Quintus rolled out of the way. The metal stung the stone inches from him. There was little room to maneuver.

He jumped onto tables and tossed clay pots, fruits, anything he could find. A powerful push from behind erupted the crowd and annoyed him. Years of training heightened his senses. He ignored the crowd noise in search of his *enemy*, hearing his steps, detecting his movements.

There. He avoided a spear and scooped up dirt, tossing it in their eyes. A third attacker swung, his blade breaking the wind, as he missed.

An open opportunity. Quintus wrapped the chain around the attacker's neck.

"Enough!" A man shouted, silencing the crowd. "What is this?"

Quintus's blindfold was removed. In front of him was a young man in shimmering bronze armor and a red cloak with the bluest eyes he'd seen. Next to him was a woman, short, like he was—unlike the blue-eyed royal, her head was down, yet her beauty was apparent.

"Elias, Nefeli," said Lysander. "The men were just having a little fun."

"It appears the slave had the last laugh," said Elias. "Execute him!"

"I just purchased him," said Kara.

Elias looked at the damage, then at Quintus, his brows furrowed. "Spartans, clean your brother's blood and wash the wounds of the man who bested you."

VASILIS

Laconia, Greece, 417 BC

"Vasilis," whispered Midas. "It is time."

He groaned, reluctantly leaving behind the warm comfort of sleep and grabbed his shield, joining Elias at the center of the small camp surrounded by the rolling hills of Laconia. The night air was crisp and carried the scent of roasting meat mixed with the sharp tang of iron as the Spartans honed their weapons, preparing themselves for another battle and the possibility of glory in death.

The three of them sat around a fire. A piece of cheese and half a hare awaited Vasilis. "What is this?"

"Food," Elias said, shining his shield with a frown and a rag.

"Where's the blood soup?" Vasilis asked, confused. He couldn't remember the last time he had tasted anything so delicate.

For Spartans, camp food was mostly blood soup, wine, and mushrooms. Leave it to Elias to turn war into a grand celebration fit for a royal.

Vasilis spent too much time on the battlefield, where he felt most comfortable. Unlike Elias, Vasilis took no wife, nor did he allow himself to get caught up in the spoils that came with being the one who would inherit the throne.

Despite his bloodline, Vasilis knew what he was not, a royal. He was an artist. His tools were his spear, shield, and kopis, the world was his canvas, and he painted it in blood. Until recently, Midas was always by his side as the leader of their group of ten that struck fear in enemies and conquered lands, spreading the reach of Sparta. This Krypteia, was organized by the king's own right-hand, Agis, who happened to be Midas' father. Regardless of lineage, Midas earned leadership, and Vasilis wanted no part of it.

"One of the men caught it." Midas nipped a piece of meat off his plate. "Everyone knows it is your favorite. After yesterday, you earned it."

"Everyone earned it. I am not special. I can't accept it," Vasilis said, though his stomach growled in protest.

"Spare me the humble act, brother. Eat it or hand it over," Midas said, pulling the plate closer to him.

Vasilis snatched the plate. "You have no honor." He closed his eyes, enjoying the richness of the cheese.

"And you have little pride," Midas said, watching Vasilis devour the plate.

"You are still brooding, Elias." Wine cleared Vasilis's throat. "We will find Nefeli."

Elias harrumphed; he folded his arms. "It is none of your business. You made your decision."

He allowed Elias's statement to simmer. "Nefeli is like a sister to me. I would have done anything to save her, but she was out of reach. Should I have lost my father's sword as well?"

"No," Elias said. His shrill blue eyes stared at Vasilis while he refilled his wine. "I should have killed him when I had the chance. When I catch him. I will cut his eyes out." He took a piece of meat off Vasilis's plate.

"Always so quick to the sword," Midas interjected. "Investigating would be more useful. Try to use less impulse and more thinking."

"I agree," Vasilis grinned.

"Why do you smile, Vasilis? You let your emotions guide you. I assure you it's going to lead you to do something you will regret," Midas raised a brow and pointed at the sack on Vasilis's waist. "And those will not help. Have you forgotten yesterday? You nearly killed our brother? I assume that wasn't your intention, or did your medicine cloud your mind?"

"Of course not," Vasilis said, unsure if his statement was true. He had to admit, Midas was right. His emotions ran higher than normal. He took a bite of the mushrooms. "My intentions are always pure, even in these trying times."

"Times are indeed trying. I hate politics." Midas pushed the blond strands of hair behind his ear. "Maybe they should bring back dual kingship. Together, we can lead Sparta to a new age."

"Never," Elias said. "We shall battle it out. Let the people decide who should be their king."

Vasilis caught Elias's eyes and his shaking leg. It was a habit he had when in doubt or was about to do something reckless.

"You can have it," Vasilis said, finishing his plate. "The kingship is tainted. It puts an unnecessary target on one's back."

"Being a leader is not made for everyone." Elias stood up. "Spartans! Tonight, we celebrate, but tomorrow we will send these Athenians straight to hell!"

Elias held his half-empty cup to the crying night sky. The soldiers echoed his sentiments. Midas handed Vasilis a cup, his blond brows raised, insisting he, too, addressed the men.

Vasilis cleared his throat. "To our fallen brothers, their death was an honorable one."

"Aye!" Midas said, holding up his cup. "May our fate be as lucky!"

The snarling and clanging metal roared with the thunder. At the moment, the pain and depression that came from his undesired position washed away with the rain.

One of Elias's men approached him, taking his ear.

Elias grinned. "We have tracked him."

The young soldier gave Vasilis his dory. "Are you sure? Vasilis questioned.

"My men are hand-selected. If they say we have cornered the general, I trust it. Now, do you trust me, brother?"

"Aye," said Vasilis. "Lead the way."

Elias led the men through the trees along a narrow path, its muddy terrain offering no obstacle to the small group of Spartans. "We should be able to cut off his route," he said with a sly grin.

Vasilis was wary of the plan, but he trusted Elias in situations such as this. If the war could be ended, it was a chance worth taking. The men split into two, positioning themselves to flank the enemy general. Vasilis waited at the edge of the peak, lying prone with his dory in hand, watching as one of the enemy riders came into view. The warriors appeared weary, their exhaustion evident after a long chase.

With a fierce cry, Vasilis used his spear to launch himself over the peak, landing on one of the enemy horses and impaling the rider. The rest of the enemies offered little resistance to the Spartan warriors, and their bodies soon littered the ground, their blood staining the dirt. Vasilis decimated the general's guard, crashing their horses into one another and forcing the general to flee on foot.

"There is nowhere left for you to run," Vasilis growled as he unsheathed his sword, Forsaken. He removed the general's helmet, only to realize in horror that he knew the young man pleading for his life.

"Markus?" Vasilis said in disbelief, finally understanding that he had fallen into a trap. It was too late. He didn't move as he embraced his inevitable death.

A sword exploded from his chest, and Vasilis spat out blood as he fell to his knees. "The gods had chosen my father, and your mother took him from us," Elias said as he licked the blood off his sword. "You know the price."

Vasilis fell forward into Midas's arms, his strength failing him. "We will spare your mother out of respect," Midas said as he gently laid Vasilis down.

With his last ounce of energy, Vasilis reached for his father's hilt, watching in horror as his brothers walked away. *This is how my father felt,* he thought, before everything faded to black.

A shimmer of light turned into an image of a young woman standing over him. She placed Forsaken on his chest, then a medallion around his neck, followed by a metal device on his forehead. "Don't die on me... I need you," she said, her voice carrying Vasilis's soul from death into the blackness.

SETH

Intrepid, 2076

C old air brushed against his skin, forcing his eyes open to a bright light, aiding his throbbing head. "Anyone there?" he said, pulling himself together.

The only response was the patting of his feet against the bone-chilling floor. He slid his trembling hand across the smooth surface of the all-white room, noticing his scars were gone. So was his armor. In its place was a white tunic. He dropped to his knees. His long-grizzled hair fell in front of his face.

"For all that became of my legacy, the gods have blessed me with the highest honor," he said as tears washed over his beard. "Angel of death, take me with you to fight amongst the greats."

A woman's voice thundered into the room. "There will not be an angel of death coming for you, and you have not been forsaken."

Seth jumped up. He looked around the room. "Your voice, I know it."

"I'm Lilith. And you're not dead," she replied, ripping through his acceptance of what awaited on the other side.

If this was not the life after, then where am I? He thought. His heart pulsated—he squeezed his fist, unable to fight the burning surge through his body. *Kara, could she have staged my death to hold me hostage?*

"I demand you un-cage me!" Seth slammed his fist against the wall, and the thud echoed throughout the room, leaving a shattered imprint behind.

A sharp horn sounded, and the room turned red. His heart paced from both adrenaline fueled by anger and anxiousness. The walls parted. He tightened his fist. *Whoever comes will either give me answers or die.*

Men dressed in all-black armor with abnormal helmets that hid their faces—they stood on either side of the doorway. He charged at them, but lightning from their weapons wrapped around him—bringing him to his knees. "The tranquilizers didn't keep you down. That's impressive," Lilith said, walking in.

She differed from Sparta. Her hair was pulled back, and she wore the same black attire as the men, but there was no doubt this was her.

"Sorry about the aggressive tactics. I don't want this for you." Lilith kneeled in front of him. "If they let go, will you behave?"

Fighting was not an option if he wanted answers. Lilith signaled, and just like that, he was free. "Where am I?" he asked, struggling to his feet.

"2076," she said, her voice timid. "I understand if—"

Seth wrapped his hand around Lilith's throat, careful not to squeeze too tight. He wanted answers. Lilith held her hand up, stopping the men from charging, saving their lives.

"False god," Seth shouted. "You deserve to die for what you've done."

"You'll kill me for saving your life... Guiding you. Without me, your legacy would be nonexistent."

"Did you help Kara kill me for your own convenience?"

"No, you did that. I'm giving you a chance at redemption. A chance to rewrite your wrongs."

"What has become of Sparta?"

Lilith placed her hand on his cheek. The world around him changed, and the walls closed in—taking him into a different yet familiar world. Everything moved too fast to be detected. The voices, sounds, and smells were foreign—then it was gone. Tears flowed as he looked into Lilith's eyes. Many of his questions were answered. However, for every answer, another question arose.

"I want to help you achieve greatness far beyond anything you've done in Sparta," Lilith said. "We need you... Help me save my world... *our* world."

"How can I? Here, I am nothing, a nobody with little knowledge of this foreign world."

"There is more that I can show you?"

Lilith started out the door. The guards parted, and he followed. "I can only show you so much. Everything you need to know will come to you after this."

They entered a room filled with admirable objects. Technology beyond any he'd seen or studied was at his fingertips. People in white greeted him with a fear he had become accustomed to—except for the woman with wide brown eyes that lit up like her welcoming smile.

With her was another. She had orange hair and bronze skin, with the same welcoming smile.

"Cruz and Tala will assist you," Lilith said, pointing at the woman with black hair in a messy bun.

"Lay there," Cruz said, pointing at the long bed with restraints.

Seth ran his hand across the leather as fine as the one back home. "What is the meaning of this?" he said, pointing at the straps.

"It's for your own protection," Tala said, strapping him in. "We're going to connect both you and Lilith with what we call a neurolink. The side effects can be intense."

It was comforting seeing Lilith being strapped in as well, unable to hide the worry on her face. She whispered something to Cruz before a device was inserted into her arm. It didn't take long for Lilith to fall asleep. *What secret was she keeping?*

"Forgive me for asking," said Seth, peeking over at Cruz sitting in front of her machine. "But Lilith appeared concerned. Should I be worried?"

"No. What she told me had nothing to do with this." Her suspicious eyes met with Tala's.

She was lying, at least that's what he suspected. But it didn't matter. What he needed awaited him in slumber. After a pinch in the arm, he'd get his answers.

His head pounded as he awoke to armored MAD agents guarding the door, with their hands hovering over their guns.

What's happened to me? He thought, looking across the room for Lilith—she was gone. He looked to where he expected the women. Instead, there was a snoring gentleman slumped over in his seat.

"Sheldon," he said with confidence, yet surprised at the familiarity he felt despite never meeting him. "Sheldon, get up!"

Sheldon sprang to his feet and put his glasses on. "It worked," he stammered. "It's a pleasure to finally meet you. My name is... you know that already. How are you feeling?"

"Like a prisoner," Seth said, slurring his words, looking at the restraints, reddening his tan skin.

"Where's the key?" Sheldon said, his frantic energy painting his face red.

Seth took a deep breath before snapping the restraints like old leather—he still had his strength.

The guards moved in. Sheldon stepped in front of them as if to save Seth.

"This will not end well," Seth said, unable to break the metal shackles on his ankles. "I wish to speak with Lilith, nothing more."

"Let's relax," said Sheldon. "I'll alert Lilith and Captain Bishop. You can put this on."

Orange light-lined walls as he walked along the sleek floors of the space station's corridor. Seth tugged on the black uniform, then passed his hand through his freshly cut brown hair. The abundance of clothing was unnecessary, as were Sheldon's pestering questions. But he was also candid, proving useful by feeding him information.

One of the occasional large windows called him. He peered out, lost in the chasm of stars surrounding this small sphere of blue and green. It was truly breathtaking.

Even at this moment, what became of Sparta plagued him. A great nation vanished in the history books only to live on as a myth and lore—the thought was disappointing. Part of him wondered if he'd ever get to see his wife and children again. What became of their lives now that he was gone and Kara lived?

Why did Lilith not share that? Surely she knew. The thought of their death was too much to accept. So, he pushed it to the back of his mind.

"We're almost there," Sheldon said.

They boarded the lift to what Sheldon called the *Cerebrum level* of the *Intrepid*. Cerebrum, as he understood it, was not unlike where the Gerousia met. But the Intrepid itself was indescribable with its many sectors to explore, and it was all in space. He struggled to wrap his head around the ordeal. *Time travel, a space station. Are the heavens real?* He found himself questioning everything he once believed,

The lift halted, and the doors hissed open. Captain Alexandra Bishop stood with her blond hair pulled back, greeting him with icy blue eyes. Lilith soon arrived with Joseph. After the trackers left, the six of them took their seats in front of the hologram.

"It's time I show you why you're here," said Lilith. "Argie, show us Kyoto, Japan, 1600, Fushimi Castle."

The hologram changed as Lilith spoke. "Your first mission is to extract Shogun Tokugawa and Mizunami Toyotomi. I've established a person of contact, Osamu Torri, a warrior with skills even you'd admire."

"Wait," Captain Bishop interrupted. "Are you seriously considering murder?"

"It's not. At least not technically," said Sheldon. "His history is written."

"Casualties are inevitable, Captain Bishop," said Lilith. "You know this better than anyone, given your galactic exploits."

"We're fighting to protect humanity."

"So are we, Alex," said Lilith. "I'm not advocating murdering anyone, but people will die. They have to if it means we get to live. Time will correct itself. Important events will happen as they should." Lilith faced him. "You must also retrieve an artifact from the Tokugawa tatami room, a blade with a special hilt. You'll know it when you see it."

"With all due respect, am I supposed to travel to a foreign land with your men? I need my men, Elias and Midas." Vasilis crossed his mind, but he found it difficult to be around him all those years. Now that he was free of the guilt, it was time to move on. Worse, who knows what his mother told him?

"Joseph?" Lilith said.

"We have enough pods for three at a time, including the jumper. As long as they check out in terms of paradoxes, I don't see why not."

"I know the history," said Lilith. "We can get you the Spartans. I'll get a team together to extract them."

"I would like to lead this mission," said Seth.

"You can't," said Joseph. "It's too great a risk."

"Don't worry," said Lilith. "My team will retrieve Elias and Midas, prepare your strategy for Japan, and focus on your training for MEV."

Why would she want a Spartan running her trillion-dollar company? I know nothing about energy, or her world. Perhaps business and politics never change.

"What about my wife and daughter?" said Seth.

"Sheldon," Lilith said.

"I'll check," Sheldon replied, removing his glasses.

Blackness consumed his eyes as he swiped his hand across the table. *Impressive*, Seth thought, as a waterfall of numbers and letters illuminated the room. The matrix stopped, and Sheldon returned. He looked at Seth. "They lived a full life."

"What does that mean?" He asked.

The looks on their faces said it all, though no one spoke a word. Joseph cleared his throat. "I'm afraid we can't. Their lives are intertwined with the timeline in ways we can't calculate. If we remove them, it could create a paradox."

All that Seth knew had changed, though he wanted a glimmer of hope with this technology. "What do I care about creating or changing a paradox? They are so far removed from this world."

"It's not just the paradox, Seth," Lilith said. "It's a chance they could get swallowed by the quantum realm. Why jeopardize their lives for selfish reasons?"

He found himself lost in his life before this. Thoughts of what he'd done to get himself killed. It didn't impact his family. Their lives were long. *If they survived to live a prosperous life in my absence, who am I to deny them*, he thought, having to accept it, as he did his role in this new world, the future, his afterlife, his redemption?

"When does my training begin?" he asked, turning to Captain Bishop.

"After you see Cruz and regain your strength at the mess hall," said Captain Bishop before exiting for the bridge.

"I'm sorry we couldn't do more for you, Seth." Lilith stood and extended her hand.

It happened again. A rush of fragmented imagery shuffled through his mind—memories, people, none that belonged to him.

"Seth," Lilith said, snapping him back. "Are you okay?"

"I'm not sure."

QUINTUS

Laconia Greece, 417 BC

Quintus spent days in pursuit of Kara, each moment draining. Despite her demanding schedule, he had to find a way to collect the intelligence he was after. Lilith tasked him and Julius with taking Midas and Elias. Kara was the key to providing the opportunity for the abduction to take place.

He lay stretched out at the edge of the vast crop field, nearly one hundred yards away from Kara's villa. Quintus gazed up at the sky in awe of a moon larger and brighter than any he had seen before.

He bit into the crisp, juicy apple, savoring its sweet tang, taking in the beauty of the night, relishing in the scent of the ripe fruit and the hum of the surrounding crops, a reminder of the simple pleasures of the world. He was free from the shackles of the arena and the brutal life of a gladiator.

Tonight was a chance to relish the moment of peace, a welcome respite from the constant strain of his mission. Quintus's heart tensed, thinking back to the day he found his wife holding his young daughter as if they were sleeping—they weren't.

The decision he made to fight back against his captures played over and over in his head. Part of him tried to justify his decision; the other blamed himself.

Still, he felt anguish as he faded to black and even more when he awoke to Lilith over him. He had a second chance, but it meant nothing without them. But Lilith, she promised to save their lives no matter what, and he would do everything to make sure it happened.

Rustling in the brush behind him broke his thought. He didn't bother with his dagger, knowing who it was that failed to sneak up on him.

"You're either careless or confident," Julius said, standing behind him. "For all you know, I could have become your enemy?"

"Confident," Quintus said as Julius took a seat next to him. "Even with that shadow trick, you won't kill me in an open field—it's not your style."

Julius's brows furrowed. "*Trick*? That's a little offensive," he said, removing a metal pipe from his waist. He lit it, took a long drag, and exhaled. The sweet smell of cannabis filled the air.

"You and your modern ways," Quintus said, gesturing to the metal pipe. "In my time, we just rolled a simple leaf."

Julius chuckled before taking another pull. "I won't argue with that," he said, "but this is a gift from a merchant from the east. The taste is much smoother, and the pipe itself is pretty amazing, don't you think?"

Quintus shook his head, still chuckling. "I suppose it's not so bad. But I can't imagine ever giving up my trusty old leaf."

"So... you don't want to take a hit?"

"Don't be stupid," Quintus said, taking the pipe. He looked at Julius, who stared off into the sky. There was no contact between them the last few days. He had the look of a conflicted man. Of course he had to be if he was working for Lilith.

Who are you really? Quintus found himself questioning.

Julius grabbed the pipe from Quintus." What have you learned since I've been gone?"

"Just how deep Seth's roots go," Quintus replied. "All of his endeavors were successful. He is as methodical as Lilith says, both revered and hated." Quintus handed him a half-bitten apple.

"Let's work it backward. Who benefited the most?" Julius took a bite.

"From what I understand, those who did are dead," Quintus replied.

"And the people who benefited were Elias and Vasilis. Both are in line for kingship—both were underneath Seth's thumb."

Quintus nodded. "Simple, yet genius."

"Time is running out," Julius said. "We need to find out when and where they die."

Approaching footsteps forced them to extinguish the pipe and hide behind a bush. A shadowy figure crept towards the house. Quintus stepped forward, and Julius grabbed his shoulder. "We must allow the timeline to play itself out. If Kara is to die, so be it."

"I do as I please." Quintus snapped away. "Lilith chose me because I understand how this world works. Do you disagree?"

"Fine, just keep both of your heads where they're supposed to be."

Quintus lunged forward with lightning speed, wrapping his arm around the assassin's neck and squeezing tightly to bring him down. The man's eyes fluttered as he struggled to break free, but Quintus was too strong. With a powerful grip, he dragged the groggy assassin towards a nearby tree. "Are you just going to watch?"

Julius let out a long sigh, and removed his belt, a sturdy leather strap adorned with silver clasps. He used it to bind the assassin's hands to a tree. Quintus ripped part of his tunic and gagged the assassin's mouth. "Wake up," he said, slapping his face.

His eyes popped open with fear. Quintus put his finger to his lips. "Answer, and you live. I will remove this now."

"Not a good idea," Julius said, attempting to stop Quintus.

"Look at him," Quintus said, gesturing to the assassin. "He is afraid. He will talk." Julius held up his arms in surrender as Quintus removed the gag.

The assassin spit in Quintus's face. "See," Julius said, removing his blade and quickly chopping off the assassin's pinky.

Quintus quickly drowned the man's screaming with his hand over his mouth. *So, this is who you are*, Quintus thought. "Perhaps you should remove his thumb so he can no longer grab his cock."

Tears flowed down the man's muffled face. "Nothing will give me more pleasure, but I am a kind man—will you speak the truth?"

The assassin nodded in compliance. Julius then removed the rag.

"Why are you going after Kara? Who sent you?" Quintus demanded, squeezing his cheeks.

"You bastard," growled the man.

"Wrong answer," Julius punched him before sliding his blade across his face.

"Ahh, it's Vasilis!" he cried. "My target is Vasilis."

"Vasilis?" said Quintus, looking at Julius.

"Who sent you?" Julius questioned.

"A hooded woman," he cried. "She kept to the dark but paid in full. I don't ask questions with so much gold."

Julius snatched the sack of gold from his waist and cut the binds. "Get out of here before I kill you.

"I assume you have a plan for letting him go," Quintus asked, watching the man stumble to freedom.

"Aye. I'll tail him," Julis said. "Keep an eye on Kara, just an eye."

"Mr. Morals, huh? Tell me, how many sacks of gold do you need?"

Julius smirked before the men parted. Quintus made his way back to the small stone house, fetching a bucket of grain and herbs. Approaching conversation forced him to take cover at the edge of the wall. *Agis?*

"Lynceus is still carrying the Elias kingship banner," said Agis. "He argues that Elias's age is not a concern. The rest of the elders are not fully on board—still, support for him grows."

"And what of Vasilis?" Kara questioned. "This division in Sparta is because half supports him, yet cling to this divinity of Seth's death."

"Preposterous," she scoffed. "Taken by the gods."

"Lysander is the safe bet," said Agis. "But the consul is not in his corner."

"Not even his brother," Kara added. "At this point. None of it matters. Vasilis may never see the throne."

Their voices moved closer to the villa's entrance. "The oracles have been wrong before. Don't let divinity guide you, Kara."

"You've heard her speak. She has never been wrong, and if they fulfill the prophecy, tell Lysander to move in on them."

"Without hesitation, my lady," said Agis as he exited.

It was quiet for a moment. Quintus was certain of the oracle they were discussing. *Lilith.* She was well known for her vast influence, but she was always cautious and meticulous in how she affected the timeline. Her actions were always subtle, like a gentle whisper through time.

Yet here he was, prepared to take a huge risk for a woman he was assigned to work for. His heart raced, replaying Julius's warnings. His time on the Intrepid, studying the culture, the history did little to prepare him for this. Kara was not a spec in time. She was reshaping the Sparta he knew for the better, making it stronger for years to come.

Kara did not deserve to die, not after all the good she's done. He turned the corner and saw Kara, who had her back against the door with her eyes closed, a small smile on her lips.

"Why haven't you left yet?" she said. Her lips thinned, replacing her smile.

"Apologies, my lady. I was just getting a head start on the day."

"It is the thick of night." She raised a brow, gesturing for him to follow her.

Quintus was met with a humble yet elegant room with marble columns and intricate carvings along the walls. He took a seat on the cushioned chairs that surrounded the sturdy table near the fire pit. A mix of sweet and earthy scents, the herbs and spices on the table. Quintus found himself drawn to the paintings of battle scenes from Spartan victories that were displayed on the walls. A large cloth obscured the purpose of the rack that sat beneath it.

"Quintus," Kara's voice brought him back. She was sitting next to him.

"Sorry, did you say something?"

"You leave every night, yet tonight you stay. Why?"

He wanted to warn her that she was in danger. But, he had a duty to Lilith, to his family, to make sure they got a second chance at life. So, he swallowed any truth he threatened to spill. "A former queen living among the enslaved."

"These are my people. I am obligated to them. Now, answer me," she said, then emptied the last drops of a bottle of wine into two cups.

"You have freed the boys, given them a home. Perhaps I want what you offer."

"Citizenship?"

"Not exactly."

Kara rubbed his chest, then tugged his braid. He smiled. "Spartan women *are* different."

"You remind me of my late husband," she said. "Young, noble, with a charm that is merely a shield to mask the pain... What pains you?"

A lump formed in his throat. He felt himself sinking into the cushions and in her eyes. She saw him for who he was, the scars that time travel could not heal. "My wife and child."

Kara dropped her hand. "What happened?" she asked, pushing a cup of wine toward him.

He drank before letting out a long sigh. "I made a deal with some bad people, and they paid the price for my arrogance."

"I am sorry to hear that. Losing a love is like losing a part of yourself." Kara took a drink, her eyes gravitating to the painting sitting above the mysterious rack. A warrior held his sword in the air, his skin covered in tribal tattoos as bright blue as the sword's hilt and shadows with glowing eyes being absorbed into the blade.

"My son is all but dead," Kara said, her eyes still focused on the painting. "The prophecy has been foretold. He will give the ultimate sacrifice for Sparta."

She knows of his death, yet she remains strong. How?

"I must find solace and rely on my strength and faith in the God Above All, or suffer in purgatory, and fail those who need me most."

"Like I have," Quintus blurted.

Kara reached up to wipe the tears he hadn't even realized had fallen from his face. She clasped his hand. "We are all broken. Forward is the only way."

Rising to her feet, she strode towards the mysterious rack, pulling back the cloth to reveal its impressive collection of weapons. Amidst the array, a leaf-shaped blade, but it was the weapon mounted at the center that drew his attention.

Without hesitation, Quintus recognized the Rhomphaia. The hilt was shaped like a majestic griffin, emitting a faint glow; its wings spread wide to form the rain guard and its radiant eyes glinting in the dim light. The griffin's head served as the pommel, while its long, elegant tail coiled around the blade, adding a touch of elegance to the deadly weapon.

"It is yours," she declared, offering the weapon to him. It is as versatile as you are. It once belonged to a warrior who came close to defeating Vasilius in his deadliest battle, yet it was that very struggle that taught him the most and changed him for the better."

"I'm honored," he said, accepting the weapon. *I'll call you Tazonia. Spine Splitter.*

A hard knock broke the atmosphere. "It's Vasilis," said Kara, throwing the rag over Quintus's sword.

Vasilis stormed in. His fine red cloak flowed with every step. Their eyes met as he placed Forsaken on the table—he turned to Kara. "Why was Agis here at this time of night?"

"You are not my husband, and if you must know, we were discussing politics."

"Really?"

"The gods and Quintus are my witnesses. Never mind my affairs. Why are you here? You have a battle tomorrow."

Quintus's eyes moved to Forsaken, the legendary sword of tales. His stomach twisted as he beheld the weapon's unique hilt— Cerberus, the three-headed hound. The length of the kopis was longer than most, measuring sixty-five cm, so he guessed. Its curved blade gleamed in the light with a deadly edge. But it was the hilt that truly caught Quintus's attention, the three snarling heads encasing the blade like a protective shell.

The tail of the beast was the pommel, adding balance to the weapon and completing the fearsome design. Quintus leaned in closer, admiring the lavish detailing of the hilt, crafted from precious gold and gems, adding to the weapon's mesmerizing beauty. As his fingers brushed over the intricate wood's grain, he noticed an odd pattern—the grain swirled in an unnatural way, as if the Cerberus itself was alive and restless within the weapon.

Vasilis paced and then snatched the rag off Quintus's sword. He looked at him, then at his mother, shaking his head. "Why is this here?"

"He earned it," said Kara. "What's wrong with you... Have you been taking mushrooms again?"

"No, mother. I'm just tired of these hypocrites. I don't want to lead *them*, not after what they did to us."

"Your father loved his brothers and served Sparta with honor and grace, as you will one day and your child, he deserves as a legacy."

Quintus stood in shock as Nero's face appeared in the small window. He couldn't believe what he was seeing. Just then, Vasilis and Kara stepped out and the momentary distraction was enough for Quintus to come to his senses.

"Vasilis, you can't just run away from this," Quintus heard Kara say as the two of them headed out.

"Go," Quintus whispered loudly, grabbing the weapon gifted to him. He swapped his blade for Vasilis by covering it with the rag, so he could escape with Forsaken. He stormed out, finding Nero, Titus, and Julius waiting for him in a narrow alleyway. Nero held the unconscious Nefili over his shoulder.

"How could you be so foolish?" Quintus scolded them.

Nero and Titus grinned. "Our brother wanted her," Tidas said. "That was the deal."

"You... he set us up to kidnap the heir's wife," Quintus said through gritted teeth. "I should—"

Julis placed a hand on Quintus's shoulder. "It reeks, but we must move."

The group ran down the alley. But it wasn't long before they were caught by Elias, who shouted for Nefeli to be brought back. In a moment of desperation, Quintus threw a nearby ingot, hitting Elias in the head and allowing Julius to grab Nefeli from Nero. They heard a crash, and Titus tripped.

"I'm alright—" his words were cut by a blade being held to his neck. Elias stood on the other side. Elias locked eyes with Quintus as he sliced ear to ear.

Nero stopped and cried a painful shout. Quintus wanted to let him die, but he knew Elias would only use him to get information from him.

"Unless you want to join your brother, we must go," Quintus said, grabbing his tunic and led them them down a rocky path.

They reached a fork in the road lit by torches. "I have made myself familiar with this area," said Quintus. "This road will take you to the chariot. By the time you reach the front gate, I will have a surprise waiting for our pursuers." he said, piling dead leaves into a small home.

"What are you doing?"

"A distraction." He tossed the torch onto the trees. "Relax, it's abandoned, now go."

Quintus darted in the opposite direction into a small village.

Julius nodded before him. Nero and an unconscious Nefeli headed down the designated road. Quintus took off in the opposite direction and found himself face to face with the legendary Midas.

A Spartan shield knocked Quintus off his feet, but he quickly regained his footing and dove feet-first into the window of a small home. The sound of an old lady shouting in fear filled the air as Quintus ran across the home and dove out of another window. He found refuge on a nearby roof, hopping from one to another until he reached the city gates.

But Julius still hadn't arrived, and with Elias and Midas closing in, Quintus was left with no choice. He sat down in a lotus position, laying both swords in front of him. Tearing his tunic, he wrapped his hands and coated them in dirt.

Maybe I was their fate, Quintus thought, as he prepared for the impending confrontation.

He stood up as they swarmed him. There was no showmanship, no pre-fight banter. He shook his head.

"Apologies," Quintus said before brushing sand into Elias's eyes, choosing to attack the giant champion first with an overhead swing of Forsaken.

Midas parried, but Quintus's left hand came with the rhomphaia. The blade's length forced Midas to stumble back; the big man moved with impossible quickness. The earth underneath his sandals felt like part of him. He could feel every movement, every shuffle. Cold energy came from both blades, but the Rhomphaia felt... good... natural.

It's a Champion sword, he thought.

He felt Elias approach from behind, sidestepping his thrust, then tossing him.

Thank the gods, Quintus thought as Nero approached with a chariot. He brushed more sand, this time hitting both men.

"It was an honor," he shouted, hopping into the back with Julius and Nefeli, who still lay unconscious. They took off as fast as they could. Quintus sighed and closed his eyes, relieved that at least this part was over.

"You will not believe this," Julius said, elbowing Quintus.

He looked up, seeing Midas use his shield to catapult Vasilis into the air. He threw his spear, grazing Julius's arm.

"I'm good," Julius said, though he winced.

Vasilis and Elias closed in. Quintus tossed barrels of wine off the back of the chariot. Elias leaped over a few. Midas stabbed one mid-stride and tossed it back. Luckily, he overthrew.

"They are machines," said Julius.

"A what?" said Nero.

"Focus," Quintus shouted.

There was nothing left. He held up Forsaken and smiled at Vasilis, knowing how much his father's blade meant to him. He tossed it in a nearby lake.

"Bastard!" Vasilis shouted before jumping in after it.

Quintus leaned his head against the cart. "Nero, I need my medallion. You have what you came for."

"Not until we return to the ship."

Just as Quinus reached for his blade, Julius mouthed. *Wait until she wakes up.*

Chaos slowed, and enough time had passed for leisure, but Quintus could not rest, an effect fighting always had on him. The orange sky soon joined the purple night sky as dawn approached. Nefeli woke, her brown hair curled in front of her wet cheeks; her eyes widened. Julius placed his finger over his mouth, then nodded at Quintus.

"Nero. Send my regards to Titus in the afterlife."

"Wait!"Nero cried out.

Quintus sliced halfway into his neck before the spinal cord resisted. He ripped the medallion from his neck and kicked him off the cart—taking hold of the horse before pulling over.

"We are not your enemy," said Julius. "We believe your husband is in danger, can I?"

Nefeli nodded. Julius removed her gag and cut the rope binding her hands and feet.

"Who sent you?" Nefeli said, revealing a small blade. "The truth, not the magic or god-talk.."

Quintus looked at Julius, then back at Nefeli. "We're from another world."

"From Egypt, or are you sky people?"

"That's enough!" Julius said. "Please, Nefeli, your husband is going to die. We were sent to stop it."

There was a pause. Her face softened. "Who are you?"

"We were hired by the elders. We work as spies," Julius said. The lie would have convinced Quintus if he didn't know the truth,

Nefeli's eyes looked them up and down. Quintus hoped she'd believe it. "I will lead you to their camp," Nefeli said. "Should you not keep your promise—you will pay."

They hiked across flat land and steep hills before taking refuge underneath a tall tree. Quintus lay on a boulder a few feet away from Julius, nursing his wound.

The entire time, there was something familiar about Nefeli. It hit him as he watched her heat the blade over the fire, staring into the sky, talking to herself. Her peculiar personality reminded him of his wife.

"What are you doing?" Quintus asked.

"Julius's wound is getting infected. Unless he wants to die, he'll allow me to help."

Julius nodded. "Thank you."

"Let's see if you feel this way afterward." She placed the blade on the wound.

Julius grunted, though careful not to scream. Nefeli tried to distract him. "Who shot the spear?"

"Vasilis," Julius grunted. "Do you know him?"

Nefeli burst into laughter. "All too well. I practically raised him, And I was the one who taught him how to throw a spear—pathetic that he missed."

"Raised him? You're a child yourself."

She pressed the blade on his wound. Julian groaned. "What was that?"

Quintus laughed at Julius's agony. "So, this spear throwing. What do you know about it?"

"I've studied the greatest philosophers in Greece. It was simple physics: force, mass, range, time, acceleration, height, distance."

"You are something." Julius smiled. "You remind me of a young woman back home."

"She must be special," Nefeli said. She looked toward Quintus. "I need more herbs."

"Something for the pain?" Julius asked.

Nefeli shook her head. "It is for protection, poppy milk mixed with something special—for kidnappers."

Julius raised a brow. "Will it kill *them*?"

Quintus eyed the bone colored milk.

"No. It will cause hallucinations."

They laughed and continued their conversation throughout the night.

MALAYA

Sparta, 413 BC

After a few seconds of disorienting darkness, Aaron's voice began to filter through, grounding her in the present. She opened her eyes, the world slowly coming into focus, to find him leaning over with an outstretched arm.

"Your chariot awaits," he said, his voice light, tinged with an unspoken concern that didn't escape her notice.

Malaya was too sick to indulge in his humor. With his steady support, she managed to stand, but the world seemed to sway unpredictably around her. A wave of nausea swept over her, an insidious tide that refused to retreat. Beads of sweat formed on her forehead, trickling down her face in tiny rivulets.

She turned away from Aaron, a futile attempt to hide her vulnerability as she succumbed to the urge to vomit. His response was immediate and caring; he held her hair back gently, his hand a comforting presence on her back.

Before she could protest, he was offering her a flask, his eyes reflecting a depth of understanding that only deepened her conflicting emotions.

She side-eyed him caught between gratitude and a lingering irritation. Yet, as she accepted the flask, her hand brushed against his, and she was reminded of the many layers to their relationship—layers she was still unraveling. He invited her into his embrace, a sanctuary she found increasingly difficult to resist, despite the turmoil swirling inside her. His arms promised a haven, a brief respite from the chaos of their current reality.

It was hard to stay mad at him. *He kept things from you,* she thought, a silent reminder to herself of the secrets and lies that had woven a complex web around her life.

Though, with the world currently spinning, the proposition looked better than the alternative. Kat would wreck her if she knew how childish she was being. They were adults. Everyone had secrets.

Aaron, sensing her hesitation, picked up the sack with a respect for her boundaries that only added to her internal conflict. She needed his help, and he was there, unconditionally. And yet, she couldn't shake off the feeling of betrayal, the knowledge of the secrets he had kept from her.

As they hiked through the rugged terrain, the surroundings were a stark contrast to the world she knew. The absence of technology, the untamed beauty of nature around them, it was both alien and strangely freeing.

Aaron moved with a confidence and familiarity contrasting his actual experience with such environments, a natural adaptability that intrigued and frustrated her in equal measure.

The further they were away from the city of Delphi, the better. Based on the vast grassy area and an endless array of giant trees, they had their work cut out for them.

After hiking miles into the night, the steep mountains of Delphi were within reach. Her legs trembled, and she sweated worse than her hot yoga class. She hated the general for guilting her on this trip, but at least she was with the man she loved—even if she was pissed. Despite her pouting ways, Aaron offered to carry her, but she simply shook her head, regrettably so.

A ride on his back sounded great right about now, she admitted.

Aaron was being nice and caring, but she wasn't caving. They created a bonfire near the mouth of a cave. Greece's wildlife was the only sounds between them.

The warm fire caressed her face, a delightful contrast to the cool, dry Greek breeze. She found herself lost in the orange-red flames, reminding her of the torches of the Villa, a club in modern Greece. Her father told her about it.

She, Kat and Emily, along with some others, took a cross-country trip to the high-class club, a blend of ancient Greek culture. She could almost hear the soft classical music fused with house giving it a unique sound to Laconia, Greece. It was old-world charm, meets cutting-edge luxury. She could taste the food, a fusion of molecular gastronomy and Mediterranean flavors—she was far from that now.

Everything happened so quickly, she thought, reminiscing.

One moment, she was waist deep in an ordinary life. Parking tickets, family and friends, people wanting something from her vying for her attention. The lab manager on her ass, assigning new projects on top of existing ones. Doing other people's work; with little time for herself.

At the time, she thought it wasn't fair, but she missed that life. She missed the time when her primary focus, despite everything, was always Project Bunge. A way to reshape humanity in a positive way. A way to observe the past. Somehow, she was now participating in it.

She trusted her mother. Lilith was a lot of things, but a thief was not one of them. They spent too many nights in the HOA lab. Malaya had given up too much of her youth—she lost so many friends. And moments that she would never get back, like prom.

No, Lilith did not steal the quantum device back from the government, not without lettering her on it.

Malaya would understand... Would she understand? Would Malaya try to stop her?

Malaya shook her head. *No, I refuse to believe it. I have been lied to all my life. Protected for my own good, but not this.*

She looked up, fighting back tears. Malaya didn't know why, but her heart ached. She bit her lip, twiddling her thumbs. She wanted to scream out at the sky, scream out at...

Their eyes met Aaron's across the fire. The red-orange flames casting a godly glow on him.

Malaya figured she had made Aaron suffer enough. "All my life, the people I loved lied to me, kept secrets when they didn't have to, not trusting me to have perspective as if I'm incapable made me feel like I wasn't truly part of this family."

She sighed. "And I took that out on you. I'm sorry."

"I understand," he said, putting his arm around her. "I'll always have your back, and I know that feeling of being left out, unsure of where you stand. Half the time I'm not sure if I know who I am. I've been lost ever since my mother died, so I lose myself in my work. I'm sorry for the role I've played in hurting you, but I love you. I know your mother loves you, too."

"I know. And thank you for being so understanding."

The warmth mingling with the cool air was unexpectedly refreshing. Malaya closed her eyes and inhaled deeply, savoring the strange tranquility of this unfamiliar land. For a fleeting moment, she wished she could stay here, frozen in time, away from the chaos.

They rose just before sunrise, the soft hues of dawn painting the sky. Without the constant hum of technology, the outdoors seemed to awaken a different part of her—a part she rarely had the chance to explore or appreciate.

The journey had been mostly smooth, yet she couldn't stop thinking about her father. What had it been like for him, making that first jump into the unknown?

He was like her in many ways—a scientist who had no business time traveling. And yet, he had convinced them he should. Unlike her, he had chosen his path. She was here because she had no choice.

"My dad would think I was a coward," she muttered, the words slipping out before she could stop them. She glanced at Aaron, unsure if she wanted him to respond. After all, he was everything she wasn't—decisive, fearless, and unshaken by the weight of the unknown.

"You're wrong," Aaron said. "You could have pushed back against the general's orders, not gone through with the training, but you did. So no, he wouldn't take you for a coward."

Malaya looked away, his words hitting deeper than she wanted to admit. The wind carried the faint scent of olives, blending with the earthiness of the trail. She let the silence linger, grounding herself in the moment.

Aaron's gaze shifted to the horizon, scanning their surroundings. "Delphi should be north of here," he said, pointing toward the uneven silhouette of the mountains.

She followed his gesture, taking in the sprawling groves of olive trees that blanketed the foot of Mt. Parnassos. It was nothing like the sparse, well-tended groves she remembered from her childhood. Here, the land was wild and untouched, its beauty preserved by a world unburdened by modern influence.

The Mediterranean herbs lead the way up the small trail, surrounded by Holm-oak, laurel, oregano, lentisk cedar, water-thyme, and arbutus. She caught Aaron harvesting oregano.

Malaya admired the way Aaron navigated the dry terrain with an ease that felt almost instinctual. How did he seem to belong so completely in every moment, like he'd lived this life a thousand times before? She wanted to ask how, to understand the layers of him that felt just out of reach. There was so much she ached to uncover, but the words stayed buried beneath her thoughts.

He caught her staring.

"What is it?" he smiled.

"Looks like you could use some help," she said, pointing her chin at the sack.

"Nah. You packed light," he replied sarcastically.

"Ha, ha," Malaya scrunched her face. "We're both new to this, but only one of us knows how to survive in the wild."

Aaron laughed, his eyes softened, and he licked his lips. "Have I told you how sexy you look in a tunic?"

Malaya's cheeks warmed. She twirled in front of him. "Who needs a thousand-dollar dress when you have ancient chic—"

Aaron yanked her by the arm, pulling her down into the tall grass. He put a hand over her mouth. A smart move, considering she was going to thrash him verbally.

He put his fingers on his lips and fanned his hand as if to signal down. She knew from basic training this meant to go prone, and based on the concerned look in his eyes, it was serious. "I don't think they saw us," he whispered.

Relief set in. She nodded. Getting caught by anyone could disrupt the timeline. If they had to engage, well, that could be worse. She could hear them getting closer—they were angry. With a combination of the language transmitter and her studying ancient Greek, she knew why they were upset.

They traveled a long way to the village of Delphi to seek answers from the oracle. It wasn't good news. If she wasn't trembling in her sandals, she'd tell them why they were stupid for listening to whoever they spoke with.

It was all made up, a hoax created to give people a false sense of security. She thought about her mother and the rumors. If she could predict the future, she should have foreseen what would happen. She should have stopped her dad from traveling—

Aaron's hand on her shoulder got her out of her head. The concern in his eyes still lingered. "They know we're here," he whispered. He slowly unsheathed a dagger from the leather holster of his tanned cloak.

Her hands trembled as she removed the axe from her holster. Aaron touched her wrist. "We wait and listen."

Malaya nodded. She closed her eyes and listened. "They're ten steps away, four of them." Several scenarios crossed her mind. There was only a ten percent chance they'd escape without a violent end. She snatched away from Aaron and jumped up, searching through the many dialects for the right one. Attic, Ionic, Aeolic, Arcadocypriot, and Doric.

She landed on Aeolic based on their vocabulary and accident. "We, like you, are travelers. Searching for answers from Delphi," she said with her arms in the air.

"We?" one man said.

"My husband and I." She signaled for Aaron to stand up. He mumbled disapprovingly under his breath. She'd ask for forgiveness later.

One of the men squinted and took a step closer with his knife pointed at Aaron. "There is something familiar about this one."

Malaya looked at him, then back at the man. "That is impossible. We come from a land far away from here, wanting to know more about this oracle. We will pay you if you show us the way."

She overheard their angry discussion about their oracle's prophetic claim that they would soon lose all that they had earned. Doing something good for someone who was scammed shouldn't alter the timeline that much. She hoped.

"Payment first, and we will show you the way," a man said with a smile.

Aaron dug into the sack tied to his waist and took out the Drachma. Their eyes widened. Aaron met one of them halfway, handing the man the silver coins of ancient Greece. As promised, they pointed them in the right direction. She turned to Aaron with her lips pressed and an exaggerated smile. Aaron rolled his eyes and shook his head.

"Not the 'I told you so' face."

"Well, I did," she said.

Her victory was short-lived. She saw Aaron's eyes widen—he heard it, too. His head snapped around along with hers as two of the four men they paid were running their way. Based on how fast they moved, these were no ordinary men.

Aaron met them head-on, surprising the men with his speed. She didn't have to spar with him to see that he was faster than Captain Winters and Sensei. Before she could think of helping, Aaron's kick lifted one of the attackers off his feet. Without looking, he grabbed the wrist of the other. She heard his wrist snap; he dropped the blade and cried in pain. Aaron towered over the man as he held up his dagger.

"Stop!" Malaya cried.

He froze and looked back at her with a concerned look. The man he kicked got up. "Look out—"

For what seemed like only a second, she pressed her eyes shut. Soon as the words left her mouth, Aaron was behind the attacker with his blade at his neck.

How?

She wanted to look away but couldn't. Aaron slit his throat and finished off the next one before she could stop him. Malaya's mouth trembled.

She was frozen in place, looking at the men lying in the blood-soaked field. Her mind went numb; she wanted to vomit and turn away, but she couldn't. He wiped his blade on the dead men's tunics before walking over to check on her.

For a moment, sound ceased to exist as she struggled to rationalize what she'd seen. Aaron... how did he? *It's the ghost radiation,* she said to herself. *Yeah, it has to be the ghost radiation having a negative effect on me.*

"How did you do that?" she said in disbelief. Aaron continued to gather their things. She grabbed his arm. "How did you do that?"

"I'll explain, but you're shaking. You need your medication."

Malaya nodded. She was stuck in the moment. Her mind relived every second in perfect detail. So much blood.

Malaya fought to keep the vomit down. Her stomach turned, remembering every slice of his blade. She reached into the hidden pocket of her tunic and grabbed the silver box. She removed a patch and placed it on her tongue. A cool sensation traveled from her spine to her head, creating an instant calming effect.

He placed a hand on her shoulder.

"Better?"

"Yeah."

"What were you going to ask me?"

She frowned and searched her mind for the question. She replayed the events of the last few moments. *Those men wanted to rob us. Aaron saved me, saved our mission. I almost got him killed. I'm glad he was able to dodge a blow from the attacker.*

"I'm sorry for distracting you. I almost got you killed," she said.

"Please don't apologize," he said. "That wasn't your fault. You were scared. I was too. Let's move forward."

Night approached. An array of wildflowers grew along the Pleisto River valley below Delphi—they were close. With the help of oil lamps and the outskirts of the quiet city, they were able to avoid any problems. As they got closer to where the traveler was, she found herself thinking more about her family.

Before she could slip into that depressive abyss, Aaron did what he always did, distract her by making her talk about her guilty, yet forbidden pleasure, anime. Given the history of the UNA and US, anime was one of the many things banned nationwide.

It took some convincing. She got him into the classics from the 2020s, like *Demon Slayer* and *Attack on Titan*. Her favorite was even older than *Naruto*, but he was in love with the *Dragon Ball* universe, and their philosophical debate stemmed from that.

"You can't be serious," Aaron stopped in his tracks. "Vegeta is not a villain."

"He's the *God of Destruction*. He literally wipes out planets. Oh, and before that, he killed people watching a tournament and ate other people from another planet." Malaya stuck her tongue out in disgust and shook her head. "Oh, and he's a narcissist. He called one of his forms Ultra Ego."

"Wow... Ms. Petty, huh? A. He was a warrior, manipulated to kill from birth. He was the product of his environment, and thanks to his friends and family, he changed. You can't hold the destruction title against him. He's there to bring balance. Not everyone can see that."

She could see why a man in his position would take that stand. Warriors will defend warriors. He saw himself in him.

Malaya scoffed. "You can't erase all the bad he did because of a few good deeds."

"A warrior is always to blame. We do the dirty work and still get overlooked." His mouth opened slightly as if he was going to say something, but he stopped and withdrew into himself like she hit a nerve.

This wasn't just about an anime. He had to do things he wasn't proud of. After seeing what he did to those men, it was clear who he was. She had to let him know it was okay. She grabbed his hand.

"Hey."

"Sorry," he said, shaking his head. "I..."

"It's okay," Malaya said. "You don't have to talk about it."

He smiled. "Thank you."

Without her realizing it, they had reached Apollo's temple.. They sat down with their oil lamps and got close enough to hide behind a stone to watch the boy.

Beautiful stone pillars encompassed the apex of what some scholars considered to be the center of the world. Sixteen lion statues lined up on the terrace as protectors of Apollo's sanctuary. Large fire bowls painted the temple red-orange. Even from this distance, it was breathtaking.

Light broke from the darkness, and her medallion vibrated, which meant the time traveler was here, at this moment. A voice cut through the air.

It was distant yet distinct, carrying a tone that resonated deep within Malaya. Her steps faltered, and she felt an inexplicable catch in her throat. The voice... it couldn't be, yet it sounded so achingly familiar.

Malaya's heart pounded with every hurrying step toward the voice, ignoring Aaron's attempts to stop her.

A flash of memory surged unbidden: a warm, comforting voice reading her bedtime stories, the same melodious tone discussing complex theories late into the night. It was a voice that had soothed her tears and shared in her laughter.

"Tell her it's from Lilith," Malaya heard her say.

For a moment, Malaya stood frozen, her mind reeling. The recognition struck like a blow to the stomach, sending a wave of shock through her body.

This can't be happening, Malaya thought. Her heart sank—disbelief, confusion, a sense of betrayal mingled with an underlying current of love and longing.

Hearing her say her name squeezed the air from her and pulled the world from underneath, making it hard to stand.

Aaron kept her up long enough to pull herself together. "I can't believe she didn't bother to hide it," Malaya said, her voice frantic. Tears welled in her eyes, blurring her vision. "Why would she... no one who knew her for light-years?"

"Wait, is that—"

"My... my mom."

QUINTUS

Laconia Greece, 417 BC

The early morning air was crisp and chilly in the woodland area a few miles from the coast. The sun was starting to rise over the trees. Quintus sat up, rubbing the sleep from his eyes as he remembered the brief battle he had been a part of the night before.

Midas and Elias would die, yet he wasn't sure how or when. Precision is what mattered most during an abstraction. Something Julius taught him. He searched his person, checking for the medallion.

Quintus gazed in wonder at the small, palm-sized medallion in his hands. The metallic surface shimmered in the morning light, its unknown magical material reminiscent of the intricate design of the Mayan calendar.

He couldn't help but be captivated by the glowing light that flowed through the ridges of the device, evidence of its life force. He knew that the color of the light indicated its strength—blue meant full, orange was faint, and red was critical. Despite their journey, it was still blue.

But it was the purpose of the medallion that truly intrigued Quintus. He knew that when the dials were turned, someone could travel to any point in the past. As long as the rules of time were not broken. He could feel the temptation gnawing at him, a part of him wanting to take a risk and see where the medallion would take him.

Nefeli stirred. Quintus quickly put the medallion back into his satchel, feeling a crumpled piece of parchment. His eyes narrowed as he read the message from Julius. Lilith had summoned him, just as she had done many times before.

Quintus huffed, unable to shake the feeling of annoyance that he felt at times when he thought of Lilith. She was as real as the tunic keeping him clothed, and just as the wool retains its natural color without the need for dyes, Lilith remained true to her nature and didn't feel the need to put on a facade to impress others.

However, her secrecy was an enigma that plagued Quintus, and he was never sure exactly what it was she had planned. And then there was Julius.

Lilith told him that Julius was a Darviant, like herself, but who was he, really? Yet another question he would not get an answer to. Since his arrival to the Intrepid, he'd been playing catch up, always one step behind.

"Bah," Quintus grunted, tearing the paper. He sighed, scanning the camp, and finding Nefeli.

Seeing her alive brought on a sense of relief, and Quintus thought about how lucky he was to have her as an ally. He thought about Nero, who put them in this position, cursing the fact that he killed the lad.

He did what he was asked, acting as he was trained. His ignorance, the way he treated slaves, kidnapping...

How could you blame a wild dog for its viciousness? Quintus thought. It wasn't regret but empathy, yet he knew if time permitted, he would sail back to the port and kill the merchant.

"What has been lost in the clouds?" Nefeli's voice broke his thoughts. He had not realized she was up. "Julius disappeared, I see," she said, scanning the area. "So, he leaves you alone with the kidnapped wife of one of the most powerful men in Sparta, hmmm?"

"I am quite sure the kidnapped wife could put in a good word for me?"

"Perhaps." She said, her lips pursed to the side, tapping her chin as piercing dark eyes that radiated intelligence and a sharpness of wit.

From his days following Kara, Quintus made it his mission to learn everything about the people within her circle. Nefeli was one of them. The striking woman wore a silk Tyrian purple dress, worn from the night before, but it was fit for a woman bred to be a royal. However, Nefeli's rigid posture and muscular tone were evidence of her lifetime of training.

Her eyes gravitate towards the Rhomphaia. "Who are you that Kara would gift a weapon of vast history?" she questioned, staring at the sword with a glint of curiosity.

The blade's intricate symbols reflected in the morning light. Now that she mentioned it, he wondered the same thing. Vasilus collected this blade after one of his many great victories, yet she gifted it to him. Why?

Before he could spit out the lie of him being a nobody, a slave looking to earn his freedom—she held up a hand.

"Your time here has been filled with falsehoods," Nefeli said. "You and Julius have made a mockery of the three most powerful men in

Sparta. And let us not forget your arrival here, where they say you managed to escape despite being bound and blindfolded by Kara herself."

Nefeli crept closer, brows depended, morning light reflecting off the thick silver jewelry around her neck. Quintus's heart pounded as he slowly reached for the sword.

She stopped. "Tizona's hilt glows because of what you are," she said, a smirk on her face. "A slayer of darkness, a man born with blood so strong that the greatest warrior trembles at the thought of facing him. You, Quintus, are a Champion."

The name Tizona reverberated through his mind, a melody he couldn't shake. As a gladiator, he'd always been a student of weapons. His life depended on it. After nearly being killed in the arena, Lilith had taken him to the future, giving him access to the world's history. He'd taken full advantage, devouring every scrap of information on weapons.

It was an old infatuation he couldn't break, no matter how hard he tried. The neurolink uploaded data directly to his brain. Some information remained elusive, but as he searched the wealth of information, it came to him.

Tizona was a famous medieval sword referenced in poems from that age. This was a Thracian sword, with no known connection to its namesake. Another mystery to add to the growing list. And to make matters worse, this girl knew he was a Champion.

However, he shouldn't have been surprised. This was a world far removed from the vale that is the future, where technology weaves an intricate web of tricks, and magic is dismissed as just another strand of illusions. People like Lilith were few in a sea of nonbelievers, but here.

"Please. You insult me with that surprised look on your face," Nefeli said. "I can assure you I know more about the Champions than you."

Quintus raised a curious brow. "What do you know?"

Nefeli's face brightened, and she gestured for Quintus to sit. "My, my, your accent is far too refined for one who's never traveled beyond Greece," she said, removing a thick silver necklace. "And the same goes for our dear friend's attire. The fabric is authentic, but there's something peculiar about it. People say I'm mad for my theories, but I ask you, traveler, how many facts does one need to disprove a theory?"

Quintus started to say something, to give an answer, but couldn't find the words.

"Exactly," Nefeli said, holding out the necklace, revealing a metallic cylinder with strange symbols that gleamed under the morning sun. "Here is another thing. That medallion you have. I have seen one like it, twice actually. A deity, *Delphi*, or so she claimed, and Lysander, who vanished at sea by the way, twice only to return with a woman with hair as red as an apple. Guess what happened to her?"

"She disappeared..." Quintus' words dragged.

"Exactly," Nefeli said. Her fingers danced across the symbols etched into the cylinder, moving with a practiced ease that spoke of long hours spent studying the artifact.

His heart raced, not of fear but excitement. *History buried some truths about Sparta*, he thought. *It was known for its military prowess, but never did they mention Nefeli, the great scholar*. He wondered briefly if this was set up by Lilith. Was she manipulating the timeline?

A soft hiss revealed a hidden compartment that slid open, revealing a long, yellowed scroll. Its stacked pages looked as though it had seen better days.

Quintus leaned in, curious despite himself, as Nefeli unrolled the map, revealing an intricate design. It depicted the surrounding area with a level of detail that he had never seen before, and he couldn't help but marvel at the work that had gone into it.

"What you see is a map passed down from the Sage seekers," Nefeli said, a note of pride creeping into her voice. "It reveals the location of a temple said to hold secrets of the gods themselves. But to reach it, we will need a Champion." She shot Quintus a meaningful look, her eyes glinting with something that looked suspiciously like hope.

The Roman gladiator stepped back, his stance defensive. "I cannot help you," he said firmly. "I know not who or what you are. And if you're as clever as you claim to be, you'd know that my hands are tied."

Nefeli let out a hearty, mischievous chuckle. "Oh, but your options are limited," she said, striding closer. "You need my husband, and as you may have noticed, I led you here. The cave is but a few miles away. We enter, unlock the door, I continue my scholarly efforts, and I promise to lead you straight to their camp. Tonight."

Quintus waved his finger with raised brows. He let out an exaggerated high-cheeked laugh, cursing himself and Julius from being in this position.

"Fine," Qintus sighed. "What choice do I have?"

Nefeli smiled. "None."

They gathered what little they had and set out on their journey. Nefeli eagerly flipped through the scroll filled with sketches, scribbles, and ancient lore. Quintus watched her with mild amusement, wondering how such a tiny person could contain so much energy. Why was Nefeli so interested in this Sage lore?

"Who do you work for?" Quintus said, dodging a sharp branch as they continued their hike.

She speed walked, dodging a few more branches, mumbling to herself. "Nefeli," he called.

"No one," she said, stopping abruptly. With the map still to her face, she walked past him in another direction for the first time after they walked straight for what seemed like hours. The sun bore down on them and the air had grown thick.

Quintus huffed.

"The question you should be asking is who I am working with," Nefeli said, breaking the long silence. There was a long pause. "Well..." Nefeli said, lowering the map.

"Are you serious?"

She held the map up to the light and continued walking. Quintus rolled his eyes. "I think I understand why Nero gagged her," he muttered.

He let out an extubated sigh. "Who are you working—"

"Kara," she blurted. "To be truthful, she warned me not to embark on this *journey*, but I could not resist the temptation to snatch the weapon you now hold and venture forth."

"And then what?"

"We have much to study. Information about the origins of the Sages, Champions, the banished gods," she paused. "Wait, why am I telling you? I imagine you and your friend will have vanished by then, so it is no problem of yours..."

She stopped and looked back at Quintus. He heard it too. Footsteps, he thought he heard them before, but figured it was an animal of the mountains. He put his hand on his lips while closing his eyes, taking a deep breath as he reached out with his heightened senses.

He could feel the world around him in ways others could not comprehend. The tiniest vibrations in the earth beneath his feet spoke to him, the rustle of leaves whispered secrets, and even the slightest shift in the air currents sent shivers down his spine.

It was his gift, though not one that he always possessed. He only discovered it after his first jump. Julius helped him understand it during their previous venture. Being a Champion came with its own gifts, but this was different.

"Four," Quintus whispered. "They stopped."

"Can you see how far?"

Quintus opened his eyes. "I can't *see* anything."

"We should keep going," she said, starting off.

With his blade at the ready, Quintus followed Nefeli. After a few more miles and a lot more mumbling, they finally stopped. Unfollowed, or so he thought. For reasons unknown, he couldn't tap into his sensory ability, another mystery for him to solve.

Facing them was a jagged mouth gaping like the jaw of some ancient beast. The cave's exterior was quiet except for the distant sound of a stream. Its walls were adorned with ancient glyphs, and the air was thick with the scent of damp earth and rotting leaves.

"We're here," Nefeli said, approaching the entrance and studying the puzzle that lay before them.

Quintus remained cautious. Goosebumps covered his skin with a sense of unease.

"May I use your sword?" she asked with an exaggerated tone.

Quintus hesitated for a moment, then handed her the weapon. Nefeli skillfully worked the puzzle, and as she inserted the sword, it roared, and the ground shook. The door of the cave rattled.

"Yes," Nefeli celebrated. "I will—"

Out leapt the harpy, a grotesque creature with wings of matted feathers, razor-sharp talons, and a piercing screech that shook Quintus to his core.

The Champion's sword appeared in his hand. He had questions, but no time to think. The monster swooped towards him with a fierce intensity, its wings beating powerfully against the air.

"This better be worth it," Quintus said, raising his sword and preparing to fight, his heart pounding in his chest.

The harpy was fast, but he was faster, and he managed to dodge its first attack. They circled each other warily, each waiting for an opening.

As the harpy swooped down on Quintus, he braced himself for the attack. He struggled to break free from the monster's grasp, but its talons were too strong. The beast cornered him against a tree, its hot breath on his face. Despite having fought creatures before, this was different. Whatever lay inside the cave, it was clear that the information about the Sages was not meant to be discovered.

Just when he thought he was done for, the harpy shrieked in pain and turned its attention to Nefeli, who had pulled out a knife. With a swift movement, Quintus ducked underneath its claws and plunged his Champion sword into the beast. Warm blue blood poured out as the sword absorbed the essence of the monster.

As Quintus and Nefeli caught their breath, they approached the cave. Four figures sprang out, clad in Athenian clothing. Two large men held weapons at the ready, while an old man in a chiton tunic and himation cloak appeared flushed and tired, likely from following them. A small boy, no older than eleven, stood next to him, sporting a similar outfit.

"Socrates?" Nefeli spat.

"Nefeli? The scholar from Sparta," Socrates replied, his voice latent with disdain. "I should have expected nothing less. Did you get clearance for this little venture?"

"What business is it of yours?"

"My apprentice and I have risked our lives for this discovery," Socrates said, taking a step forward.

Nefeli rolled her eyes. "So you'd let a child into your lecture halls, but not a woman. Fascinating."

"Plato is no mere child. In some ways, he is like you. Like you, he has shown great potential and, unlike you, he knows his place," Socrates said with a twinkle in his eye. "Now, step aside."

The two guards by his side advanced, their armor glistening in the sun. Plato tugged on his teacher's tunic. "That may not be necessary, or wise."

Socrates ignored the child's warning, and one of the large guards attacked Quintus. "Run inside," Quintus yelled to Nefeli. "I'll hold them off."

She took off into the cave as Quintus made easy work of the guard, while the other cowered in fear, watching as he defeated his mate.

An upset Socrates lunged at Quintus, but he stopped the frail man and flicked him on the nose.

"Wait your turn," Quintus said with a smile. He looked past the irate scholar to the frightened child and smiled. "Plato, is it?" The boy nodded. "Go inside. Nefeli won't mind. Guard! Accompany him."

Socrates's mouth dropped open. Plato and the guard waited for his approval. "Don't just stand there, fool," the scholar said to the guard. "Take the boy."

He turned his annoyed expression back to Quintus. "You can unhand me now," he said, snatching away.

As Nefeli and Plato returned, glowing with their newfound knowledge, Socrates ran inside the cave. Quintus and Nefeli left, and as they walked away, they could hear Socrates yelling around inside.

Quintus asked what she found, but she fired back with questions about where he was from. "It appears we both have our secrets," he said.

"I will tell you this. The cave confirmed that Champions are chosen by Uranus to lead and fight against evil. "

"Like the Sages?"

"Yes," Nefeli said. "The reason for the existence of Champions was to defend against the Sages."

"To kill them."

Nefeli shook her head. "The Sages are immortal beings. They cannot be killed."

Quintus's throat tightened at the thought of a creature walking the earth. Nefeli had to be mistaken. Immortality was not possible, yet part of him knew there was not an exaggeration with their power. After fighting that beast, it was clear. Lilith needed the Champions; he was one, and the other was here, in Sparta.

As promised, Nefeli led him to the camp. He hid as Nefeli approached one of the men. He couldn't make out what they were saying, but he knew it wasn't good. The aura of the camp and the body language suggested tragedy—he was right. Nefeli dropped to her knees, sobbing. The soldier walked away.

Quintus rushed to her side. She looked at him with watery eyes. "He's gone..."

"Who?"

It took a minute for it to register. *Vasilis is dead.* The warm breeze kissed his skin. His stomach twisted as he watched on his aching knees. *How could such a tragedy happen on a beautiful day?*

It was then he realized he made a mistake.

Something felt... off.

A sack covered his head, and his hands were bound—metal pressed against his neck. "You dare return."

Elias? Did she set me up?

"He saved my life." Nefeli cried. "He killed my capturers."

"Why didn't he just kill them in Sparta?"

"They had something that belonged to his wife."

"Kara would be upset if you kill him," Midas said.

"Why bother?" said Nefeli. "You are king now. Put an heir in me."

King? But how? Quintus felt the tension in the air. He remembered how he was at that age, what he had done. Now he was at the mercy of a child.

"We should honor our fallen brother," said Nefeli. "Here, I just made this."

"So be it," Elias said. "To Vasilis."

The small camp of men jeered, but grief filled Quintus's heart, for he knew the pain Kara must have felt, even if she accepted his fate.

In a few moments, laughter filled the air. *Nefeli's drink was working.*

Nefeli adjusted his tunic. "I will come back for you," she whispered to Quintus.

Their voices became distant until they faded; he wasn't sure how much time had passed, but the cool air signaled night. Clanking armor surrounded Quintus, soon followed by grunts and the thump of their bodies hitting the floor. The men didn't stand a chance.

Am I next?

The ropes came off, then the rag. Lysander stood in front of him. He looked around at the carnage, then at Lysander. His warriors walked toward him, covered in blood. "Elias and Midas are clinging to life."

"Was this on Lilith's orders or Kara's?" Quintus asked, standing up.

"Mine," Lysander replied, handing Quintus his sword. "Now take them and never return."

LILITH

Intrepid, 2076

A hollowed robotic voice fought its way through the ringing. "Alpha Aries requesting access."

Lilith rubbed the grogginess from her face, but not the twisted feeling in her stomach. The dream happened again, but it felt so real. She could still smell the fumes from the burning engine before the plane crash.

The horrid screams rang in her ear, and her mother's horrified face broke her heart. She was so close she could touch her, maybe save her.

What if it wasn't a dream?

Thanks to her training, her powers were growing at an exponential rate. Maybe this was her powers manifesting beyond her own comprehension. Experiments and data suggest ghost radiation could be responsible for the growth. Though she couldn't help but wonder if the dagger was having an effect.

Time travel prevents any jumper from jumping to a place where they exist. So, she knew it was scientifically impossible to be there with her mother during the crash. After all, she was home and found out the same way the rest of the world did when the UNA televised it.

Lilith shook her head, as if to shake the thought away. *Of course, it was a dream.*

"I have an update on the boys' progress," Seth said, unfolding a tablet. He paused, his brown eyes raised with concern. "Are you okay?"

"Yes, why?" she replied, though the throbbing pain in her head said otherwise. She grabbed the tablet from him.

"I can tell something is wrong. You know it's a sixth sense of mine," he said, tapping his temple. A witty smile formed under his neatly trimmed beard. "Besides, your hand is shaking. Perhaps you can use—"

"A drink," she blurted, stretching out her fingers to stop the trembling.

Of course, he could feel something. Lilith groaned softly, regretting the necessity to bond with him psychically. It worked by accelerating his learning curve.

"Your computers calculated their attribute potential. Midas and Elias's limits far exceeded these numbers." Seth said from behind the bar. "These numbers are wrong; I imagine you'd agree once you see them for yourself."

From the moment he was extracted, she had no foresight. She thought it was unique to Seth, from the psychic link, but the same happened to everyone removed from their timeline and brought into hers.

Lilith sat at her desk to analyze the data. Their testing was beyond peak human abilities, beyond any athlete, even those who were genetically enhanced. *They will prove very useful.* She wasn't surprised, given all she learned about warriors throughout time.

Darviants was the name modern science gave to anyone with special abilities, the unexplained. Lilith, however, learned that there was so much more, particularly those men and women with the blood of their gods coursing through their veins. With the addition of Midas and Elias, she had two more on her side. Seth was a man of his word, and these boys were exceptional. Still, they were a wildcard, especially Seth.

Fragments of her consciousness linked with his. The parts of her she needed him to know, but there were other complications. Lilith continued scrolling through the tablet. "How are those headaches?"

"Better than yours, I imagine," he said, handing her a drink. "The medication helps."

"What about the fragmented images?"

"I haven't had them," his tone drifted. He walked toward the large window overlooking the earth.

Good. She thought, relieved the medication was working. It helped suppress the subconsciousness that would otherwise reveal more than what she needed him to know.

What are you thinking, Seth? She stood up, following his gaze.

He sighed before turning back to her. She quickly shifted her focus back to the tablet.

Seth's wrist beeped. "Elias and Midas are waiting."

Lilith nodded and handed back the tablet before seeing him out. After a long shower, she suited up and pulled her hair into a tight ponytail. She placed her hand on the desk scanner.

The drawer opened to the shimmering gold sun-shaped metal attached to a midnight-black pommel with a grip made for her—the *Sun Dagger*, they called it.

Was it fate? she thought. Her mind drifted to the day she met Mei, an old scientist from Norway with an eerie resemblance to Lilith's grandmother.

Lilith remembered sitting on a park bench waiting for Malaya with sunglasses and a wide-brim hat concealing her identity. However, this woman, Mei, not only recognized her but knew about Project Bungee and what they needed to harness antimatter and negative energy, otherwise known as ghost radiation. She handed her a metallic element she promised would solve their problem—she was right.

Lilith unsheathed the dagger, letting the gold blade made up of the same mysterious metal take its turn to shine. She held it, knowing one thing that wasn't a mystery; everything came with a price. Today, the stranger's price rang loud in her head.

Someday, you will harness the gifts of this dagger. In the same way, your daughter will use the metal to unlock time. When she does, you will send her to unlock my daughter.

Lilith's eyes glanced inside her desk at the old parchment that held the coordinates. She tucked the sheathed dagger underneath her jacket before boarding the lift to the top deck of the space station. She walked past the trackers into the command room, where her senior staff waited for her arrival.

It was a simple room with silver and white panels on the wall. The earth's blue glow provided a soft hue to the room. Everyone except for Alex, who had a meeting with her crew.

"Nice of you to join us," Quintus said, taking a seat. Sheldon sat across from him and Joseph, Rose next to Sheldon. "Are the Spartans behind you?"

"No. But they will arrive soon," Lilith said, taking her seat at the head of the table. "Unfortunately, you won't be here, so your fandom will have to wait until the time is right. I'm not ready to have that conversation about what you did to them, not yet."

"How are we doing in the public relations department?" She asked snidely, partly knowing what Rose was about to say.

Rose cleared her throat. Her mechanical arm decompressed. "The support isn't just coming from the public. Four of the six governors have come out publicly demanding President Ross meet with the new UNA leader."

All she needed was the people, but to have leaders of the Sectors wake up was an unintended blessing. Pressuring the government and developing an alliance was key. With Empress Maki in her pocket, the transition of power will be seamless.

Maybe now was the right time for them to meet.

"Things aren't looking so good under Maki," Rose said. "Kakashi hasn't been very forthcoming. Rumors are blaming Kakashi for the bombing, and he's keeping Maki out of the public eye. So meeting with the president now wouldn't be a good idea."

Lilith nodded. "It'll make them look desperate and weak in the eyes of the other families, who'll have a reason to take them both out."

There was a long pause before Lilith spoke. "We will use this to our advantage. Have Ghost use the platform, tell the believers that the savior is coming, do not revolt, at least not yet."

Rose nodded.

"Rose, please call your husband and activate the security plans. Things are going to go south in New Japan. Be careful."

"Understood," Rose said as the doors closed behind her.

Lilith adjusted herself. "Speaking of allies. Have you heard anything from our contacts?"

"Yes, actually. I received a message not too long ago." Joseph said, scanning his tablet. He tried to wipe the worry from his face.

"What is it?"

"They're sending Malaya to Japan... with the Spartan."

"Dammit," Lilith said, leaning back in her chair. "I need a drink."

Sheldon brought her a Malta. It was a perfect balance of condensed milk and malt. Sheldon knew her like a book. He was lacking a mother figure—he found one in her, and he was like a son to her. Malaya and her father would frown at the thought of adding ice. A smile followed the thought. She tried not to, but she missed them. Unfortunately, both her father and daughter were fighting for the other side.

More than anything, Lilith wanted to tell her daughter the truth, but after Mexico, she couldn't risk it, though the magic in the medication helped Malaya in ways she couldn't—it also hindered her. Yet, here they were, using Malaya.

Even with her growing abilities. There were so many uncalculated changes. One of those miscalculations was the number of people impacted by the radiation leakage in the atmosphere. Governors implemented a quarantine protocol for parts of the country. People got sick, and others also gained abilities. Unfortunately, HOA only had a few locations across the world, but it wasn't enough.

She needed to move quickly to prevent the worst-case scenario, Darviants being used as weapons—she needed to do something.

"Sheldon," said Lilith. "I need you to contact the headmistress and headmasters at every school and have them mask results. We can't afford the government exposing the truth about Darviants. Also, have our lab work on contriving measures for the ghost radiation, for both us and leakage."

Joseph exited.

It didn't take long for the Spartans to arrive. Sheldon hurried to fetch Seth his favorite wine. She secretly hated how devout Sheldon became to Seth, but he was an extension of her, even if she wouldn't admit it out loud. Seth took his seat at the opposite head while Elias sat next to her and Midas across from him.

The two young Spartans' acclimations came without complications. They cut their hair to prove their commitment and wore the uniforms assigned to them—something every group on the Intrepid adhered to.

Since they were travelers, they wore a dark crimson jacket with a gold stripe across its shoulder and cuff. The colors not only paid homage to the power they held in Sparta, a small token of gratitude, but it meant something more.

These warriors held a higher rank among the other crews, third overall, thanks to their vast absorption of knowledge and prowess. Only members of the Military Astronaut Defense ranked higher, recognized by their black uniform with silver stripes, and the senior staff who wore purple and gold.

Lilith cleared her throat. "Everyone has completed the training and has received the briefing. So I'll make this quick."

A holographic image appeared in front of everyone. "Your mission is an extraction. Location: seventeenth century Japan. You will take the head of the Tokugawa clan, the Shogun himself, Ieyasu Tokugawa and Mizunami Toyotomi."

Seth's face looked concerned before he even spoke. "The Tokugawas just came out of a war. Their senses will be heightened. Perhaps posing as weapons dealers is a great cover, but it could be troublesome."

Lilith leaned back in her chair. He was right about the Tokugawa's, but it was too late now. She did all she could and made the right alliances. "We have an inside clan. Osamu Torri, who will aid in the extraction. You will meet with him and go over the plan. It's important that you trust me the way I trust you."

There was a pause. "I would be more trusting if I knew the entire plan," said Seth, his voice deep and gruff, like a battle-hardened warrior from ancient Greece.

"Everyone is on a need-to-know basis, but I'll tell you this. Mizunami and Ieyasu are two vital pieces to my plan. I've edited the text in the Kojiki, promising them a savior who will rise here in this world, unite the people, and give way to those willing to fight against the tyrants that are the UNA."

Seth raised a brow. "Kojiki, huh... That is the Japanese holy book, correct? Is that not blasphemous?"

"It's not exactly a holy book," Lilith's brows furrowed, feeling slightly offended. "And I simply added a few lines."

Seth twirled his drink. "Such a complex plan. Could you not contact Ieyasu in his youth, tell him you will see him again in the future, and make your proposal, then?"

"Time would not allow it," Sheldon interjected, charging the display to algorithms of time. "Ieyasu is too important to time itself. His life is marked in ink, as we call it, so any disruption would be monstrous, but after sixteen hundred, well... things are a bit murky with his history."

"That's why we need to bring Ieyasu here," said Lilith. "We need him to see the future and make a deal..."

Elias tapped on the table, his sinister, rich blue eyes staring at her, waiting for her to tell him to speak. He was like a caged beast, ready to be unleashed. That fury drove him, but if not tamed, he could be dangerous. Luckily, he had Midas and Seth and a soft spot for her.

Lilith turned her head. "What is it, Elias?"

"You brought us here to make a difference," he said. His voice was equally as menacing, no matter how relaxed and calm his tone was. "We cannot do that if you are going to handcuff us."

Sheldon cleared his throat. "Sorry, but it's not her that's restricting you. It's time itself."

"I'm addressing Lilith," Elias said, causing Sheldon to withdraw in his seat.

"Sheldon's right," Lilith said. "The lessons about time fluxes and paradoxes were not to keep you busy. You have to use caution."

"We will be as careful as possible," said Midas, his green eyes cut at Elias. "We don't need to kill unnecessarily." The baby-faced blond wasn't as intimidating as his six-foot-five bulky frame suggested.

"Elias is correct," said Seth. "Matters of this magnitude require more. We are infiltrating a man whose paranoia aided in his victory. You can't be so confident that he won't spot Osamu's treachery—"

"What about the Great Guard?" Elias interrupted. "Kasumi is a formidable warrior, and so is Inoichi, a Champion of his own time if I understand correctly."

"Yes, he is," Seth said, a twinge of excitement in his voice. "There will be bloodshed. It is necessary, even at the Tokugawa's expense. You must prepare for the worst."

Lilith narrowed her eyes as she watched Seth give his speech. She knew he was a savage, but that's exactly why she chose him. He possessed a raw power, a gift so strong that it struck fear into those who knew they couldn't control him. He also had a drive to do whatever it took to get things done, even if it meant killing a friend. The thought sent chills down her spine. She could see it in his intense glare as he continued to motivate, the thrill of taking on a Champion burning in his eyes.

But Lilith couldn't let him forget the bigger picture. What would happen if there were no Champions in that time period? Who would stop the others if someone woke another Sage? They would not have a Champion or anyone to control it. Inoichi, Midas, Quintus, Vasilis, and the other Champions meant more to history than Seth could ever know—more than what he needed to know.

Lilith cursed herself for not considering how dangerous someone like Seth could be, but she needed to remind him who was in control.

A mocking laugh escaped her lips as she felt her blood boil. "You don't get it. We have to tread lightly. If time itself doesn't stop you, then you'll risk creating a cataclysmic time flux. So let me ask you, Seth. What kingdom will you inherit, then?"

A force surged through her body, causing the table to tremble beneath her. Lilith wasn't surprised; these tremors and visions happened often. But as the visions flooded her mind, She saw labs filled with children and adults being probed and experimented on, families being torn apart by war and death, and so much bloodshed. It was the catastrophe she was trying to prevent.—even if it meant being the villain. She could not let Seth risk it all.

A hand on her shoulder brought her back. She looked into Sheldon's eyes. "Try to relax."

"Right." Lilith exhaled, her cheek warm from tears, ignoring the concerned stares from the others. She wiped them away and held out her hand, calling for the cup of Malta. Like a puck across ice, the cup slid across the table into her hand. What was left of it cooled her body and her tone.

Lilith looked into each of their eyes. "The Tokugawa family is untouchable. Do everything you can to avoid killing, no matter their status."

"Aye," said Seth, pouring himself another drink.

"And what about these hilts?" Midas asked.

"My research is almost complete, but I need two of them in order to test my theory. So it's important to do all you can, within the rules of time, to get your hands on them."

"You haven't shared much about this *next phase*," Seth said with a smile.

Lilith shot him a stern glance. "I have to see how Japan plays out first."

Sheldon briefed them on the divergences while Lilith took a trip to a secret spot inside the very bottom of Intrepid. A clear bubble away from everyone, surrounded by everything space had to offer. The cold silence was addicting. This was where she'd come to pray. She untucked her cross and prayed, but today, she came to do something more. She needed to test the Sun Dagger. The dagger required part of her. She poked her thumb; a drop of blood covered the tip.

Lilith closed her eyes, feeling the emptiness of the universe and time converge within her, becoming a part of her essence. A faint tremor ran through her body. She felt it travel from the pit of her stomach to the palms of her hands and into the dagger.

"Come on," she whispered, gritting her teeth. Sweat trickled down her back.

A beam of light burst from the tip of the dagger, opening a small vortex. Lilith's face lit up with joy as she watched it expand, growing large enough to accommodate more than one person.

"Yes!" she cried out.

At her command, the vortex closed. Time was now a part of her, and she couldn't explain how or why, but it was. Science could never fully comprehend her powers or those of the Darviants, but she was now something greater. All her research had paid off, and the dagger seemed to amplify her abilities. She wondered if she could create a vortex without it, but for now, it would suffice.

Lilith returned to her quarters and spoke into her journal. A villain's monologue of sorts. She smiled at the thought. The doctor had been right. It was therapeutic. It was the only way for her to release all her secrets and thoughts, like talking to Jeff. She sat on the edge of her bed, wishing he was there to witness it all coming together. Despite a station filled with hundreds of people, she felt alone.

"Angie, close log, that's all for today," Lilith said. "Call Sheldon."

A holographic image of Sheldon appeared. "It worked," she said, grinning from ear to ear. "I just needed to rest, but it seems to drain my other abilities temporarily."

"So that's the only downside, huh," said Sheldon. "I guess we have a more efficient way to send you and Quintus to Scandinavia."

"Yes, we do, and possibly horizontally through time. Maybe I wouldn't be late for the meeting anymore," Lilith said. The thought of Malaya crossed her mind, and she knew she needed to give her daughter a chance before proceeding. "Sheldon, I have to go."

"Angie, open a secure feed," she commanded. "Call Malaya."

The transmission was faulty, but she could see Malaya, the pain swirling inside her cinnamon eyes. "Mami. Where, where are you?"

"You know I can't tell you that."

"Okay, just tell me you're being held against your will? Tell me the UNA is blackmailing you." She pleaded.

Her eyes watered and she cleared the lump in her throat. "I'm sorry for what I've put you through."

"I don't want your apologies," Malaya whispered. Her voice cracked, holding back her tears. "Come home, please, the Cabinet—"

"I can't do that."

"So, why did you call me?"

"To give you another chan—"

"Stop," Malaya interrupted. Her anger was prevalent. "You have everyone fooled, Mom, even yourself, but what you did was murder the emperor for the sins of his father. There is no justifying that."

"I lived it, bodies littering the street, staring down the barrel of a gun, defenseless, unable to control my gifts. We survived that, only to see my mother years later get executed—in the name of Kasimoto."

This was the first time in years she openly spoke about it. But it didn't bother her the way it used to. The day was still fresh in her mind. Of course, even if she wanted to, she couldn't forget. She wished her mother had listened to her warnings, her premonitions, and stayed home. So yes, this was revenge and so much more.

"Akai Kasimoto wasn't innocent. He was a monster who was on his way to washing his hands in blood. The Darviants were weaponized and tortured, all in the name of a dictator who would have risen. A dictator unlike anything history has seen, and I had to stop it, even if lives are lost."

"Oh, I get it, and since you're one of them... a *Darviant,* right? A telepath, is it... like the few in HOA?" she said, not shying away from the sarcasm. "So, enlighten me, Lilith. Did you see their faces? Do you have names?"

Lilith felt the tears stream. "I can't do that. It hasn't happened because of me. It won't happen. Even if I showed you, you wouldn't believe me. You haven't believed in anything in a long time."

"My beliefs have nothing to do with this. If Papa was here, maybe he could have stopped you," Malaya's voice drifted. "Wait... Who else helped you? Uncle Joseph? Shay? Grandpa?"

"Your uncle and aunt have nothing to do with this. Focus your energy and time on finding him, please. Don't go to Japan and keep Shay sane by being there for her."

I'm sorry for what we've done by keeping you in the dark, but it was to protect you from this vast impracticality. The medicine, removing you from HOA and not telling you the truth about.

Malaya was unwilling to give her the benefit of the doubt. Who can blame her? Telling her the truth now was fruitless. It wasn't time. The least she could do was give her a choice to fight with her.

"This is bigger than you know," Lilith said. "I'll tell you everything—no more secrets, but you have to choose. Me or them?"

"Nothing is bigger than time itself. So, keep your secrets. I refuse to sit back and watch you kill innocent people. I will find you and everyone helping you."

Lilith wiped the wetness from her face. "Okay, catch me if you can."

INOICHI

Edo, Japan 1601

An aroma of sweet green peas and rice made its way into his room, along with his younger brother, Fukumatsumaru, who was still wrapped in bandages, an honorable testimony to his fight on the front line. The Battle of Sekigahara haunted them, taking many lives, but earned his brother the name Tadayoshi. Though, he will always be Fukumatsumaru in Inoichi's heart.

Fukumatsumaru wasn't always a willing fighter, but he was special. And Inoichi suspected another war, and he'd need his brother by his side. "Nobuyasu, I mean Inoichi-sama," he said with a dimpled, suspicious smile. "Before you do your painting thing, I have a gift for you."

"I don't think I need another gift from you." Inoichi's thick brows furrowed. "Not after the last one."

"I promise this one doesn't bite unless you ask," he hurried out and then quickly returned with nothing.

"Well, on with it."

Fukumatsumaru brushed his loose black strands behind his ear, then whistled. He rubbed his hands together as a tall, elegantly dressed woman walked in. Inoichi's jaw dropped as she slowly undressed.

"Stop," he commanded, turning away. "Take her away immediately."

"Big brother, you don't understand. This is a high-ranking oiran with very *special* talents."

"Then you take her. I do not desire a courtesan," he growled, aggressively tying his long, fine hair into a knot.

"You know I can't. I'm attempting to purify myself."

"Yet you defile me."

"Very well, very well," Fukumatsumaru said, resting a hand on Inoichi's shoulder. "I admit I can be forceful at times, but my intentions are always in good faith."

"I know you mean well." Inoichi turned to face his brother. "So take this woman as a gift from me to you."

"A joke," Fukumatsumaru said, walking toward the woman. "You are not married yet, and you're already a changed man."

"My brother is in love," said Fukumatsumaru. "As for me, I never invest too much of myself into anyone, for you risk losing yourself." He looked back at Inoichi. "I shall see you at the ceremony, big brother. Can't wait to tell Kasumi and Hidetada about this."

Inoichi grunted. The thought of including more siblings in this torture twisted this stomach. He grabbed his paintbrush and canvas.

Sunrays shone perfectly on the cherry blossom where people sat and ate while children ran freely in the courtyard—the perfect muse for a perfect day. By sundown, he'd marry the woman he was destined to be with. A smile crossed his face, sliding wet paint against the canvas.

The perfect gift, he thought, painting his final stroke.

"Inoichi!" His father said, storming into his room.

"Father," Inoichi said through gritted teeth, forcing a deep bow.

"Mother," he said, softening his voice as she took her usual place behind his father. Her head was normally lowered; however, on this day, she stood with it held high.

"Pillagers have entered the Torri village," his father said. "I advise you to postpone this marriage and travel there immediately. Torri Osamu will assist you on your voyage."

"Why not send a small army and slaughter these pillagers? We are Tokugawa, soon to be the shogunate, feared from Mikawa to Kai; even the elders recognize us as the most powerful! Yet, you would send the heir for small matters on the day of my wedding. Say what really bothers you, Father."

Wrinkles on his father's forehead and the bone in his wide jaw protruded. "You are arrogant. Your decisions are brash. What you are doing is unruly; matters of the heart do not belong in politics."

"The history between the Tokugawa and Toyotomi, is just that, history," said Inoichi. "Look beyond blood and violence; see why our union is good for not just our nation but generations to come. Perhaps you're afraid of an eight-year-old?"

His father's flaring nostrils warned that he crossed the line. "Do not forget who you are speaking with! I fear no one! Yet, I don't underestimate anyone. That boy will grow into a man and demand his position."

"Father, you gave up land and power to settle in Edo. Was that not a risk? I am doing the same, but differently. This is a peaceful solution. When Toyotomi Hideyori comes of age, he can marry Senhime. She is only a few years younger; I'm sure my brother will not protest."

Ieyasu's eyes no longer flamed with rage. It was a solid plan; his father appreciated that. "You think you know it all? Your ignorance must have made you forget what your sister did. The price she paid for ignorance and love."

Inoichi clenched his teeth and fought back the redness climbing the surface of his face. He looked over at his mother, unable to hide the pain in hers. *How could he still blame her, and worse, use the massacre as a tactic to win a fruitless argument...? Tasteless.*

"Ieyasu," his mother said, her voice low and soft. "Must you befoul *Tokuhime* at every turn? She is still your daughter."

"I don't recall asking for your input," his father whipped his head around, forcing her to bow and take a step back. "And it's Kasumi now. She lost the privilege of Tokuhime... I could never forgive her for what she's done — nor will I ever forget. Allowing her to serve as a *Great Guard* was merciful because she was my daughter. Otherwise, she would have been killed."

Ieyasu faced Inoichi. He took a step forward. "If you are foolish enough to go through with this marriage, I will choose Hidetada as the next Shogun.

"You can't," said Inoichi, squeezing his fist. "It's my birthright.

"Birthright?" His father scoffed. "The title is not yet official, but I assure you, if you empower those Kojiki wielders, I will strip you of yours," his father said. "Tell Mizunami to ask their kami for power—not my son!" Ieyasu stormed out, his bodyguards and servants tailing him.

Inoichi stared out the window. From his room, the villagers seemed so small, yet, despite the castle, he felt just as powerless. *Would he destroy their lineage out of fear of losing power?*

"I admire your strength," his mother said in a low tone—careful not to let his father hear. "You and your sister share that."

"We get it from you."

He saw his mother light up. It wasn't something he'd seen from her lately. So much death and sadness. His father had changed, not just the snow in his beard, but he consumed power like he had food. There was a different fire in his eyes. After all, he had won a great war.

For all his achievements, he lost part of who he was. His mother bore the weight of it more than she should. Consequently, part of who she was, disappeared. Though she was still there for them when they needed her. She grabbed Inoichi's hand—she smiled again. The sun hit her eyes, painting them a glowing light brown.

"You are the greater leader. Your father knows this. Everyone knows this, but I am no one to advise on matters of the heart?" she stared at his painting.

"I was guided by a friend, a woman, not of this world. She told me of all the women, it was I who was destined to marry your father. Despite the warnings of who he'd become, I still advised him, loved him, and gave him more than he would care to admit in the name of our nation to strengthen the Tokugawa reign. You must ask yourself, is Mizunami worth it?"

"Lady Saigo, may I speak to Inoichi?"

Osamu stood behind the sliding wooden doors. The translucent paper imaged him as he scratched the middle of his black, messy ponytail. Inoichi waved him in.

Osamu's farewell to Lady Saigo was a silent affair, marked by a respectful kiss on her hand. As she departed, he lingered in the doorway, his fingers absentmindedly tracing the contours of the unusual medallion concealed beneath his unkempt beard, his gaze distant and laden with unspoken thoughts.

Inoichi watched, a sense of unease crept upon him. *Perhaps it was more serious than I thought.*

The jovial warrior Inoichi once knew was replaced by a weathered man lost in contemplation. This was a side of Osamu only present during battle or strategy sessions—not the man who dubbed him the Branch Slayer.

Inoichi drifted for a moment that felt like ages ago when Osamu trained him and his brothers to channel their kai as a weapon. Inoichi's attempts were often met with failure, his concentration broken by the slightest distractions, leading to a particularly memorable incident.

In a moment of unchecked anger, Inoichi took his rage out on a nearby tree, snapping a branch that swung around to strike him across the face, leaving a welt that would scar over time.

Osamu, witnessing this, could not contain his amusement, gave Inoichi a nickname that would stick for the rest of the season, and longer. *Nobuyasu the Branch-Slayer.*

He would often mock his temperament, but that rage helped them all with the Battle of Sekigahara just two seasons ago. Yet today, on the day of his wedding, Osamu could not fain a smile.

Times were difficult, Inoichi understood that. Every clan involved felt the effects of the war. The Torii Clan was no different.

Lives were lost, and loyalties were tested. Osamu and his younger brother Ryu, who fought with the intensity of his red hair, were instrumental in the victory for the Tokugawa.

Ryu fled soon after in pursuit of enlightenment, though rumors suggest he could not bear the sudden weight of becoming clan leader. With Ryu gone, Osamu did his best to keep the Torri intact, though political differences drove the clan apart.

Osamu finally stopped fumbling with his odd medallion and stepped further inside the room. "Your father advised you to stop the wedding on the clan's behalf."

"Do you agree?"

"No. I informed your father that the men were not strangers, but exiled men looking for revenge."

Relief washed over Inoichi. He could not bear anyone else expressing their disappointment. "What of Ryu?" he asked. "Have you found him?"

"No. And his absence is being felt throughout the village. I fear unrest, which is why I have come to deliver this news personally." Osamu dropped his eyes. "I admit I took advantage of your father's lack of interest in your union. I requested your father send Hidetada and Tadayoshi to guard the village in my absence."

Inoichi waved a dismissive hand. "Father would not allow them to attend."

"For what it is worth, *gomen nasai*." Osamu squared his shoulders toward Inoichi and offered a deep bow. "I have also arranged for men from the west to arrive tonight. They will meet with your father to discuss an alliance."

"I should return after the ceremony then," Inoichi said

"And disappoint your bride? No. Allow these matters to rest in the hands of your father. I will arrive late after their introduction… do not worry, I will inform Mizunami."

"Good."

"I will leave you to get ready. Time is of the essence," Osamu bowed. "Excellent painting. Mizunami will love it."

Inoichi asked a servant to grab his painting and take it to where they'd have dinner. He finished combing his hair and pulled it back into a tight, long ponytail before searching for his father.

There was no chance of him changing his mind, but part of Inoihci hoped to appeal to his father's softer side and get his blessing.

Inoichi found him in his favorite room, decorated with gold, jewels, and artifacts. Some were expensive, while others were priceless, some purchased, some had been taken as a reminder of his victories, and others given as gifts.

His father stood with his back to the door; his hand hovered over a lonely wooden box. Its carvings were unique, with a story too elaborate to believe for some. Most of its lore was kept inside the castle walls. No one had opened it until now.

"There's a tale of elite warriors from all over the world who sacrificed themselves to stop a threat far greater than any god or kami," his father said, opening the box. He turned around, holding out the hilt. The stone faced man from before had softened. He looked more like the father he knew than his commander.

"Their power was otherworldly," his father continued, "and it is rumored that the carrier of this hilt could wield such power. It was a gift from my father to me, Divine Wind. Its divinity brought him luck. I can't say the same. Perhaps since I am not a believer, but for you, it may."

Inoichi grabbed it and bowed. *"Arigato gozaimasu,"* he said with widened eyes, running his hand across the metal.

It was odd to see a tsuka coming out of this foreign box. Scales of black serpents spiraled from the pommel, forming their head around the empty guard.

The tales it must have, he pondered, unable to break his gaze. For a moment, he thought he saw a faint glow emerge from their eyes.

"Your mother will not attend your ceremony," his father's sharp words cut through him, snapping his head up.

Inoichi swallowed the anger. He would have been foolish to expect anything else. "I understand, but at least I could have one of my brothers by my side."

"No. "I asked Fukumatsumaruu to remain to meet with Osamu's guest," his father said, walking past him.

Without giving Inoichi a chance to respond, his father slid the door closed.

Inoichi squeezed the hilt, feeling its ridges pressing against his skin. He wanted to throw it. *How can he get angry when it was expected? He will not have this day.* He took a deep breath and tucked it inside his robe.

Miles away, people gathered on this beautiful day to honor a union between the Tokugawa and Toyotomi. As always, her beauty radiated unparalleled even by the sun—she deserved this day.

After their ceremony and celebrations, he changed into his gold surcoat while Mizunami changed into her cherry and white kimono. Her hair was held up with a metal stick, and her bangs hung to her cheeks. Samurai trailed them as they strolled along the firefly-lit stone path boarded by stout trees.

"Why are you carrying that old scroll?" asked Inoichi.

"It's the original Kojiki," she said. Her voice was always low, as if afraid to let people hear what she thought. "It was given to me as a gift. I was unaware of your concern."

"Your faith can only take you so far."

"That is odd, since Shinto is your family's tradition, which adopted philosophies from the Kojiki," she said, withdrawing her scroll into her robe. "Where is this coming from?"

Inoichi frowned, stopping just before they reached the garden with a small pond. "My father... he threatened to take it all away if I did not postpone our wedding, but his true intentions were to stop it entirely. I can't help but recall what he did to Kasumi."

Mizunami lifted his chin and moved the strands of black hair from his face. "If she were still heir, my family would not have supported our marriage. They expected me to marry a male shogun."

"Is power all you want of me?" Inoichi questioned, vehemently turning away.

"Of course not. You know better than that. It was a joke. You are always so tense, but I apologize. I want you to understand the strength that lies between us. You are a man with exceptional gifts who will someday serve as a prominent leader, and together, we will reshape this nation."

"How can you be so sure?"

"Faith," she smiled. "I must see your wedding gift."

"Close your eyes," he said, putting his hands over her face. And escorted her toward the end of the garden. In front of it was his canvas; he stood between Mizunami and the painting. "Open them."

Mizunami gasped. He smiled, but it faded, realizing it wasn't the look he had hoped. "Yatagarasu," she said, forcing him to turn around.

His stomach sank as he, too, stared at the three-legged crow sitting atop his painting. Its eyes glowed gray in a darkness that replaced his bright sky and blackened, hollowed vessels replaced the joyous people.

Inoichi's mouth trembled a bit before he finally mustered the words. "This, this was not my painting."

A vibrant sensation inside his robe forced him to look down. He started to remove the hilt, but three Tokugawa samurai interrupted. "Forgive the intrusion, but your sister is missing. She left her armor behind and hasn't been seen since sunset. Shall I deploy a search squad?"

"The crow, the painting, and now your sister." Mizunami touched his cheek. "You should tighten security."

Inoichi scoffed, pressing his brows.

"Forgive me," she whispered, dropping her eyes.

"Send as many as you can. Cover as much ground as possible," he commanded the soldier. "I will be right behind you."

Osamu approached, looking at the samurai passing him by. "Sending those men is unnecessary."

"It is necessary. There are strangers at the castle. Kasumi would not have left it unguarded. Fukumatsumaruu cannot handle things... *my mother*." Inoichi turned to Mizunami.

Mizunami knelt and placed her hand on the ground. "There is something wrong... the earth, it's crying — you must go.

"Perhaps you two are overreacting," Osamu said, placing his hand on Inoichi's shoulder, stopping him. He looked at Mizunami. "What you feel could be from the war. Bodies are still being buried."

Inoichi looked into Osamu's eyes, his face scrunched. "What is going on?"

Screams broke through from the distance—Osamu removed his hand. "Can I trust you to take care of Mizunami?" Inoichi questioned.

"Of course."

Osamu's assurance gave him confidence. He kissed his bride and darted toward the castle, taking a shortcut using the trees to his advantage. It was a technique his sister taught them. This time, he was alone in his race.

As he drew closer, the scent of fire became stronger. He climbed atop the castle wall, seeing men and women lying motionless, drowning in their blood—pure carnage like he had never seen.

VASILIS

Island off the Coast of New Seattle, 2076

Blinding light replaced the darkness. *Is this death?* Vasilis thought, the pain of his brother's betrayal left him motionless. As he came to, a young woman with soft brown skin stared at him with concern in her eyes.

"Malaya, get back," he heard another woman say.

With what little strength he could muster, his eyes searched the room, finding an older woman with hair as white as her long coat. Her stern face looked as if she had never seen sunlight. She commanded a younger woman with pink hair tucked under a white hat.

"Nurse Joy, log."

"Yes, Dr. Gray," Nurse Joy said. "Male, age eighteen, six foot two, one-hundred eighty-five pounds of pure golden—"

"Annie-Mae! Please stay focused." Dr. Gray interrupted.

"Of course." Her wide green eyes lowered.

"Let me help," Malaya said.

"I understand you are concerned, but you are compromising my OR," Dr. Gray said, stepping in front of her. "Please, let us do our job."

Malaya sighed, taking a seat.

"Computer, scan!" Dr. Gray said, leaning over him.

"Nanobots have ceased the internal hemorrhage," said Nurse Joy. "Preparing to remove the man-skirt for further inspection."

"Focus!" chastised the white-haired woman. "There will be no man-skirt removal. Thankfully, his body responded remarkably well to the nanobots, but we can't take it lightly. Besides, there is time for that later."

They both laughed.

Maybe this was Elysium, Vasilis thought.

Malaya peaked over Dr. Gray's shoulder. "Doc, I believe he is experiencing anesthesia awareness."

Dr. Gray hovered a hand over Vasilis, revealing a combination of light and letters. *This must be a witch healer,* he thought, realizing he was trapped inside a device. *Perhaps these were Hades's temptresses.*

Vasilis tried to move, to speak, but he was as weak as a child starved of food. He knew the feeling from his days in the Agoge, but this... His heart raced as thoughts of his friends' betrayal fueled him. In that moment, he realized that shackles on his wrist and ankles pinned him down.

What have they done to me? Their betrayal left me at the mercy of people from another world. Did I truly deserve this? Why, mother? Why did you leave me to bear your sins?

He broke one hand free and slammed his fist into the device encasing him, inciting panic on the faces of his enemy. If not for the pain, he'd relish in their fear.

"Increase the dosage," Dr. Gray said.

A sharp pain in his arm sent him spiraling into a groggy haze as voices around him became distorted and the room spun out of control.

As the darkness consumed him, Vasilis could only hope that this was all just a nightmare, one that he would soon awaken from. But deep down, he feared that this was reality. He could not escape.

Blades of grass tickled Vasilis's skin, sending shivers down his spine as feeling slowly returned to his body. Despite this, he still couldn't move his limbs. "Sixty seconds until his awakening." He recognized the voice as Malaya's, the temptress.

Vasilis slightly opened one eye, seeing two men dressed in black armor unlike any he'd seen, armed with black sticks with glowing blue tips. *Who were these men, and what kind of magic did they possess?*

"Twenty seconds before his awakening," Malaya said.

You mean ten seconds, Vasilis corrected, feeling some tingling in his fingers.

The fake deity spoke again. "Cloak the aircraft and stand by."

Aircraft? He cracked his other eye open.

A large triangular black machine slowly disappeared, like a chameleon blending into nature. The two warriors vanished with it, leaving Malaya alone, talking to herself.

"Hodge, what about the translator?" Malaya whispered, looking around nervously.

What an odd woman, he thought, *crazed perhaps?*

Five, Vasilis thought, feeling in his arms and legs returned, bringing forth a glint of hope. *Zero.*

The sun emerged from behind the clouds, shining brighter and warmer than he could remember. He rose to his feet, brushing the dirt from his pteryges—the traditional Spartan leather strips hanging like a skirt from his armor, each one etched with symbols of battles fought and victories won.

This is embarrassing, he thought, analyzing the odd tight cloth hugging his manhood and the blue tunic made from unfamiliar material. He brushed the bronze hair from his face.

Browsing the landscape, he found a woman in a dress with her arms folded, leaning against a large tree shaded by purple leaves. The sun brightened her captivating brown eyes.

It was her, back in Sparta, he thought, walking toward her, stopping close enough to smell her sweet fragrance.

"I know you have many questions," she said.

Vasilis extended a flat palm, placing it on top of her head, extending to his nose. She slapped his hand and jumped back. "What's wrong with you? Keep your hands to yourself."

"Sorry, it's just you're tall for a woman," he said, looking her up and down, sensing her fear and anger. "And yes, I have many questions. How or why am I here?"

"I don't know how to say this. So, I'll just say it—we saved your life."

"Saved me?"

Vasilis gazed at the forest beyond the meadow, rubbing his chest for the rest of his life before this moment, but he felt no scars—except for the newest addition.

"We decided to leave that one," Malaya said.

Why this one? To honor the shame of death at the hands of those I loved. But death will forever live across my chest.

"A sword came out of my chest, yet I'm alive," he said. "Am I cursed to live out my days atoning for my actions?" He looked away.

"No," she replied, taking a step forward. "Your perspective is yours alone, but I ask that you think of it as a fresh start."

He nodded, his eyes still roaming. "Gratitude, woman."

She frowned. "Woman?"

"Have I offended you? Are you not a woman?"

"It's my sex, not my name. You will address me as—"

"Malaya," he interrupted. "Yes, I heard. So, *woman* Malaya, where am I? Are you a god?" He tilted his head and rubbed his chin. "No, you can't be. I met a goddess once. They are *confident*—you are not. So, tell me, am I dead? If so, where is my father?"

I am sure they have prepared a formal response for this, but I need real answers. If she lies—

"You are on an island in the year 2076. Yes, I am a goddess. No, you are not dead, but I'm sure your father is smiling down upon you as we speak, and it's just Malaya, thanks," Malaya said. A nervous smile covered her face before she randomly whispered to herself.

Vasilis raised a brow. *She seems ill, like those who sit in the darkness speaking to themselves.* He heard another voice, someone speaking back to her, making him second guess which one of them was the ill one. The voice was faint, but whoever it was, was smart. They told her to calm down and ignore his attempt to upset her. *Who are these people?*

"You are an odd woman, Malaya."

Malaya took a deep breath. "Do you understand when I say the future... 2076?"

"Yes, I do. You are referring to time travel."

A surprised look covered her face.

"My close friend, Nefeli, spoke of such things… She would be dead now, I suppose." He paused for a moment, thinking back to the days Nefeli teased him, yet took time to teach him things. Of course, he pretended not to care just to upset her. Everything had changed. He got older, and she married the man who killed him, a man he once called a friend.

He looked around the vast landscape of grass and tall trees. *Elias and Midas's betrayal brought me to this unknown place.* His brows hardened. He needed answers, and Malaya was going to give them to him one way or another.

"Where is this *future*?" he asked. "Why have I been captured? Real answers. Carefully, for these words may be your last."

"You should show a little more gratitude to the woman that saved your life, or—"

"Or what?"

Malaya glanced in the direction of where the ship and warriors had disappeared. Vasilis raised a brow, hearing yet another voice in her ear. *"Would your mother be so brash? Play the role."*

Malaya grunted softly, turning to him with soft eyes. "My apologies," she said in a forced angelic tone, brushing up against him.

Vasilis nearly laughed at her failed efforts, but he kept composed. "Who are you?"

"I'll show you." Malaya signaled for him to follow her down a rocky dirt path.

He didn't move. She was going to earn his trust.

Malaya turned back around. "What is it? Don't tell me this big, strong Spartan man is afraid of being alone with a woman?" she said, a sly grin on her face.

"No. You are not a skilled liar. Terrible, actually. I will not go with you until you tell me the truth."

Malaya rolled her eyes. "What truth?"

"Well, you are a woman with very little muscle except for the one on your backside. With that, I know you could not have brought me here alone," he said, walking closer to Malaya. "And your clothes, though they are strangely enticing, you look comfortable. Not alluring like a temptress, or in any way for that matter." He was close enough to feel the anger radiate from her body. "In fact, your appeal is so bad you would make a terrible whore."

The muscle in her jaw protruded, and her eyebrows deepened.

"You are angry?" Vasilis smirked. "Perhaps I am wrong. Maybe you will make for a great whore since I do like my women with a—" Vasilis reached behind her, "strong backbone."

"Hell no!" Malaya growled, thrusting her knee into his manhood, sending him to his knees. She shook her head. "Unbelievable. Thousands of years, and men have yet to evolve. If you want answers, you better control yourself, or I will cut you."

Vasilis groaned as Malaya stormed off. Pain raided through his body. "Where are you going?" He pulled himself up and hobbled behind her.

They reached a small wooden house that blended with the towering trees and endless greenery. Vasilis stared in awe at its simple yet charming appearance. Inside was clean with a fragrance of burning logs. A table in the center of the room held a bowl of fresh apples, reminding Vasilis of his mother's home. He made his way to the cushioned chair and reached for a shiny red apple.

"What do you know about the Oracle of Delphi?" Malaya asked.

A glint of curiosity caused him to pause. *How much could she have known? Did she know about Lilith?*

"I've only heard stories," he said, attempting to sink his teeth into it.

"You're lying." Malaya ripped the apple from his hand.

"You are vile, woman," Vasilis said, reaching for another, but she snatched the bowl.

"I could say the same about you," Malaya said. "Tell me the truth."

"My memory is a bit hazy. Time travel and hunger do that to me," Vasilis put a fake smile, eyeing the bowl in her hand.

"Fine." Malaya rolled her eyes before she sat the bowl down.

"Thank you," he said, taking a bite of the sweet, tangy fruit. "I will show you my gratitude by being forthright," he said, with his mouth full. "Unlike you, the oracle has proven herself over time. Her knowledge and power earned her favor amongst the people—including those in power."

"Power? Malaya questioned. "She is no oracle. She knows all because she's from the future. She's a manipulator."

"You talk as if you know the oracle. Who are you to judge her? And how are you any different? Did you not save me to use me?"

"I am different, and I'm not using you. You have a connection to her, and I know because," Malaya paused. "I'm her daughter."

He paused mid-bite. Her words sent a chill down his spine. *All of Llith's tales were about her. This was who she boasted about?* Vasilis thought, looking into her eyes, seeing the resemblance. Not to her mother, but to his own pain. A pain in her eyes, one he was familiar with. One that he felt after losing his father. Her mother may not have passed, but they were lost to one another.

"She's put billions of lives at risk, including yours," said Malaya. She then paused, seeking an edge. "Those men who killed you are working with her."

Vasilis spat out the fruit. "What?"

"Like I said, a liar and manipulator."

"Elias and Midas are—are here?"

"They were taken from your timeline the next day—Lilith took them."

Malaya sat next to him and poured a bottle of wine into an odd-shaped glass. Vasilis smiled to himself, staring at the wine bottle—its art reminded him of Nefeli's sculptures.

"It's called a glass cup," Malaya said. "In my time, we have mastered this technique and more."

Vasilis drank the finely aged wine from the glass, peering into the wilderness. Brief moments of silence allowed him to think. He looked at Malaya, then his hands before removing his tunic. He walked over to the mirror, scanning his blemish-free body.

"They're dead because of you," Vasilis said. "You took me away from my mother and my people. The traitors—they must pay, and because you've captured me, you let them off easy!"

"You were going to die!"

"Perhaps I welcome the afterlife! You had no right. You're no god!"

"I'm not, but I can send you back so you can die, or you can stay and exalt your revenge here."

Everything—everyone—is gone. Vasilis's eyes widened. He passed his hands through his hair, then balled his fist, trying to fight the pain weighing on his soul. Staying here, getting revenge was the only way to lift it. If she was lying, it was a risk worth taking.

"Can you really give me a chance to say goodbye?"

"I can," Malaya said. "Only after we find my mom and your... former friends."

Vasilis let out an exasperated breath. "Okay, but I must speak to the man in your head, your superior.

"What?"

"Someone was speaking to you," said Vasilis. "Perhaps they were in that ship, the one that became invisible."

"How could you have possibly heard them?"

"I suppose there are many impossible things you will learn about me," he smiled. "Now, may I speak with the man in your head, please?"

Malaya nodded. "General Williams," she said to herself. "The subject would like a word."

"It's just Vasilis," he smirked.

General Williams strode into the room, his blue uniform crisp and with badges and decorations earned from years of service. Despite his impeccable appearance, there was something deadly about him. His eyes, sharp and piercing, commanded attention, and it was clear that he was a warrior through and through.

"I don't like being summoned, so this must be important," General Williams said in a voice that was at once smooth and powerful. There was something familiar about him, something that reminded Vasilis of his mentor and father figure, Seth.

"Well, Son, did she make a mistake with you, or can you give us something useful?" General Williams said before taking a seat.

"You have made a mistake if you think she can catch Lilith," Vasilis said, looking over at Malaya.

"You dick," Malaya said, taking a step forward, stopping once General Williams raised his hand.

"She is reluctant to see her opponent for who she truly is," said Vasilis. "She claims to know her, the oracle, but refutes how powerful she is. Yet, I am required to believe she can help me?"

"Really?" Malaya said. "Are you actually going to stand there and try to negotiate when their lives are at risk? Maybe I was wrong."

"I have information," said Vasilis. "And it's apparent I know your mother better than you."

The older gentleman rubbed his forehead. "At the moment, what Ms. Grant believes about her mother is the least of my concern. I just want to catch Lilith, so I'm asking in good faith that you tell us what you know. The information will determine how much we help you."

"Good faith," Vasilis repeated. There was much he could tell them, but he had to be sure they could do what they promised. "Okay, but I will need my sword. It holds valuable information."

"Alright, Son. This had better be good. Bring the boy his sword," General Williams said into his shirt.

"Is that wise general," Malaya said, keeping her eyes on Vasilis.

"It's the only way I can show you," said Vasilis. "Your mother often worked on her personal affairs in her free time. I memorized some numbers once and took them to Nefeli and a scholar she studied with."

Forsaken was close. He could feel its energy. His stomach sank when he held it for the first time. "Thank you," he said before unwrapping an old strip of leather from around the hilt, laying it flat across the table. These symbols were foreign, even to Vasilis.

"These are Nefeli's notes. She had her own code. Just in case the enemy got hold of it."

"What is it?" General Williams questioned, looking at Malaya for the answer.

"Acrophony in its purest form," Malaya said, passing her hands over the symbols. "A formula value system... a writing system using attic numerals."

Vasilis cleared his throat. "Nefeli said it was impossible to figure out. She needed more time, saying it's a—"

"Puzzle," said Malaya, with an intrigued smile on her face. "She's a genius."

"Well," said General Williams, stuffing a fruit in his pocket. "Unless you speak ancient Greek in code, this is going to take some time—I'll take this to the lab."

"No." Malaya grabbed a marker off the general's shirt. "She decoded it. They just didn't understand it."

The wheels were still turning in her head—her eyes looking off to the side. She started mumbling to herself. Malaya worked fast, adapting to the language with each passing line. *Lilith was right. She is amazing.*

"These are coordinates to Japan, and there's a name, Kojiki," Malaya said. "I saw this before."

"What does this mean?" Vasilis said, his eyes following General Williams. They both stared at Malaya.

Malaya pressed the device on her wrist. A blast of light surfaced, and an image floated above her wrist. *Did she have magic like her mother?*

The light was sucked back into the device. "Ghost's last stream mentioned something about a liberator of the people prophesied in the Kojiki. None of it makes sense, nor does it tell us what she wants."

"You are a genius, but you sure as hell are naïve," General Williams said, standing up.

"Excuse me, sir."

"It makes all the sense in the world. Your mama wants control," he said, walking toward the window. "Who can blame her? We all know what those sons of bitches did to your grandmother."

"What happened to her grandmother?" Vasilis asked.

"None of your business," Malaya said. "Sir, it doesn't make any sense. She's worked alongside them."

"Of course, for the betterment of the environment and her pockets... Your pockets, but this is next-level terrorism." He looked at Vasilis.

Vasilis could tell Malaya's mind was still working something out. Her thumb rubbed across her fingers—she started to mumble again.

"Sir," Malaya said. "The Edo period. That's where she's going. Emily said there was a minor flux. She thought it was nothing but—" Her wrist glowed again. "The Battle of Sekigahara in 1600. Yes, that's it. I know her target, Tokugawa Inoichi."

MALAYA

Island off the Coast of New Seattle, 2076

The first rays of dawn crept through the sheer curtains of the modest cabin bedroom, casting a haunting, pale light that seemed too gentle for the torment it revealed. Malaya, entangled in the sheets, was a prisoner in her own bed, her body writhing as she fought to escape the clutches of a relentless nightmare.

Her father, once a robust figure with dark skin as rich and absorbing as a Blue Nile gem, with a smile that outshone the brightest neon, was transformed into a ghastly apparition. His once vibrant complexion was now deathly pale, his body scrawny, a mere shadow of the man he used to be.

He stood before her, a vision of decay, his hands trembling as they reached out in a silent, desperate plea. His eyes hollow, yet sad, begged her to save him. But all Malaya could do was stare, frozen in horror, as the life withered away from him, leaving nothing but a haunting echo of despair in its wake.

Malaya's heart raced as she suddenly sat up in bed, gasping for air. The scent of copper and burning hair lingered in the air, a foul ghostly smell that intensified her nausea.

The nightmare of her father's death, a scene replayed too often in her dreams, had become all too familiar, haunting her even in this peaceful setting.

"You had the dream again, didn't you?" he said, his deep brown eyes full of concern.

She nodded, as tears rolled down her cheeks. Her mother's betrayal cut deep, and it was too much for her to bear.

Malaya's gaze drifted to the slit in the curtain of the palm trees. Her mind wandered back to a piece of advice she received from a therapist when she was younger. She had been told that life's stressors often dredge up past traumas, manifesting them in the form of dreams... well, nightmares.

Aaron handed her a cup of tea. She smiled and took a drink. Only now realizing he was fully dressed, ready to train. He tied his locks into a ponytail before sitting next to her.

"You don't have to stay," Malaya said. "I'll join you after I shower."

"Nah," said Aaron. "The others can wait. Talk to me."

As Malaya lay her head in Aaron's lap, her thoughts were drawn back to the recurring nightmare. She remembered a therapist once telling her that life's stresses often resurface past traumas through dreams.

This insight echoed in her mind now, as the vivid nightmare of her father's death seemed to be a direct result of the overwhelming tension she was currently facing.

Aaron's presence was a calming force. She felt grounded as she lay there, finding comfort in his warmth and silence. After a while, she sat up, her heart still heavy.

"You should go," she said, her voice a soft whisper.

"How about I cook you breakfast instead?" Aaron suggested with a smile, a glimmer of playfulness in his eyes. "Unless you want to…"

"Don't be a douche," Malaya retorted, a faint smile breaking through her pained expression, knowing that if she cooked, the cabin was likely to burn down. She was fortunate to be with someone who was skilled in the kitchen.

Today was turkey bacon, fried to a crisp, and the sweet smell of his French toast filled the air. Any other day, they'd eat with the others, but today, she was glad it was just the two of them. She needed a quiet breakfast fee from discussing their mission.

Still, Malaya couldn't shake the feeling of being trapped, stranded on this remote island. Her mother's actions had left her here, under the watchful eye of General Williams and the Cabinet, as they prepared to jump to feudal Japan. The mere thought of it sent chills down her spine as she struggled to comprehend exactly what Lilith planned to do.

"Catch me if you can."

Malaya couldn't shake the feeling that her mother was leading her on a wild goose chase, manipulating her with a false prophecy.

The weight of the situation was heavy on her shoulders, and she couldn't help but feel like a pawn in her mother's game. Darviants, magic—none of it made sense. The impalpability of it all forced an incredulous smile onto her face. It was all too much to wrap her head around.

Everyone else fell for it; she stuffed her mouth with another sweet maple bite.

"What is it?" Aaron's voice brought her out of her thoughts.

Malaya looked at him, grateful for his presence. She was so caught up in her own stuff that she forgot they had been thrown into this training together. She couldn't imagine going through this alone.

The training was rigorous, and she had to adapt on the fly to the unfamiliar culture of feudal Japan, which she had known nothing about just a week ago. At least she had Aaron there with her.

The island had its issues, of course. Constant monitoring, for one, though it made sense given this was a covert military training ground for the most elite soldiers. General Williams thought it was best for them to stay here, which made sense, but it was who she was here with that was the problem. Right now, she was not going to waste a thought on him.

"I just...I can't believe any of this," Malaya said, shaking her head. "It's all so unbelievable. I feel like I'm in a dream, or a nightmare."

Aaron nodded in agreement. "Yeah, I know what you mean. But we have to keep moving forward. We have to stop Lilith before it's too late."

Malaya took a deep breath, trying to steady her nerves. She knew he was right. They couldn't let her mother destroy everything they held dear. They had to stop her, no matter the cost.

"You know who is special?" Aaron said, suddenly changing the subject.

"Me?" she said with an exaggerated smile.

Aaron laughed. "Yes you, but Vasilis."

Vasilis. The mere thought of him made her blood boil. He was insufferable, his arrogance making him unbearable to be around. But deep down, Malaya knew he was suffering, even if he wouldn't admit it. Unfortunately, he had answers to questions about her mom, though he wasn't always forthcoming.

Aaron continued, "He's tested off the charts and broke every record held by any agent, even mine."

Malaya scoffed. "There's an explanation for everything. He's able to shut down bodily functions and fire the entire reserve of catecholamines, like you and other peak humans. A combined rush of noradrenaline and adrenaline maximizes his strength and speed. The amount coursing through his bloodstream lasts longer than most. It's unique, but it isn't anything science can't explain."

Aaron smiled at her. "You have an explanation for everything."

"Don't be condescending," she smiled, stuffing the last piece of sweet bread into her mouth.

After breakfast, Malaya came out of the shower feeling refreshed and ready for the jump. She had already chosen her outfit: a stunning cherry blossom pink kimono with a purple yukata and woven straw sandals. As she walked out of her room, Aaron nodded in approval.

"This has Natwat written all over it. The man has style, I'll give him that," he said, rubbing his beard.

Malaya raised an eyebrow. "You think I should have worn something more basic?"

"It would have allowed you to blend in better," Aaron said.

Malaya laughed. "It is a festival. A bi-racial *gaijin* in 1601 Edo Japan. Yeah, I'm pretty sure I'll stick out no matter what. So, I might as well—" "Do it *in style*," they said simultaneously, mimicking Natwat.

They headed for the shore before sunrise. Vasilis had James and Esther out there for hours. After sunrise, like always, Aaron wanted to be early for his eight a.m. appointment with Dr. Gray. Malaya went into the woods to practice archery. She needed time to herself.

She launched another arrow, missing her target yet again. *How do they expect me to pull this off?* Her mind drifted to Aaron. He was a natural at blending in. It was a shame Aaron couldn't join them, though it made sense, given he was still recovering from the rash on his arm.

Dr. Gray had suggested it was due to prolonged radiation exposure, but Malaya couldn't help but wonder if there was more to it. They were in Sparta at the same time and she had healed. Malaya shrugged the thought away. Her aunt Shay didn't seem to care, tasking Aaron with tracking down her uncle instead.

Maybe he could find more answers about the missing, Malaya thought. After a last-ditch effort to get this archery thing right, she joined the others.

"It took you long enough," Esther said. Malaya turned to see her friend trotting toward her. "Wow, you did it," she said with wide eyes. For days, Esther talked about cutting her hair, and she did. She chopped off her long brown hair, leaving a short wavy bob.

"Rocking, right?" Esther said, modeling her new look.

"Of course."

Esther sized her. "This was a solid cover," she said, unable to hide her eagerness. "The brain power of Aaron and Natwat, amazing... Where's your tomahawk? And your bow?"

"Natwat packed it for me yesterday. In fact, he packed everything we needed. It's all on Mantis."

Esther nodded. "The fact they entrusted us with a mission this critical, freaking time travel."

"Yeah, it's wicked," Malaya said, doing her best to share her friend's enthusiasm.

"Crap," Esther said. "I almost forgot something. I'll be back."

"O... kay..."

The time had come. She hurried back to the others. Having James and Esther come into the festival as performers was genius. She was the star, an archer who lost a great love traveling this dangerous world alone. They didn't spare any detail. Esther, along with Vasilis and James, wore all black, acting as stagehand.

"Hey brainy," James said. "Before we make this leap, I have to ask." He lowered his voice. She was sure he was going to say something insulting. "You ready to give up that Hershey kiss for Godiva?"

"Always the dick, huh, James? I'd wreck you, except I would hate to give you the benefit of me touching you. Maybe I should tell Aaron." Malaya started to walk away.

"Sorry," James pleaded. "I'm messing with you. Aaron's my guy."

The words sounded sincere enough to stop her. He walked closer, looking back as if he were being followed. "To be honest, I'm scared shitless. I've been wanting to ask you how—how is it?" He didn't have that same cocky smile—he was nervous.

"Trust me, it's not that bad. It's like—" Malaya paused. "Close your eyes."

"I always knew this day would come," James snickered.

"I'm telling Aaron," Malaya said.

"Okay, okay, geesh. Don't get so raged."

He closed his eyes, and so did she, taking a long, deep breath. "Imagine you're on a rollercoaster, the squeezing feeling in your stomach as it ascended, the pause... then there's a sudden rush of descension that leaves you weightless."

Malaya punched him, her hand bouncing off his thin, muscular shoulder. "That's it, that's the feeling."

"James, it's time," Esther yelled, standing in front of the second Mantis. James brushed her off, waving his hand over his shoulder. "Before I go, I wanna apologize. I didn't say it before, but I am responsible for what happened between you and your mother. If only—"

"Don't. She played us all. Go ahead before Esther kills you. I'll see you in the quantum room. Oh, and James...thanks."

James smiled. "Oh, my god. Did we just bloom a friendship?" he said, covering his heart as he jogged backwards.

"Never," Malaya said with a smile.

Aaron jogged over. The submarine had arrived. She tiptoed to kiss him. "Thank you for being so amazing. Go ahead. I have something to take care of before I leave."

"You sure you don't want me to stay?" Aaron said, somehow hearing the ATV pull up behind him.

"I don't want you to be late for your mission. My aunt... she can be a little... difficult."

"So I've heard," he hugged her, squeezing her like he had never before. "See you soon. I love you."

"I love you too," she said, watching him shake Vasilis's hand before boarding the Mantis.

Vasilis walked toward her. "Looks like we have company."

"No. I have company," Malaya said, walking toward the waiting agent. "You wait for our ride."

Malaya stormed out of the cabin, ignoring their calls, hopping on the ATV and driving herself to shore. *It's been way too long, and they still haven't found one lead. They can't do this without me.*

The submersible aircraft, *Flying Mantis*, waited by the shore. The dome-shaped roof retracted, and she stormed inside, brushing past the pilot without so much as a peripheral glance. Vasilis sat next to Emily. He dozed off while she sat at the table, scribbling notes—she couldn't hear a thing. Malaya stormed toward her and pressed a button on the table.

"Hey, I was listening to that," Emily said.

"Sorry, I'm just so agitated."

"I couldn't tell," Emily smirked, pushing back her caramel blond hair.

Vasilis jumped up. "What's with you?"

"Shut up, this doesn't concern you," Malaya snapped.

"Well, perhaps you should keep your voice down," he replied, moving and giving them his back.

Malaya rolled her eyes and grunted in disgust before lowering her voice. Not because he asked, but it wasn't any of his business.

"The Cabin's more focused on the symptoms and not the disease. I need to be here tracking her down. You'd think they'd grant me the opportunity after divulging so much information. Extracting another person seems fruitless. Vasilis didn't give us much to go on. What do they think another hot-headed warrior erased from history will give us at this point?"

"I'm still here," he mumbled.

Emily cracked a smile; Malaya wasn't the least bit amused. "Don't make me lie to you," said Emily. "I empathize with everything you're going through, but they're right. Extracting him is more important. It'll throw a wrench into her plans and force her out of hiding."

"No." Malaya shook her head. "You don't know her like I do. She'll have a backup plan to her backup plan."

"You're right, but you're also not thinking straight. You haven't been for a while now. Here's your proof." Emily pointed behind her.

Kat turned and placed one arm behind the chair, her head tilted, her green-tipped ponytail drooped like her face. "You didn't notice me."

Malaya looked at Kat, her eyes softening with a mixture of affection and longing. "That just means you're amazing at your job," she said, her voice laced with a warmth that reached beyond mere words.

As they embraced, Malaya felt a surge of gratitude and comfort. Despite the chaos surrounding them, this moment of connection with an old friend was a reminder of the simpler times they had shared.

Releasing from the hug, Malaya studied Kat's face, noting the subtle signs of fatigue beneath her resilient exterior. "How'd you get stuck driving a Mantis?" she asked, a playful smile tugging at her lips.

"I volunteered," said Kat. "I wanted to see you before you left. Plus, this is one of a kind." Her eyes gleamed. "You look amazing, wrecked, but amazing."

"Uh, thanks."

Kat nudged her. "C'mon, you know what I mean. Don't let those shadow assholes upset you. If they don't listen, take charge. Ask yourself, how much do you really *need* them?"

At this point, nothing was going her way. She was no closer to finding her mother, and they had all the resources. Maybe doing things for her was the *best* way, the only way. "Thanks, Kat."

"How are things out there?" Malaya said, looking back at Emily, who resumed listening to her music, writing with intent.

They walked toward the front of the ship and sat across from one another. "Whispers of a rebellion against the U.NA."

"None bigger than your family, though."

"I hate to admit it, but New Seattle doesn't have those problems because of my family. They kept the city in order. The people need the internet. UNA can't keep Americans from having what we want."

Malaya sighed. "Maybe."

"Anywho, your mom, she's a martyr," said Kat. "Support is growing for her. People are taking to the streets claiming to be part of it, the movement, her movement, *Ghost*."

"These people are going to get themselves killed, and for what? A false agenda. If they had listened to me, they could have drawn her out of hiding and turned the public against her. Who knows what the new UNA leader will do to silence them?"

"You haven't heard," Kat lowered her voice. She pressed her watch.

A news feed emerged, lighting the small cockpit. Men and women were being removed from an abandoned, old-school car shop. The last one of its kind since the ban on privately owned emissions vehicles.

"They're blaming an anti-communism group for the missing scientist, MEV bombing, even the assassination. Apparently, they're linked to an *inspiring extremist* group who call themselves the Brotherhood of Freedom. And the media is shifting the assassination to an inside job. It's getting crazy out there."

A spontaneous laugh escaped Malaya. "Anarchy. This is what she wanted." She started to relax, seeing Kat's perplexed gaze. "She doesn't even care, uprooting peace to reshape the world in her image. You know, she told me she was doing this to prevent some new threat to humanity. She's the threat."

"The real question is, who is feeding the media?" Kat grabbed her hand. "I guess it's up to us to stop her now, isn't it? Understand, you're not alone."

Malaya did her best impression of a smile. The surface of her watch flashed green. "I have to take this." Kat stepped out.

The Cabinet's afraid of her. They'd go so far as to create a False Flag narrative, framing innocent people, though? I have to stop her, Malaya thought.

"Malaya!" Emily shouted, waving her over. "You've been so distracted that you had me trying to decipher this, something you would have figured out weeks ago. I need your help."

She pointed at the unraveled papyrus lying across the table. It was something they found hidden underneath Vasilis's sword's strap. Another coded message. She had, in fact, forgotten about it. "Vasilis. Does this mean anything to you?"

"None of my business, remember?"

"Useless prick." Malaya pursed her lips to the side and sat next to Emily. Perhaps if she had taken time to decipher the message, she could have noticed its conspicuous detail.

"A *Sage*," Malaya said confident, yet puzzled by the message coded in ancient Greek. "Cursed and bound to this world... destruction... anarchy, Elvir." Malaya continued to read, though mostly to herself in a mumble. "This is bull crap." She rolled her eyes, pushing it away. "Magic, relics, gods. How is this supposed to help me?"

"Wait," Emily said. "You mumbled something about Scandinavia. Right?"

Malaya shrugged.

Emily rolled up the papyrus and swiped her hand across the desk's surface. Luminous aqua pages sprouted from its holographic interface.

"Got it," she said before crumbling the other pages.

"The stories of the Sage Elvir can be traced to Scandinavia, and there are hundreds of tales about gods...or deities cast down to Earth, Aigons."

Malaya rolled her eyes. Emily looked back at her. "I get it. To you, it's elaborate, but—"

"At least we have a location," Malaya finished Emily's statement.

They smiled. It was just like the old days before their careers drove them apart. In some twisted way, her mother brought them back together.

The door hissed. Natwat strolled in. His loafers clanked off the sleek metal floor of the control room. "Ladies."

He never looked their way. Instead, he headed toward the table further behind them, housing the assortment of weapons. Malaya looked at Emily before opting to join him. "So what'd they say?"

"Perhaps if you didn't storm out, you would have heard their proposal," he snapped, never taking his eyes off the weapons. "It was bad enough they dragged me out of bed denying me my morning Joe, and after your outburst, the president chewed me a new one—you embarrassed me."

His tone sent chills down her spine. Malaya looked back at Emily, who threw herself back into her work. "I-I'm so sorry, it's just with everything going on, it's just, I have no excuse. You've been so amazing during all of this."

Natwat was one of two who volunteered to head this operation, a.k.a. babysitting. He wasn't a complete stranger either, having worked with Lilith before. The Cabinet felt better having one of their own looking after them. Attorney General Randal Mayor, who also served under her grandfather, was the other volunteer.

Shay opted to stay back and assist the agency with leads. Tracking down her husband took precedence over anything. Jose took over the business, spending his time in New York near the new location. There was no chance of Malaya playing a role in her game. She didn't care much for the family business at this point.

"Luckily for you, your mother is a wanted criminal," Natwat teased. "And I'm forgiving."

"Thank you." Malaya smiled and hugged his neck before staring back at the weapons table.

"Back to business," Natwat said, dropping the sack and laying out some of the equipment. "This is some of what you asked for: Medical herbs, gold, and a pipe."

He frowned, his lips peeking between her kimono. "And you already have on your light armor. Geesh, are you taking a trip to Japan or planning a heist?"

"Ha-ha, very funny," said Malaya, checking the rest of the equipment. "This coming from the man who demanded they pack my beats and pancakes." She tossed him the food orb, a hand-sized wooden ball.

"Touché," he said, dropping it into the sack.

Natwat turned his attention back to the weapons. "Bamboo wood and leather, what a magnificent design," he picked it up. "You know, despite the structural changes in height, the core of what makes a yumi hasn't changed in hundreds of years. With proper care, it can last many generations. This is the one."

"Looks like the gangs all here," Kat said, entering the craft and taking her seat in the pilot's chair.

"Ladies and gentle-man, strap up. This is going to be a bumpy ride, considering this is my first time piloting this bad boy with people."

Malaya led the way for the confused and frightened looks. "Here we go."

The three of them reclined in their seats. Malaya looked to her left and right. "Once we dock, that's it. I'm off to a new world. It may be a while before I see you guys again."

"You'll only be gone for a few days," Emily said, drifting off. "For every two days spent in Japan, only a day passes here. Though, it's not one-hundred percent."

"Right, a few days."

MIDAS

Shimōsa Province, Japan, 1601

The roar of an angry river filled Midas' ears as he stumbled along its bank, the mist from the churning water cooling his warm, fair-skinned face. The thin air at high altitude made it hard to breathe, but that was the least of his worries. Violent bouts of vomiting and explosive diarrhea had taken their toll on him, but fortunately, the river provided a place to relieve himself. He was grateful to be alone for the moment, but he needed to find Elias and Seth.

He scanned the dark clouds of this foreign land for any signs of human life. He checked the gold medallion given to him by Lilith's team, the blue light still chasing the metallic grooves. He stuffed the medallion back into the pocket of his odd, uncomfortable attire suited for this time.

The river's roar grew louder, the mist thickening as the water churned more violently. Midas pressed on, his feet sinking into the soft, damp earth as he trudged forward. The scent of damp earth mixed with the scent of the river, and the dampness of his clothes clung to his skin.

Infiltrating foreign lands was something Midas had done since Seth made him part of his Krypteia at thirteen. He accepted what he was: a natural killer, a weapon, a tool, a rather large tool with unique gifts bestowed upon him by the gods. Ischyró was a title given to him at birth, with many interpretations.

For those in Sparta, it meant one thing: Champion. He even carried a Champion's weapon, Forspoken, the twin sword of Vasilis' Forsaken. Like all Champions, it carried the same destiny affiliated with its carrier—protecting Sparta from a great evil. Its lore is shrouded in mystery and legend, evading Midas.

Perhaps they could have been more creative with the name, he admitted. It did not matter. Midas had lost the sword, and by way of Lysander's blade, he lost his life. It was poetic, given how he bore the burden of killing a man he loved like a brother.

The son of the great Agis, protector of Mother Sparta, is nothing more than shit Helot. The sardonic smile that adorned his face belied the bitter irony of his situation.

No matter what Lilith said, he was an elite warrior turned glorified Helot. Like a slave, he wore clothes assigned to him. On Intrepid, it was uniform with too many layers. For this mission, it was something familiar, a chlamys, though it differed from the robes back home.

The cream-colored ensemble restricted his movements by wrapping around his elbows instead of the waist. The waraji was a familiar welcome, like in Sparta; the sandals woven from straw, wrapping around his ankles, binding the sole were heavy, though much lighter than those on the *Intrepid*.

Also, like a slave, he was fulfilling the tasks of a master, hoping to ingratiate himself into their society. And he wielded his master's weapon, a spear, which had its benefits. Modern technology hid the spear in one bracer, while the other hid his shield.

Midas soon spotted Elias splashing river water on his face. "How's the water?"

"Weird tasting."

Midas smirked. "Where's your father?"

"Further down, he found an old stone path," Elias said, tossing him a sack and ragged cloak before they set off for Seth.

They found him passing his hand over beaded square stones of an old building.

"It's a shrine," Midas said, not quite understanding how he knew—it just came to him. It seemed to happen more and more.

His mind was full. He could remember events of his past he had forgotten and some things he wanted to forget.

There were things in his mind about places he never visited. There were objects he never touched, people he never met, and technology he never used. It was all there, neatly filed and color-coded. This was yet another gift afforded to them by Lilith and her people.

Seth smiled. "We are really here... in the past, or is it our future?"

"Technically—" Midas started.

"Does it matter?" Elias said, a hint of annoyance in his tone. "Let us get this over with."

"So eager to return to their world, son?" Seth asked. "Trapped in that space station. We are warriors, or have you already forgotten who you are?"

"No, father. I am not interested in exploring this world, no matter how beautiful it is. Time is not on our side."

Rainfall followed them until they reached a fork on the rustic path. The research was correct almost to the stone, which meant the Torii castle was down the path on the right side. They had an inside man waiting for them.

"There is a Shinto shrine up this hill." He pointed to his left, revealing a piece of itself underneath his cloak. "Go introduce yourself. Give them a Spartan welcome to their new reality."

Seth seemed to embrace this mission as if this was just another adventure, him leading an invasion of a foreign land, readying to face the unimaginable, but it wasn't—nor was what he was asking him to do.

That was often the case back home, but no one spoke up. Why would they? He was Seth the Conquer, a great warrior who conquered man, land, and beasts.

"That is not necessary," said Midas. "We are all on the same side."

"Since when does it matter?" said Elias. "This is nothing new to us."

"It is a place of worship," Midas said.

"Mental warfare is always a necessary tactic," said Seth. "Just like we did back home."

"Back home, there were four of us."

Elias threw his arms up. "So, the truth appears."

Yes, this was an uncomfortable truth. Vasilis was like a brother to them. He'd died because they stabbed him in the back. What would the gods say? How could they fight alongside the elite warriors for all eternity?

Does such a thing exist? He asked himself that question more often lately, though he dared not utter the words out loud.

Seth paced for a short time as they argued. Until he had enough. His voice expressed the anger on his face. "Now is not the time."

"I am not a child anymore. You will treat me as your equal," Midas said, unwilling to back down this time. He promised not just himself, but Vasilis's spirit. "Why are we even here, truly?"

"Lilith told us why," Elias said. "Leave it and be grateful that she saved us. Besides, have you forgotten Kara killed my father and Lysander killed us? "

"Why are you speaking as if your father is not standing next to you? And why should I be grateful? Lysander, for all we know, Lilith could have planned all of it. She's hiding something."

"Watch your tongue!"

Seth stepped between them. "This is fruitless. You want to be treated like a man. Well, here it is. I loved Vasilis and his father. Vasilius was my best friend, my family, and you know what? When my hand was forced, I killed him. Just like Elias's hands were forced. Let us not forget you could have stopped Elias, so your hands are red as well."

"This is our new world," Seth declared, his voice steely as he made a broad, encompassing gesture with his arm, as if claiming the land before them. "A chance to start over. Now, you have a choice. Either you end us, here and now, and then yourself, if that's what your honor dictates. Or," his eyes bore into Midas with an unyielding intensity, "you get up that hill and do your job."

Midas tightened his jaws. *Job, like a damn Helot,* he thought, trying to hide his discontent as their eyes met.

Seth grabbed the back of Midas' neck—they touched foreheads. "Don't forget, I love you, and I saved you too, but this is not the time, kid. Leave history as it is."

A crushing knot formed in Midas's throat. He wanted to say something, anything, but what could he say? Seth was right. He was no better than any of them and no worse than Lysander, who killed them in their sleep.

Midas clenched his jaw. "Understood."

Seth released him, and they took the path towards the shrine. From here on, his focus was on the mission. "If their gods matter so much to you, wait until after they pray," he said before they parted.

Midas grunted.

"Welcome back, brother." Elias's laughter rang as he jumped on Midas' back before continuing through the crisp morning breeze.

A red torii welcomed worshippers. Today, it welcomed the men who would take their lives. They made their way to a man in an all-white robe leading a small group of people, who washed their hands and clapped before bowing.

Elias kicked in the door, startling everyone inside as he led the way down the path. He slowly unsheathed his kopis and pointed it at the man. "Kneel before your new masters."

"This is sacred ground!" the man said, his voice trembling. "Who are you?"

"Did you not hear me? I am your master." Elias looked back at Midas. "Are these translators working?"

Midas shrugged. He looked around at the scared faces. Despite his trembling voice, the man in the robe showed no fear.

"Kneel," Midas said, almost pleading.

"I will never," the man said, his chest out.

The vein on the side of Elias's head expanded—he smiled. Midas knew this look Elias had in his sinister, deep blue eyes. "Elias, wait!"

It was too late. Elias slit the man's neck before he could blink. Blood spewed everywhere, and so did the screams. Elias embraced the horror and stalked his next victim.

"He flinched for a weapon," Elias said before leading the way to the shrine's innermost chamber.

"He did not flinch."

"Okay, he did not flinch, but he also did not kneel. Besides, it is one body, brother."

"Paradoxes, Elias. Paradigm shifts. We cannot afford to alter their world. Do you want to disappoint Lilith?"

"Fine. No more fighting unless absolutely necessary."

Midas forced open the two enormous iron doors that creaked open. There was a cold chill bathed his body. The cold always came when he tapped into the strength that was that of a Champion. There was a river of energy or power beyond his own, or that of a human. The river was cold, and infinite, but his reach was limited.

Despite his unnatural strength, like his late mother would have mentioned, the tip of his fingers ache. They stopped after seeing a kneeling man with a wide, muscular back and dragon tattoo—a messy bun with long black strands of hair that flowed like a river. They almost didn't see the second man. A younger samurai, placing a vase filled with white flowers next to a bronze Buddha statue. He was thinner than the first samurai, with the top of his head shaved.

In front of them were odd foreign objects and an empty rack where a katana would have been. The object was a bronze artifact that was that of shapes, inside of shapes. The same symbols he saw in the scroll of the sages. The kneeling man didn't move. He stayed in a trance-like meditation. He opened his palm on the second samurai. The young man smirked and crossed his arms, leaning against the wall.

"You're already on your knees. Now turn to your master," said Elias.

"What have you done?" His voice growled.

Elias smiled. "Nothing, just a simple introduction."

Midas nudged Elias. "He was going to attack. We did what was necessary."

"That was a mistake," said the younger samurai.

"Nakamaro-kun, tend to our people."

"Of course, Lord Osamu." He gave him a slight bow and grabbed a handful of nuts. He threw them in his mouth as he strolled past them, as casual as a walk in the park.

An auric white light formed around the kneeling man—his hair changed from black to white. There was a slight rumble, like the engine on the Intrepid, but there was no engine. And a sudden odor of death filled the room.

"Tricks are for children," Elias said, charging the man.

Even with his speed, Elias found himself at the end of a radiant fist to the chest, sending him flying back the way they came.

Midas didn't wait. He attacked his blind spot, throwing a punch—the white-haired warrior grabbed his wrist and tossed Midas as if he were not six-foot-six and two-hundred-and-seventy pounds.

In Sparta, they faced warriors with great power, but this man—this warrior—was different.

The man grabbed the spiked kanabo. He came down with it. Midas activated the metal shield from his brace just in time.

"You are dead," he heard Elias say.

He attacked with unrelenting rage and speed. Yet the warrior caught him once more with a punch, then a devastating kick.

Midas saw an opening. He grabbed the distracted warrior in a bear hug and drove them both through the concrete wall—they landed outside.

Both men were quick to their feet.

"Easy, kid!" Seth shouted from inside the shrine with his sword in one hand, surrendering with the other. He kicked Elias until he woke up.

"You must be Torii Osamu. I am Seth. Lilith sent us."

Osamu turned to Seth, careful not to lower power or his guard. "You and your men have disrespected sacred grounds."

"Apologies cannot express how sorry I am. It is a misunderstanding. You have fought admirably, but if you choose to continue this fight, you will not defeat all three of us. I can assure you, Midas and Elias are the least of your worries. I urge you to focus on the future Lilith promised."

Osamu looked at the groggy Elias, then back at Seth. "A misunderstanding," his tone tempered, and he bore an impassive expression despite the underlying tension of a looming fight.

In tandem with his words, his hair transitioned from white to black, reflecting a return to a more controlled—less powerful state.

The shirtless warrior turned and escorted them to the castle. Seth continued to apologize on his son's behalf. This was Seth at his best. Send the knives to open the wound while he bandages them. Osamu welcomed them into his home with supper and a place to sleep.

Midas's restless mind kept him awake and wandering the castle grounds. *Not long ago, I was in another time and place. Now this,* he thought, walking a pathway illuminated by moonlight and lanterns.

He heard voices coming from behind the two large sliding doors. Curiosity forced him to peek through a crack where Osamu kneeled at the head table, speaking with two other men. He held a white cup; its steam penetrated his nostrils. Whatever was in his cup carried a flowery aroma with a hint of the sea.

Sakura, Midas somehow knew.

The others passed around a masu box. *Sake,* he suspected. He didn't recognize the man in the blue kimono but remembered the man sitting across from him, Ikeda—they met at dinner. The old man wore the same brown pants and a green kimono with a wakizashi at his waist.

"Out with it, Ikeda, you are not one to hold back your tongue," said Osamu.

"You have disgraced your family and your men," Ikeda's naturally strangled voice carried throughout the room.

Osamu's shoulders dropped as he placed his empty cup down. His lips curled into a wry smile.

"Do not dismiss me," said Ikeda. "Why didn't you slay these *gaijin*?"

"Perhaps if Ryu did not take Kusanagi—" another man said before Ikeda interrupted.

"Nakamaro! That's enough. Do not speak that name within these walls."

"It is okay, uncle," Osamu said. "To answer your question. All my life, I have taken risks. It was the only way to ascend once Uncle Kamako left. Our clan's future was at risk, but our pride kept us from speaking about it. The travelers are a means to an end. Their leader has given us an irrefutable opportunity of immortality—personal vendettas no longer matter."

"The *gaijin* gave us great detail of the castle," said Nakamaro. "Should we continue with the plan?"

Midas ducked underneath the entrance. Osamu's guests drew their swords. "Excuse my intrusion," he said after a deep bow. "I wanted to apologize again for our inexcusable behavior." He removed two gold royal coins. "Please accept these for the damage and the man's family."

"Teo," said Ikeda. "His name was Saito Teo. You should forever remember it. And how dare you attempt—"

Osamu put his hand up. "A man can only do what he can, uncle. This gift is generous. It will more than cover the building. This will also aid Saito's family. Please sit."

Midas squeezed into the space at the table, opting for tea instead of sake. Its smooth, lightly salted taste was different. At least the tension of a looming battle was familiar and calming as their tea.

"I must ask you something personal if I am to trust you," said Midas. "Your clan fought alongside the Tokugawa, tilting the Battle of Sekigahara in their favor. Why betray them now?"

Judging by their reaction, it was a sensitive subject. Nothing about Osamu spoke of a traitor. He knew a traitor when he saw one. After all, he saw a traitor in his own reflection.

"Ieyasu is a visionary. He and my father shared ideologies." Osamu smiled. "My father died for those ideologies, but he left me a message." His smile disappeared. "Ieyasu wanted something more, something darker. The power of a Sage."

Midas begged the obvious question. "What is a Sage?"

"Demons with incredible power. They were slain and trapped long ago by fierce warriors who scattered each soul across the world. Such a creature lies here, feeding on death, growing in power..." His voice trailed, and so too did his gaze, as if something was calling him. He cleared his throat. "My father made a mistake by not stopping his friend who seeks this power. I will not allow any man to rule with absolute power—your leader can help."

Osamu's story about a Sage reminded him of a child's tale back home about false gods who dared challenge the Greek gods, but they failed. To help keep Mother Sparta safe, the gods birthed the Champions. He was one of them—Vasilis was the other. The elders told them that Sparta would someday need the Champions to defeat a great evil. He would not live out that destiny—neither would his dead friend.

"Lilith promised to spare the Tokugawa's, which played a role in my agreement, so here we are." Osamu poured Midas more tea. "I respect you coming here tonight. You are an honorable man."

Would an honorable man stab his friend in the back? Or watch another slice the throat of a holy man?

"No. I am nothing more than a soldier following orders," Midas said, taking a sip of tea.

After a momentary pause, Nakamaro spread out a map of the place they would soon invade. "My men will start a fire at the outer ring," Nakamaro said, tracing his finger around the outer perimeter. "This will force the guards to lower the bridge, giving us an opening to storm the castle's village."

"You will split off again at this point," said Osamu. "Take a small group through the back entrance. I will bring our target to the extraction point. You will be pinned between the outer and inner ward, so we must move quickly. This is where our new alliance will open the gate from the inside."

"The second gate is key," Ikeda said after guzzling the last of his sake. "If the *gaijin* can open it, we could overtake the castle. If not, we risk spreading our forces too thin, which could mean—"

"You will have to rely on the trailing force for support," said Midas.

"Hai... We must hold," said Nakamaro. "If you fail, we will be vulnerable."

"Failure is not in our blood. Seth will stay close to the Shogun, undoubtedly drawing men toward him. He will keep him safe—he has to."

Osamu nodded. "Inform me in the morning. Seth and I will head early to Edo. I need to ensure my nieces and nephews are secure. Your friend should get some rest. In the morning, explore what Edo has to offer. You may like it here."

Midas nodded and headed back to his room, where Elias pretended to be asleep. He nudged him. "How long were you listening?"

"Long enough to know things will not go as planned."

"And Seth?"

"Who do you think gave them a detailed vision of the castle?" Elias said, turning his back.

"Of course," Midas smirked. "For the sake of your new life in their world, let's hope your instincts are wrong."

LILITH

Intrepid, 2076

In the vastness of space, Lilith lay in her quarters, phone in hand, wrestling with the unwelcome necessity of sleep, a trait she shared with her father—a curse she may have passed on to the rest of her family. God knows she did worse.

Malaya had officially traveled through time, and got the upper hand on Lilith, a credit to her. A contrasting mix of pride and anger filled Lilith. The Cabinet had one of her other Champions, which would be a problem given Lilith's need for four. Malaya had no idea what she was doing, but if all goes right with the next phase of her plan, Lilith would have Ieyasu Tokugawa. Perhaps even his son, Inoichi, giving her a fourth Champion.

Still, the weight of her daughter doing the very thing that got her father killed was a burden Lilith struggled to bear. It was supposed to be you and me, Jeff. I wish I trusted her more.

A pang twisted in her stomach at the echo of her and Malaya's conversation. The resolve burning in Malaya's eyes—the pain. Her own daughter was helping the enemy—the Cabinet. It was youthful naivety intertwined with justifiable hurt on Malaya's part—Lilith blamed herself.

Wiping Malaya's memory, suppressing her powers, the thought chiseled with a painful precision, sculpting a hollow within her solid conviction. Like a sculptor who realized their masterpiece had a flaw in its core, Lilith faced the imperfections of her own making.

If she was being honest, what she put Malaya through was just the beginning. Her daughter had no idea what was to come.

Lilith swiped to a family picture with her mother, father, and herself when she was thirteen. "What would you think of me now, mama?" she whispered the question that could never be answered.

"I wish I knew what you told Malaya," she added. "Was it something to help me save them... to save her? There is so much I don't understand about all this... magic, Champions, the Sages... my vision. There's something missing."

After a long look at the picture of her mother, she kept in a locket. As she drifted off, her subconscious carried her to a time years before her mother's death—before her father became president, before she came into her abilities. A time when she was naïve to the true evil humans were capable of. When death stood on the steps of her home. She closed her eyes, trying to sleep.

A violent rumble woke her to chandeliers hanging over her bed—she looked around, recognizing where she was. Her childhood home. Another rumble knocked over the display of dolls. Roaring from an engine nearly drowned out her parents screaming her name as they made their way to her bedroom.

"They broke through the border patrol!" her mother said.

"Lilith, we have to go to the safe zone now!" her father exclaimed. He grabbed her by the arm.

Another blast shook the foundation, and with it, more tears. She tried but couldn't control them. The sound of someone kicking in the door made her numb. Death was knocking on their front door.

They're here. Lilith thought, her heart pounding with the rumbling of the tank. She knew that's what it was, who it was. The UNA had made its way across the coastline.

She remembered the warnings in school about the threat that was the UNA. Invaders, and the praise of Seattle's borders, yet here they were.

We're going to die. The panicking thought flooded her mind.

"It's going to be ok," her mother promised, removing her gun from its holster. And her father grabbed the rifle. "We're going to be ok."

Her voice was always soothed, but not this time. This time, her words were hollow. The door opened to large armed men dressed in black fatigues, their faces hidden behind helmets. To Lilith's relief, she saw the American flag patch on their right shoulder.

Shields expanded from their wrists; it protected them but couldn't mask the horrific screams and rapid gunfire. The soldiers escorted them through what was West Mercer Island. Another loud blast shook the ground.

"We're almost there," a soldier yelled.

"Loaded and ready to roll," the soldier yelled, giving the thumbs up to the driver of the green Unimog truck. "Be safe, Mr. and Mrs. Castillo."

"You too, Sgt. Mayor," her father replied.

"Thank you for everything, Randall," her mother said, pulling Lilith close. "It's ok honey, we're safe now."

"Look out!" a soldier yelled.

Lilith and her family were thrown from the truck. Her ears rang, eyes watered, and smog made it difficult to see. A hand grabbed her by her neck and began shouting in a foreign language; the ringing in her ears made it difficult to make out, though it was clear who he was from the UNA patch on his uniform. His face was hard and angry—spit flew from his mouth as he continued to shout.

As she closed her eyes and took a deep breath, the sudden blast of the gun echoed in her ears, accompanied by a blinding flash of white light. The ringing slowly faded into a brief silence. It wasn't long before a voice broke through the darkness.

She opened her eyes to find a TV reporting the grave news that changed her life forever.

"CNN's field reporter Angela Castillo's chopper shot down by UNA. The reporter was presumed dead, survived by her husband, Senator Jose Castillo, and her young daughter."

A phone rang. She looked around the empty house. It rang again. She reached into her pockets and answered. "Hello."

"You should have told her..." a voice hissed from the other side, a mix of her mother's and something else.

Lilith tried to run to the nearest door. "Problems are not solved alone, you need help..." the voice echoed before she pushed the door open.

Another white light flashed, and she was in her old office, laptop open to a global webcast, of the tragic moment that reshaped the fabric of her being.

She desperately attempted to shift her position, but her arms were tightly bound to the chair, rendering her immobile.

There she sat, forced to see her mother and the crash survivors detained at gunpoint by the UNA, and the camera captured their fear, causing a global shockwave.

Tears flowed down her face, knowing what was next. In that moment, the sound of the trigger being pulled forced Lilith's eyes closed. She screamed through the gag, trying to break free.

"You need her—" her mother's voice became clearer.

Lilith woke, gasping for air. Her stomach was in knots at the haunting memory. Despite how badly she wanted to suppress the memory buried with the best modern medicine money could buy, she could never forget what happened that night.

After what the UNA did, she was going to make them pay. She would be the dormant virus that meticulously corrupted the system that ran the world. With Quintus, Midas, Elias, and Seth, she was one step closer to getting closer to avenging her mother and protecting the Darviants from the evil that threatened their existence.

For now, she needed a drink and to dive into her research. So, she got up, strapped on her boots and uniform, making her way to the meeting room.

As she entered, the sight of Seth's meticulously crafted strategy maps spread across one wall reminded her of his unparalleled skill in plotting their course through the murky waters of their war. His plans were always several steps ahead, a chess master in a game where the stakes were life itself. Because of him, she was going to take down the shogun and win the Great War in Japan.

Dominated by an oval table big enough to accommodate about thirteen people, it had a distinct head where Lilith normally sat, indicating her position of authority. The table itself was equipped with the Lucy AI interface, allowing for seamless integration of data and communication.

Along the sleek panel walls was what she came for, a full bar stocked with an array of beverages. She reached into the fridge for a Malta; she grabbed a glass and some condensed milk. Glass in hand, Lilith took a long pour of dark rum in her Malta and leche mix.

Lilith sat at the table and programmed Lucy, pulling up her private data. She took a long sip of the sweet pleasure. The smokiness of the rum blended well with the Malta, and warmed her body as she glanced at the information she organized in categories, specifically the Champions and Sages.

She thought about a meeting she had with Elias. He was a bit unhinged and misunderstood. A warrior gifted with speed that could make Hermes envious. At least he had Midas, a Champion and leader who deserved a second chance at life. Who, admittedly, did not seem to love this world as much as Elias, or Quintus, for that matter. Another Champion and trustworthy who was more than a gladiator, but at the end of the day he was just that—a gladiator. He and Midas were her safeguard against the Sage, Elvir.

Her plan was set, the Kojiki, Japan's Records of Ancient Matter, would ensure Mizunami would be accepted as the rightful ruler of Japan, slowly unraveling the UNA.

Waking Elvir was next. An immortal being, part of the Seven Sages who once ruled the world with powers that made the gods tremble—according to legend. Even the rum couldn't dull the chill that ran down her spine at the thought. But she needed his power, if she was to sway the war, ensuring the Tokugawa reign ends earlier than history knew.

Lilith studied the data, displaying the division among Darviants. Telepaths, Elementals, Technopaths, and Feralmorphs, each wielding distinct powers Yet, a nagging thought resurfaced. What made the Champions different?

The door slid open, breaking her focus. Sheldon, bathed in the tablet's glow, hesitated at the threshold, his presence stirring the air with a familiar, chaotic energy.

"Sheldon," Lilith's voice carried a mix of authority and surprise. His gaze lifted, briefly meeting hers, a flicker of apology in his blue eyes before darting away.

"Apologies, I wasn't expecting to find anyone at work," he stammered with his nervous habit of adjusting his glasses. "But of course, Lilith Castillo-Grant's dedication knows no bounds..." His voice trailed off, attention captured by the data dancing across the screens. "What is all of this?" he whispered, almost to himself.

Lilith masked her irritation, her voice even, "Categorizing Darviants."

Sheldon's interest deepened, eyes scanning the screens, lost in thought. Lilith observed, her initial annoyance softening slightly. His work ethic was not lost on her. A technopath, with the ability to interact with AI interfaces and analyze data better than other Darviants in the HOA. His obsession with all things history, wars, ancient warriors, relics, and lore made him perfect for her team.

After a pause filled with unspoken thoughts, Sheldon's voice broke the silence. "This is wrong," he murmured, his concern barely louder than a whisper.

Lilith's patience snapped. "Excuse me?" she challenged, her tone sharper than intended.

Sheldon recoiled, his apology swift, "Sorry, it's just..." He met her gaze, his eyes pleading for understanding. "May I?"

Lilith let out an irritated sigh, gesturing for Sheldon to proceed. He eagerly took over, fingers flying across the interface, the display lighting up with blue and purple flashes. As he navigated the data, he didn't just sort the Darviants. He unveiled a complex hierarchy that turned their understanding on its head.

Watching the colors shift and settle, Lilith realized Sheldon was doing more than solving puzzles—he was challenging their entire perspective. The room, now bathed in the glow of their newfound knowledge, seemed to pulse with potential. As he stepped back, and the colorful hues painted the room, the picture became a work of inquisitive art.

"Explain," Lilith asked, curiosity piqued.

"Well," Sheldon began. "With your data and a slew of other information gathered throughout time, I—"

"Sheldon..." Lilith growled, annoyed. "Get to the point."

"Sorry." He cleared his throat. "Our understanding of Darviants has been too simplistic. We aren't a uniform group differentiated only by our abilities. There's an underlying structure, a complex hierarchy, that we've completely missed. U-Class is the pinnacle of Darviants, followed by the formidable S-Class, the versatile A-Class, and the widespread B-Class."

Lilith nodded. Yet, at the hierarchy's pinnacle were the Champions, unmatched and unparalleled. But the question remained—what set them apart?

"What about the Champions," she looked at Sheldon, his lips curled into a smile. "What?"

"That's precisely why I'm here," he revealed, excitement underlining his words. "The Sky Knights, twin warriors, believed to be among the Champions."

Lilith rolled her eyes, skepticism written all over her face.

Sheldon, catching her expression, laughed nervously. "I'll have Lucy present their story. It might shed some light on our... conundrum."

He adjusted Lucy's settings to storytelling mode, a feature rarely used but perfect for this moment. Sheldon was dramatic in that way, an amusing trait she related to.

As the room dimmed, Lucy's voice filled the space, not as the AI they were accustomed to but as a storyteller from ages past.

"In an era untamed and vast, there lived two warriors, whispered in legend as the Sky Knights. Their tale was not one of mythical birthright, but of a legacy self-forged. Bound by a connection deeper than blood, their strength seemed to surge from the heavens itself."

Lilith listened, drawn in by the unfolding saga. The narrative hinted at a power reminiscent of ghost radiation, tied to their celestial swords and an innate, frost-like strength.

"They hailed from distant lands, their paths laden with trials. Yet, it was their unity, their combined might and shared chill of power, described as drawing from an ice god above, that marked them as extraordinary."

Lilith caught Sheldon watching as if he was the telepath. "They spoke of a cold that empowered them, a direct link to the ice god's strength in the skies."

Lucy's tale painted the Sky Knights as beacons of hope, embodying the ideals of unity and resolve beyond personal glory, touched with the divine purpose by the sky God. Their legacy, as Lucy told, served as a reminder of the power of unity and purpose of Champions.

As Lucy's voice faded, leaving a thoughtful silence, Lilith pondered the parallels between these legendary brothers and the other Champions she knew of. She finished her drink in contemplation.

After a while, Lilith realized what made Champions different from other Darviants. "Champions draw in ghost radiation," she concluded.

Sheldon nodded. "Other Darviants, like myself, we tap into the internal power gifted to us by GR," he added, completing her thought.

"Exactly. This changes everything," Lilith whispered, more to herself than to Sheldon.

The weight of her tasks, her goals, suddenly shifted. It wasn't just about gathering Darviants. or fighting against the UNA anymore. It was about understanding the roles these Champions played in the grand scheme of things, about guiding them, protecting them. Before tonight, she saw Champions as adversaries of the Sages, but they served a greater purpose in the buried history of these supernatural beings.

Once she awakened Elvir and tipped the scales of war in her favor, effectively sealing the UNA's fate, she was determined to unravel the true essence of the Champions' purpose.

This also made one other thing clear—she needed Vasilis on her side now more than ever. He and Midas had a purpose: to guard the Vessel, but she had Quintus.

Could they seal Elvir alone? She allowed the thought to linger, recalling something she read about the purpose of each Champion.

Champions were bound by an unspoken oath to fight alongside one another to ensure to shield humanity from the Sages' malevolent grasp. None of that mattered at the moment. She needed Forsaken in order to actually wake Elvir.

They have Vasilis, she thought. She could use her connections to take him. Maybe Malaya did her a favor.

For now, she would rely on the fact that Malaya was in the SUV. Lilith thought back to the nightmare. Perhaps it was her subconscious pushing forth the guilt of what she did to Malaya. For a moment, Lilith allowed her mind to drift back, thinking there was a lesson—a message that she needed her daughter—needed her powers. She didn't need Malaya, not now at least.

She's not ready.

What she needed to do was make sure she stopped the Cabinet from using her again. What she needed was to ensure she threw them off her trail.

Before Lilith could articulate her next thought, the door chimed. It was her brother-in-law Joseph who entered hastily, his expression etched with seriousness. The mood in the room shifted instantaneously, a sense of urgency palpable in the air.

Lilith and Sheldon turned their attention to Joseph. "What is it?" Lilith asked sharply.

Joseph hesitated briefly, as if weighing his words. "It's Malaya," he finally said, his tone laced with concern. Lilith felt her heart race. "She's in Japan."

MALAYA

Japan, 1601

"James," Malaya whispered loudly, looking around. "Ester, Vasilis?"

Where can they be? They must be close by. It was the first time the DCC sent so many individuals at once. There were bound to be inaccuracies.

"Spaghettification? No. Stay positive, Malaya," she said, pushing through the blend of towering trees and neon green brush.

Scattered rays of sunlight warmed her brown skin just enough to calm the chills, another side effect from time travel.

Or was it fear?

She was in yet another foreign place, only this time, she was alone. Her stomach turned at the realization. The earthy smell of vegetation didn't help.

She heard leaves crunching, but the steps were small and quick. *Must be a fox*, she thought, before rambling to herself as a myriad of possibilities clouded her mind.

Malaya collapsed against a boulder, pain throbbing through her skull. Another episode was coming, and she knew it. She fumbled for her medication packet, her fingers trembling as she tore off a strip and placed it on her tongue, bracing herself for the familiar rush of atto-energy. It flooded her senses like the first rays of sunlight breaking through a stormy sky, clearing her mind and easing her pain.

She drew in slow breaths, a technique she learned from Sensei. With everything going on, it helped, though not as often as she would have liked. Of course, he'd tell her to meditate or pray to her God—neither was pragmatic. Her medication and the breathing technique came in handy for now. She opened her eyes.

A new sense of calm allowed her to see where she was. Sun rays splashed the greenery, breathing life into the vibrant blend of blues, purples, and reds. For a moment, she was lost in the beauty of it all. The distant sound of chatter brought her back to reality. The language transmitter created a chaos of Japanese and English, making it difficult to understand whoever was close enough to hear clanking armor.

She stumbled forward, her feet catching on branches. She peeked around the tree and saw a group of nine samurai dressed in dark blue heavy metal plates with red accents. They were armed to the teeth, and they meant business.

Samurai. She gulped, the fear making its way from the pit of her stomach as she thought about everything that could go wrong—there was no one to protect her.

In Sparta, she had Aaron. On *Intrepid*, she had Winters and her family. But here, in Japan, she was a sitting duck. She braced herself for whatever was to come, knowing that her life was in danger.

Their dialect finally became clear. "A priest murdered on sacred grounds, blasphemy," she heard a warrior say. "Dead, like we should have done with the foreigners at our castle."

One of them cursed. "We are Torii, are we not? Osamu is—"

"Do not question Osamu!" another shouted, his voice thundered, bringing the men to a halt. He wore a blue and red kabuto with a jibaori surcoat, their leader Malaya guessed.

"Apologies, Ikeda-sama," the soldier said, metal clanking as he bowed.

"They will pay..." Ikeda said, and they began walking.

Malaya's heart raced as she frantically searched through her bag, hoping to find something—anything—to defend herself. Her hand finally landed on her father's tomahawk. She struggled to remove the sheath in her panic.

Realizing she couldn't fight them off, she reached for a wooden ball—the MRE Natwat packed her—pancakes and strawberry syrup. Wasting no time, she mixed the syrup with dirt and smeared it on herself.

She tore her clothes with the edge of her tomahawk, creating lacerations on her stomach and legs. Finding the perfect spot, she played opossum, using a shallow breathing technique taught to her by Captain Winters, hoping to trick the samurai.

As the samurai knelt to examine the fresh dirt on a nearby boulder, Malaya's heart pounded in her chest. She reminded herself that they couldn't catch her in a race, desperately trying to convince herself that she would be okay. Just as she began to relax, one of the samurai noticed her and they approached.

"Oh, an archer," a soldier shouted, sheathing his sword. "What do you think happened to her?"

"Rape, most likely."

"These *gaijin*, wrong place, wrong time," another said.

"Let's go," Ikeda said, moving ahead.

Malaya breathed a sigh of relief, but it was short-lived. A warm hand touched her, searching for signs of life. She fought the urge to panic, hoping they couldn't see the goosebumps covering her skin.

"She's still warm," one said, touching her face. "A look would not hurt."

Guess you can't factor in perverts. Malaya slammed her tomahawk into his wrist. The bladed edge sliced through his flesh with a nauseating crunch that would have made her vomit if she wasn't so scared. She rolled over, daring not to look at the damage she did.

With her sack in hand, she sprinted in the opposite direction, still able to hear his anguished screams.

Don't look back, she reminded herself, hearing the knocking of their bows, as she was already a few yards away. *Soldiers don't look back.*

She looked back. Her stomach sank seeing her; a young little girl, hiding behind a tiny boulder. Those were the steps she heard earlier. Saving her wasn't an option or else she'd risk creating a time flux. *History had to play out, right?*

"Darn my morals!" Malaya said. She ran back and tossed the frozen girl over her shoulder and ran, her long brown hair brushing Malaya's face.

She increased the distance when pain shot through her leg mid-stride. She looked down and saw an arrow piercing her left leg. Another whistle passed her ear. Malaya shouted in agony as blood poured out.

The little girl screamed. Fighting through the pain. Malaya pulled her behind a tree. "Run."

"I can't."

An arrow whistled by Malaya. "What's your name?" she said through gritted teeth, her heart raced.

"Reika," the girl said, her voice trembling. "They call me Re."

"Re, you are strong. I believe in you. Now run and survive... please."

She nodded and ran into the bushes.

Malaya struggled to break the arrow free, but the pain was too great, and she quickly surrounded.

Ikeda grabbed her face, and two others held her arms. "Who are you, *gaijin*?"

Two masked warriors appeared behind him, hidden in the shadows of the forest. When Ikeda realized what she was looking at, it was too late. An arrow hit his armored leg; a spear nipped his helmet as he ducked to attend to his wound. "Get them!"

The warriors attacked the other samurai. If Malaya didn't know any better, she would think the attacker looked straight out of a manga. The other wore leather armor over a kimono and a fox mask underneath a straw hat, wielding a double-edged chained kunai.

"Protect your leader!" the samurai shouted.

The two warriors were swift, unified, and graceful, using the trees, making it hard to keep up with them. They forced the samurai into the center before cutting down samurai with shurikens and elegant chained blades. Malaya wasn't sure if she should be afraid or relieved—she knew she had to escape.

"We will not quit!" one samurai said.

Malaya watched as the rhythmic strikes disarmed him before laying waste to the others. Ikeda was quicker than expected. He fled before

Malaya realized. The two warriors disappeared just as suddenly as they appeared.

"This way!" a man shouted.

Clanking forced her to run. She grabbed her bag and tomahawk, then strapped the bow across her back. Momentary relief took over after discovering the other medallion that was tucked safely inside her hidden pocket.

For some strange reason, she noticed the gem on her neck shining brighter than ever. Its scintillation was unlike anything she'd seen. *Focus, Malaya.* She took one more step.

Gravity pulled her down a grassy hill. She tumbled off a small cliff—a dirt road broke her fall. Excruciating pain pinned her to the ground. She turned her head. Through her hazing vision, she saw her dislocated shoulder. "Esther... James... Vasilis..." she whispered before passing out.

"Not so fast," said a small middle-aged woman, forcing Malaya to lie back down on the wooden bed. "You fell quite the distance."

"Hideaki, bring me some water," she added, turning to an old white-haired man.

"Where am I?" Malaya said, touching her bandages and analyzing the tiny rustic room.

"You speak Japanese," Hideaki said, handing the woman a cloth. "Azmani, I told you she would know Japanese. Now I can go help myself to some sake."

Good, at least the language transmitter is working, she thought.

"Don't mind Hideaki. He's an old fool. My name is Azmani."

"Nice to meet you, but I have to go," Malaya said, wondering if her words came out as groggy as she felt.

"You need rest."

"No, no, I really should get going."

"There aren't any manners in your country, are there?" Azmani said, with a smile as flawless as her skin and jet-black hair.

"I apologize. My name is Maria, a traveling stage performer," Malaya said, bowing her head. "*Dōmo arigato gozaimasu*, but I have to find my friends for the festival."

"It ended yesterday."

"What?" The words knocked her back onto the bed. *It was my only shot at Inoichi. What am I going to do?*

"As I have said, quite a fall."

Azmani placed a towel on Malaya's head. "By the way, most of your belongings were stolen. However, we found a small sack."

"And my friends. Where are they?"

"No friends, my dear, just you. We brought you here to my restaurant."

Overwhelming fatigue forced her body to rest—her mind could not. Finding her team was imperative, and so was getting an audience with the second most powerful man in Japan.

"Azmani, would it be ok if I spoke with your staff? Maybe they saw them or heard something?"

A corner smile wrinkled Azmani's face. "Aren't you lucky to be in the best sake shop in all of central Kyoto? Sure, you may retrieve all the information you need, but not without earning it. This is a great season for us. I only have one other worker. I think you will find working here of great use."

Work? I guess it's the best way for me to get information. How difficult could it be?

"I appreciate the offer... I'll take it."

"Good. But first, you rest."

Malaya's injuries healed sooner than expected, and she was soon thrust into the heart of all that this side of Japan had to offer.

From the outside, Azmani's shop wasn't unlike any other shop in the history books, with its thatched roof and wooden exterior. A simple wooden sign hung over the door with two lanterns on either side. But inside, it was a different story.

Lanterns lined the walls, masking the smell of alcohol with a sweet, earthy scent. The walls were adorned with paintings of rice fields, sake brewers, and poems. A tantalizing blend of fermented rice and baked goods welcomed customers from miles away.

Everyday eyes seemed glued on her, not in the way she was used to. At home, she was the life of the party, Malaya Castillo-Grant. But here, she was a foreigner, lost in a place she had no business being.

Malaya pushed her way through the throng of impatient customers vying for a seat. Azmani had left her under the watchful eyes of Hideaki and Cho, who ran the shop in her absence. The kindly old farmer had granted Malaya a much-needed break from her serving duties.

As soon as she made it through the wooden door into the back, leaving the noise and clamor of the customers—their chatter, laughter, and the clinking of cups—gave her a headache. Malaya kicked off her thin, worn shoes and let out a sigh of relief. The fabric of her kimono chafed against her skin, leaving red marks where it rubbed against her arms and legs.

Kat would be disappointed with my detective skills, she found herself thinking about her failed efforts.

Some days brought larger crowds, but Malaya saw no sign of Lilith or her friends. Or anyone from Edo, for that matter. As much as she thought about leaving, it wouldn't make sense to do so now.

Traveling alone in a foreign land fresh from war wasn't the best idea, especially not after what happened when she first arrived. Chills crept up her spine at the thought of what she had to do to survive. How she'd almost...

"Okay, okay…" Hideaki said, backing into the kitchen. "Maria, dear, you are being summoned," he said in a commanding tone. He took another step inside, looking over his shoulder before letting the wooden door shut. "The other one is upset you are still on break."

Malaya rolled her eyes at the mention of the mean-spirited Cho. "What's with her?"

Hideaki waved a hand. "Ah, Cho is an overachiever, the oldest of ten children. She left home to work, to learn, so anyone who does not fit her standard. Well…" he raised his arms and shrugged. She noticed a tattoo of a symbol on his wrist. She'd seen it before.

She was too tired to ask and didn't want Cho to storm in. Malaya slipped on her shoes, hurried to the bar, and grabbed a pitcher of sake.

"Over here," a man shouted, waving his hand at her like she was… a waitress.

She huffed and walked over to the table of three chatting. His accent was different from the others. A gift from the language transmitter deciphered dialects and accents within seconds. *Edo? Maybe.* She cleared her throat, interrupting the conversation.

"Are you from Edo?" she asked. The man ignored her. "Sir," she called again, the man continued to ignore her. "Ugh."

Desperate for something, anything that could find her friends, she slammed her hand on the table, finally getting his attention. "I am looking for my friends. Your accent it…it's from Edo, right?" She ignored the blank stares as she continued to ramble. "Have you heard any stories about travelers from a foreign land? They came around the time of the festival—"

The man stood up, towering over Malaya. She stopped talking. His thick brows narrowed as he removed coins from his pocket and slammed it on the table. He called her rude as he and his friends stalked away. She looked over her shoulder at the gawking eyes and a searing glare from Cho. Luckily, she was too busy to scold her.

"Sorry," Malaya muttered, embarrassed. She quickly moved on to the next customer, pouring another cup.

While working, Malaya's mind wandered, comparing her present reality to her past life. She had always balanced two contrasting worlds. There was the exhilaration of scientific discovery and the allure of high society.

She often spent her days in the lab, unraveling complex mysteries, her mind burning with the thrill of potential breakthroughs.

Yet, evenings would find her amidst the glittering elite, where she effortlessly mingled, relishing the luxurious comfort and reverence that came with her social status.

It was a dual existence that she had mastered—the scientist by day, mingling with intellectuals and innovators, pushing the boundaries of knowledge—the socialite by night, gracing glamorous events, where every detail was catered to her liking.

Now, stranded in a time and place so different, she longed not just for the comforts and recognition of her old life, but for the familiar sense of purpose she felt in her scientific pursuits. The contrast was stark—the certainty and control she once wielded in both domains of her life were now replaced with unpredictability and inconspicuousness.

In her world, she was a figure of control and influence, and if she was being honest, losing control, more than the absence of luxury, unsettled her the most.

In Malaya's eyes, these people were oppressed, never knowing what true freedom was like thanks to the stronghold of the most notorious rulers history has ever seen. Yet, they were content, happy even. There was an inspiring strength to them.

Despite her admiration for the people, the feeling wasn't reciprocated. They treated her like an outsider, and getting people to talk to her was impossible. That rude customer didn't help.

On the other hand, part of her relished the experience of working a job outside of a lab, in a sake shop in seventeenth-century Japan, of all places. Even amidst the literal chaos of the world shattering around her, she found herself enjoying the experience.

"Maria!" Cho barked, snapping her back to her duties. "We have more customers. Please try to stay focused."

Malaya felt her annoyance bubble up but quickly squashed it. Working with Cho was a hazard of this job. She couldn't afford to make enemies here, not when she was so far away from home. She grabbed the drinks and made her way through the small crowd, feeling Cho's eyes drilling a hole into her back.

She wasn't much older than Malaya, twenty-one, maybe, but she was a pro with how she handled the job. She always wore her jet-black hair parted in the middle and pulled back into a bun, which only accentuated her intense gaze.

As she set down the drinks, Cho rushed past her, serving her third table in less than fifteen minutes. "You are moving too slow," Cho scolded. "If you want these people to like you, move faster and smile."

Malaya gritted her teeth, fighting the urge to roll her eyes. She'd been told she suffers from RBF; resting-bitch-face. It wasn't a problem before.

Maybe they're the problem, she thought as she continued failed efforts to keep up.

Her mind kept wandering back to Lilith and the betrayal that had driven them apart—that drove her here. She wondered if her mother was watching her from some hidden corner, laughing at her struggles.

Cho noticed her hesitation and pounced on it. "Come on, Maria, you can do better than that," she said, her eyes glinting with annoyance. "You need to smile. Like this." She flashed a fake grin that made her look like a clown.

Malaya felt a surge of anger and embarrassment. She didn't want to play this game of false niceties, but she knew she had no choice. Azamani was nice enough to give her a place to live, and a place to work. Playing nice was the best she could do. She put on her own fake smile and forced herself to move faster, serving the customers with robotic efficiency.

Malaya glanced down at Cho's arm as she handed her a towel. "Cho, where did you get that?" she asked, unable to hide the curiosity in her voice of a woman in this age having a tattoo.

Cho's face grew tense, and she quickly pulled her arm back. "It's none of your business," she muttered.

"Whatever," Malaya mumbled as she left Cho to close the shop.

Later that night, Malaya sat in the steaming water, her muscles loosening as she let out a content sigh. She had grown accustomed to this routine over the past few days, though she missed the luxury of a shower back home. But with the constant stress of working and hoping her friends would show up, she welcomed the comfort of sulking in a hot bath.

At least she had a sketchbook. She started to draw as her mind drifted to the day she arrived, the day Azmani and that mysterious person saved her. She flipped to that page and it hit her.

Cho's arm, the marking, it's the same one. Her eyes widened in surprise. She remembered seeing that same marking on Azmani's arm. *What would Kat do?*

Malaya slipped out of the tub and got dressed, making her way through the rest of the house. She walked down the hallway, scanning the walls for any sign of a hidden room.

"What are you doing, Malaya?" she said to herself, feeling foolish for expecting a secret passage to open up like some Indiana Jones movie.

She stopped at a blank section of the wall and pressed her hand against it, feeling for any seams or cracks.

Symbols lit on up: hieroglyphics. It was a puzzle, an intricate and complex maze of symbols and glyphs that she would have to solve if she wanted to enter.

At first glance, they seemed to be nothing more than a jumbled mess of lines and curves. But as she studied them more closely, she began to see patterns emerge—certain symbols that appeared more frequently than others, certain lines that seemed to connect in particular ways.

Malaya traced the symbols with her finger, trying to make sense of the puzzle. She tried different combinations, testing out different sequences of symbols to see if they would unlock the door.

But each time, she was met with failure—the door remained resolutely shut, and the symbols seemed to mock her with their incomprehensible complexity.

She took breaks to rest her mind, studying the symbols and trying to find meaning in their shapes and curves. And then, finally, it happened—a sudden flash of insight, as the symbols suddenly seemed to click into place, forming a coherent message.

With trembling fingers, she traced the symbols once more, feeling the satisfying click of the lock as she worked. And then, with a final flourish, she traced the last symbol, and the wall shifted, revealing a hidden passage. Taking a deep breath, Malaya stepped inside, her heart racing with anticipation.

The air was musty, and the walls were covered in strange writing and texts. The passage led to a small room filled with ancient texts and artifacts. She scanned the walls, searching for any clue as to the significance of the marking on Azmani and Cho's arms.

Instead, she found a story about a lost people who sought dark power and caused the end of an era. Giant beasts slain by warriors wielding powerful weapons. She shrugged off the fairytale and pressed on, deeper into the room until she found a symbol she recognized from an ancient Spartan text she and Emily had decoded on Vasilis's sword. It was drawn on a scroll sitting atop a table, sitting next to a steaming cup of tea—

"What are you doing here?" Cho demanded. "You're not supposed to be in here."

Malaya's stomach sank. She looked around, searching for a lie. "I, uh..."

"It is okay, Cho," Azmani's voice shot from the darkness. Malaya nearly jumped out of her skin.

"Crap," she said, grabbing her heart and turning to see Azmani stepping out of the shadows.

"It's time we share some truths."

ELIAS

Edo, Japan, 1601

Thick smoke covered the half-moon, chaotic cries so loud that it would send a lesser man into a guilt so deep it'd leave him naked in the mind. For Elias, who wore the Torii armor, this was music to his ears. Midas tugged the rope. A rumbling cough soon followed.

"Relax. Do you want to give us up before getting wet?" Elias asked, one leg hanging in the well. "It's my fault. You appear to still be suffering from a hangover. Was it the girls in the sake shop?"

Elias chuckled. Midas ignored him and continued to stare into the deep, dark hole. "Seriously. What's your issue? Please explain before Ares comes and shits on our day."

"You heard the story of Yuurimi?"

Elias shrugged. "Humor me."

"The spirit of Okiku, a servant who died here? She comes out with jet-black hair and a white robe, counting her ten plates, but she never arrives. She always stops at nine."

"Oh, her." His voice perked up as a lazy smile painted his sunless face. "Do not worry, that happened in Himeji Castle, this is Edo Castle. Come on."

The men slowly lowered themselves into what felt like an endless abyss of frigid water; chills surged through their bodies. Elias led them, using the moonlight that streaked along the wall as a guide. They valiantly swam to where Sheldon told them to follow. It wasn't long before the light disappeared, and a brisk gust of wind hit him as they popped up on the other side where a cave awaited.

"I can't see my hand."

"Then you'll appreciate this," Midas said, revealing a glow stick.

"You bastard. Lilith would have us air-locked if she found out."

The rules were clear. They were to travel light, with minimal technology, no matter how enticing. If anyone found the tech, it could create a flux and unforeseen aberrations. Elias wanted to adhere to every rule, ensuring his place in the hierarchy of the Intrepid. Yes, his father was promised a kingdom here, but he wanted to start his own life, fresh, in their world. Lilith's world.

"Calm down *idiôtēs*," Midas said. "It has a rapid biodegradable enzyme."

"Oh," Elias said, relieved but not surprised. Midas was never as stupid as his blonde hair suggested.

"I have something else for you." Midas handed Elias two six-inch metal sticks.

"Spears with microbial corrosion?"

"Yes."

"Nice."

Elias could see the intense look on Midas' face, and he wondered what he was thinking. They once shared the same dreams and philosophies, but things were changing. Why did they have to? Elias started to countdown, doing his best imitation of the black-haired women from the stories. He got to eight before they reached their destination.

"Nine," a voice cried just before they sank.

"Who was that?"

"That was really good."

"It wasn't me," Elias said, looking back and seeing what he thought was the shadow of another person. "We must hurry and get this over with. I have to get out of Japan."

The cries of slain men and the intense heat from burning fires carried across the moat, adding to the chaos as people leaped to their deaths. A hunger churned in the pit of Elias's stomach, and his spine tingled with anticipation as he spotted those who would satisfy his desire. With swift strides, he raced across the once-healthy garden toward the entrance gate.

"Too slow," Elias snarled, sidestepping an attacker. One after another, his foes fell victim to his speed and rage, fueling his blade with each life taken. The expression on their faces was both glorious and empowering as he carved a bloody path through the guards, clearing the way to the gate. "Hurry, our army awaits."

Elias helped Midas lift the gate, allowing a flood of Torri men to pour in. Ikeda greeted them, his gaze fixed on Elias's blood-drenched armor. His brow raised in shock, unable to hide his surprise.

"Does Osamu have the target?" Elias said, grabbing a Torri helmet and fitting it atop his dark brown braids.

"No word yet," Ikeda said.

Their clan was few in numbers, but he admired their furious nature, while the cohesiveness in which they fought reminded him of home, though there were some memories he wanted to forget. Fighting, however, was what he lived for. Most of the Tokugawa men retired inside of the fortified castle.

"Let's move before the Tokugawa cavalry arrives." Elias led thirteen warriors past the guards and chaos.

"If you do not want to die, pay attention," Elias said. "We will take point and create a wall with our shields. Press against us and push forward no matter what. With your spears, the narrow hall, your grit, and trust in one another. We shall become victorious!"

The Spartans revealed two metal sticks that expanded into a dory. Their vanguard unfolded like a fan with steel plates connecting until it formed a hoplon shield.

"It's unnatural," Ikeda said. His words echoed the shock on everyone's face.

"Yeah? Well, it shall keep you alive," Midas said, opening the door—as Osamu promised.

To Elias's surprise, Seth appeared, stumbling into them, holding the side of his neck; blood covered his hand to elbow. "Father! What happened?"

"Ieyasu… and his son…" he said, his voice low. "I need medical attention. I'm returning to base."

Elias placed his hand on his father's shoulder. Seth looked into his eyes. "Son, I messed up."

"Don't talk," Elias said. "Go. We will finish the mission."

Midas turned to Ikeda. "We require a few men to escort him to an emergency extraction point."

What have you done, father? The decisions you make tend to have dire consequences. Heat rose inside him, but he had to focus.

The wooden floors creaked, alerting the wakizashi-wielding samu-rai who bunched together in a narrow hall. Without hesitation, the Spartans rammed their large shields into them.

"Push!" said Elias.

The spears followed, and with it, a mountain of bodies piled up. Midas collapsed his side with ease, forcing the last of the samurai to retreat through the wooden door. "Barricade the entrance. You're up."

Elias removed his helmet and brushed his hair back, following them into the small room with more sliding doors. "Honey, I'm home!"

Redwood squares held storied paintings, which made the ceiling, and gold trim bordered the walls. There were other doors painted with gardens and gods. This was a room fit for a king, lavish in ways that paled in comparison to the *Intrepid* simulators.

"What a room?" Midas said, echoing his thoughts.

"There he is, the man of the hour!" Elias pointed at Inoichi, who sat in a tranquil lotus position on the elevated platform. "My com-pliments to your designer, and apologies for not removing my shoes. Forgive my laziness, and time, well... she can be a bitch..."

Elias's heart sank as he saw the two lifeless bodies of Inoichi's father and brother. The anger and frustration boiled inside him, threatening to consume him. *Ieyasu Tokugawa... dead... Κατάρα.*

He clenched his teeth, struggling to contain the wave of emotions surging through him.

Seth couldn't resist testing his power, and now they were all going to pay the price. Elias had seen it happen before in Sparta, and it had cost him and Midas dearly. And now, history was repeating itself. *Lilith warned us. She only had one request. What will become of us now?*

"Inoichi. Apologies for what my father has done. Out of respect, we will not attack."

Elias shortened the dory back into its stick form. Inoichi didn't respond. He knelt beside his father and brother, his hands covered in blood, his eyes red. Elias knew that no words could console him, no apology could erase the pain of losing his loved ones.

"We are looking for a hilt," Elias said. "It is special to a woman I hold dear to my heart. Please. Point us in the right direction, and we will leave."

Inoichi remained silent.

The men behind Elias protested, "Tokugawa, I promised you our return!" Ikeda shouted, marching toward Inoichi, leaping over the platform, his sword overhead.

At first glance, Inoichi appeared unmoved, not even a flinch. But Elias smirked as he saw Inoichi quickly push up the guard of his sword with his thumb, drawing it and striking at Ikeda. He barely blocked it. Elias's eyes widened as Inoichi unsheathed his sword with lightning-fast reflexes, striking at Ikeda with precise movements.

Despite the initial shock, Elias recognized the familiar power and speed of a Champion. Lilith had chosen not to recruit Inoichi, but Elias knew his prowess was undeniable. He himself had struggled to keep up with Midas and Vasilis, always feeling at a disadvantage with his smaller stature. But Inoichi moved with an effortless grace that made Elias envious.

Ikeda's face showed that he had seen such moves before, but Inoichi's movements were something else entirely. It was like watching a dance, with each step calculated and executed with precision. Elias couldn't help but feel a sense of awe and admiration for the Champion.

"Iaido, good," Ikeda said. "But I have experience!"

"Without discipline, experience can only take you so far. You lack honor! Even less than the company you keep." Inoichi straightened his stance, clutching his sword with both hands. "But do not worry, for you will receive it in death."

Ikeda slashed at Inoichi, but the Champion moved with such fluidity that it seemed as though he knew the attack was coming. In one swift move, Inoichi plunged his sword into Ikeda's abdomen, the clanging of metal ringing out in the room. The thumping of the Tokugawa samurai who had entered the room soon overlapped the sound.

Elias's heart raced as they were suddenly surrounded. Two of them stood out, wearing mostly gold armor—the Torri men. They looked at each other, their expressions unreadable.

"Golden Dragons," one of the Torri said.

Chaos ensued, with Spartans attacking and the Torri and Tokugawa slamming into one another, decorating priceless art with blood. But the Golden Dragons had their eyes set on the Spartans. A blue aura transferred from one of the golden armor to the katana—the others' katana glowed a fire red.

Darviants, he thought. The Spartans' short swords would have to do. In this chaos, they had the advantage. The Spartan armor was no match for their weapons. If only Midas had his sword—Forspoken would have evened the odds. But Midas still had his power. He slammed his shield into one of them, sending him into the other. Elias finished them both before they could stand.

Elias tried to keep an eye on Inoichi, still hoping to retrieve the hilt. Amid the battle, Osamu entered the room, holding Mizunami Toyotomi over his shoulder. Inoichi's eyes widened. "Osamu! You will pay for your treachery. Let her go!"

Inoichi's draw speed left Elias in awe. It was fast, as his legend suggested, with flawless technique. He knew Ikeda's men didn't stand a chance. Midas rushed to help, but waves of samurai kept coming.

"Inoichi!" Mizunami said before Osamu covered her mouth.

"You do not understand yet," Osamu warned. "Inoichi, please."

"Phílos, we need to get to the center. It's the extraction point," Midas shouted. The closer they got to the center, the more his medallion glowed.

"It's over, Hetáire," said Elias.

Inoichi looked up, realizing the thumping had stopped—the Tokugawa were dead. More Torri warriors stood watch by the door. Inoichi drew his secondary sword in preparation, charging Elias. Inoichi's sword sliced through his dory, splitting it.

Midas threw his dory, cutting the side of his knee. Elias saw an opening crashing his shield into his head. Bloody gushed from both wounds, but it wasn't enough. Inoichi's unorthodox style proved troublesome for them, forcing them to take refuge behind their shields—unable to predict his moves.

"I will not die today." Inoichi used Elias's shield to accelerate and propel himself towards Midas, successfully causing him to fall over a pile of bodies.

"You're good, but don't underestimate me!"

Elias tried to keep Inoichi distracted, though the continuing screams of Mizunami proved to fuel his rage. Elias saw Inoichi's brother, Hidetada, running into the room.

"Now, Midas!" Elias said, diverting Inoichi's attention.

Midas grabbed his spear and chucked it, hitting Hidetada in the shoulder.

"Brother, no!" Inoichi exclaimed, giving Elias the opening he needed. He thrust his sword into Inoichi's back.

"We have to go!" Osamu said, standing at the extraction point.

"I said don't underestimate me," Elias said, stalking Inoichi, who crashed into a painting of a crow, leaving a streak of blood. "I was going to let you live, but you made this difficult."

"Stop!" Midas said. "You know our instructions. We must not cause unnecessary effects. Your father has done enough. Do you want to upset Lilith?"

Elias stopped. Though part of him felt it was already too late. If Inoichi died, this could be over for them, but the hilt could be their saving grace. He knelt in front of Inoichi. "The hilt, where is it?"

Inoichi spat blood into Elias's face.

He looked at him with a smile. "We will take great care of your girl. Won't we, Osamu?"

Osamu turned to Inoichi. "I'm sorry."

"I'm not," Elias said, just as Midas pressed the medallion.

MALAYA

Japan, 1601

Malaya sat at the polished wooden bar, tracing the grooves in the cool wood grain, replaying the moments before. The bar was usually bustling with customers, but tonight, it was quiet except for the soft crackling of the torches and the clanking of cups as Azmani tended to the bar. The faint aroma of cedar and sandalwood filled the air.

Azmani walked over, the wooden floorboards creaking beneath her steps; a half-smile formed slight wrinkles at the corners of her mouth. Behind the warm smile and concerned eyes was something darker: a highly skilled warrior trained in the arts of stealth, deception, and murder.

"Try this," Azmani said. "It's my special sake. You need it."

Malaya took a sip, cringing at the bitterness. "That's terrible?" She teased.

Azmani chuckled. "See, Cho was right. You lack culture."

Malaya cringed hearing her name, thankful she wasn't around to make things worse. Azmani hovered over Malaya. *An assassin with honor,* Malaya replayed the words Azamni spoke moments ago as if it eased.

"I need more answers," Malaya said, hoping to get some clarity.

Azmani's response was firm but gentle. "I have told you all I can. More than you needed to know. We have a saying: a guest who opens the host's closet to search for hidden treasures is like a thief who sneaks into a farmer's field to steal fruits. Both are unwelcome and deserve no reward."

"I'm sorry," Malaya said. "I've been here for days, getting nowhere. I want to find my friends, speak to the Shogun, and save my people. But all this magic talk... I can't make sense of it."

"Your mind is clouded by disbelief, and that's why you struggle," Azmani interrupted, her tone gentle but firm. "The people here can see you're not authentic. You must earn their trust by being what they need you to be. Don't apologize for that."

Azmani stood up and left Malaya alone in the bar. "I ll help you be what you need to be."

Malaya sat, trying to make sense of Azmani's words. Her mind wandered to her mother—who was she, really? Not the savior portrayed in the media, nor the loving mother who raised her.

Was it possible she planned all of this? The thought sent shivers through her body, but it wasn't impossible. After all, she wore a mask for years, and now Malaya needed to do the same. She took a drink, and with each drop, she found it easier to digest.

Over the next two weeks, she worked and trained with Azmani. No, she wasn't buying any of the fabled tales she spoke of, but Malaya appreciated the rich history of her culture. Azmani had her secrets, but not like Sensei, who was stoic and guarded. There was a kind of sternness like a mother, her mother.

Night after night, she tried to adhere to Azmani's advice, though the idea of resorting to tired old clichés, such as batting her eyelashes and smiling to get what she wanted, made her skin crawl. It felt like a compromise of her very being, but she knew it was necessary. With her fluent Japanese and light brown skin, she quickly became a familiar face to the locals, especially the men. The attention made her stomach churn with disgust, but she had to keep up the facade.

"Maria," someone called out, his words slurred with alcohol, but Malaya knew who it was: Seki. "I have something for you."

Azmani stepped in, a stern look on her face. "Now Seki, she's told you a hundred times."

The other men burst into raucous laughter, teasing Seki. He was a large man with dark, short hair, and she could see that he had once been handsome. Unfortunately, the years of heavy drinking had left their mark on his face, and the man's features were now bloated and weathered. It was a shame, but there was something charming about his infectious sense of humor.

Malaya smiled. "What is it?"

He tried to compose himself as he walked over. "Would you accompany me to dinner tomorrow night?" His head nodded toward the small partition separating one area of the shop from the rest.

It was a dense wooden screen that marked a boundary between two worlds. The world of the everyday drinkers and the world of the powerful political figures. Azmani discouraged her from engaging with those on the other side, even when they crossed over, but they were the people she needed to talk to.

What would Kat do? What would her mother do?

"Yes," Malaya said.

"She said yes, you fools," Seki shouted, rejoining his friends.

Azamni popped up, catching Malaya's gaze, a slight depression in her brows. "What exactly did you agree to?"

Azmani would be gone tomorrow night, which meant there was no need to upset her. "Dinner," Malaya said.

"Okay..."

"It will be fine."

"It's not you. I am worried about. It's him," said Azmani. "You are going to break his heart."

Malaya smiled. "I am sure he knows it is as friends," she said, loud enough for him to hear.

He raised a glass. "A pretty woman on my arm is all I ask."

The following night, Malaya wore her hair in a simple tight bun and dressed herself in a fine white silk kimono wrapped in black vines, a gift from Azmani. She grabbed her tomahawk, just in case. She found a spot inside her kimono, a built-in slot for a weapon.

"A ninja kimono," she smiled. "Thank you, Azmani."

She met Seki out front, trying to avoid Hikeada and Cho, who were supposed to be back by now.

Seki gave her a wide smile and bowed. "You will be the most beautiful woman there."

"Thank you," she bowed slightly, before stepping through the partition and into a different world.

The overwhelming smell of sake mixed with an expensive sweet fragrance added to the luxurious decor and bright lanterns that cast an inviting glow struck her. Silk wall tapestries depicted stunning landscapes, and the tables were made of dark, polished wood that reflected the light in a way that made them appear to glow from within.

The men in the room were just as ornate, with elaborate silk kimonos and perfectly styled hair. There were women, lots of beautiful women, almost three for every man. Enough to make her sick, but she was too determined to let them distract her.

She followed Seki, taking a seat at a table with men who wore black kamishimo with purple patterns. It was an upper sleeveless garment that was starched to make the shoulders stand out and show they were a clan.

It wasn't long before the men didn't notice her. It became clear Seki wanted to impress them. He once belonged to the men, but now he was... alone.

Part of her felt bad for him and happy she was able to help. This wasn't any different from a man bringing a beautiful woman to a boardroom gathering, hoping to impress the boys, a lesson she learned from her mom.

Disgusting, she found herself thinking. *And sad to see how not much had changed.* The corporate world wasn't her thing, and neither was this, but she knew it was best to play the role. *Quiet, smiling, and unassuming.* Malaya repeated in her mind like a formula.

The food soon arrived. The waitress brought steaming bowls of soup. A combination of spice and fish filled her nose. She smiled and looked inside, seeing eyeballs attached to the fleshy gelatinous cheeks of a fish head swimming in yellow liquid and green vegetables. Her stomach turned—she noticed the men watching.

It was like time stood still, waiting for her. So, she swallowed the vile threatening to embarrass her and took down a slurp from the spoon. Its salty-sweet sauce warmed her empty stomach. She found herself tasting the buttery fish.

Before long, she overheard their stories. The bushy browed man was the leader. He spoke about a murder at a temple. Then it hit her. She thought back to when she first arrived and how the samurai were talking about a group of gajin that murdered someone at the temple. She couldn't help but wonder if it was connected. Before she knew it, her mouth opened.

"These gajin... how did they look?" Malaya blurted, instantly regretting it.

Silence, complete and utter silence, with raised brows and suspicious gazes. One of the men shot an angered look at Seki. His thick brown eyebrows deepened with anger. "Does this woman not know her place?"

"He does not speak for me," Malaya said.

"Apparently not," the thick-brow man said, ignoring Malaya, his eyes fixed on Seki. "We allowed you here despite your recent transgressions in the hope that you were still one of us, but it appears—"

"She knows her place," Seki said. "She is nothing more than a woman who sought to use my status to get a word with the shogun..."

Malaya felt the anger rising in her as Seki continued to belittle her. She snapped. "The four of you are an insignificant waste of atoms, an inebriated bunch of detestable idiots. The world would have been better off if your mother swallowed—"

"Marie," Seki shouted through clenched teeth, face flushed with embarrassment, as were the others. "Do you know who this is?"

Malaya stood up. "I couldn't care less."

"Well, you should," the man shouted, his voice thundered in the nearly quiet room except for the other women who mocked her in whispered tones.

She wished they could feel her verbal wrath, but her knotted stomach and fear creeping up her spine at the sight of the angry clan leader stopped her.

"Are you so weak that you would hit a woman?" she blurted, despite the fear.

The general sucked his teeth. "No, I am a dignified gentleman. She will take care of you for me."

Malaya sidestepped a punch that whistled past her face, surprising the woman who caught herself on the table but not before knocking over a few drinks. A benefit from Azmani's training, no doubt. It felt good for a second until a blow to her back knocked her off balance.

She turned to see another woman before Malaya could attack before she could make a move. Thin muscular arms wrapped around her neck. Malaya dropped her chin and grabbed her attacker's wrist and elbow, giving her enough room to parry away and sling the thin woman into the other. Just like Sensei taught her.

She stared at the two attackers dressed in clad kimonos, taking their fighting stance as the men cheered them on, as if they couldn't be more disgusting. Malaya's heart pounded with rapid beats of fear and anxiousness. She prepared for this, right?

One attacked, and Malaya dodged one punch after another until landing one of her own, southpaw, in the attacker's ribs—something Winters taught her. Yes, she was prepared.

A dulling pain shot through her jaw and changed her mind. She crashed into a table, then onto the floor. She tried to stand, but a kick to the stomach made that impossible. Through her ringing ears, she could hear the cheers. Her vision blurred then turned white.

Get up, she heard a woman say; for a moment she thought it was Azmani—the voice spoke again. *Get up*. The voice echoed—her grandmother flashed in her vision. *Get up!* She shouted.

The kicks stopped. When she opened her eyes, the two women were on the floor, groaning in pain. All gawking eyes with draped jaws stared at her. She looked around for the person who helped to tell them thanks, but no one claimed the damage.

She struggled to her feet, and the women weren't too far behind. Malaya readied for one more round, hoping whoever it was would help her now. They both attacked and in a flash, Cho appeared with both their wrists in her grasp.

"You two, out!" she said, releasing them. They bowed and walked away. Malaya knew then she had to be the one to stop them before.

Cho stood and turned around, anger in her eyes as she looked at Malaya. "You too. Azmani is waiting."

Malaya's mouth opened to say something, but she stopped and bowed before returning to the other side.

Azmani stood behind the bar with a half-smile and a drink ready. "I knew you could not help yourself, but did I not warn you?"

Malaya nodded and flopped down. "I'm s—"

Azmani put up a finger. "No apologies. You did exactly what you needed to. You are not ready, but that could have gone worse. Perhaps you may get answers sooner than you think."

Malaya followed her gaze to a mysterious fair-skinned man who walked from the side of the screen. His six-foot-six broad frame and oceanic eyes silenced the room. He removed his hood. His blond hair was braided neatly, along with an undercut that was unusual. She hadn't seen him, but maybe he was surrounded by women. She turned back to the bar, daring not to drool over him like the other women.

Cho wasn't far behind. She stepped behind the bar as he sat. "Sorry for the inconvenience," she said, aiming a side-eye stare at Malaya out of the corner of her eye, begging her to say something.

How could she say anything other than thank you? So, she took the nonverbal jab.

"No problem, beautiful," the mystery man said in perfect Japanese. Too perfect, Malaya thought as he continued to speak. "Four bottles of your best chintashu."

"Of course," Cho said, blushing like a teenager.

It was the first time Malaya saw her smile, genuinely smiling outside of the mocking grins and laughter during their training sessions. Unfortunately, she was too fascinated by the large man a few seats down to make fun of her.

After Cho left to the back, the handsome stranger glanced over at Malaya. She turned away quickly. Hoping he didn't catch her staring.

"Maria, is it?" he said.

Crap, Malaya thought as she turned to him, embarrassed. "Yes."

"Well... Maria. That was quite a display you put on back there."

It hit her. There was something familiar about him. The way he said her name twice as if he didn't believe her and the way he looked at her...

Could this be someone working for my mother? A Spartan? What are the odds? Why would they be here? Crap, could I be exposed?

He continued to stare, almost baiting her to come over. *What would Kat do?* Malaya thought, not dropping her gaze. *She'd take the risk.*

Malaya walked over, taking a seat next to him. Determined to not make the same unflattering mistake she made with Vasilis. "Portuguese wine? Interesting," she said. "*Você fala Português?*"

"*Sim*, but I don't speak it in public," he said in Portuguese before switching back to Japanese. "It's unsettling for the locals. Antonio." He smiled through his blond stubble beard, extending his hand.

"Where are you from, *Maria*?"

The question pinned her to the seat. "That's difficult to answer. I spend most of my days traveling. I came here for the festival."

"From where I was sitting, it looks like you came here to find trouble."

"What about you, Antonio? What trouble are you going to get into?" She held his deep green eyes, trying to read on him. This was harder than she thought.

"Ahem," Cho interrupted. "Your wine, sir."

"Thank you very much," he said, bowing his head before handing her a gold coin. "Keep the difference."

I have to stop him. He could have answers about my mother, but I have to be subtle. She cleared her throat and forced a half-smile. "You should join me; we can have a fun evening."

A fun evening? Great Malaya, now you sound like a whore.

"I wish I could, but I have an early trip to Edo tomorrow, but this drink is on me," he said, placing another coin in front of Malaya, covering his head with his cloak. "Hope to see you again."

"Darn it," Malaya said, pushing the coin away.

"The emperor's crest engraved coin. How?" Cho asked, examining the coin.

"Why, what... does it mean?"

"There aren't many people walking around with one, especially outside of the castle. And he had two."

Malaya watched Antonio pass to the exit, eyeballing a woman from her chest to her eyes. "Typical." Malaya shook her head and turned her attention to her sake. *I should have gone after him—*

"May I?" a woman asked.

Malaya shrugged, not taking her eyes off the full cup of sake in front of her, but she could see the girl sizing her up from the corner of her eye.

"I haven't seen you around here," the stranger said, taking a seat.

Malaya continued to try to ignore the women's presence. "Apparently, you haven't been here enough."

"Your Japanese is impressive. You must be very special to Azmani to be wearing such fine clothing."

"I like to think I am quite special," Malaya snapped, then she paused. *Wait... Who the heck is this?*

After Antonio, she couldn't help but think this woman might be a pawn. She was someone who clearly knew more than she should. Most of the people she encountered thus far were far reserved, especially the locals. Yet she was forward, introducing, prying.

Needing to get a better look, Malaya turned her head and met the woman, who was either friend or foe. Her eyes were deep and soulful, mysterious, a rich brown that spoke without ever saying a word.

Her long, deep brown hair cascaded down her back in a silken waterfall, catching the torchlight in a way that made it seem as if it were on fire.

Cho burst from the back, wooden mug in hand. "Here you go, *shishou,*" she said, sitting down the cup.

Shishou? As in master? Malaya's eyes darted to Kasumi, then back to Cho.

"I see you've met Maria," Cho said, cutting her eyes at Malaya.

Kasumi squinted. "Hmmm, not officially. She is not much of a talker."

"She does complain a lot," Cho said.

Before Malaya could reply, Cho was rushing back to work. Kasumi smiled and looked at Malaya. "So, *Maria,* a little birdy told me you are seeking an audience with Tokugawa Inoichi. Why is that?"

The statement caught Malaya off guard. She looked over her shoulder at Cho, who watched them closely. "Seems like Cho is the one with the big mouth," Malaya mumbled as she shifted in her seat.

"Who said Cho told me anything?"

She had a point. A black Latina working in a sake shop wasn't exactly inconspicuous.

"Well," Malaya said. "I wanted to perform for his grace. His acknowledgment would bring me and my family great pride."

Kasumi smiled and took a drink. "You perform as a server?" she teased.

Malaya looked over at Cho again, who responded with a childish, cynical smirk. She shook off her annoyance in favor of Kasumi. "No, not as a server, as a stage performer, an archer, to be specific."

"You must be amazing, considering you traveled all this way for the festival," she said, side-eyeing Malaya as she drank. "Lucky for you, my father is a man of great power. Since you obviously missed it, perhaps I could grant you an audience."

"Why me?"

Kasumi leaned over. "Cho spoke very highly of you."

"No..." Malaya chuckled in disbelief. "Really?"

Kasumi nodded. "Speak any word of this, and I will deny it—"

Kasumi jumped back just as Cho walked past them toward the back, a curious look on her face. Malaya shared the curiosity, though it was more disbelief in her case. Cho made her life hell, yet she had something nice to say about her to her... *teacher*.

Malaya had almost forgotten. She glanced at Kasumi, turning away a man who offered to buy her a drink. Who was this girl? She was offering to help her a few moments after she met Antonio, a man who, just moments before, was hanging with some of the most powerful men in Japan. *Something doesn't feel right.*

"Kasumi," Malaya called. "Why are you so willing to help a stranger? And don't tell me it's because someone put in a good word. That's not how things work?"

"You, a stranger in a new world, suddenly know how things work... Interesting." Kasumi chuckled and took a drink.

Malaya stammered. "Well... yeah."

Kasumi placed the mug down and relaxed on the bar. "Well, I do have a motive."

"Exactly," Malaya snapped.

"I am on a mission and require your expertise...."

Malaya's face pinched with confusion. "My expertise?"

"An *archer*...."

"Oh, right," Malaya smiled, hoping her false confidence wasn't palpable.

"You help me, and I shall aid you in your efforts closer to the heir to the shogunate," Kasumi said. "Do you agree?"

"Sure," she said through clenched teeth.

"Good," she shot up from her seat. "We will set out to Edo in a few days' time." She removed a coin and placed it on the counter.

Malaya watched her carefully from the corner of her eye, hoping to find a sign she was of the Iga Clan, the ninja guild Azmani belonged to—the symbol of eternity. She hoped she had found the other woman who helped save her life, but she didn't. There was no tattoo. Malaya shook her head slightly, disappointed.

Kasumi started to leave.

"Wait," Malaya yelled, heading toward Kasumi. She checked over her shoulder, her voice near a whisper. "What's the mission?"

"You will find out," she said in a reassuring tone. "I shall see you soon."

Malaya tried to rest, but couldn't shake the thought of Kasumi and, more importantly, Antonio, for the next few hours. It was still early, but she knew that if he was leaving for Edo, he would likely be at the port. She needed a closer look, but distance was the problem. Leaving now was her only option.

She quickly changed into a black kimono and hakama pants, tucking her small axe into her obi belt and securing it tightly against her waist. With the bar full, Cho busy, and Azmani gone, she could sneak out without a problem, but she knew that she could never be too safe.

She tiptoed on the woven rush floors, making her way around the house to the foyer, where she grabbed a lantern. As she opened the door, Azmani stood on the other side, scaring her out of her skin.

"Have you not had enough trouble for one night?"

It took a moment for her to gather herself. "You heard about that?" Azmani's brows raised at the silly question. "Of course you did."

"It has been established that I know all things," Azmani teased. "It is best if you tell me the truth."

Malaya filled her in. To her surprise, Azmani encouraged her to find the answers, but she would not go alone. Azmani led the way to the port, where they camped out, waiting for Antonio to arrive.

Azmani handed her a flask of water while they sat and watched. "I believe our paths were destined to cross. As do all my students, including your new friend," she said.

"Cho and I are hardly friends."

Azmani smiled. "Not Cho, dear, Kasumi."

"Your student..."

"Please tell me you are not surprised.

"Honestly... No."

"As I was saying. Like her, you have amazing gifts and a good heart, but you will be tested."

"Like now," Malaya said, seeing movement just as the sun rose.

"That's him," she said, pointing at Antonio, who was with a crew of men, but not all Japanese but one. He wore a cloak. Azmani assured the hiring of local sailors was very common.

Other than that, there wasn't anything abnormal about the situation. She felt like an idiot for thinking she could solve anything but an equation. On their way back, Azmani did her best to repair Malaya's broken pride.

Her mother's shadow lingered heavily in the back of her mind. The weight of the fragile time-line, a vase slipping through her finger. Perhaps she wasn't enough, perhaps she was in over her head.

Malaya reached for a fish that hung over the fire. "I can't do this... none of this." Her voice filled with melancholy.

Azmani stung the back of her hand with a thin branch. "You can. And you will. What the mind commands, the body follows, and what the mind believes, the body believes. Believe in success. Believe you will save those who require saving. Then you will save them."

But who will save me? she thought.

KASUMI

Kyoto, Japan, 1601

The Indian ivory pieces clanked against one another as Azmani-sensei added yet another victim to her pile. Kasumi let out a loud sigh, keeping her eyes on the faded wooden checkerboard.

She could feel her sensei staring at her, with her insufferable smirk and her insufferable white hair that was held up with a chopstick. The iron wind chime rattled in the breeze, irritating her even more. A relic intended to ward off evil proved futile, considering Azmani's presence sitting across from her.

Kasumi's fingers hovered before moving her most prized piece, their queen, Joōryū. With every detail intricately carved from ivory, the queen dragon was a representation of Azmani-sensei's teachings, embodying wisdom, strength, and strategic insight.

Today, she was to be sacrificed.

Kasumi moved her queen, never lifting her head, not caring for Azmani's impassive expression. She could almost hear her lips part with a cynical smirk, creating a peng of doubt in Kasumi.

She's been spending more and more time at the back of Azmani's sake shop, assisting with her garden, and keeping an eye on this *gaijin*, Maria.

Kasumi watched her underneath her straw hat. Maria was holding a water clay jar with both arms and repeatedly jumping onto a tree stump. The stump was nearly half her size, but she made the jump every time.

She appeared out of nowhere, nearly getting herself killed by some of the most notorious samurai in Japan. Barely escaping with her life, Azmani not only took her in, gave her a job at the shop, a place to live, but she was bent on teaching this stranger. Surprisingly, she even managed to win over Cho—she disdained everyone.

Even the sun, hanging low on the horizon, its light filtered through the towering trees, enveloped her brown skin in its warm, golden hue.

Who was this girl, the archer who claimed she wanted to seek counsel with Tokugawa Ieyasu? The question lingered in the air. Soon she would have an answer about this, archer.

"If you were to spend more time on the game than on our guess, you could be winning," Azmani said, snapping her back to the game.

Kasumi ignored the snide remark. "How long?"

"She's been at it since dawn. Perhaps I might get those fat thighs—back in shape. Though, I must admit, her explosiveness is quite impressive. Almost as explosive as your losing streak."

Kasumi sighed, finally looking up. "I meant, how long will you waste your time in training her? A shinobi is a lifelong commitment. What can a few weeks accomplish?"

Azmani leaned back, arms folded. "One can learn a lot from a person in a few weeks, and even more for themselves."

Kasumi shook her head. "Why?"

"Why not?"

"I am no longer a child, sensei. I do not require riddles."

Azmani unfolded her arms and took another of Kasumi's black pieces.

"Ehh," Kasumi squealed in surprised.

She followed Azmani's gaze, shifting to her guest. Who had removed her kimono from her drenched body?

"Earlier this week," Azmani began, "Himiko had a dream with a salamander. Then, Malaya shows up."

"Oh." Kasumi rolled her eyes. "The self-proclaimed god dreamt of the sacred salamander. I recall begging and then fighting earning my way into Iga, and the scared salamander did not show until after, but her..."

"Envy is such an unbecoming shade on you."

Kasumi laughed, moving her queen again. "Hardly. You asked me to help her, but I do not see how it benefits me?

"Helping her without a personal gain? Perhaps I am wrong to ask a fox to guard a henhouse out of the goodness of its heart."

"*Nee*... I am simply attempting to understand it all," Kasumi said, making another move. "Check."

"Check?" Azmani snapped. She rubbed her chin, trying to figure a way out, how to save her king.

Kasumi smirked seeing her sensei's expression shift, if only for a moment. "Oh no, checkmate?"

Azmani brushed off Kasumi's gloating. "Not everyone is the hero of the story," she said, her tone brimmed with purpose. "Sure, you may be the hero in your story, but you may be the sword in hers."

"So, you would have me be her stepping stone?"

"Occasionally, one must play the role of queen to the king. Even if the queen is more capable than the king, she must do what it takes to not just win, but stay in the game."

Azmani moved Kasumi's queen, sacrificing it, and saving the king. She moved both pieces until black won the game.

"Yay, I won. You owe me a free round of sake." Kasumi crossed her arms, pinching her eyes close.

"Oh, wait a moment," Azmani said.

"I never ask you to touch my pieces." Kasumi stuck her tongue out, and further turned her body. She fought the urge to smile, peeking at Azmani with the corner of her eyes.

Azmani waved a dismissive gesture. "Oh, fine, but you're cleaning the pieces."

Their attention was suddenly seized by a burst of water. They found Maria on all fours amidst the shattered jars, its pieces scattered around the vegetable garden.

"Maria, that was my grandmothers!"

"It was?"

Azmani smiled. "No," she teased.

Kasumi cleared her throat, capturing Azmani's attention. "Sensei," she began, her voice—a once confident force—now quivered, diminished by the shadows of doubt that lingered in her mind. "How much time do I have left?"

Azmani looked over at Maria, then back at her. The grass rustled in the winds, mirroring the inner conflict that was also present within Kasumi.

For years, Kasumi wrestled with the intricate threads of her existence, entangled in a world that thrived on chaos and bloodshed. A Christian at heart, she carried prayers whispered under her breath to the one God who had gifted humanity with a sacrifice.

Yet, in equal measure, she honored the teachings of Shinto and Buddhism, where the divine was not distant but walked among mortals, leaving their marks as blessings and curses alike.

Within her burned the power of Inari's kitsune, a feral gift that both exalted and burdened her. This duality, a believer wielding the wrath of a god, gnawed at her soul. Her faith taught her to forgive, to seek peace, yet her gift demanded sustenance—fed on the essence of those who reduced others to shadows of themselves. Her existence, a contradiction forged by gods and sharpened by the sins of men.

In her quiet moments, Kasumi drifted into the tides of her thoughts, wondering how, after all these years, the world had remained an unyielding mirror of its former self. The faces may have changed, the battles shifted, but the essence of it all—the weight of existence, the gnawing emptiness—persisted, unbroken. No triumph, no fleeting solace had truly filled the hollow chambers of her soul, a void untouched by time or victory.

Death remained an inevitable fate, a constant cycle of life. Even more so, for those who dared oppose the shogun's rule—their lives ended sooner as they found themselves either broken in spirit or body. Weariness had taken root in her, sporting a seed of doubt in her purpose—the kitsune's purpose.

She was tired of serving as a shield for Ieyasu, the Shogun—a man she once revered as her father. The tendrils of tumultuous conflict branched within, threatening to consume her time in this realm should she continue to wield her power.

Azmani finally broke the silence, likely confirming Kasumi's fears. "The Tenge within you grows stronger with every transformation. I suspect you have reached your limits," she squinted, tilting her head.

Kasumi avoided her eyes.

"You knew this," Azmani said.

"I suspected the dangers, but the nine tails—"

Azmani held up a hand. She leaned in, lowering her voice to a whisper. "If you continue to use her powers," her tone carried a mix of annoyance and finality. "She will consume you."

"I see," Kasumi mumbled in defeat.

Hearing the words spoken aloud only served to water the seeds of doubt, sown by her own fatigue. Countless battles had been fought, numerous foes of varying strength and power had fallen by her hands, often with considerable assistance.

Yet, she was no closer to finding the answers she sought. The only path forward seemed to be achieving the next and final transformation, but was that possible here?

She had journeyed to many places and trained with the greatest fighters, yet she had plateaued like a boulder yearning to ascend into a mountain.

"No one has ever reached eight tails," Azmani's voice reassured, a coat of comforting warmth and certainty embracing her fully. "What you have done is remarkable. You should be proud of that. Retire, and lead Iga. The Christians can fend for themselves... I turn sixty soon. The Iga clan needs change."

Kasumi paused, absorbing the weight of Azmani's words. "I am twenty-eight..." she began, her voice trailing off as she grappled with the enormity of what was being asked of her.

"A battle-worn, twenty-eight," Azmani added.

The idea of retirement, of leading Iga at such a young age, felt like a mantle too vast to bear. Beyond that, there were so many questions left unanswered.

"I'm not ready," Kasumi confessed, a tinge of vulnerability in her voice that she seldom allowed others to hear, but Azmani-sensei was not just anyone. "Something is missing..." The admission was more to herself than to Azmani, a recognition of the internal void that achievements and titles could not fill.

"Life is full of holes," Azmani said. "Rain sometimes misses its mark, but a bucket still gets filled." She held up a finger. "If the bucket is too full, it will overflow. That is the danger."

A pregnant pause hung in the air, broken only by the distant sounds of the wind and the occasional grunt from Azmani's guest.

"Have you seen it?" Azmani asked, her gaze probing yet gentle, breaking the heavy silence.

Kasumi understood immediately what "it" referred to—the kitsune, a living embodiment of the ethereal creature that had once appeared to her after she ascended the eight tails of knowledge.

In this stage of her transformation, Kasumi witnessed the manifestation of the kitsune that had shown itself during a tumultuous battle, guiding her to rescue people trapped in a burning home. Since then, however, it had remained elusive, evading her sight no matter the mission or circumstance.

"No," Kasumi said flatly, not hiding her disappointment.

"If I am being honest, I want you to stop searching for more knowledge. Whatever secrets Inari and this kitsune does not want you to know should stay hidden," Azmani said. "But you must remember, even the most elusive spirits reveal themselves when the time is right. Do not rush. You have your entire life ahead. Patience is a virtue, and perhaps there are lessons to be learned in this moment of waiting."

"Thank you, Sensei," Kasumi said, her voice steadying with a measure of respect despite her disappointment.

No one outside of Inahime could understand, but even she had moved on with her life. Perhaps Japan was no longer a place for her, if she were going to be the bucket in the season of overflow. She bowed deeply, choosing to drown her sorrows at the bar.

Kasumi drank deep into the night. Her thoughts lingered. The kitsune spirit within howled for action, thirsting for blood—not tonight.

Thoughts of Maria flitted through her mind, the untouched innocence in her eyes. How could an ordinary human ever grasp the complexities and truths of this world?

"Should I help her?" Kasumi pondered.

Kasumi watched as her index fingernail elongated and sharpened—a visible mark of the Tenge, the were-beast.

Her sharp nail etched into the surface of the table. *Maria, Mother of Christ*, she thought, tracing the unfamiliar name. *Could this be the sign I seek?*

The pursuit of the final Tenge tail demanded that she consider every possibility, even those beyond the bounds of her faith. The local priest might condemn such thoughts, but she was no ordinary Christian, and this was no ordinary quest.

She could become a creature as real as the magic that swirled around her, far beyond what she once imagined. Now a stranger from somewhere unknown was thrust into their world, one where magic and the unseen ruled in the shadows.

The more she drank, the heavier the weight of Japan's suffering bore down on her; the nation itself felt more oppressive than ever before.

Yet, the true nature of their suffering seemed obscured to its people. She had glimpsed what true freedom looked like, having seen it with her own eyes across the waters.

For years, she had been the savior of her people, the *hero of legend*. Yet, there was always another challenge to face, another villain to outwit, another evil to vanquish, another monster waiting in the shadows. And at times, she feared the monster lurked within herself.

In that moment, she made her decision. Her destiny lay beyond, in the pursuit of the nine tails of kno—a quest that Genzo, who longed passed, desired in his heart but could not reach. And that Inahime, despite her potential, had forsaken for the roles of wife and mother.

It was a path of solitude and sacrifice, but it was hers to walk. For in the pursuit of the Tenge's true purpose, she sought not only enlightenment but a liberation so profound that it promised to unshackle the very essence of her being.

She was closer than either of them, yet the true power was an evasive puzzle with a piece separated by an unknown chasm calling her to find it. Perhaps it was not the wisest decision to make. Some may call her selfish—she had been called worse. All that mattered was discovering the true purpose of the Tenge.

The following morning, Kasumi stumbled out of her room, the horizon still cradling the sun's impending rise. Drawn by the sound of laughter, she navigated through the rustic corridors of Azmani's sake shop, now a makeshift home, to the garden where the day's first magic unfolded.

There, amidst the early light, Maria was a makeshift steed on all fours, a child perched gleefully on her back, their laughter a melody to the dawn.

Nearby, Maria, adorned in old hakama pants tied with a simple brown rope, transformed into a spirited horse, her playful neighs chasing another delighted child.

"Cho would find this amusing," Kasumi couldn't help but exclaim, her voice slicing through the morning's tranquility.

Maria concealed her surprise, promptly turning her gaze towards Kasumi with a blend of astonishment and reverence. "Cho is seldom amused by anything," she responded, her smile lingering as she bowed.

"Good morning, Maria-san," Kasumi returned the gesture. The formalities of their world were never far behind, even in moments of levity.

"We will play later," Maria said, sending the children scattering.

"Azmani tasked me with guiding you in meditation," Kasumi shared.

Maria acknowledged with a nod, her gaze briefly catching on the two mats laid out before them, an invitation to tranquility.

They knelt, facing the sun, the ritual beginning. "Sensai mentioned you struggle with quieting your mind?" Kasumi inquired, her voice a soft nudge towards the day's lesson.

Maria confessed to her battles, the medication she feared, and the longing for peace that seemed just beyond grasp.

Kasumi listened, her acknowledgment a simple nod, her focus unwavering. "The red morning sun is our ally, its energy a catalyst for the body and soul. The earth beneath our feet, another. Both are essential."

Skepticism briefly danced across Maria's features.

"You are a nonbeliever?" Kasumi questioned.

"No. I mean, yes," Maria stammered. "I'm willing to try," she assured her openness to learn shone brighter.

Kasumi exhaled. "Imagine a vast room, surrounded by empty chests. Begin to fill these chests—one with the past, another with the future. This room is eternal, fill as many chests as you desire. Now, place time and matter into another. You wield the control, holding the keys. Your mind belongs solely to you."

Maria's confusion surfaced. "Time and matter. How do you—"

"I'm sorry," Kasumi said. "That is, perhaps beyond your understanding."

Maria nodded.

"Let's begin with the concept of ki, the life force that binds and powers all. Close your eyes, breathe... slowly...'

"I don't know if—"

"Shhh..."

Over the years, the kitsune taught her various concepts and dreams, establishing a reciprocal exchange of learning and help. However, there always remained a barrier, a divide she feared might never be bridged.

The ki energy within her had always been the source of her transformations, and it was during her most advanced kitsune transformations that she began to truly perceive the ki.

She was just one example of encompassing ki, but her brother, Inoichi, had a ki far greater in his base form than any warrior she faced.

Maria sighed.

Kasumi opened one eye. She knew the struggle, her first time truly meditating... *Genzo.*

A brief smile crossed her face. He was gone, but his memory and lessons lived on within her. And she would teach Maria, exuding the same patience as he did with her.

"Ki is within you," Kasumi began, "it is all around you. To harness it, one must reach inward and outward simultaneously. Anchor your spirit to something pure, something or someone that ignites a spark of positivity within you. Hold on to this vision with clarity and intention, for it shall be the beacon that guides your focus and shapes the ki flowing through and around you."

Kasumi's words seemed to linger in the air, a profound silence enveloping them as she hoped Maria absorbed the teaching. The air was filled with the promise of untapped energy. It was a moment of revelation, a bridge between understanding and application, marking the beginning of a deeper journey.

"My mind is so still, it's working." A bright smile illuminated Maria's face as she opened her eyes, awash with newfound calm. "How did you learn this?"

The question seemed to weigh heavily on Kasumi, a complexity shadowing her expression, one that Maria appeared to grasp intuitively.

"I learned it from a good friend I lost. His name was Hojo Genzo."

"I'm sorry to hear that," Maria said, sincerity clear in her voice.

Kasumi shook her head. "Thank you. I've lost many over the years, including my mother."

Maria's gaze shifted away, a clear indication that the topic of mothers was a tender one for her as well. Kasumi placed her hand on Maria's knee, offering silent support.

"My life is complicated," she confessed. "It seems the more I do, the more things unravel for the worse. I have to tell you something."

Silence hung between them. Kasumi had a feeling that Maria was hiding something, but she respected the importance of keeping secrets. Yet, she did not stop Maria from confessing.

"My name is not Maria. It's actually Malaya. I took the name because I needed to protect myself, but now I don't know. You're so nice, unlike Cho," she mumbled. "I can't keep lying to the truth is—"

"Please," Kasumi interjected. "Malaya-kun, your heart is kind. Soon enough, you will tell me the truth I require."

Oddly enough, Kasumi felt a bond with Malaya, whose life seemed to be unraveling for the worse. It was a feeling she knew all too well, a recognition of the circle of life. Sometimes, it's the decisions that defy the norm that have the power to change everything.

If she wanted to reach the ninth tail and fulfill her destiny, She needed to change. *I need to do the impossible—bond with the kitsune and achieve the ninth tail.*

"Malaya-kun, I think we will be friends."

MALAYA

Kyoto, Japan, 1601

Days turned into weeks, each one marked by the relentless demands of training. Cho's sparring sessions left Malaya with purple bruises, while Kasumi's meditation exercises seemed to twist her brain into knots. At least they let her sleep in. Though the guest bed of this era was far from luxurious, Malaya found solace in the exhaustion that came from daily training, made sleeping easy.

Unfortunately, time did not offer a break from the haunting dreams she kept to herself. At first, the dreams centered around her father—his death. Yet lately, they shifted to her mother. It was a repetitive dream that always began within the walls of a rustic cabin, its location yet uncertain.

Even more unsettling was the presence of Angela, her grandmother, standing alongside a man who seemed to be either a priest or a monk. The two were locked in a heated argument, with Malaya caught helplessly in the middle.

Then an earthquake would ensue. The priest opened his mouth, unleashing a torrent of purple smoke and ethereal sparkles, enveloping the room before plunging Malaya into a void of white.

Voices beckoned from all directions as the white transformed into countless doors, each leading to a different realm—magical, fantastical, with symbols spanning various religions and mythologies. One door shimmered with an otherworldly allure, promising boundless tranquility amidst gleaming radiance.

But none captivated her like the weathered facade of the door before her, whispering tales of forgotten glory decorated with symbols both foreign and vaguely familiar. Every attempt to open it ended with her waking up.

As the whispers of her dream faded into the back of her mind, Malaya woke with the remnants of her unsettling visions clinging to her thoughts like cobwebs in the morning light. Shaking off the leftover unease, she rose, intending to free her mind. A good run always helped clear her mind. It was more effective than attempting meditation.

The forest floor crunched beneath Malaya's feet. The weight of the heavy sack served as a constant reminder of her burdens. Dodging the familiar obstacles that littered the trail, she moved with practiced grace, each maneuver a testament to her training under Azmani's watchful eye.

Azmani's teachings echoed in her mind, urging her to perceive the looming branches not as harmless obstacles, but as potential threats lying in wait. She followed her guidance, never allowing her gaze to linger too long on any one target, instead seeing them through the periphery of her vision, feeling their presence like the whisper of a passing breeze.

With each duck, sidestep, and jump, Malaya danced through the forest, her movements fluid and precise. In her mind, she envisioned the branches as tendrils of her mother's reach, her presence lurking in the shadows of time, ready to strike at any moment.

Unlike the slow, gradual changes of nature's canopy, her mother's influence was swift and unforgiving, a force to be reckoned with. At the moment, there was nothing she could do about it.

As she approached the hot spring, a haze formed beneath her feet, and the distinct smell of sulfur filled the air. Dropping her sack, Malaya noticed a rabbit nearby, its ears perked up in curiosity. She froze momentarily, remembering a previous encounter.

One day, Cho had accompanied Malaya to the spring, where she encountered what seemed to be the same evil fluffy brown rabbit. That day, it hopped toward them, and Malaya, startled, ran, tripping over a branch and bruising her ribs in the process. Cho got a kick out of it. This time, however, the mischievous rabbit hopped in the opposite direction. Malaya breathed a sigh of relief.

After disrobing, she sank into the warm water, allowing its soothing embrace to wash away her tensions. In the distance, there was a stunning evergreen, a gift from nature to humanity, that added to the beauty of the surroundings.

Being in Japan brought some sense of freedom and a purpose in an otherwise stagnant situation. The people she had met, the lessons learned—they all seemed to weave together, shaping her existence in unexpected ways. And her mother has begun to pull the threat that would unravel an entire timeline.

She will unleash war upon these people, Malaya thought, *sweeping away lives like a mound of ash in the wake of a relentless storm.*

It had been nearly a month, and still, there was no word from them. They were strangers in Japan, their portal had to have landed near Kyoto. *So why was it taking them so long?*

Malaya's mind drifted back to the day in the bar when she had met Antonio. *That had to be Midas,* she thought, recalling the green-eyed blond man who towered over everyone. He was one of the Spartans working with her mother. And what was she going to do about it?

"I need to find my friends and Vasilis," Malaya muttered to herself, pulling on her clothes. "Maybe that brute was to blame."

Malaya sighed. *That's not fair, Malaya.*

Nothing about time travel was absolute, and she could blame no one but time travel's and technology's inaccuracies. Vasilis was a lot of things, but he wasn't to blame for this.

After all, the imperfections of technology was how her father got trapped in 3,000 BC. It could be worse for them.

She shook away the thought of what Esther and James could be going through if they were alone. At least they were soldiers. She wasn't.

Malaya made her way back to Azmani's, readying for her shift. Usually, she'd take a trip into town and ask questions, but she was drawing suspicion from the locals. Over the last few days, all she had was hope. Hope that they were all together and making their way to her.

Patience, not hope however, had been the steady hand guiding her through the uncertainties, but anxiety was the shadow lurking in the corners, threatening to engulf her in its darkness.

And there was another problem. The mysterious mission she was set to go on with Kasumi. *What if they came to the shop, and she was gone?*

The shop was abnormally loud. "More wine!" she heard the familiar voice shout, forcing her to take a peek.

Vasilis sat with his arms over a drunken Esther. "More wine!" James echoed with his arm on the shoulder of a man wearing a red kimono and charcoal pants, who was equally inebriated.

You have got to be kidding me, she thought, storming from the back. "What are you doing?"

"Malaya, you're alive," Esther shouted, squeezing what little anger she had out of her.

Everyone surrounded her. Their breath reeked of booze. "Where were you?" she demanded, though they were likely too drunk to answer sensibly. "We agreed to meet at the city center, a popular location. And this is the most popular shop in town."

"Well, we met Ryu, and he hates mainstream commercial shops," James slurred. "He knows the best hole-in-the-wall shop."

Ryu nodded; he wasn't a local for sure. She would have remembered seeing his messy copper bangs and the elegant hilt on his hip that rivaled Forsaken.

Vasilis put his arm around Malaya, his words slurred. "Ryu here wanted nothing more than to return home and beg his brother's forgiveness for leaving his clan. I encouraged him to follow his dreams and continue west to the place. What was it? Oh, Fukuyama."

Malaya shrugged Vasilis off. He held up his drink. "To Ryu!"

Everyone echoed him. James and Esther gravitated to him. "Malaya," James said. "Vasilis here is a great man, a real leader. We'll follow him to the ends of the earth."

"That's great," Malaya said. "While you guys were having the best time of your life, I was putting in work! Following leads. A *Midas* lead at that!"

"You found him?" Vasilis said without a slur. The name appeared to sober him up.

"I don't know. I don't think so. All I know is that my lead is heading to Edo tonight, and so are we."

"Can I join this party?" said Kasumi, holding a bag.

"Yes, yes, you may." The fire in Vasilis's eyes disappeared.

Azmani was generous, giving them more than enough food for their journey and horses on what was a short trip to Edo. Luck was on her side now that she had her team and Kasumi. Lilith continued to stay one step ahead, but for the first time, she felt optimistic nothing was going to get in her way.

VASILIS

Edo Japan, 1601

Kasumi didn't allow leisure time. Her command was absolute, her tenacity endless, and Vasilis loved it. The route to Edo was a grueling one, the *Tōkaidō Path*, Kasumi called it. An eastern sea route with various ancient routes buried by the fast-flowing rivers.

Despite it all, Vasilis believed the gods seemed to be in their favor. The water was forgiving, and the weather was ideal. Part of him feared it was the calm before the storm.

After all, in less than a year, the Tokugawa clan won the war and secured their newly gained land. Point and check permits differed from the freedom of Greece.

Kasumi always cautioned them to stay back while she somehow got them past each one. Her father's clout reached even the most remote of land. The samurai even seemed to fear her once they realized who she was—they were lucky.

Horseback cut the week-long trip down. They were only a day from Edo now. Malaya was more determined than usual, but Kasumi decided to rest in what they learned was the Shizuoka Prefecture. This was one of the more complete posts with accommodation, porter stations to horse stables, and lodging. A perfect area to regain our strength.

An endless colonnade of pine trees cast a welcomed shadow, and so too, did the impressive giant trees. Kasumi said they'd rest at the temple, which was the home of a monk she knew well.

James reached out to help Malaya off her horse. She hesitated for a moment. Gesturing her thanks with a smile accepted his help. Vasilis thought to do the same thing. James was a modern man. He knew what women of this era wanted.

Perhaps Kasumi would accept the gesture, Vasilis convinced himself.

Unfortunately, when he attempted to aid the beauty, she was already down.

Esther smirked, seeing Vasilis's disappointment. She walked over to Kasumi. "What are those trees called?"

"They're called siga. That large one is sacred," Kasumi said, pointing at one with a large rope around it. "It is thousands of years old."

"Mt Fuji is beautiful," James said, gazing at the snow peak mountain before turning to Malaya with a lazy smile that wasn't returned.

"*Hai*. For hundreds of years, Fuji served as a sacred site for Shinto."

They reached the large two-story red temple. Two monks greeted them at the door and led them inside the large room with white walls and a sweet aroma mixed with wood.

Kasumi bowed to the young man waiting at the end of the room. He wore a fine purple robe with an equally fine staff that shone like his clean, bald head.

Though young, he exuded wisdom and experience beyond his years. Vasilis couldn't help but notice the simplicity of the young monk's attire and demeanor, a reflection of the Buddhist teachings of humility and detachment from worldly possessions. Something that once existed in Sparta, or so he was told. As Kasumi straightened up, Vasilis felt a sense of reverence for this young monk and the wisdom he embodied.

"Lady Kasumi," he said with a deep bow.

"You know I'm no lady, Shoto." Shoto smiled. "I see you brought friends."

"Yes. Malaya, James, Esther, and what's your name again, kid?" Kasumi smirked.

Vasilis blushed. "*Kid...*"

James laughed out loud. "He's Vasilis."

Shoto bowed, and they echoed the gesture. He and Kasumi spoke briefly, leading to them being welcomed to dinner and a night's stay.

After dinner, Vasilis took a self-guided tour around the small village. Wild deer and other animals gathered down the nearly empty street. The few remaining merchants scolded the street dogs, who seemed alarmed.

He smiled, thinking about his people back home, the Helots, hard-working people who did so without complaint and barely any clothes. They were the true backbone of Sparta—the means to a wealthy, powerful empire. This place felt like home.

"This place is majestic," said James, walking behind Vasilis with a lantern in one hand and kiseru pipe in the other—a habit he recently picked up. "I wouldn't mind staying here forever," said James.

"Aye, neither would I. This world has a magic your world lacks. That is one thing I miss about home."

"Home." James took a puff from the tobacco strings. "Too bad staying here isn't a realistic option. Besides the scientific issues, my nephew needs me. He just made division-one football, a young black man without a father... Yeah, I have to be there for him." He passed the pipe to Vasilis.

"Congratulations. Seems like you are close with your family."

"Thanks. Close is one way to put it, but if I'm being honest." James paused. "I think I hate my father, actually. He's always away. I mean, I get it, given his line of work. You know, he wanted to do this—time travel. He played a role in making this possible. He sacrificed a lot, part of himself. I've seen him change for the worse and for what? He'll never get the opportunity to do this. Yet, here I am, living his dream, time traveling... rambling. Sorry."

"It is okay." Vasilis handed him the pipe back. "I'm sure you miss your home... your family, but I can do without going back. Unfortunately, too many people rely on me—well, us."

"You mean you and *Esther*?"

"Yes. Esther won't say it, but she does so much work at Synagogue."

"And you travel to Miami helping those less fortunate, not just your nephew," Vasilis said.

James raised a brow. "I have read your profile. I like to know who I battle with."

James nodded.

"From what I researched, it's not the utopia the books suggest," Vasilis said, lighting the pipe in the lantern.

"You're right. While it's not Sparta, children are still struggling, just differently. Lilith... she's shaking things up. Between me and you, what she's doing is not the horror story our government made it cut to be.

Anyone who studied history knows what the UNA did, what they took. What she's doing is a welcomed change, a risk worth taking, but destroying the fabric of time..."

"So, they believe Lilith is a liberator—interesting."

James shrugged. "I still have a duty to fight for the timeline... Dang, we're out of smoke. Let's take a walk."

A deer jetted past James. He stumbled into a stranger. "Careful," the man said. "Shoto asked me to escort you. This area can be... confusing."

He looked like Shoto, but with hair that draped from underneath a straw hat. His robe was even finer, though their staff equaled in gold.

James looked at Vasilis, who shrugged. "Who are you?"

"My name is Todoroki, Shoto's twin brother. To ensure you don't get lost, I will stay a few paces behind."

"What we say stays here," James said.

Todoroki nodded. Vasilis and James walked deep into the forest. Siga trees covered parts of the cloudy night sky. Moss covered part of the land. The deeper they entered the forest, the greener the plantation became, but the darker the forest became—Vasilis stopped.

"If you're going to murder me, this is far enough."

"Man, Esther and Malaya have big mouths—they actually narked."

"What?"

"You know, ratting us out. You know what—it doesn't matter." He removed two small glass containers.

The smaller one glowed sky-blue, while the larger one glowed red. James peaked over his shoulder at the trailing monk and lowered his voice. "You put me on to the mushrooms. Well, this is better."

Vasilis grabbed the red container. "What is it?"

James flashed a grin, the container catching the light. "This, my friend, is 'Superman.' A new spin on DMT– you know, dimethyltryptamine."

Vasilis's confusion deepened. "And that is...?"

"A dimethyltryptamine that enhances human awareness. Not that you need to be any more super, but it puts you in the zone."

"In the zone?"

"Once released into the bloodstream, it focuses your consciousness into a state of heightened perception. It takes you to the plight of human sensation. Too much and everything will appear motionless, but with the correct amount—well, yeah, you'll be *slaughtered*. Try it."

Vasilis drank half of each bottle as directed. A few seconds later, he saw a child run past him.

"Help!" the boy cried.

Vasilis snapped his head toward James. "Did you see that?"

James shrugged.

Vasilis ran after the child into the forest, ignoring James's call, not caring about the trees closing in on him or how dark the forest had become. Why should he?

The lantern seemed to glow brighter than before, maybe brighter than the sun and the forest—it called to him. The trees spoke to him; their winds sent chills up his spine. This was euphoria, even beyond the mushroom.

"Snakes!" James shouted, forcing Vasilis to turn around.

He didn't see snakes, but he suddenly felt tingling up his arm and neck—he smiled at the sensation. He looked down at his legs—spiders were everywhere.

A frantic Vasilis tried to brush them off, but cockroaches joined in, crawling in between his toes. "Help," the boy cried, reminding Vasilis of why he was there. Vasilis tried to follow the voice, but the monk grabbed his arm. "We should go."

"No, I have to save him." Vasilis snatched away, and with great speed, he followed the boy's voice into the marsh. The air tasted like decaying vegetation or rotting corpses—either way, death filled the air. He called out for the boy.

"There... is no kid," James said, wheezing underneath a thick tree.

"I know what I saw," Vasilis said as things came into focus.

The drug was wearing off, so he thought, which changed when he saw a fox with multiple tails. It moved so quickly it was hard to keep track, but it stopped to look back as if playing a game of tag before disappearing into the darkness. "Sorry, I can't play fox. I have a kid to save."

He turned back to see a thin woman with flawless ghostly skin hugging her knees. Markings were the only thing that covered her body. Her long black hair twisted in vines, covered her face.

"James, are you seeing this?" Vasilis stammered. James didn't reply. He looked back to see his friend waist-deep in the swamp, eyes glued on the pale woman.

"Vasilis..." James said, his voice distant and lifeless. "We should save her."

Vasilis saw this before in a village back home. Midas and Elias were tasked with conquering the village, but not without its fair share of problems, one being a powerful witch doctor that nearly drove Midas and Elias off a cliff.

If not for the elder from Laconia, they would have died then. Maybe it would have been for the best, Vasilis found himself thinking before bringing his attention back to his friend.

"James! Snap out of it!" Vasilis shouted.

Where's the monk? Maybe he could help? Vasilis eyes darted across the darkness, finding a source of light—flaming purple eyes from something in a tree. It cawed, spreading its wings.

Purple light cascaded from its wings as it flew away, shining a light on enormous wolves with sky-blue aura. They darted away. A glowing frog jumped on him, startling him. He swiped away. When he looked up, a three-headed hound appeared.

All the animals were standing still, waiting for him to take the lead in a game of tag. *What in Hades is this?* "James!" Vasilis shouted, watching him inch closer to the pale woman. "Stop!"

"Vasilis!" the monk called, turning him from James, seeing him favor his ribs and his robe stained with blood. "Let me help."

"It's too late for me. Get your friend, lead your team and get out!"

Vasilis pushed through the thick swampy water and grabbed James. At that moment, the woman looked up. Her eyes were abnormally large, her nose was small like a cat. She opened her mouth to a black void, teeth jagged and a deafening screech.

She leaped into the air toward the two men who escaped before the nude woman could reach them. They ran with animals, which helped them out of the forest and to the temple.

When they looked back, the animals were gone, so was the woman. Malaya, Esther, Kasumi, and Shoto were outside.

"Get the weapons!" James said, trying to catch his breath.

"The monk, we-we have to save him," said Vasilis. "He's under attack by the swamp lady-monster!"

Malaya walked up to Vasilis. "Are you high?"

Vasilis pulled his head back. "No, I mean, yes, we were... but not anymore. Why are you acting like my mother?"

Kasumi stepped closer. "What monk?"

As they explained, Malaya and Esther laughed in amusement. Kasumi and Shoto, however, seemed more intrigued. "I had a twin brother," said Shoto, "but he died years ago."

"There's your proof," Malaya said. "You were wrecked."

Vasilis frowned. "How do you explain the two of us seeing the same thing?"

"You saw what you told one another you saw, creating one experience."

"We know what we saw," said James.

"Malaya. What if this opened a portal to another realm?" Kasumi said.

"If you saw my brother, you were in danger," said Shoto. "Someone or something was or is praying on you—"

"I will not disrespect your beliefs," said Malaya, "but they were on drugs. End of story. Both of you get some sleep."

"Wait," said Kasumi. "Before you two sleep this off, I want to try it... Do you have more?"

James dug into his drenched pocket for two more glowing bottles. Esther smiled. "I want in."

They washed up, and the four of them enjoyed the euphoric sensation of Superman without the horrors of the forest.

After breakfast, they stormed out, making it to the busy street of Edo by twilight. They made their way across the now-empty central market. Small shops bunched together, bordering a narrow road. They veered off onto a pathway surrounded by monstrous bamboo trees before coming to a stop across a water garden.

Kasumi was quiet the entire way despite them asking her where she was taking them, especially Esther. "We need answers, Kasumi," Esther said as they all took cover behind a boulder. "We had our fun, but a mission is a mission. Why are we here?"

Kasumi pointed at a small cherry wood tower. "Innocent people are being held captive.""So," Malaya said. "Why would we risk our lives for people we don't know?"

"What she really meant was, could their interference cause a paradox?" James whispered to Vasilis.

Malaya shot him a death stare.

"I am usually a great judge of character," Kasumi said, looking at Vasilis. "I knew you would help, and I swore a vow to protect the innocent. Tomorrow, these people are going to be executed for their Christian beliefs. They don't deserve to die."

"Forgive me for being blunt," said James. "But we barely know you."

"That is true. However, you have seen what I can do and I promise I am your best option to seek council with Tokugawa Ieyasu."

She didn't trust them either. Vasilis understood that, given he lacked trust in Malaya. This was the only way to prove our worth. He crouched next to Kasumi. "Get us in. That is all we need."

"What are your thoughts?" Kasumi asked.

This was a noble mission. But I can't let this stop me from catching Elias and Midas, Vasilis thought. *We need to do this now.* "Why are my thoughts important?"

"Because they are," Kasumi shot back.

Vasilis sighed. "Religion is too complex for one man to judge another. So, punishing those who believe differently makes you no less evil than the very people you proclaim to hate."

"I agree," Kasumi smiled, reaching out her hand

Vasilis was reluctant, looking at James for answers.

"Shake her hand, idiot," Malaya whispered, walking behind him.

"Right." Vasilis accepted her soft, warm hand.

"Is it customary for it to last this long?" Kasumi said, directing her eyes at their hands.

"Apologies."

A smile covered her face as she tied her dark brown hair into a bun. "I will take you all in as prisoners."

"It's risky, but it may work," said Esther

"We should recon first—" Malaya said before wincing in pain, trying her best not to make noise. Kasumi rushed over. "Are you okay?"

"Yeah, and no. I lost my medication a while back. It, uh, keeps me focused."

"This is pointless," Vasilis said. "We are warriors. We need not have time for tricks and plans. Malaya, you are in poor condition. I say we attack. Use the element of surprise."

"Control yourself, Vasilis," Malaya said in a loud whisper.

"You want to play games like your mother because you are no warrior. We are."

"I agree," said James. "We've wasted enough time."

"Fine," said Esther.

Kasumi lowered her fox mask while everyone covered their faces with rags. Malaya did so without taking her angered eyes off Vasilis—this wasn't the end of this conversation.

"There's only one way in," Malaya said. "We have to climb."

Kasumi grabbed one of Malaya's bows and tied a metal claw at the end. "All you have to do is shoot this arrow. I will distract them while the three of you free the prisoners."

"On with it," said Vasilis.

Kasumi gave Malaya the weapon and Esther gave her false encouragement. "Three floors. Across the Moët, past the trees... easy peasy, lemon squeezy."

"It shouldn't be a problem for someone as skilled as Malaya," said Kasumi.

Malaya sighed. "Fine. You can stop. We all know I can't make that shot."

"It's good to know I'm not the only one keeping secrets," Kasumi said. "Since we are being honest. I do not think I can make that shot, either."

"You can, and you will," Esther said. "You have the skill, and Malaya can tell you how."

"Right, just simple geometry," Malaya said, perching her lips to the side, rubbing her thumb around one another.

It was a familiar look, but something was different. Her eyes squinted, her movements ridged. She was fighting through her pain, an admirable quality in an otherwise annoying girl. Malaya adjusted Kasumi before pointing toward the building. "Shoot it, there."

Kasumi raised the bow and let out a long breath before releasing the arrow—hitting the target. "Wow," she said, echoing the sentiment of the others.

"Shall we?" Vasilis said, being the first to traverse the rope.

Kasumi sprang onto the second floor and Malaya worked her way onto the third floor. Vasilis led Esther and James as they hid on either side of the door. Vasilis waited, despite his eagerness to fight, but he knew his true enemy would taste his blade soon enough. *Elias, I'm coming for you.*

James opened the door to several Christians kneeling next to one another, five on each side. Around them stood at least twenty samurai. If Midas and Elias were by his side, this would be a race to a body count without risking the captives.

Unfortunately, James and Esther were novices. There was also the problem of the kopis. A short blade meant they needed to keep this fight inside, which risked the lives of their ten captives.

This is not Sparta, and I am wasting time.

Vasilis ran into the cramped hall—James and Esther followed. He dropped seven samurai before James could even finish his first man, but three more replaced the fallen.

Esther fought well, though her focus was freeing the prisoners. Vasilis knew if he didn't do something, they were going to get themselves killed.

Kasumi rushed in, whipping her chained blades—her movements were flawless and masterful as they found their mark.

"Look!" a man shouted. Armor clanked as the samurai ran for the exit.

Confusion clouded Vasilis's thoughts as he noticed their adversaries retreating. *Why are they fleeing?*

Without a second thought, he dashed outside, leaving Esther and James behind, each embroiled in their own battles. It wasn't a decision made lightly. Vasilis trusted in their capabilities, believing they could handle themselves against the remaining forces.

An instinctual understanding gripped him, like a wolf sensing its prey miles away through the dense forest. *Elias and Midas could amidst those people.*

Vasilis's pulse raced as he scanned the chaotic aftermath of their infiltration. "We must go, now!" His voice was urgent, a command born of desperation as he caught sight of Malaya weaving through the debris towards him.

Malaya's pace faltered, her gaze darting around the scene. "Wait, where are James and Esther?" The confusion in her voice pierced the haze of battle, anchoring Vasilis back to a grim reality.

"What do you mean?" A cold dread settled over Vasilis, heavier than the air, thick with dust and echoes of conflict. His heart plummeted, sending a ripple of panic through his veins. *Why did I leave them?* The question gnawed at him. Midas's emotional warning from the night before echoed like a premonition unheeded.

A scream filled with agony shocked Vasilis to his bones. "Malaya," he called, following her cries.

As he reached the origins of the sound, Vasilis paused, seeing Malaya hovering over Esther and James's bloody bodies.

James's eyes were open but quickly fading. Vasilis dare not say anything. In that one moment, he was reborn as another man, a lesser man. He had failed, again.

James rubbed Malaya's tearing face. "Beautiful."

"We can still save them!" shouted Vasilis. "The medallions we can send them—"

"They're gone..."

"I refuse." He took Malaya's hand and handed her the medallions. "Reprogram them, an emergency extraction, please!"

It only took her a few seconds, but a portal opened and swallowed their two fallen friends. Vasilis looked back, smelling smoke. "Tokugawa castle is on fire. We're too late."

"What? My family!" Kasumi shouted, dropping her mask and sprinting through the bamboo.

"Family..." Vasilis said.

Malaya ran after Kasumi, Vasilis followed. She ran across the stub tree pathway, ignoring everything around her. They made it to a bridge into the entrance of the castle grounds where guards lay lifeless.

"Kasumi, wait!" Malaya shouted, before slowing down—she ogled at the gory trail of bodies.

The sight was sickening, even for Vasilis, but the smell of iron was potently familiar. He knew who did this. He held his sword at the ready.

"Mama, Papa," Kasumi cried, rushing into the castle.

They followed her up upstairs, inside the castle. Vasilis kept Malaya close. She held her mouth, stepping over the mountain of samurai left in the narrow hall—where Kasumi found her family her father and brother slain.

"Kasumi," said a faint voice.

"Hideyoshi! You're alive," Kasumi cried.

Malaya rushed over. "It's just his shoulder."

"Help Inoichi," he muttered.

Kasumi rushed over to Inoichi. "Ino... don't die... I'm here. Malaya, he's barely breathing. Please use your magic. Send Ino with James and Esther. Wherever that was."

"We will," Vasilis said, looking at Malaya.

Malaya took out another medallion. A gold coin fell to the floor. She picked it up and paused, appearing lost in thought.

"What is it?" Vasilis asked.

"He had a map of Norway, Scandinavia." Tears formed in her eyes. "I could have stopped him."

"Who?"

"The guy," Malaya stammered. "Antonio, I think he was working with Lilith." She kneeled next to Inoichi with the small paper and ink stick, quickly scribbling a message and handing it to Vasilis. "Hold on to this."

Vasilis didn't protest. "Are you going to Scandinavia without knowing the year?"

"I know it's in the ninth century, during King Harold's reign. I'll have to take the chance. I can't lose this opportunity to catch her."

"Eight-seventy-one," Vasilis said, picking up Inoichi. "The code Nefeli created in Sparta, the one you asked about on Mantis. That has to be the year and where you'll find Elvir."

KASUMI

Germanic Kingdom, 871 AD

"Please, do not die."

Kasumi sprang from her sleep, gasping for air, her face slick with sweat and the acrid scent of smoke stinging her nose. She clutched her kunai, the chain attached to it clinking in the stillness of the night.

Her heart raced, pounding against her chest like a thundering stampede as thoughts of her family haunted her dreams. Seeing them laying in their own blood grasping for life.

"Fukumatsumaru," she choked on his name as her breath caught in her throat. She fought to keep the tears at bay.

Her youngest brother was but a boy, who should have enjoyed the spoils of not being an heir, fighting battles, having to worry about dying by the blade's end. Yet he died in his home by the blade of a coward, traitors.

She shuddered, testing the weight of her chain—their voices and laughter now just echoes in the forest's emptiness. Even now, the pungent smell of ash tainted the earthy scene around her, a reminder of what she'd left behind.

"This was your choice, Kasumi," she whispered, moving through her familiar kata forms to calm her mind.

Most of her life had been shaped by others' commands–how to live, whom to marry, which men to kill. All to strengthen the Tokugawa clan. Now her father was dead, along with the warriors she'd trained, fought beside, grown with.

Nothing truly dies, she reminded herself.

The chained kunai spun in her hands, its motion fluid like embers carried on the wind—dancing, unpredictable, yet guided by purpose. It was a reminder of the fire within her, not a blaze of destruction, but a tempered flame—a controlled fury, honed into precision and strength.

The essence of all living things surrounded her, a silent rhythm woven into the chain itself, bound by the lingering warmth of a lover long gone. Teachings from a former lover who had been her anchor, showing her how to master its feral rage rather than succumb to it. Through him, the fire remained hers alone, every choice shaped by her will, not devoured by the flame. *Mine alone.*

She rose quietly, careful not to disturb Malaya and Vasilis. The journey ahead would be long, and they would need their rest.

A misjudged step betrayed her presence, leaves crunching beneath her feet. She cursed softly. Even years of shinobi training couldn't fully prepare her for this foreign terrain.

The thick trees towered, devouring the moonlight that filtered it into blue shadows. Something watched her; she felt it in the way the forest held its breath. Then, movement. A fox, its coat lighter than those of her homeland, emerged from the darkness. The kitsune stirred within her, responding to its presence.

The fox darted behind a tree, its movements deliberate, almost beckoning. Kasumi followed, drawn by an instinct deeper than thought. Each step carried her further from her companions, yet she could not stop. This was no mere chance—the gods often spoke through such signs. But could their voices still echo in this foreign world, untethered by time? Or was this an endless mission, a futile grasp at something forever out of reach?

Perhaps I am alone in this new world? She thought, emerging into a clearing. Her breath hitched at the sight before her.

Red leaves shimmered as if kissed by celestial lips, their hues blurring the boundary between mortal earth and divine sky. Kneeling, she traced the rough bark of an ancient tree, her silent prayer rising with the wind.

How am I to embrace this new world, new mission?

A warmth touched her hand—the fox, its tongue brushing her fingers. Their eyes met, yellow locking with yellow, and the Kitsune's power surged through her, a recognition that bound them. Was it more than a connection? Was it an affirmation of the Tenge's vital role in saving this strange new world?

Kasumi sighed, unable to shake an ache that lingered—a hollow echo of what she had lost, of the world she had chosen to leave behind, and the love she might never find again.

"God," she whispered, "I am lost. Show me the way. Something is missing—"

The crunch of leaves snapped her focus. She spun, weapon ready, the mask of steel slipping into place.

"It's me," Vasilis said.

The fox vanished as she exhaled. "I could have killed you," she said, turning back.

"I doubt it," he replied, confidence dancing in his dimpled smile. Beneath the moon's glow, his sharp gaze bridged the gap between their worlds, carrying an aura both mysterious and alluring.

"Why did you follow me?" Kasumi asked.

"I was worried," he said, as if it were obvious.

"Hm. I am surprised you were able to wake after the mushrooms you took."

"That?" Vasilis shrugged. "It was nothing. I have done worse." His brows furrowed. "What truly disturbed me was the leaves crunching." He grinned.

She cracked an embarrassing smile at his jest.

She stood silent as Vasilis stepped closer, his brown eyes scanning her features with quiet intensity. She didn't move, held by his gaze.

"Perhaps you could use mushrooms to help you sleep," he said, a hint of teasing in his voice. "Wandering off in the middle of the night in a strange land doesn't seem wise." He raised a brow, a small smile playing on his lips. "I'd be happy to find some for you, if you like."

"It is fine," she replied, though touched by the gesture.

Vasilis ran his fingers through his deep bronze hair. "After the other night, if you need to talk—"

"I am fine, really," she said, trying to sound as reassuring as possible. "Thank you."

A brief silence hung between them, broken only by the rustling leaves.

"May I ask you a question?" Kasumi said.

Vasilis raised a brow. "Depends…"

"About Malaya."

His brows furrowed as his face twisted in a way that a child would when told to eat their vegetables. "As you will."

Kasumi did her best not to laugh. "The night at the monastery when we all took mushrooms. Did Malaya take any?"

Vasilis scoffed, his eyes rolled. "No. Of course not. Malaya is…" His head swayed side-to-side as he searched for the word. Perhaps not to offend. "How should I put it? An old hag trapped in a young pestering girl's body."

Kasumi laughed harder than she expected to. She took a deep breath, collecting herself. "That night, we all took them. She, too, heard voices."

Vasilis head tilted. "Are you sure it was her and not you?"

Kasumi nodded.

"Perhaps her consciousness is opening up," Vasilis said. "In her world, people only believe in what they can see."

"Consciousness? That was deeper than what I would have thought coming from a child. Maybe you're more than meets the eye," she teased.

Vasilis's mouth dropped open.

"Move!" A large voice shouted in the distance, interrupting them.

Groans reverberated in the forest. They exchanged glances, their eyes filled with a silent understanding that only warriors possess. They followed the sound and discovered a group of men and women, chained together and huddled like cattle, being led by a gang of burly, bearded men wielding axes.

Kasumi's stomach churned at the sight before her. Her trembling hands clenched into fists, the inner kitsune awakening with a familiar, unsettling stir.

The horror of slavery, a scene she had confronted time and again throughout her life, never became easier to stomach. She had devoted much of her existence to liberating those crushed under the oppressive weight of tyrants who deemed themselves superior.

Azmani's became an echo through time. "No matter how much time passes or places traveled, there will always be those who devalue life."

She recalled the night her life had changed—the night she had first felt the kitsune's fury course through her veins. The night she lost herself to the feral rage of the Tenege's purpose.

After a journey fraught with peril, where every step was a battle against her own failing body and the life she carried, her path had led her to an unexpected crossroads. It was not just a physical journey, but a spiritual one that had ended in bloodshed, a confrontation guided by a desperate need for survival.

It was a night defined by darkness, not just in the sky but within the hearts of those who, blinded by their own ideals, hunted down those of the Christian faith. She remembered she and Inahime sought refuge, only to find themselves trapped in chaos and violence.

Screams pierced the night, and the glint of steel was the only light. She recalled the fire that was kindled by the need to protect, transforming her from a frightened woman into a vessel of divine wrath.

The kitsune within her, a spirit of destruction had awakened fully that night, driven by a rage that was foreign, yet intimately hers. As the kitsune unleashed its power, she had become an observer within her own body, a passenger to the horror that unfolded. The line between self-preservation, a mother, and the kitsune's rage merged into a singular force of retribution.

Lives were ended, blood was spilled, and in the aftermath, she was left with the haunting knowledge of what she had become. It was not just the spirit's fury that had propelled her; it was her own desire to stop the cycle of suffering, to protect those she loved and to assert her own existence against the tide of darkness.

Over the years, she had shattered countless chains, yet the cycle of oppression seemed endless. But it was her desire to stop the horror that drove her to break many chains, but it was never enough.

She glanced at Vasilis, his face darkening with a mix of emotions she recognized in herself. Unable to watch these people suffer for another second, Kasumi reached for her kunai, ready to strike.

Vasilis placed a hand on her shoulder, his grip gentle but firm, easy to fall into if circumstances were different. "You don't have to do this," he said, his voice low and calming. "I lost my father in battle as well. I know how it feels, the need to spill blood, but it doesn't relieve the pain. That is not your problem. These are not your people."

Kasumi paused, her fingers loosening their grip on the kunai. But he was wrong. It wasn't the death of her father. She would always help those who could not help themselves. Standing idly by while others were being treated like objects was unbearable. She took a deep breath and looked at Vasilis.

"I have to do this," she said, her voice steady. "For them and for myself."

"There are over fifty men..."

At that moment, she saw the fox again, dancing around the last man, an Asian monk. *A bonsō. This is why you appeared to me.*

Her thoughts drifted to the significance of the fox's presence. It wasn't just a chance encounter—it was a manifestation of the power she had unlocked—the eight tail of knowledge.

It was during the chaos of battle that she first witnessed the occurrence, when a fox suddenly appeared amidst the carnage, captivating her attention, navigating through the turmoil until she reached a burning home.

Even now, she could still hear the screams. The fox had vanished, but she ran inside to discover a family whose home bore the symbol of their faith, a cross, on the wall.

Back then, she had not truly grasped what her newfound power was, but now part of her wondered if this connected to selflessness—the eight tail of enlightenment.

Perhaps the fox is the manifestation of the transformation. Could this be generosity in a form?

"Kasumi," Vasilis' voice broke through her reverie, his touch grounding her in the present moment. "Did you hear me?"

She nodded, her gaze unwavering as she met his eyes. "Yes, but it doesn't matter. You see that man?" She gestured towards the monk. "I am being called to save him. If you do not wish to help, I understand."

Vasilis hesitated for a moment, the weight of her words hanging heavily between them. Then, with a resigned sigh, he nodded, his grip tightening on the hilt of his blade.

"Fine," Vasilis said. "I will cut down the chain holder in the front. That should give everyone a chance to run. You can go after the monk."

"And when they chase you?"

Vasilis laughed. "Speed is never a problem for me. I move quite fast."

"Really? That can be a problem for me," she said with a devilish smile.

Vasilis blushed, his mouth agape.

"We must move, now," she said before he could say anything.

She slipped on her fox mask as Vasilis leaped from the brush, arms raised in surrender.

"Hey!" Vasilis called. "Does anyone know where I can get ale?"

As the men surged forward, their cries slicing through the tense air, Vasilis sprang into action. His movements were a blur, a fluidity and speed that Kasumi recognized all too well. It was a prowess mirrored only in memories of her brother, Inoichi, whose own extraordinary abilities had once left her in awe.

Despite the chasm of time and space that now lay between Vasilis and her brother, his combat style was unique to his training, but his exceptional speed and strength bore an uncanny resemblance to Inoichi's.

Was Vasilis also one touched by the divine, blessed with abilities beyond the ordinary?

The question lingered in her mind as the kitsune within her stirred, sensing a kinship to Vasilis' power. As he swiftly dispatched the first warrior and shattered the chains, his movements were more than just skilled; they were imbued with an almost supernatural grace.

Kasumi watched, her warrior's eye noting every move, every decision. The way Vasilis wielded his sword was not merely practiced; it was as if the blade was an extension of his very being—a trait she had seen only in those favored by the gods.

As she watched Vasilis, Kasumi couldn't help but feel a deep connection, not just to the man himself, but to the path she walked, intertwined with beings of extraordinary fate.

Within a few moments Vasilis was running, leading the men away, opening the door for her to help the monk she was called to save. He had fallen to his knees, his robes tattered and smeared with mud, but he was alive.

Despite her small stature, she assisted the taller man, albeit awkwardly, as she began to drag him to safety.

"Are you okay?" she asked, hoping he spoke Japanese. "Yes," he replied in Japanese.

Amidst the quiet, Kasumi could make out the distant shouts of men, their voices filled with both anger and agony. *At least the monk was safe.*

"What is your name? How did you learn Japanese?" she asked, hoping to distract him from the chaos.

"Ji, from Tiantai, China, by way of the Wudang Mountains," he said. "I learned Japanese as a child, with a Japanese Bhikkhu... Saichō."

Kasumi's breath caught, hearing the Wudang Mountains, a place she visited in an effort to harness the Tenge gift. Genzo, her love who had long since passed, had written her from the place, as he too sought to harness the Tenge. She vividly remembered the man, whose eyes shone like golden orbs, radiating an aura of immense power that could rival that of a god on earth.

Here she was, having traveled through time, connecting with someone from the exact place she had studied.

The thought of the fox that had led her there crossed Kasumi's mind. The purpose of it all.

"I can sense your mind and spirit," the monk's soft, yet deep voice grounded her. "They are at war. It happens often with those blessed with divine gifts—the Tenge gift." His words shook Kasumi to her core, though she dared not show it. "Navigating the murky waters of your own existence and human instincts with the untamed forces within can be a tiresome journey."

Kasumi felt a profound urge to ask him so many questions. The wise keeps quiet and listens, she recalled her father's teaching. So she swallowed and listened to him speak.

"Learning to coexist with the beast within, acknowledging its strength while maintaining the compassion and wisdom of their human heart. Your gift, the kitsune, led you to me. You truly have unlocked the Eight-Tails-of-Knowledge, Generosity and selflessness. However, you must understand that the divine have their own mission that may conflict with your own. You need not find a god walking among us to get the answers. Perhaps I can accompany you—"

She heard a thump and a grunt. Peeking over her shoulder, she saw an arrow's tip dripping blood and the insides of the monk. "No!"

"Please, do not be sad," Ji's voice was a whisper as he struggled to speak.

"I—" Her voice faltered, caught in the grip of unspoken words she struggled to release.

Tears traced a warm path down her cheeks. The reason for her tears eluded her. Perhaps it was the relentless burden of this world, the weight of expectations and the sting of losses, leaving her feeling hollow. In that fleeting moment, the overwhelming burden threatened to crush her.

Kasumi halted the flow of blood from the arrow wound, leaving the tip embedded to prevent further bleeding.

As she cradled him, she saw him clearly for the first time: his eyes, a gentle shade of brown, held a youthful innocence, not unlike her brothers. Yet here he lay dying, a casualty of her inability to save him—just one more life slipping through her desperate grasp.

"I am sorry I failed you," she cried, holding him in her arms. Her plea was both for him and her family.

Ji's voice was thick with the familiar warmth of death. "You have failed no one," he assured, his breath ragged. "Your journey... is unique. You are destined to bring change, yet there is much you must learn."

Kasumi's eyes brimmed with confusion and fear. "How can I be saved? Why am I chosen?"

"You are no ordinary being," Ji whispered, a flicker of strength returning to his voice. "Your life will change the world, but..." he coughed. "You must be brave...The universe is sorrowful yet transient. To find your love... to achieve stability and peace is through Nirvana."

The state of bliss reached by the Arhants and Buddhas, he thought. "This is all too much. Am I going to die? What do I need to do? Are you saying my soulmate is alive on the side?"

"I have not said that he exists after death, and I have not said that he does not exist."

A turmoil of questions raged in her mind. *Does that mean Nirvana is outside of this realm? Does it transcend both being and non-being?* "Please speak clearly. I do not understand. Does he exist?" She cried.

There was only silence as his chest stilled, and the light in his eyes faded to a distant memory.

The monk's final words seared into her consciousness, igniting a dim light of solemn hope amidst the engulfing abyss of despair.

Vasilis's distant shouts pierced the bubble of her sorrow, pulling her back to the grim reality. Masking her emotions, she rose, her warrior facade firmly in place as she met his gaze. Vasilis, maintaining a respectful distance, offered her a silent acknowledgment. His eyes masked any sign of having witnessed her vulnerability. It was an unspoken gesture of respect, not typical of a warrior, yet deeply gentle.

"We have to go," Vasilis's voice cut through the lingering silence, firm yet not devoid of concern.

Together, they hastened back toward the camp, pausing only upon reaching the river's edge. Kasumi cleansed her face and hands of the day's brutal reminders, then collapsed onto the grass, finding solace in the rare patch of beauty in the shadowed forest.

Questions raced through her mind as she prepared to embark on a journey through time, seeking divine wisdom to bring new hope to a world destined to endure more darkness before the dawn.

Vasilis settled beside her, his presence a silent comfort. "Do you want to talk...or—"

"I just want to lie here," she said.

LILITH

Intrepid, 2076 AD

Lilith struggled to wrap her hands around it, but she was up for the challenge. She could taste the salty fluids running down her face. Beads of sweat continued down her chest and exposed back, glistening in the Caribbean sun. Her grunts echoed. She was winded and in pain, but she enjoyed it.

"Harder, harder!" Alex shouted, standing next to her. "Now wave... hammer... and stop. Battle ropes down!"

The ropes fell onto the white sand of a crystal blue ocean that reminded Lilith of her childhood. She couldn't remember the last time she took a vacation. This was as close as she would get. With the second workout of the day complete, she didn't have much energy for anything else—Alex made sure of that.

Lilith caught her breath. Her hands rested on her hips, her white bathing suit still wet. At her command, the room transformed back into its normal state, a silver and white contemporary ultramodern suite fitted with different programs, though still a work in progress.

"I still can't believe you imported real Caribbean sand," said Alex, who wore spandex shorts and a sports bra, showing off her toned physique.

"Go big or go home." Lilith threw a towel at her. "Let's hit the showers. I'm sure dinner is coming soon."

"Delivery? I need to hang out with you more often."

"You really do."

After the shower, they ate dinner. It was too long since she spent time with Alex, one of the few childhood friends she still had. More importantly, Alex was one of the few people she trusted, which was a substantial part of her life—now more than ever. Her inner circle was small; trustworthy, but incomplete.

"Japan was a success," Alex said.

Lilith's face said otherwise. She gulped her water.

"No, no Japan success?" Alex questioned, going for her cup.

"Seth messed up, in his own words. He killed Ieyasu Tokugawa."

"What!"

"Yes, he created massive damage to the timeline."

"So, what's the plan? You always have a plan. Wasn't that what you told Malaya when you bested her in chess?" Alex's face pinked? "I'm sorry."

"No need to apologize," Lilith said, massaging her temples. "This wasn't where I imagined we'd be, but Malaya's emotional, thoughtless, selfish decision brought us here, and now Seth."

Monitoring the timeline was all they could do after Seth's screw-up. The river of time wanted to flow correctly, so she knew certain events needed to play out for that to happen—time wasn't on her side.

"I wish I had more answers than *backup* plans," Lilith said.

"That's why you should have sent me," replied Alex.

"No, you have done more than enough. Your team is the backbone of this operation. I can't and won't ask for more than that."

"Thank you. With that said." She unfolded a screen and slid it across the table. "The ground team you wanted changed their mind," she smiled. "They'll arrive in Japan tonight and are awaiting orders."

It was an audacious plan. One with several stages that will undermine the UNA. Sure, she had some control of UNA with Sato as a partner, but she wanted a full collapse. Her focus was Japan, the heart of the Alliance. With the government in disarray, she needed to stir the people so that they would seek a new leader. That's when the mystical shogun will appear.

"What changed their minds? Why help now?" she said, swiping through the profiles, trying to keep from smiling. This was a pleasant development, one she had hoped for. She knew going to Japan had to be optional. They needed to want it.

"The revolution. Even with the pro-UNA supporters emerging, they want to help."

"These new recruits, do you trust them?" Lilith replied, handing the screen back. "If we can't, I don't want them around."

"That's why I need you to interview them. I need the sight. Don't worry. They will be secured."

"Secured, as in hands, tied and blindfolded?" Lilith said, handing her back the tablet.

"They understand what they are getting into."

"Thank you for everything," Lilith said, wanting to make it known what this meant to her.

The Military Astronauts Defense had given everything to Lilith's cause—to save humanity. At times it seemed surreal, but it was her reality, *their* reality. People were taking risks, in the case of MAD, their intergalactic exploits could only serve as a cover for so long. If discovered, they would face charges of treason. These brave men and women believed in Lilith's. It was a tall order, and Lilith knew the risk involved. She had liquidated assets to ensure the families of the MAD agents were taken care of, leaving only MEV Inc. as her sole possession.

They both agreed not to discuss anything related to the mission until after dinner. Instead, they dwelled in the old days. After dessert, it was back to business.

Lilith swiped through her agenda to a full schedule, color-coded and complete with meeting times and some names she didn't recognize. "Sometimes, I'm not sure if I'm the boss or Sheldon."

"I need these four at the top. Seth first, but separate these Spartans. I can only take so much."

"I'll have a team escort Seth first thing tomorrow morning, just in case."

"There's no need." Lilith continued analyzing the list.

Lilith lay in her bed. At her command, the diamonds from her earrings spiraled above her. Tomorrow's agenda weighed on her until she dozed off. The following day, Lilith woke with soreness from the night before, readying herself for what was more exhausting. She sat in her office wearing a black and white pencil dress, her desk more cluttered than usual.

"Angie, send a draft email titled *Midas's homework.*"

"Sent."

The door chimed, and two guards let Seth in, who wore a black shirt and black jeans and boots. He looked back at the guards, then sat in front of Lilith.

"So, I'm being summoned to... what do your people call it... the principal's office?" Seth smiled.

He looked different beyond the trimmed beard and groomed hair. He knew this conversation was coming, and so did she, but it still didn't stop the butterflies. Seth, however, was confident, almost to the point of arrogance. That would change.

"Even a lion must feel the rage of mother nature," she said, hoping to wipe the smile off his face. "You believe this is a game, Seth?"

"I believe I did what I could."

"You murdered the one person I told you not to. Do you even understand the consequences of your actions? The targets you put on our backs. It was selfish, barbaric—"

"It was unavoidable!" Seth stood.

The door slid open, and two armed soldiers came in, pointing rifles.

"Out now," Lilith commanded. "Angie, seal this room; mute audio." The diamonds from her earrings swung faster until she stopped them with her hand. "Sit down."

Seth obeyed. That smile returned. *Was he enjoying this?*

"Seth, you wanted to know the full story? Well, here it is. I was going to offer him an extension of his life. Since he was going to die at age seventy-three, I was going to give him an extra fifty years, more or less. In exchange, he would rule present Japan. A hero sent by the gods. The savior that the sacred Kojiki predicted."

"No one believes in myth and legends in your time. And there is no savior in these scripts.

"Not yet. I added them."

A grin covered his face. "How evil of you."

"Someone needs to be the bad guy to save humanity from themselves. And if DNA backs the myth. It will bring hope to desperate people."

"And the girl?"

"With my gold. She was going to control the Toyotomi."

"Leave no stone unturned. I can learn a lot from you so... What now?" He asked, leaning forward. "How do we fix this situation?"

"*I* will subdue the situation. You're getting benched."

"What? You need me."

It was true. Lilith needed his expertise. He offered power that could not be replicated, but she valued loyalty over everything else. And Seth betrayed that.

There was something dark within him, and she felt responsible, but always had a choice to make. He made the wrong choice once again. Seth's presence was a reminder of her own failure. She needed him gone. There were other ways he could be useful. A way he could regain her trust.

"I will give you the opportunity for redemption. As promised, you will run a kingdom. *My* kingdom, MEV."

"What are you saying?"

"I'm breaking up my shares between you, Malaya, and my father. You will have all the luxuries of the modern world."

"No. If the shares are divided into thirds, your father and daughter will only look to override my authority."

"She will not, and I will ensure you can operate with the freedom to do what you see fit. To expand what is now *our* kingdom."

Seth sighed as he leaned back and folded his arms. Lilith could feel a migraine coming along. Seth seemed to be a magnet for headaches—more than the others. Yes, it was a risky move, but this welcomed an added distraction for her pursuits and a way he could regain her trust.

"I agree," he finally said, making the rest of their meeting less painful.

Mizunami was next. Lilith stood as she timidly walked in, her bowed head dragged like her navy-blue kimono. This was the first time they met face to face, but not the first time Lilith saw her. She watched from a distance as Mizunami got acclimated to this strange world—as much as technology would allow. With everything she'd been through so far, Lilith wanted to make a good first impression. After all, she did have her kidnapped.

"Welcome, I'm Lilith," she said with a deep bow. "And despite the circumstances, I mean you no harm. You are safe."

Mizunami returned the gesture before setting. She peeked at the relics and souvenirs decorating the small room. "I-I've never seen a woman in charge."

"It is common in this world. I want you to know I'm not your enemy. And I understand that you've been through a lot. There is much to sort in your mind, which is why I brought you here to help you further."

Lilith reached for her hand. Mizunami withdrew. "I've heard what you can do, Lilith-sama."

"I beg you to let me bring clarity so that you can truly understand the situation beyond the information you already received."

"Then tell me, with your words."

Lilith smiled. Mizunami appeared timid, but she had an inner strength waiting to be unlocked—this was part of why she chose her. "As it currently stands, the Tokugawa and Toyotomi Clan teamed with allies to crush Osamu and the Torri clan."

"Too many lives were lost," Mizna said, keeping her soft tone. "I will not assist you."

"Many more will perish, including your brother," Lilith said, forcing Mizunami to look up. "It happened in 1615. Your brother weds Hidetada's daughter, but it does not stop the Tokugawa clan from slaughtering your people."

"Little brother…" Mizunami's voice trailed as did her mind, but she snapped back. "How do I know your words are true?"

"Because I've offered you to show the truth. As you said, you know what I am capable of. I need you. The past and present need you. Osamu will be by your side every step of the way. Once he returns, you will take your place as Shogun in this world."

"Osamu, he—"

"It is important to understand that he sacrificed everything to save your life—he loves you, Mizunami, but he also loves his clan. In return, you must not destroy the Torri. I promise their clan will be on your side, but the Tokugawa betrayal shouldn't go unnoticed. This is an opportunity to have your clan claim what their victory earned them. Ieyasu took the kingdom from your father after his death… honor him."

Mizunami frowned at Lilith's disappointment. *If she allowed me to show her, this would be much easier.*

"Don't just take my words for it," Lilith said. "I will offer you unlimited resources. I want you to see the oppression of your people. Millions, no billions of lives are at stake, and you can help save them."

Mizunami's brows deepened. "Why me? How can I help in your time? I was raised to be one way only, to serve, not lead."

"I know your secret, what you are capable of. I am here to tell you that your abilities are a gift—not a burden. And I will take you out of that shell and shape you into the leader your people need—a true savior. Not like me."

Lilith reached for her hand. "I just need you to trust me."

Mizunami let a tear roll down her face. Even if she couldn't use her powers, it was an obvious conflict brewing inside her, asking that plaguing question, the same question that haunted Lilith. *Who is evil at this point?*

Mizunami wiped the tears from her face. "I cannot help you. Because of you, Inoichi is dead. I... I do not have the strength."

"What if... if I told you—" Lilith paused. *This could change everything if she knows. Then what's stopping her from finding him, consequently leading the Cabinet right to me? But I need her and him.*

"Inoichi is alive, brainwashed, and manipulated into working for those trying to keep this broken world the way it is, and they are my enemy... *our* enemy." Lilith sat back. "There will come a time when you see him again. When you do, it's up to you to make him see your point of view. That is, if your perspective aligns with my goals. Go, think about it."

Once Mizunami stepped out, Lilith took medicine for her headache. She realized the slight yet dulling pain was brought on by Jumpers. The Jumpers' natural barrier fogged her sight. There were no shortcuts with them. They had to buy into her cause. To ease her pain, she met with Alex's people between Jumpers. Reading them was the scent of morning dew.

Is this my new existence? Trapped in meetings without adventure. Lilith thought after the MAD agent left.

Elias was next.

He strutted in with slides, gray joggers, and a white sweater. Elias embraced the modern world more than every jumper. Reading his share of military books to gaming, he wasn't just a soldier—this was his passion.

"Lilith," Elias said, his voice almost brittle. He knew this meeting would not be a pleasant one.

"I've missed our periodic visit," she said, to his surprise. "You haven't been avoiding me?"

"Never. I took solace in preparation for life outside the Intrepid." He lowered his head. "I know I messed up killing those people. It surprised you wanted to meet."

Lilith smiled. "Eli, what makes you think I want you to leave? Betrayal will get you air-locked and launched into space."

Elias looked up, then smiled. "I'd understand if it were true."

"See, there's that smile," she said. "But I have to be honest. I can't downplay the loss of life, but who am I to judge? At the end of the day, my hands are bloodier than everyone else's."

Lilith reached out for his hand. He hesitated, but he accepted it. "You are under my wing. You're one of us now. And prison... that is the last place for someone like you—you need help."

"What do you mean, *help*? I murdered a man in cold blood, a religious leader, and I felt nothing. It was like swatting a fly." He slowly withdrew his hand. "There is a special place in your hell for a man like me, isn't there?"

"It's not for me to say, but I doubt what you did was of your choosing. You lack control. And that's why you will see a doctor every other day to set you on the road to recovery. A psychologist, someone who can help you control those impulses, that rage."

Elias folded his arms and looked off, seeping into his mind. It was the only way she knew how to help. Underneath the blood thirst, Elias was just a boy drowned by the demons he struggled to slay. She granted him that moment. It took a minute before he spoke.

"So, I'm getting benched, like father."

"You are, but only for the short term. I need you to recover and get back out there. For now, speak to Midas. He'll prepare you for the next phase."

Of the three, only Midas knew about her Scandinavian backup plan, and he prepared accordingly. Compartmentalizing was the key to keeping her own secrets, which scared her, but no one mastered it the way she had.

"One more thing, it's about the *Golden Dragons*. Was it just two?"

"Nah, I am sure they are the Tokugawa's secret weapons. Warriors with abilities are not uncommon in the ancient world. Your world has forgotten."

"Thank you, Eli."

My suspicion is right. I will need more firepower. I have to risk it.

After taking the last of the meetings, she retreated to her quarters, needing a break before Quintus. Thankfully, he always took his time to look his very best, often resulting in him being fashionably late.

This time, he wore black jeans, held up by suspenders, and a black undone button-up shirt with rolled-up sleeves. His gold Cuban link and watch glistened like his smile and greased-up dirty blond hair he had pulled back.

"Are you going to South Beach, or are you attending a meeting with your boss?"

"I was hoping you would join me. I hear the sushi there is splendid," he said, placing a bottle of fine Brandy on her desk.

"You're speaking to the *former* richest person in the world. You can't impress me if you tried." Lilith slapped her head right after the words left her mouth.

"Wanna bet?" he said.

"I set myself up with that one."

Quintus cleared his throat. "So, what's Plan B?"

There's that question again. Lilith grabbed Brandy and walked to the bar.

They weren't wrong. She always has a plan, B, C, and D if necessary. With Scandinavia on the agenda, things had to be flawless—especially after Japan. Fixing Seth's screw-up was a plan she already set in motion with Mizunami, though that wasn't something he, nor anyone else, needed to worry about. Finding this Sage meant everything. It was her only priority. Therefore, it was theirs.

She remembered how the Sage was just a folklore in the back of her mind. The Aigons and their Champions battle with demigods of their own creation, the Sages, who once walked among the people—something she would never forget—Jeff's log made sure she wouldn't.

It had been a while since she last listened to his recordings—once was enough. His logs discussed the lore surrounding the Taino, an ancient indigenous people who had a connection to the banished gods and the Sages. She spent her free time studying the legend of the Sages. Now she was preparing to uncover one.

"I'm moving forward with Scandinavia," Lilith said, placing two brandy-filled glasses on the table: one garnished with cherry juice and orange, the other straight brandy on the rocks. The amber liquid swirled in the crystal, catching the light like secrets she had yet to unveil.

She paused, savoring a sip of *Les Remarquables de Martell.* The warmth spread, reminding her of afternoons spent peeking into her father's study, watching him pour the same drink during meetings. She was too young to understand the weight of their discussions, but even then, she had recognized power in the way he moved, the way the brandy seemed to grant him authority. She'd soaked in every detail, her small hands gripping the edge of the doorframe, eavesdropping when she shouldn't have.

Now, the ritual was hers, the flavor a tether to a time when she was learning to command a room without ever stepping inside it.

Lilith slid Quintus a note that included a map. He took a drink of his cocktail before swiping his hand across the screen. The more he read, the more he drank, his brow furrowing as he absorbed her plans.

He slid the note back to her and rubbed his newly shaved cleft chin, his fingers lingering as if testing a new identity. She could tell he wasn't quite used to the look yet, but they both knew it was necessary.

"How can you be sure any of this is true?" he asked, his skepticism laced with curiosity.

"Osamu," she said, the name rolling off her tongue with measured precision. She took another sip, letting the brandy's heat steady her resolve. "He's been hiding a secret—his true ability, which ties him to this legend. And his brother was thought to be a Champion."

"Fair enough."

"The Viking will not make this easy."

"Neither was kidnapping Elias and Midas, but you made it happen. Besides, I will eventually join you. Now that we don't have Kofi, we will rely on Elias and Midas. I will also send you two emails, one labeled Elvir, the other labeled MEV."

"*MEV?*"

"Yes. If it comes to that, you'll finally get to meet the man you admire as my Plan B."

"What about Malaya?"

"Malaya will move how and when I want her to. Right now, she's chasing the carrot. When she's ready, they will take over."

The gravity of the situation loomed through the quietness. Quintus poured them another glass. Lilith broke the silence. "I'm looking into new recruits from Scandinavia, with new Jumpers, aside from the Sage. So, I can't hold your hand during the transition to MEV. You have plenty of resources, and Rose will be there to help you along the way."

"Lending me your kingdom, I can easily build my own kingdom ...is it just trust?" He tilted his head, then smiled. "C'mon, you want me. Just give in to your fantasy."

She pinched her nose. *This guy.* "Quintus. I like my coffee black."

"Have you ever tried Greek lattes?"

"Don't make me tell your wife."

They both chuckled, but the wind was let out of the room. Quintus looked down at his glass. Lilith refilled his cup. "Quintus, I just want you to know I'm not holding your family hostage. This is brain surgery. It requires precision. I promise, when the time is right, I will bring them back."

"I know." He gulped down what was left. "May I ask you a question, my lady?"

"Just one."

"You have all this power. Why haven't you brought him back? I know I would have."

"I tried." Lilith leaned back in her chair. "But I can't find Jeff late enough. There's a gap in which I lose him. I never get to see him again. Time doesn't let me save everyone. She's a bitch, and she wants it her way all the time and has it her way *most* of the time."

The room was quiet again. Quintus refilled both cups, pouring the last of the bottle. "How's Kara?"

"Kara? Kara's one of the strongest women I know... she did just fine."

"To Jeffrey and Valentina, then. Wherever they are."

They tapped glasses and drank. At this point, Lilith was feeling the brandy's effects, and her emotions were high. Though her tongue felt heavy, so did the burden she carried. "I'm no saint. I'm not God, but if I could save everyone and sacrifice myself, I would, in a heartbeat."

"I know."

KASUMI

Germany, 871 AD

The waterfall roared as Vasilis stepped out of it, his nude, chiseled body lathered with moisture. He flicked back his long bronze-brown hair; their eyes locked as he combed his hair back with both hands.

Even from atop the tree where she slept, Kasumi made no attempt to hide her curiosity, nor did he attempt to cover himself, not that he had any reason to.

She smirked, and her eyes moved to Malaya, who sat on the opposite side of the tree, doing her best to avoid the bright morning sun. Her arms were still crossed and a slight wrinkle was present on her forehead.

Kasumi sat next to her in a lotus position. "We will venture as far as the sun reaches. You have my blade... I will track down your mother."

The news was more bitter than a Nigauri melon. Malaya's own mother was behind the attack on Edo Castle. On one hand, Kasumi felt she didn't owe Malaya anything.

On the other hand, Malaya had Azmani's blessing, a rare feat given her sensei's usual reluctance to accept outsiders. Then again, Malaya had consistently demonstrated fearless compassion.

Kasumi had witnessed it firsthand in the forest when Malaya rescued the child. There were also the Christians she had helped save, despite losing her friends in the process.

She had her own motivations for doing so, Kasumi thought. *No, capturing her mother is the correct course of action. There is no honor in soiling my word as a woman.*

Kasumi's gaze trailed Malaya's, noticing how her eyes flickered away with a blend of disdain and a faint blush coloring her cheeks. This shift occurred just as Vasilis emerged from behind the brush, casually reaching for his kimono.

Kasumi felt a twinge of disappointment as he wrapped the garment around himself, concealing his form. Malaya seemed to pick up on Kasumi's subtle reaction, giving a scoff and contorting her face in sheer disgust.

"Are you still upset?" Vasilis voice cut through the awkward silence.

Malaya rolled her eyes. Kasumi let out an exasperated sigh, predicting the firestorm that would occur.

"Am I still upset?" Malaya growled. "You are abandoning two women in the middle of nowhere. Correction, in the middle of the Viking age."

"You are mad, woman. Your lack of respect for authority and discipline is shameful. We have our orders."

"Screw General Williams and his orders," Malaya blurted. "We have the timeline at stake. I need to reach Hamberg, and your one, and only job was to–"

"Track Lilith Castillo-Grant," Vasilis interrupted, "and report back to the general."

Malaya sprang to her feet. "This is not Sparta! He is not your commander."

"Neither are you, Castillo-Grant—"

"Spartan?" Kasumi exclaimed.

Vasilis frowned as he gave Malaya a nasty look. "I was going to tell you, but the time" Kasumi turned her back.

"It wasn't proper. Those men who attacked... I admit, I once called them brothers. I fought and bled next to them... until they stabbed me in the back."

Kasumi raised her hand. "You owe me nothing." She swallowed the knot in her throat. "I understand. The actions of a few men do not represent all of Greece. But I would still like you to go look after my brother. I will look after Malaya." She kept her back turned, not wanting to see the sorrowful look in his eyes that would only reopen a still-fresh wound.

"As you wish, my lady."

The resounding boom reverberated through the dense forest, so deafening that Kasumi was certain even the mountains had heard it.

Startled birds took flight and the woodland creatures scurried deep into the lush greenery. Kasumi turned to look, feeling a twinge of regret, but he was gone; he had vanished.

Somehow, his departure rekindled a feeling deep within the pit of her stomach, a feeling she thought was impossible. Finding out that Vasilis was a Spartan somewhat alleviated the growing warmth she had begun to feel towards him. A part of her was actually relieved he was gone—she needed to focus on her mission.

Distractions from such feelings were not what the gods intended. She reminded herself of this, although the question burning in the back of her mind lingered.

Who was she to predict what God wanted? Either way, being away from Vasilis was probably for the best.

Kasumi settled herself by the tree and drifted off. It was night by the time she woke. Malaya slumped over a tree; the poor girl nurtured her for most of the day.

"We should go," Kasumi said, waking her.

A full moon peeked through the tall trees, lighting the marsh, whose driftwood nested insects. Kasumi hurled clear liquid before they made their way through a swamp. Their wet hair clung to their faces as they did with one another.

"Malaya..." Kasumi murmured, her voice barely a whisper before she collapsed.

She woke atop a grassy hill, finding Malaya sitting on its edge, mumbling in an unfamiliar language.

Malaya looked over her shoulder and rushed to her. "Are you well?"

Kasumi raised a brow. "No... Your accent has changed, and where are we?"

Malaya stammered. "Where do I start?"

"From the beginning. You speak in your strange accent. I need more rest."

Malaya's face flushed with concern. "The ghost radiation must be affecting you."

Kasumi grabbed her stomach and rested on the grass as Malaya did her best to explain. *Time travel,* the words still seemed unreal, yet here they were, in a foreign land over eight hundred years in the past.

Part of her was excited about the unexpected yet impossible feat. The other part of her, of course, still mourned her family. *What will become of them?*

What would become of Inoichi? She wanted to ask if he would be safe.

Malaya was visibly distressed, her demeanor teetering on the edge of panic. She was a portrait of worry and confusion, barely hiding the turmoil within. Despite the chaotic whispers surrounding her mental state, she refused to acknowledge the issue she was facing.

"You mentioned your technology," said Kasumi, hoping to help Malaya focus on one problem at a time. "The broken language transmitter. Will it be a problem?"

"Yes. We'll have trouble communicating with the locals. I don't have my medicine, so solving that problem is an issue all its own, and then there's nightfall. I don't know the weather patterns here..." Her voice trailed and her eyes closed. She started mumbling to herself again.

"I think you should rest. I will gather what we need for a fire."

Malaya jumped up. "No. I can do it. I am well versed in survival."

"The point is not just survival, but rather for you to gather your thoughts so you can solve this issue."

"I can do both. You should focus on recovering."

"Understood. After you collect the firewood, lean them onto those two trees, but do not make the fire too close to it."

Kasumi couldn't help but smirk, observing Malaya's intense focus as she shed her drenched kimono, revealing tight black pants made from a peculiarly sturdy material. Mirroring her actions, Kasumi discarded her own soaked garment, clad only in her light underclothes, settled into a cross-legged position on the welcoming grass, seeking solace and stability in her posture.

Her attention lingered on Malaya, who seemed lost in her own world, meandering through the surrounding trees. Confusion and distress were carved into her features, and her murmurs floated in the air, forming words Kasumi couldn't decipher. This unfamiliar sight kindled a blend of worry and intrigue within her.

Sensing an opportunity to ease Malaya's turmoil, Kasumi gestured invitingly, encouraging her to join in meditation. It was an offer of solace, extending the kind of support that transcended the barriers of language and confusion.

"Channel your anger, recognize its presence," Kasumi guided gently, her voice steady and calm. "Transform it into your strength... Now, take a deep breath, let it flow slowly, like a tranquil stream..."

Nature guided their silence until Malaya spoke. "I've figured out a solution to our communication barrier," she announced, her hands diving into her bag with eager haste. After a brief, frenzied search, she triumphantly presented her findings. "This might seem a bit unorthodox, but I need you to remove something from my... mind." She held up a compass alongside a peculiar stone.

"This metal," Malaya began, her excitement palpable as she handed the items to Kasumi, "has properties that will draw out what we need." She then gently took Kasumi's wrist, guiding her hand to the side of her own head. "Start here," she instructed, placing the stone against her temple. "Slide it across and don't stop for any reason. What we're after are called liquid-nanos."

Liquid-nanos... Kasumi's reaction was a mix of astonishment and skepticism, her mouth agape before she regained her composure. A fleeting thought of her brother, Hidetada, flashed through her mind—the same relentless determination she now saw in Malaya. She hadn't bid him farewell.

"Are you ready?" Malaya's voice yanked Kasumi back to the present.

With a soft chuckle, Kasumi responded, "In my time, I've witnessed countless injuries, numerous lives lost, but never have I encountered someone so ready to extract something from their own mind."

Malaya quickly fashioned a biting block by wrapping a cloth around a stick. She bit down and nodded as she lay softly on the dirt.

Nervously, Kasumi followed the given instructions, her hands steady despite the gravity of what they were about to do. As she began the delicate procedure, she sought to offer comfort to Malaya, who was visibly struggling with the pain.

"Try to focus on the waterfall in the distance," Kasumi whispered softly. "Imagine its serene flow, the cool mist against your skin, the sound of water crashing down—let it take you away from here."

Before long, a lump the size of a youngberry emerged, causing her body to tremble uncontrollably. The initially berry-shaped mass morphed, eerily following the stone's guided path until it reached the inner corner of her eye. Malaya's cries pierced the silence, startling birds into the darkening sky as droplets of blood splashed onto Kasumi's face.

"Don't stop," Malaya grunted.

Kasumi swallowed hard against the bile rising in her throat, the grotesque scene before her twisting her stomach. She had witnessed countless wounds and inflicted many more. Yet, the sight that unfolded was unlike any battlefield horror she had encountered. The object in her hand glimmered with a metallic sheen, writhing and twisting upon the stone. A shudder of horror escaped her lips.

"A-a metal centipede! Oeee!" she exclaimed, her voice a mix of awe and disgust. The cold sweat that dotted her brow and the tremor in her hands were foreign. The world, it seemed, still held surprises that could unsettle even her seasoned soul.

Malaya, meanwhile, appeared surprisingly nonchalant, even as she panted from the ordeal. "That was easy," she breathed out.

Her command of Japanese carried a heavy accent but conveyed her meaning clearly, explaining her technology. Liquid-metal devices, made up of smaller devices called nanites, together they made up this modern marvel.

Kasumi nodded, though she didn't quite grasp everything. It was nearly impossible to listen to anything when she couldn't pry her eyes off the thin, needle-like creature about the size of a fingertip. The centipede shifted from solid to liquid as it squirmed around the rock—she flinched at the odd sight.

Malaya pressed on the centipede's head, causing its liquid form to eerily split into two. "You're going to place one in your ear," she warned, her palm open, the light glinting off the liquid creature.

Kasumi hesitated, questioning her life choices at that moment. Her mind flashed back to the battle with the warrior whose arms twisted and struck with the lethal grace of snakes. Even facing that unearthly foe had not left her as unsettled as the task at hand.

"You will be fine," Malaya assured, her voice a comforting blend of concern and confidence. "A small pinch, some discomfort, but nothing more..."

Taking a deep breath, Kasumi reminded herself of her strength. *I am a ninja. I am strong,* she thought, allowing the creature to slither onto her finger. She froze as the cold device twirled around her finger, its touch foreign, yet fascinating.

"Oee," she said, squirming, thinking about what was about to happen.

She slowly put the creature near her ear. Its spindly legs tickled as they entered, probing and prodding along the sensitive skin. She could feel it worming its way inward, metal limbs scratching along the inside of her ear in a way that made her entire body shiver. It was like a frozen needle piercing her mind. An icy chill shot through her head. Her eyes watered at the sharp sensation.

Then, in an instant, it was over. The creature nestled itself in her mind, as if it was always there. Lightheaded, Kasumi wondered if it worked.

"Did... it... work?" Kasumi questioned. Her tongue felt heavy, like a drunken night after too much sake.

Malaya pursed her lips, a spark of mischief lighting up her eyes. "Got it," she smiled broadly. "So, any new updates from the future waiting in your inbox? How's the Wi-Fi signal in there?"

Kasumi blinked twice, a puzzled expression washing over her face as she echoed Malaya's words. "What does it mean?"

With a nonchalant shrug, Malaya grinned. "Nothing really. Just making sure the connection's alive and kicking."

They exchanged smiles, bridging the chasm between their worlds. Yet, as swiftly as the smiles came, the weight of their situation descended upon them, a stark reminder of their purpose. It was time to press forward, to continue their journey through this unfamiliar terrain.

In this unfamiliar terrain, Kasumi felt an intuitive nudge guiding them, a blend of curiosity and caution. The landscape, though foreign, sparked a flicker of recognition within her.

Emerald pines and towering oaks whispered of her childhood in Japan, of running through similar woods with her brothers, weaving tales of samurais and mythical battles. Silently hoping she could fight alongside her warrior husband—a wistful echo of simpler, sun-drenched days.

Yet, here, the looming snow-capped peaks dwarfed even the memories of the Japanese Alps, introducing a majestic but cold truth far removed from her past's warm familiarity.

Amidst this ancient European wilderness, with its unfamiliar cadence of bird calls and the distant murmur of a rushing river, Kasumi found herself adrift in novelty. She thought of Inhamie, her sister in all but blood, their battles with one another, the treachery, and forgiveness.

Despite the echoes of home in the woods' embrace, the vast expanse before her was a stark canvas of uncharted mysteries. Her shinobi training kept her steps light and senses sharp; a samurai displaced in time and space, yet ever vigilant. The world around her brimmed with the unknown dangers and discoveries alike.

"We should move. Follow the river. It is our best option," her voice carried the weight of a decision made.

"I disagree," Malaya let out a quick retort. "We should go opposite the river."

The counterproposal lingered between them like an unsolved riddle. In Malaya's determined gaze, Kasumi recognized a familiar brand of stubbornness, one that mirrored the expressions of her sisters back home.

Each memory of their shared stubborn moments, the petty squabbles, and some far greater born from clashing wills, danced through her mind. She recalled her own willful stands, the ones that led to unnecessary conflicts, and the lessons painfully learned from them.

But Malaya wasn't her sister, and this was far from the familiar disputes of home. That life was gone. This was a mission with stakes far higher than any familial argument, set in a world neither of them could claim as their own. She had to trust her, or at the very least trust the gods to lead.

Kasumi understood the weight of leadership and the cost of learning from one's mistakes. *Perhaps sensei was right,* she thought. *I am simply a sword in her story.*

Kasumi shrugged. "Fine," she conceded, her voice laced with understanding. "This is your mission, But we stay vigilant, and at the first sign of trouble, we reconsider our path."

Malaya nodded curtly, taking the lead.

As they navigated the dense dirt and gravel, Kasumi's thoughts wandered back to her family, her life before, and her mother. *"Neko ni koban,"* the words echoed, embodying her late mother's philosophy. The idea of giving *gold to a cat* sparked a laugh deep within her, though only a smile surfaced as she carefully placed her feet among the rocks.

The memories of her past, once so vivid and tangible, now seemed to fade into the distance as they ventured into the night of an unknown world.

She reminisced about a younger version of herself, a stubborn girl by a different name brandishing a samurai's wooden sword, her joy mixing with her brothers' as they absorbed the lessons of bushido. The aroma of wet rice fields, sprawling endlessly and spilling over the hills, floated through her memory.

"Over there, that's the main road," Malaya's voice cut through the silence, pulling Kasumi from the depths of her memories as they stood at what felt like the edge of the world. "Civilization shouldn't be too far."

"Yes, but we have spent all our energy searching for a road that could lead us anywhere."

"Your logic is understandable. Yes, following a river is a survival tactic, but I'm on a mission that requires precise decisions. We should find the coast. Hamburg is the goal."

Kasumi nodded. "I will follow your lead."

As they moved forward, Kasumi noticed Malaya's pace slowing, an unusual hesitancy in her steps. Under the dim light of the evening sky, she could see Malaya shivering, a visible tremor that seemed out of place with the mild chill. The air around them felt heavy with an unspoken dread that whispered its horrors through the leaves.

"Jesus Christ!" Malaya gasped, horror etched across her face.

"I thought you said you were an atheist?"

"Really, Kasumi, now? And that's not what I said," Malaya retorted, but her immediate focus shifted back to the horror that had halted their steps.

They stood frozen, staring at the pile of dismembered bodies scattered across the blood-stained road, the victims predominantly male. The air hung heavy with the scent of death, and Malaya, overwhelmed by the ghastly scene, vomited.

Even Kasumi, hardened by countless battles, felt a surge of nausea but suppressed it, placing her hand over her mouth as a wave of dread washed over her.

Approaching a small, lifeless form apart from the others, Kasumi squatted down beside a boy. With a gentle touch, she closed his eyes, her heart heavy with an unspoken grief. A grief tugging at memories of war and death.

It was as if they had stepped into the heart of a decaying forest, where the air was heavy with the scent of rot and the silence was simply just the beginning to the unknown.

For the first time, Kasumi felt the kitsune stir within, a sensation like the first light from a storm crackling along her spine—a warning of impending danger. Perhaps from whoever left these people behind.

Could they still be close? The kitsune, her unseen guardian spirit, had never steered her wrong, its instincts sharp and flawless.

"Something's off," Kasumi murmured, her voice barely above a whisper.

"No crap," Malaya said between retching.

"These bodies are lined up in a pattern. We should change clothes, take what we can, and go."

"Are you insane? Do you know what types of diseases a corpse can have? Tuberculosis, Hepatitis B and C, Creutzfeldt-Jakob—"

"We have no other choice," Kasumi's whisper carried an unwavering command. "We must blend in."

"Option B is taking this trail." Malaya pointed at a thin dirt path that was barely visible if not for a few cut branches. "Look, you're right. But we need to move, and stripping dead people is out of the question."

"Fine, this is your mission," Kasumi said, mostly to herself. "But if we die, I will abandon my afterlife and kick your ass in your heaven."

"You're the Christian."

"Oh, I suspect God has a different location planned for me."

"You and I both, sister."

Soon after they started, using the brush and darkness as their cloak, Kasumi caught a glimpse of something—or rather, someone—unsettling.

Ahead, a group of well-built men, their blond hair braided in a style that spoke of their origin, moved with a purpose that Kasumi instantly recognized as dangerous. Without a second thought, she reached out, her hand firmly grasping Malaya, pulling her down into the shadows with her.

"Vikings," Malaya whispered. Dread and intrigue filled her tone. "Look at the size of that one."

He was one of the tallest men Kasumi had seen, and here they were a few meters from their grasp. She saw the horror on Malaya's face and wondered if she had to tap into the kitsune to ensure she survived. She turned her attention back to the Viking with broad shoulders and long brown hair.

"How large do you think he is?" Kasumi asked.

"Six-nine from the size of his arms and legs, two hundred and eighty pounds."

Kasumi raised a brow, confusion evident on her face. *Six-nine? What manner of measurement is that?* Before she could press for an explanation, her attention snapped to a new urgency in the area.

"Rollo!" another man called out, catching the attention of the tall figure. "Our scouts found bodies."

"*Nani?* What are the chances?" Malaya whispered, her voice trembling. "Is... is time trying to kill us?"

Kasumi looked at Malaya. "What do you mean time is trying to kill us?"

"If my memory serves me correctly—and it always does—the man down there is Rollo the Walker, a renowned Viking. If they catch us—"

"We shall not put his legend to the test—" Kasumi's grip tightened on Malaya's wrist as a branch cracked beneath her feet, an accidental betrayal of their presence.

At that moment, Kasumi and Rollo locked eyes. Without hesitation, she tugged Malaya away from the looming threat. Fear propelled them forward just as droplets of rain fell from the sky—a favor from the kami, perhaps, as the rain blurred their hastily made tracks.

The scent of wet earth filled the air as they plunged deeper into the wilderness, the underbrush growing denser with each step. Soon, they found themselves within the refuge of a forest, surrounded by trees that stretched towards the heavens, a natural fortress of towering trunks and shadow.

In this momentary pause from their relentless escape, Kasumi turned her attention to Malaya, her voice laced with concern. "How are your wounds?"

"They're fine," Malaya responded, though her breath was short. "I just need water." She paused. "If we continue this way—no, maybe we should—" Her voice faded into silence, her eyes scanning their surroundings in search of an answer.

Kasumi caught the uncertainty in Malaya's rapid glances, watching as she began to mumble. It was as if her words wove through tangled thoughts as she struggled to map out their next move.

Placing a reassuring hand on Malaya's shoulder, Kasumi gently brought her back to the moment. "Your mind is wandering again. We need to rest and meditate."

"But those men—"

"Will not find us here," Kasumi assured firmly.

Settling down beneath a tree, the air around them changed, carrying the fresh scent of impending rain.

For Kasumi, the rain evoked memories of her little brother, stirring a deep ache within her. She braced herself as the emotional tide rose, waves of pain threatening to wash over her once more.

"I'm sorry for your loss," Malaya whispered back, her voice a soft echo of empathy in the quiet that surrounded them. "You've been so great at helping me, I never took the time out to listen to you. So please..."

Kasumi felt a knot form in her throat at Malaya's kind gesture. "I never imagined him dying in battle. He was different, not a fighter," she sighed. "I suppose such a naïve thought is not very warrior-like of me."

"No," Malaya smiled. "You sound like an older sister. I don't know what it's like to have a sibling, but I can understand, to some degree, what it's like to mourn someone you love..."

An eerie silence hung over them for a moment. Kasumi understood that death was a natural course of life, a continuing path that leads from one existence to the next, much like the lotus flower that blooms pristine from the mud. So, she chose to live for those who passed on to the next life, learning lessons in route to the path of enlightenment—to live for those who could not.

Yet the pain of loss lingers like a deep wound that never truly heals, Kasumi thought.

"I'm so sorry, Kasumi," Malaya's voice was a gentle nudge to Kasumi.

Kasumi fanned a smile. "There was nothing you could do." With a tender gesture, she reached for Malaya's hand. "You saved Inoichi, right? Are you sure he is safe?"

"More than safe." Her tone was emphatic and reassuring. "He will get the help he needs from the world's finest physicians." Her eyes lowered and her tone sobered. "I have to be honest. My world is not safe. We are on the brink of war."

A fire of frustration burned within Kasumi at the mention of another world at war. She understood all too well the human nature of fighting for power. After all, she had wielded the divine gift and curse of a kami, *the Tenge,* as her sword in countless battles in the name of Ieyasu Tokugawa.

"I understand," Kasumi said, her voice flat, laden with the weight of surrender. "My country has been entangled in conflict for centuries. Now, presumed dead, I can only hope my family succeeds where I could not—may they finally bring lasting peace."

Malaya smiled. "Over two hundred and sixty years of peace, to be exact," her voice carried a power of reassurance.

For a moment, it warmed Kasumi with pride, then filled her with sadness at the thought of how much blood soiled the earth to secure peace. *A sad truth to the perils of war, indeed*, she thought.

"You said your home is at war," Kasumi said. "But you described it as a paradise. How could both be true?"

"When a multi billionaire attempts to play god, things like war are not far behind. She has time on her side, years of planning—"

"And now you have the advantage. You will not let her beat you twice."

"I hope you're right."

"None of that," Kasumi said, standing straight and reaching out her hand. "Believe you'll make sure that doesn't happen,". "We just have to get to Hamburg, right?"

Malaya nodded, a silent agreement sealed between them, accepting her help. Together, they ventured into the gloomy embrace of the morning. Dark clouds churned overhead, threatening rain that never fell. Instead, bitter winds sliced through the air, doing little to alleviate the chill of their damp clothing.

Kasumi's ears, sensitive to the slightest rustle, picked up an odd noise. She halted, her hand raised for silence. "Did you hear that?" she whispered, her voice barely carrying over the wind.

"Yeah, what was it?" Malaya whispered.

Their eyes traced the dense wet greenery bordering their path.

Before Kasumi could respond, chaos erupted. A screaming man burst from the forest, his form a blur of motion as he stumbled onto the trail and collapsed onto his hands and knees.

Words failed him, but his long, dark brown face was a canvas of fear and desperation. He scrambled to rise, his long, brawny arms flailing, grasping at a nearby tree for support. But as quickly as he had appeared, he vanished, pulled back into the forest's shadowy depths as if he had never been.

They stared at one another. "Run!" shouted Malaya.

A surge of primal fear propelled them forward, their feet pounding the earth in a desperate gallop. The identity of their pursuer mattered little; the instinct to flee overwhelmed all else. Kasumi spotted the naked man lying in the dirt.

"He must have run into a tree," Malaya said, attempting to help him.

"Leave him!" Kasumi shouted.

"I can't," she said, checking the side of his neck. "He's still breathing."

"Good. Now we can leave," Kasumi insisted, urgency lacing her words.

But as the man stirred, a chill ran down Kasumi's spine. Observing him more closely, his formidable size seemed to engulf them, much like the shadows of fear darkening his eyes.

Laughter, distant yet chilling, broke through the silence. "The Franks," Malaya murmured, a note of fear in her voice.

"There," the man rasped, pointing weakly away from them. "Sorry," he breathed out, the word barely leaving his lips before his feigned frailty transformed into aggression.

With swift, surprising strength, he swung at them, his arm a blur. The impact felt like a boulder crashing into Kasumi, darkness swiftly overtaking her senses.

"Here, over here," the man's voice, now clear and betraying, called out to the unseen others as darkness claimed her.

INOICHI

Island, 2076

The cabin door flew open with a bang as Vasilis burst through, the morning's heavy rain still clinging to him like a second skin after his daily run. "Time!" he shouted, his voice echoing against the wooden walls furnished with this world's finest training equipment, ancient armor stands that hinted at the cabin's militant purpose.

Inoichi scoffed. "Only fifty miles today," he responded without missing a beat. His body hung from a bar, methodically performing sit-ups in a rhythm that matched the drip of water from Vasilis's clothes.

"I see you're still hanging around," Vasilis mocked, a smug grin spreading across his face as he delighted in his own humor.

Inoichi merely closed his eyes tighter, a silent plea for patience as he tried to drown out the bad jokes with the focus on his training. He never counted, only worked in durations.

"Not even a smile, huh? Bah, you're no fun. So... How many have you done?"

Counting, in his view, imposed limits—boundaries on what could be achieved. His life, marked by the divine gift that made him a formidable force on the battlefield, was a testament to transcending limits. The gift, though not fully understood, set him apart, bathed him with a power that felt both invincible and burdensome. It was this power that defined his existence as Ieyasu Tokugawa's son, turning him into a weapon in countless battles for supremacy.

Yet, his power failed him as did his father's ability to spot infiltrators among his men. Seth, a Spartan warrior with unmatched prowess, was the serpent who crept into their midst, shattering all illusions of invincibility. His deadly strike ended the life of Inoichi's father, the great Ieyasu, altering Inoichi's destiny.

Inoichi tensed at the thought, his muscles burned, but the fire in his belly of the night his father died was scorching with the desire for vengeance. A concept that never drove Inoichi before now, seemed a distant, almost irrelevant pursuit. He was a man out of time, centuries removed from his world, his battles, and his revenge.

Perhaps Seth was dead, wounded severely in their last encounter. Inoichi often told himself.

Still, the absence of a clear conclusion to their conflict left Inoichi in a liminal space, caught between the desire for vengeance and the realization of its uselessness.

"In the art of body and mind," Inoichi began after a long silence, "a true samurai does not rely on mere numbers of repetition, but instead," he recited through reps. "The ceaseless flow of time and the relentless perseverance to exceed one's limits."

"Good thing I'm no samurai," Vasilis replied. "You are always so grumpy."

Inoichi could hear him rummaging through the refrigerator. "Of course, a brute Spartan would lack appreciation of intricate techniques."

With a swift motion, he lowered himself and snatched a towel, his footsteps barely audible as they met the soft surface. Sunlight broke into the cabin, filling the room with an orange glow, a stark contrast to the emptiness Inoichi felt since arriving. Absent was the life he was forced to leave behind. His brother, his mother, his sisters—his wife. He wiped his face and readied himself for his kata, needing to push the futile thoughts behind him, for now.

As time unfolded in their newfound world, the rivalry with Vasilis only deepened, sharpening with each training session. Vasilis trained him in wrestling, the shield and spear. While Inoichi taught him *Kendo: The Way of the Sword,* with its many arts of dueling. Then there was *Bushido: The Way of the Warrior,* a code that emphasized the importance of duty, courage, and especially honor in the lives of the warrior.

It was a code of conduct that encouraged selflessness and loyalty. A code Inoichi lived by. He tried to teach Vasilis to lean on technique over physical prowess.

Philosophical differences led to arguments over tactics and strategy. Inoichi would never admit it out loud, but it was refreshing. He couldn't think of the last time someone challenged him, both physically and mentally.

Vasilis laughed, undoubtedly spitting out whatever unhealthy mess he stuffed in his mouth. "Your kata and dancing technique will get you killed in a true battle."

Inoichi smirked. "Perhaps you would like for me to teach you a very painful lesson."

He could hear Vasilis's chewing cease, "Shall we take this outside?"

They decided not to take their weapons, but Inoichi grabbed his tactical watch, and turned to a news station. He was a samurai, a warrior first, but he understood the benefits of learning the political and business climate of this world.

The Cabinet agreed it was best if the two travelers were in familiar elements. It was still a prison, except it was located on an off-grid island in the Pacific Ocean. Still, it was a refreshing escape from the SUV. It didn't hurt that the Cabinet provided them with the spoils they both requested.

The advanced technology of this world allowed them to train in different elements, similar to the war room on SUV, but Vasilsi was right in suggesting they take things outside. Even with all the technology, their new *home* was not the smartest place to spar.

Vasilis opened the cabin door.

Bryce Bennett stood on the other side, a scowling look on his square face. It was surprising to see someone of Bryce's status watching over them, but the SIA leader made it clear that he had no interest in leaving the assets under the watchful eye of anyone else.

At twenty years old, Bryce was two years Inoichi's senior, continuing the trend of young operatives in this world. Inoichi had a deep admiration for the way this world trained its children to be warriors from a young age.

The war between nations killed millions, forcing children to grow up faster than they should, a familiar finality to a horrific symphony of war. It was no surprise Bryce showed little fear. He had only arrived a day ago, but Inoichi imagined he was watching them from afar. The six foot four agent was a man with a strong jaw and few words until today.

There was a moment of silence and Inoichi realized what was coming from his watch. A broadcast of the National memorial for James and Esther, although publicly they were branded as Delta Force operatives. Inoichi shut off the watch, seeing the pain in Bryce's eyes.

"For weeks, you two have walked around as if you belong," Bryce snapped. "My other agents were in awe of you because of your... *gifts*. They may have forgotten what you've done, but I haven't. This is not Japan or Sparta. You are no heir to any throne. Here, in the year 2076, on my island, you are nothing more than pawns in a game none of us enjoy playing. Instead of enjoying the spoils and sparring, how about you use the resources provided for you and find answers?"

Vasilis took a step forward. Inoichi sighed and prepared to step in if necessary. "You harbor these feelings of envy because we peak humans. We are superior—"

"You think?" Bryce laughed and shook his head in disbelief. He cleared his throat, regaining his composure. His blond brows deepened. "You don't get it, do you? Neither of you do. James and Esther were more than soldiers. They helped people. They were a son and daughter, uncle, sister, brother, and now they're dead. Dead! And for what?"

His angered eyes shot toward Vasilis. "You left Malaya in god damn Germany. What do you think is going to happen to her? Yet you're here living the life, and we are no closer to finding Lilith the reason for all this shit. And you... Inoichi Tokugawa. You come off soft-spoken and honorable, but you are nothing more than a spoiled, entitled son of a dictator who is hiding something. Both of you are."

Inoichi stood between them, not caring about either of their scowling looks. No matter how elite Bryce was, he could not defeat Vasilis—he didn't care.

"Vasilis," Inoichi said. "Perhaps meditation would be best. Bryce, you are welcome to join us."

Bryce scoffed and stormed out. Inoichi wanted to tell Bryce that he was right. They were hiding something, but he was wrong about them not caring. James, the former SIA leader and Agent Esther Brovovich were two casualties of time traveling to a world so far removed from their own. Inoichi empathized with them. He heard they fought bravely and prayed their spirits would be born in a place free from war.

Inoichi led the mediation as they waited for the agent who arrived everyday around the same time, Katherine Bennett. She was a relatively new recruit, a lower-ranking operative who happened to be Bryce's sister. Like her brother, she had green eyes and a background in clandestine operations and specialized in intelligence, but the similarities ended there.

Katherine wore her blond hair braided in a style that reminded Inoichi of the warriors from the western lands. Vikings, he learned they were called. She had painted green tips, a contrast to her blond locks. She sat near the window overlooking the beach, her black boots crossed at the ankle as she sipped coffee and watched the news on her tablet. Despite her position as an SIA operative, she seemed almost reluctant to wear the logo on her jacket, as if she weren't entirely proud of what it represented.

"Ino, you were right, MEV just moved back into *Forbes Top 25*," Katherine said after the door shut behind her. "The new mysterious CEO is making waves..." Katherine's voice drifted along with her mind.

Inoichi stared at her for a moment as she sat quietly, lost in thought. There was something different about her. She was forthcoming, as if she did not adhere to any restrictions. In some ways, she reminded him of his sister, especially when she called him Ino.

One day, he hoped to thank both Malaya and his sister for saving his life. If she was alive. *No, she has to be alive*, he thought, cruising himself, knowing one thing that Kasumi was is a survivor.

Kasumi was a warrior, after all, maybe the greatest he'd ever seen. Much of what he knew about the power within was taught to him by her, mostly in secret with Hidetada along with them. Her compassion and warmth were like that of a mother, yet their father had so much hatred for her, for reasons Inoichi cared little to understand.

Why should he? Kasumi had atoned for her sins. Her punishment would have broken any of his other sisters and some of his brothers. No matter what she had gone through, she found a way to persevere. He remembered his mother once said that Kasumi was a sword that had been tempered and polished by fire. Yet, she was like a lotus flower, blooming in the midst of muddy waters.

"Katherine," Inoichi called, breaking her trance. "What has you lost in thought?"

She looked back at him with a smile. "I was just thinking we should take your talents to Wall Street; make us some real money."

She's lying, he thought, continuing to punch the dummy.

Katherine raised a brow. "You should probably take it easy on that one," she warned. "It's the last one they'll send over. I get it. You're strong, but as the saying goes. *With great power comes great responsibility*. Try to hold back... and smile for a change."

Katherine turned back to her tablet. "Hey, Ino, can you quiet down a bit?" She said, waving her gloved hand at him. "MEV's new mysterious partner is about to make his first public appearance."

A woman's voice introduced a man, Achilles Teresi. As he spoke, chills surged through Inoichi's body. *That voice, it couldn't be.*

"Katherine, display your feed!"

"Why? It's just some□"

"Hurry!"

"No need to get so crazed. I didn't think you would be that interested," she said, pulling the video from the tablet and expanding it to a hologram.

Flashes of that fateful night surged through Inoichi's mind. If he hadn't witnessed it firsthand, he would have dismissed the idea that one man could single-handedly take down one of the most fearsome warriors in Japan, the shogun... his father.

His heart broke all over again thinking about his brother. He didn't deserve to die. He was not a fighter, not like the Inoihci. No matter how bad he wished it to be a nightmare, the tragedy, that voice, was etched into Inoichi's memory. The pain was a constant reminder that he was too late to save them.

"It's-it's him," Inoichi muttered.

Vasilis burst into the room. "It can't be!"

Katherine raised a brow. "What a minute. How do you two know Achilles Teresi?"

The words fell from Inoichi's lips like shards of metal, each syllable cutting through the air. "He murdered my brother and father," he uttered through gritted teeth, his voice a low growl. Every muscle in his body tensed, coiled like a spring, as he inched closer to Vasilis, his eyes burning with an intensity that could melt steel.

"He's family," Vasilis replied, taking a step forward. "He wouldn't have acted without reason. He must have been manipulated, tricked, or blackmailed."

"Or he is a treacherous coward who deserves to die," Inoichi replied, his tone calm compared to the storm that raged in Vasilis, who stood tall with clenched fists.

"Hold on!" Katherine interjected, stepping between them. "You two need to calm down—"

"Hands up," Bryce shouted, pointing his gun at Vasilis, then at Inoichi.

From what Inoichi learned of this world, it was an excessive measure to have a gun drawn on two unarmed men. Yet, history has proven that abuse of power is human nature. Neither he nor Vasilis were ordinary men. There was no doubt in Inoichi's mind that Bryce's decision to draw his weapon was made in haste.

No, this was a culmination of days spent in unease, watching, waiting, and wondering what it would take to subdue such beings if the need arose.

They were warriors with abilities far greater than any one man should have to face alone. Bryce was inferior and afraid despite his authoritative title, and his weapon made him feel safe.

Inoichi's thoughts returned to a piece of wisdom he'd encountered, a truth spoken by a poet from an era long passed named Nas. *People fear what they don't understand and hate what they can't conquer.*

Standing before them was proof of that, an echo of a dark history. Inoichi and Vasilis exchanged glances, a quiet understanding shared between them. They both knew this world, these people feared them.

Bryce's voice, firm with the weight of command, broke the tension, albeit momentarily. "Don't take another step," he warned, his resolve clear but his hands betraying a slight tremble. The authority of his position clashed with the visceral fear of the unknown powers he faced.

"Relax, Bryce," Katherine said. She placed a gentle hand on her brother's shoulder, a silent plea for peace that seemed to reach him. "Something freaked them out. They are warriors, after all. No reason to get your panties in a bunch."

Bryce's shoulder relaxed as he lowered the weapon, easing the tension that once filled the room. "You need to remember I am your commanding officer, *Sergeant* Bennett," his tone softened as he reluctantly holstered his gun.

"Right, sorry," Katherine rolled her eyes. "Let's just give them some time, *Commander*."

Bryce took a long look at them before allowing Katherine to drag him out the door. "I'll have you placed in cryo," she whispered, mocking Bryce.

"That's why your voice is deeper than mine," Bryce retorted.

"My cock's bigger too."

"Screw you, Kat. I hope you stay in New York," he replied, closing the door.

Inoichi and Vasilis were left alone. "I must go after him," Inoichi said. "I know what he means to you. For that, I will let you say your piece, and then I will kill him."

"I will not let you do that," said Vasilis. "There has to be a reason why he did it. Maybe he was brainwashed, or maybe it wasn't really him. You and I both know what this world is, what they can do, their machines... technology. No, there has to be a reason or some sort of explanation."

Inoihci sighed. "If it wasn't him, we will find out. But if it was, and he did it for his own gain, there's no excuse for murder, and he will pay."

Vasilis grumbled. "It will not come to that, but we need to be sure before we take any actions."

Inoichi nodded in agreement. He needed to meditate, so he kneeled in front of the fireplace. Though it was hard to ignore Vasilis rummaging through the icebox, using food to suppress his anger. Katherine sat at the table, going through documents or communicating with someone. Whatever she was doing had her pacing in silence.

Katherine finally broke the long silence, her voice no higher than a whisper. "If you two believe Achelis to be a traveler from the past, I need as much information about him as you can think of."

Inoichi remained still, his skepticism a heavy cloak. "How do we know you won't use it against us?" he asked, the question laced with caution. "You haven't been entirely transparent about who you are, nor where your loyalties lie."

A weighted pause stretched between them, the air thick with unspoken thoughts. Inoichi's eyes remained closed, yet his mind raced, analyzing every possible outcome.

"There is no way for you to truly know," Katherine admitted, her voice steady, reflecting a sincerity that caught Inoichi off guard. "But I will tell you everything you wish to know. And if, in the end, you still feel you cannot trust me, I understand. However, the truth is, we are bound by a common thread in this mangled pile of shit. We need each other."

Inoichi settled beside Vasilis and Katherine, a silent specter drawn to the flickering candle of truth she was about to reveal. As Katherine unwound the threads of her identity, Inoichi felt as if he were watching ink spill across parchment, the dark fluid of her words sketching a picture of intrigue, betrayal, and hidden daggers.

Katherine was not merely a detective. She was an artist of deception, painting her strokes within the very gallery she sought to expose. Her canvas was one of murder and corruption, a landscape callused by the scars of dark secrets.

Now, Inoichi and Vasilis found themselves at the epicenter in this grim portrait, figures pulled into the foreground of a scene they had not anticipated. So were those who killed his brother and father—the Spartans that destroyed his home.

Katherine leaned forward. "At the center of it all was one woman, Lilith Castillo-Grant."

"This is our way off the island," said Inoichi. "We can use this information as leverage."

"Ha!" Katherine scoffed, almost mockingly. "They will not let either of you off without an escort."

"Or a cover," Vasilis said.

There was a tense pause. Katherine sat there, thinking. "Okay," she finally said. "Natwat could help."

"Can we trust him?" Inoichi questioned.

Vasilis nodded in agreement. "I believe we can."

"We aren't telling him everything," Katherine said. "Just enough to get you off the island. I leave for New York in a month. I have a...meeting with a contact. I'll arrange a meeting with Natwat to discuss strategy before you meet with General Williams."

Contact? What are you hiding? Inoichi thought. *Rather, who are you hiding?*

Katherine's revelation—that she was, in fact, an investigator of truths—slotted the last piece into the puzzle for Inoichi. From her initial appearance, an air of mystery clung to her, her demeanor marked by a keen intelligence and a certain craftiness, Inoichi recognized.

She possesses the makings of a formidable shinobi, he thought, keeping this observation about Katherine in the front of his mind. Despite the enigma she presented, she had honored her commitments. He respected her for that.

A month later, the meeting with Natwat gave them the opening to meet with General Williams. It wasn't often the general traveled to the island. Natwat rode with them a few miles away from where their cabin to another at the end of the road boarded by tall trees. Inside was full of smoke and simple, with only a chair and a bowl of fruit.

General Williams sat drinking whiskey from an old bottle and smoking a cigar. "I don't know if Natwat or Vasilis here warned you, but I hate being summoned."

"He knows," said Vasilis.

"I assure you this will not take up much of your time," said Inoichi.

"What can I do you for?" He said, putting out the cigar.

"We are ready to be more forthcoming," said Inoichi.

General Williams nodded. "Well, spit it out."

"Get us off this island," Vasilis demanded. "In return, we will tell you the truth about Achilles Teresi."

There was a brief pause. Inoichi thought he saw a glint of shock on the general's face, but it was hard to tell.

General Williams stood up. He cocked his head and grinned, suspiciously. "What reason do you have to travel our world? If it's women or men you want. I can arrange."

"Well, since you asked—" Vasilis started.

"Neither," Inoichi snapped.

"Fine," Vasilis shook his head and refocused. "Sir, imagine being a prisoner in every way without the title itself. That is what we are. Why? Because of someone else's actions. Have I not given you information? The least you can do for me... for us, is grant us the opportunity to see the great city of New York."

"The neurolinks have opened our eyes to the world," Inoichi added. "We understand you are an honorable man and one of great influence, who is also well-traveled. Would it not behoove you to have warriors with experience of the world beyond SUV or this island."

"Cut the shit," General Williams snapped. "This ain't about me at all."

The words struck Inoichi in the stomach. He could see the same disappointment in Vasilis.

"You're young," General Williams continued. "I get it. You want to travel the world, shit. New York isn't the worst place to travel. Tell you what. Give me something to go on. Something palpable, and we might have a deal."

"Teresi is from Sparta," Vasilis said before Inoichi could answer. "That's all I can tell you.."

"I'll be damned," General Williams replied. Inoihci was certain he was shocked and amused. "Consider your one-time trip to New York booked under one more condition."

Inoichi looked at Vasilis, then at General Williams. "What is it?"

"You work for me and catch Malaya."

KASUMI

Germany, 871 AD

Slowly, Kasumi's awareness crept back, the world around her coming into hesitant focus. Shadows of men in boiled leather chest plates moved at the edge of her vision, their figures blurred and indistinct as they searched, fortunately, looking away from her for the moment.

"Malaya," she whispered, quickly spotting her lying unconscious.

Using the shade of darkness, Kasumi picked herself up and dragged Malaya to a nearby tree as the men approached. With Malaya safe, she knew what she had to do. Kasumi called their attention.

"Looks like we found an unexpected gift," said a bald, sturdy man with a brown cloak. "I was looking forward to seeing someone bleed, and we ran into a little cunt."

A burst of soft laughter rumbled around the group of ten.

"You may get your wish," Kasumi replied, staggering, wielding her chained kunai.

"You speak our tongue...interesting. What to do with you now?"

"Cut off her nipples and stuff them in her mouth," one man shouted

"Stuff her ass," said another.

Kasumi's chain spun faster with every insult. "I'll kill you two first."

I'll make sure to keep my rotations brief and concise. Kasumi tried to convince herself that she would defeat them, even as the fogginess clouded her thoughts.

As her chain spun, the tip of the kunai lightly grazed the leaves on the ground, creating a faint scratching sound, the sound of death.

They would find no mercy here.

The sensation was all too familiar yet unwelcome, stirring memories Kasumi preferred remained dormant. The inner beast, her kitsune essence, recognized in Japanese folklore as a Tenge, one destined to transform, was stirring. This ancient heritage likely fueled her swift recovery and her unsettling craving for blood.

In times past, she might have relished the challenge these men presented. But now, she acknowledged with a grim acceptance, the curse's weight bore heavily upon her. Reaching the Eighth-Tail-of-Knowledge had brought immense power, yet it teetered on the edge of overwhelming her very being.

Azmani's warning echoed ominously in her mind, "Should you transform, there's no telling if the bloodshed could be halted." The gravity of his words weighed heavily on her.

Malaya's safety was paramount. Despite Kasumi's efforts to suppress the beast, her senses sharpened, a cold, empowering chill cascaded over her skin, fortifying it against the impending danger. She could not transform.

Fighting as a human would have to do—

The leaves crunched behind her. As a glint of spiked metal flashed in the corner of her eye, she instinctively ducked, avoiding the club aiming for her head.

With precise agility, she countered, driving her shoulder hard into the attacker's burly chest. The momentum allowed her to plunge her bo-shuriken deep into his knee. The Iron rod spared no one. A gruesome crunch signaled the shattering of bone, a howl of pain followed.

Cruel laughter came from the surrounding men, an eerie tune to the unfolding violence. As he clumsily dropped the club, reaching for his injured knee, she seized the moment. A forceful head-butt shattered his nose, sending him reeling backward, he dropped his weapon giving her the space and time she needed for the rod to find his neck.

One-by-one the mocking grins of her attackers disappeared, replaced with a grim expression. There would be no teasing of a fallen friend, or a song about how they had taken two women. The only song would be the one of death, Kasumi would be the composer.

She met the gaze of each adversary, extending an unspoken invitation through the silent language of her fingers.

Driven by a warrior's rage and wounded pride—they charged her with blind fury. The one with the silver arm bands came first, Kasumi marked him as the leader. His axe came up, baiting her to entangle it with her chain. She accepted the invitation, coiling her chain around his weapon and wrenching it from his grasp with a forceful pull.

He closed the distance, a forbidden step in this dance, predictably a dagger appeared.

Same trick, a different man. Kasumi tossed the opposite end of the chain into his face, the iron ball smashed his forehead, a melodic thud just before he crumpled to the ground.

Two others joined, an axe and a sword were their instruments of choice. Kasumi moved with grace, throwing the bo-shuriken, but he blocked it with his chain-mail—she never meant to kill him. She simply wanted to create a chance to meet the swordsmen head-on.

Kasumi's chained shuriken sang the melody before she yanked the man's axe to the ground. She eyed the weapon. It was larger than she was accustomed to, but it would have to do.

Her Tenge gift allowed Kasumi to hear the rest of the men charging, which meant their dance would have to end soon. Unfortunately for them, a few seconds was all she needed.

In the end, they were mere brutes—warriors and murderers of the defenseless—unversed in the art of pitched battles where she was forged into a soldier. There was a difference. Today, they would receive their brutal lesson.

He swung in a short, conservative thrust, offering her more respect than she anticipated. His mistake. Nimble footwork allowed Kasumi to close the gap between them, masterfully maneuvering her axe down his blade, to knock the swordsmen off balance.

Her kunai sliced his hand to the bone, forcing him to drop the sword. She looped the chain around his neck, securing him in place, ending their dance. Kasumi had barely broken a sweat.

The kitsune's snarls and barks were louder than ever. Singing for more battles, more blood with a power that roared like an orchestra reaching its crescendo. It was like a drug her body craved, and she did her best to keep it at bay.

Control, control, she told herself, yet the Tenge cries suggested, *we can kill them all. Malaya would be safe.*

Kasumi closed her eyes, the high of the kitsune taking over. However, the moment was short-lived.

Malaya stumbled forward. "We yield," she said in surender.

Kasumi snapped her neck toward the time traveler. "Why did you come out? They did not spot you. You have a mission. I am no one, remember?"

"Take them both," the leader said, signaling his men.

"I don't think so—" Kasumi felt a pinch in her neck.

She removed a dart—and darkness soon took over.

Malaya, Kasumi thought, fighting through dizziness. She looked around and realized she was naked. She trembled, frantically tugging on the metal brace around her neck. And the steel chains that bound her naked body to dozens of other humans.

"Malaya!" She spotted her friend, who was just as exposed.

"Relax, sweet bunny, no one stuffed ya with their carrot," a girl said. Her voice was unusually cheerful and high, given they were being held captive. "The same goes for brown bunny over there."

Unlike the others, she was chainless, playing with paint in the air as if it were her canvas. A black tunic covered half her body, and her fallen dirty gold hair covered her ghostly face. "The boys just wanted a peek. Norman won't let them ruin their best merchandise."

"Take these. The boys want you looking pretty."

She tossed Kasumi two brown tunics with horrible patch jobs and paint all over them.

Kasumi covered Malaya. She woke her, easing her into their compromising situation. After a few tears, she was as calm as one could be. The pale girl did not help matters. "Hey, brown bunny, everything's going to be okay," she said, blowing Malaya a kiss.

"Brown bunny?" Malaya questioned, looking at Kasumi for answers.

The girl tapped her forehead. "They joked about your bunny, saying they had never seen one with so little hair," she giggled, throwing her head back, revealing her thin face and colorless pupils.

"You're blind?" questioned Malaya.

"Can't see a lick. Well, I do see something," she said, putting her red-colored finger up to her mouth. "Shhh."

"I'm Malaya. This is Kasumi," she said. "And you are?"

"Where are my manners? The name is Hildegard... Hilda for short," she said, holding out her red hand. "Oh, I'm going to get you ladies something to eat."

The camp was littered with men. Kasumi scanned the camp as Hilda walked away. It was spread out in a large flat area right outside of the forest. She could hear the drunken men fighting and joking as if they were in a bar and not hoarding slaves.

Anger rose as she realized these were the same men from the black forest. Some of the slaves made it to freedom, and now they were slaves.

From the smoke in the air and laughter, they were near the fire. *Malaya was right*, she thought, *Vasilis should have stayed*. He, like her, was a warrior and would have made a difference.

The other option was to unleash the kitsune within her. Even the thought caused it to stir, restless and eager. But with so many warriors gathered here, she would need to draw upon too much of its power—perhaps three tails or more. She dared not risk it. This camp brought haunting memories of another time, another place, where she lost control. The kitsune had been unleashed, and more than forty samurai fell to its fury.

No, I can't risk the innocent. I must find a way.

"You should have let me fight," she said in Japanese.

"You would have died."

"You dishonor us both. Now, we are slaves. I would rather be dead."

"Not sure what she said, but she sounds angry," Hilda said with a smile, dropping food and water in front of them. "I like you."

Kasumi reluctantly accepted the food. "I cannot say the same."

They ate, forcing down the bread and unfamiliar plain meat. Water made it easier to swallow. "I can get us out of here," said Malaya.

"Shhh," said Hilda. "No one speaks of escape. If you try." She slid her finger across her throat.

Some of the other slaves gave them sour expressions. Freedom was not an option around here. They could lay and accept their fate; she would not. Kasumi rolled her eyes and turned to Malaya.

"Speak in my native tongue," she said in Japanese.

"There are sixteen possible ways to escape. Fifteen will get us killed and raped, not sure in which order."

"That only leaves one. What is it?"

"Probability is low, but it involves outside help," Malaya explained, careful not to draw attention to them from the others or the men.

"No, that is not a good idea," said Kasumi. "I have another—"

"Pssst, Hilda, can you call Norman?" Malaya said, interrupting her. "My throat is sore."

"I hope whatever you are planning doesn't get ya killed. Norman! Chocolate bunny wants you."

"Your wounds," Kasumi started before looking at Malaya, who had completely healed. "How?"

Malaya shrugged. "Maybe it's the... "

She trailed off as Norman hobbled toward them. "What do you want?"

"Your food tastes horrible. Back home, I am the town's greatest cook. I'm sure no one else can claim that. Because you did not touch us, I offer that gift to you."

"I will not give you the chance to poison us."

"I'll taste it first."

"This food does taste like shit." Norman rubbed his beard. "Perhaps you can be useful with one eye. Hilda proved the blind have many... *talents*." He let off a robust laugh.

Kasumi pulled on the chain around her neck. It was becoming a habit at his point. She slipped out the wrist knot but kept the appearance she was still tied. All of her training flooded her mind, the days she spent in the Iga mountain, learning how to escape situations like this.

She took a deep breath and centered herself, recalling the discipline and focus that she had learned in the monastery with the Shaolin, a journey that was meant to see her used as a weapon, instead, her quest opened her eyes to a new world.

Kasuumi was ready to strike, but something within cautioned her not to thwart Malaya's plan, no matter how irrational it was. In truth, Kasumi had another reason, a nagging feeling that could not be dismissed. *Perhaps there was something divine at work.*

"I'll need my sack," Malaya said. "And a blanket. It's cold."

"Fine." He grabbed Malaya's arm, leading her away. "Do not try anything stupid."

With clenched jaws, Kasumi watched Norman forcefully remove the woman, turning the *hare away* from the fire.

Malaya dug into Kasumi's sack and grabbed some herbs. She dropped them into the fire and used the wet blanket to hover over it, allowing smoke to build.

"Who let this cunt out?" said one man.

"Get her away from the fire!" Norman shouted. His face twisted in anger.

The soldier grabbed Malaya, moving the blanket. A mushroom of white smoke filled the night sky, and a large fire followed.

"You bitch!" An armored man's gauntlet crashed against Malaya's cheek, sending her sprawling to the ground. Gasping for air, she barely had a moment to recover before a boot slammed into her stomach. She doubled over in agony, clutching her stomach. Kasumi saw the man draw back a fist, his eyes gleaming with malice.

"What are you trying to pull?" he growled, his voice dripping with venomous intent.

"Forget the girl," Norman shouted, practically saving Malaya. "Put it out. Quickly!" His men stomped the flames, but their boots caught fire. "Lock her up now."

A man dragged Malaya by her hair. Kasumi tugged on the chain, watching helplessly. "Should we put her in the cage?"

"No," said Norman, yanking another slave along. "That's for him."

It was him, the man who put us here.

After caging the man, Norman picked Malaya up and then slapped her back into the dirt. "Can we have some fun with her, captain?"

"No," Kasumi shouted, rising to her feet.

Hilda shoved her back down. "Don't."

"What are you doing?" Kasumi raged. "I'm going to kill you."

"You're making me jealous," Hilda said, ignoring her threat, turning toward the men she exposed herself to. "I thought I was your fun girl. Besides, she can't take you, and she's no good if you damage her."

"You're right," said Norman, dragging Malaya back to Kasumi. "Another move like that, and I will let my men have their way with her—while you watch."

Kasumi looked at Malaya. "Was this part of your plan?"

Malaya lay quietly, staring into the starless black sky. Tears streamed down her face as the three men had their way with Hilda. All Kasumi could do was hold her, for all of her smarts, it was easy to forget how young she was.

Time passed, and the horror ended. Hilda returned, joyful as when she left. Malaya jumped up. "I'm so sorry."

"Sorry?" Kasumi snapped. "She smiles as if she enjoyed it. Why do you think she's free? I swear I would open your belly myself."

Hilda didn't seem to care at all. Her white eyes scanned the night sky, ignoring Kasumi. It was an empty threat, but Hilda infuriated her. She met women, girls like Hilda, who loved to give themselves away for a better life, for better things.

She was around it most of her youth, the many women who threw themselves at her father. It was disgusting. Women could be better than that. Yet, here Malaya was empathizing for her.

"Green is in the air..." Hilda's voice trembled with fear. "The color of... death. Death is here—"

A flood of armored men with large shields surprised the drunken Franks. "Rollo and the Vikings," Malaya exclaimed.

Shouts erupted, the men fought, and the slaves panicked, pulling everyone in different directions. The rope came off her wrist. "Everyone, calm down," Kasumi shouted. "We must work together."

"Hilda," Malaya shouted. "She can help."

Kasumi looked back; she was gone. "Your *friend* will not save you again. Everyone else, stay low, move together."

They moved as one, doing their best to avoid the battle. Those who did not listen were cut down. "Kasumi look," Malaya shouted. Hilda was heading toward them.

"I'm going to kill her," Kasumi said.

"Hey bunnies, how are you leavin' without this?" She said, holding up keys, slowly approaching. "I'm going to free you now. Please don't cut me open."

"Just free us."

Now free, Kasumi guided the others to safety, fending off attackers. A voice called out for help. From the corner of her eye, she spotted Malaya walking toward the man in the cage.

Malaya kneeled, locking eyes with the desperate man before dropping the key in front of him.

We need our weapons. Kasumi led the way, trying not to draw attention to themselves. Men begged for death, crawling for help. Malaya was frozen, staring at the bloody chaos.

"Malaya! Our weapons."

"I see them." She snapped out of it and ran toward the weapons.

"Wait!" Kasumi ran after her.

Fleeing men knocked them over, trampling over Kasumi. Boots slammed against her ribs, taking the wind out of her. Bodies piled over her.

She looked up, searching for Malaya in the chaos. She found her being held captive by Norman. She fought relentlessly, holding the wood of the axe as his burling arms pushed down.

Kasumi's vision faded, her breathing shallowed and left her body. Flashes of her life flooded her mind, a child she would never hold, a love she would never know, friends she would never make, a destiny she would never fulfill. Was this how she was going to die? Life being choked out of her. No glory.

The kitsune inside of her snarled, wanting out of the cage. So she let her out.

A flood of energy jolted her. She moved men twice her size. She had room to breathe. *I need to get to Malaya.* Then Rollo appeared. He hovered over her with his great hammer. She was too weak to fight back. *Here I come, Fukumatsumaru.*

"Save your tribe," Rollo said, helping her up.

"Thank you," she said before he disappeared into battle.

She ran toward Malaya, though the distance was too great. Malaya could no longer fight Norman off.

Suddenly, his eyes widened—an arrow protruded from his neck. He dropped the axe, falling to his knees. Malaya gasped for air, Kasumi rushed over, so did Hilda.

A slim, well-built deep brown skin woman stood over Norman's fallen body holding a spear. Her skin was smooth and swarthy, filled with white markings. "You three come with me. Now," she demanded, heading into the darkness.

JOSE

New York, 2076 AD

J ose stumbled out of bed in the crisp, early morning, his mind heavy with the weight of recent events. He yearned for his favorite coffee spot in New York, the only place that printed newspapers, an old habit instilled in him by his great-grandfather. Given the hacks and breaches, it was best to go back to the nearly ancient ways of getting the news.

The constant travel between New Seattle and New York was exhausting, but a walk to his coffee spot would help him clear his head. Though he couldn't rest until he found a way to help his granddaughter, Malaya.

At least New York hadn't changed much. Sure, some cf the tall buildings have changed over time, but it was still busier than ever. His heart skipped a beat as he thought he saw Malaya on an eclectic scooter.

"Fuck off!" she shouted as he stumbled back.

His stomach twisted at the thought of Malaya alone in the past. The Cabinet was displeased with her recklessness, and Jose couldn't blame them. Malaya had sent a warrior from Japan to the present day, an act that could have grave consequences. Having one of those warriors was one thing, but two.

Jose prayed the young men could adjust to their society. Though, being confined to an island surrounded by the world's elite was hardly the best way to welcome him. At least he had Vasilis to help him acclimate.

When he returned without Malaya, he was interrogated and handled things well. Jose was grateful that Vasilis provided a small glimmer of when he returned with information on Malaya's whereabouts—Germany, in the year 871 AD.

Malaya had been gone for over a month, and his mind was plagued with negative thoughts. Jose's blood ran cold at the thought of how much time had passed. He was no scientist, but he understood the laws of time travel. For every day spent in the past, two days went by in the present.

The deafening siren of an ambulance flying overhead roared past him. It was still an odd sight. Flying cars were restricted to AI-driven emergency vehicles. No thanks to a restriction he helped implement with the treaty he signed with the UNA. To this day, he didn't understand why they wanted to ground Americans. Censoring and limiting the internet was understandable, but why cars?

It was a question he never cared to ask the old UNA emperor. The memory of how he lost control of the war was sickening, especially given the control he and Diamond Wolf had during the transitional period.

Maybe control was too strong of a word, but Red always had his fingers in everything, which left Jose, even as president, feeling more like a puppet than a master. And now he was losing control of his family.

From the start, part of him knew that sending Malaya was a bad idea, though for very different reasons. He couldn't have thought she would go rogue. Then again, she was a Castillo, and a Grant—it was in her blood. He stepped off the sidewalk to let a woman and her child pass.

Not a day went by that he didn't think himself stupid for underestimating her. How naïve could he have been to think that she wouldn't take matters into her own hands?

After all, it was Lilith who had taken things too far, putting him and Malaya in an impossible position. They were going to arrest her, and Malaya would be the one to do it.

Bradley's words replayed in his mind. *There is no stone I will not turn to bring in a terrorist.* His stomach twisted as he thought about that day. It would come. It had to happen.

He hated that Lilith felt like she couldn't come to him. If she told him her plans, their plans, would he have listened? Not likely. He would have talked her out of whatever crusade she was planning. Something he failed at with his wife...

"MEV Inc.'s grand tour begins again this weekend. Tickets for Zeus are running out..." a voice from a billboard forced him to look up.

It was him. Achilles Teresi, MEV's newest majority owner, advertising the company's public opening. In only a brief amount of time, he changed things dramatically. To the displeasure of the board, MEV entered foreign territory with weaponry and a blatantly transparent business relationship with the UNA.

Aside from the well-traveled Greek aristocrat, no one knew who he was. The model of perfection, the online magazines called him. Jose knew better. It was all a facade, a carefully constructed persona designed to hide the true nature of the man. Jose knew better than most what that was like. He, too, was a man of power and influence, with skeletons buried in places no one could find.

The whine of passing cars and the buzz of UNA drones blending into a white noise that he barely registered. A crowd of people blocked the entrance of the restaurant. *This is getting out of control.*

The number of protestors had grown over the weeks since the public opening. So did the support for Lilith. But this, this was the largest crowd yet, and the sun had barely come up.

Protestors on one side called themselves Ghost. But they were not the super hackers, helping his daughter, the murderers responsible for the UNA emperor's death. They were followers of *a new movement* who hid behind all-white attire and Ghostface masks.

Then, there was the Brotherhood of Freedom. They wore no masks, just a tactical vest with corresponding attire and plenty of rage. They resembled a militia with a sign that read:

Government Conspiracy, False Arrest, and *Down with MEV.*

Given the size of the crowds, news crews were sure to be on their way. Jose hid behind the collar of his tan trench coat and brown fedora. He sighed and pushed through the mob, feeling the pain these people felt. BOF was a necessary scapegoat...

A gentleman bumped into him. "Sorry, sir," the boy said. "You should watch where you're going, old man."

Careful not to reveal himself, Jose looked up, recognizing the rude Samaritan as the son of an Alpha Kings member and student at HOA Herman Burns. *Why was he in New York?*

"Yeah, you know us old folk," Jose said. "We lose our balance."

"Just watch it," the boy added, suspicion latent in his tone, eyes glancing at Jose's coat pocket.

Jose tilted his head before turning back toward the café. The bell jingled as he entered, leaving behind the noise from the mob in favor of the sweet smell of fried food and coffee grounds. He greeted the only two people sitting at the booth table.

Thomas and Benito, two older gentlemen that sat there every day. They greeted him as Mr. President, which always made him smile and tilt his hat.

Jose grabbed a paper from the stand before taking his seat at the bar, sinking into the soft leather stool, allowing the quiet intimacy to wash over him. The savory aroma of *carne de sada* sizzling on the grill blended with the buttery scent of fried eggs and nutty aroma of cooking tortillas.

"You're late, Mr. President," said the barista, Carlo, his voice sarcastic and bright as his bald spot. He was about fifteen years Jose's senior. His café was known for its Baleadas; it was a historical landmark that withstood the industrial shifts that overtook New York through the decades. "Will it be the usual?"

"*Sí,*" Jose replied, removing his hat and sunglasses.

Carlo raised his thick, snowy brows. "I'll make it a double. You look like hell."

Jose smirked. "*Gracias.*"

Carlo stood at the coffee machine talking to Jose, complaining about the pesky protestors. It wasn't long into their conversation before the bold, sweet steam of *café con leche* warmed his nostrils.

Today, the smell took Jose back to a time when he wasn't a silver fox but a wolf in sheep's clothing; a young, history-making thirty-five-year-old leader of the free world.

It was his first day, but he had prepared for it for a decade. President was a long way from MIT, but a reward he earned after surviving tortuous weeks spent in captivity across enemy lines. He was a soldier with scars that had healed on the surface, but there were others that would never heal.

Those men who tortured him long paid their dues. They did not stand a chance, not with him. If he had a soul, perhaps those unsuspecting pawns would still be alive.

Instead, he unleashed the beast within and reigned hell on all those responsible for his capture, making sure no trace of them or their lineage was left behind. The ordeal made him the champion of the people, but he was something more, something darker.

He was a monster who deserved to die in what is now known as Cupid City. His survival got the attention of those working in the shadows who saw him as a way out of the third world war.

On his first day as president, he walked to the west wing into the White House mess for a *café con leche*. "You don't have to come down here, Mr. President. We deliver," said the man behind the counter, his thick brow raised and voice bright as the blond hair.

Jose leaned in to get a look at his name tag. "Well, Carlo, I don't mind being around the people," he said, basking in the steamy sweetness.

He made his way back to the Oval Office. An agent opened the door, and a cloud of cigar smoke replaced the smell of his coffee. Snakeskin boots were propped up on the table. His stomach turned, knowing exactly who it was.

"Red," Jose stammered. He took a deep breath. "I wasn't expecting you so early."

Red put his feet down and put the cigar out on the table. "Mr. President, you know how long we have been waiting for this moment."

Red stood wearing an all-black long-sleeve shirt with tan buttons and black slim jeans, a belt with a large buckle with shining stones wrapped around his waist.

In the few times they met face to face, Jose never saw him without that belt. His wool coat was thrown on the chair along with his cowboy hat that sat at the far end of the table, making himself right at home. Jose wondered how many presidents he got in that seat. How many didn't do what he asked and ended up dead?

"I imagine you have news."

"I do," Red said in his heavy Mexican accent. His lone gold tooth shone as he smiled. "Russia is out and the UNA borders are forming. India remains protected, their natural borders saved them. Apparently, the bloodshed is not worth it, so the two parties signed a treaty. With air battle eliminated, the UNA only have to focus on two fronts, Europe and America. Africa will hold, for now, strict borders have made most of the countries hard to access. Europe will soon fall."

It's the USSR all over again. How did we allow a simple Asian alliance to get out of control? It's that AI, what's it called, Heaven's Net... Nukes kept humans in check without it His thoughts trailed off.

Jose frowned and gritted his teeth. "So, the bloodshed on our soil is acceptable? It's still a war zone on the west coast."

"A war zone? No." He swayed his head back in mocking amusement. "You lost that battle, along with Alaska and parts of Canada," he said nonchalantly. "Don't worry. The south has guns, it will be fine. Come, sit."

Red gestured toward the chair, taking a step back. Jose took a seat on the plush, velvet-upholstered chair, a piece he had imported specifically for its exquisite craftsmanship and comfort.

Jose was not naïve.

He knew the Oval Office would never truly be his; at least he got to choose the furniture. His gaze found the painting that once belonged to Angela. He mocked her for spending so much money on what he called a simple painting, but he understood why she loved it.

It was a quiet, empty beach at dawn. The sky is just beginning to lighten, with shades of pink and orange peeking through the clouds. It was a tranquil piece of art, but there was also a sense of nothingness to all, with the smooth and untouched sand, except for a few footprints leading down to the water's edge.

The ocean was calm, with small waves lapping gently at the shore. In the distance sat a solitary sailboat could be seen on the horizon. At that moment, the weight of it all hit him. The love of his life was gone, this ongoing tension, this war was to blame. If he could stop more blood from being shed, he would. That's what Angela would have wanted.

"We have the power to stop people from dying and set a precedent for the rest of the world."

"*Órále güey*, don't tell me you're getting cold feet. You know the plan, *our* plan. This is not a request. It is something that must happen. Think of it as divine providence... as our destiny." He felt Red's hands slam on his shoulder. "When this is all said and done, guess who will be revered as a hero? Imagine being the only president, the only leader of any country to defeat the big bad without Russia."

"Ugh..." Jose shrugged him off.

Red raised his arms in surrender. "Our tech and weapons make them unstoppable, our private force taking down key points. This is *our* dream. You want to end this war, do you not?"

"*Si, si,* of course," Jose replied.

"You of all people know that sometimes you have to be evil to do good,"

"*Pai, tu sabes que?*" Jose said, his voice lessening its grit. "I thought... back then, what I was doing was a good thing. Those who I killed deserved it, ya know? There was a time when I cared for human life. Taking a few meant saving the many, pure utilitarianism." Jose sighed. "That was until I saw, truly saw, what I had done, who I had become. How can you save the world with the blood of children on your hands?"

Joe shifted in the seat. Part of him hoped he'd get a response, but his smarter side knew exactly where Red stood.

"Utilitarianism ignores the way that utility is distributed, implying that trading off someone's pain to achieve the greater good of everyone else is acceptable. I admire your will to want to change," Red said flatly, collecting his hat and coat. "But, someone has to be the monster for the greater good... So, don't forget who you represent..."

Diamond Wolf. Jose looked down at his forearm; his white shirt covered what lay underneath.

A tattoo of a wolf with piercing eyes that seem to stare straight through anyone who looks at it, while its teeth bared in a fierce snarl. It was more of a branding than a tattoo.

A buzz in his pocket was a thankful interruption. He stuck his hand inside his coat, removing a silver pocket watch. "Carlo, I-I have to go," Jose said, leaving behind his coffee and a tip. He rushed outside, scanning the crowd, though he knew Herman would be long gone.

Bright lights from cameras and mics were in his face, asking him questions about the new CEO and the mob outside of the building.

Dammit, he thought, readying himself for a response, but Carlo came out with his broom, sweeping a path for Jose.

The cameras and murmurs were behind him Carlo handed him his coffee and a bag, likely with his baleada. "Couldn't let you leave without it, Mr. President."

They exchanged smiles before security escorted Jose the rest of the way. He took the elevator to his penthouse office in the Apollo building. He walked past Achilles's office; it was supposed to be Lilith's. Emma, his assistant, looked up with a smile. He nodded and continued past the empty boardroom to his office.

Jose removed the watch, tracing his fingers across the shiny silver before opening it. A red screen shone, requesting a thumbprint. He took a deep breath before placing his thump onto it. A message from Headmistress Babcock played.

"I've received word that House of Angela's remote locations in England, South Africa, and Canada are preparing to shut down. Seattle is surely next. I'm fearful, for these children are in danger. What will happen if the others find out the truth about the few Darviants? I've done all I can. It's up to you now..." The message started to scramble, erasing itself, leaving behind a blackened screen.

With a sigh, Jose grabbed the framed portrait of him, his wife Angela, and a young Lilith. He stared at it, feeling the weight of Lilith's decision. HOA was closing, and his hands were all but tied. Angela took the reins from her mother protecting Darviants; House of Angela was that place. Now, Lilith's decision to put Teresi in jeopardized everything their family had worked for.

None of it made sense. *Why put someone in power who didn't align with your vision... unless he did?* The thought made Jose sick. He couldn't imagine this is what Lilith wanted, but she chose this man.

He wanted to do more than his power would allow. A boardroom and war weren't that much different. He had to remind himself that force would not win this battle. *This Teresi was no warrior. He was a suit, moving with finesse.*

"Mr. Castillo," Arya's voice brought him back. "Your ten o'clock is here."

"Send her in."

Jose placed the watch inside his desk and the picture back on the bookshelf. He swiped his hand across his desk and pressed the command control to open the windows. The blinds slid back, letting in the morning light just before his appointment walked in.

"Welcome to New York, Katherine," Jose said.

MALAYA

Germany, 871

As they made their way through the dense forest, the silence between them stretched, heavy with unspoken thoughts. Malaya's mind lingered on the slain bodies, a grim reality she was living in.

So much death, she thought, her body suddenly rebelling against the images that haunted her as she doubled over, using a hand to support her wobbling legs while she vomited.

Wiping her mouth with the back of her hand, she tried to steady her breathing, to push the nausea and the images away.

"Grab what you can," Zoya instructed, dragging Malaya back to the present as she pulled sacks hidden behind a rock. "These are things I've collected along the way before those savages captured my husband."

Zoya's pause was pregnant with anticipation, her gaze sweeping over the three women with an intensity that felt almost tangible. "I must ask you something," her voice filled with both hope and a tinge of desperation. "Have either of you seen a man so tall he could touch the stars, his skin dark and beautiful as the night sky?"

The question lingered in the air, and Malaya felt a sudden tightening in her chest. *Tall enough to where he'd stand out. Could it have been?* Her mind raced back to the day she and Kasumi were captured. A tall, muscular black man had been part of their entrapment, and she paid him back by leaving him in that cage—a detail that now gnawed at her conscience.

Was that him? Did I trap her husband?

Snapped back to reality by a gentle nudge, Malaya found herself momentarily lost. "Huh?" she managed, confused.

"I was telling our savior here that I didn't see a thing," Hilda interjected, a dismissive wave of her hand accompanying her words.

Zoya's hopeful eyes, illuminated by the flicker of her oil lamp, turned to Malaya. "Have you?"

"Uh—" Malaya stammered, caught off guard by the question that was forcing her to lie. She played ignorant. "Have I what?"

"Nothing," Kasumi interjected, staring at Malaya as she handed her a sack. "My friend has been through a lot, but we will help you find him. Right?"

"Yea-yeah," Malaya said as her hands trembled. "We'll do what we can to help you find him."

Zoya's forehead puckered. "If he was not with you, then he would have been taken by the Viking to Scandinavia."

Malaya and Kasumi exchanged looks. "That's where we're going," said Malaya.

"We shall travel together," said Zoya. "Let's go."

"Right," said Malaya.

As their journey began, Zoya led the way, Hilda by her side. Malaya stayed behind with Kasumi.

"There's a lot of blue," Hilda said, tilting her head. "Blue is a good color, calming. Perhaps our journey will be more pleasant."

"Perhaps..." Zoya's voice trailed off. "Did you not say you were blind?" Her curiosity echoed the silent questions hanging between Malaya and Kasumi.

This wasn't the first instance of Hilda discussing colors as though she could see them. There had been several moments when Hilda claimed to perceive certain hues, each time linking them to emotions or sensations.

"Am I not allowed to perceive colors?" Hilda questioned, as if it were obvious.

"Hm." Zoya replied simply, picking up her pace.

A sense of unease stirred in Malaya's stomach. She put on a mask of composure, hiding the guilt that threatened to spill from her features. "Eventually, I have to tell her, right?" she whispered to Kasumi.

"Yes, go tell her," Kasumi retorted, "and she will slit your throat. That curved blade is perfect for it."

"That's not funny."

"No, but both are equally true."

"You two should pick up your pace," Zoya said. "We must set up camp. We can start again at first light."

The starlit night wasn't enough to help Malaya sleep. Death plagued her, James and Esther haunted her, and so did the replaying of the dead bodies piled atop one another... that child. She may have left a man to endure the same fate. And here she was, lying next to his wife, the woman who saved her life.

Maybe this was all a mistake. She let the tears stream down her face. *Maybe I'm the monster, and my mother is the savior. Maybe if she got Elvir, things would change for the better.* The tears slowed as the stars flickered until they disappeared into blackness—that's when she saw the lonely girl crying for help.

Malaya ran until the darkness swallowed her, making it impossible to see. She looked around, finding a glint of light and the voice calling from beyond it. With trembling hands, she walked toward the desperate plea. When she was close enough, she reached out.

"Help!" a girl shouted.

Malaya jumped up, panting. She rubbed her face, then slowly scanned the camp. "I'm losing my... mind..."

There she stood, off in the brush, her eyes glowing red, like her hair. She nudged Kasumi. "Are you up?"

"Of course," she grumbled. "I often lay awake with my eyes closed."

"Now is not the time. There's a girl. She needs our help," Malaya said, pointing at the girl.

Kasumi looked. "I see no one. You need to rest your mind. Perhaps we should—"

"No, I don't need meditation," she said, realizing she raised her voice when Hilda and Zoya awoke.

"Now Kasumi, no means no," Hilda mumbled.

Kasumi grunted something before lying down.

"I know what I saw."

Zoya sat next to Malaya. Her heart pounded. She tried not to avoid her sad eyes, but it was difficult. "You are not well," said Zoya. "If you want to unburden yourself, you may."

Malaya looked over at Kasumi, hoping she'd save her, but she was out cold. *Telling her the truth now would not make things better. There's an eighty-five percent chance the Vikings took her husband to Scandinavia.*

"My medication is gone, and without it—"

"You're free," said Zoya. "I heard what you said about the girl. I can hear your cries when you sleep—we all can."

"I-I'm sorry."

"You should not apologize for being who you are. Embrace it. You are too busy living in here," Zoya tapped the side of her temple. "Get out of your head. Accept there are not always answers for the unexplained nor the unexplored. The problem is, you are a nonbeliever, yet you have something special."

Zoya handed her a waterskin laced with herbs. "My husband, he was like us, *gifted*. He also needed to quiet his mind. This is from my home. It should help you—and *us* get some sleep."

"Thank you," she said before taking a large gulp. The earthy taste blended well with the cool water. They sat there for a while, contempt in silence.

The calming effect came rapidly, but the wandering girl lingered in her mind.

Malaya's eyes darted into the brush, waiting for the girl to call out for help–nothing. *Special?* She thought, staring at the bottle. *What am I if I'm hallucinating?*

Malaya removed her tomahawk. She passed her hand over her gift, the last gift her mother gave her—a reminder of her father. The red gem sat inconspicuously in the slot; its chain dangled around the belly of the hatchet.

I thought I was going to lose you. She thought, placing it around her neck.

A surge of energy rushed over her. The gem always seemed to find the faintest of light in the darkest of moments. She remembered when it first happened in Sparta with Aaron. She smiled at the thought that her father wore it around his neck.

Malaya looked up at the endless array of stars, wondering if there was anything beyond that. She sighed before downing the bittersweet liquid that helped her drift off to sleep.

Malaya was jolted awake by screams piercing the quiet of the night. Instinctively, her hand flew to her tomahawk, her mind racing with thoughts of the girl crying out for help. But as her eyes adjusted to the dim light, she saw it was Hilda, curled up on the ground, her head buried between her knees in distress. Malaya, along with the others, hurried over to her side. "What's wrong?"

"The light," Hilda cried, lifting her head, pointing at the bright morning sky. "I lost my covering..."

Malaya rummaged through a sack, saying nothing. She looked at her leg before unwrapping the blood-stained cloth. "Zoya, your blade." She split the blood-stained rag and wrapped Hilda's eyes. "Better?"

"Thank you, ladies. Sorry I scared ya." She touched the wrap and turned in Malaya's direction. "Guess we're blood sisters now."

"Oh, sorry about that. I had to think fast," said Malaya.

"You did good," Zoya's tone carried a hint of admiration. Malaya couldn't help but smile. Zoya turned to Hilda. "Why did you remove your covering?"

"I didn't. I..." Hilda started. Her face reddened like she was embarrassed.

Kasumi placed her hand on Hilda's shoulder. "Whatever it is, we will not judge you."

"Sometimes I wander in my sleep. I have woken up in different places, or I find my way back. It's like another person has control, like I'm in another world, like a dream, but it feels so real. In these dreams, I can see where I have been..." Her voice trailed. "I know it sounds—"

"Wonderful," Zoya said. "But we must go now that we have the light. Are you well enough to travel?"

Hilda smiled. "Yes. Freedom awaits!"

Malaya and Kasumi helped Hilda to her feet, and they began their journey.

The day turned into night quickly, and the days thereafter. She was no closer to finding her mother or the girl. *Maybe she didn't exist.*

Still, it didn't stop her from hearing that cry for help, nor the dreams. *This could be post-traumatic stress syndrome, considering everything that happened.*

She'd studied enough to know the symptoms. Maybe this was the result of not having her pills. With them, she didn't dream, let alone hear voices or hallucinate. She chuckled to herself. Here she was, hiking in the middle of ninth-century Germany, questioning her sanity and her decisions along the way.

Fatigue was setting in from their long journey. She'd forgotten just how long it's been since the last time they saw a human. There was the gracious farmer who traded some shoes for Japanese short-grain rice.

Since then, food and water. Most of what Zoya gave them was traded away, including the weapons she found. And there was the time their hidden sack was swiped during their visit to a small village. They were down to just rags, relying on streams, hunting, and Hilda's determination to get them what they needed–by any means.

"Kasumi, why are you still brooding?" asked Hilda after they left their last pit stop.

"I do not brood. Your lack of pride and dignity concerns me."

"Hey, that was days ago," said Hilda, grazing the thin trees as they exited the woodlands. "I had Malaya's support before she forgot her tongue. What was it she said?"

Hilda placed her finger under her chin. "Oh yeah, I remember." She cleared her throat to impersonate Malaya. "While I do not agree with her tactics, statistically, it was the most favorable outcome."

Kasumi reached inside the pocket of her oversized stitched-up rags for two old daggers. "Is this what you call beneficial?"

"Yeah, one for each tit," Hilda said, grabbing herself.

"You must admit, that was pretty clever," Zoya said, with a smile forcing Kasumi to do the same.

Malaya's teeth shone through the dirt that covered her face. It was the first time she'd gotten some relief. "We have a sack full of supplies—that's all that matters now," the voice erased her smile.

Even in daylight, the girl's voice called out. At night, it was louder. She wondered if anyone else heard her. If they did, no one said anything—neither did she. Their focus needed to be on finding the riverbank.

"Wait," Zoya said, kneeling, examining the soil. She closed her brown eyes. The breeze brushed back her thin, bronze dreadlocks. "The River Albis is not much further. Telling by your tired look, we should probably stop."

"No."

Dusk and a large hill were ahead of them. They arrived atop the hill. A dense blue, endless red, and pink painted the sky. At the bottom, soft purple made up the vegetation. Malaya marveled at the sea of mauve calluna covering the heath. Flowers in this cool air? It must be late summer.

"Why'd we stop?" Hilda asked.

"It's beautiful," said Kasumi. "Reminds me of home. The land is covered with—"

"Wait!" Malaya shouted, seeing the girl from the woods.

She darted down the hill after the girl, leaving the others at her back. She sprinted through the field, not caring where she was. It was just like her dream. She ran through thick trees, twigs, and branches, not caring about the inevitable cuts on her arms and legs or the darkening forest.

"I know you're scared. Please, let me help you—" She lost her footing and stumbled into a stump. Her vision blurred before it blackened.

"Malaya," she heard a voice call out.

She opened her eyes to Kasumi and Hilda hovering over her while Zoya stood with arms folded and face pinched in anger.

"I am happy you are alive," said Zoya. "Now I can kill you."

"Where's the girl?" said Hilda, helping to hold Malaya up.

"There is no girl," Zoya's voice was stern like her face. "We are lost, like her mind."

"There was, I—"

"Please," a hallowing voice echoed.

Malaya looked around. The girl's voice seemed so clear it was sickening. Sweat dripped down her face as the cool breeze countered her burning skin. "Did you hear that?" Malaya questioned.

"Yes," Zoya said, the same shocked expression as the others.

"Please what?" Hilda shouted.

"Quiet," Kasumi urged. "We know nothing of who or what we are dealing with."

"Black," Hilda said. "I see black with sparks of blue."

"What does that mean?" Kasumi asked.

"Death and despair. She needs us."

"No," Zoya whispered. Her eyes cut to Malaya. "We do not follow evil. We go the opposite direction."

If looks could kill, she'd be dead. Kasumi stepped in front of Zoya. "We should help. We can help."

Zoya took a deep breath. "We find this girl, rescue her, and then we go."

They all agreed.

Silence accompanied their movements through the slim trees. Zoya led alongside Hilda, who claimed to see a trail of black and blue. Malaya struggled to believe anything beyond what she saw or heard. It did not matter since she deduced the voice came from the direction in which they were headed. The uncertainty of their future weighed on Malaya.

The air suddenly became dense and dry, as if they were in a high-altitude landscape. However, Malaya knew that was geographically impossible. It wasn't cold, yet goose bumps covered her skin. They stopped at a long-standing timbered fence stretching past the end of the heath.

"Do you feel that?" Zoya asked Kasumi.

"Yes. There is something mystical at play," Kasumi said.

Malaya scoffed. "No. We are in an unfamiliar area where the air and climate itself change. It's natural philosophy, not magic—"

Kasumi and Zoya shot a look at Malaya as if to tell her to shut up, so she did.

They all looked out at the small house with a flickering porch lamp. A lone wooden chair stood facing the flowers, with a small table next to it. Wood and stone formed the sturdy house. There was a tall young man collecting wood with a ginger braid that draped across his burgundy tunic.

He spotted them. "Father! We have visitors," he said, carefully putting down the logs and raising his arms. "You can come out."

"What do we do now?" said Malaya.

"We fight only if necessary," said Kasumi, leading the way.

A man stepped outside, his white beard as robust as his stature. He was bigger than Rollo, with a goatee that hung to his belly. "Inside Gier," he said, never taking his eyes off them.

"Father," Gier pleaded.

The man's white eyebrows deepened — Gier hurried inside. "Put your weapons down, women! Or I'll have my axe put them down for you!" His voice burrowed through the wilderness as he brandished a two-handed axe.

No one moved. He took a step forward. "Heed my warning. This does not have to be your fate."

"Why aren't we running?" Hilda questioned.

"We've come for the girl in the woods!" said Malaya.

The tension in his face changed to confusion. Before he could respond, the door behind him opened. An elderly woman appeared. "Sigurd, lay your axe before you hurt someone," said the woman, whose skin hung like her silver hair. "These women are not here to see you."

"Come ladies, ignore my angry son," she said, waving them in.

Malaya raised a brow, staring into the eyes of a woman with an uncanny resemblance to her great-grandmother. *This is all so odd.*

Sigurd slammed his axe into a tree stump, splitting it in two. "Gier! Let's go! Your brother is taking too long," he said, storming toward the women.

They guarded themselves until he passed. Gier was right behind him. "It's okay, ladies. My grandmother is the sweetest woman you'd ever meet. And I'm sorry about my father."

"Gier!" Sigurd shouted, hurrying his son.

Malaya walked ahead of everyone. *The construct is unbelievable*, she thought, admiring the classic ninth-century home. Small windows and scrolls decorated the walls.

Crates and barrels under the stairway stored their food. Large pieces of fish roasted over the squared fire pit in the middle of the room. The elderly woman led them inside, sitting in a chair at the center of the room.

"Pardon my manners. My name is Mei. Sit-sit," she said, waving her hand. "As a token of my apology, I offer you a drink."

Zoya stood as the others filled the three large wooden chairs, disparately chugging down water from the ceramic cups. "Pull a chair from the back, dear," said Mei, pointing past the bookshelf.

These cups are from ancient Greece, Spartan? Malaya thought, smiling at her.

"No, thank you." Zoya grabbed the fourth pot.

Mei looked at Kasumi. "Please help yourself, one for each of you."

"So long without fish." Kasumi quickly grabbed a piece and took a bite. Her eyes rolled as she sank into her chair. "I do not know how I survived."

"You honor us, I am Zoya. The fish eater is Kasumi from the east, Hildegard of Hesse, and Malaya—"

"I knew a Hildegard once. Can I call you Hilda?"

"Sure gray, you can call me whatever you like as long as you keep feeding us."

Mei smiled. "My true name is Sigrun. Mei is a name the town's people gave me."

"Sigrun, as in the priestess who sacrificed herself so that her brother could win a war?" Hilda said with her mouth full.

Everyone directed their attention to Hilda, sharing the same confused look as Malaya. "Oh." Mei laughed. "The stories have evolved over time and those stories into other stories, like the one about four female warriors wandering the forest."

"I hate folktales," said Zoya.

"I know a story about an African warrior who hated folktales," Mei smiled, taking a sip of wine. "The truth is no folktale, but it is long and dark, one for a later time."

"Well, gray, if your stories mean more fish, count me in," said Hilda.

"Sorry about her," said Malaya. "Thank you for your graciousness."

"It is fine. Hilda is a joy. My concern is you. You came here chasing a young girl with hair of fire, calling for your help. Her cries grew louder the closer you got to this place. Stop me if I speak a lie."

They stopped eating; her crow's feet formed as she grinned at their shock. Malaya cleared her throat. "Where's the girl?"

"The girl," Mei repeated. Her pupils flickered gold as the flames lit her wrinkled face. "Well, she's here, of course, buried underground."

JOSE

New York, 2076

J ose watched as Katherine's green eyes peered out the oversized windows of Jose's office that looked over Fifth Avenue, which sat on the grave of the former Rockefeller Center. Agent Katherine Bennett was always so confident, and her unwavering determination was second to none.

He couldn't help but feel a sense of relief wash over him. She was one of very few people he trusted completely, and the only one he could truly rely on to get to the bottom of things. But there was something different about Katherine. Maybe it was the way she reminded him of himself when he was younger, or maybe it was the fact that he had taken her under his wing from the day she graduated from HOA admiration? Respect? No, it was more than that. Jose realized he had come to care for Katherine like she was his own daughter.

For more than a year, Agent Bennett operated undercover for Jose and trained the Elite Eight, a group of teenage operatives. He remembered when being a teenager didn't involve working covert missions. In this broken world, someone like Jose needed a team he could trust and train for any form of operation. This required special talent and time.

The Elite Eight were handpicked from the greatest boarding school for the gifted, HOA. His wife, Angela, had never intended for her school to become so prestigious. It had been a passion project for children who never fit in, orphans, more importantly, a place for Darviants, the special humans with supernatural gifts who needed protection from a world that didn't understand them. However, after he became president, the school became something more. HOA became a destination for the most talented and powerful students. Katherine was one of them.

Over the past year, some questionable events had occurred, and Bradley was somehow involved. He was now in charge of Project Bungee, and Jose knew better than to think it was all a coincidence. *I knew time travel would be trouble.*

Today, Katherine was going to either prove or dispel his suspicions. She removed the hoodie and pulled down the face cover of the dark brown cowl neck jacket. Her eyes gravitated toward the family portrait. "Lilith looks a lot like her mom."

"They have more in common than looks," Jose said, softly rubbing his wedding ring.

"Yup," she said, making her way to his desk.

"I have something for you." She brushed the loose strands from her blond braids behind her ear before removing manila folders from her leather handbag. "Reports from some crypto-accounts."

"Not many of those around anymore," Jose said, ruffling through the files. "This account has several aliases attached. Please tell me you made sense of all this."

"Mr. C, c'mon, it's me here," she said with confidence. "I have two names, General Bradley Williams and this man." Katherine slid another folder to Jose. "Orenthal James Diya."

Jose examined the files with a raised brow. "Commander James Diya's father..."

It didn't take long for Jose to connect the dots. Orenthal, Bradley, and the others on the account belonged to the Alpha Kings. Jeff Grant's name was missing. Jeff was part of the Alpha Kings; he knew that much, and by extension, Orenthal's name was attached to the antimatter project. Despite the abundance of currency transactions, there was only one that Katherine highlighted. "There was a payment to Rattlesnake five years ago, to that three sixteen account."

The transaction happened before Jeff's death, and Orenthal dropped out of the project a year before that. "Mr. C, I have to ask." Her words dragged, almost as if she didn't want to approach a suspension they both shared. "Do you think that maybe Mr. Grant's death wasn't an accident?"

The springs in Jose's chair creaked as he leaned back and folded his arms. "Several people would have killed for Jeff's data, even a friend," he sighed. "The confirmation by Rattlesnake was the exact dollar amount Orenthal put into Bradley's personal account."

Katherine handed him more files. "General Williams has been digging into Lilith's disappearance fourteen years ago."

"That son of a bitch." Jose shot forward, and the springs snapped back into place. "James's death wasn't anyone's fault. He was a soldier on assignment. Orenthal had to know his son was at risk, no different from Esther, or Malaya, for that matter."

"Sir, do you actually think General Williams and Orenthal are working together on some revenge plot?"

Jose tapped on the desk. Wouldn't he have gone after Malaya if it were revenge? There was something deeper at play. It had nothing to do with Orenthal's son's death.

"Sir," Katherine called again.

"Sorry." Jose slid the papers back to Katherine. "There had been a lot of questions asked about Lilith's disappearance back then." He took a deep breath. "I was one of few people who knew, though I wasn't told by either Lilith or Jeff. I kept silent, but now I am forced to break the promise I had kept to myself for so long."

Katherine tilted her head. "What are you saying?"

Jose sat quietly, reluctant to utter the words, but he had no other choice. "Jeff owed some people, some bad people, the Alpha Kings. He must have thought he and Lilith outsmarted everyone, but I knew their secret."

"Apparently, so did Orenthal," Katherine added.

"Yeah. Look. No one knows who this Rattlesnake is, but if he worked for the Alpha Kings, if Bradley hired him, then he was dangerous—"

"Mr. C, the suspense... it's tenser than a tightrope walker in a windstorm, sir."

Jose exhaled before telling a secret his daughter and son-in-law had kept hidden for over a decade. "Lilith and Jeff... had... another child."

"Holy shit," Kat blurted loudly before quickly lowering voice. "Shit, shit shit. Does Malaya know who she... or he is?"

"It was something her parents wanted to keep a secret for the child's safety. My guess... to protect him from the Alpha Kings. The child's identity remains a mystery, but it won't stay that way for long, not with Bradley lurking."

Why do the kings want their child so badly? Unless they think the child is a Darviant.

"Sir," Katherine said. "What do you need me to do?"

"Nothing yet. You have enough on your plate. Speaking of, what have you learned about Black Mamba?"

"He's a ghost." She handed him more files. "Not one of the Lilith followers, but his history only dates back fifteen years. The woman he remembers as his mother doesn't exist. And his name, Aaron Walker, well, that name belonged to an eight-year-old who died in a house fire in 2065."

"Damn, I knew there was something off about him. And this entire time, he's been lying to my granddaughter."

"Shay was actually the one who performed the screening process, and sir, there's more," Katherine said, removing a USB from her brown calf boots. "Aaron's been working with Lilith."

They quickly cleared the folders off the desk. Jose placed the USB into its port. He opened the software, and countless messages appeared, sorted, and filtered by date and location. Jose opened the most recent message pinged from the island.

Tell Lilith the Cabinet knows about Scandinavia, but not the weapon.

Jose removed the drive. He held onto it for a while. "Apprehending Shay won't do any good. The Cabinet would just assume they were all in on it, and Malaya would be in danger, but Aaron. Well, I could have him brought in for questioning."

"Good thing he's here in New York."

"Why am I just hearing about this?"

"You haven't been answering, sir. Have you checked your messages?"

Jose looked at his phone. It blinked red. No, he hadn't. "Why are they here?"

"Turns out Mr. Teresi is someone they both know very well."

"You mean, he's—"

"A traveler, from Vasilis's time. And according to Inoichi, he murdered his father, perhaps at Lilith's request. Be careful, sir."

"Great work, Bennett," he said before bidding her goodbye. "I'll keep in touch."

That was the shift the Continuum warned us about. Had Lilith really become reckless enough to kill a prominent political figure in two different timelines? Was President Ross next?

They weren't any closer to finding answers. No one knew who really murdered the emperor. Now this, he thought, staring at Aaron's profile. What purpose did he serve? Did she know he was dating Malaya?

Jose's mind wandered as Aaron's picture stared back at him. "Shit," he said, feeling the weight of his actions in his trembling hands. "That can't be him," his heart pounded. He placed a call.

"Cryo Access Code, POTUS 20J32C47," he whispered, hoping what he thought wasn't true. "Arsenal Program... Status update, prisoner Arnold Reeves, codename, Arsenal."

The room spun. He let the phone fall from his hand. *Lilith... Wh-what have you done? Aaron Walker is Arsenal.*

The thought brought images of his early days as president. Red called in one of his favors by requesting Jose greenlight a clandestine operation with his prodigy, Arnold Reeves, as the leader. He knew from the time he met Arnold, Red's driver, that he was special. Of all the members in the Shadow Elite Program, Arsenal was the strongest, most loyal, and the most dangerous. Because of who he was and his power, Jose placed him in cryo—over thirty years ago. That explains why he doesn't look a day over thirty.

Jose cursed himself. Knowing one day Red could find out the truth, his lie, and wake him, but what was the connection to Lilith? A knock at the door startled him. "Open."

"Sir, are you okay?" Arya said, her voice sultry and deep like her golden skin.

"Yes, thank you." He forced a smile. "Come in, come in."

"Of course," she said. Her curls bounced with her blue and white striped swing dress. "I got Kat's message. Here's the burner."

"Pair of yours," he said, examining the glasses.

"Of course."

"Good," he said. She started to leave before he stopped her. "Tell Emma to set up a sit down with Mr. Teresi after the meeting."

"Yes, sir."

"Also, I'll need you to fill in for me at the meeting. I have some things I need to take care of."

The door clicked shut. Jose rested his chin on his hands, his mind racing. He fiddled with his glasses, opening and closing them as he fought the urge to make the call. The weight of his decision pressed on him—this deal could save his family and give him a way back in, at least for now.

He stood and poured a bottle of Malta into a glass, then spiked it with a generous splash of rum. After draining the glass, he stared at its empty bottom, his resolve hardening. Finally, he slipped on his glasses and made the call.

It didn't take Red's hologram long to plant himself in his office. Surprisingly, nothing changed about him — not a thing. He had an old, rugged aura to him. His tan skin had a youthful look to it. As always, he wore a thick mustache and short, curly hair. He looked around Jose's office. "So, this is the work of your baby girl, huh?" he said, with that same charming bright smile he often used to mask darkness within. Jose knew Red better than most. "Oh, how they grow up so fast."

"I want back in," said Jose.

"Just like that. No small talk, huh? No, how are you doing, Red? Sorry for leaving."

"I earned my way out."

"Yes, twenty-five years, four months, and three days ago. Now, I'm just supposed to open my arms."

"I need back in. I'm sure you know that, watching from the shadows."

"We don't need you."

"I have an asset you may be interested in."

"Oh?"

"Ammunition." Red shrugged, pretending to not know who Jose was referring to. "Don't bullshit me, Red. You know who, the kid, Arnold Reeves."

The gold in his eyes burned with interest. His nonchalant tone changed. Now he was paying attention. "I thought he was dead. Why didn't you kill him?"

"Doesn't matter, but don't expect history to repeat itself." Jose knew he had him. One thing he and Red shared was the need to tie up any loose ends.

"What does he remember?" questioned Red.

"Not a damn thing. He's been washed. Still, he's doing what he does best."

"If he gets his memories back."

"I know…" The blinking light from his phone called for his attention. Another missed call from Katherine. "Don't worry. I have it handled."

"Fine," Red said with a golden grin. "You're back in."

"We'll keep in touch." Jose removed the glasses, the hologram disappeared, and he crushed the glasses. He grabbed his phone to call the Continuum.

"Is there an update on Malaya?"

MALAYA

Germany, 871 AD

B *uried?* Malaya tried to shake away the idea that any of them heard the voice of a dead girl, which made little sense. It was like something out of a horror movie. Malaya couldn't ignore the wide eyes stares fixated on Mei. She had to admit that she was surprised too.

However, Malaya knew for certain that ghosts, spirits, entities, or anything paranormal were nothing more than a manifestation, hallucination, or illusion created by the human mind. *People saw ghosts because of a tendency to perceive patterns and shapes, even when they don't exist.*

"Her physical body and mind are motionless," Mei said, "but her spirit remains unrest. You are not the first to seek the girl. Many have come searching, but none could save her."

"She-she's dead?" Malaya said in a soft tone.

"No, and yes," Mei said.

"I don't understand," Kasumi said, beating Malaya to the punch.

"Back then, my skin was youthful and invigilating just like yours," she said with a smile. "A time of great change in the world. Yet I was stuck in a village unwilling to change or forgive. You see, Sigrunn was born different. Like each one of you, she had the ability to tap into great power, but that power, it came from a dark place, a curse she did not deserve…"

Her gold eyes wandered, water filled them, but she didn't let a tear fall. Mei cleared her throat. "I couldn't help her, not as a mother should have, not as I could now…" her voice trailed. So did the look in her flickering gold eyes.

Regardless of what Malaya thought, Mei believed what she was saying. Malaya's stomach knotted at hearing the helplessness in a mother's voice, seeing her pain.

Zoya cleared her throat. "Mei, what happened to Sigrunn?"

"She was unable to control her power. Because of that, many died, and fear reigned over the town." Mei let out a long sigh. "My people demanded death from the abomination. Even gods of foreign lands called for her life. How dare they ask me to take my own daughter's life? I could not. I would not."

There was another pause. Crackling from the fire thundered over the quietness.

"My defiance saw me trick the gods," Mei continued. "I used my life force and help from some allies to place my daughter in a prolonged sleep."

Chills covered Malaya's body. *A barbiturate-induced coma. That's not possible—not in this time period.*

Mei looked into the fire, lost in its flames. "We searched for a cure wherever and whenever we could find it. We even ventured into Tartarus itself, to the banks of the river, seeking help from Styx. Even the daughter of Oceanus and Tethy could not help..." She trailed off, her unusual gold eyes flickered with sorrow. Nothing worked. "And now... now we can't wake her."

The women allowed the silence to linger. They watched the fire burn the wood to ash as they were lost in thought.

"You mentioned *your people*. Who are your people?" Zoya questioned.

"That is a long story for another time," Mei said. "One with wine."

"She was gifted," Hilda said.

"You all have gifts yet to be explored," Mei said, looking at each of the women. "Hilda, your vision goes beyond your sight of color, a gift that *will* improve... soon. Malaya, your gift is one of many generations, and Kasumi, you have a power deep inside you, let the fox free—"

"Mei," Zoya interrupted. "You are gracious, and we are honored, but we did not come here for a reading."

"Of course. Forgive me, child. My mind often wanders." Mei smiled. "Perhaps you will keep an old lady company. The men will hunt all night. Please stay, wash out back. I have extra clothing."

Though her story lacked pragmatism, it was far from murder. It was more of an old woman suffering from dementia, believing her loved one was still alive. "We'll stay," Malaya said. The others agreed.

The lake looked exactly how she imagined, without the morning fog. No one else seemed to care about the eeriness of it all. The invitation to cleanse themselves was all that mattered. Zoya helped Hilda to the water. Kasumi took her time coming out. This was the first time in a long time they weren't in a rush.

"I'll join you in a bit," Malaya said, admiring the bright night sky filled with more planets and galaxies than she had ever seen.

She allowed herself to get swept away. Understanding why people believed in something more than themselves, just like she once did. Malaya decided not to waste the opportunity to use nature for essential purposes. It was also a chance to avoid Zoya a little longer.

Malaya felt Kasumi's disappointing stare while she collected rocks and materials to build a filter—it was the perfect constructive distraction.

It didn't take Kasumi long to hover over her. She spoke in a low voice in Japanese. "Are you experiencing shame?"

Malaya scoffed. "No. We need a filter. I have crushed charcoal from Harz, this rag, stone, sand, and leaves. When I'm done, we'll have fresh water no matter what."

"That's wonderful," replied Kasumi. "The water we had to drink before here was horrible, but must I remind you, you are a bad liar. Why are you burying your head in your toys?"

"Not a toy. A filter."

Kasumi exhaled before sitting down. "I know the feeling, that burden of blame. My actions cost me more than my title. The Great Guard was my punishment after I chose love. I tried to tell myself that choosing love was the right thing. In truth, I was being selfish–and my mother paid the ultimate price."

"I'm sorry to hear that. And you're right, but it's not just the guilt—it's everything," Malaya confessed, struggling to finish the filter, shoving the useless collection of debris aside. "I feel like I'm losing my mind. I can't organize my thoughts. You know I woke up remembering what I ate as a toddler. Without my meds, I'm useless."

"Stubborn, indeed," Kasumi acknowledged. "And maybe a bit unusual, but far from useless. Your medication was merely clouding your consciousness, obscuring your true vision. It's time to stop resisting it."

"I'll try," Malaya said. "You've had my back through all of this despite everything you've lost. How-how are you so strong?"

"My strength comes from me leaving my faith in the hands of the gods. Family and everything else falls into place, but my loved ones, their memories, are my anchor, especially my mother. She is a source of my strength."

"You sound a lot like Vasilis."

Kasumi smiled. "You mean he sounds a lot like me?"

"Either way, you two have something in common: family. I don't know if I have any trustworthy family. My father's dead, and my grandfather has his own secrets. My mother, she's one step away from destroying our world."

For a moment, the splashing from the water was the only sound.

"You and I are not that different," said Kasumi. "I barely knew my father. Yes, he was there in the flesh, but he was hardly the man I admired growing up. Perhaps I am the one to blame. I'm surprised I cried when he passed."

"However, it's best to just focus on the happy moments," Kasumi forced a smile. "You must hold on to them. I know things are bad, but look at what you've done. You've saved my brother and me. Yet, here you are dwelling."

"I don't mean to."

"I know, and you'll learn." Kasumi tossed a pebble back and forth in her hand, then tossed it to Malaya—she dropped it.

"What happy memory comes to mind at this moment?" Kasumi said, picking up the filter and tossing it.

Malaya caught it. "Breakfast with my boyfriend. It was the most normal, simple thing in my life."

Kasumi smiled. "I knew Vasilis was a good man."

Malaya frowned. "It's not him. His name is Aaron."

"My apologies." Kasumi stood up. "I hope in the future, this moment is one of your happy moments, just as it has become for me."

Kasumi held out her hand. Malaya smiled, accepting it graciously, feeling a warmth she missed. It was like she gained a new family member. She rubbed her gem—a new habit she established.

"Are you ladies coming?" Hilda shouted. "Or is Brown Bunny scared to wet the bald bunny?"

"Trust me, there's no bald bunny anymore," Malaya said. They both laughed.

She dropped the filter. It thumped as it hit the ground. Before she could investigate, Kasumi dragged her toward the lake. "This is crap," Malaya said, dipping her foot in before getting undressed. "It's freezing cold water."

"Crap? What an odd choice of words," Zoya said, her wet dreadlocks pressed to her body.

"It's an expression," Malaya quivered, submerging herself into the water.

Hilda moved closer to Malaya. "Mind taking this off?"

"Of course not."

Hilda's smile and porcelain skin glistened like never before. Malaya smiled back, realizing how precious these moments were. Even with all the horrible things going on. This was a memorable moment. If only Hilda could see how happy she was. "I'll help you wash. Go down on three."

"Never thought I'd hear you say that," Hilda teased.

Malaya smiled. "Three!" She dipped Hilda's head, washing the remaining dried blood from her face.

In the moment Hilda arose, Malaya gently brushed aside the golden locks that framed her face, her heart seizing in a mix of disbelief and awe. Gone was the murky veil that had clouded Hilda's vision, replaced now by a mesmerizing sea of clear, blue depths that seemed to hold stories untold, mirroring Malaya's own stunned silence.

A tender smile graced Hilda's lips, soft and serene, a whisper in time that carried the promise of newfound beginnings. "Beautiful," she murmured in a melodic tone that mirrored the tranquil, calming breeze.

To say there was something different about Hilda would be akin to observing the transition from a tumultuous storm to the serene calm of an idyllic spring day. Malaya's breath hitched before she spoke with the weight of uncertainty her next words would carry.

"Can you... see?" she managed, the words tumbling out, tinged with a hope so fierce it made her voice quiver. "She can see!" she exclaimed louder, a crescendo of joy and wonder in her voice that echoed the miracle before them.

"I can see!" Hildegard shouted; tears streamed from her face as everyone rejoiced. "Is this your doing?"

The revelation hung in the air, a testament to the miraculous, painting the moment with strokes of awe and joy. It was a declaration that reverberated through their very beings, igniting a spark of hope and wonder.

They were not just witnesses to Hilda's healing but participants in a moment that transcended the ordinary, a beautiful testament to the extraordinary unfolding before their eyes.

The revelation hung in the air, a palpable presence that filled this moment, Hilda's moment with awe and joy. Deep within them, the confirmation echoed in the well of the unknown with hope and awe. In this moment of clear vision, Zoya, Kasumi, and Malaya found themselves not just witnesses to Hilda's transformation, but active participants of the remarkable event unfolding right before their eyes.

"Was it the water?" Hilda questioned, her newfound vision scanning the faces of her friends for answers, her voice tinged with curiosity and a hint of disbelief.

"No dear," a soft, soothing voice drifted through the air, turning their collective gaze towards its source. Mei, the elderly woman who invited them in, stood on the grass, observing them with the tenderness of a mother.

With the grace of a seasoned Sage, she stepped forward. "Your journey brought you here, but there is nothing special about the water, only who's in it," she smiled. "Perhaps the gods have blessed you as you all have blessed me. Now come, I have your clothes."

Mei handed the finely woven aqua tunics to them, her attention momentarily caught by the shimmering red stone hanging from Malaya's neck.

"Lovely rune," the elderly woman remarked, a touch of emotion coloring her voice. "Where did you get it?"

Malaya's eyes briefly dropped before she met Mei's gaze again. "From my father, post mortem."

"It's a gift from beyond the grave, then. Both it, and its bearer, are truly special. You will discover the hidden truths in both. Perhaps you have already discovered one," she inclined her head toward Hildegard.

A hint of confusion crossed Malaya's face as she offered a half-hearted smile. "Thank you..."

The weight of recent events sent Malaya's mind racing, spinning through a vortex of impossibilities.

As she watched Hildagard stand a little taller, speaking with new-found eloquence and clarity of sight, Malaya's skepticism clashed with the miracle before her eyes.

Miracle? Malaya's stomach churned with the whirlwind of what she had just witnessed. Her fingers trembled as they delicately traced the intricate carvings on the stone rune pendant against her skin.

She gazed into the stone, and for the first time, she saw traces of light with unfamiliar symbols swimming within its misty current. Perhaps she was losing her mind, and the sickness of ghost radiation exposure that took her father was causing her to see things that weren't there.

Could there be unrecognized medical properties waiting to be discovered by research? Did her mother, or her father for that matter, gift this to her in hopes she uncovered this scientific marvel?

A chill swept through her, not from the cold air, but from the sudden realization of her ignorance. There was a vast terrain of unknowns she had yet to navigate, and the pendant in her grasp was the compass pointing toward uncharted territory.

Despite her scientific mind trying to rationalize the day's events as mere anomalies, Malaya couldn't escape the nagging suspicion that Mei held keys to doors she had yet to open.

Did Mei know? Malaya thought. *No, that's impossible.*

Was it, though, after what she just witnessed?

Malaya found herself looking around for the elderly woman who had invited them. She realized she had vanished, causing even more chaos on this already chaotic day.

"Have any of you seen Mei?"

They looked around, confused looks on all their faces.

Zoya gestured for the women to come close. "There's something odd about this place," she remarked, more like a question than a statement.

Malaya could see she was trying to keep her composure, but it was clear she was shaken.

"A miracle just happened," Zoya continued, "and this woman acted as if she had seen it all before. And while this is the least of oddness. How did she get all our sizes perfectly?"

Malaya stayed quiet.

"I sense something as well," Kasumi added, "but I am not sure of what it is, but I know it is not dangerous."

"I couldn't care less about your opinions," Hildegard stated, her refined tone making her almost unrecognizable. "I have been awakened. That is enough for me."

Awakened, Malaya allowed the words to dance in her mind, a bit unsure of what to make of what was happening. She had so many questions, but dare not spoil this moment.

"I'm with Hilda," Malaya said. "It doesn't matter how strange this place, or Mei, is. We focus on the good, right Kasumi?"

Kasumi nodded.

Malaya tried to fight the curiosity that plagued her. This place is beyond strange. No matter how hard she tries, nothing explains Hilda regaining her sight, or the sudden shift in personality.

Malaya walked toward the water. She stopped when something hit her foot. The filter. She picked it up. Now, how did you get over here? She remembered the hollow sound it made when it fell. "I'll be right back."

She circled back to where it fell and brushed away the debris, revealing an engraved metal hatch. The lettering was unlike any she'd seen. "The other side," she said, surprising herself with how quickly she figured it out. "But what does the rest say?"

"This is the way to the other side," Mei said, startling Malaya. The torch she held lit her smile. "Impressive. Why don't you explore your curiosity? See what is on the other side?"

A familiar voice sent chills down Malaya's spine. This time, she knew no one heard her. Her stomach sank. This is not happening. What is going on?

"Why would we do that, old woman?" said Zoya, sneaking up behind Mei with the others.

"I think I have to," Malaya found herself saying, driven by an inexplicable pull towards the hatch.

"Take this dear," Mei said. She handed Malaya the torch. "Your answer is in there."

Malaya opened the hatch and held the fire over the dark abyss, a staircase winding down. Zoya's hand on her shoulder was both a restraint and a question. "What are you doing?"

"I'm not sure," Malaya replied.

Kasumi stepped forward. "We will not let you do it alone," she said, her resolve clear.

Hildegard peered into the darkness, her recent return to sight making her hesitant. "I just regained my sight, I am not keen on embracing the dark once more."

"You can stay, Hildegard," Kasumi said, grabbing the torch from Malaya and handing her the tomahawk. "I will go first. " Without another word, she started down the stairs.

Malaya turned to Zoya. "Will you stay with Hilegard?"

Zoya nodded. "Of course. It is best. I will make sure this hatch does not close."

Malaya nodded her thanks and let out a shivering sigh before she followed Kaumi into the darkness."

KAT

New Seattle, 2076

“**M**a’am, this is a restricted area!”

Kat shot past the runway operator. “Call President Castillo!” she yelled into her watch.

A MEV jet waited for her at the end of the runway, and so did unarmed security guards, making it a little more difficult to reach her destination. “C’mon, pick up.”

Jose’s hologram finally appeared after a few tries. “It’s o-three hundred hours, Ms. Bennett. This better be good.”

“Tell them I’m authorized to use the company jet!”

“Is this what you called me for? Don’t you have your own clearance?”

"Please, it's a matter of life and death."

Their expressions changed once everyone noticed who she was talking to. His face was enough to create a path to the jet. "Computer, secure this room."

"What is going on, Bennett?"

"Winters is Rattlesnake," she said. "And he may have traced the signal back to my phone."

"You sent the signal to your personal phone? There is a lot you have to learn. You may be in danger. I'll do what I can to protect you."

"Thank you, but that's not the only thing. I know who Lilith's child is."

Jose popped up, carrying her with him as he got dressed. Kat knew the risk, the possible punishment, but this was bigger than her career. The jet trembled as it took off, pressing Katherine to her seat, reminding her of her fear of flying. Jose took a deep breath.

"Who is it?"

"A student at HOA, I know him—"

Jose interrupted, "Don't, don't say the name... Why are you calling? Get Susanne on the line."

"I've already contacted Headmistress Babcock and Sensei, sir. The Fat family will arrive soon and secure safe passage to the UNA. I'll activate the Elite Eight to make sure the cargo is secure."

"No, no, *I* can protect him. They're just children, and the UNA is not safe." Jose dragged his hand across his face, unable to wipe away the anguish.

This was a side of him Kat hadn't seen. A wolf was taking over. No, she didn't know what he was capable of, but this wasn't his era anymore.

"Sir, if I don't do everything in my power to protect him, I could never look Malaya in her eyes again."

"Understood. Take only the team leaders," he said, his tone back to normal. "I'll have a chat with Bradley again, and I'll work on other options for the kid, albeit extreme."

"It's not a Castillo plan if it's not extreme, sir."

"Make preparations with Sensei for a meet up. Have Emily Benoit and Natwat Hodges contact me. We'll keep in touch."

"Yes, sir, Kat out." She pressed the service button. "Please send in tea. I need to calm my mind."

Kat contacted the Elite Eight's young squadron leader, Dreamer, a title passed down after the original retired. She also added the sergeant first class cyber-runner, Dean, who gathered as much information on Jin's family as they could—no stone was ever left unturned. She wanted to know all about the Fat's and their last visits to the states. He was a replacement for the B Squadron leader and her twin sister, who was on an undercover assignment at MEV.

Her phone beeped, and she allowed a halo feed to run across her glasses. An update from Mr. Castillo, along with his orders.

It had been a while since she had an extraction. Unlike before, this one was personal. However, she knew better than to allow her feelings to cloud her judgment. She arrived at the park around noon. The sun was already beaming with heat. She expected the target to arrive within the hour, so she went over her notes.

"It's been a while, huh boy?" she said, stroking the black fur of her Pitbull, Sniper. He gave her a quick lick; he was always stingy with his affection.

"You ready?" she asked, pulling her green-tipped braids into a ponytail before removing the tablet from Sniper's backpack. "Go play until it's time."

Kat zipped up her cowl-necked leather jacket before pressing down on the sunglasses. She pressed her tragus. "Confirm your position."

"Positioned west side rooftop, confirmed," said Dreamer.

"I have this location in a bubble," said Dean. "We're on ice. I have the target in sight, less than a klick away."

"The Fats are meeting someone," said Dreamer. "He's wearing a long tan coat, sunglasses, and a gray fedora. I can't make out his face."

Kat called Sniper over to attach the tablet back to his backpack. "Come only if I blow the whistle, understood, boy?"

"I'm going to check it out, she said. "Approaching the north entrance of Nature's Diner, watch my six."

"Copy... Uh, Kat, a van just dropped off two armed men on the west side of the alley."

"Shit, this was supposed to be clean. Do they look like Ghost or Freedom?"

"Neither, but I have a shot."

"Negative. Keep your firearm cold until further notice. We can't risk civilian casualties."

"I'll incapacitate for now if needed."

"Are you sure your gift has that kind of range?"

"Yup, as long as they're in my sight, I can trigger their melatonin then night-night."

Kids like Dreamer and Dean were the Elite Eight secrets, hand-selected by Jose and Kat from HOA before the SIA could sink their fangs into them.

Whispers circulated about a group of gifted children, the secret HOA faction known as *the few*, but science labeled them *Darviants*, and the black market labeled them an asset.

No one knew how they got their abilities, but there were not many. Some speculated three hundred, maybe less. She'd worked with a Darviant before, trained under one—now she was leading them.

As she got within a few yards of the diner, a man jumped up and pointed a gun at the cashier, hidden behind a Yankees cap and sunglasses.

Kat pressed the emblem on her sunglasses, activating the helmet to conceal her identity.

"Why don't you stay back and let the cops handle this," said Dean. "I'll unscramble the signals and dispatch help."

"Besides, the target is less than five hundred yards away," added Dreamer.

"I got this," she said, activating the voice modulator. She placed a black chip onto the doors, disintegrating the glass. "Drop your god-damn weapon."

The gunman turned and opened fire. A particle wave brushed past her, blasting the firearm from her hand, shattering a glass display. Horrid screams made it to the streets.

The sweaty man frantically pivoted back and forth, aiming the gun at the trembling, frozen bystanders.

Kat could see the gun wasn't recharging. *He doesn't know how to use it.* She protracted the two metal batons from her wristband, ignoring Dreamer and Dean's warnings.

"Where did you get a military-grade weapon?"

He didn't respond. Instead, he pressed the trigger. He looked at once—it didn't fire.

"You said this would work," the gunman shouted before attacking Kat.

She ducked underneath his wild swing, slamming her baton into his knee—the bone shattered on contact. The final hit was to his throat. She stood over the gunman, who angrily cursed whoever gave it to him.

"Now tell me. A, where did you get a military-grade weapon? And B, of all the places to steal bandwidth, why a diner?"

Crushing throats and then asking questions, probably not the smartest thing. Batman would approve. She allowed a few seconds as he held his neck in pain. The man's eyes looked toward the Fat's. Before he could say anything, the man sitting at their table shot him. Smoke radiated from his skull around his eyes, blackened from the plasma burning him from the inside.

Kat jumped back and drew a secondary firearm, pointing it at the man in the trench coat, holding Mrs. Fat at gunpoint. Based on the glowing square around his collar, he was also wearing an identity morpher.

The man tapped Jin's mother on the head with his gun. "I only need one of them," he said in a modulated voice. "Lower your weapon if you want her to make it out alive."

"The target is about to arrive," said Dreamer. "I recommend you wrap things up."

"Copy," Kat said, still looking at the gunman. "You're stirring a big pot of shit with the UNA trying to take these two," she said, lowering her weapon. "Trust me, this place will be surrounded by more than just cops. So, let's make a deal."

"There's no deal to be made, Agent Bennett," he said, slowly backing out through a back exit.

Shit.

Kat looked around at the horrid faces. "Help is on the way," she said, bursting through the rear doors. Although there were no signs of any help, not even from the androids, thanks to Dean scrambling their signal.

This was well-planned and professional, but who? She thought, trying to catch up to the kidnapper.

"Dreamer, I need a location on the Fats?"

"Heading east toward a black suburban. I can't take down the assailant."

"Shit." Kat ran after them, weaving through the clean alleyway, knocking over clear plastic trash cans.

"The target just arrived. Sensei is engaged with the assailant."

Though the crowd of people made it difficult, she could see Sensei fighting the gunman, apparently having things under control, while Jordan and Jin watched from inside the car.

"Watch out," Dreamer warned.

Kat dodged a fist. She went for a counter, but the assailant passed out. She smirked. "Good work, Dreamer—"

A hulking arm squeezed her neck. The smoking skull branding was one she recognized on one other person.

Just before the blackness took over, Sniper attacked him, loosening his grip.

"Move, boy," Kat said before activating the voltage on her batons. She pressed them against his neck and left him for someone else to clean him up.

"Are you okay?" Dreamer said.

"Peachy," she said, dragging herself across the street. "Target in sight. Prepare for extraction."

"On it," Dreamer replied.

"I'm back, moving to EZ," said Dean. "This was intense."

Kat took a moment to catch her breath. "Yes, go,"

"Extraction zone is ready," Dreamer said.

Before she reached Sensei, the assailant opened fire, hitting him twice.

"Call the paramedics. Sensei is down!" she cried as chaos ensued, making it impossible to get a clean shot.

"You have to go after them," Jin pleaded. "Please… I'll stay with him."

"Paramedics are on the route. So am I," said Dreamer.

Siper ran over. Kat removed a needle from her belt and jabbed into Sensei's leg, hoping the nanobots could clot the wound in time.

Sensei grabbed her wrist. "Take… the boy."

The van arrived. "Let's go, Jordan," said Kat.

"What?" Jordan refused. "I'm not in danger. His parents are, and I can't leave Sensei."

"Leave now, boy!" Sensei said.

"Sensei—"

"Now!" Sensei repeated.

Both Jordan and Kat watched Sensei refuse help from the paramedics. Instead, choosing to climb in the truck under his own will. The partition window slid open.

"You guys okay?" Dreamer said, looking back.

"Yeah, we're fine. Great work out there."

"Is that Jayden?" Jordan asked.

"In the flesh, but it's Dreamer now," he said.

Jordan lowered his voice. "So, Dreamer is part of the Elite Eight?"

"Can't say," Kat replied, converting the helmet back into sunglasses. "Sniper, come here, boy."

He gave her a quick lick.

"Fair enough. Can you at least tell me why I'm being taken?"

"I'm not at liberty to disclose any information." Kat removed the tablet from Sniper's backpack. She tried her best to ignore Jordan's pleading eyes.

"C'mon, Kat, this isn't the time. You can't force me to leave my friend and say you can't tell. Why am I your target?"

"Kat, he would like to speak with you," Dreamer interrupted, giving Kat an excuse to leave.

"At least tell me where you're taking me."

"Puget Sound."

"Why?"

"You know the answer," she said, closing the partition.

"This is bullshit!"

She wanted to tell him he deserved to know, but it wasn't the time or her place. "You wanted to speak to me, sir."

"Congratulations on a successful mission, Agent Bennett," said Jose.

"Successful is a stretch."

"You extracted the target."

"Yeah, and Captain Winters was there. He murdered a man in cold blood, shot Sensei, and one of his men nearly killed me. Oh, and they kidnapped the ambassadors."

The surprised look on his face was telling. "Winters? How do you know him?" Jose said.

"While I was in a chokehold, I recognized the smoking skull branding on an assailant's arm. The only other time I saw it was on Captain Winters during a training session. And this guy in all black, he knew my name, sir. The way he fought off Sensei reminded me of Winters, but the move he did with the gun gave it away. He definitely orchestrated the whole thing, including a botched robbery."

If his hologram could emit fumes, it would, despite how calm he tried to be. "What would Winters want with UNA Ambassadors?"

"I don't know, sir, but I will find out."

"No. You need to get Jordan to the SUV."

"I'm not sure I can go back there."

"Don't worry, you'll have clearance," Jose said. "I'll be with you shortly. I'm stepping off the jet as we speak."

"I've informed Shay and Natwat of your arrival," he continued. "Shay doesn't know we're on to her, nor does she know who Jordan is. I want to keep it that way, at least until I arrive. Natwat and Emily will join you all in the Quantum Room. Vasilis and Inoichi will meet with us as well. Take him there, no stops."

How did he get them out of jail? She thought. "Understood, sir."

Jose continued filling her in on the plan. The van stopped at the port; a fairy awaited them. Jordan probed Kat, but she did what was asked by giving him little to no answers. Dreamer handed Jordan ear mufflers and a blindfold.

"You can't be serious," Jordan said.

"I'll help you," Kat said, making sure he couldn't see or hear a thing.

After inserting her command, a dome formed over the fairy before they submerged. Kat avoided as many people as she could while escorting Jordan to the Quantum Room. Everyone was there. Jose wasn't far behind.

Emily dismissed the other members of the Continuum. Kat watched Jose eyeball Jordan from head to toe with a sense of pride and relief.

"You should sit," Jose said, looking at Shay and Jordan. "What I'm about to say will make you question everything."

Kat filled everyone in on Williams's search into the Castillo-Grant family. "I found out what that secret was. Whose secret it was."

Jose cleared his throat. "They had another child, a boy who was supposed to pledge his loyalty to Alpha Kings when he came of age. But Lilith knew the dangers. She knew what would come of him if they knew he existed." He looked at Jordan. "It's you, son."

"Remarkable," Natwat said, staring a hole into Jordan.

Shay looked over at Jordan with tears wetting her face. "I'm your aunt..." she said, hugging him.

Kat tried but couldn't fight the overwhelming weight of her contagious emotions. She wiped a tear, waiting for Jordan to say something, anything. He was understandably speechless. Just seconds ago, he had nothing, no one, and now he has it all, yet they want to take it away.

"I, uh..." Jordan cleared his throat. "I'm not sure what to say. I want to be angry, but I'm not. Part of me understands, and I have so many questions, but it doesn't look like I'll have the time."

"No, you won't," said Jose. "These people will look for you everywhere, but there is one place they cannot find you."

Kat looked at Vasilis and Inoichi.

"No," said Shay. "We can protect him."

"We can't," said Jose. "No one can, not here, not now. Inform Lilith. Let her know the damage she caused. You didn't think I had Aaron arrested without linking it all back to you and the Raging Bull Program, did you?"

Aaron was the former leader of the elite branch of SIA. After James and Esther died, her brother Bryce was their new leader. She wondered if the unit was cursed. Kat paid close attention to Shay Taylor; information is in the details.

Kat saw her brown eyes widen just a bit before a slight smile crossed her smooth, ebony face. *She was impressed.*

Jose continued to explain why this was the only way to protect Jordan.

"No one other than Williams and his men has access to the quantum portal, and even he will be restricted. The other Cabinet members are in Washington."

"Since Vasilis and Inoichi have already agreed to head a recovery mission for Malaya, I can oversee things with Emily and the Continuum," said Natwat.

"I don't see why not," Emily stammered, actively avoiding Shay. "The coordinates are all set. And we have enough energy and medallions to send multiple people back. I'll get my team in here to finish up."

"Then we have a plan," said Jose.

"Jordan will need to prepare properly for this trip," Natwat added.

"Can you bring the thing we talked about from my room?" said Kat. "It's essential, sir."

"Of course."

Jose created time for them, so everyone had to rush to prepare. Jose and Kat walked toward Inoichi and Vasilis. Both men came ready for their journey in all-black hooded cloaks and a sack of provisions, including armor and swords.

Jose bowed toward them. "I've told you before, and I'll tell you again. I'm sorry for what my daughter has done to your lives, but I know you two are honorable men. And I'll need you two to watch over him while we figure things out here."

"I'm not a kid who needs a babysitter," said Jordan. "But I have to admit, if I'm going to have sitters, a samurai and a Spartan isn't bad."

"I like this kid," said Vasilis. "After everything you've done since bringing us back, it's the least I can do."

"Malaya saved my life," Inoichi said with a firm term. "It will be my honor to protect her brother. Have either of you tracked my love?"

Jose turned to Kat. "Maybe you and Natwat can take Inoichi with you and update him on what's going on. Shay and I need to spend some time with Jordan."

"Understood, sir."

After speaking with the Continuum, Natwat handed Kat the backpack. "It's all there," he said. "Wait until they get ready to leave. Jose's not going to like this."

Kat nodded before she called Inoichi.

Natwat leaned into her. "How are we going to explain this?"

"Rip the bandaid off," Kat said.

Natwat took a deep breath as he unfolded his tablet and started searching. "Some time ago, there was an announcement. A woman who claims to be the true power in Japan," he said with a cautious and caring tone, like a father breaking bad news to his child. "She says her blood is pure. This news caused quite a stir as the young woman claimed and proved to be part of a rare royal bloodline. She calls herself Toyotomi Mizunami, the new shogun."

Natwat handed Inoichi the tablet. "Is she your wife?"

Inoichi's eyes widened, lost in a combination of sadness and hope. "I-I..." he stammered, watching the news feed. "She looks the same, but somehow very different. Her eyes."

It was the first time Kat saw him smile—it lasted the entire feed. He was a different person at that moment. When the feed ended, she placed her hand on his shoulder. "I will do my best to look into her after you're gone. If you want, you can take some time—"

"No, I'm fine," he said abruptly, handing the tablet back. He slid the black hood over his head, hiding his eyes behind its shadow. "Thank you, Katherine, and Dr. Hodge," he said with a deep bow. "We have wasted enough time. I should help Jordan prepare for the mission."

Kat watched Jordan take it all in. She could see the resemblance not just to Malaya, but to their mother and father. He took the news well.

Malaya should have been here.

Jordan's spirit was admirable. So was his dedication, as evident by his retro Viking look. He had a touch of realism and a bit of cosplay. Kat picked up the rust-colored ventail helmet. "You don't think this is a bit much?" she questioned, placing it on his head.

"Say what you want, but I'm ready," he said. He stood up, admiring the well-crafted short blade before sheathing it.

"Have to admit, you look good in a tunic," Kat smiled.

"Gotta admit, I kinda look good in everything," he said with a raised brow and dimpled smile.

Kat stepped closer to him; she grabbed his hand. "You don't have to do that. If you're hurting, no one will—"

"It's time!" Emily shouted.

Jordan withdrew. He smirked. "I'm good, Kat."

"Well, I'm not," she sighed before walking with him.

They all stood in front of the large spiraled metal door. Kat removed a steel box from her backpack. She secretly handed it to Vasilis. "I need you to give this to her."

He looked over her shoulder and lowered his voice. "Who allowed you to give me this?"

"Don't worry, I have connections."

"What is it... if you don't mind me asking?"

"A reminder that our friendship and that our world still exists."

Kat handed Inoichi two extra medallions. "Natwat said these are absolutely necessary. It's the only way you'll bring your sister back with you."

Jordan kept that confident smile, making it difficult to tell if he felt anything other than what he wanted you to think he was feeling.

"Malaya is going to need you," said Kat. "Tell her I love her when you see her."

"I will,"

"See you later, Jordan Grant-Castillo."

"Has a nice ring to it," Jordan said. They both smiled.

"Get back, Katherine," said Natwat.

The doors slowly opened to a multitude of colors that swallowed them. The moment they disappeared, SIA agents stormed the room. "Katherine Bennett, Shay Taylor, and Jose Castillo, you are all under arrest!"

MALAYA

Germany, 871

As Malaya stepped into the shadowy tunnel, the cold, wet mud squelched under the boots provided by Mei, sending a shiver up her spine. Glancing back, she saw Zoya and Hildegard's silhouettes framed against the dim light,

Hilda got her sight back. She thought, toying with the idea of calling it a miracle, but she held back. *There has to be a plausible explanation.*

She pushed the thought aside and welcomed the comforting warmth of happiness that flowed through her, countering the chilly dampness of the tunnel. Her mind focused on the mission ahead.

Kasumi carried the torch, its flickering flame casting eerie shadows in the cool space that reeked of damp concrete.

Malaya's hand shook uncontrollably on Kasumi's shoulder. By every account, there should only be eight steps. She counted, though the dripping made it difficult. Still, once in a while, she heard more, felt something more.

"I can't believe I'm doing this," Malaya whispered. "None of this makes sense."

"I have come to believe that there exists a realm of mystery within us and around us, where even our own actions and choices whisper of magic unfathomable," Kasumi replied, her gaze set on the uncertain path ahead, barely illuminated by the torchlight extending no more than a yard in front of them. She paused thoughtfully, then added, "And in guiding us here, Mei seems to have intended for us to confront this realm, to perhaps understand or embrace the mysteries it holds."

So did that girl, Malaya thought, unsure of anything at this point. Hearing Kasumi speak was a stark reminder of how different they were. Malaya knew could never accept things as they are.

There is always an answer. Malaya thought.

Though she found herself grappling with uncertainty, a feeling that was foreign to her. Accustomed to having answers, this perilous journey from one world to another brought forth more questions.

Deep down, she knew she was out of her depth, though admitting it out loud was another matter. Maybe relying on others was the best option. Her decisions had nearly cost her and Kasumi their lives, and now, here they were, navigating through a godforsaken tunnel.

Yet, the idea of turning back seemed impossible; a stirring within her insisted that she was meant to be here.

Was it fate? She briefly entertained the thought before dismissing it. How could fate have any sway in a world where she had the power to control time—

"Closer." An eerily soft, yet familiar, voice crept through the silent darkness of the tunnel.

The hair on the back of Malaya's neck stood up as chills surged through her body. Her eyes widened; she was sure they would pop out of her head. Kasumi stopped.

"Did you hear that?" Malaya questions, trying to keep her fear in check.

"Yeah..." Kasumi replied, she gasped, freezing momentarily.

Malaya trembled. "What?" she whispered.

"I saw something."

The pause that followed was heavy with suspense, the darkness around them seeming to thicken. Malaya's grip tightened on whatever she held, her knuckles white, as the torch flickered, casting long shadows that danced across the walls.

Malaya searched the floor, finding a twig. Kasumi burned and tossed it in front of them, lighting part of the hall. In its black eye glaze, Malaya saw something twisted, part human, with horns.

Its swift movement strayed away from the light, deeper into the abyss.

Kasumi grabbed Malaya's tomahawk, swinging wildly into black. "Ah, die," she shouted, swinging the torch, guiding them through the darkness.

"Thank God," Malaya said as they arrived at a circular bronze door. "Bring the light closer."

As the torchlight washed over the door, it revealed symbols that danced eerily familiar in Malaya's memory—like those from her dream. She felt a pull to them, like a planet to its sun, drawn by the gravitational force. The symbols seemed to hold a key, a secret that was just beyond her grasp, yet she needed to uncover.

"It's some sort of puzzle or code," she murmured, her mind racing. "Can you not see this... the numbers?"

"The number must be for your eyes only," Kasumi said, handing Malaya the torch. "This is your journey."

Malaya stared at the cryptic aged bronze door, a sense of anticipation stirring within her. She'd unraveled more puzzles in her lifetime than the stars scattered across the night sky—a comparison not lost on her as she considered the vastness of mysteries she loved to solve.

For Malaya, tackling a problem was like an artist wielding a brush on a canvas, each stroke deliberate and purposeful. With the finesse of a master painter, she approached the intricate puzzle before her, blending the hues of logic and intuition to craft a seamless masterpiece of solutions. This challenge was no different.

Semi-circles, acute angles, and ancient inscriptions formed a mesmerizing mosaic, an enigmatic tapestry that seemed to defy earthly explanation. It was this unfathomable complexity that had enabled her to decipher the mysteries of time travel.

Now, with fluid yet delicate movements, she navigated the intricate patterns with practiced ease, her fingers tracing the contours of ancient glowing letters like a seasoned scribe.

With each twist and turn, she edged closer to unlocking the puzzle's secrets, her determination unwavering in the face of its enigmatic allure. Numbers materialized above the symbols, as if her subconscious was guiding her, revealing the sequence she needed to follow.

The door moved, its ancient gears grinding in harmony with the rhythm of Malaya's heartbeat. As the pathway beyond the door started to reveal itself, Malaya's anticipation crescendoed. The thrill of discovery, the allure of the unknown, and the sheer joy of solving yet another puzzle filled her with a familiar sense of inebriation.

As they emerged from the narrow pathway, the dimly lit chamber unfolded before them, revealing its ancient secrets. The air was thick with the scent of aged stone mixed with a faint, unplaceable fragrance, reminiscent of old parchment and dried herbs. The walls, lined with intricate carvings that seemed to dance in the flickering torchlight, told stories long forgotten by time.

At the chamber's heart lay another opening, drawing Malaya and her companions toward a sight both wondrous and unsettling. There, suspended in the air above a metal table etched with symbols that shimmered under the torch's glow, slept a girl with strawberry blond hair.

"Impossible," Malaya whispered, her voice barely audible over the sound of her racing heartbeat.

The girl floated as if cradled by invisible hands, her hair fanning out in a halo of soft light that seemed to emanate from within her. Her red tunic, vibrant against the muted tones of the chamber, was untouched by time. The fabric clung to her form in a perfect fit, its gold trim catching the light with every subtle movement of the air, as if it, too, was part of some enchantment. The craftsmanship spoke of a bygone era where artistry and she dare think—magic—intertwined, making the impossible seem mundane.

"What did Mei put in our drinks?" Malaya said. "It's Japan all over again." She took a step forward, but Kasumi grabbed her wrist.

"Don't move," Kasumi urged. "There may be a trap."

The girl sat up, calling out. "We need to help her." Malaya pulled away, running across the path into the large room without a second thought.

"What are you talking about?" Kasumi shouted.

The door slammed shut behind Malaya with a resounding echo, sealing her fate. She pounded on the metal, desperation clear in each thud, but the other side remained silent, as if she had been swallowed by another world entirely. With a slow and steady breath, Malaya slowly turned, facing the unknown that awaited her.

The chamber revealed itself in the flickering light from torches mounted on the walls, each flame casting long, dancing shadows that played across the ancient stone. Strange symbols were etched near the torches, their meanings lost to time, yet suggesting a purpose far beyond mere decoration.

The room, despite its evident age, was in a state of impeccable preservation—as if dust and decay were held at bay by some unseen force, or perhaps, they dared not encroach upon this sacred space. Shelves laden with scrolls and artifacts lined the walls, whispering tales of forgotten knowledge and power that once thrived within this hidden sanctum.

In the center of the room, a girl sat hugging her knees, her presence an enigma. Malaya approached cautiously, each step echoing softly in the vastness of the chamber.

An unsettling sensation washed over her, a palpable yet familiar shift in the atmosphere akin to traveling through a portal sent a shiver down her spine.

Standing beside the girl, Malaya hesitated, the air thick with the tension of a thousand unasked questions. The girl remained motionless, her silence as heavy as the stone that surrounded them.

"You're safe now," Malaya said, trying to convince the girl of something she wasn't sure was true.

"You can't help me," the girl said in a hollow voice. "I'm out of time."

"What do you mean?"

"You can hear me?" She lifted her head—hope gleamed in her mesmerizing gray eyes and alluring pasty face.

Malaya hoped the girl didn't catch her staring at her cold blue lips. "You can see me too," the girl said, peering at Malaya's medallion, her freckled nose crinkled. "You're out of time too."

"Out of time?" Malaya said, rubbing it. "Time? You're out of your timeline... a traveler?"

"Yes, a traveler, but not through time. I exist between realms; this is the other side, yet you're here..." Her voice trailed.

"You're not one of them, yet you have the gift," the girl said. She stood up. She was about four inches shorter, but only a few years younger than Malaya. Her voice was angelic and wise. "It was you who heard my calls. I was wrong. You are the only one who could help me, and I will repay you."

"Repay me, how? Who are you? How did you get here?"

"All of your answers will come in time," said the girl. "I see you are still so confused, but I will give you a token of gratitude. Elvir will bring death as he always has. My mother warned me about his power, our power, but there is a great smithing god, Cykius. You must find him in the land they call Egersund, but I warn you. He is sleeping. You must wake him in order to get what you need."

A loud bang on the door startled Malaya. "My friends will help," she said, starting for the door. A growl coming from the other side made her rethink her decision to leave this delusional girl.

Malaya turned around to the girl standing so close she could feel her cold breath. She grabbed the medallion.

"We must go," she said.

Before Malayas could protest, an intense light forced her to close her eyes. She hoped it was all a dream, and she'd awake in her apartment next to Aaron. She looked over to find Kasumi.

"What happened?"

"You have some explaining to do," said Kasumi, pointing.

Sigurd was on his knees, surrounded by his family, as he hugged the girl. This time she was more... physical. "That's Sigrunn," Hildegard said with a smile. "Back from the dead."

His son Geir cradled the frail Sigrunn, her long hair dragging across the cobblestone floor. The family made their way back to their home, but something held Mayala in place–gold coins. But it wasn't the actual gold that pulled her, it was the slight fluorescent glow from one of the coins.

Kasumi and Sigurd followed her gaze. He tugged at his beard with a smile. "Looking to get paid for your services, aye?"

"No, it's not that," she said almost to herself. "Why does..."

"It have light?" Sigurd finished her sentence. "Aigon technology. Do you understand that term?" She nodded, her eyes lost in its light. He flipped her the coin. "Keep it, consider it payment."

LILITH

Norway, 871

"Now it's your turn," Elias shouted, holding his blade, peering past Lilith at Quintus.

With anger and tears in his deep blue eyes, he started for Quintus, but Lilith immobilized him. He struggled to break free. It was useless, given the control she now had.

She had feared this moment, but letting him fight Quintus was unthinkable, even if she understood his anger. His father's abandonment was one wound; seeing his best friend align with the man who kidnapped his wife was another. Yet, he stood by his side—for her. His loyalty was rare, as was the simmering rage that now fueled his strength.

"Look friend, I did you a favor," said Quintus. "Your wife wanted you dead."

Lilith frowned. "Quintus," she sighed. "Elias, Nefeli's life was better without you in it. I know it's hard to accept, but it was. Trust me, I know the feeling. I also had to accept the harsh reality that my son's life was better without me."

Elias stopped pushing against her. She let him go. His sword dropped to his side, and he dropped to his knees. "My father has moved on with the life you gave him, so has my mother and my sister, Nefeli. I knew she was not happy. What is my purpose? Am I anything to anyone if I am alive?"

Lilith knelt beside him. Her trembling hand touched his shoulder. "You are important to me, Elias."

"We are on the same side," Quintus said. "For what it is worth, you have my sincere apologies. That grief you feel. That loss, use it to give you strength. You need not your father or a woman to validate who you are. Did you not just see what we did together?"

Quintus reached out his hand, and Elias grabbed it. Midas picked up his blade and handed it to him. "Let's see this through the end for eternal happiness, brother."

"Your father may not respect or value you. We do," Lilith said.

Elias dug into his pocket for the medication. It helped ease the anger and sadness.

Lilith and her men left the black sand of Iceland with answers and even more questions. They sailed and hiked to the outskirts of Norway to a settlement shrouded in mystery all its own.

History told the story of a hidden village rooted in magic. If she was going to unlock the Sage, she needed to enlist the help of a famed sailor who knew the sea and Iceland better than anyone.

Empty houses circled an enormous mead hall. The aroma of food made its way out. So did the humming from the singing.

"Try to blend in," said Lilith, "and keep your eyes open."

Quintus opened the door. No one batted an eye as the four strangers entered the crowded longhouse. It reminded her of an inn their family visited during vacations in Colorado. Though it was more work than a vacation—work that allowed her to travel to places like this. The craftsmanship was unlike any she'd seen in other parts of the country. These were the outcasts, enjoying life away from everyone else.

"There he is," she said, finding a man pounding down drinks. He was tall even as he sat on the stool with wide shoulders that lay underneath a shabby gray shirt.

"Are you sure?" Quintus asked. "He doesn't look knowledgeable."

"Yes."

She removed her hood and took a deep breath before sitting next to him. He glanced over at her before chugging down whatever was in his cup.

Lilith cleared her throat. "Are you Raven?"

He scoffed and asked for another drink that he chugged, then wiped the drippings from his long gold and white beard.

"I am. At least I was, but you can call me Floki," he said. His high voice contradicted his stature.

Lilith looked from the corner of her eye at someone by the entrance. "Floki, I've come here—"

"No."

"Floki, I need your help."

"I said no!" He slammed his hands on the table, rattling the drinks.

The music stopped. Quintus walked over, and Midas and Elias raised from their seats.

Lilith stopped them before opening a map and placing it in front of Floki.

He side-eyed the map and the three men she stopped—he sighed. "I have given so much I cannot help anyone, not anymore," he removed a glove from his right hand—three fingers were missing. "One for each raven, I suppose. That was the cost and so much more. So, no, I will not help you."

A random, wide smile crossed his face. "But you can enjoy Caitlin's amazing ale during your stay in the village of the free!"

People cheered, and the music strummed. Floki called for another drink.

Lilith grabbed his arm. "Please," she said, hoping to read his memories.

Floki snatched away before she could see anything. "Are you mad, woman?"

"You have no idea," she replied through gritted teeth.

Lilith unrolled a parchment paper. "These symbols, they speak of a Vessel. You know the island. You've seen what we saw. I know this because I know so much about you."

Floki tilted his head with a raised brow. "Please, tell me more."

"I can't say much, but your legend grows beyond Norway, Floki."

"Liar. I am no one but a lowly cripple. No money, no magic, no legend."

Lilith waved Quintus over. Floki peeked across his shoulder. He gazed down at the box Quintus sat next to him.

"All I'm asking is for a little help," Lilith said. "I did not come empty-handed."

Quintus opened it to the most precious jewels she had—the last of them.

Floki's eyes widened. "You know the way to a Viking's heart."

"What can you tell me about the caves of Víðgelmir, Elvir, and the Vessel? Anything will help."

"Shhh," Floki raised his long finger to his mouth. He reached for the box.

Quintus snatched it away. "Information first."

Floki smiled. He slid the hood over his head. "You and your friend should come with me. The others must stay."

They followed him into a hut filled with relics he claimed warded off the evil spirits. After all, he upset his gods. "All of my friends have abandoned me. My wife is gone, so has my son..." his voice trailed. He grabbed a wooden toy, and tears streamed from his face. "They took Pjóogarour away from us. My daughter is gone, swallowed by the land. That place is not what they think. The gods truly walked on the island..."

His voice spoke of the loneliness and sacrifices he made for one goal, but the success wasn't worth it, not for him. He found the riches Iceland had to offer and the fame that came along with it.

Yet, here he was, left with nothing. Through his story, she realized they were alike in that way. So were those responsible for the Sage she was ready to wake, the Aigons. Their flaws and faults resulted in them being banished from the world of the gods. Their creation brought her an outcast, herself looking for help from another.

"The god you're looking for, Elvir. He is not to be awakened without *the* blacksmith and the Vessel. Those caves held the key to a door that leads to another world. The Vessel is here, but you will never find them."

Floki laughed so hard he snorted.

Was he enjoying this antagonizing me? Okay, if you won't give me what I want—I'll take it. Lilith reached for his hand. He allowed her to grab it. Flashes of white light and scrambled images were all she saw. She released him and he laughed.

"A Seer who cannot see," Floki said, still laughing. "I am a mystery."

"Dick." Lilith stood up.

Floki grabbed her wrist. "You cannot get into the otherworld without passing the first door. After door number one lies door number two, and you can't get by without this."

He reached into his pocket and placed something in her hand. "This is the key to open door number two, but it doesn't matter because you will never find the other clues."

"Help me."

He eyed her with a smirk. "You have heard two clues... the legendary Blacksmith is the Gatekeeper. Without him, you can't enter the sealed chamber."

The second door.

The chair creaked as he stood, towering over her. He looked into her eyes, then down at her chest.

Lilith rolled her eyes. *You have got to be kidding me.*

"Do not think I fancy you," Floki said. "I see you have the Nazarene around your neck. Like your Jesus, you must walk through water."

"He walked on water."

"Oops." He snickered and worked his way to a hysterical laugh.

Lilith stormed out. A surge of dizziness hit her. She stumbled a bit. *Get yourself together,* she told herself, hearing footsteps behind her.

"Are you okay?" Quintus said.

Maybe I'm overusing the dagger.

"I don't know. Maybe I shouldn't have tried to read the mind of a lunatic."

"You should rest more," Elias said, joining them, Midas at his side.

"So... Will he help us?" Midas said.

"No!" Floki said, followed by a hysterical laugh.

"He's helped as much as he could."

"Do you want me to get the jewels back?" questioned Midas.

"No. He gave us this..." She opened her palm, showing them the shimmering purple stone, though she wasn't sure where to use it. "He also said the Blacksmith and Vessel from that story in the caves are here."

"Amongst these people?" Elias asked.

"Pssst," someone exclaimed, interrupting their conversation.

A short man waved them over. With him was a woman, just as short. There was something alluring about them. Maybe it was their plush hand-woven garments or the radiant emeralds around their necks.

Lilith signaled for the others to stay back as she approached the two locals. "How can I help you?"

"We could not help but overhear you speaking with our old friend," the woman said.

Lilith looked back, still hearing Floki's manic laugh. "Yeah, he was interesting."

"Forgive him," the man said. "He has not been the same since returning from the island of the gods. It is a shame what he lost, but the gods could not stop him from the wealth he obtained."

"All things come with a sacrifice," the woman said.

"So, you believe him?" Lilith said, unable to hide the surprise in her voice.

"Indeed, we do," the woman said. "He is the reason we are here. We can trade with the richest of men. We have so much because of him. He brought us here, though he would never admit it. Sadly, he is losing his mind, but I think it is the magic from the island calling him back home where he belongs."

"I'm sorry, but who are you?" Lilith questioned.

"Hallveig Fróðadóttir. This is my love, Ingólfr Arnarson."

"My friends, they call me Arn," Ingólfr smiled through his perfectly trimmed copper beard.

The names, she recognized them, but could she trust him? Lilith reached for their hands. They looked at one another before allowing her to see the power they had—one history failed to record.

"You are a strong one, aren't you?" said Ingólfr. "Whatever you saw, do not tell us."

"At least now you know we mean you no harm," said Hallveig. "We want to help you."

"Why would you do that?"

"We need you to take us to the island. Allow us to begin our settlement away from King Harold and Norse gods."

"Settlement?" Lilith questioned.

"Yes, all of us here," said Ingólfr. "No one wants the crippled or crazy, and those of us with certain gifts are often hunted. We would go ourselves. We have boats, large boats, but we are not navigators. As you've seen, Raven is not the man he was, and we want to show him that his sacrifice meant everything to us."

"I see," said Lilith. "What can you tell me about the Vessel or Blacksmith?"

"There are rumors of a man with a blacksmithing gift like no other," said Hallveig. "Three of them arrived here years ago. His name is a mystery, but he is the youngest of the three. The eldest bears a mark of those cursed to carry the soul of a demon—"

The Vessel.

"We can take you to the Blacksmith, but you must swear by All-Father that you will help us. One mother to another."

Lilith nodded. "I swear."

A massive carriage awaited Lilith and her men. There was enough room for the four of them and more. Things were going right. The morning fog covered the land, so too did the eerie feeling. She needed to rest. The three of them encouraged her to sleep.

Just as she dozed off, a surge of uncertainty warmed her veins. A flash of light took her away to a place nearby. She heard a voice; it was deep yet sweet, with a familiar tone that warmed her heart. Then she saw his face, the one she missed so much. He was there, in Scandinavia, so close she could touch him.

"Jordan," she cried, sure that the words echoed through the wilderness.

She felt herself reaching for air as she jumped awake in the darkness of the star-filled sky. The carriage had stopped. They stared at her. "How long?"

"Too long," said Quintus.

"She's fine," said Midas. "You can continue."

Elias lowered his voice. "Who's Jordan?"

Was there any reason for her to hide this from them? She thought as their eyes caringly stared at her. "He's my son, and he's here."

They looked exactly how she expected, though the surprised look didn't last long. Elias was the first to speak. "I think I speak for everyone when I say that we are used to you keeping secrets."

"But a child," said Quintus. "By the look on your face, I assume no one knew."

"Yeah, and now the wrong people know," Lilith said. "He will be here, but he's not alone."

She looked at the three of them, hoping the names she said would not provoke a reaction. "Inoichi and Vasilis will be with him."

"What?" Elias said, his anger dragging the word from his gritted teeth. "If they are here for us, I will kill them before they get to you."

"No, we can't waste time fighting, not when we're so close," she said. "Follow the leads."

Lilith sent the three men to follow the leads. She needed time to gather herself. *Jordan*, she thought, rubbing her head. She needed to focus and track these three blacksmiths, and two of them needed to go with her—no matter what. *A blacksmith with a gift. He must have to be the Gatekeeper. The key to the entrance. Maybe the other one is a Darviant, maybe even the Vessel. What about the third? I can't imagine he's just an average Joe. She* let out a long sigh. *One problem at a time, Lilith.*

"Don't kill anyone," she blurted out, realizing she got lost in thought.

Lilith leaned back against the rough bark of a tree, relishing in the quiet rustling of leaves. It had been a while since she had heard the peaceful sound of nature without any interruptions. Suddenly, her serene moment was shattered by the sight of three wolves racing past her; their size and ferocity made her heart nearly jump out of her chest. These wolves were abnormally large. As they disappeared from view, Lilith saw Midas returning, his face contorted in dismay.

"You must come!" Midas shouted. "Elias is losing control!"

"I thought you had him handled."

"He hasn't killed anyone yet."

Lilith rushed behind Midas into a small, rustic house. Elias hammered away at an elderly man.

"That's enough!" she shouted, grabbing Elias by the hood of his cloak. "Go, walk whatever it is off, redirect that negative energy. We have to set sail once we get the boy."

Elias grunted and left. She walked over to the decrepit man tied to a chair. "I'm sorry about my friend here. He's a bit too aggressive."

The man held his head up, proud that he was not broke. A trait reminiscent of her father—she admired it. Lilith raised her arm slowly, feeling the surrounding energy pulsate through her body. Midas ducked underneath the short wooden entrance. "Are you sure you want to do this? Are you strong enough?"

It was the strongest she had ever felt. Midas was right to be concerned. She had to be careful. Using too much of her power was costly. "I'm fine." She closed a fist and pulled the chair toward her.

Lilith smiled. It was always special to see the shock on their faces, but he wasn't—not even a flinch.

The man shook his head in shame. "You are quite the gifted, aren't you," he said, his voice brittle but calm. "I have seen your kind before, Mature yet beautiful. Men are at their beck and call. You witches and huldras are all the same; you murder those who oppose you—"

Screaming from outside interrupted the hovering old man. She felt a tug on her shoulder that snapped her out of her daze and forced her to release him. His body dropped, the chair shattering as he hit the floor with a thud. His eyes lost their confidence. Instead, he looked at her like the monster he described.

"Faramond!" a young man burst into the room, helping up the old man, untying him from the chair. "You all have done so much, but you can stop protecting me. It's my turn."

Anger filled his eyes, and he stared at the three of them. Midas and Quintus stepped in front of Lilith with their weapons drawn.

Quintus pointed at him with his sword. "Was death something you had planned today?"

"Wait," Lilith held up a hand, as she recalled reading about a Darviant of this time with the ability to manipulate mass.

There was a boy, estimated to be in his late teens or early twenties, who was rumored to possess the bloodline of Wayland, the Norse smithing-god. He was both feared and revered, but his life was cut short—a few days from now, if she remembered correctly. That was because the king of Norway perceived him to be a threat.

He was on the list Sheldon gave her. *Darviants to look out for*, he had called it, and it clicked.

"You must be Trahen the Blacksmith?"

"Yes," Trahen replied, holding a short, thin piece of metal.

A thin white aura surrounded the metal, and it slowly transformed into a metallic hatchet. "You will pay for what you've done to these people."

"No need for anyone else to get hurt," Lilith said. "We just need your help."

"Why would I help you after what you did to this place, these people?"

"We didn't kill anyone. Yes, there were some things broken, some injuries. You weren't here to stop it, but you can save them from someone far worse."

Trahen didn't lower his weapon. It was obvious he felt threatened. "It's not me you need to worry about. The reign of King Harold will see this village and all its history burned, women and children slaughtered."

"She has the sight," said the old man.

"If so, she knows I'm not the blacksmith they are looking for."

"Not exactly," Lilith said. She looked at Midas. He knew exactly what to do.

Midas closed his eyes and replicated himself. Even if it had limitations, like limiting his strength, it was useful.

Before Trahen could raise his weapon, Midas stood on either side, holding him in place.

The man tried but couldn't move. Lilith made sure of it, sitting him back down in the seat. She looked at Trahen, who no longer struggled to break free.

"Take off your clothes," Lilith demanded.

"What? No!" said Trahen.

"I wish it didn't have to be this way."

With a wave, the young man's trousers and shirt fell, displaying his muscular physique under his sweaty, dirty body.

"Impressive."

Trahen's face flushed in red. Midas rolled his eyes. But she needed to know for sure if he bore the Sage's seal—he didn't. *He must be the youngest. If he wasn't the Vessel, then he had to be the Gatekeeper.*

"Bring him when he's finished," she said before meeting the others by the carriage.

"It's not him, is it?" asked Quintus.

"No," she replied.

Ingólfr and Hallveig lowered their heads.

"You two did great," said Lilith. "I will hold up my end of the bargain."

"I see," said Ingólfr.

Lilith heard a cursing Trahen struggling to break free from Midas. "Sorry," she said, before tapping his head, knocking him unconscious.

They loaded the boy in the back with them. She needed to get Jordan somewhere safe, and she also needed the Vessel. Lilith plotted her next plan before they left Norway, with the confidence her elaborate scheme would work. After days of planning and rest, everything was in place.

The day had come for them to set sail for Iceland. Ingólfr and Hallveig loaded up dozens of people from the village—Floki wasn't one of them. They promised him they would return.

After all, they were part of her plan. As for now, she needed to get back to Iceland and the cave. Their long journey meant time was not on her side.

They found a place to lie low as the others settled. Within a few days, she returned to the cave. She held up a decoder to the metal door, needed to decipher the alchemic labyrinth puzzle that hid what was beyond it.

"Dammit," Lilith said, slamming the decoder. The screen fluttered before blackening. *All the tech money can buy, and I can't decipher this.*"

Lilith leaned against the iron door, sliding down slightly as she tapped her head against its cold surface.

The eclipse was imminent, and yet she was no closer to unlocking the door. A spontaneous smile broke across her face as she realized that no amount of technology could accomplish this task; she needed the one person who could solve any puzzle.

"After all this, I still need her," she murmured to herself, the irony not lost on her.

KASUMI

Germany, 871 AD

Bathed in the tranquil silence of pre-dawn, Kasumi sought refuge within Mei's dwelling, where a celestial art made up the ceiling that whispered tales of long-forgotten mysteries. The world outside was veiled in darkness, not just as a silent witness to the threshold of day and night, but the witness to the miracles over the last few nights.

Inside, crackling flames cast a light, inviting shadows to dance against the wall to the silent strum of turmoil twisting Kasumi's thoughts. She had seen many things in her twenty-eight years, but nothing compared to what hadhappened since arriving in Germany.

Kasumi sat alone, cup of tea in hand, watching the shadows around stretch and bend, as if reaching out to grasp the truths she was struggling to comprehend. Hlidegard, Malaya, and Zoya slept, but she could not.

Since arriving, something stirred the Kitsune unlike before, almost as if it was crying out for Kasumi, but she did not know how to respond. In truth, she was too worried about Malaya, who had not spoken a word of what happened. It was almost as if she withdrew into herself.

Denial, she thought, but she could not approach the subject.

Who was Malaya Castillo-Grant? A girl that could wake the dead yet did not believe anything that did not have reason.

Kasumi sighed and sipped her tea, losing herself in her own thoughts.

The sound of creaking floorboards echoed through the room as a large shadow emerged on the wall, gradually diminishing as it moved closer around the corner. Part of her hoping it was Malaya. She could have an excuse to bombard her with questions.

It was not Malaya.

Instead, it was the woman, Mei, who had taken them in, and in return, the gods blessed her with the return of her daughter. Mei smiled her wrinkled smile and asked Kasumi for permission to sit down in her own chair. Kasumi nodded matter-of-factly before helping the old small woman sit.

"Would you like some tea?" Kasumi asked, driven still by the ways of her world, a life she chose to leave behind, but some habits are hard to break.

"No, dear, it is quite alright." Mei replied, gesturing for Kasumi to sit. "I have come to speak with you."

"Oh," was the only word Kasumi managed, caught off guard by the unsuspecting announcement.

"I will not bore you with pleasantries," Mei's tone shifted with the flames, serious and commanding. "You have come to my home harboring secrets of who you truly are. The feral, divine power within you has you unrest, afraid, curious. Please feel free to stop me when I am wrong."

Kasumi sat quite dumbfounded. The air grew thick with anticipation, the kind that precedes a storm. For what Mei had revealed was so profound that even the Kitsune quieted.

"Fox got your tongue, perhaps?" Mei said. Her words hit Kasumi's heart with the ferocity of a drum.

Kasumi's grip tightened on her cup, the warmth of the tea no longer reaching her. Mei's insight into her soul was unnerving, yet it stirred something within her—a longing for answers, for understanding.

"Who are you?" Kasumi finally managed.

"Mei, of course," the old woman quibbled as if she was enjoying this. "Perhaps you want to know how I knew you three were coming? Or How I know that, you know how I know none of it compares to the real question you need answers to?"

Kasumi started to speak, but truly did not know what to say to this woman sitting before her. An enigma who spoke in riddles, yet she knew, somehow Mei held answers.

"I can tell so much is happening in your thought cage." Mei chuckled, her laughter echoing softly in the quiet space. "Forgive me. Some habits, inherited from my parents, are hard to shed. We've always reveled in the intricate dance between deities and mortals, and even among the gods themselves. This is the very reason you find yourself here, Kasumi. It's why each of you has been drawn to this moment."

Kasumi shifted in her seat.

"Your paths are etched with the potential for greatness, shaped by the decisions you make. Consider Malaya, for instance. Unaware of her true essence, she stands at the precipice of discovery. The role she has played thus far is but a prelude." her voice softened. "Oblivious to the realms of magic now, soon her Magical Pores will awaken, altering her destiny in ways not unlike her father's, a man who sacrificed for a world he did not belong to. And you..."

Mei's golden eyes locked on Kasumi. "You struggle with purpose, but what you fail to realize is that you have been serving that purpose most of your life. You have been, and will always be, a protector, Kasumi." She paused. "Or should I say, Furihime Tokugawa?"

In that moment, Kasumi's heart skipped a beat and lodged itself in her throat, leaving her breathless. Her stomach turned as the name danced around in her head like a forgotten tune.

She took a moment. Her training taught her to mask her emotions. But the mention of her old name unearthed memories she thought she had buried deep. She had not heard the name, or even thought of the girl that was for some time. That girl died with Genzo.

Kasumi's mouth trembled before she asked a question she was not sure she wanted the answer to.

"Furihime Tokugawa is a shadow of my past." She steadied her voice as best as she could. "But you speak of purposes and destinies as if they are written in the stars, unchangeable. I've learned that fate is not so rigid. It bends under the weight of our choices."

"I knew I was wise to choose you first," Mei said, her tone filled with pride. "You are correct, my dear. The future is not set in stone. It is fluid like a stream, its path guided by nature, changing with movements of the earth, only the stream does not have a choice on which path it takes. We all have free will, and some paths are more illuminated than others. Like the stream we are guided by forces beyond our understanding, Only God knows what lies at the end of each path. Some of us can only see one."

"You said *God*, as in one."

"Yes, the God Above All."

"I am aware of God, Yahweh," she said, drawing the cross from beneath her tunic. "And I know of the other divine beings—the Elohim."

Kasumi adjusted herself in her seat. "But in my homeland, worshiping the singular God is prohibited." her voice faded into silence, her gaze lost in the dance of shadows on the wall. Memories of a harrowing night she longed to erase yet couldn't forget resurfaced.

As darkness cloaked the camp, Kasumi recalled the unspeakable acts inflicted upon the faithful of the one true God by the Oni King. Despite the fire's warmth, a shiver ran through her as she thought of that night long ago, when she and her friends had faced the monster and his Demon Clan.

Even now, his shadow lingered, reaching out from beyond the grave—a haunting reminder of a power so vast it echoed through time. The memories of that night stood in stark contrast to the warmth of her new life, a new path.

Mei's voice brought her back. "Do not let the past trouble you so much."

"You said that I was a protector all my life. That is not true."

"No need to deny it, child. Oni was the first of your many battles, but that thirst for quest still thrives within the Tenge inside."

As Kasumi met Mei's gaze, her heart quickened, a tide of recognition sweeping through her. Those same golden eyes, which had once guided her amidst the tranquil mountains of China, now held her own, carrying the weight of wisdom and stillness.

They brought to mind the Monk, whose teachings had deepened her bond with the Tenge, unlocking abilities she had not known lay dormant within her. In that moment, she began to understand—truths could be found within many paths.

And then there was Himiko, spoken of in hushed tones as divine, her eyes reflecting that same ancient wisdom. The presence of such beings always stirred the Tenge within her, whispering of truths she had yet to fully comprehend.

It was a connection, a lineage of power that transcended time, and now, it seemed, had led her to Mei. The realization dawned on her that the journey of understanding her Tenge, of unraveling its mysteries, was far from over. It was a path intertwined with beings of extraordinary power. Perhaps Mei was the latest guide on this path, holding answers Kasumi had long sought.

The silence between them was filled with unasked questions, with the Kitsune inside her stirring, ready for the truths that Mei might reveal.

"Who are you?" Kasumi asked, her voice a mix of urgency. "Really, no games or mysterious talk, please..."

The chair creaked as Mei leaned forward, her golden eyes shimmering a bit brighter when she smiled. Kasumi watched intently, her tea momentarily forgotten, as Mei revealed truths that seemed to stretch the fabric of reality itself.

"I am a being once removed from time and space, with a heritage linked to the realm made for the divine. Some may call them gods and others the progeny of angels. No matter the name, they are above man." Mei's eyes stared off for a moment, lost in the weight of her own history.

Kasumi's grip tightened around her cup, the warmth of the tea no longer comforting as she tried to grasp the vastness of Mei's existence.

"I have lived as a ruler, a queen, commanded armies, started wars, and saved humanity from many more. I have been revered and feared, hunted, loved, and cursed. I am Sigrunn, timekeeper of the once-revered Aigons—divine beings akin to the Kami revered in Shinto, the Orishas of Yoruba spirituality, the gods of Greece and Norse mythology, the deities of the Taino, and countless others." Mei's voice carried a mixture of pride and melancholy, echoing the loneliness of her long journey.

Kasumi felt a chill despite the fire's warmth, the air thick with the history and power emanating from Mei. The mention of Kami and other gods drew a line connecting Mei's past to Kasumi's own spiritual understanding, yet the expanse between them seemed vast.

"Some have called me and those of the Aigon bloodline, fallen gods," Mei scoffed, the term seemingly offensive. "An ambitious title, considering what truly happened."

Kasumi swallowed, her throat dry. The revelation that Mei was not just a witness but a participant in the history of gods and men reshaped her understanding of the world. She set her cup down, the sound barely audible over the crackling fire. Her mind raced with questions.

"Fallen gods," Kasumi repeated softly, her voice a whisper against the magnitude of Mei's confession.

"The Sages," Mei continued, the name escaping her lips. "It was our own fault..." Her voice carried a grim tone, merging with the shadows dancing across her features. "After the Cataclysm that flooded the Earth, my ancestors endowed these gifted mortals with the power to shape reality, to bend the elements and harness magic at their will. Bestowed with the essence of the divine, seven immensely powerful beings became gods amongst men, ruling entire regions of the old world. But with great power comes the potential for corruption. Assisted by a dark source, these entities became immortal, forever altering the natural course of an already chaotic world."

Mei's revelation of the Sages sent a chill down Kasumi's spine recalling the tales of the Shadows of Yomi, the might and wisdom of seven great mortals that were more than human but less than god were legendary. So was the tale of their downfall. Their quest for knowledge led them down a path of darkness, the same as Mei's story.

"All magic requires a balance," Mei said, her eyes drifting once more. "The Champions were born, some say centuries too late, but those Fourteen defeated the Sages, insuring balance within the human realm."

Kasumi's mind raced as she connected the dots. "How did you, your ancestors, become the fallen gods?"

"The other gods decided it after learning the Sages could be reborn. It was our punishment. We live amongst those we birthed, destined to find a way to reverse their immortal curse."

Kasumi sighed, still not understanding what any of this had to do with her. She was no Champion, nor a Sage. "Mei, please forgive my bluntness, but what does that have to do with me?"

"Dawn is approaching," Mei said. "The others will wake soon, and there is no better time to connect than now. Perhaps the way to the Awakened State is out there."

Kasumi lowered her head. "I have mediated plenty. Still, nothing." She looked up. Mei was gone, vanished as quickly as flame under a slight blow.

Kasumi thought about searching for her, but changed her mind. If a god told her answers lay within the earth, who was she to go against it? Grabbing one of Mei's blankets, she made her way outside, seeking the serene guidance of nature near the pond that awakened Hildegard's other half. A few meters away sat the dungeon where Sigrun had been brought back to life.

Perhaps this is the place for answers, she thought, crossing her legs and closing her eyes. She would absorb the energy before walking on the earth, feet to dirt becoming one with nature.

Leaves crunched behind her, snapping her eyes open. She turned her head to find no one. "Sorry to startle you," a resounding deep voice forced her head around to a man standing before her, with hair so bright it rivaled the sky before dawn.

His shoulders were wide as large tree trunks and his arms large as boulders. Yet, there was a warmth in his eyes, a gentleness with an air of innocence like a boy who had not taken a life. More than that, he valued it.

Kasumi stayed seated. "You should be careful who you sneak up on."

"My grandmother told me that I could help you."

Kasumi opened one eye. "Help me how..." Now sooner than the words left his mouth, Mei came to mind.

Was he supposed to provide the answers? She thought.

"You are a Tenge, struggling with understanding the path the gods set before you. Unless I am mistaken," he said mockingly.

Kasumi thought to say something snide, but held her tongue for once. If he was to help her, barking would not get her fed. "You are correct," she said, her tone even.

The faint, ethereal glow of pre-dawn cast subtle shadows across his boyish face. "I am capable of seeing paths," he began. He made a gesture toward the empty spot on her blanket.

Kasumi nodded her approval.

"I am what many call a seer." The large boy shifted to face Kasumi, a bit too close for her taste. She backed away a bit. He instead did not get the hint but held out his large hands as if to ask her to place hers in them.

"I do not wish to have my fortune told."

"I apologize for the confusion," he said, lowering his hands. "My intention wasn't merely to reveal the path of mortals, but to explore those divine in nature. For you, specifically, I can unveil the Tenge's past, helping you grasp its true purpose. This knowledge will aid you in navigating the tumultuous future," his voice resonated with the depth of someone who had traversed many lifetimes. "The journey of the Tenge extends beyond mere power or transformative states. It encompasses understanding the cycles of existence, the equilibrium between creation and destruction, and the delicate barrier that divides our reality from realms unseen."

Kasumi hesitated, the shadows of past battles flickering across her mind. "How do I know this path won't lead me into darkness I cannot escape?""You don't." He held out his hands once more. "All you need to do is take a leap of faith."

His words tugged at her heart. Kasumi's eyes shot up, locking onto his. She was mistaken; he was not the innocent, she thought, but wise beyond his years. "I do not allow men to touch me without knowing their names."

"I do not wish to touch you," he snapped. His face flushed the same red as his hair. Kasumi took pride in this, feeling hse took back some power. He cleared his throat. "I am Gavdarr, Seer of the Divine."

"I am Kasumi, just Kasumi," she said, placing her hand in his.

"How is this supposed to work?"

"By letting go," Gavdarr said, standing up. "Let go of your preconceptions, your fears, and your doubts. Embrace the present moment, for it is all we truly have. And in doing so, you'll see the threads of time, how they intersect and diverge, and how you can influence them, just as they influence you."

His voice resonated with an ethereal quality as he wove the narrative, his hands clasping Kasumi's gently, grounding her for the journey they were about to embark upon.

"Close your eyes, Kasumi, and let your spirit be the vessel through which the ancient truths flow."

As Kasumi closed her eyes, a soft luminance enveloped them, the world around her dissipating into a mist of light. She felt herself lifted, transcending realms, her essence guided by Gavdarr's unseen force.

They arrived in a celestial expanse, where the fabric of time rippled like water under a gentle breeze. Here, the cosmos unfolded in layers of vibrant hues, each strand of color a testament to the eons that shaped the universe.

"In the dawn of ages," Gavdarr's voice echoed around her, "when chaos and order danced in eternal embrace, Inari, the deity of harmony and balance, foresaw a rift in the weave of destiny. The Sages, ingrained with the essence of creation, bore the potential to tip the scales towards an irreversible chaos."

Kasumi's vision swirled, drawing her into a moment frozen in time where Inari, in her divine majesty, stood at the precipice of creation. Her form was both magnificent and terrifying, a beacon of light against the shadow of impending doom.

"Against the counsel of her celestial kin, Inari chose a path of intervention. She reached out to the Aigons, beings of time and space, to forge a covenant that would echo through the ages."

The scene shifted, revealing Inari and the Aigons in a sacred conclave, their figures casting long shadows across the fabric of time. From Inari's essence, a spark ignited, weaving into existence the lineage of the Tenge—a force destined to counterbalance the might of the Sages.

Kasumi watched, her spirit afloat amidst the cosmic tapestry, as the Tenge's purpose was sown into the heart of the world. Each thread represented a choice, a potential path that the Tenge could take—a protector, a guardian of the delicate equilibrium between creation and destruction.

"You must wield your power with caution," Gavdarr added, his voice a gentle reminder in the vastness of her vision. "The Tenge, while a gift, bears the weight of wisdom and restraint. The Sages, lost to their thirst for knowledge, strayed from their purpose, leading to their downfall. You have seen this happen with other Tenge and you must not repeat their mistakes."

Kasumi felt the essence of the pact, the solemn promise between Inari and the Aigons, envelop her being. It was a legacy of guardianship, an eternal vow to uphold the balance of the universe.

"As you tread the path of the Tenge," Gavdarr's voice faded, bringing Kasumi back to the present, "remember the origins of your power."

Slowly, the celestial expanse dissolved, the colors fading into the soft glow of dawn. Kasumi opened her eyes, the remnants of the divine journey lingering in her soul. She understood now—the depth of her lineage, the purpose of her power, and the path she must walk to reach the Awakened State.

Gavdarr smiled, a knowing glint in his eyes. "The past is the foundation upon which the future is built. Embrace your legacy, and let it guide you towards the enlightenment you seek."

Kasumi absorbed his words, a sense of clarity beginning to dawn within her. With this newfound knowledge, she was ready to face the trials ahead, her spirit aligned with the ancient pact that bound her destiny to the will of the divine.

"So, my training...?"

"I can imagine with my father and Grandmother. it will not be traditional," Gavdarr confirmed, standing up. "Consider this: if time is a river, most only touch its surface. But you must learn to navigate its depths, to see beyond the immediate, to perceive the possibilities that lie within each moment. This is how you'll break the veil, not by force, but by understanding."

As Gavdarr disappeared back into the early morning light, Kasumi felt a peace she hadn't known in a long time. She remained seated, the first rays of the sun warming her face, pondering the journey ahead. She understood she would be exploring the depths of her own being and the nature of the universe itself. She also wondered if her friends would have the same sense of clarity.

VASILIS

Germany, 871

The gods lie. Eternal youth wasn't what Vasilis thought it would be. Although he wasn't immortal, it didn't stop the feeling in his gut. He turned nineteen today, at least according to science. It was his fourth era, thousands of years after his birth. Yet here he was, experiencing what he shouldn't have, or perhaps what he should.

The boulder he sat on felt the same, and so did the bright green grass on his feet that covered the land as far as he could see. Even the white peaks that sprouted from the grass still took his breath away. Large valleys and fresh rivers were like home, calm to the point it was asleep, but this wasn't a dream, or a simulator.

As usual, he sharpened his weapons to pass the time. Incichi blessed the carcass he slew before dressing it. Jordan lay a few feet away on a bash of flowers, staring into the blue sky. It was something he'd done ever since they arrived. Today, it was daisies.

"Perhaps I can find the man you seek if I lay next to you," Vasilis said, lying in the opposite direction, their eyes locked in on the eagle chasing the falcon.

"I love eagles. Eagles are life," Jordan said.

"Yes, the world is wonderful because it is a creation of the gods."

"Thales of Miletus?"

"Correct," Vasilis smirked. His intellect continued to impress him.

Throughout their journey, Jordan did nothing more than comply. Both Vasilis and Inoichi could tell his heart was absent. They understood, given the both of them lost their fathers, but unlike the two warriors, Jordan never had never basked in his father's warmth, never absorbed the wisdom of his words, nor felt the guiding pressure of a loving hand—pressure meant to mold, not break, to transform coal into diamonds under the weight of expectations and love.

"Boy!" Inoichi shouted, snapping Jordan out of his sky gazing. "A boy with ears lives forever."

"Sorry, I don't know who that is, Mr. Tokugawa."

"Tokugawa Inoichi. Now come learn how to prepare your food."

Vasilis grabbed the Elk by its hind legs while Inoichi removed its organs, saving most of it for the road. They followed the river, trading meat and valuables from their sack along the way. Inoichi kept to himself when he wasn't instructing the boy. It was an admirable quality in Inoichi. Vasilis did what he could, but lacked the same tenacity for teaching.

The nights were quiet. For Jordan, it was a bit unsettling. He would become chatty and tremble in his sleep. At the moment, he was not sleeping. Vasilis did not mind the conversation.

Being here, the distance between him and the busy sounds and lights of the modern world—here, he was the expert. Refreshing nature aside, Germany did not wield any pleasing results. Not after a few run-ins with angry locals and fruitless results. A dull night was a welcoming one. It didn't hurt that it was Vasilis's birthday.

"Where are the Vikings?" Jordan said as he tossed a piece of meat into the fire.

"Don't waste meat," Vasilis said, grabbing the meat out of the fire. "This is not your era. You can starve to death in the real world."

"My bad. I was just expecting more."

"Be careful of what you ask for. You will get your adventure soon enough," Inoichi said, tossing a berry into his mouth.

A soft, angelic voice ended the conversation. With Forsaken in hand, Vasilis stood up. No words needed to be said—their eyes did all the talking. There was a chance it was a trap, but morally, they couldn't object. Inoichi agreed to stay and guard the boy and valuables.

Lantern in hand, Vasilis walked into the black forest. A light shined through the slim trees. It's not a fire, he thought, hearing his heartbeat over the sounds of gravel crumbling beneath his feet.

"Please, help us," pleaded a girl, sending bumps down his spine.

He poked his head around a tree, seeing a girl kneeling over a motionless body with a bright white aura radiating from her hands. She called for help again. The frigid air didn't stop his hands from sweating. How do I get myself into these situations?

The girl looked up. Her unusual gray eyes pleaded for help. "A snake bit him," she said as the lights from her hand dwindled. "Please help."

He rubbed his hand through his air and scratched his forehead.

Natwat prepared them well. They had more than they needed for survival, including a universal antivenom.

"I can help." He lifted the man over his shoulder. "He's a big one," Vasilis said in a failed attempt to lighten the mood. "What is your name?"

"Sigrunn."

"Don't worry, Sigrunn. We will help him."

Inoichi and Jordan had questions as he placed the stranger by the fire. He explained what little he knew. Jordan brought the vial, and Vasilis helped him drink it, but the man was not well. The girl kept saying it was her fault.

Vasilis looked into her worried eyes, then at the fallen red-haired stranger, whose face was covered in cuts and old bruises. *There was no way she could have done this.*

"What happened?" Inoichi said, looking at the girl. "The truth."

She wiped her eyes. "A group of men. They wanted me and Gier. He... he stopped them."

"You said it was a snake," Vasilis exclaimed.

"It-it was. There was one among them with a gift of a serpent—one that extended from his arm."

Vasilis looked to Inoichi, hoping the fire to fight was in his eyes. "Should we go after them?"

"No," said Inoichi. "General Williams gave us our orders. You are a man of medicine. I will take the boy and scavenge for what you need to help this man, can you not?"

Vasilis nodded and gave them the simple list of things he'd need. He watched his mother cure disease and close the worst wounds. She taught him to do the same. While he didn't share her same gift, Vasilis did what he could to ensure the wounds did not get infected. Inoichi encouraged Jordan and Sigrunn to do something that avoided both him and Inoichi, sleep.

As the sun began to rise, they discussed strategy and tried to figure out what would happen with the girl if Gier didn't make it. Time seemed to crawl as they did what they could, given the circumstances.

"Thank you," Vasilis heard the red-haired man grumble. Sigrunn jumped up and rushed to his aid—helping him to his feet. Jordan wasn't far behind.

Inoichi scanned Gier's bruises down to his worn boots with his usual scolding look of agitation and distrust. "He recovered rather quickly, given how close he was to the edge of death. Wouldn't you say so, Spartan?"

"Aye."

"We need answers," Inoichi said sharply. "It is the least you can do after we saved your life."

"We?"

"Shut up, idiot."

"Guys," Jordan said, stepping between them. "Relax."

Gier looked down at Sigrunn. She nodded. "Vasilis saw my light, so there is no point in hiding anything. To eye such a bright light, you must have God's blood."

Grier looked at Vasilis, then at Inoichi. "Both are half-bloods, like you."

"No one is quite like me," she said. Her voice was nearly a whisper.

"Sorry." Grier sighed before he looked at Inoichi. "We are Aigons who come from a protected village hidden in the fog of enchantment. Sigrunn has something special latent within her, a power so great people wish to harness it for themselves. However, if she loses control—"

"Lies," Inoichi said the words out loud, but his body language and facial expression told a different story.

Sigrunn tilted her head. "Your mouth speaks it, but your eyes do not lie. You believe him. If you are afraid—"

"I am not."

"Good, because I cannot bear hurting any more people. My mother sacrificed enough so that I would not. It aged her so. If she continues, I fear we will lose her."

"What is this latent power?" asked Jordan.

"I am what they call a Vessel to a great evil, born with the seal. Our history is extensive and complicated. My mother fell in love and did what was taboo—"

"Mating outside of your clan?" Inoichi interrupted. His tone was no longer defensive.

"Yes," said Gier. "The blood of our people and that of mortals should not mix. At least, that is what was told."

Inoichi pressed for more answers. As they continued to share their story, thoughts of his old life came back to Vasilis. The stories of the gods mating with mortals.

According to Sparta, there were two families that were descended from the twins, Eurysthenes and Procles, the descendants of the demi-god Heracles. His family were part of the Agiads, as was Elias's mother, Vasilis's aunt Vashty, his father's sister, and Midas, formerly of the Eurypontids. It was both fantastical and yet real. Still, it was a large pill to swallow, but the stories of his own people weren't that far from hers. *Banished gods... a hidden realm... Vessels of a great power. What if it is all connected?*

Inoichi frowned. "You say you are searching for others like you? Aigons, as if they can prevent the inevitable. Age and death are a part of life. Nothing will change that."

Sigrunn showed them a well-aged parchment with a coded message. "It's a coded message from my people. It was my grandfather's. We lost the means to fully translate its meaning, but we believe it holds the key to rejuvenation. It tells the story of Idunn, the goddess of fertility."

"She's a myth. All of it is," said Jordan. "Look, I'm not closed-minded. I understand divinity, but this is bullshit."

"My family's history is not false, child," said Sigrunn.

"I didn't mean it like that," said Jordan. "I apologize. It's just that nothing is forever, but if it's coded, I can help. I love puzzles."

She gave him a dirty look but handed it to him, anyway. Jordan scanned the parchment, passing his finger over it. "This could help. It's fragmented. *Healing of the land, Idunn, Bragi's wife, Tiazi the giant,* and *Loki.*"

Vasilis raised his brow. He actually discovered the coded key.

"Wait, I think I know this story," said Jordan. "Tiazi abducts Idunn, sending the Norse gods into a panic. Loki saves her, then shape shifts into a falcon to escape. Tiazi does the same, but as an eagle and chases him."

"This symbol," said Inoichi, breaking Jordan's joy. "An eagle, why?" He pointed at the end of the message. "In your story, the antagonist turns into an eagle."

"Good point," Vasilis said. "My gods have the nectar of immortality. When the father of my gods was an infant, an eagle brought it to Zeus. Even his daughter, Hebe, turns into an eagle."

"The golden eagle is also tied to my gods, the Tengu," added Inoichi.

The fire in Jordan's eyes returned. "Garuda also resembles an eagle in both Hinduism and Buddhism—he's also tied to the elixir of immortality. The Bible also refers to someone's youth to be renewed, like an eagle."

"The Danes of Denmark," Gier said. "There are Danes with eagles on their shields. It is said they were inspired by gods."

"Why panic?" Inoichi said. "Why did the gods care for a god of Vanir?"

Jordan's face lit up. "Because her apples helped the Norse gods stay young."

"A continuous rejuvenation process," said Vasilis.

"That's the key," said Sigrunn. "I need to find the apples for mama."

"No, not apples," said Jordan. "They use the word *Epli*, meaning small berries or nuts. In the story, Loki turns Idunn into a nut so that he can better hold her as a falcon."

"So, your gods must have these nuts," said Vasilis.

"It seems that way," said Gier.

"Amazing," said Sigrunn, staring at Jordan.

Vasilis patted Jordan on the back. Even so, he didn't seem gratified. "I'm sorry I can't decode the entire message. If Malaya were here, she would have—"

Sigrunn interrupted him. "Malaya? I have met someone of the same name."

Everyone froze. Jordan shared the same wide-eyed look. This was no coincidence, but they had to be sure.

Sigrunn continued. "She woke me from my long sleep. She traveled with three other women, Hildegard, Zoya, and Kasumi—"

"Kasumi," both Vasilis and Inoichi said simultaneously.

Inoichi's frown wiped the grin from Vasilis's face—he pushed him aside. "Where are they?"

"Likely near what the Saxons called Norpweg. Who are they to you?"

"Malaya is..." Jordan trailed.

"His sister," Vasilis said. "And Kasumi is Inoichi's sister."

"Will you come with us to Norway?" Jordan's nervousness shone through his smile. "Malaya's wicked smart. She can decode this for sure."

"I cannot," said Sigrunn, knocking the joy from Jordan's face.

"So, I guess we're going our separate ways," he said.

"Our paths will cross again, Jordan," said Sigrunn.

She kissed him on the cheek before they parted.

Vasilis teased Jordan en route to their destination. It took the last of their gold to secure safe passage to Norway. Most tried to avoid the Viking Sea. The merchant ship wasn't much, but the crew was sturdy.

Vasilis found a sense of peace at sea. So much had happened since his death, his awakening, but he felt more sleep than ever.

This world was vast, with much left to be explored—even within himself. His mentor and his former friends played for the other team. At least he had Inoichi to understand this complicated new life.

His wife was on the other side, with those responsible for the death of his family. And his sister was surely tied to Malaya by now. At this point, the title of good or bad was just a matter of perspective.

Norway was the opposite of Germany. Where the soil was rich, mud and gravel made up Norway. The land was hard, brittle, and dry. Much like most of the people they came across. They covered themselves with cloaks, pushed fast, and didn't overstay their welcome. Sigrunn's information was accurate.

The village was easily found. They were sure to stay hidden behind, but asking for Elvir made people take notice. Canderyn's name also rang a bell for some. Black mud slushed underneath their boots as they walked through the village of homes made of wood and stone.

"This was far too easy, Spartan," said Inoichi.

"I don't like it either," Vasilis said, keeping Jordan close to him.

They spotted rows of cattle and villagers gathering at the center. The people seemed to be preparing for a journey.

"Old man," said Vasilis, spotting a man peeking out his door. "We have just arrived. What is going on?"

The man was skin and bones. "Uppsala," he said, closing himself in.

They looked at Jordan, who seemed to know more about this era than most.

Jordan was horrified. "A religious pilgrimage. They travel to a mountain and sacrifice for seventy-two days."

"I see," said Vasilis. "So they will sacrifice the cattle. That's not uncommon."

He could tell there was more to it. Jordan pressed his lips.

"Well..." said Inoichi. "Spit it out"

"They also sacrifice humans. This is a bad time to be here," Jordan said.

Inoichi grabbed the boy, taking him into an alley. Vasilis followed. Vikings carried sacs on their shoulders as they passed by—rows of men followed. The old man's sign led them into his home. He had no windows, but the inside was grim. There were dried bones on his walls, odd stones, and statues. The young men kept close to one another; they allowed the strange man to lead the way, passing hanging objects.

"Please sit, the old man said. "You should wait until the men leave."

"No. What the f-" Jordan started before Inoichi grabbed his mouth.

"The boy is not well in the head," said Inoichi. "Thank you, grandfather."

"Tonight is a special evening. An awakening is coming. A fellow seer awaits."

"Seer? Who?" questioned Vasilis.

"Wait and see for yourself."

After thanking the old man, they found it easy to blend in with the leftovers.

So they did. By nightfall, most of the village had left, but a group of red-cloaked men and women stood behind. They gathered around an enormous fire, filling the air with smoke.

They drank, sang, and passed mushrooms around in the form of a drink. The ritual seemed ancient, sending chills down Vasilis's spine. He was tempted to take part, but after Japan, Vasilis did not dare risk Jordan's life.

Two men sat next to them, one tall, a redhead with pale white skin and a large braid. A brown-haired man with a mustache and goatee sat on the opposite side.

A shirtless man with white face paint stood up. "I am Arn, and tonight we welcome a god that will bless us with wisdom. First, a worthy man must step up. One with prestige to his name, so the rest of us can be worthy of his presence."

No one stepped forward. Everyone looked around at one another, murmuring.

"Damn this. I want to see him," the brown-haired young man said before standing up. "My name is Trahen. I am a famous blacksmith. I demand his presence."

From the shadows, a man emerged. He must have been seven feet, at least. His arms and shoulders were godly, and his braid complemented any skilled warrior—a god even. So was the hilt on his waist. A faint glow in its carvings surged through the text carved into the center of the massive blade. He unsheathed his sword, swinging it in the air. Inoichi and Vasilis looked at one another.

"My name is Elvir."

SETH

New York, 2076

Dawn usually accompanied ungodly hours at MEV, making sleep a loathing necessity. There was a renewed level of respect for Lilith's work ethic. However, for the first time since arriving on Earth, he stood over his penthouse balcony basking in the New York skyline. Maki was in his ear, and while they usually talked business, she made him promise to watch the sunrise.

The view reminded him of how big the world was, how little he was compared to it, and what little power he held, even with the UNA Empress on his side.

Maki made things simple. She made this abnormal world feel normal. Maki didn't know it, but they shared an unspoken bond. Tragedy granted the UNA Empress everything, but it was Lilith who put her in that position, Lilith who manipulated as much of her life as she did with his.

"You sound exhausted," he said, running his fingers across the carvings of the antique Greek table. "I see. Well, that's the thing about power. Someone is always trying to take it." He paced with the phone to his ear, butterflies fluttering in his stomach like a teen speaking to a girl in the meadow.

"No experience at all, just a lover of history... My favorite? My home of Laconia, Greece... Their history is rich. I feel most connected to its story, especially Sparta."

Their sacred kinship allowed him to connect with her in a way he could have never imagined, but not enough to reveal his true self. Instead, he wore the mask of Achilles Teresi as well as his three-piece suit. His new identity helped him compartmentalize his thoughts.

Here, he wasn't a warrior, just a conquer. Like the silver tie tucked behind his blue vest, what he revealed about himself stood out just enough to get Maki's attention. Achilles was more than a mask; in many ways, it was a new beginning—a past etched in his history as lore. This new world offered a fresh start and so much more — he was ready to embrace it.

Seth cleared his throat. "Speaking of history, because of our last conversation, I did some digging into your father's death. It seems Ghost never had a history of assassination. It's hard for me to believe they single-handedly pulled off a job of that scale."

A knock on the door grabbed his attention. "I'm afraid I must go... *Mata au made*," he said before removing the earpiece.

The doorman escorted him to the elevator. He could hear the choppers' soft whining blades as he opened the door to the launch pad. As always, he tipped him handsomely, including some extra bandwidth. "Don't tell anyone, kid," he said before boarding the self-piloting chopper.

He programmed the destination, and the chopper took flight to MEV Inc.

Below, protestors gathered, filling the block between MEV and Carlo's Café. Two groups protested, neither truly understanding how right they were nor how little control their words had. Things were different with him. Achilles Teresi controlled a multi-Trillion-dollar corporation and took it to new heights. Despite the pushback from the board, MEV earned the title of the most profitable tech company in the last thirty days.

The rooftop helped him avoid the chaos below. His penthouse office sat across from Jose's, separated by the conference room. It had Lilith's touch, from the window overlooking the sunset to the stocked minibar, state-of-the-art appliances, and designer furniture. He had grown used to it, the spoils of running the company.

Despite his best attempts to avoid dwelling on the past, there was still an unfillable void within him. He reached into his desk for his medication, needing to avoid the inevitable migraines. They were growing worse. The medicine dissolved on his tongue. He washed the residue down with a drink.

"Good morning, Mr. Teresi," said Emma, his assistant. Her deep olive cheeks widened with a smile as golden as her silken wavy hair. She was excellent at her job; it was expected, considering where she came from.

Emma, like her twin sister Arya, was gifted children from the House of Angela. They were early recruits for a special program, unlike many others who were kept hidden behind the fortress built to contain their abilities. Many of the institutions across the world interned these children's talents, but not anymore, not at the expense of MEV. If he was going to conquer this new world, he'd need more than money.

He needed weapons and a team, much like he had in Sparta, the Krypteia. He cut the funding, forcing the International Intern Program to close—some of the schools themselves were next.

As he combed through his agenda, Emma interrupted. "Mrs. Albright is here to see you."

The meeting doesn't start for another hour, he thought, looking at his watch. He closed the files with a swipe of his hand. "Send her in."

Rose's heels hammered as she barged in. "Shutting down the House of Angela wasn't part of her plan."

"I did MEV a favor. HOA was draining the company."

"Do I□" she lowered her voice, tugging on the straight skirt and box jacket of her designer black suit. "Do I need to remind you of why you're here?"

"No, I'll remind you." He stood up and walked toward Rose. "I was groomed, handpicked by Lilith to run her kingdom. She deserves to regain her wealth tenfold. In return, I will regain her trust, and I will not allow anyone to get in my way."

"Your contravene behavior was predictable," said Rose. "You fail to realize you don't have any true power."

"You are nothing more than a glorified babysitter," he replied. "Go back to the Intrepid and twiddle your thumbs. If Lilith wants to speak, she needs to contact me herself."

The fire ran from her hair into her eyes. Servo noises came from her prosthetic arm as she squeezed the wood on the back of the chair, cracking it. "Don't be stupid. The gods will not favor you," he said, brushing past her toward the restroom. See yourself out."

Rose cleared her throat. "Consequences of your decisions will have dire repercussions... Seth," she said, exiting his office.

Seth, a name he hadn't heard in what seemed an eternity. The demobilizing headache happened again, causing him to drop to one knee—he closed his eyes. Fragmented memories clawed their way to the front, flashing one after the other.

Images of people he'd known, a life he never knew but felt familiar. This time, there was something new: a faceless woman calling him home to Delphi.

"Mr. Teresi," he heard Emma shout, rushing into his office. "Here," she said, holding his head and placing the patch on his tongue.

Within seconds, the pain was gone, along with the faceless woman, for now. Seth picked himself up, walking to the long white daybed. "You had something for me?" he asked, laying down.

"It can wait, sir."

Seth gently grabbed her wrist. "It's ok."

Emma nodded. She took a deep breath before she spoke. "You've taken a wicked PR hit after shutting down the HOA. It's a smart move to mentor some of the elite students. New Seattle is a great start, sir." She unfolded her tablet, swiping her hand across the clear surface. A young student from New Seattle's HOA appeared along with his profile. "This is Yuk Fat, a.k.a. Jin, the one you've been asking for."

"Good work, kid. I'll take it from here," he said, swiping through his profile.

Yuk Fat was someone he saw during the flashes brought on by the headaches, though he was much younger. *It must be destiny*, he thought, reading his profile and spending the moments before the meeting researching everything about him.

The Fat family had connections with the UNA, in addition to a rich history that dates back to the Wu Kingdom. Through research and connections, he learned about Yuk Fat's gift of vast perception and the ability to read an enemy is a priceless tool.

However, Sensei, his relative, was of great interest. He was vocal about the HOA shutdown. If Yuk Fat were to join his Krypteia, Sensei was the key. He'd have to make some calls to see if he could be persuaded, but that had to wait. It was time for the emergency meeting.

Seth sat at the head of the twelve-seat table; the walls were made of glass, allowing the light inside the room. Jose was late, but the other board members bombarded the company lawyer with questions, but he refused to answer. *Was this the day Malaya would claim her share? Why else was Rose here?*

Rose walked in with a man a little taller and a lot younger than Seth. He removed his charcoal coat and handed it to the lawyer, then reached out his hand. "It's an honor to finally meet you... Mr. Teresi," he said. A smile covered his round, clean-shaven face. "I'm Liam Clare."

As Seth's gaze landed on the brown-framed glasses perched on his nose, something felt off. It wasn't just their style but the way the light passed unaltered through the lenses, lacking the slight distortion prescription lenses would impose.

Was he wearing them for style? Seth pondered. *Perhaps, but with Rose barely holding back her smirk, it was something more.*

He grabbed Liam's hand. Callus made up his grip, which was as strong as his cleft chin. "Pleasure's all mine, kid."

They waited for a few more minutes for Jose, but his assistant sat in for him. "Mr. Clare will act as a silent partner for now," said the lawyer. "Shadowing Mr. Teresi for the time being." These were the only words that mattered in their long rumble.

Murmurs filled the room as the meeting progressed—heat rose through Seth's spine. *Silent partner? Was this Lilith assigning me a babysitter? How dare she undermine me?* Seth looked at his watch. He felt the headache coming on. "You all continue without me. I will send Emma in my place; I have an urgent matter to take care of."

Seth shaded the windows before he reached into the desk for his medication. He placed the patch on his tongue and rested until a knock awoke him. "Come in," he grunted.

"Sorry to barge in, but I got a little worried since you didn't show up for our meeting," Jose said, walking straight toward the bar. "Red or white?"

"Apologies, I had something I needed to take care of... Red." *Was he part of this? Did he know who Liam was?*

"I'm gonna be frank with you," Jose said, handing him the glass. He paused, his expression turning more serious. "Word around is that your recent decisions haven't exactly been... universally popular."

Seth couldn't help but smirk. "What can I say? I have a long history of upsetting people. You were saying."

"It appears you've overstepped, Mr. Teresi," Jose said as he took a seat. "What you fail to realize is that Lilith is always two steps ahead—Liam, or whoever he was, is proof. All of this could have been avoided if you hadn't run wild with power."

"Lilith? I doubt she's pulling any strings from a UNA cell. This is the board members trying to regain power."

"Let's not play games. They didn't contact Malaya. We both know she is missing."

Seth smiled. "Malaya missing? With all due respect, Mr. Castillo, I appreciate your concern, but I can handle my affairs. You said you were going to be frank. So, tell me, why are you here?"

"I know you're not Achilles Teresi," he said, almost like he'd always known, but he didn't. Yet he spoke with such confidence. "I want you to help me help my daughter. All I'm asking is for you to tell me where she is. Do it as an offering to save yourself." Jose leaned forward.

"Everyone involved will understand. You were Lilith's bishop, a useful piece to keep her enemies at bay."

Lilith's bishop? Could she have set me up to take the fall for everything while Liam took over? Seth took a drink, looking into the eyes of a man who spoke of desperation, but his eyes told a different story. *This was a game to him; the apple didn't fall far from the tree.* Seth cleared his throat.

"Considering the vast resources you have at your disposal. I'd imagine if you had anything more than hearsay, you would have me apprehended. Mr. Castillo, I truly apologize that you've wasted your time." Seth walked toward the door; Jose followed him without hesitation. "If you don't mind, I have an engagement I must attend."

"Maybe I'm mistaken, but I'd tread carefully, Mr. Teresi," Jose said. "You never know when your past may come back to haunt you."

Was that a threat? How much did he know? Was he working with Liam? Questions needed to be answered. He'd get them soon enough.

Seth slid his hands down his face before staring at the bar. There wasn't enough alcohol to drown this problem. Before sending Emma home, he asked that she arrange a meeting with MEV's newest shareholder.

As requested, Liam met him atop the helipad before taking a trip to his penthouse. On the ride, Liam was more forthcoming than Seth expected, opening up about his time spent on Intrepid, promises that were made, and why he chose to follow Lilith. He gave just enough to reel Seth in—she had him trained well.

Although his role didn't request total secrecy, he was hiding something—they all were. It was what Lilith wanted. The question was, what secret was Liam hiding?

They stepped off the chopper to an empty rooftop. A doorman was usually there to greet him. Seth escorted Liam to the elevator.

"Are you going to kill me?" Liam smirked.

"No, this suit is much too expensive to get bloody."

The elevator doors opened to the foyer. Seth smiled as Liam marveled at the statues on either side of the hall. "Perhaps you served as inspiration for one of these elite warriors," he said, placing his palm on his door scanner.

"After you—" Steel pressed against Seth's neck. He stared into the eyes of a young man he'd long since forgotten.

"Relax, friend," Liam started, but his words were cut short by a blade pressing against his neck.

"No friend, you relax," a stranger's voice said.

"Julius?" Liam said. "It's me—"

"Shut up," the man said. "We're here for him. Stay calm."

"Enough said. I don't know him well enough to die," said Liam.

"Inoichi, stop," said a young blonde woman dressed in black, appearing from the shadows, a gun in her hand pointed at Inoichi. "This was not part of the deal."

Just as she stepped forward, so too did another. His presence sent chills through Seth. *How, how is this possible?*

At that moment, the blade at his neck no longer mattered. Perhaps he deserved it. He did everything in his power to stop the words from pouring out of his gaping mouth, but thoughts clouded his mind.

"Vasilis, what are you doing?" questioned Inoichi. "You two were supposed to stay hidden."

"I told you, not like this," Vasilis said, unsheathing his sword. "This is not your way. Remove your weapon from his throat. We need answers. Seth can give them to us."

"Listen to him, kid," said Seth. "And he's right. I can explain everything, but I am not the man you think I am."

"You think I lack honor?" Inoichi questioned, ignoring Seth. "I made you a promise. I intend to keep it."

The blade loosened on his neck, though his throat was still tight. He fought hard to suppress the anger and thoughts of betrayal. *Jose, he must have known. He must be working with Lilith. She did this. Bringing an enemy to my home, and Vasilis—*

"Seth!" Vasilis shouted, breaking him from his thoughts.

Before any words left his mouth, a light shone through his balcony window. Without warning, men dressed in black slid down ropes, landing on his patio. Inoichi pushed the blade harder into Seth's neck. "Are these your men?"

"No. More intruders," Seth said.

"They're with me," said the young blond, walking toward the balcony and sliding the door open.

"Arrest him," she said, pointing in Seth's direction.

A smile covered his face, relieved he'd be taken away from this horror. Inoichi dropped his guard. Liam took advantage, removing the blade from his own neck, disarming Julius, and forcing his arm behind his back. The men pointed their rifles and walked toward him, led by a tall blond. *Bennett* was stamped across his black vest. His green eyes pierced Vasilis and Julius.

"Put your blades down! Agent Aaron Walker, we are under orders to apprehend you. Please come quietly."

"Under what grounds?" Aaron questioned, staring past the men at the blond. "Katherine!"

"Impersonating a government officer," she said. "Take him."

The room fell quiet. Seth looked at Aaron's puzzled face as three of Bennett's men escorted him onto the balcony. "Mr. Teresi, I apologize on behalf of the Special Intelligence Agency and the United States government," said Agent Bennett. "For the rest of you, put your hands behind your back and come with me. That's an order!"

"What the fuck?" said Katherine. "Do you have any idea who this man is?"

"You will respect me as your commanding officer. My authority is just that. I walked in on you, losing control. When we—"

"Perhaps there's a reasonable explanation for all of this," said Liam.

"I know you! Quintus!" Vasilis shouted, rushing Liam.

Seth stepped aside. *Quintus, huh? What other warriors are you hiding, Lilith?*

Liam released Inoichi and sidestepped Vasilis, grabbing hold of his hoodie, wrapping him in it—sending him crashing into Inoichi. *He's swift. Impressive*, Seth thought.

Vasilis freed himself, readying to attack Liam until Bryce pointed his gun at him. "Stop! Or I will paint this floor with your brains."

Rage fueled Vasilis's eyes as he charged at Bryce. Inoichi launched at Vasilis, but a rifle was quickly pointed at him. However, Seth was able to stop him — they locked eyes. "I'm sorry for the confusion, kid," he said, wishing he could tell him more.

"Sir, please step aside," Bryce shouted. Another soldier came in from the balcony.

"Vasilis means you no harm, Agent Bennett," Seth placed his hand on Vasilis's shoulder. "He was just bested by a superior warrior. There is no room for anger, only improvement, isn't that right?"

Seth could see Vasilis's jaw protruding in anger, but he was calm. "Perhaps we can discuss this at another time," he whispered.

"Good, now that we all have properly met," said Liam. "Perhaps we can enjoy the spoils of Mr. Teresi's wealth."

"No time for that, sir," said Agent Bennett. "Arrest these two."

They handcuffed Vasilis and Inoichi. Vasilis shook his head in shame. He said nothing. The desperate look in his eyes said everything as they escorted him out. "Vasilis saved your life," said Inoichi, walking past Seth in handcuffs.

"Quiet," Bryce commanded. "And Mr. Teresi, you can expect a formal apology from my commander."

"Actually, get me the general," said Seth.

The door shut behind them, letting some of the tension out of the room. "So, Quintus, how do you know Vasilis?" he questioned, turning around... nothing.

A slight rumble shook the penthouse. A light beaming from the upstairs bathroom called his attention. He leaped up stairs onto the next story. He pushed the bathroom door open—Liam was gone.

GENERAL WILLIAMS

New York, 2076

B radly held his pipe by the shank, looking over at his wife, making sure she was still asleep. He slipped out a vintage flip-top from behind his black vest that was tucked in his white buttoned shirt.

"Alice?" Bradley questioned in a deep, low tone—sparking the flame to light his bowl.

"Don't even think about it. Not in the cockpit, especially tobacco." Alice said, shimming in her chair, her eyes remaining closed.

"What happened to the hum putting you to sleep?"

"Beauty resting. Who still does that anyway?" she said, passing her hand over her long, ombre silver hair.

Bradly's forehead tightened as he slid the lighter into his blue jeans. "Approaching destination, helipad clear," said the AI.

He stroked his neatly cut pepper beard. "Land on Apollo... you should have worn the red dress. Black is so—"

"Classy?" she said, interrupting him.

Alice held Bradly's arm as he escorted her to the elevator while another helicopter landed behind them. Secret service agents ran to catch up with the couple. Bradley's phone rang. He kissed her hand, ignoring it.

"Honey, meet Agent—"

"To the bar," said Alice, interrupting him. Heading for the elevator. "Just keep your distance. I have a date with Stephanie."

"Take five," said Bradley, directing his men with his nose.

He took a deep breath, opening the projection. "This better be good, Castillo. I have a bottle with my name on it."

"I painfully underestimated you this time."

"Jose, what the heck are you talking about? You sniffing cocaine?"

Jose's voice was barely a whisper. "You know what I'm referring to. Stop playing games. Going after Lilith is understandable, but you're crossing the line chasing my family. If you keep searching under rocks that don't concern you, you will get stung."

A smirk crossed Williams's face. "Taking matters into your own hands again? We crossed this bridge before. It didn't end well."

"This old record again?"

"We had a plan!" Williams looked around and lowered his voice. "You threw our life's work down the drain."

"People were dying, Brad. I had to sign that peace treaty."

"It's war. People die. You know goddamn well it was about Angie. You had instructions, and you took things personally."

"Red just wanted—"

Bradley interrupted him. "*We*, Jose. It wasn't just about Red. You and I had a plan. We had the UNA where we wanted them, and you blinked."

"Let it go, Bradley. I know about everything, the Alpha King's obsession with my family. They wanted something from Jeff and Lilith... *someone*."

Williams tried not to show any expression, not wanting to give Jose any indication that he was right. Jeff owed the A.K. someone special. Malaya was off the table. She was too far gone and not special beyond her intelligence.

Malaya wasn't a *Darviant*.

Jeff outsmarted them; he died. Instead of getting financially backed by A.K, Lilith turned to the government and Bradley. The deal shut out Orenthal and the A.K, but snakes always reappear. Orenthal was not a man to let things go, coming after Williams, forcing him to join A.K—of course, Lilith didn't know. But he kept to the shadows, stalking his prey. And if Jose wasn't careful, he'd get his family caught in the crossfire of a man more powerful than either of them thought he could be. A mistake Bradley would never make.

"I know about Rattlesnake, how you sent him after Jeff, and your real plans with Project Bungee," Jose continued. "Again, leave my family out of it, or I will expose you."

Williams shook his head, tired of Jose's holier-than-thou stance and his threats.

Back then, even with World War III in full swing, they held all the power. They all reaped the benefits of power, and no one forced their hand. And it was up to him to protect the Republic. Catching his terrorist child was going to do that, but that could wait. At the moment, he needed to set his friend straight. "You know I had to beg Red not to kill you. I had to give up our entire private force in the process. You, of all people, understand what that cost us. Maybe you've forgotten or can't see from the high horse you're sitting on."

Jose scoffed. "You don't need a private force, Bradley. You have the goddamn US military at your command."

"That's not the point," Williams said through gritted teeth, trying not to go above a whisper. "We could have brought the UNA to their knees—"

"I arrested Agent Walker," Jose blurted.

"What?"

"He was working for Lilith."

Williams paused, furious, but not wanting to show it. *That kid held back info...what's his name... Bryce Bennett? No wonder he brought his entire squad for a simple shadow job.*

After Katherine asked for permission to spy on Teresi in New York, Williams was inclined to send Bryce to secretly shadow his sister. Regardless of how competent Katherine proved to be, he couldn't allow historical figures out of his sight.

A soldier spying on a spy. Thought I left this shit behind. I should have known he was no ordinary soldier. Williams shook his head at the thought of someone working under his nose yet taking other orders from Williams's best friend. *Aaron Walker, a fucking traitor. Unbelievable.*

Both he and Jose reloaded for another round. Jose was the first to speak. "I have a file over his head. I also have Red back in my corner."

Bradley can't hide the shock on his face. *How is this possible? Red is back?* He looked around. Suddenly, every shadow seemed menacing. He looked down at his arm. His Diamond Wolf tattoo was slightly faded, but his bruise was fresh. No one was more powerful than Red, not even Lilith. He led the secret private force, manipulating both sides of World War III. "What do you want?"

"Stop searching for Lilith's child. Call off your dogs."

"The US military will not get involved. No harm will come to the child."

Jose nodded, then his image disappeared. Bradley turned to throw his phone, but stopped midway. "This is not over." He signaled his serviceman to accompany him on the elevator. He watched the numbers rapidly dwell down before he realized the elevator had reached its destination.

The door rang, alerting the staff to the VIP entrance, where a young woman greeted the men. She escorted them up a wide red-carpeted stairway to a large, dimly lit room that shimmered with a rose gold decorum. The lights hovered over the glass bar and tables—that looked over the common area.

"Scott, do your thing," Bradley said, to no response. His guard disappeared into the crowd, awaiting instructions. The blond host gesturing drew Bradley's attention.

"Mr. Teresi is waiting for you at the end booth, sir," she said.

Teresi's son was a young man with black jeans that were destroyed at the knees and a hooded black leather jacket. He took a shot, then slammed the glass on the table. The men locked eyes as they passed, a look that was familiar to Bradley, the eyes of battle.

Achilles Teresi stood up to greet. "General Williams, I presume. It's an honor to finally meet you in person, sir," Teresi said, folding his brown tie as they sat.

"Likewise," said Williams, blatantly looking back at the young man.

"Forgive my son. The kid is a knucklehead. Please have a seat."

"I'm sure he's a good kid."

"Not even close. I should send him with you."

Williams snickered as the waitress held her tablet, waiting for their order. "Scotch," said Williams. "I could use a strong kid like him."

"The 2020 collection. That was an interesting year. And I'll have my wine."

Teresi exposed his diamond face watch underneath the sleeve of his tailored emerald suit to pass her a hundred-dollar bill. "Lilith never held any expense, and neither should I."

The waitress nodded. "An exquisite vintage, sir," both men watched her walk off in her tight white dress.

"Almost too damn real," said Williams, taking a sip of his water. "With Lilith's taste, she's going to hate the place I'm going to send her."

Teresi cleared his throat. "Now, General, an apology over the phone would have sufficed. I imagine you're an extremely busy man."

"None of that now, son. That was an embarrassing moment for us. I'm here to set things right."

"For us both, what was that about?"

"Just a case of mistaken identity." Williams was lucky the New York press didn't catch wind.

"I see. I also imagine MEV's new weapon program raises your interest." Teresi took a sip of water.

Williams nodded and smiled slightly. Teresi's weapons program could help the US military fight and protect the Republic against threats in the shadows. Williams was impressed, but not surprised, that Teresi knew exactly what he would want, but this was about Lilith. He must know where she is.

I have to flip him, but he's good, really good.

After all, Teresi's meteoric rise afforded him a reach that rivaled some of the most influential people in the world. He couldn't have gotten there without doing his homework. Williams leaned in. "I believe our business can be mutually beneficial."

Teresi smiled and looked down at his watch. "And what do I need?"

"A successor. My intel informed me of your search for a kid with a certain set of skills—endless potential. I think they said, *gifted.*"

Teresi laughed, pointing at the general and rubbing his beard right after. "Spying is a dirty trick, so is chasing a person for a project she started."

The drinks arrived. "Anything else, sir?" she asked with a generic smile.

"Yes, a steak for us both," said Teresi. "Await further instructions after this meeting."

"Anything you need, sir," she added.

"I'm straight," Bradley said, waving her off before taking a large gulp of his drink. "I'm a Florida boy. We don't take bullshit. Tell you what... I can provide you with a kid with unquestioned loyalty."

"Any type of skills or abilities? Even a Darviant?"

"Who knows, anything is possible."

"And all you want is first access to my weapons program?"

"Not exactly. You know what I want."

"I know what you want? We shall see." Teresi vaguely brandished his teeth. "There's a kid named Yuk Fat, a prodigy out of New Seattle's HOA," he said before sipping his wine.

"The Fat family Complicates things."

"I don't care about complications... Perhaps I don't know what you want. He has parents, doesn't he?"

"Yes, the son of UNA ambassadors. I have an agent who can be very persuasive. He would make Yuk extremely motivated once he's done."

Let's see if kidnapping parents crosses your line, He thought.

Bradley drank the rest of his drink, eyeing Teresi. He folded his sleeves back, exposing the tattoos that covered him from his wrist back to his back.

"Intel has it that you know Rose Albright. She's a fellow business peer of yours, but how do you know this, Osamu?"

"I have connections, General, and the kid is not enough," Teresi said, never losing focus. "I plan to establish my own company in my homeland of Greece, but I need funding. I also want to meet this agent of yours, you know, the one who is going to kidnap. You need to put big boy chips down if you're trying to make big boy moves."

Williams took out his pipe and lit it, gaining Teresi's attention. "Here's a big boy move for you. You're gonna tell me where Lilith is, or I will arrest you for treason."

Teresi laughed out loud as he cut a piece of his steak. He ate it and shook his head with a smile, exposing the gnashed-up meat. Teresi pointed at Williams with his fork. "I never took you as one to underestimate, General, but you allowed Lilith to swipe the device and get away—that'll be the last assumption I make. Thanks to your show the other night. I had to hire some thugs in my corner."

The gulping sound of Williams taking a drink seemed to echo. Williams peaked over at Shaw. Teresi continued cutting. "I'll kill you where you sit before you can call your friend by the bar, then I'll kill him—I'm sure your wife at bar two wouldn't want that. My men tend to make a mess of things," he said, placing the next bite in his mouth.

That's it, the eyes of a veteran, both he and his son, Williams thought. "Fair enough. Get me in touch with her, and I'll get you in touch with my agent. But I want to speak to her now."

"I want a call from them by the end of the week. Oh, and the boy, Yuk Fat—make the arrangements." Teresi stood up and cleaned his mouth. "Maria, take him to the VIP lounge and grant him access to the Meta Reality. He needs to make an important call. I'll be in touch, General."

"Is Achilles Teresi even your real name?"

Teresi smiled and said in a low tone, "My real name is Seth the Conqueror."

Maria sat Williams in a secluded dark room with a red gel ball at its center. She took a white box out of the wall and gestured for him to sit. "Have a seat, relax... the gel will not stick, but you must allow yourself to sink."

"Can I just have a freaking regular chair?" he asked slowly, allowing himself to be submerged into the cold red gel up to his neck.

"Relax," said Maria with perkiness in her voice. She opened a steel box and removed a silver mechanical scorpion.

He felt a pinch as it latched onto his neck. His vision blurred. It was like they strapped him to a high-speed train without breaks. He felt his mind—no, his very consciousness—leaving his body, taking him to a virtual world, one that he could feel. Bradley soon stabilized as he arrived in a completely white space.

"Come out and play," Bradley's voice echoed into the white abyss. "Come on!" He shouted at the continued blinking light on top of a lone door.

Lilith's image flickered in front of Williams until she became solid in a white dress. If he didn't know better, he would mistake her for a goddess.

"I don't get a *beso?*" said Bradley, spreading his arms. "I tried to picture your facial expression, and this is all I get? Nonchalant. I'm disappointed."

"Cute, did you come up with all that on your own? Or do you think of me when you're in bed with Alice?"

"Maybe I'll try that with Malaya," he said with a semi-smile. "It's over Castillo. I have you cornered, but I'm seeking reconciliation." Bradley slowly closed the buttons on his sleeves. "We have the same enemy. For that, I'll bring you back on board. No harm, no foul. You have the UNA in Chaos."

He didn't know if she would take the bait, but he had to try. One part was true: the death of the emperor lit a fire under the people across the globe. Outside of Russia and India, which were never conquered, protests erupted throughout Eurasia. They are tired of the UNA's iron hand, tired of oppression–but Lilith is the bigger fish for now.

Lilith passed her hands through her hair, dropping it to one side. "It feels so real, doesn't it? More real than your empty threats and vague promises. See, your arrogance is your downfall. You believe in *your* power."

She walked up to him and passed her hand over his beard. "Real power is what I have. Power that I weld at my fingertips," she said, walking away.

His brows knitted. "You owe me!" He said, pounding his chest. "Orenthal and the Alpha Kings wanted you dead, along with Jeff. I convinced him to spare you, and this... this is how you repay me? Jeff made an oath. You and I both know it's not just a fraternity. You know what they are capable of. You and your daddy are so much alike."

Williams sighed. "I had to fix it. I gave Malaya a chance when *they* wanted a Grant-Castillo for themselves, the *special* Castillo's." He shook his head. "You reaped the benefits of my help. I did it despite the secret you kept from us. And you have the balls to lecture me about power..." Bradley raised his arm, his voice more strident, pointing at Lilith. "I'll show you what power is."

Lilith buried her hand in her hair once more, returning his half-smile. "So, the cat's out of the bag. I always felt something, but I was never in real danger. You needed me and Malaya."

"You arrogant bitch! You think you have untraceable secrets. I know more than you think I know, your connections, your inside agents. Your secret child."

The surrounding space flickered colors, her iris mixed red and black, locking eyes with him. The open area changed to gray. "Why wait? I'll show you real power now. Take a look at your news feed, and you'll see what this arrogant bitch is capable of."

The room changed back to white. "And the next time you mention my children, I'll end you."

Bradley woke up from virtual reality. The heliograph television feed displayed the podium, which was located at a park in Japan—where a large crowd gathered.

Rose Albright stood wearing a charcoal suit with Osamu Torri, who wore his hair over his shoulders, with an all-black suit with a long brown coat. They stood beside a young woman dressed in an elegant and oversized red kimono. Pink cherry blossoms decorated her kimono and a samurai sword at her hip with gold trims.

Rose stepped up, taking center stage. "In my hand, I hold the original and authentic Kojiki. As history tells, the leader that was promised is not chosen, but inherited by law."

Whispers could be heard through the TV as Rose handed the mic to Osamu, who spoke in Japanese. "Carbon footprints of this scroll and DNA analysis provided by Mrs. Albright's company, Albright Prosthetics, proved who: the leader of Japan and the United Nations Alliance. The results have been sent to all the major countries, and reports are accessible to the public."

Both Osamu and Rose stepped back, giving the young woman a bow as she allowed her to take the mic. Her kimono flowed across the stage.

"I am Toyotomi Mizunami, and I declare myself shogun and the rightful commander of the military. I denounce the false government. My bloodline is pure, and I will free my people from oppression. I command the immediate arrest of the false leaders of this nation, and the complete surrender with the rest of the United Nations Alliance. Yes, this is a declaration of war."

ELIAS

New Seattle, 2076

Using Lilith's hypersonic plane might have been a mistake, Elias realized too late. The opportunity had been too tempting to pass up for a guest in this new world, despite the risks. As they plummeted through the night sky, the surrounding clouds a blur of darkness, the reality of their situation became starkly apparent.

Midas, overwhelmed, slumped over, his eyes rolling back in distress. In stark contrast, the twins, Arya and Emma, found exhilaration in the chaos, their laughter ringing out uncontrollably.

Amidst them, the MEV interns stood out with their badges and crisp business attire—a facade of maturity that the night's events were quickly unraveling. Elias wondered, not for the first time, what this journey would reveal about them all.

Arya grabbed the oxygen mask and placed it around Midas mouth; while Emma slapped his face, his head and undercut blond hair snapped back.

"Hyper drive mode has concluded," said the AI, "Switching to ultra jets."

Elias grabbed the oxygen mask, taking deep breaths of the cold air. "Computer, pictures of Greece." The cabin changed from exterior view to summer beaches of modern Greece. Most of which was from Athens. "Computer, Laconia, Greece."

"Well, that's petty of you Eli, the landscape didn't do anything to you," said Emma, twisting her curly brown hair.

"Athens University was his rival. Give him a break," Ayra said while continuing to shake Midas until he came too. She gave him a perfect smile, along with her freckles that were perfectly scattered across her nose and cheeks. "Besides, you hate the Rams for always winning the Super Bowl."

Emma crossed her legs and leaned back. "I guess. So what do you think, Eli? You got the hyper rush?"

"No rush or high," Elias replied. "Just a headache."

It took less than an hour to travel from New York to Seattle, using Lilith's hypersonic plane. It was a modern marvel, although Elias thought it looked like a groin cup with v-shaped wings.

Here they sat, thousands of years in the future, with the nieces of Elias's boss.

Ironic, Elias thought. *I went from challenging for a throne to working for someone, from carriages to jets.* He looked at the twins, wondering if they knew who he was before this.

Did they know he worked for Lilith?

He wouldn't be surprised, given the prestigious blood that ran through their veins. There was something special about Lilith's family—there was a prodigy everywhere.

"I feel high," Midas said with a smile, his large frame sinking into the seat.

"That's not the only way you can get high," Elias said with a grin.

"Oh?" Emma placed one hand across her breast in shock.

Midas chuckled. "Careful. Where we're from, girls are married as soon as they come of age."

"Uh huh, really?" Arya said, snapping off her phone from her magnetized necklace. The little device was rolled together, no longer than a finger. Her phone's translucent frame glowed a soft green as she scrolled through it. "Wow, the age of consent is *fifteen* in Greece." She raised her dark brown brows. "Careful, Ems, I don't know if the old man can take them."

She referred to the old secret service agent at the back of the plane. "I mean... it's only a three-year difference than here, plus I'll be eighteen soon enough," Emma eyed Elias, like a predator would its prey.

Their mother was an American politician of sorts, and their father was Joseph, who they knew very well. *I know where their missing 'father' is... how odd.* Elias thought as he pulled his black hood over the cornrows.

He was thankful for her braiding his earlier in the flight and to Midas for providing an undercut shaving, but getting on Lilith's bad side by fraternizing with her niece was not on his agenda. He peeled an apple with his knife as the plane trembled. The cabin changed to the exterior view camera as they approached the airport.

At night, New Seattle was more beautiful than ever. It was as if the gods came down as stars descending from the skies, painting new skyscrapers. New York was a mixture of the old and the new, while

Seattle was *new*. It reminded him of home, in a way. *A city built on the ruins of the old.*

A neuro machine planted a wealth of information in his head, equivalent to a modern middle schooler; he studied history in his free time. He reread the history of Sparta over and over, the rise and the fall. Seattle was one of the home fronts during the war.

Its famous space needle was one of the few staples to survive. They built a metal net-like structure around it, with the names of the fallen rising to the sky. The memorial was taller than the tower itself.

Thoughts of the life before this one washed over him. He was used to death, losing men—that was war. It never spilled into the city, not like their war did. The honor of a mutual battlefield was lost over time and the result cost millions of lives.

"Please prepare for landing," said the AI. Elias placed his seatbelt over his black destroyed jeans that matched his leather jacket.

"Where can we get a drink around here?" Midas said.

The twins looked at one another. "We're not old enough to drink," they said simultaneously.

"But," said Emma. "We know about an internet speakeasy."

Midas and Elias looked at one another, confused. "As long as we can get a drink," Midas spoke for the both of them.

"Cool," said Arya, "But Midas may have to buy you a drink," she teased.

"Midas is my same age!" Elias exclaimed, sinking into his seat once he realized it was another height joke. At home, five-foot-six inches wasn't that small. But here, he may as well have been an Oompa Loompa.

It rained on the way to the hidden bar, and the silver automated electric car took them. Everything is so clean. The wet streets took the color of the city. From what he read on the flight, every night, there was a color of choice.

Tonight it was green, though they made sure all colors were included, no matter the national or political mood. It was a uniform, the government's uniform. In this world, artificial grass and trees were planted in specific locations, cars were turned on and off on a whim, many self-operating.

Littering was a fine, and a habitual offender would see a cell. The wrong words spoken out loud to the wrong person could cost you your career. New Seattle was different.

Lilith was right. This is no utopia; it was a nightmare. Elias always got philosophical once he had a drink, and after the disaster they created in Japan, he knew there was more to come.

Elias and Midas shared a curious look as the twins spoke a password into a sliding hatch of a steel door. It was like a mobster movie in the 1920s.

They instantly felt underdressed and out of place. Midas fared better, with fitted khaki pants, white shirt and an olive long coat. The twins coughed as they swiped smoke from their faces.

Beyond the loud music and dim lights were marble floors and elegant chandeliers. The lounge was filled with suits, the worst type of people, people like his father, low-lives in high places, people like him.

The live rock band was the only one that was out of place, David and the something, Elias didn't hear, nor cared to listen.

Midas and Elias sat at the bar. The twins disappeared into the crowd with some women. As the liquor faded from his system, his problems returned. "Hey, Goldilocks," Elias called the bartender in all black with a gold-tipped wide mohawk, faded at the sides.

It would have been a strange sight if not for the neurolink, internet, and the stuff he's heard about the flamboyant style of New York.

"Welcome, gentleman," said the bartender. "Anything in particular?"

"The strongest you have," said Elias.

He poured both of them two shots of a clear liquor. He took it down. It was bitter, worse than the sake he had in ancient Japan. "Taste like piss," Elias said. "I'll take another."

Flashes of his father stumbling out of Edo Castle crossed his mind. The shogun's blood covered his face. Elias knew he messed up, yet he did not appear to learn from his mistakes. "Can't believe I'm benched, all because of father," Elias said, taking down another shot to piss tasting liquor. "And now he continues to make moves in his own interest."

"Lilith will not go back on her word. If she says you are in the games, as they say, then you are." Midas took down the shot, his face squeezed. "Shit. It really does taste like piss." He raised his hand for another. "I cannot believe Vasilis survived."

His name knotted Elias's stomach. "No wonder Inoichi came for father. He had all the right to seek vengeance for what he did. I would know. I did the same and failed."

"Keep your voice down. And your father is still alive."

"That is not the point!" Elias exclaimed in a loud whisper.

The bartender cut into their dance. "You guys are obviously not from around here. I can smell fresh meat from a mile away."

"You can say that," Midas said. "We are from Greece."

Elias just grunted.

"Ohh, *gēraskō d' aieí pollá didaskómenos,*" said the bartender, puffing out his chest.

The translator changed it to: *"I grow old always learning many things, English of all things."*

"So stop learning," Elias said in ancient Greek, turning to Midas.

"Oh, a scholar of the old," said the bartender. "I'm a scholar myself. A detective. I like to call myself a man with many hats."

"We are Tsakonian, from the mountains of Greece."

"The ancient people descend from the lost Spartans."

"We are Spartans," Elias snapped. Midas shot him a quick look. Elias shrugged.

"Then you are the last Spartans," said the bartender.

Elias was quick to continue the conversation with Midas, but more discreetly, as discreet as one could get in a place with loud music and chatter. "It was Kara's intent that matters. She tried to murder him."

"It is what it is. Vasilis was a brother."

"You could have stopped me, so get off your high horse."

"How long are you guys staying for?" asked the bartender.

Elias scrunched his face. Midas leaned toward him. "Bartenders are like therapists for modern humans who would rather drown their sorrows in a bottle than talk to a professional."

"Well, how rude? I didn't even introduce myself," he said, adjusting the long gold tie he wore tucked behind his black vest. "My name is Roberto Clemente." He had a newly developed yet slight Spanish accent when he said it.

"Like the Puerto Rican baseball player?" Midas asked with a contagious smile.

"Right, but from the Dominican Republic," the bartender said.

Elias squinted slightly.

"I'm Midas, this is my partner Elias... and to answer your question, we will not be here long, friend," Midas said. "We were invited here by..." Midas trailed off.

Elias followed his eyes, only now realizing the twins were gone. If fraternizing would get him in trouble, losing them would get them air-locked.

"Oh, here they come," Midas said in relief.

The twins arrived with two other people. A pretty young blond and equally handsome blond male with a strong jaw.

Elias pushed past the fog inebriation, remembering the *people of interest* during their briefing. Arya spoke in her usual soft tone, introducing their two new friends, but Elias knew. *Katherine and Bryce Bennett, Special Intelligence Agents.*

He remembered what Lilith had told them. She had a vision, leading a raid against her. *I could do her a favor by eliminating a problem.*

Elias looked out of the corner of his eye, wondering if Midas was thinking the same thing. He wasn't.

Instead, he extended his large hand to Bryce and encouraged Elias to follow. He grunted quietly, accepting his firm grip, and stared into the pale green eyes of a man who could put Lilith in a Black Site prison.

"Pleasure to meet you," Kat said. "Emma tells me a lot about you two."

"Everything is true," Midas said with a large smile.

Elias nodded. Emma snatched off his hoodie. "Stop trying to be tall, dark, and handsome. You have two out of three, naturally."

"He does." Kat bit her lip, holding back her smile.

Arya pulled Emma before she could sit on Elias's lap. "Let's go. Kat's going to help us with our work."

"Jack, fix them up with the Greek spirit you imported. I have a feeling they are into the *ancient* stuff."

Elias bit down on his jaw while maintaining a smile. *She knows... I would hate to kill such a pretty woman.*

"Right, I forgot about that bottle," the bartender said, his russet-brown cheeks flushed with guilt. Kat and the twins went up the stairs. Midas and Bryce spawned off into conversation. Based on their chummy nature, it was genuine, but Elias knew Midas well enough to know it was a way to keep the potential enemy close.

Elias turned his attention to the suspicious bartender. "Jack, huh?"

"I like to have fun. Telling the same origin story to hundreds of customers gets old fast."

Jack placed a clear, perfectly square ice-cube into the small chilled glass. He took out a clear labeled bottle. He tapped it with his ring before pouring it with a smile. "Go ahead, Spartan, try it."

Elias's eyes widened as the cold liquor danced in his mouth. The distinct yet familiar sweet, nutty flavor brought back memories of Hecktor, Vasilis, and Midas as children, stealing *Mastika*.

"Where did you get this?" Elias demanded.

"Greece, the island of Chios."

Mastichiades villages, Elias thought. "Midas, come taste this."

"Wow," said Midas, this is better than I remember. "We need—"

"Prosecco wine," Jack said, interrupting him with a bottle already in hand.

The three men smiled, and they instantly became the best of friends. They cleared bottle after bottle in a short amount of time. Jack handed them a DMT called Superman. "This will alter your mind." Red and blue flowed within the capsule that he and Midas popped into their mouths.

Within minutes, Elias's problems and the voices were gone. The world was a party. Mother nature tamed. She was his bitch, but there was nothing mind-altering about the drug.

Elias looked at Jack. "When will it kick in?"

"You'll know," he flashed a white smile.

From his peripheral, Elias saw a suited man whisper something into Bryce's ear. He closed his eyes to tap into one of his many talents, his keen sense of hearing. "Tedesco," Elias overheard.

It was translated from German into ancient Greek thanks to the language transmitter. Bryce gave Jack a nod, and he went to the back. Elias noticed he grabbed something. *A gun?*

"Let them in," Bryce told the suit.

"But they are with the Villari family, Mr. Bennett," said the suit.

"Father or uncle is not home, so I'm in charge. Let them in."

A tall woman walked in. Though, from the muscular physique and masculine facial features, Elias wasn't sure. She wore a suit along with everyone that entered after her. Bryce and a few of his guys met them at the door.

Jack returned with a different look in his eye. "Problems?" Midas questioned.

"Yasmin 'Four Fingers' Tedesco," Jack said. "No problem, just rivals, that's all, business."

Their presence cleared the bar of everyone except for Midas, Elias, and a woman. They continued to drink. Odd thoughts came to mind, both in the past and now. Thoughts of his father and his loyalty. Thoughts of the modern human, how soft they had become.

Seattle's citizens once fought bravely, fighting off enemies in their own backyard. Now... They're fixated on other people's lives instead of working together as a community; marrying robots, population decreases.

Elias shook his head. He knew so much about their world, yet they knew so little about human nature. No longer did they eat real meat—everything was fake. They didn't know any truths, nor did they care to know. Instead, they lived with simultaneous contradictory beliefs.

They are doomed, Elias thought. *It's the thirteenth hour. They just don't know yet.*

"Shit, this drug really isn't working," Elias said to Midas, taking down another drink, trying to stay out of his own head. "Has it kicked in for you?"

Midas shook his head. One of Yasmin's men kept hitting on the girl, but she brushed him off. It was like he didn't get the rejection. Midas's face reddened. The drunken suit grabbed her arm. They gazed at one another. Midas took one last shot and got up.

"Finally, I was getting bored," Elias said.

"Unhand her." Midas's voice was a loud grumbled that cut through the crowd.

"Shit. I don't care if you're six or eight feet." The guy flashed his gun.

Midas flashed a smile, and Elias started to laugh. His laugh spiraled uncontrollably until it was maniacal. Everyone on both sides stood.

"Let's take it down a notch, guys. Leave your sets at the door," Jack said.

He walked past both men and the girl and stopped at Yasmin. He leaned on the bar, elbow on the table, hand on his elbow, and a smile on his face. Elias grabbed her drink, mixed it with the olive stick, and chugged it. The room gasped.

"Elias?" Bryce said from afar.

A news feed erupted from everyone's phones and glasses. The tv screen flashed. *The United Nations of Asia declared war. Japan is revolting, and World War IV is possible.* Mutters spread around the room. A woman gave a slight scream, and another cried.

It has begun, he thought.

Elias smiled and ate the olive off the stick, then jammed it into her eyeball. She cried as she fell to the floor.

Everyone shouted in horror.

Elias turned to the man standing in front of Midas and stabbed the man in the back with his knife. Midas grabbed his gun before he fell, shooting the man next to Elias.

Ten other men took out their firearms. Elias and Midas jumped over the counter. Midas took the women with him. Bullets flew as both mafia rivals exchanged fire. Jack stood over them with an AR-15, shooting it with precision and confidence. *A soldier.* Elias suddenly noticed his muscular build.

Darkness took over for a split second. Lights flashed as the world around him sputtered—he knew it—Superman kicked in.

It hit him harder than any Kryptonian ever could. Lapses in time made it difficult to keep up as spots of his life were voided.

At one moment, he was in a bar fight. The lights went out. He was in a car accident, joined a gang, rioted, bought a blade to a gunfight, and got a tattoo.

His phone woke him. The early morning sun burst into a room he didn't remember going to. He struggled to sit up partly from a booming headache, and the two arms draped over him. The same girl from the bar and the girl he stabbed in the eye.

What in the Hades? He thought, seeing the one-eyed girl with a robotic eye—he could tell by the surrounding metal. The tone of his phone rang loud in his head this time. "This ring... it's her!"

He scrambled to look for the phone, but his room was filled with money. He swept away until he heard the phone fall on the rug.

A pain in his rear end grabbed his attention. He grabbed his phone and looked at his butt chicks in the mirror. He had the names *Yasmin, Jack, Midas, Betty, and Erika* tattooed on his rear. "What the heck..." he looked down at the phone.

It reads secure line-on. It scanned his face. *Phase 2 is on. Return home, you're back, from Jessica.*

"Lilith!"

OSAMU

Hyogo, Japan, 2076

Osamu winced as blood traced the ridges of his ribs. The tattoo artist wiped it away, then pressed the needle back into his skin—a sharp, euphoric rhythm. Vibrant cherry blossoms bloomed, merging with the intricate dragon sprawling across his back, a living testament to his path as a samurai.

"Oh, we're almost done, you big baby," Akame, at least that was what they called her. He wasn't sure if it was her anime tag, as they called it nowadays. Most people in the UNA had a virtual name as well.

She handed him Tom, a fat gray cat that helped him relax. The cat purred as she put the final touches on his tattoo. The doors burst open, and in came her boyfriend, a tall black man from some island called Honduras.

They argued as Osamu looked for his shirt. He eyed her out of the corner of his eyes. He didn't speak any English, only some local language, but his translator translated well as they argued about his social score.

In the UNA, rights were granted based on merit. If you were a good and compliant citizen, then you were granted rights. They allowed them to use cabs, discounts, and even their digital money at times.

He slipped on his black collar shirt, then looked at his tattoo one last time in the large mirror. His hair was getting long, dark black, shoulder length, but today it was pulled up into a messy, silky black knot. His beard was low and neat, accentuating his square jaw.

"I'm getting big," he told no one in particular.

Although he was still in Japan, this world was far from the land his ancestors roamed. He had gained weight since living in this strange new world, a combination of amazing food and his addiction to heavy weights at the gym.

He passed his fingers over his abs, the sakura leaves that represented the countless tales embedded within each stroke of ink.

Akame shouted, her voice a potent blend of passion and power that sent a shiver down his spine. She was impossibly beautiful, her plus-sized figure radiating confidence that only amplified her allure. Her perfectly sculpted curves and glowing face, framed by cascading, shimmering blue hair, exuded vitality and undeniable charm.

There was nothing better than a toxic woman. *I guess that is my toxic. What do they say? Toxic trait.*

He closed his shirt and tucked it into his black pants, then threw on an olive green long coat. The man grabbed her hands.

Osamu felt the instant surge within. He closed his eyes, allowing the chains of his inner beast to resonate. It was a consistent reminder of his curse. He was a vessel to a Sage, and there was no changing that.

As he placed his brown gloves on, the man increased his tone, now bordering on a shout.

"That's enough," Osamu told him in Japanese.

"Mind your business," he returned flawlessly.

Osamu fiddled with his glove and sauntered towards him. The man released her, squaring his shoulders. "You don't know who I am, man," he said, his voice filled with humor.

"It's okay," said Akame. "He's dangerous. I got him."

"You think you're dangerous?" Osamu crept forward, his gaze unrelenting. "My eyes have seen the underworld. I've been there and back, and the demons accept me."

Osamu head-butted him, and his nose burst open, spreading blood everywhere. The man stumbled back, and Osamu tossed him out the door with ease.

"Stand by that table," Osamu commanded Akame. She complied.

The inner monster at this point was shrieking; even during this time period, he could feel it. He could feel him. He stood by the security keypad. "What's the code?"

"One two three four," she said, still wide-eyed.

He shook his head and entered it. A gate fell. The man rushed to the gate, rattling it in place. "Let me in! Are you scared now?"

"The gate is not for you, but for me," Osamu said as he walked up to Akame.

They locked eyes, and then he kissed her. She moaned, her body clinging onto his. He lifted her onto the table as the second gate came down, like a partition in a limo. The man shouted as it slowly closed, and Osamu had his way with her.

Like clockwork, his UAV was right on time. A holographic landing pad appeared at the rear of the ink shop. The UAV hovered, its loud humming echoing among the tall, clean buildings. By this time, her boyfriend was sitting in his car. He opened his door when an armored man jumped out of the UAV, pointing smart rifles in all directions, especially at him.

"Is that a Bugatti?" said Akame. "You're like a billionaire?"

"Yes, I am." He kissed her hand and gave her his dimpled smirk as he guided her onto the vehicle.

"I'll have some tea," he told the driver.

The flight from Kobe to Himeji Castle was a short one, but he took the time to continue his research. His target: BleachStone, a multinational investment company based in Japan with roots in the Middle East. His task was simple: murder everyone. He worked hand in hand with Ghost, the mystical hacker guild. As always, no stone was left unturned. And every stone would be dealt with.

As Akame succumbed to slumber, Osamu's gaze fixated upon his own wiki page titled "Torii Tadamasa."

An overwhelming sense of pathos enveloped him, for there it stood, a footnote in history. A mere four lines. Tadamasa was a name long relinquished that now resonated like an ancient whisper. The Torri clan faded into history, but he couldn't allow it despite his father's sacrifice. His father had given his life, holding down a fort against insurmountable odds.

Inoichi's father, Ieyasu Tokugawa, was able to gain the time he required to win the Battle of Sekigahara. Regardless of the lands awarded to the Tokugawa, Osamu betrayed them, and Ieyasu paid the ultimate price. He wanted to be Tadamasa the honorable again, but today required Osamu the villain.

Osamu closed the page and watched a blue dot moving on a map. Seth's tracker moved to New York, the same location he had been in for weeks. This wasn't part of his mission, but he tracked him anyway; he didn't trust him.

Lilith held something from them, a secret about Seth, or perhaps it was the fact that Seth killed Ieyasu. He closed out the last page, which was the profile of the would-be assassin. *Focus.* Who could be powerful or skilled enough to murder the cabin?

"Arriving, sir," said the AI pilot.

Out the window stood his former home, Harima Province, which was now part of Hyogo Prefecture. Heralded as Himeji-jo, or the ethereal White Heron Castle, it stood as one of Japan's few remaining fortresses, meticulously preserved through the ebbing tides of time. Its brilliant white walls were perched atop a formidable hill, commanding a majestic presence.

He remembered spending most of his youth between his family's estate down in the bailey and the motte up in the castle with his father.

Noh theater, martial arts, and festivals were regular occurrences, along with his training as a samurai. The UAV hovered on the trimmed lawn as Akame and Osamu hopped off. He waved them off, and they disappeared into the night sky.

The drop-off was far from the main castle; they couldn't risk the attention, even though they had everyone in their pocket.

Sure, Japan was under the regime's thumb, but the people's fighting spirit was not dead. What started as a forced Asian alliance turned into a fight for freedom. And Osamu would do whatever it takes.

They strolled down a labyrinthine passage. By now, the sakura trees had lost most of their pink hue, but they still amazed Akame. Concealed by fortified walls, the path wound its way cunningly, devised to confound and hinder invading forces.

They made their way to the core, a formidable Main Keep soaring six stories tall, its wooden form exuding an air of grandeur.

Soldiers scrambled out of Osamu's way, their boots echoing on the smooth wooden floor. "Another stray?" said Mizunami, standing and gathering her kimono.

Osamu walked closer, with Akame in one hand and Tom, the cat, in the other arm. The cat hopped off his arm.

"Akame, this is—"

"Toyotomi, Mizunami," Akame said, interpreting him. "The Shogun."

She turned to Osamu, eyes wide. "You're her right-hand man... I thought I recognized you. I'm kidnapped."

"Osamu, you didn't tell her?" Mizunami came closer, the firelight casting a glow on her pale skin. "You have been recruited. Wasn't this what you wanted? You spoke to one of our recruiters."

"Oh, yes, I guess." Akame cleared her throat. "I was thinking more of low-level crime. You know, like sneaking some fantasy books into the children's library. You know, classic ones like Tolkien, Brando-Sando, etc."

Mizunami smiled, scrunching her nose and linking arms with her. "Everything is fine. You're not kidnapped. You're the farm girl, right?"

Osamu grabbed the tablet off the table. "Former forensic arson investigator, graduated top of your class, only to turn tail and pursue your passion for art, creating a fallout with your parents, although you have made amends. Speaking of parents, both are former teachers who were imprisoned by the UNA. They were also former political activists... Did I miss anything?"

She shook her head with a numb expression. Mizunami sat her down by the table. "Don't mind Osamu. He has a cold, business heart." She sat behind the table, shifting her focus to the laptop.

"What does that even mean?" Osamu shook his head, lighting a cigar. "You are extremely skilled and require your... particular skill sets."

"Our leader requires a dangerous assignment-"

"Your leader?!" Akame whispered. "I knew there was another player. The Shogun is a figurehead. No offense, Shogun."

Mizunami shot Osamu a glance. He rubbed his forehead. "So, you are a conspiracy theorist?"

"Yes, definitely."

"Well, you're about to be part of a conspiracy," Osamu said. "We require a fire to look natural. An accident."

"Wait, don't you want to send a message?" Akame said.

"Not all moves are for the public. This organization is a powerful player in the underworld. We don't need to create enemies in the shadows."

"Why?"

"Because this is an assassin's guild."

"There are a lot of assassins around the world."

Osamu adjusted himself on a chair across from her. "You are on a need-to-know basis. Just know this is an important domino to fall, if not the most important. We trust you; you would not be here if we didn't. But our operation is compartmentalized."

"No one person can take down the entire operation."

He nodded, then stood up, pouring her a drink of sweet sake. She shifted uncomfortably in her chair; he could tell his aura made her uncomfortable.

Power has that odd effect.

But she wasn't like the others. There was something about this woman that turned his insides, unlike other women—a slight power. They were of a similar age, both in their early thirties, and both from completely different upbringings. He was born into power; she was a simple farm girl.

"I'll do it."

"We can't guarantee your safety. There is a risk."

"I understand."

Mizunami slid a black briefcase across the table. The leather scratched on the silent castle. Osamu handed it to Akame. "Repeat after me. Knowledge is power."

"Knowledge is power." It scanned her, the handle glowing green for a moment.

"Welcome. Now, you will work with an engineer. We require a large fire, enough to take down a corporate building."

Mizunami turned the laptop around. There was a digital blueprint of a mid-height office building fitted with black glass.

At the top of the blueprint was their emblem: a circle with a rod and a smaller circle connected to the rod's center. "The fire will start from the basement, making its way up. This operation has been planned for months. They are having a meeting at the end of the night. Everyone in the building is guilty, and everyone must perish."

"That's dark," Akame looked down.

"It's a dark world," said Mizunami. "But rest assured, there are no innocents here."

"But didn't you say assassins? Why not kill them directly?"

"They are the assassins, honey. They just wear suits."

"But fire?"

Osamu spoke up. "The fire is just for the cover-up. I will personally deal with everyone inside."

Soldiers were speaking loudly down the hall, interrupting his train of thought. Osamu stood up, adjusting his coat and straightening it. He sat back down. "My men will escort you to the basement."

"Actually, I will escort her," Mizunami said.

"Out of the question."

"Excuse me?"

"You are too important to risk."

"I wasn't asking, sir." Mizunami stood up. "I'm powerful; I can defend myself. If I'm going to become a proper General, I need to be out in the field."

"This is not back in the day."

"It is for me."

"Our leader will not be pleased."

Mizunami smiled a dimpled smile. "I'll take responsibility."

Akame cleared her throat. "I don't need any engineer; I can rig this tonight."

Osamu nodded, then looked at his watch. It read 2:47 am. "You have seventeen hours before the party starts."

A little over an hour of sleep was all he could muster. It was the perfect hour, anyway; sunrise was at 4:38 am, and he was raised to rise before the sun. He made his way to the river that ran down between the bailey and motte.

Even with the summer humid morning, the water was brisk. He folded his clothes at its rocky edge and embraced the cold, as his father taught him. The time between darkness and light was the best time for a samurai to focus his mind and body. This task was a bloody one but a necessary one.

Lilith planted her own myth in the Japanese sacred Kojiki scroll. The text was the source of many historical accounts and mythology alike. Mizunami's clan was always more driven by it than the Tokugawa, thus replacing them in history was and is important.

Lilith's new section added the hero of freedom. A person who would free them from oppression. One who would match the blood of the parchment. Mizunami added her blood to the school in 1602, then returned to the present to claim her prize.

It worked, although many didn't believe in her, but all just wanted a reason to fight. All for a vision. A vision that saw the entire American cabin murdered, a new world war, and Darvients used as tools.

Yes, the assassin must be dealt with personally. But not only the killer, the entire organization had to burn. We can't risk it.

"Sorry to interrupt, but I can't sleep," Akame said with a bow.

Osamu stood up from the water. The early light glazing off his leather-tattooed skin. She eyed him from head to toe, then blushed. He made his way to the edge, then signaled for her to come closer. She obeyed.

He passed the back of his finger over her cheeks. "Why are you throwing me off my game?"

She shrugged. He allowed himself to grab a handful of her hair, exposing her neck. He kissed it, then shuffled rocks aside with his feet. They both looked down. She understood where her knees would go. So she complied.

As night cast its shadow, Osamu made his way to the financial district of Hyogo, parking their vehicle just opposite the sleek black glass building.

They observed the departure of the employees, leaving behind only the senior staff, just as ghosts orchestrated, while Mizunami and Akame blended into the corporate landscape, clad in gray business suits.

Osamu stood out from the mundane; black tactical pants tailored to perfection, embedded within were rectangular plates of metal resembling a samurai's haidate—thigh protectors.

The individual pieces of armor gave smart bullets trouble. A similar samurai-inspired armor protected his arms, complemented by a white armored vest. The white armored vest served as a deliberate target, diverting attention away from his head, left unprotected without a helmet. A helmet, after all, did not suit him. It was a striking fusion of modern technology with the echoes of ancient traditions.

By this time, everyone in the area was gone; there was very little nightlife. His iron kanabo magnetically snapped onto his backplate. A kanabo wasn't for everyone; the spiked club was heavy and tall enough to reach his chest despite his hundred and eight-two centimeters. They made it inside the sliding doors. Their enormous lobby was empty. Mizunami dropped sand as their boots echoed. There was only one woman at the desk.

"Ghost, where in..." he whispered.

"Got you. Shutdown is commencing. We need a few," said Ghost in his head.

"We are closed," said the woman at the desk.

Osamu lifted his Shemagh tactical scarf, covering his mouth. It wasn't bulletproof, but at least it was blade-proof.

"I said, we are... wait." The woman drew a gun.

Mizunami pointed her finger at her, and an explosion of sand erupted. Osamu held Akame while the glass shattered around them. Slabs of steel came down as the emergency armor came down, sealing them inside. The power was next to go, and only the emergency light provided illumination.

"Akame, let's go."

Osamu gave Mizunami a grave look. She looked him in the eye.

"I will protect her with my life."

"Just be safe."

She nodded, and they headed towards the basement.

He peeked over the desk and saw the woman lying on the floor, a pool of blood around her head. The stairs were dark, and the flashing light didn't help. The door swung open with little regard. Amateurs, he thought.

With a fluid motion, he drew a .22 caliber pistol from his abdomen and placed two shots in their head. The caliber was small, but the suppressor made it quiet. The closest to movie-quiet you can get. The last thing he needed was a building filled with assassins coming down on him at once.

He switched to three hundred blackout. Another quiet, smart pistol, with a brace he could shoulder. Two more minutes, he told himself. He kept his back to the wall, ascending the stairs.

Ghost assured him the first three floors were empty, so he skipped them completely. He entered the door on the fourth floor. There was a long corridor with at least fifteen assassins in suits standing in the hallway, and they were now staring at him.

They all drew, and a hail of bullets erupted. Osamu fell back, kicking the door closed.

Bullets tore right through the door, spraying in all directions. There was a slight curve for the bullets as they looked for their targets, but their direction was limited by the laws of physics.

A flash of pain came over him. One of the bullets hit his shoulder, but the armor held. Returning fire, he ran up the stairs. More warriors appeared from the upper floor. Bullets came from all directions as he was pinned on the stairs. Sweat came down his face despite the headband, along with black smoke.

Osamu pulled the pin off the grenade and tossed it towards the lower door.

"Grenade!" someone shouted.

It exploded, releasing a pink gel that turned into foam. It grew and grew until it filled the entire door frame and part of the stairs.

I should have waited for Aaron, he thought, just as his timer expired. And just like that, the shot was silenced.

"Smart firearms deactivated."

"Thanks, Ghost." Osamu stood up, removing the Iron Kanabo from his back. "I should have waited for the timer to go off... I need more practice." His club clanged as he dragged it up the stairs like a tired man going to work.

An assassin appeared before he could reach the door; he instantly swung the club, bashing his head. It crashed on the wall, creating a crushing, wet sound. He pulled the club out of the concrete wall.

There was another man on the floor, his face horrified. Osamu lifted the club. "Wait."

Osamu calmed down, crushing his skull. He grabbed both bodies, dragging them inside the large office space.

Ten assassins waited, eyes widened, a variety of melee weapons in hand. He dropped their comrades.

For a moment, they just stared at one another. Of course, the corpses didn't scare them, so Osamu released his inner monster. His hair turned bright white, the smell of decay and death taking over the room. There was a visible white aura around his skin, but they attacked anyway, and unlike the movies, they attacked at the same time.

The spiked kanabo, throughout history, was probably the least known and most underestimated martial arts weapon in the Japanese arsenal. It was all about weight management. A dance with your enemy, pushing enemy weapons, and using the extra weight on the backswing to back up and avoid getting hit.

Some swings required holding the club from both ends. Osamu did all of this, but there was very little need. His enhanced speed and strength were more than enough, combined with his healing from the ghost radiation. A positive effect of time traveling with the medallion. It wasn't instant, but everything helped.

The last assassin dropped without much trouble. Osamu already had his eyes fixed on the last door. It was a double wood door, fit for the boss. The infamous assassin named Force.

He opened the double doors wide. But there was no monster, only a little kid in the corner, facing the wall. She was blonde with brown skin, Middle Eastern, he guessed.

"Come, it's okay." She turned around; her eyes were large with dark circles underneath them as if she hadn't slept in weeks. "I don't want to anymore."

"It's okay. I will not hurt you." The smoke was thick at this point, so he started coaxing. "Come, we need to leave. I will not hurt you."

"But I will hurt you." Her eyes glowed yellow. She was a force.

They are using young Darvients, he thought. Then he was transported. No longer was he in a burning office building; instead, he was in a golden hall. It was bathed in ethereal light, its grandeur unmatched, a sight that both captivates and humbles. An expansive space with gleaming golden pillars that reached towards the heavens. There were men and women eating and fighting as far as the eye could see.

Viking? But two old men sat close to him. They sat on thrones. One had a large hammer. *Mjölnir.*

"This can't be real."

Thor and Odin stood up.

She is manipulating my mind. Force is a telepath of sorts. He knew there was one moment before she killed him where he stood.

His stomach turned, knowing what he had to do. He further unleashed the monster.

"Ōtakemaru!" His head automatically swung back, and then he swung his club. Then, he was back, and Force had her face crushed in.

Osamu started laughing. He noticed his white hair was now down his back, and his hand had claws. Fire was all around him now, and he loved it.

"No... No!" His hand retreated, and his hands and skin returned to normal. He fell to his knees, the smoke filling his lungs. Sand burst down from the rooftop.

A Medical UAV hovered with its side door open. Mizunami and Akame tossed him a rope. He grabbed on and was pulled up. The fire department was already on the scene, along with local police, mostly made up of drones.

Mizunami's soldiers pulled him up. Akame put water in his mouth. Mizunami was talking to him, but he couldn't hear her, or rather, he didn't want to. All he could think about was the Sage and how close he came to taking over his body.

He wasn't sure if all sages could do this or if it was just him, also known as Ōtakemaru in Japan. The Sage was supposed to be locked away. *So how... It doesn't matter. I can never unleash him. I can never endanger the world again. Even if it costs me my life.*

VASILIS

Scandinavia, 871

"False god!" Vasilis shouted, watching the giant flail his sword. The young man next to him was taken aback.

"What are you doing?" Trahen said over the growing chatter.

"Out of my business," Vasilis said, throwing his hood back and springing to his feet.

He looked around at the torch-carrying cult members, whose red cloaks made up most of the large circle. They whispered, but didn't make any sudden movements.

He's mine. He took his first step—Inoichi grabbed him.

"Who said you get to have all the fun?"

"I made the noise. I get to silence it." Vasilis snatched away.

"Make it quick. We still have to find Malaya." Inoichi frowned. He leaned against the tree and folded his arms.

Vasilis smirked. He looked at Jordan. "Keep your eyes open."

Arn, the host of this gathering, grabbed a spear and said. "How dare you?" There was something unusual about him, but Vasilis couldn't decide what it was. "I will kill you myself, peasant."

Vasilis smiled, never taking his eye off the giant. "If that were true, you would have done it by now," he said, removing his cloak and revealing his Spartan armor.

"What type of god doesn't know how to wield a sword?" Vasilis said. "Perhaps you have them fooled, but I see you are nothing more than a farm boy. I am a warrior, one with true god's blood."

The giant's laugh erupted, shaking those around the fire. "Very well, I will take your head, warrior."

Arn dropped to his knees. "He is not worthy. We shall kill him for you. Please take the blacksmith with you to the other world."

"No," the giant said, spiking his sword to the ground. "Better yet, I will kill him with my bare hands."

"No weapons? That's fine with me," Vasilis said, tossing Forsaken to Jordan—giving him a wink and removing his armor.

The false god did the same, revealing tattoos that covered his entire body, starting from the top of his massive bald head. Two braids draped from his long beard, decorated with seashells.

Arn looked up; fury covered his face. Vasilis raised his brow. *What angle are you two playing? Are they working with another?* He thought, though it didn't matter, the result would still be the same.

He rushed Vasilis, his movements as wild as his punches, and then he saw it, the slight pause to square himself. Vasilis kept his arms up, chin tucked in, flowing with the wind. *Southpaw, huh? He's left-hand-ed.*

Memories of his training with his father and his pet, Little Bear, returned to him, and so did his time in the Agoge. Fights against Midas, Elias, and Hecktor, dreaming of becoming men and fighting alongside one another.

Despite tainted friendships, he kept his childhood in a separate container. He had Inoichi to thank for that. Though he would never admit it, the samurai was skilled, honest, and someone he could trust.

Living on an island, training, and time traveling had that effect on him. It also didn't hurt that they shared a common enemy in his former friends, Elias and Midas.

Vasilis could hear the crowd growing restless over his thoughts. He evaded Elvir more than he fought. Inoichi's annoying glare made it all the more fun. The giant's movements slowed, and he was panting.

Keep coming, Vasilis thought. *How much do you have left? Thirty seconds.*

"You are a winded god," Vasilis said. "Guess what? Now we fight."

With two clean shots, the giant's legs wobbled. He had him, but not enough. Vasilis lifted him off the ground.

"That's enough, Spartan," said Inoichi. "There's no need for death."

Vasilis looked over. The giant took advantage, elbowing him in his mouth. Vasilis replied with a knee, swallowing the blood pooling inside his mouth. He grabbed him again.

"No," Inoichi shouted.

It meant nothing this time. The driving urge to toss the cult leader toward the blade meant more. Elvir stumbled, struggling to catch his balance. He put a hand up at the last minute, but the blade was unforgiving; it sliced through his hand and half his neck.

A woman with a red cloak screamed in agony. "Loft-den, no! You killed my brother, asshole!"

Vasilis ignored her and the restless crowd, who grew in anger. Instead, he smiled at a black-cloaked spectator.

"You fool," Inoichi said. He pushed Vasilis hard enough to knock him down, taking an arrow in the arm.

Black mud splashed into his face. He looked up, seeing the dark-haired beauty he first met in Japan. If not for the slight pounding of adrenaline, his heart would have skipped a beat. He smiled, uncaring about the blood on his teeth. "Kasumi, nice to see you again."

"You silly boy," Kasumi said, running past him toward Inoichi, who was struggling on the floor with both Arn and the woman.

As chaos grew, the rain poured harder. Vasilis frowned as he watched her run toward Arn, who stood with Inoichi's sword in hand, kicking him in the face.

What have I done? Vasilis thought, looking around, finding Jordan running—his hood fell off.

"Jordan!" A girl screamed. "What in seven hells!"

"Malaya?" He tilted his head as she ran past him.

A large black cloak crept behind Jordan. "Jordan, look out!" Vasilis said, getting up and running toward him. The man grabbed him, lifting him off the ground. His hood came off, revealing his blond undercut braid.

"Midas," he exclaimed. His stomach sank, anchoring him in place, seeing his old friend. The man who had walked away and left him for dead.

Another red cloak revealed himself. He was tall, shirtless, and built like a Greek statue. The stranger wore a gold ornament around his long neck and one on his head.

"Trahen, look out!" The stranger shouted, removing a dagger from the animal hide wrapped around the waist of his purple pants.

Trahen threw an axe at a cloaked man, who dodged it with ease. He picked up another wooden stick—it turned into an axe. "Find Canderyn," he shouted, readying himself for the black-cloaked figure moving swiftly through the chaos.

A rumble took most of the people's attention. The slaves returned, running downhill from a stampede of Vikings. The village center erupted into chaos. Even then, Vasilis couldn't stop his gaze off the man heading for Trahen, who tossed the axe.

The cloaked man moved, his hood falling back. He knew who it was even before seeing his face, but he had to be sure. It was as if time slowed for Vasilis. All he could see were the deep blue eyes of the man who took his life.

"Elias!" The name tore from Vasilis's throat, laden with the weight of memories and betrayal. It was a shout that carried with it the ghost of a dull ache in his back, a reminder of the cold dagger that had rewritten their destinies.

It was difficult to see anything beyond the chaos, but he knew what he wanted, who he wanted. The man he once called brother, the man who stabbed him in the back.

"Help!" Jordan shouted, breaking him from his rage.

Before he could come to his rescue, Kasumi had her chains wrapped around his former friend's neck, forcing him to release Jordan. He sprinted to safety, though the victory was short-lived. Confusion reigned over the village, but Elias called Vasilis's attention. They locked eyes from a distance. Elias stood atop a chariot. Every inch of skin was covered with blood and dirt covered his face, yet his blue eyes and victorious smile shone in the darkness. They were escaping with Trahen.

"Elias!"

The screams and cries faded into the background as flashes of his last days in Sparta crossed his mind. He failed to protect Nefeli from Quintus, and he'd failed again. His eyes moved to Malaya, who used her body to cover Jordan from the arrows that rained the sky.

"Brother!" a redhead man shouted, snapping him back to reality. He followed his gaze to Trahen. The towering man slammed into Vasilis's back, knocking him back to the ground, his head hitting a stone. His ears rang, and the world spun.

Bodies fell over him, and arrows pierced Vikings left and right. He struggled for freedom. He climbed over the tight group of men, struggling to breathe or cope with the thought that he would not catch Elias or protect Malaya. Malaya's cry of pain sent a surge of energy through his body.

Protecting her was part of his assignment, but he needed to kill Elias. He pushed the bodies off in time enough to spot Elias in the distance. Vasilis started to run toward his enemy, but her cries held him. He turned to see an arrow sticking from her back.

The large red-haired man who knocked him over saved Malaya from taking another. He lifted and carried Malaya. "Get up, boy," he shouted at Jordan, who was unharmed and capable of running on his own.

Inoichi was being helped up by a blonde woman and Kasumi. They didn't need his help after all. The word spun as he tried to move–falling to his knee. He grabbed his head. Out of the darkness, he saw a pair of yellow eyes. They glowed in the rain, like a wolf hunting in the dark forest–or a fox. He extended his arms, trying to avoid the animal.

It was then that it—the fox grabbed him. Kasumi pulled Vasilis just as more Vikings flooded the area. She ordered everyone to follow.

A remarkable recovery by Inoichi allowed the group to quicken their pace. Vasilis suspected a mild concussion, but it was clear he was fine. They followed Canderyn, who led them through thick vegetation that soon turned into a small hidden path leading to a cabin built alongside a mountain. Grass made up the rooftop. Its entrance lived inside layered rocks, making their home nearly invisible.

Everyone shared the same marveled look as Canderyn welcomed them inside. He encouraged them to enjoy the fire, food, and water. His gentle voice and welcoming nature were a contrast to the rugged look of the man.

"We thank you," Inoichi grunted, removing his vanguard. Blood poured from it, soaking the land.

"Let me help you close your wound, little brother," Kasumi said.

"I should probably help—"

"I'll help," Malaya said, interrupting him and brushing past Vasilis, avoiding him as if he were diseased.

"I'm fine, thanks for asking," Vasilis said sarcastically before grabbing a bowl of cherries.

He found a wooden stool some feet away from the others near a window. Its frame was made of hard, thick wood with metal hinges, a way to provide some secrecy. Rain continued to patter against the window. Of course he understood the need to keep things hidden.

Part of him hated what he did back there, but he would not say it out loud or apologize for it. That's who he was, a warrior by nature. Take the lives of those who threaten to take yours.

If a man draws his sword, be the one to make the fatal strike. That is what he was taught by his father, by Seth, by Sparta. It's how his ancestors survived and how his failure to live up to that code got him killed. He would do it again if he had to, but he wouldn't waste as much time.

"Hey, V," Jordan's voice broke the tension. He stood there, uncomfortably holding Forsaken. "Here you go."

"You did good back there," Vasilis said, followed by a pat on the back.

Jordan smiled and nodded before turning away.

"I believe an introduction is in order!" Canderyn said.

Everyone looked on as he introduced himself, which came with a story. Vasilis cleared his throat. "I do not mean to interrupt your grand tale, but..."

"You did it anyway," Malaya interjected. "Please ignore this child."

"Here we go again." Vasilis rolled his eyes and tapped the back of his head on the stone.

Malaya removed her tomahawk from the worn belt of her equally worn trousers. "That little stunt you pulled back there almost got Jordan killed on top of the fact that he's even here. Tell me again, I must have missed something. How the heck is this better than all the power my family has back home?"

Vasilis' jaw tightened. "Must I repeat myself? This is for the best. Jordan is fine. You may not be aware as usual, but the world you left has changed. The kid was in danger—is in danger, so your grandfather trusted me—" Inoichi cleared his throat. Vasilis smiled. "*Us* to look after him."

"Not if you're dead," Malaya snapped, marching toward him with her weapon drawn. Her blue tunic, once vibrant, now looked as though it had seen better days. Vasilis was caught between an urge to laugh and the instinct to unsheathe his sword.

Was she truly mad enough to make me disarm her? Vasilis wondered, bracing himself for the worst.

To his relief, Hildegard ripped the axe from her hand. "Careful, Malaya, you may hurt someone," she said before fading to the back of the elegant room with the others.

Arguments had woven themselves into the very fabric of many relationships, a testament to the fire and clash of wills that defined interactions. But this time, as he stood there, witnessing the ferocity in Malaya's stance, Vasilis felt a shift in the air—a palpable change that unsettled him more than he cared to admit. She was different now, transformed in a way that went beyond mere anger or defiance.

Even without knowing the full weight of the secrets he harbored, Malaya's actions spoke volumes of her love for the boy. A love so profound—so strong that it could pierce the toughest armor—a love he once had for his brothers. Seeing her unwavering stance evoked a twinge of guilt and respect that nearly stopped him from responding.

Vasilis looked at Jordan, who did not seem to be affected. He may have enjoyed the thrill. Malaya, while justified, was overreacting. He needed to put her in her place. With that thought, he hardened his resolve.

"Will you relax?" Vasilis began. "Jordan has yet to complain. Believe me, this will make for a great song." He folded his arm and winked at Jordan.

"You smug asshole. If not for Inoichi, you would be dead. Kasumi saved Jordan—you just don't learn," Malaya said, unrelenting anger marking every word as she stood in front of Vasilis. "You're more selfish than I thought."

"Selfish? Ha! This entire ordeal is based on your family's problems. Let's see. Your mother waged war, has my mentor in her pocket, who killed their father," Vasilis shouted, pointing at Inoichi and Kasumi. "Oh, and she's currently looking for some god-like warrior!"

"Granted, you saved my life, but I didn't ask for this!" He pointed at his chest. "I have sacrificed. While you were in a Benz, I was trying to hold on to dying comrades."

Malaya glanced around, changing her tone. "Dammit, Vasilis. Watch your tongue. You're not home."

Vasilis grit his teeth, the tension in his jaw betraying the calm he fought hard to maintain. "I know strategy, woman," he snarled, his voice a low rumble, matching her tone.

The effort to keep his rising anger in check was palpable, a visible muscle twitching in his cheek. He stood his ground, eyes blazing with a mix of defiance. "Look at what happened. I revealed the rats hiding in the shadows. We have a direction now. You head back. That's the deal. You all are welcome, by the way."

"Please, I'm not going anywhere. You expect him to keep his word? That's your issue. You'd rather take orders than take charge, like a real man. So, screw your orders, and screw General Williams."

"Who says we can trust you, *Castillo*—"

Something hit Vasilis on his forehead. He looked down at the rock. "Imbecile," Inoichi said, signaling for silence.

It was then Vasilis felt it too, a presence, followed by the crunch of deadwood just outside the door. Everyone grabbed a weapon—Malaya huddled with Jordan, who held the tomahawk.

"Who goes there?" asked Inoichi, his voice more menacing than usual.

"Brother?" said the man outside the door. "Are you in there? I am alone."

Canderyn brushed past everyone. "Ylorb, you're alive!" he bellowed, embracing the man Vasilis recognized from the fight.

This time, he held an enormous sword wrapped in cloth. "I was not able to save Trahen."

Canderyn introduced him to everyone as his stepbrother, Ylorb, a lanky man with shaggy hair and a soft voice. He spoke about their life and how Trahen's father took them in as young boys. By trade or by fate, they were all blacksmiths, so he said.

Three brothers, three blacksmiths. That could not be a coincidence. Vasilis thought, unable to take his eyes off the unassuming guest.

Ylorb raised a thick, black brow as he looked at Malaya. "I saw you take an arrow to the back. How are you walking?"

"I'm a fast healer," Malaya said. "Plus, I wore armor."

Inoichi stood, joining the conversation. "I remember you now. You were sitting next to Arn. You are part of that cult."

"Yes, that was I. And I admit, we are all Seers, waiting for the awakening of Elvir."

"You were raised a pure blacksmith," said Canderyn. He grabbed the sword from his hands. "What is this? You are not a man of the sword."

He unwrapped it. Vasilis instantly recognized the eloquent metal shimmering through the dirt. The gold trim on the Viking hilt reflected the fire well, giving it a unique tingle. "A Champion sword," Vasilis said, inspecting the engraved text.

+VLFBERH+T.

His translator helped him read it as *Ulfberht.*

Ylorb's face darkened, still avoiding his eyes. "The *false god* who Vasilis killed was Loft-den Gamle Frodesdatter, brother of Hallveig Frodesdatter, wife of Ingólfr Arnarson," he looked at Vasilis. "You should remember all the lives you destroy."

"Perhaps it was the god's will, punishment for deceiving the people," Vasilis said.

"Loft was just doing as Arnarson asked of him, a favor that Trahen was a part of," Ylorb said drily.

"Trahen? What does our brother have to do with this?" Canderyn demanded, stepping closer to him.

"A foreign Seer came to Arnarson for help, seeking the truth about the *Sage* Elvir and all that surrounds his lore, including the legendary Vessel," Ylorb said.

Malaya and Kasumi looked at one another.

"Vessel?" Vasilis said.

"Elvir is not a man but an entity," Ylorb continued. "This entity is what some call a spirit, and the spirit requires a Vessel."

"I think it's storytime," Jordan said.

Ylorb smirked. "Elvir was once a man. He, along with seven others, traveled the world, helping humanity. They worshiped their gods that history has forgotten, the Aigons. These Aigons granted them powers to further assist humans. They collectively became known as the Seven Sages. Like many men before them, they sought more power, and they found it. A dark being granted them the ultimate power of immortality."

"Just another fantasy story," Malaya said.

"Allow him to continue," Inoichi said.

"Gods from other realms took notice, many from foreign religions, even Odin himself. The Aigon were forced to pay for their actions. They were exiled to and forced to live as humans."

"And what happened to the Sages?" Jordan said.

"They were sealed by Champions of the gods," Ylorb said in a low tone. "For every Sage, there were two Champions, fourteen in total, that wielded great power. Together, they defeated the Sages by sealing their essence away for eternity. They are locked away and protected by Gatekeepers, a faceless group shrouded in mystery, sworn to protect the foundation on which the Sages lay."

"Are the Champions selected at random?" Kasumi asked.

"Yes, they are selected by the gods," Ylorb replied. "Born to do one thing, protect man against the Sages should they ever awake."

Kasumi's brows furrowed as if solving a puzzle. "The Champions cannot be random if the Sages are spread throughout the world. Champions must be born local to that Sage. Am I correct?"

Ylorb nodded. "So the legend says."

Local to the Sages. Vasilis thought. *My father... Myself... Midas.*

"So V and Ino must be Champions then," Jordan said.

"The loft was part of the act. It wasn't supposed to happen this way—everything went wrong."

"So your brother, he's working with this Seer?" Malaya questioned.

Ylorb came closer to the fire. "No, he knows the man they seek. He means to hide him. That's why he stood up, to make sure no one else did."

"You and this *Elvir*... I want to save our brother," Canderyn said, clearly upset. "Nothing else matters."

"Elias will make him pay for his betrayal," said Vasilis. "Your brother, I mean."

"The Viking ran us out of the village," said Ylorb. "I fear Trahen is not our only concern," Inoichi said, his hand on his empty scabbard that once held Divine Wind. "We must seek Arnarson as well. He has a sword of great value." It seems the kick was harder than he expected. "That Arn, he took my sword."

"That's a family heirloom," said Kasumi, who sat between Jordan and Hildegard.

"It must be part of Lilith's plans," said Malaya. The name seemed to unease Jordan.

"Who is Lilith?" Canderyn questioned.

"Lilith. She-she's the seer," said Ylorb. "You know her?"

Before Malaya could answer, Inoichi spoke. "Emily warned us. She wants our hilts."

"Lilith continues with her fairy tales," said Malaya.

"She attempted to steal Forsaken back home," added Vasilis.

Everyone was quiet, taking in all the information. *Her mother made her move. Now it was time for Malaya to make hers*, Vasilis thought, watching the look on her face, the one she made when she was searching for a solution.

"Emily's intel is trustworthy. We go after the hilt at first light," said Malaya.

Ylorb assured them that Arn would go to a village called Etne. Trahen, on the other hand, was last seen heading east. "We must not wait until first light. We will lose track of them, Elias—"

"Lilith is more important than your stupid vendetta," Malaya interrupted

"Vasilis is right," said Kasumi. "We should pursue both. We split the group and reunite in five days at Etne."

"I called Team Kasumi," Vasilis said.

"I owe Malaya my life," Inoichi said. "I will not leave her side." His eyes narrowed as he addressed the blacksmith. "Ylorb will show us the way, won't you?"

"Of course."

"Canderyn, you will come with us," said Kasumi. "We will locate your brother. Hildegard will come with me."

"We just reunited, yet you choose to go with strangers," Inoichi protested before storming off.

"Don't worry, little brother. Vasilis will take care of me!" Kasumi teased.

Vasilis and Inoichi took Jordan with them to hunt, telling Malaya they needed to spend tonight as part of their training. The truth was, they did more than hunt, feeling the need to warn Jordan about how Malaya would take the news, the truth of who he was. It was one thing for her to have mentored Jordan all these years. But, to discover a secret such as this was akin to the unbridled strike of lightning that would truly rock Malaya's foundation as a tumultuous storm of emotions would sure to follow.

A pang of sorrow filled Vasilis. For all her bluster and bouts of being, frankly, a bit of a terror—mean might even be putting it mildly—the thought of her grappling with such a monumental family secret bordered on the absurd.

After supper, everyone had fallen asleep. Vasilis took watch. Part of him wished he could sleep with the same ease. Vasilis placed the black box Kat gave him next to Malaya just as the sun began to rise. He stared at her, hugged up next to Hildegard. For reasons unknown, Vasilis found himself wanting to pass his hand through her hair, but dared not.

He turned to Kasumi, who was still lying down, eyes glued on him. "She doesn't bite once you get to know her," she said.

"I beg to differ." Vasilis smiled. "I dare not test her."

They both chuckled. He found himself drawn into her eyes, the flames from the flickered making them even more beautiful than he remembered, and a different color brown. *I must have hit my head harder than I thought.*

Kasumi cleared her throat and moved closer to him. "I never thanked you for the other night. My soul was in shambles after everything that happened. I was in a really dark place." She paused. "I guess what I am saying is… thank you for not asking. Some things are better left unsaid."

As if it were second nature, he placed his hand over hers. His mother had taught him about offering comfort and solace to a patient, but this was to a troubled soul. His heart raced once he realized what he had done, but Kasumi didn't move. Her eyes flicked down at their hands, then back up to the fire and Malaya. Did her pinky finger graze his? Or was it just his imagination?

He cleared his throat, following her gaze. "I just hope it all ends differently for her than it did for all of us."

"Then you weren't paying attention."

KASUMI

Scandinavian, 871

Kasumi watched as Malaya and Inoichi disappeared into the horizon, like stars consumed by the advancing dawn. A quiet ache stirred within her, longing for moments unspoken, for words left unloosed like arrows resting in a quiver. Yet, she could not ask him to remain—he was the steadfast oak, bound by honor, unshaken in his loyalty.

She allowed herself a fleeting smile, the kind one gives to a passing memory. To tell him how much she admired him would be to strike glass with a hammer.

His pride would splinter like fragile ice, she thought.

The following night was full of clouds and conversation that was nearing drowned out by the rain. Fortunately, the rain had ceased, though the strategizing was just beginning. They braced for an impending journey, potentially culminating in a battle.

Beside her stood a Spartan warrior, Vasilis, with skin the color of whose handsomeness and prowess matched any she had encountered. Despite her unfamiliarity with him, his aura bore a comforting resemblance to someone she had once lost.

Then there was the large man with fiery red hair, an enigma in his own right. *Could he be relied upon in a fight?* That remained to be seen.

It did not matter; she was ready to fight with them if it meant getting their brother back. She had a power within that helped her defeat many men, women, and monsters alike.

As they navigated the wet, dense terrain of this unfamiliar world, Kasumi's thoughts drifted to Canderyn. He was a man of few words, his demeanor marked by a quiet kindness. Though reserved, his profound love for his brother was unmistakable—a sentiment Kasumi could deeply relate to.

She had a chance to do something for someone that she couldn't do for herself—save a brother. Vasilis, however, was on a different mission; he was engaging with everyone, smiling despite the situation. The night passed quickly.

Kasumi drifted to sleep only to be awakened by a chiming metal—just before sunrise. She jumped to find Vasilis staring at her. "Sorry, did I wake you?"

"No," Kasumi said, barely able to get a half-smile from Vasilis.

"Ah, so you dream best with your eyes open too," he teased.

Different body, same mind. She smiled, reminding her of this feeling back home for a love she once knew. A man just as charming who hid his emotions just the same. "So, you make others laugh, but are too afraid to smile at yourself."

"Perhaps I smile internally," he replied, his smile bleak.

"Or, you could just be afraid—"

"I am Vasilis," he interrupted, keeping his voice to a whisper. "A *Spartan* warrior, I have faced things you can only imagine. Thus, I do not fear."

"Then you are stupid," said Kasumi.

"Stupid enough to think you were..." Vasilis paused and started striking the metal faster. He stopped. "You know, Inoichi warned me about your tongue."

"And Malaya warned me about you," she smiled. "I'll try again."

"As you should."

"If you keep talking, you'll quickly realize my kunai is sharper than my tongue," she said. "When I said you were afraid, it was not to offend but to bring forth a possible conflict, a demon you have not slain."

"You're right," Vasilis said, staring at his blade. "But I have tamed it."

Kasumi nodded. He was a lot like she thought he would be, and at the same time, not at all. Vasilis stood up, putting the cloak over his shoulders. She did the same. The morning was not going to be pleasant, and they could not stay here for long.

"How much sleep is required with you Scandinavians?" Kasumi asked, nudging Canderyn.

"I'm not from here," said Canderyn, his eyes barely open, a voice a low growl. He reached for a bone that lay next to him, scavenging for meat.

"A perfect time to tell us that," said Hildegard as she stretched. "If you're not from here, then where are you from?"

Canderyn paused. The sun reflected the emptiness in his emerald gaze as he stared at the gray sky.

Was he searching for a lie to tell? Kasumi thought.

"Part of me feels unsettled," he said, his tone somber. "I cannot recall the last time I saw my brother before yesterday. He had been on his own for some time, searching for..." he paused.

"For what?" questioned Kasumi.

"I am sorry." Canderyn shook away whatever was plaguing him. "My mind tends to wander. Please forgive me. I did not imagine seeing him in such chaos."

"And we will save him," Vasilis said, tossing them tanned wool cloaks. "We should keep our heads down. Oh, and Inoichi wanted you to have this." He dug into his sack and removed a folded black cloth. "In the future, they call it a *ninja outfit*."

Kasumi smiled. "Back home, we call it shozoku, but it's nothing like this," she said, unfolding the all-black clothing—the material was lighter than any she'd ever worn. "It weighs nothing."

"Their world is advanced," Vasilis added. "It is nearly impenetrable like my—"

"Quiet," Kasumi urged, seeing two growling wolves.

Their eyes spoke of hunger and pain, but these were no ordinary wolves. Its deep growl nearly shook the ground. Standing on its forelegs, the wolf clearly towered over the red-haired Canderyn. Her heart pounded despite her trying her best to keep calm. She, like many other children, heard the stories about the Hokkaido wolf from their land. She never saw one, but she imagined this was what it looked like.

"We will tread carefully," Vasilis warned. "No one move."

"What beautiful animals," Hildegard said, taking a step forward. "You must be hungry. "

The wolves barked as if to agree, then they charged toward them. With nothing left to do, they grabbed their belongings and ran into the wilderness, doing their best to dodge trees and debris. No matter how fast they ran, the wolves kept up.

Why have they not caught us by now? Kasumi thought. *They have plenty of chances. Something is off.*

Rain started to pour, creating puddles of water, making it more difficult to escape. "We need to find high ground!" Kasumi said, knowing they would tire before the wolves. If that happened, who knows if they'd survived?

In short time, they found a large boulder to climb and readied their weapons–the wolves didn't show. They waited in silence for what seemed like an eternity, waiting for the beasts—perhaps waiting for death.

"My apologies," said Hildegard. "I was not expecting them to eat us."

Canderyn laughed; it became contagious. When it was clear the wolves were not returning, they decided to continue their journey, though something told Kasumi it wasn't the end of it.

Candyern was the first to jump down. "I am somewhat familiar with the area. I will guide our way back..." his voice trailed. They all followed his wide-eyed gaze, finding the danger that quieted him. With the rain gone, morning blanketed the forest, giving way to the wolves' eyes, glowing like orbs of molten gold in the mist.

Vasilis stepped in front of Kasumi. "I'll take care of this one," he whispered. "I have fought a canius dirus once before." He climbed down slowly.

"No. Fighting them should not be an option," Kasumi said. "We are a threat to their home."

Hildegard's gaze tore into Kasumi, and Kasumi knew then what was being asked of her. She hesitated for a moment, her heart pounding in her chest. The secret she guarded was a heavy burden to bear, and the risk of revealing her true nature to the others was great. She took a deep breath, and like a fox slipping into the shadows, she pulled her mask over her face.

The kitsune spirit, long dormant within her, stirred to life. Kasumi felt its presence; a faint whisper in her ear urged her to embrace its power.

For years, she had felt the connection to the animals around her, hearing their voices and understanding their needs. She had always known she was different, special in a way that set her apart. But it was only with Mei's guidance that she had learned to control the kitsune within her.

As the wolves emerged from the shadows, their growls echoed. Kasumi stood her ground. She could feel the tension in her muscles as she prepared to defend herself, but as she did, she felt a strange vibration coursing through her body.

The wolves circled them. More emerged from the evergreen forest. The moment slowed. She felt everything. The cold mud on her feet. Vasilis's warm hand on her body. Without warning, five tails sprouted from her back, each one crackling with fiery energy.

The noise startled everyone, but no one knew where it came from. With the right eyes, the aura they emitted was powerful enough to light a path through the darkness.

Vasilis was too distracted by his blood thirst to notice the transformation anyway, but Kasumi knew that only a select few would be able to see the aura of the kitsune. Those who did were rare individuals, attuned to the magical forces that coursed through the world.

"*What are you?*" The voice of a boy questioned, coming directly from the wolf.

The snot wasn't moving. It never did when she heard the voices, but this was different. This did not feel like an animal. They did not talk with the same coherence or speech despite how much she understood them. It was like her speaking their language, but he was speaking hers directly to her.

"*I'm like you, only different,*" said Kasumi. "*We do not want to hurt you.*"

The inner fox in her disagreed. The kitsune and okami were natural enemies. It snarled, wanting to shred them with its claws. She twisted her neck, pushing down the urge, still not having the control she wanted. "*Just tell us what you want?*"

"*Everything,*" the wolf replied.

"Are we going to attack or not?" Vasilis whispered, keeping his eyes on the beasts.

"*Tell your boyfriend to put the weapon down,*" the wolf warned, his growl growing louder. "*My pack will devour him.*"

"*He's not my...*" Kasumi started. "*Why are you doing this?*"

"*We are tired of running,*" he replied. "*We are too powerful to continue to play nice...*"

Kasumi closed her eyes, calling on the god Inari to unlock more power. It was both a gift, and a curse, given that the kitsune wanted full control, but it needed to yield to Inari. It was an ongoing battle.

The more power she gained, the more danger her friends were in. *Control.* She inhaled deeply, allowing more air to flow into her body. Her orange-red cloak became more visible to the human eye as she felt her face changing behind the fox mask.

She growled, releasing all what she stored. She crept closer to the young wolf, her radiant claws at the ready. The low growl turned into snaps, startling Vasilis and Canderyn.

"What is that?" Vasilis said.

"She is fine. Stay away from her," Hildegard warned.

Canderyn's eyes widened, his mouth with a slight agape. The wolves, snapping and growling, crept closer.

"I'm the fox of the Tokugawa clan," Kasumi said, though she continued to not surrender full control. "We are descendants of the Genji clan, and wielder of a great power. Who is the pack leader?"

They retreated into the forest, and behind a large brush, a black wolf lurked. His eyes were brighter than any gold her father found in Toi, with his size and clearly the Alpha. The wolf's size was unmistakable even before it emerged from the shadows. Its aura stirred a primal urge within Kasumi, threatening to overwhelm her human form. She hurriedly transformed back to avoid losing herself to the beast.

Kasumi looked at Hildegard and sighed. "We need Hilda," she said through clenched teeth.

"Who is Hilda?" Vasilis said, backing up as the wolves slowly approached.

"Are you sure?" Hildegard replayed.

"Yes, I'm sure. I must know if he is trustworthy."

"She's still upset with you. Please, try to be nice."

"No promises."

Kasumi sighed, wishing she didn't need her. Hilda had not been seen since Malaya's blood cured her blindness. As a result, she unlocked a power within, giving birth to Hildegard, proving Mei was right. Something inside each of them would arise—it had.

If they were going to get answers, Kasumi needed the version of Hildegard, who did anything and anyone she wanted. Though even she had to admit Hilda saved them, more than once. And she was the only one who could decipher the wolves' true intentions. Still, she hated that Hilda would be around for at least a day.

Within seconds, Hilda's eyes whitened like the clouds. A half-smile replaced the bleakness as she glanced at Kasumi and Vasilis. "I see a lot of pink between you two."

"Not now." Kasumi gritted her teeth, feeling Vasilis and Canderyn's urge to stare at her.

"Oops, was I not supposed to tell?" Hilda said sarcastically.

"Focus. I need your gift."

"Of course, since you asked so nicely."

"Please," Kasumi said through gritted teeth. "What do you see?"

"Nothing."

"Hilda!"

"Okay, okay." Hilda cleared her throat. "Brown, lots of brown... they are afraid."

Kasumi urged the men to lower their weapons, and though hesitant, they obeyed.

"Show us your true self. See that we mean you no harm," she said.

In an instant, the wolf was gone, replaced by a man with coiled black hair and deep brown skin that glowed with an almost ethereal smoothness. Kasumi's breath hitched.

She had heard whispers of the fabled werewolves, but witnessing their power firsthand was something else entirely. Memories surged through her like an unrelenting tide, dragging with them thoughts of her family and the companions who had set out with her long ago on this transformative journey.

If only Genzo and Inahime could see this.

The powers of the kitsune and the werewolf—two beings rooted in the ancient lore of the Tenge—could not have been more different.

Through trial and reflection, Kasumi had come to understand the intricate nature of werecreature abilities.

Her kitsune powers, tied to the none tails of knowledge, were precise and consuming, reshaping both her body and mind. But every transformation stole fragments of her identity, bending her will to the divine being that lingered within her. The werewolf's transformation, by contrast, was raw and feral—a primal force unleashed without hesitation or restraint.

A memory ignited, vivid and searing: the moment she lost her power. The revelation had struck like a thunderclap, shattering her understanding of herself and the world. *All Tenge are bound together,* the old man had said, his voice echoing in the hollow depths of her despair. *They are drawn to one another, like stars pulled by the same unseen force.*

Could that connection transcend even the boundaries of space and time?

Sigurd, the imposing son of Mei the Revered, had unveiled to her the profound complexity of werebeasts throughout history.

"Legend has it," Sigurd's voice boomed into the night, "that wolves reign supreme in the werecreature hierarchy. Their lineage traces directly back to the divine blood, honored by the Olympian gods, and those of the Norse, and my ancestors, the Aigons. Some merely stand on hind legs, but others, like my ancestors, undergo a complete transformation into wolves. "

Could these beings be descendants of the Aigons? Are they kin to both Mei and Sigurd? The warrior within her yearned to measure their might. *If they are,* she thought. *I cannot put my allies at risk. I must control myself.*

"Leave us," the leader ordered his pack to depart.

Turning to face Kasumi and her companions, the transformation in the leader's demeanor was palpable. His golden eyes, previously burned with the fire of command, softened, revealing a glint of humility.

"My apologies," he said, his voice lowering to a respectful tone as he bowed slightly. "I hope my nudity does not offend.

"Not in the slightest," Hilda said, walking toward the man-wolf—Kasumi pulled her back.

"Good. I am..." His voice trailed along with his gaze that landed on Canderyn. "Cykius? I thought it might be you, the stories of your sacrifice, but your eyes are so... *green*. What happened to you?"

Confusion clouded the expression of the red-haired Northman, his eyes darting around in surprise. "You confuse me with another. That is not my name."

The Alpha's eyes darted back to them, then back to Canderyn, tracing his features. "I see," he said, disappointment evident in his tone. "Perhaps I am the confused one."

Vasilis took a step forward, his tone deeper than usual and his stance straighter—protective even. "Who are you?" he demanded.

The man stared at Canderyn a little longer before facing Vasilis. "I am Rafik, leader of these direwolves. And you are..."

"Vasilis of—"

"Greece." Rafik interrupted. His eyes scanned Kasumi as she stepped between the men. "Why are you in these lands..." He paused, his nostrils twitching as he inhaled the air around her. "kitsune," the words floated in the cool wind to her ears.

The stillness inside the Tenge was palpable, the same quietness she always experienced around the Aigons. A silent confirmation that Rafik was a god amongst men, an Aigon.

"We are lost," Kasumi confessed. "We did not mean to trespass. It was your pack that chased us here."

Rafik's voice held an unexpected gravity, betraying his youthful appearance. 'They were only following their teachings; killing was never their intention. These are just kids, still boys and girls at heart,' he said, his words echoing with a wisdom that seemed far beyond his years.

"Why were they so afraid?" Kasumi asked.

"Men have taken our village," a girl said out of the shadows.

Long spiraling brown hair that covered the breast of her bronze nude body. Her hardened eyes and tone betrayed her soft beautiful face. "While Rafik was away, this woman, a *powerful* woman, and her men destroyed our home and kidnapped the human we were sworn to protect—"

"Jamila," Rafik interrupted.

"A powerful woman?" Vasilis said, bolted toward them. "Who exactly was she?"

"Why do you care?" said Rafik.

"Hilda?" Kasumi said.

"Green spills from her," Hilda said. "She is telling the truth."

"We are hunting her and those men, at least we were, until your *children* chased us off," said Vasilis. "Allow her to tell us her story. Perhaps we can help."

Rafik shrugged. There was a look on his face, as if he wanted something in return.

"We have exotic food, many you have never tasted," Kasumi said, opening a sack and showing them the delectables.

Rafik nodded. Jamila explained how the people who stormed the village destroyed much of their cattle, displaying great power, too powerful for them—forcing them to flee. "The woman, they called her a Seer. We are not sure how she knew about things even though we did not, but she did. She knew he was a mage blacksmith with the blood of a different god."

Canderyn's red brow raised. "A blacksmith?"

"Yes," Rafik said. "I guess our paths were meant to cross after all. We swore to protect the boy when he came of a certain age. He came to us some time ago. "

"You must take us," said Kasumi. "I believe we can help you."

"Please," said Canderyn.

"We will not be returning," Rafik said abruptly.

"But—" Jamila started.

"Quiet," Rafik growled. "That part of our life has concluded. Get the others. We will continue the next phase of our journey. Others need our help, so we must make it to the island." He looked at Canderyn with a concerning glare. He looked at the others. "Tell you what. I will show you the way. For the rest of the food, of course."

Vasilis grunted as Hilda happily handed over what she had for the necessary information. Kasumi led the way to the village, which they hoped would give them answers.

Cykius? She thought, unable to get Rafik and Canderyn's meeting out of her head.

Kasumi slowed enough for Vasilis to catch up. "Why do you suppose Rafik thought he knew Canderyn?"

"The better question is. Why did Canderyn pretend like he did not know Rafik? How in Hades did he know who I was?"

A thud followed by Hilda's concerned cry for help forced them to stop. "Canderyn has fallen ill."

"Not now," Vasilis said, digging through his sack. "Stand back, please."

He knelt over him, removing a small bottle with a wooden cork, then lifted Canderyn's head, dumping the pink liquid down his throat.

A healer. Kasumi smiled, watching Vasilis.

"Canderyn needs to rest," Vasilis said.

They all agreed to cease travels for the moment and look after Canderyn. Kasumi and Vasilis sat together on a flat, grassy boulder. Vasilis crushed herbs in a medicine bowl.

"Perhaps we should be making sure Hilda doesn't take advantage of Canderyn," said Kasumi.

They both laughed.

"Are you going to tell me where you learned that skill?" Kasumi asked as he continued to crush the herbs.

"My mother. Though she was much better than I am. Then again, I am more brawn than brains, right?"

"Malaya was teasing and clearly mistaken."

"I miss her," Vasilis admitted, shocking Kasumi.

He had not talked about his family other than the men who betrayed him. There was a long pause before Kasumi spoke. "I miss my mother as well. She and I were close. Perhaps like you and yours."

"Aye. But they ruined any chance of me ever seeing her again."

His aura changed as he smashed the leaves harder. She knew this would happen, as it did many times before. No matter the conversation, Midas and Elias were at the forefront of his mind, driving his rage and hunger for violence. There was something more, sadness.

"You don't want to kill them because they killed you, but because they left her alone."

Vasilis didn't respond. Kasumi placed her hand on his shoulder. "You love them still, so it is not as easy as you think."

He looked into her eyes. "It has to be."

She reached for his hand, feeling his pain, his confliction. The battle between love and hate, a struggle was one she knew all too well. She owed it to him to tell him everything, how she fought her way back from it all. He confided in her, allowing her to see the side others did not see.

Chills went down her spine as she touched his face; she could see the bumps on his skin.

"You're up, Vasilis!" Hilda said, skipping toward them. She had a vile grin after they pulled them away from one another. "Hope I wasn't interrupting."

"What's with you, Hildegard?" Vasilis questioned.

She twirled her hair. "Well, if you want to know—"

Kasumi interrupted. "I am sure Canderyn is more important."

A crimson violet sky christened the sunset. It was time for them to move. Canderyn did his best to push forward as they started their journey with Vasilis, aiding the mysterious Northman. Kasumi led them to a large valley Rafik described. Patches of bright green dividing brown gravel. At its center was a small village with a few simple homes made of wood stacked on top of each other.

Kasumi turned to Hilda and Canderyn. "You two stay here."

Vasilis unsheathed his sword. "Shall we?"

Kasumi pulled down her fox mask and followed him into the abandoned village. A guarded wooden house sat away from the village center. Kasumi signaled Vasilis to attack from the bottom—she'd take the top.

She lightly sprinted and scaled the house, leaping on the rooftop, then jumping on the guard's neck. She disarmed him quicker than he realized he was being attacked. Within seconds, he was unconscious.

Vasilis smirked, pointing at the guard he knocked out. Kasumi nodded and held up her hand... three, two, one. They rushed inside.

No one, not the Blacksmith or the two men responsible for taking him. "Dammit," Vasilis shouted, kicking the broken wooden chair. He tossed the table, looking for something else to break, slamming his hand on the straw bed.

"Quiet, they can still be close."

"No, they're gone."

Kasumi sighed. *He was right.*

After securing the guards with ropes, Kasumi and Vasilis moved them discreetly into the woods. As they planned their next move, aware that Lilith remained a step ahead in the race to the Blacksmith, Kasumi's attention fell on a dagger resting on the counter beside scattered tea leaves. Thinking they might be useful, she pocketed both.

A storm loomed overhead as Lilith closed in, making their target ever more elusive. Seeking refuge, they settled in an abandoned village—a quiet reprieve from the wilderness. Amidst the stillness, Canderyn's illness demanded care, and Vasilis, with his unexpected skill in healing, provided it with quiet efficiency.

Kasumi found herself drawn to Vasilis, his presence like an echo of her own fractured soul. He, too, hid his pain behind strength, embodying tales where love and compassion overcame darkness. In him, she saw a reminder of the person she once was—before battle and betrayal left their scars.

Driven by unbridled attraction, she approached his dwelling. Dispensing with formalities, she bypassed the customary knock and stepped inside. The house, its larger furniture a quiet testament to his presence, felt as empty as their hearts. She found him on the bed, his back a silent barrier to the world.

"You must not sulk over what we cannot control," Kasumi said, sitting next to him. "Sadness is just one step closer to death, and you have plenty to live for. If you need to *not* talk..."

Vasilis lifted his head, a contagious smile on his face, and eyes that drew her in to kiss him. For a moment, the pain was all gone. She could feel it leave him as it did her.

Their embrace lasted well into the night, lost in each other's arms until the morning light. The weight of their past lifted, and in that moment, they found solace in the promise of a new beginning. It was a blissful feeling she could only describe as... perfect.

MALAYA

Scandinavia, 871

What aren't they telling me? Malaya wondered, turning the small wooden box Vasilis had given her over in her hands.

Guilt gnawed at her for the way she had lashed out at him—but he deserved it. He had been a jerk, abandoning her and Kasumi when they needed him most. They were kidnapped, nearly killed.

He's selfish, she decided, her grip tightening on the box.

"When are you going to open it?" Jordan asked.

It was the first time he spoke to her. Probably not by choice, given how Inoichi emphasized the importance of Jordan learning to navigate as part of his training. She couldn't focus, anxiety was eating at her. Inoichi was taking forever to tell her the truth. To tell her why Jordan was here.

Part of her wanted Jordan to be as anxious as she was—he wasn't. He was clearly better at this time traveling than she was. And then there was the box.

"I'm not sure I want to open it," Malaya said, placing the box in the sack.

"I wonder if she kept her promise to look for Jin's parents."

"Kat's resourceful, and determined. She'll find Jin's parents."

Jordan nodded. "She is resourceful. I give her that. She got me here."

"Tell me—" she paused, keeping her voice low. Inoichi would not like her probing him. He did his best to make sure that didn't happen, but Jordan, well, he was no Inoichi. "Why are you here?"

Jordan raised a brow. "I have strict orders to not say. It's not gonna be easy to hear, though I really wish I could." His brown eyes lowered. "Try to relax. Inoichi will tell you when the time is right, sorry."

She wasn't sure if it was the dreaded puppy dog look, but the moment the words left his mouth, so did the anxiousness.

Malaya sighed, tilting her head up. The vast expanse of ninth century Scandinavia was clear and beautiful. The clouds drifted lazily, casting their shadows upon the earth, while the sun's warm embrace enveloped her form. With a gentle sigh, she let herself become lost in the beauty of the world around her.

As the day drew to a close, the sun's warmth began to fade, leaving behind a gentle breeze that whispered across the grassy fields. Yet Malaya's feet ached, a reminder of the miles she had journeyed across the rolling hills and rugged terrain.

The beauty that had once entranced her now bore a hint of dread, a subtle reminder that danger lurked in the shadows. If Germany taught her one thing, it was that danger came quickly, furious, and without warning—especially at night. Although the horrors of the past few weeks hunted her, there was too much on the line.

"The world needs me," she mumbled to herself, trying to remain steadfast in her resolve. She laughed. "Wow, that sounds silly saying that out loud."

Inoichi stayed stride for stride with Ylorb after promising no harm would come to her. He didn't trust the stranger. Though, aside from his long frame and muscular physique, nothing about him was intimidating. Still, if she had to put money on who'd win in a fight, she may have to bet on the soft-spoken, often quiet Norwegian native. *It was always the quiet ones.*

Ylorb did take a liking to Jordan, everyone seemed to. He had a magnetic personality, but Inoichi wasn't a fan of them being so chummy.

"Leave the boy alone," Inoichi said, seeing the two of them whisper. "He must focus on the journey ahead. Whatever it is you need to speak about can wait."

"Relax, Ino," said Jordan.

"You lack trust, traveler," Ylorb added in his deep, rhythmic, yet soft tone. "I am loyal to my word."

"Yet you whispered to that *stranger* a few miles back," Inoichi said, undeterred by his suspicions.

"Ah, she knew the way of the wild. We shall be grateful for her warning of the night creatures not conquered by man alone."

Inoichi stopped. "I am more than a man. Fabled creatures do not concern me. You do."

"Understood. Trust does not come easy, but I am a man who seeks to protect his people from a danger beyond this world. I will do so no matter what and I imagine you can understand that having a sister, can't you?"

"We all can," Jordan said, looking at Malaya as if he could sense her doubt in him as well.

Malaya rolled her eyes. "If my mother felt that way, we wouldn't be here."

"What if she does?" said Jordan.

"Excuse me?" Malaya questioned, feeling lightheaded. Heat warmed her body.

It was the same feeling she got in her dreams. The ones where she was in a cabin with her mother. The dream where she saw her grandmother. She shook it off and started walking.

"Maybe Lilith has her reasons," Jordan said.

Malaya tried to ignore him. *What does he know?*

Jordan continued. "Not everything is black and white, imagine being..."

His voice hollowed. Malaya's legs and eyelids weakened. *My medication.* It had been so long since she had it. She wondered if it was in the box, but that wonder would soon turn into blackness.

A familiar smell awoke her. She recognized the fire burning in the middle of the rustic, empty house.

Sigrun's house. How did I get here?

Hollowed whispers echoed through the house, pulling her toward the backdoor. She picked herself up, and a white flash absorbed the room—her heart sank.

Before she knew it, she was facing the door where she found Sigrun. The door opened to a room with black flamed wall torches.

Beyond the door lay a chamber illuminated by torches flickering with black flames. Carvings adorned the walls, depicting a saga of humans and gods locked in fierce combat, guided by fourteen valiant warriors, both male and female.

"Malaya," a voice, faint yet hauntingly familiar, jolted her from her reverie, sending shivers down her spine.

Her gaze drifted toward a couple dressed in radiant white robes—James and Esther. A surge of emotion welled up inside her as she stumbled toward them with trembling hands. Their embrace offered solace in the midst of surreal surroundings. Though she knew it was not real, their presence felt tangible, grounding her in a realm of uncertainty. "James, Esther," she cried. "Are you—"

"Happy?" Esther interjected, sharing a knowing glance with James.

He flashed a mischievous grin. "Hey stupid, don't be so sad," he teased, eliciting a bittersweet laugh from Malaya.

"You're obviously confused," Esther added, elbowing James gently.

Malaya chuckled through her tears. "You have no idea. But where are we?"

"Paradise," James proclaimed with a serene smile.

The scene shifted once more, revealing a familiar door glowing with ethereal light. She remembered the door from her dreams. *How is any of this possible?*

Unlike her dreams, this door opened to an ascending golden staircase ascending into the clouds, James and Esther led the way.

"You have to go," said Esther. "So do we."

"I have so many questions."

"The questions you have will soon be answered," James assured her. "There are things about yourself you have yet to discover."

"Allow yourself to be free," added Esther. "Accept the unknown, tap into what lies within, and only then will you—"

James grabbed Esther. "Sorry, we really have to go now." He walked her upstairs beyond the gates.

"Tell her you're sorry!" Esther said before an intense light forced Malaya's eyes closed.

Malaya's eyes snapped open, revealing a scene bathed in the faint glow of a starlit sky above. The ground beneath her was hard and cold, the unmistakable scent of earth mingling with the tension in the air.

"Protect her," Inoichi's voice cut through the night, his figure silhouetted against the sparse light as he engaged in a fierce battle with a group of men not far from where she lay.

This surrealness of it all seemed like a nightmare unfolding in real-time. Frantically, she reached for her tomahawk, only to find it missing, a realization that sent a pang of helplessness through her.

"You're awake," Jordan's face appeared above her, his expression a mix of concern and surprise. "Terrible timing, maybe not." His words floated down to her, an odd comfort amid the chaos.

"What's happening..."Malaya's voice faded, her focus fixed on a towering figure charging through the night.

Its massive silhouette, outlined by dim light, moved with a deceptive grace with skin, rough and mottled as ancient tree bark, seemed to merge with the shadows, its glowing eyes targeting them with predatory malice. Its grotesque face, twisted in rage and mouth agape in a silent roar, struck a primal fear in Malaya. This creature was a relic of a wilder world, a stark reminder of an era when such horrors claimed dominion over the land.

"It can't be," she murmured, disbelief coloring her tone.

"Jordan, Malaya, watch out!" Ylorb's warning cry pierced the moment just before darkness claimed her once more, the world around her dissolving into oblivion.

Thunder woke her. This has to be a dream, she thought, seeing Kasumi and Sigrunn struggling with the sails. It was pouring rain as it did when they left Mei and journeyed to Egersund. Sigurd did his best to handle the wheel. Zoya and Hildegard sat in front of her, powering through the tenacious waves.She remembered that. How could she forget it?

"Row!" Zoya shouted, forcing Malaya to grab her unmanned oar.

Tell her you're sorry. Esther's words replayed in her mind. Anger and sadness covered Zoya's wet face. "Sorry!" Malaya shouted. "I'm so sorry."

"Your apologies are fruitless," Zoya said over the loud rain. "You could have saved a man, but you locked him in a cage, leaving him for dead. And you lied to me about it." Her voice cracked with the thunder. "My husband was a good man before. We needed help to save him—if he dies, you will pay with your life."

The storm swiftly vanished, taking everyone except Zoya, who sat on the edge looking back at Malaya. "I must find him," she said, then jumped into the water.

"Wait!" Malaya reached out for Zoya, but fell into the ocean.

Malaya's eyes slowly fluttered open, momentarily disoriented. Her hand trembled. Still feeling the guilt of keeping that secret from Zoya. Guilty that she was a liar just like her mother, and now her friend might be dead. She gazed around the dimly lit room.

The walls were made of thick timber logs, and a faint musty smell hung in the air. The bed beneath her felt unusual—its frame of rough-hewn timber stark against the softness of the straw-filled mattress and rough linen sheets.

Attempting to ground herself, she swung her legs over the side, only to pause at the unexpected distance her feet were from the floor. The bed was notably tall, a reminder of the rare luxury single beds represented in this era, seemingly designed for someone of considerable height.

Looking down, she caught Jordan's gaze from far below. "Welcome to Etne, Hordaland," he called up to her with a grin.

"How the heck did y'all get me up here?" she asked, her voice a mix of confusion and accusation.

"Inoichi carried you the entire way, with ease, I might add."

Malaya found Inoichi guarding the entrance of the room. "Thank you."

"No need to thank me. Are you well?"

Malaya nodded.

The crisp, cool air carried the scent of wood smoke as she took a moment to gather herself. She heard the rustle of leaves as a gentle breeze caressed the nearby window. The distant murmur of people was just outside the door of the small house.

As she rose to her feet, she realized she was in the midst of a large village, surrounded by wooden houses and a bustling marketplace.

"What happened to you back there?" Jordan asked.

Inoichi placed a hand on his shoulder. "Leave her."

"It's okay," Malaya said, giving Inoichi a gentle nod.

Inoichi crossed his arms and leaned back. "You can explain in time, or not at all."

"Time." Malaya's eyes widened. She frantically searched around the neck of her tunic. "Where is the medallion?"

"Ylorb must have taken it!" Inoichi exclaimed.

"Relax," said Jordan. He handed her the necklace with the medallion attached to it. "You guys have trust issues."

"Where's Ylorb, anyway?" Malaya asked.

"Bringing back the thieves if he values his life," said Inoichi. "He's been gone too long. I should have known better."

It was a wonder how fast Ylorb was able to track down Arn. After taking Divine Wind from Inoichi in the midst of chaos, he has a substantial head start. *I wouldn't be surprised if all this was my mom. Sure, the katana looked expensive, but it seems too much like a coincidence. I sound like Ino.*

Jordan stood up. "Maybe he's in trouble."

"Or maybe he is playing a role."Inoichi continued.

Malaya found herself nodding in agreement.

"If not for Ylorb, I would've been dead! Malaya would be dead."

Inoichi scoffed. "He merely stumbled into the fray, then tried to escape. If not for the Vikings wasting my time, I would have defeated that creature myself."

"Yes, but you were tied up, and he didn't *escape*. He led us here."

"This could be a trap," Inoichi said, clearly annoyed.

More happened during her time-lapse than she could have imagined. *Two attacks simultaneously... Could Norway be this dangerous? If Ylorb saved my life, I need to thank him—*

"Bro," Jordan grunted. "You're tense. I'm going to find Ylorb."

Malaya grabbed his wrist. "Wait."

"It's cool," he said. "Just get some food and relax. Inoichi has something to tell you, anyway."

Once again, his words silenced that urge to worry. She let him go and turned her attention to Ino, who had a look of shock on his face.

"You do have something to tell me. Why is Jordan here?" She started to feel weak again.

Inoichi helped her stand. "You should not worry so much. At least not until you get food."

He gave his version of a smile, a slight curl in the lips, and disappeared towards the kitchen. Apparently, Ylorb was able to land this empty home—*of a friend*. Inoichi soon returned with the sweet, nutty aroma of the steaming honey bread, and freshwater to watch it down.

She dug into it, ignoring the heat, savoring its grainy sweetness, almost forgotten about the hallucinations. She paused, realizing how foolish she must have looked—Inoichi quickly looked away.

"Thank you," Malaya said.

"It's I who should be thanking you. The opportunity never arose to thank you formally. You risked it all to save my life. I am in your debt." He gave her a deep bow, then relaxed on the wood chair. "You are not the uptight girl Vasilis described."

If she wasn't so hungry, she would be fuming. "That jerk," she said with a mouth full of bread.

Inoichi sighed. "We are not that different. I have been hiding a great secret from you. It is time you know the truth."

Butterflies and anxiousness replaced hunger. She sat the bread down. "Yes..."

"Jordan. He's... your... brother."

Inoichi's voice blended into the throbbing yet suffocating pounding of her heart. It felt as if someone was inside her stomping her heart down into her stomach until she vomited it out. Inoichi tried to help her. She shrugged him off and pushed him away. She started out of the house until Jordan slammed into her.

"He's in trouble," Jordan said before taking off into the darkest part of the city.

Homes were as broken as its residence. They followed him into the rustling grass on the outskirts of civilization. Ocean waves replaced the voices of the townspeople. They peaked through the brush near the water. Ylorb was in a standoff with two men, apparently losing the fight—one of them was Arn.

"We have to help him," said Jordan.

"Quiet idiot," Inoichi whispered. "This could be a trap..."

Inoichi was right. This could be a trap. If Ylorb was supposed to bring Jordan, maybe this was to lure him here. Then again, Ylorb saved their lives. *Whoever wanted him needs him alive, that could mean—*

"I know you are afraid, little one," the woman said, as if she heard them. "I promise your safety. If you do not come out, Arn will kill him."

Arn drew his blade. "Hallveig, dear—"

"Wait!" Jordan shouted, jumping from the brush before Malaya could grab him.

Inoichi and Malaya readied themselves for a fight, revealing themselves.

"Smart boy," Arn looked to breathe a sigh of relief, not hesitating to sheathe his blade. "We are not here to fight."

"But here you are, fighting Ylorb," Inoichi said, an axe at the ready, a weapon he gathered along the journey.

Arn spat at Ylorbs feet. "Ylorb knows our situation. He is supposed to be a brother of the great Elvir."

"His greed could be the end of our lives and that of our family," Hallveig added. "Kill us if you like. We will die for our family. We only took this sword as the payment for our voyage to Iceland. The captain is expecting us by the docks."

Inoichi looked at Malaya. "They are afraid and for that I see no fault."

Jordan clamped down on his weapon. His eyes darted toward Inoichi. "Wait, what are you saying?"

Inoichi continued. "We do not wish to be the cause of death unless deemed necessary. That could all change if I do not get Divine Wind back."

Arn walked the sword over to Inoichi and lowered his head. Malaya pulled Inoichi to the side.

"Look," Malaya whispered. "I think you might be right. This could be a setup, but we can use this to our advantage. If she's going through all this, why not go? We could take her down once and for all. She's been manipulating me for too long. This might sound crazy, but maybe I can convince her to stop all this before it's too late."

Inoichi nodded slightly. "I will not stand in your way. I understand what it is like to be the child of someone who would stop at nothing to ensure their vision of the world come true, no matter who they hurt. So, we will continue to pretend to be one step behind and allow them to lead us to her."

Malaya nodded, though not with much confidence. She thought she had got the jump on her and ended up in Germany. She had a better feeling about this. "Oh, you should probably apologize to Ylorb by the way. He's a victim in all of this, too."

Inoichi cleared his throat and walked over to Ylorb. "My apologies. You lead us to Divine Wind, and I have not forgotten your heroics during our journey."

Jordan smiled a gloating smile. "Now what?"

"You have your sword, and we still have no way of getting back to our family," Arn said.

"We will give you the silver to pay for your trip," Malaya said.

"And we will accompany you," Inoichi added. "Let us go back to the village."

Malaya and Jordan sat in the small house together with a group of strangers. For all they knew, these strangers could want them dead. Having Inoichi there helped ease the worry, but Malaya doubted he could take on three people. Luckily, they had Ylorb. At least he was sleeping. The other three strangers gave them some privacy. The down time gave Malaya and Jordan time to discuss their lives and what brought them to this moment.

Malaya sat in stunned silence as Jordan recounted the story of Lilith's visits to the orphanage. Despite her anger at their mother for stealing her time travel device, she couldn't help but feel a strange sense of relief at the thought of her long-lost brother finding a connection to their family.

Jordan's eyes sparkled with tears as he talked about finally having a family. Malaya felt a lump form in her throat as she realized the significance of what he was saying.

For so long, Jordan had felt alone in the world, but now he had something that he had never known before, a family.

As she listened to him talk, Malaya's mind raced. How could their parents have kept such a massive secret from them? The anger that had been simmering inside of her boiled over, and she felt a fierce sense of betrayal, again. After everything had happened, she was still uncovering lies and omitted truths about her family.

How could she have hidden the fact that she had a son for so long? And why had Dad never mentioned it?

But amidst the anger, there was a glimmer of hope. Jordan was happy, and that was all that mattered. For the first time in her life, Malaya felt a sense of connection to someone who shared her blood, and it was a feeling that she had never experienced before.

Malaya looked at Jordan, and for a moment, all the anger and confusion melted away. She saw her father's eyes staring back at her and felt a pang of sadness. He had died four years prior, and she missed him terribly. But looking at Jordan, she saw a piece of him that she had never known existed. A part of him that she could now share with her brother.

"Malaya... you okay?" Jordan asked, noticing her staring.

She shook herself from her thoughts. "Yes, I am. I think you should have this." She handed him the tomahawk. "It was from Papa's first jump. It's a Taino relic."

Jordan hesitated. "I can't."

Malaya took a page from Jordan's book and tilted her mouth in sadness until he accepted it. "Besides, I have this rune Mom gave me." She showed him the lively shimmering stone around her neck.

"You think it's magic?" Jordan asked.

Malaya looked around cautiously. "Yes," she whispered. "If I take this off, you'll see me age hundreds of years until I turn to dust."

"Wow, you are a jerk," Jordan teased.

Malaya's lips curled up into a warm smile. "Let's go check on Ino."

He sat in a lotus position, looking out at the stars. "I'm worried about the others," Malaya whispered to Inoichi. "We said five days. Here we are, on day six."

"Vasilis is too stubborn to die," he said keeping his eyes closed, "and my sister is relentless. I am sure they are fine. It is you I am worried about." He opened his eyes and hopped up. "Come, I will show you some kata to bring your mind to ease."

By morning, they all gathered by the busy coast. Today was the day their friends needed to show, or they would have to travel without them. A cargo cart guided by a hooded person headed straight toward them.

"That's them," Malaya said, seeing Vasilis peek from underneath the large cloth. Kasumi and Hildegard were with him.

After everyone embraced, including the Norse brothers, Canderyn, and Ylorb, they caught everyone up. Malaya rolled her eyes at the thought of them seeing werewolves. She was sure they were mistaken, but arguing about the generic impossibilities would get her nowhere.

Besides, she was still in awe of everything that had happened over the last few nights. Between the tea-leaf willow and dagger Kasumi found and Ylorb's confirmation that it was native to Iceland, her suspicion was all but confirmed. *All signs point to Iceland.*

It wasn't long before two knarr ships arrived. Malaya sighed in relief that she didn't have to row again. She'd be okay with never seeing a row boat. They separated into groups and split the supplies.

Inoichi, Kasumi, Canderyn, and Ylorb boarded the long ship captained by Arn's brother, Hjörleifr Hróðmarsson. The others sailed with a man they said was Byzantine Italian. His long dirty blond hair fell from his hood, an even longer beard hung just above the jewelry around his neck.

What kind of Scandinavian sailor wears a gold cross? Malaya thought, though it was hardly the only abnormality. The Italian also wore an unusual jewel that held the paludamentum cape strapped across his right shoulder.

Hours passed, but Malaya still hadn't found the right words for Vasilis, though he didn't seem to care much either way. He sat at the front of the ship and talked to Jordan about him and Kasumi. And there was the continuation of the elaborate adventure they had with Canderyn and Hildagard, who wasn't much help. Although, it wasn't surprising given her vast beliefs.

After what happened in Germany, who could blame her? Limitations or not, Hildagard got her sight back. It was a miracle if such a thing existed. Malaya found herself contemplating the *what-ifs. Not having my medication is having an incalculable impact—*

"Hey ugly," Vasilis said, standing behind her. "There is something I must tell you—"

"Wait," the ship's captain said, randomly. He held a fluorescent yellow ball. "Save your stories for later. You will have plenty of time."

Malaya felt a vibration from the medallion, then the power shut off. "The medallions!"

Jordan tried to run. The captain grabbed him and stuck a needle in his neck—Jordan slumped in his arms. "Sorry, friend."

Malaya tried to move but couldn't. Vasilis dashed toward the captain, who drew a plasma pistol, blasting him with an energy wave.

"You always seem to be a step too late," he said. He looked at Malaya. "Apologies, my lady, but your mother had no plans for him being here. This was no place for a family reunion."

"Quintus!" shouted Vasilis. "Don't hurt him." "He is safe," Quintus replied. " Jordan is going home."

Before Malaya could make a move, a singularity appeared. Hildegard was close enough to latch onto his leg before they vanished.

KASUMI

Coast of Scandinavia, 871

Beneath the vast, open sky, the sea stretched into infinity, a boundless canvas mirroring her own expanding thoughts. Just as sails unfurl to catch the breath of the wind, so too did her mind open, embracing the solitude that surrounded her.

It was here, amidst the hushed whisper of waves, that she could truly ponder the monk's parting gift of wisdom.

"I am here to save you," Kasumi whispered into the wind, giving voice to the memory. "Not the other way around. You are a special child. Your life will someday change the world." The words hung heavy in the cool breeze, mingling with the mist spray of salt.

Kasumi sat, pouring her thoughts onto fine aurulent paper bound in a sturdy maroon cover, its carved symbols mysteries she imagined Malaya would one day unravel.

The journal was a gift from Mei, a divine being walking among mortals, who, with her progeny, had revealed the key to the awakened state—the ninth tail of enlightenment.

Kasumi now understood the kitsune's role in the eternal dance between mortals and celestial beings, a delicate balance where gods set the rhythm. Inari, the kami she worshiped, had ensured mortals wielded a sword to match the Champion's shield against the immortal Sages.

Understanding the kitsune's purpose, Kasumi would never allow herself to reach the Awakened State because she feared her own purpose in this realm would be cut short. She was to be a hero, perhaps a legend of time.

As she continued to write, Kasumi wondered if the monk was referring to the final transformation as he spoke of her existence with a serene juxtaposition of noble warriors and divine purpose. She sought to uncover the meaning of those words, to capture their powerful message into something meaningful and enduring.

Kasumi knew that the journey she was on was more than a mere voyage across the sea. It was a transformative odyssey.

The eight tails of knowledge granted her some access to divine knowledge, one she wrote on a scroll back in Japan. But it also granted her recognition of text as one of the benefits. She relayed the words, her mind lost in thought.

The universe is sorrowful yet transient. You must be brave... To find your love... to achieve stability and peace is through Nirvana. Is he saying my love is on the other side? Or is he talking about Vasilis? No, I am far from at peace.

She sipped her tea, allowing a statement to sink into her soul. *Life is marked by loss and pain.*

She wrote:

The notion of transience... that nothing in life endures. The impermanence of all things—living and unliving alike—is the essence of existence itself. It unveils a universe both wondrous and sorrowful, where beauty and suffering intertwine, and all is bound to the ceaseless tide of change.

It calls us to ponder the fleeting nature of our days, to see in life's ephemerality not despair, but purpose. For in this transitory world, meaning is not found in permanence, but in the delicate threads we weave, knowing they, too, shall fade.

"To achieve stability and peace is through Nirvana."

She wrote:

The idea implies that true peace and stability can only be found through the attainment of this state of enlightenment—Nirvana. By freeing oneself from the cycle of suffering, from samsara, and achieving inner peace and wisdom, one can reach a stable and lasting sense of tranquility.

"I have not said that he exists after death, and I have not said that he does not exist."

Humans know nothing.

Kasumi dropped the quill. Did he suggest that Nirvana transcends this realm?

The monk's last words were an invitation to embrace the complexity of life and remain open to the infinite possibilities of existence, even in the face of uncertainty and suffering.

Her hands covered her face. A knot formed in her throat as she held back tears. Despite being on a ship full of humans, she felt alone, and the monk's words felt as destined as ever. The same questions still lingered, but there was no one to answer them.

How much more of the world's pain and suffering must I endure?

It seemed endless.

The words brought back memories of the abducted Christians in Japan. Their priest preached the gospel of Jesus Christ, a forbidden act, but his story left a lasting impression on her.

She wrote:

Jesus' sacrifice stands as a profound act of love—selfless, empathetic, and compassionate. By bearing the pain of others, he showed deep concern for all, transcending status and position. It was a redemptive act, a commitment to the greater good, seeking to transform the world.

Kasumi pondered out loud. "Reminds me of Nirvana. Different religions but–"

Malaya's moans broke Kasumi's focus. Her eyes fluttered as a twinge of sympathy settled in. She hesitated, hand hovering, reluctant to wake her friend from nightmares that left her so fragile, so exposed. The last time, the terror that gripped Malaya made waking her feel cruel.

Peace eluded Malaya, especially after Jordan's abduction. Kasumi couldn't recall the last time Malaya had eaten or spoken without the weight of their shared grief. Days had passed, yet there had been a fleeting smile—a moment of happiness so unexpected it felt jarring.

Kasumi recognized the effort it took for Malaya to don that mask, a facade crafted to shield her pain from those who cared too deeply. It wasn't merely a barrier but a fortress, one that Malaya retreated behind, hoping to conceal the depth of her suffering.

Kasumi knew the weight of such a mask, the exhaustion that came with pretending the shadows weren't looming just at the edge of one's vision, pressing on the cracks of a fragile mind.

To Kasumi, it was evident that Malaya's smiles were as much a defiance as they were a defense—a battle cry against the darkness that threatened to consume her. But behind her confidence was a dark truth.

She watched Malaya, knowing she wasn't merely dreaming. She was reliving each moment of her trauma with a vividness that left scars on her soul. Each night was a journey back through memories that clawed at her, demanding to be felt, to be acknowledged.

Someday, Kasumi thought, *You will conquer and harness this burden, as did I and use it as a gift.*

Kasumi brushed her hair back in frustration, calling Malaya again. Vasilis woke up instead, an unintended but pleasant surprise. He forced a smile onto his groggy face. Kasumi knew it was a mask, a terrible one at that.

After what happened to Jordan, he'd drowned himself in sorrow and whatever substance he could find–to an extent, everyone did. He got up and took a few steps toward Kasumi, accidentally nudging Malaya—waking her. They both looked at one another, preparing for the worst.

"Move, you orc," Malaya mumbled, to their relief.

There was no comeback. Instead, Vasilis quietly made his way to Kasumi and gave her a kiss on the cheek. It was cold and lifeless, like the ocean in a light breeze. She watched as he sauntered to the front of the ship. No matter how hard he tried, Vasilis could not unburden himself.

Kasumi did what she could to console him, including an invitation to swim with her as a challenge. He lost the race, not for lack of skill, but neither his heart nor mind was in it, so she swam alone. She looked back at Malaya.

"You're going to get sick," Malaya said, before she could ask whether or not she was okay. She tossed Kasumi a towel. "That water must be freezing."

"I run hot," Kasumi smiled as she wrung out her fine dark brown hair. "The birds did not return today."

Malaya frowned in confusion. "I imagine that's good news."

"Yes. It means we are going to make landfall soon."

Iceland was still two days away and the Faroe Islands were the halfway mark. After the hard rain and rough waters, they welcomed the island. The couple invited them to stay in the place they called Sunnbøur, a village by the coast.

Kasumi looked out towards the island as the boat approached. It was a stark contrast to the harsh and rocky terrain of Norway. The Faroe Islands were lush with greenery, and the rolling hills seemed to beckon her closer. As they docked, she took in the sight of the village.

Sunnbøur was small, but it was bustling with activity. The houses were quaint and colorful, with sloping roofs that made them look like they belonged in a fairy tale. A few children were running around, chasing each other and giggling.

Kasumi smiled at the sight, feeling a bit of the sorrow that had weighed on her heart, if only for a moment. It was a reminder that there was still innocence and joy in the world.

As they stepped off the boat and onto the dock, the village residents greeted them warmly. Kasumi couldn't help but feel grateful for their kindness, yet she held her suspicion about the convenience of it all. They were all aware that this could be a trap. But, if Lilith wanted any of them dead, she had plenty of opportunity to do it.

At that moment, she made up her mind. With everything that happened, Kasumi wanted to take this time and spend it with Inoichi.

They broke off into groups. Hildagard and Canderyn, and though Kasumi tried to get Malaya to room with her, she insisted on being alone. Inoichi would not allow it, so he opted to room with her. Vasilis found the first place where he could get inebriated.

She understood why and had faith he'd come out of it when he was ready. The best thing she could do was allow him to grieve. A time would come when he would need to face reality.

As for Kasumi, she took the time to herself. She set up a small table at the beach's edge, underneath the white sky that hid the sun except for a few intervals of light. The makeshift table was low to the ground, with two neatly folded cloths on either side.

This adventure was her personal mission to remind herself of where she came from and who she was before the horrors of her life washed it away. As promised, Inoichi arrived with an oversized fur draped over his shoulder, paired with a black coat and trousers that spoke of foreign influence.

Kasumi smiled, as she couldn't help but notice the attention to detail in the fabric's quality and the way he carried himself in the outfit, a testament to his stylish taste.

Despite the bitter wind, Inoichi seemed unfazed, striding confidently towards Kasumi's makeshift table. For most of the voyage, Kasumi spent her time carving Japanese-style saucer bowls and cups, a gift passed down from her mother—she taught Malaya.

"Interesting," Inoichi said in Japanese.

Kasumi scoffed at the mild compliment. She knelt, then let out a deep exhale, placing her hands on her thighs. "Malaya's a worthy student. She and I hand-carved everything," she said calmly, masking her disappointment. "The painted fox was her artistry."

Inoichi bowed. *"Dōmo arigatōgozaimashita."*

Inoichi sat with his back firm, hands on his knees, in front of two small colorful fish laid on his plate—cleaned, sliced, and seasoned to perfection, just as Kasumi had requested. "I remember the look on your face when I first brought you this kind of fish," Inoichi said before pouring Kasumi some sake.

She smiled, pleasantly surprised at the gesture. He tucked a single strand of hair that had escaped his short ponytail, then took a bite of fish. His eyes widened in apparent delight. "This has seasoning," Inoichi remarked.

Kasumi nodded as he took another bite with his chopsticks. "Vasilis. He says it closely resembles *future* food."

"It does, and you'll have it soon enough. Your excitement for their world is growing tiresome."

"I've mourned our losses, Ino, but now I look forward. I yearn for freedom that sees an end to this meaningless circle of birth and death. There has to be a reason behind everything."

"You sound like Fukumatsumaru," Inoichi said in a somber tone.

Though she looked forward, a smile covered her face as they found themselves engulfed in conversation about their brother. She knew their paths would cross once more. However, she wanted to see what the future beholds.

"Sister, if you believe the modern world will have your answers, you are mistaken," said Inoichi. "They are an advanced world, yet they are further away from the truth."

"Perhaps they are rediscovering themselves, as I have. You know, for a while, emptiness was all I felt. Vasilis filled that void. I hope you approve."

Inoichi looked up briefly, brows furrowed with discomfort, then continued to eat. The ocean carried the conversation for some time.

Until Malaya was brought into the conversation. He saw it too, the eyes of pain. The eyes of a mind close to breaking.

"Just give her space, allow her the freedom to figure out her own demons."

Kasumi just nodded, fighting her first instinct to assist a person in need. Watching her younger brother enjoy his meal warmed her heart. They have been through so much and have lost so many. For him, this was a good sign, considering his past reactions.

"I was saving the last of their spices for a special occasion."

"Lost at sea," Inoichi said before taking another bite.

The warm sun kissed Kasumi's face as she beamed. "Baby brother, was that an attempt at a joke? I'll accept it. I am glad your mood changed for the better—"

"There it is," Inoichi wiped his mouth. "Your true intentions come to light. This was about my feelings for Mizunami."

"We have learned enough to know that Lilith will have a trap set in place. I must know your emotions are under control. If not, I'm here to—"

Inoichi slammed his cup. "Lilith has control of Mizunami, somehow. I will stop at nothing to retrieve my wife. So there is nothing further to discuss."

"What if she is not being controlled? Now sit," Kasumi commanded.

"You seem to forget your role, woman."

"My role is your sister. You are so young, just twenty-two. With much to learn."

"You are six years older, yet you lecture me about understanding love and betrayal. The only thing you understand well is having a lover fighting on the other side."

Kasumi's mouth trembled, unable to find the words to combat Inoichi. *Shedding tears on a wound,* Kasumi thought, recalling her shameful past.

She remembered the beauty of the sweet spring air and singing birds that failed to compare to Ōta Ujifusa. Their fathers were sworn enemies, forbidding them to see one another.

One day, as she sat with her love—the Hōjō clan invaded their father's camp, taking many lives. When Tokugaswa Ieyasu got word that the two of them were together, he was convinced Genzo was part of his father's plan—Kasumi knew better. He branded Genzo a traitor and blamed her for her naïve nature.

She could still remember Genzo's eyes once the blade protruded from his back, out of his chest, her own brother wielding the sword. She didn't blame Ino; his clan was the enemy and the aggressor. But Genzo wasn't part of the attack and was searching for Kasumi.

Tears were not enough to express her pain. However, her father felt little sorrow. He stripped her of her surname, rewrote her place in history, forbidding her to marry or have children, and sentenced her to life in the Great Guard. Tokugawa Furihime was dead, and Fuma Kasumi was born.

Death will be your only freedom, were his final words. In twisted poetry, their older sister wed the eldest son of Hōjō, Ujinao.

Their father was right. Here she was, as he promised—*dead and happy.* Yet, her brother spoke as if he knew.

"You know a little of my past, but you don't know what I've been through the past few months."

"I am still the heir, and you will not dishonor me."

"You have done enough dishonoring for the both of us when you killed my betrothed." She regretted the words as it left her mouth, but she was interrupted before she could take them back.

"Did you not want change?" Vasilis interjected, his voice carrying from the beach as he approached. "Letting go of the past, the words of regret—they meant nothing."

Inoichi's reaction was immediate, a storm brewing in his eyes before they locked onto Vasilis. "This is a family affair," he countered, his voice a low rumble of warning thunder. "Stay out of it before I lose my temper." The air seemed to thicken around them, charged with the imminent threat of a tempest.

Vasilis, never relenting, stood undeterred, meeting the storm with the calm of the eye. His stubbornness and resolve were sexy, but it could and has gotten him in trouble.

Kasumi watched as the two men she loved stared at one another. Two men, cut from the same cloth separated by bloodline and time, otherwise they would be brothers. Neither warrior wanted to give an inch to the other. Kasumi, recognizing that the two individuals' egos were too sensitive to be challenged by a woman, opted to simply observe without getting involved.

Her inner warrior couldn't help but speculate on the winner, curious about the ultimate outcome. Of course, the other side of her, the more sensible side, hoped at least one of them would be the bigger man. They needed to be on the same page after all, infighting would not help them achieve their ultimate goal.

"I yield, oh noble prince," Vasilis retorted, his words laced with sarcasm, striking like lightning against the darkening sky of Inoichi's patience. His defiance, a whirlwind stirring in the calm before the storm, threatened to unleash the torrent of emotions brewing beneath their tense exchange.

The moment Inoichi turned, the tension cracked like sharp thunder, leaving a silence that echoed with the words left unsaid. Kasumi, caught in the crossfire of wills, sought solace in the small comfort of her own touch, passing hands over her face and through her hair in a gesture that spoke volumes of her inner turmoil.

Vasilis, seizing the moment, helped himself to Inoichi's vacated spot. "It's remarkable," he said, his voice soft and caring as he passed a hand over every edge of the carvings. He picked up the fox's head. "Perfection, like you."

Her anger disappeared. This was the side of Vasilis, unknown to others, like his eye for detail. He was thoughtful, with a soft touch, and often knew what to say. Though there were times his youth took the best of him, all he needed was a chance.

Kasumi smiled, then poured him something to drink in his cup. He took a sip. "I love Japan, but sake is not for me."

"Perhaps you are still a boy in a man's body?"

"Lucky for you, it's not physical." Vasilis forced a smile as he lightly twirled the sake. His mind seemed busy.

"Please forgive my brother. He's just—"

"Complex," said Vasilis. "It took me some time to understand Ino. I know he will come around."

"We need him as much as he needs us. Malaya does as well."

"She obviously wanted to be alone."

The sound of water blowing through the air grabbed her attention. She stood to look at the animal inside the ocean. Vasilis held her from behind.

"It's called a blow-hole," he whispered in her ear.

"How romantic," Kasumi teased. "Didn't you call it a kētŏs?"

"A sea creature," Vasilis replied. The warmth of his breath left her with chills. "It's called a whale in the future." They clasped hands and stood in silence for a while, enjoying the tranquility of nature she hadn't been able to in some time.

Before long, they found themselves back in their underdeck, in a loving, blissful embrace until they woke the next morning readying for their journey.

Everyone gathered at the dock and boarded the ship, but Kasumi couldn't take her eyes off the whale that was following them. To her, the whale symbolized something more than just a magnificent creature of the sea. It represented the unknown and the unexpected, a reminder that anything could happen on this journey.

As they sailed, the whale continued to follow them. Kasumi and Vasilis watched in awe as it breached the water and shimmered in the sunlight. The sight of the whale filled Kasumi with a sense of wonder and reassurance. Even in the midst of uncertainty and danger, there was still beauty and grace in the world.

KASUMI

Iceland, 871

A horn sounded, startling Kasumi.

"Land!" the captain shouted.

The journey was long and challenging. As they neared their destination, everyone gathered on deck to witness the sight of the land ahead. The jagged black rocks lined the coast were a stark contrast to the white sails of the ship, and the black sand on the beach seemed to absorb all the light around it.

Arnarson and his wife, Hallveig, dropped to their knees and picked up handfuls of the black sand. "I never truly thought we would return."

"Iceland," said Malaya.

"Have you been here?" Kasumi said.

"No," Malaya said.

Arnarson and the crew removed the rest of the supplies. Kasumi approached them with two large sacks. She passed one to Arnarson. He nodded his thanks.

"We must take leave imminently," said Hallveig, her gaze sweeping over the group before settling on Malaya.

"Yes, we must hurry," Arn added, stepping forward with Hallveig. Together, they approached Malaya, who was visibly shivering in the cold. "Malaya, we send you our regards and may you have the favor of the gods."

Malaya looked up, a mixture of surprise and gratitude flickering in her eyes. The moment, brief as it was, bridged the distance between them, offering a sliver of warmth in the icy air.

As they departed, the uncertainty of what to do next increased. Everyone had gathered, with Kasumi standing at the front. Malaya hugged herself as the frigid cold greeted them.

Beyond them stood a forest with a dense tangled mass of towering trees, its tangled undergrowth and towering trees cast an eerie darkness, blocking out even the faintest rays of sunlight.

Canderyn took a few timid steps forward, surveying the landscape. "There is something familiar, no..." his deep calm voice trailed, "enchanted by this land." His lost green eyes searched the mountainous backdrop that was tipped with snow.

They needed to get their bearings. Kasumi took command. Even though their beliefs were different, Lilith was the one common factor, and it united them. "First, we need to gather our supplies and lose any trace of our presence in the wilderness. We can't let her guide us like sheep."

"We have to beat Lilith to this Elvir so that we can control him ourselves," said Vasilis.

"No. We must find our brother," Ylorb said, locking eyes with Canderyn, who agreed.

"Lilith is our objective," Inoichi said, his voice stern and unrelenting. "We have orders to stop her. We do that and we prevent everything."

"Inoichi is right," Malaya said, her arms folded. "Believing in the nonsensical tales and myths of some immortal being is nothing more than a result of groupthink, common tropes that exist in many cultures... spirits, artifacts, monsters. It's all just superstition and irrational fear-mongering. There has to be a rational and logical explanation."

"Believe it or not," Ylorb said. "My brother is still in danger."

"Calm down," Inoichi interjected. "We will find Lilith and your brother."

"Yet we stand here without a path," the towering Northman brushed past Inoichi.

Kasumi put her hand up to stop her brother from going after him. "I got it," she said, dropping the sack to chase Ylorb. She grabbed him by his tunic, spinning him around. His imposing size dwarfed her.

The difference in their heights was stark—she was barely five feet tall while he towered over her by more than a foot. But she didn't falter as she met his gaze.

"We all want the same thing, Ylorb," Kasumi said. "I will do whatever it takes to get your brother back. Both you and Canderyn have my word. So you will go back, continue to keep your mouth closed, and follow our lead. Understood?"

Ylorb's mouth opened, but no words came out. Suddenly, Canderyn burst into laughter, his voice echoing across the empty dock.

"Size means nothing," he joked, shaking his head. "You heard the lady, little brother. Do not be so hasty."

Kasumi fixed her attention toward the two men she loved. "Inoichi, Vasilis, prepare your armor. Ylorb and Canderyn will scout the area."

Canderyn and Ylorb disappeared into the depths of the forest. Vasilis and Inoichi returned to the ships.

We are in over our heads. Kasumi opened the sack and removed Inoichi's gift, a blue, full-body shinobi garment, and a cloth holding several weapons.

"Why so many pockets?" Malaya asked, touching Kasumi's garment. "Navy blue? I always assumed a ninja wore black?"

"Kasumi!" Malaya called.

"Oh, sorry. The pockets hold offensive and defensive weapons, twelve in total," Kasumi said, filling her pockets with shuriken and small, dark balls. "A shinobi must become the shadow. Blue is best, black is more visible in dim light, and your world's technology gives me the ability to have both."

"Transitional fabric."

"I'm not wearing a straw hat, though," Malaya said, her voice carrying a hint of amusement.

Kasumi chuckled softly. "No, no straw hats here," she replied, her gaze drifting toward the serene landscape surrounding them.

The empty black sand beach of Iceland stretched before them, the air heavy with an eerie quietness. It was the kind of calm that usually preceded a storm, the calm that hinted at impending chaos and turmoil. Despite the breathtaking beauty of the scenery, there was an unsettling feeling lingering in the air.

"I expected more from Lilith," Kasumi continued. "Something is not right—"

Before Malaya could respond, the sudden appearance of Canderyn and Ylorb, their expressions filled with urgency, brought the storm.

"Run!" they shouted in unison, their voices echoing through the stillness of the forest.

Kasumi handed Malaya a dagger. She froze for a moment. Before Malaya could fully grasp the gravity of their predicament, an arrow, swift as the strike of a hunting hawk, sliced through the air, narrowly missing Malaya's face.

Instinctively, Kasumi pushed Malaya down, taking an arrow to her hip—her shuriken stopped it. Another arrow nearly missed, landing in the sand. Kasumi picked it up. They both recognized the design.

"We need to move!" Kasumi shouted.

Dozens of armed Vikings stormed the beachfront, flanked by two figures, their presence unmistakable. Among them was Zoya, a once-friend of Kasumi's, her beauty a sharp contrast to the grim purpose in her eyes. Beside her loomed a menacing figure, his ebony frame giving way to his singular intent—to exact revenge on Malaya for past transgressions.

"Halt," Zoya's command pierced the chaos, her bow already drawn. With lethal precision, she released an arrow, finding its mark in Ylorb's leg, eliciting a cry of agony. The arrow grazed his leg, causing blood but still only a flesh wond.

"He will survive. The next, however, will ensure someone dies."

"Do as she says." Inoichi's authoritative voice cut through the tension, his figure a symbol of unwavering resolve as he advanced, his Divine Wind blade gleaming in the dim light.

Vasilis, clad in his formidable black Spartan armor, stood by his side, ready for whatever confrontation lay ahead. "What do you want?" He demanded.

"We came for the brother," Zoya declared, her gaze fixed on Malaya.

Kasumi looked over at Canderyn and Ylorb. It was clear Ylorb was the target.

"Zoya, I'm sorry," Malaya pleaded. "Please leave him and come with me so we can talk."

"You lost that opportunity long ago. You are lucky my husband does not kill you. As I have said, we want the brother. This will not be a battle. No one has to die." She signaled her husband to pick up the limping Ylorb.

"No," Canderyn said, attacking Taznit—to no avail.

The large warrior disarmed the inexperienced fighter before slamming him into the sand. He picked up Ylorb and walked toward his wife.

"We have what we came for," said Zoya. "Do not move, or blood will flow." With a wave of her hand, the warriors sprinted toward the forest.

"I won't lose another person!" Malaya said, sprinting after them.

"Wait," Kasumi called out, trying to run after her—struggling to keep up.

An arrow from their fleeing enemy hit Kasumi under her ribs—her shuriken didn't block it. She stumbled before her body gave out. Every breath was like a dagger to her lungs. Her vision blurred, but the kitsune's fury would not allow her to die so easily. She could only watch as Malaya tackled the Viking, but he twisted out of her grasp and wrestled her off of him. Giving him the upper hand.

The long bearded Norseman was disarmed, but he didn't need his weapon. The Viking's attacks were relentless, each blow delivered with precision and brute force. He landed a series of punishing kicks to Malaya's ribs, each one a thunderous echo of his intent to subdue without killing.

"Yield," he implored with an edge of desperation in his voice. "I wish to take you for myself, not kill you."

Kasumi called out to Malaya. The Viking stopped locking eyes with her. "I will take you," he snarled. "Two is better than one."

Just as he turned back to Malaya, in a brief moment of clarity amidst the chaos, Kasumi locked eyes with her friend, recognizing the resolve in Malaya picked herself up.

Her stance was a reflection of Wing Chun's principles. With new-found strength, Malaya deflected the Viking's attack with precision, but his brute force overwhelmed her.

The blow sent her crashing to the ground, blood trickling from her mouth. He glared down at her, massaging his bruised jaw. With a ruthless grip, he seized a handful of her hair, eliciting a cry of pain. In a desperate bid for survival, Malaya swiftly turned the tables, striking his head with a nearby stone. Blood and dirt mingled on his face as he staggered back, momentarily stunned.

Undeterred, he launched himself at her once more, grabbing her dagger, and hurling her to the ground. To Kasumi's surprise, Malaya used Jujutsu to mount him. Despite the Viking's desperate grasp at her dagger, aiming it at her throat in a last-ditch effort to control the fight, Malaya's survival instincts took over.

Kasumi saw it then, the glimmer of something fierce and untamed flickering within Malaya, a spark that threatened to engulf her whole.

A primal battle cry came out of her as she turned the dagger onto his chest. Piercing his blue tunic, past his chin mail. His eyes widened.

"I yield," he cried weakly, "I yield. I..." The blade disappeared into his chest, and his eyes drifted to the cloudy sky.

Only Malaya's breathing could be heard. She fell over. Streams of moist dirt fell from her eyes as she looked at her bloody hands.

"Malaya, no!" Kasumi's cry shattered the tense air, a desperate plea from one friend to another, a beacon of hope in the encroaching darkness. But it was too late. The deed was done, and the light in Malaya's eyes dimmed, overshadowed by the grim resolve of one who has crossed a line from which there was no return.

He was going to kill her or worse if she didn't kill him first—Malaya had to make a choice, She told herself.

The kitsune growled in support of Malaya—he deserved it. But Malaya was no killer and wished to spare her friend from the burden of becoming one.

"Kasumi!" Vasilis called out as he rushed to her side.

"I will be fine. Help Malaya."

Vasilis helped her up, doing the best he could to stop her from trembling. With help from Inoichi, they made their way back to Canderyn and set up camp.

Losing Ylorb and what Malaya had done weighed on everyone. Inoichi stitched Kasumi while Vasilis did what he could for the injured Canderyn and Malaya. He could stitch her wounds, but there was no stitching the scar Malaya now bore—she was one of them now. A killer.

Kasumi joined Vasilis and Malaya by the fire just as he finished treating her external wounds. She locked eyes with Vasilis, leading him to Malaya. What he thought was a suggestion at first glance turned into a demand with her piercing gaze.

If this team is going to bond, they must learn to lean upon one another; trust was also key. Malaya needed more than Kasumi. She needed to see the side of Vasilis that Kasumi knew was within him.

Vasilis cleared his throat.

"Back in Sparta, there were once acutely four of us. His name was Hector. A bully turned brother in arms. During the Agoge, stealing from the slaves was a rite of passage. Hector was the worst at it."

A smile crossed Vasilis's face, and the fire danced in his eyes. "So we followed him at night, ensuring he wasn't caught or punished. We warned him—never go for the children. Children startle too easily. He went for the cheese instead, but the boy shouted. Out of fear, Hector stabbed him. The boy lived, but his father and brothers came for us. We dragged Hector away and fled. Yet I... I stayed. I always had to stand apart, to prove myself. The different are always cast aside. I turned to strike the father with a farm stick—but he ran into the blade."

Inoichi and Canderyn join them around the fire. Malaya looked over at Vasilis. Her eyes watered.

"I was crushed, shocked. I was waiting to get berated, but it never came. I was just praised, but I could not shake the boy. I left that kid without a father. Hector was the only one who came to me and, ironically, told me words from the king, my father. A Spartan is not just a warrior—he is a fighter, but it takes more to be a fighter. Years later, Hector died in battle, an honorable death worthy of any warrior."

A knot formed in Kasumi's neck. She moved next to Malaya, and Vasilis joined her. He wiped the tears from her cheek.

Vasilis continued, "You are a Spartan, Malaya, a fighter. Heck, we are all Spartans."

"Was the last part necessary?" Kasumi asked.

Malaya chuckled. "He's so corny."

They all mustered a laugh.

"We will get all of our comrades back," Inoichi said.

"No matter the cost," Kasumi said as Malaya laid her head on her shoulder.

MALAYA

Iceland, 871

Above, the northern lights loomed. A scarlet hue drowned the other colors across the night sky—a haunting reminder of the deed that left her hands stained with a permanent crimson. Underneath the veil of darkness, Malaya sat near the fire and sleeping friends, its flames and their warmth failed to thaw the icy coldness she felt within. A coldness that made sleep evasive for fear of what the darkness would bring.

Stars scattered across the sky, silent witnesses to the act that stained her hands. Each one served as a reminder of how insignificant she was in the expanse of the cosmos.

What was one life but a microcosm in the macrocosm of the universe?

Yet, the weight of a life she had taken weighed her down with the force of a thousand tons, making it hard to breathe, let alone lay her head to rest.

"He was going to kill you," Kasumi's words echoed in her mind.

Yet louder, drowning the flames, were the pleas of a helpless man. "I yield," he cried.

Her tongue felt heavy, and nausea took over as she replayed the sound of the bone crunch and his skin break as she drove the blade into his heart.

She rose, staggering from the weight of her dark thoughts. She stumbled away from her sleeping friends, who sought refuge in the embrace of sleep. Their breaths were soft against the quiet of the night as she sought solace, her back pressed against the chill of a nearby boulder. Its cold surface, a parity to the dark thoughts that consumed her.

With every ounce of willpower, she attempted to purge the dark thoughts that consumed her. But despite her efforts, all she could do was retch, expelling everything she had eaten until her stomach was empty. Yet, despite the physical purge, the darkness persisted, clinging to her like a shadow.

Part of her wanted to pray for forgiveness, but to who? The God she had forsaken.

"How could you forgive me?" she asked the God she had once believed in; the only reply was the waves crashing against their boat.

Her eyes started to burn, and her mouth trembled. "Please forgive me," she begged, collapsing under the weight of her guilt.

Forgiveness felt like a distant dream, a flickering star beyond her reach. She couldn't bring herself to deserve it, not after what she had done, not after becoming this stranger to herself.

In that moment, despair wrapped around her like a suffocating blanket underneath the biting cold of Iceland's chill.

She stood apart from her friends, unable to bear the weight of their empathy. They were warriors, their hands stained with blood, but for them, it was a mark of honor, a testament to their strength.

Yet for her, it was a stain of shame, a reminder of the darkness lurking within. They embraced their roles without hesitation, while she struggled to recognize the person she had become. Unable to bear the cold, Malaya dragged herself back to the fire.

As dawn broke faster than Malaya anticipated, she found herself wishing she could simply sink into the dirt where she belonged.

She watched as Kasumi picked up the pieces left from the bonfire. Needing a distraction, Malaya inquired. "Why ash?" she said, watching Kasumi collect and pour ash into a pouch.

"It has many uses," Kasumi said. "One being melting snow, cleaning, and my favorite, throwing it into an enemy's eyes. Isn't that right, Vasilis?"

Vasilis nodded in agreement, his focus on cleaning Forsaken and his armor using ash and water, proof of the practicality of their ability to maximize their resources.

A hand on her shoulder grabbed her attention. She turned to find Inoichi's stern face staring into her eyes. "After the ashes," he said solemnly, "there was nothing left, but not everything was lost."

As Canderyn led them up the icy terrain, Malaya trailed behind the others, aiming for isolation. As much as one can get hiking up a massive glacial mountain, still unable to fathom how fast life could turn one person upside down.

In the blink of an eye, she lost Jordan, Hildegard, and her best lead in Ylorb. Lilith was running circles around her, dangling a carrot in front of her.

The more she thought about it, the more her journey felt mapped out. Everything from the alleged error that landed them in Germany to the boat she selected. Now, here she was, a murderer. And without her medication, her mind relived that hateful moment.

She wished the frigid cold could numb the pain. She wished the roaring winds would drown the sound of him gargling in his blood. Her blood-stained hands trembled, even as she hid them inside her pocket.

I had no choice. I did what I had to do, what she made me do, Malaya repeated to herself. *If this is what I've become, what will happen to Jordan? She's poison, controlling. There's no telling what she'll do to Jordan. Will he become like her? Would she even give him a choice?*

She watched Kasumi and the others press onward. Each of them made the most of their situation in their own way—a lesson Malaya knew she needed to heed.

Determined not to let her mind wander, Malaya made a firm commitment in that moment to avoid dwelling on what had happened. Despite the horrors she had faced, she had survived, and she refused to let her mind linger on the darkness that threatened to consume her. Instead, she focused on why they were here.

Canderyn's insistence on following his gut instinct was troubling. *Was it truly more important to him than locating his own brother?*

The suspicion lingered in her mind, mirrored by Inoichi's unwavering glare directed at Canderyn. She could see Inoichi slowing to match her pace.

"Why are we entrusting your mission to a Norseman who seems indifferent to finding his own brother?" Inoichi's voice was barely above a whisper.

Malaya sighed softly, the words carrying on the chilly breeze. "I wish there were another option," she admitted quietly, "but Canderyn is our only lead."

"For better or worse, we always have a choice," Inoihci replied, "but even if one made the incorrect choice, that choice does not define who they are. Unless we allow it."

Malaya's brow furrowed. "This isn't about Canderyn is it?"

"You've mourned," Inoichi's tone was firm. "Now it's time to focus. Your brother is safe, safer than facing Vikings or traversing treacherous terrain. If this Elvir truly embodies the evil of legend, we must prevent your mother from aiding him at all costs. The fate of the timeline hangs in the balance, and we cannot succeed without you."

As their ascent transformed the rocky and rocky landscape of the mountainous plain into a snowy terrain, a sudden gust of wind whipped through the air, carrying with it a flurry of snow that obscured their vision.

It was as if the mountain itself rebelled against their ascent, a random blizzard descending upon them out of nowhere, as if determined to push them back down.

Amidst the swirling snowflakes, they caught glimpses of oddly placed graves atop the mountain, their markers barely visible through the thickening storm.

For a moment, Malaya thought she saw skeletal remains peeking through the snow, a chilling sight that sent shivers down her spine.

Then, just as quickly as it had come, the blizzard subsided, leaving behind a transformed landscape. The graves disappeared beneath a fresh blanket of snow, and in their place, a rocky charcoal path emerged, winding its way upward.

As they neared the summit, at the end of the stone path stood a snow-dusted wooden building. Icicles hung from the roof, glinting like teeth in the torchlight, as if the enigmatic lodge hungered for their arrival.

The lodge seemed to grow from the mountainside itself, its weathered wood blending seamlessly with the snow-laden landscape. Smoke curled from the chimney, dissipating into the twilight sky. The runic dwelling was both inviting and unsettling, a beacon of shelter in the wilderness that somehow felt not quite of this world.

As they approached, the wind carried the faint strains of music and laughter, a jarring contrast to the eerie stillness of the mountain.

Glancing around, Malaya saw the others wore the same perplexed expressions as her. Their breath misted in the frigid air. They knew they had little choice but to seek refuge within, yet a sense of trepidation settled over them like a heavy cloak. The enigmatic abode held secrets, and they were about to step across its threshold into the unknown.

VASILIS

Iceland, 871

A rush of welcomed heat, accompanied by the aroma of smoke, met them as Canderyn led them inside. The pungent scent of ale and roasted meat followed closely behind, as did the eyes laced with apprehension gravitating toward them.

Inoichi grunted, an echo of the unspoken trepidation shared amongst the five strangers entering the mysterious lodge. Vasilis brushed the snow off of his shoulders, allowing the hood of the cloud to drop.

They entered the hypnotic enchantment of what lay beyond the large black wooden door—and a fine door, it was. The fine carpentry continued, with carved wooden furniture decorated the spacy lit area, resembling a rustic inn. Two long staircases rose on both sides, which led to twelve doors with intricate carvings of ancient symbols and runes. Furs and shields hung from the rafters, filling the high ceiling.

"This had to take years to build," Malaya said to Kasumi.

Kasumi just nodded, staying close behind Canderyn who was making his way towards one of the two women serving drinks. There was a roaring fire at the center, casting dancing shadows on the rough-hewn walls. The space was filled with the low murmur of conversation, punctuated by the occasional burst of laughter and the clinking of tankards.

Vasilis's gaze swept the room for exits and any armed individuals. His attention was drawn to a group of burly Vikings by the fire, their faces weathered from the harsh Icelandic climate, focused on a man skillfully playing a lute.

No weapons, he noted.

The cheerful melody that filled the air was a testament to the enduring power of music to unite people across cultures and times. Some of the Vikings nodded in appreciation, while others tapped their feet to the rhythm.

At the bar, farmers and other locals sought refuge from the biting cold outside. They nursed their drinks, with some savoring the rich, frothy ale, while one drunk requested *black death* from the auburn-haired girl. She, noticeably younger and shorter than the other woman, swiftly catered to the request, pouring the drink into a horn.

The red-haired bartender waved them over, her demeanor as welcoming as if this were a tavern in Athens, and not a lodge in the middle of nowhere. "You must have come from the mainland," she observed, pouring each a drink. "Take a seat. I imagine your journey was a weary one."

The others sat without hesitation while Inoichi refused to sit or drink. "We have, in fact, come a long way on the hunch of this *man* who thinks what we're looking for is here."

"Forgive my friend," said Vasilis. "He does not mean to be rude. He is weary. What he means to say—"

"This feels like a trap," Inoichi interrupted. "Let us get this fight on already."

The music stopped; everyone was paying attention. "My tongue is not heavy, and my instincts are never wrong. What is this place?"

"Inoichi, please." Malaya pleaded, placing her hand on Inoichi's shoulder, seeing the men at the end of the bar rising. He was tall and stout, with a long auburn braid and a scar.

Kasumi rushed to his side. "Yes, little brother, please relax."

"No, this could be Lilith's trap, and you all are part of it."

Vasilis didn't admit it out loud, but he could be right. This entire situation was odd, and the location was odd, and the people were odd. But it didn't matter. Lilith could scream all she wants, but the plan always crumbles once someone gets punched in the face, and there wasn't a face he had lost to. Sure, he lost battles, but never a duel or a scrimmage with some barbarians.

At the end of the day, only one thing mattered, and that was revenge. Elias and Midas would pay for their betrayal, and Lilith for her role in it. Although he must admit, the thought of imprisoning Lilith turned his stomach. Not for her sake, but for Malaya and Jordan.

Vasilis crossed his arms and hung back at the rear, keeping an eye on everyone. He eyed Malaya, who was trying to settle down Inoichi to no avail. When the situation arises and her mother is cornered, could she bring her in? Could she even endure it? Questions for another time.

When the time came, Lilith and all of her warriors would fall—they were certain of it. This belief was not born from a place of underestimation or overconfident bravado, but from a meticulously crafted certainty. It was the essence of retribution—a righteous return for wrongs endured, a thirst for justice that coursed through Vasilis's veins with untamable rage. Revenge was a joy so sweet, so profound, so intoxicating, that it rivaled only one other pleasure in its ecstasy.

Nearly a year had passed, yet the stench of betrayal, like an infected wound, lingered—an odor no time could cleanse. The memory of a dagger—wielded by those he once embraced as kin, ignited an insatiable desire within him—a craving not for food, water, but for the all-consuming quench of vengeance.

Tonight, he mused, might just grant him that dark desire. If indeed this night was a trap, he would soon face those who wronged him.

Vasilis dreamed of defeating Elias, replaying the duel in his head countless times. He considered every scenario: one-on-one, two-on-two, or even two-on-three.

Elias, though not a Champion, was not to be underestimated. Vasilis recognized that the warrior possessed a divine favor of a different sort. With a sword and spear in hand, Elias moved like a demon unleashed, his prowess unmatched—his speed a force that seemed to slice through the air itself. In wrestling, Elias was the best when Vasilis held back—his technique and agility were masterful. There were times when Vasilis showed restraint when sparring for fear of killing his allies. Perhaps if he had known the fate that lay ahead, he would have killed them all.

A Champion's strength and speed surpassed mortals, fueled by an innate thirst for battle, and the man he once called his brother had been sharpened by two Champions to become steel incarnate, a blade forged to cleave through the very essence of earth and bone.

There was Midas, son of Agis, a Champion who matched Vasilis balanced speed and power, with overwhelming might and brawn with a speed that defied his large frame. Beyond physical strength, Midas possessed a keen intellect for combat, positioning him as the most formidable warrior Vasilis had encountered, with Seth being the only exception. This unique blend of power, agility, and strategic intelligence made Midas an unparalleled force on the battlefield..

Yet, the presence of Inoichi shifted the balance. Besides Vasilis, Inoichi's technique and agility shone as their greatest asset. His divine athleticism, superior even to that of any mere mortal, promised an edge if and when the confrontation happened. With Inoichi by his side, they could win. Yes, this would do. Elias would perish by his father's blade, Forsaken.

A small boy snapped Vasilis out of his thoughts.

"I hear angry voices, mama, " he said, hobbling down the stairs and wiping his eyes. "Is everything okay?"

Inoichi's face changed from angry to embarrassed. It was the first time Vasilis saw him look any other way than intense. The bartender walked around and knelt in front of the boy.

"These are just visitors looking for a place to stay the night."

"Okay," the boy looked over at his mom and then at Inoichi. "nice sword, can I—"

"No," the bartender interrupted. "You must go back to sleep. I will be up shortly."

Inoichi softened his stance. "My apologies..."

"Caitlin," said the bartender. "and that is my sister Ama. her eyes gestured at the younger bartender. Her gaze then shifted to Malaya's bloody hands.

Malaya snatched them back quickly. Caitlin nodded at the men around. They sat down, and the music started playing again. She smiled at Inoichi. "If you and your friends stay the night, perhaps I'll be a little more forgiving."

"We can use the rest," Kasumi said. appreciation lace on her voice.

Vasilis shrugged. "Where else are we going to go?"

Malaya sat a sack of gold on the counter, which Caitlin refused. "You can rest for tonight. Be out by morning."

"Brother!" Canderyn shouted, forcing them to all look up as he ran toward Ylorb.

His lanky brother was more disheveled than ever. His thick, dark brown hair was matted and danced past his shoulders. He wore the same filthy tunic, with his leg wrapped in a bloody cloth.

"You were supposed to be resting," Caitlin said. trying to help Ylorb sit.

Inoichi was right behind her. "How are you here?"

"I barely escaped. I'm sure they want me dead, but it's you she wants." Ylorb looked at his brother.

"I don't understand."

They all exchanged looks. There was an unspoken understanding that Canderyn played them all. Vasilis never believed his instincts led them here. Based on Inoichi's clenched jaws and fists, he didn't believe it either. *He knew his brother was here. He knew Lilith would be here, and he led them into this trap. None of it makes sense—*

"Was this a ploy?" Vasilis said. "You claim to not have any memories of this place, yet you bring us here?"

"Wait," said Malaya. "If that were true and this is a trap, why not take Canderyn in the first place?"

"They knew we would give chase," said Inoichi.

Canderyn sighed. "Something led me here, and I followed it. Inoichi was right to not trust me, all of you were."

"No. This... this is Lilith's fault," Malaya said. "We are all pawns."

"Lilith?" Caitlin asked, her face distraught as she looked around. "Please keep your voices down and follow me." She escorted them back to her bar, where there was a hidden room. The room was plain, with a straw bed and a chest. A white wolf's pelt decorated the wooden floor. Her voice was just above a whisper.

"My husband, he tried to oppose Lilith, but it did not end well for him."

"Is he..." Kasumi said.

"No, but he's been badly wounded. He is being looked after back at the village. I cannot say the same for the others."

"Why would she do this?" Kasumi asked.

"The thirteenth door. It lies beyond the cave. it's said the soul of a Sage is trapped. This building was first bilt as a place of worship. But many died trying to free him. The original family fell into debt, and my grandfather bought it, turning into a place for drink and sleep, rather than death," said Caitlin. She revealed the entrance underneath the pelt. It was a simple latch with a lock. "Between our fighters and magic, we couldn't hold her off. My spies tell me she has passed the first door, but she cannot pass the next door if she does—"

"If Lilith is inside, We must go now," Inoichi said, interrupting her. "Show us."

"And if it *is* a trap?" said Caitlin. "You'll end up like my husband or the others. Besides, my spies also tell me she is gone. She can vanish and reappear at will. Lilith needed more missing pieces. She has the vessel and one sword. She is retrieving the other as we speak, because the missing sword is on this island."

They all looked at one another. She warned us not to follow her. She said to seal the hatch as they will find another way out once.

"If this is Lilith, she could be waiting for us," said Kasumi. "But if we have Canderyn..."

"Then she doesn't have the Vessel," said Vasilis.

Kasumi addressed everyone. "Tonight we rest. Tomorrow, we will find her."

Malaya nodded. "It's not like she has anywhere to go, and poison is not her style."

Despite the peculiarity of this situation, he yearned for camaraderie. As a Spartan, Vasilis was well-acquainted with the camaraderie and simple joys of communal gatherings.

Yet, there was something uniquely captivating about this tavern, perched high on a snowy mountain in a land far from his own.

The laughter, the music, and the shared pursuit of warmth and companionship in a harsh world resonated with him, echoing the universal human desire for connection and belonging.

Vasilis grabbed the drunk man's horn cup, who was now asleep. "Fine. Let's drink!"

INOICHI

Iceland, 871

The smooth wooden floor was cold to his touch as he knelt. A warm flame burned on the lantern in front of him, a contrast to the icy wind that threatened to break down the sliding doors.

Inoichi ripped open his kimono. Sweat trickled down his abdomen. His hands trembled as he picked up the black tanto. He unsheathed it.

A raven was handcrafted onto his tsuba and seppa that led into the blade. The blade was forged with a fine blue hue—it will do.

He placed the blade against his abdomen. *I hope I honor you father.*

He didn't even hear the footsteps, but the door burst open. It was Furihime. "Brother, stop!" But it was too late; his brain had given the command. It was as if his hands were moving on their own. He shoved the blade into his belly.

Inoichi shouted as he woke. Snow fell off his beard as he brushed it off. *Where am I?*

The realization was slow to creep back into his mind. He was sitting behind the tavern in Iceland, in a timeline he didn't belong to, chasing the woman responsible for the death of his family. He adjusted himself, shifting the chopped firewood he used as a bench. He leaned back when a sweet voice opened his eyes again.

"You plan to kill yourself, stranger?" The woman said, placing a torch on the wall. "There are more interesting ways to die than in the cold, on some mountain, in the middle of nowhere."

He appraised the young woman with a discerning gaze. She was a petite, fair-skinned beauty, a vision of otherworldly allure framed by cascades of chestnut locks that shimmered like molten gold in the moonlight. The curve of her hips beneath the woolen dress tantalized, he admitted, though the modest cut left much to the imagination.

"Not at all," Inoichi finally replied. "I tend to run hot. Besides, the cold has never bothered me, anyway."

"You run hot, aye?"

He could feel his face flush. Inoichi cleared his throat. "Apologies, I don't think we have met, my lady. My name is Inoichi."

"Ama."

Her attire marked her as a working maiden—a dark blue ankle-length frock, the fabric coarse but well-made. Over it, she wore a full-length brown apron, the front and back panels connected by sturdy shoulder straps and fastened with a pair of intricately wrought brooches. Her apron, stained and scuffed, bore the tale of a tavern wench, but somehow she wore it with quiet dignity.

Inoichi couldn't help but draw a parallel between Ama's alluring presence and that of his wife, whose betrayal had left him bleeding and shattered like a withered blade easily broken.

The memory of Mizunami's treacherous act, the cold steel of the blade she shoved in his back, seared his heart like branding iron. *Perhaps the ale must be getting to me.*

"You work here? On a cold mountain in the middle of nowhere?"

Ama smiled. "Yes, it's not my first option, but there are few options on this island. Besides, this place would fall apart without my cooking."

"You cook, clean, and serve; you're the full package."

"More like a thrall."

Inoichi's expression betrayed his confusion. She continued.

"A person in bondage."

"We are all in bondage. One way or another."

"May I?" she gestured to the space next to him.

"You're a thrall to that dream you were having. My mother was a seer. So if you wish me to decipher the meaning..." she trailed off.

"I am...but there isn't anything to decipher. It was a nightmare of a life long forgotten, of a person long dead.

The statement was true enough, but he couldn't shake off how realistic this dream was. It was as if he was there again, attempting to take his own life over honor.

To this day, he had no idea how he survived. Once Kasumi entered that room, he didn't wake for half a fortnight. Every time he asked her how he was saved, she gave him a different answer, one always laced with jest.

"Well, if you want to talk, I'm here for you after I'm done with work. It shouldn't take long for the owner to get drunk and pass out."

"I look forward to it."

She grabbed a few pieces of firewood, her hand passing over him, close enough to smell her sweet scent. Ama piled the wood in front of him.

"Oh please, don't trouble yourself, my lady."

"It's nothing. I don't want you to freeze to death before I return."

She started the fire with the torch from the wall and returned to work. The fire soon raged. Inoichi continued feeding it until it was large enough to grab others' attention.

"Mind if I join you?" said one man.

Inoichi just grunted.

Others continued to pour in. Some Norsemen, he guessed some might be Swedish and Danes, hardened warriors and soft-spoken farmers. Many cultures convened in a realm that defied existence, adding yet another enigma to the tapestry of the unknown that is magic.

Inoichi released a weary sigh as the last drops of ale vanished from his cup. "I should have asked Ama for another," he muttered to himself.

Unfortunately, before he could dwell further, someone approached to fill it up. The problem was not the ale being poured; it was that the warrior was pouring it.

"Fill up, brother!" Vasilis shouted, using an oversized horn to pour and fill Inoichi's large wooden mug to the brim. "Tonight we drink in Jordan's name!"

Inoichi had no quarrels with Vasilis per se, but he could only take so much of his extroverted personality. Silence was addicting for him, and he required it to recharge. But somehow, Inoichi had drawn out a small crowd.

As Vasilis's enthusiasm filled the air, Inoichi rushed to drink it down, eager to avoid a spill. The liquid hit his tongue, and he recoiled, his senses assaulted by an overly sweetened taste that seemed to claw at his throat. He almost spat it out. "What in the gods' name is this?"

"Mead, brewed with local honey," came the reply.

"Too sweet," he said, pinching his face.

"It does taste like bee piss. But it is stronger than Ale."

Inoichi chugged the entire mug, riling up the men and women around him. They cheered and handed him another. He just wanted to get it over with, then move on to a more quiet place, but it seemed peace was out of the question for now.

"Hurry and drink so that I can have something better," Inoichi said, his desire for respite evident in his voice.

Vasilis chugged it down, still managing to elicit cheers, albeit with slightly less enthusiasm this time. Nevertheless, he laughed, belched, and joked with the best of them. Despite his outward demeanor as a fool, Vasilis was a prince, surrounded by the best Greek scholars of the time, some of the greatest minds in all of history. Even a fool like him had to pick up a thing or two.

As the crowd dwindled, Inoichi and Vasilis sat quietly for a moment, enveloped by the hushed conversation around them.

Inoichi lowered his voice to a whisper. "What are your thoughts on this, Ylorb? Why him, and why now?"

"Let us figure that out on the morrow," Vasilis said, taking a bite from a piece of bread dripping with honey. "At least he is safe and in our possession."

"By then, it could be too late, you fool."

"Fine, but drink this," he said, handing Inoichi a mug.

"What is it?" Inoichi asked, examining the light, yet creamy white liquid with a subtle nutty aroma.

"Something to loosen you up," Vasilis said with a devilish smile. "I heard it is called Poppy Tea."

Inoichi took it down in one shot.

Vasilis's eyes widened. "Idiot. That was a potent drink meant to be shared."

"What? What does it have?"

Vasilis chuckled nervously. "A poppy plant..."

"As in opium?"

"And... I added mushrooms," he said, followed by another chuckle.

"You imbecile. Why didn't you warn me?"

"You looked thirsty," quipped Vasilis.

Inoichi grunted. "No matter. My shoulder has been bothering me, and I can hold my drink either way."

"We shall see," he said, disappearing into the hall.

Vasilis soon returned with more, this time for himself. Despite the Spartan's wishes, Inoichi found himself unable to control his tongue. He began to recount the entire situation aloud, whether Vasilis wanted to hear it or not. Inoichi delved into everything that had transpired over the past few weeks, from Norway to Malaya's journey in Germany. He discussed the red cloak followers of Elvir, Vasilis killing the fake Elvir, someone Lilith planted, Jordan's kidnapping, and now Ylorb's involvement.

Inoichi leaned back against the wall of the tavern. "Why has Ylorb returned?"

"Why not?" Vasilis replied. "If Lilith believes he's the vessel..." he took a sip of his tea. "Of course she would set him free as a way to trap us."

Of course he could state the obvious, Inoichi thought. "Lilith believed Trahen was the vessel. If not, why take him? Now she seems to have changed her mind?"

Vasilis groaned. "Too much to think about on such a joyous night." Inoichi glared at the brute with an annoyed blank stare. Vasilis sighed.

"So there is a link to the three brothers. The gods favor them. So your question is, why not take all three and be done with it?"

Inoichi just nodded.

Vasilis continued after filling Inoichi's drink. "The same could have been said with Jordan. Why not take every person she needed? To that, I say opportunity. It is, after all, much easier to pick us off one by one. Kidnapping a group of people with two Champions is not an easy feat."

"Yet, it has been done," Inoichi said more firmly than he intended. "She had the opportunity to take them both on the beach. Kasumi knew Lilith would strike in Iceland; the breadcrumbs were obvious. And she outmaneuvered us anyway."

"I'm surprised you allow your baby sister to lead this band of misfits."

Inoichi crossed his arms. "Kasumi is a seasoned warrior. A rare cross of samurai, ninja, and shinobi. She has taken down some of the most powerful warlords. I, on the other hand, was bred for pitched battles and duels. I'm well aware of my strengths and weaknesses."

"Aren't ninja and shinobi the same?"

"Simply, a shinobi is a spy, whereas a ninja is an assassin."

They both sat in silence, allowing their thoughts to simmer in the cold wind. A man began to sing, his voice thinner than expected.

None of this set right with me. Inoichi thought, his eyes wandering into the sky, transfixed as the Aurora's ethereal dance painted the obsidian canvas.

Ribbons of luminescence twisted, unfurling in tendrils of emerald, ruby, and sapphire. It flashed and burned across the skies. The celestial display flowed like a river of light, colors bleeding seamlessly. Iridescent curtains billowed, fading to stardust before rekindling anew—a visual symphony that whispered of realms unseen and unknowable yearnings. Some of the locals had taken notice and decided to sacrifice a ghost to the gods.

It seemed like more were outside than inside the tavern. Song, paint, and chats were bellowed while drinks were handed out. They spoke of a rare lunar occurrence.

How they knew evaded him? But he yearned to paint the event.

"Lilith's actions don't make sense. Why didn't she plan Canderyn's capture as well?"

"Who is to say her plan is not already in play?"

This brought Inoichi's head up, meeting Vasilis's eyes. Vasilis continued.

"Who is to say Lilith's plan was not this tavern? Separate us, get us drinking."

Suddenly, the number of Norsemen, Swedish, and Danes around them seemed more alarming than before. Not all were drinking. Some used the time to sharpen swords, clean swords, some lacking any rust. Most men were strong and sturdy, not unconditioned farmers. Inoichi's heart skipped a beat when he realized Kasumi and Malaya were inside. And where was that Canderyn?

Vasilis smiled as he followed Inoichi's mental estimation. "Even drunk, we take them. These farmers just like to play Viking."

Vasilis's voice carried louder than Inoichi would have liked. Some of the men looked over. One wide-shouldered man spoke up. "You have something to say, Eastman?" Directing his thick voice at Inoichi.

"I said it," Vasilis said, standing up.

The man stood up. He was taller than Vasilis, with tan skin, a long auburn braid, no beard, and a scar that ran across his chin. *An ugly bastard.*

"I challenge you to wrestling!"

The word that came out of his mouth was *pale*. Inoichi assumed it was the Greek word for wrestling.

The crowd chanted, "Glima."

Their word, he mused. *These translators are exceptional*. Despite the man speaking another language, the crowd didn't notice his lips moving differently. *The brain only saw what it believed*.

As he concentrated on Vasilis, the words began to filter into his ears. Among them, he recognized Vasilis saying an unfamiliar word, "*orthopale*."

"In a square," one shouted.

"*Hólmganga á fang!*" said another.

The crowd chanted this phrase, forming a square of men with shields. Vasilis took off his shirt and tied his hair back. He bounced next to him, throwing his arms out.

"Skills only. I want to see a match of wits," Inoichi whispered to Vasilis.

Vasilis nodded. It was the only way a Champion could train. He was always forced to match his opponent's strength and speed, careful not to overwhelm him. So he was sure Vasilis knew how to. After the rules were stated, the match began.

Vasilis was disciplined, with strategic thinking and explosive move sets, while the Viking used technique, balance, and leveraging. He was skilled but relied on endurance and power, none of which Vasilis was short of. In fact, Vasilis took on six men before tiring.

It wasn't until Vasilis began to shrink that Inoichi's attention peaked. The man-child moved at an incredible speed. Soon enough, Malaya and Kasumi joined them. Both were no taller than toddlers, yet they retained their ninja attire. Canderyn was there as well, adorned in gold godly attire along with his brother Trehen. He only knew who he was because Canderyn continued to call his name. The bunch played, their names echoing through the forest.

The diminutive party danced, hands intertwined, as hues of red engulfed the surrounding woods. They played on, oblivious to the encroaching flames, their laughter a symphony amidst the crackle of burning leaves, enticing baby Inoichi to play. They stopped, a worried yet understanding expression crossing her face. They gazed at one another, then proceeded to push. They squatted, strained, and pushed until treasure littered the burning forest floor.

Inoichi took a step back. When he looked, they had all transformed. A fox, two wolves, a two-headed dog, and a frog. It was then they noticed the fire urging him for help, but what was he to do? What can a... crow do? The animals all hopped onto his enormous black wings, taking off before the fire engulfed them.

The flame was so close, so close, he could feel it in his hand.

"My hand? I'm no longer a crow?"

"No, only a young idiot samurai who can't hold his ale," Vasilis the human said.

"You are a human?"

"Aye, and he needs water," said a young voice. What was her name... Ama?

She escorted him back to his wooden throne of chop logs, away from the flames.

"I saw animals," Inoichi said, taking a cup of water.

"Spirit guides. They lead you to your destiny. Tell no one, you will decipher it once you're upright." Ama placed a cold rag on his forehead.

As the night wore on, the rituals continued, and Vasilis replaced his water with ale. Intervals of consciousness washed over him like waves on the sand. He remembered his sister taking Vasilis away, thanks to the gods. He would make him pay in the morning. He remembered getting into a fight, then... then Malaya. No, she wasn't a memory; she was here with him, changing his towels and feeding him water.

"Malaya?" one side of her lips pitched upward in a half-hearted smile.

"You scared me for a second. Vasilis said you were having a negative mind ride. Whatever that means."

"The Eastman wakes. Inoichi the Feared! A true drengr!" said one Viking, his horn cup in the sky. Inoichi recognized him as the first man Vasilis wrestled. Some of the crows cheered, their horn cups in the sky. Ama was at the Viking's side. He remembered that it was her brother, whose name he can't remember. "*Skol*!" she shouted, wooden cup in hand.

With few options, Inoichi lifted the horn cup that was handed to him. But before he could drink it, Malaya took it away.

"I think he's had enough for the night."

The crowd was not pleased. "She wants him sober to fuck!" shouted one. The crowd cheered again.

Inoichi stood up. "Mind your tongue, boy, or meet me in the square with shield and sword." The young man sat, but so did Inoichi as the world spun. He made his way back to his feet.

"Malaya, we've only known each other for a few fortnights. But you are like a sister to me. You saved my life and defended my honor."

"Thank you, Ino," she placed an arm on his shoulder. "It means a lot to me."

"I am aware my mind is clouded by ale, but I mean it."

"I know. You are a brother to me as well."

"Yet, I failed to protect Jordan."

She wiped the sweat off his face. "It's not your fault."

Inoichi stood on his throne, the chopped pieces of wood falling to the sides. "This is my sister! If anyone touches her, I will send them to Valhalla!"

He stumbled his way down. Malaya caught him before he fell. "Thanks, Ino, now I'm really not getting laid."

"I will sleep with you," said a drunk man on the floor.

"No thank you, I jest."

Inoichi kicked him. Then, he noticed the singer playing the lute.

"Singer, bring it here," he called out.

The man hesitated, but floundered towards him and handed it over. It was simple, a dark wood, with Dane lettering.

"I have something to say," Inoichi declared.

Malaya took a step back, surprised more than anything.

First, a poem, or as my people call it, a haiku.

He rang the lute, its sound taking control of the crowd. His voice was deep and powerful, with a golden undertone that brightened the darkest of minds.

Blood-soaked blade

Beneath falling cherry blossoms

Spring's arrival

He allowed the crowd to digest it. Ama repeated it, then lifted her cup. "Inoichi would best any man in flyting. Dare, and challenge his words!"

The crowd just nodded, no one daring to challenge him in a poetic battle, so he continued with *Shadow of the Shinobi*. It spoke of a harrowing journey through the abyss of war's shadow, where despair clung like a shade, and the seductive call of death beckoned with irresistible allure. Yet amidst the bleakness, the song whispered of the firm spirit of the warrior, a light of resilience that refused to be swallowed by the darkest of nights.

A shadow lurking in the moonlit night
A blade stained with blood
Playing a sorrowful tune
Carried by the wind
The days of battle have passed
Cherry blossom petals dance and scatter
In the heart of the shinobi
A ray of hope shines through

He rang the lute until the end, displaying his mastery of the instrument. There was emotion at the tips of his fingers. Inoichi embraced the roar of the crowd, then he ran around a corner to retch.

With the corner of his eye, he saw Ama hurry to his side. She made her way to Malaya, who already seemed to know her.

Malaya rubbed his back as things became more and more violent. He felt a cold draft wash over him, the cloud of his mind fading. He rinsed his mouth with water, then splashed his face.

"I feel... better," Inoichi said, his eyes meeting Ama's.

"Good, because I'm ready to continue our conversation in private," Ama said with a wink.

Malaya cleared her throat; her eyes spoke of a burning question.

Inoichi wiped his chin. "She knows, Malaya. And I am of a clear mind now."

"So she knows you're married?"

They both nodded.

"Malaya," Inoichi's voice was low, with a firm yet gentle touch. "I understand your culture, and it is respectable. But Japanese women, and as I have learned, Norse women, see relationships differently. A one-night stand with a lover is just that. Most Japanese women do not consider it as being unfaithful. And Mizunami is one of them. I hope you can respect our culture."

Malaya just nodded. He grabbed her by the back of her neck and kissed her on the forehead. He leaned in.

"I meant what I said. Get some rest; tomorrow we will end this."

She pursed her lips and nodded. The drunk man on the floor lifted his head again. "My offer stands, hazelnut," his words a sneer.

Malaya kicked him in his groaning, spreading a smile across Inoichi's face.

MALAYA

Iceland, 871

The bitter wind forced Malaya back inside the inn. She entered through the back door, pulling her fur cloak—which she had bought from a drunken trader—close around her.

At this point, the rest of the drunks were passed out across the tables, while most of the other settlers were finding their mates for the night. The same could be said for those who she traveled with, who had all vanished into their rooms.

Malaya made her way to the bar, smelling Inoichi's drink before handing it to Caitlin.

"God, that smells like death," she said, the edges of her lips curling downward.

The bartender just smiled. "Burned wine, some call it black death. A potent drink, frozen several times to add strength. But your boyfriend added his own ingredients."

"Boyfriend?"

"The young, handsome one with light hair."

"Vasilis is not my boyfriend." I could barely call him a friend, she added in her mind.

"Oh, it was just the way he looked at you."

"You mean with distaste? He has eyes for Kasumi. And I like it that way. My boyfriend is…"

She trailed off as anger boiled in her belly. Caitlin caught on to her expression.

"Perhaps ale? So we can later curse the bastard."

Malaya forced a faux smile. "That would be nice. But I reserved some mead with your father. It was going fast, and I wanted something at the end of the night to help me sleep."

She turned, spotting her father at the other end of the bar. The old, short man hobbled back and forth, serving a group of women surrounded by men.

"Papa, where is the mead I put aside for the girl, eh?"

The man grabbed a drink, wiped his gray beard with his sleeve, and slid it towards Malaya. She sniffed it.

"Sorry, this is ale. I reserved mead."

"Aye, girl, and the mead is gone. I saved you ale instead."

Malaya laughed. "But I reserved mead. You don't remember my reservation?"

"Yes, I do, but the mead is gone."

"But the reservation keeps the mead here; that's why you have the reservation."

"I understand how reservations work."

The old man grunted.

"I don't think you do. If you did, I'd have mead. Anyone can take a reservation, but you have to hold the reservation. And that is the important part of the reservation, the holding," Malaya countered.

The man sighed, his wrinkled face souring even more. "Let me go speak to the owner, see if there's anything we can do."

The old man brought out a hand mirror, square with silver vines adorning the edges. He carried on a fake conversation with himself, mumbling and smiling as he nodded. Malaya pressed her lips together, crossing her arms. Upon his return, he placed both hands on the table.

"Apologies. There isn't anything we can do."

"What a fierce conversation you were having back there. Glad you fought so hard for me."

The old man nodded. "Well, we do have this mead here, don't we?" He gestured to Inoichi's drink.

"Yes, I think I will, because I'm about to beat the hell out of this old man."

Malaya downed it in one gulp. Caitlin stood wide-eyed, handing her water from a block of ice they kept in a barrel.

Nearby, there was a stream that ran only in spring, now frozen over. She rarely indulged in drinking, able to count on one hand the occasions she had done so in public or around anyone other than Aaron. She simply didn't trust her tipsy self. Drinking always opened her door faster than Kramer, sending her straight to Aaron's bed. The thought of him at her mother's side only fueled her need for a few more drinks of ale.

A blond woman sat next to her, and the three held a conversation for some time, moving from topic to topic. Her head was soon spinning, and her mind was wild with thoughts.

"Caitlin, once this ale drops, make sure I don't wrap myself in one of those warrior's belts."

The bartender nodded and smiled. Malaya followed her field of vision, spotting a few Vikings entering the inn from the back door. She remembered one of them, the hot jumbo-sized Viking who had wrestled Vasilis. He was hot in a rugged, logger type of way, with a square jaw, broad shoulders, and large hands that were scarred like the rest of him.

"Save me as well," Malaya said, almost to herself. She turned around before he caught her staring. At least, she hoped.

"How would you lady like to die? Caitlin said.

The question made her heart skip a beat. When she turned, Caitlin was cleaning a cup, watching the men settle. "I want to go with a blade in my belly and one in my hand, cutting down my foe. In my dreams, my lover is at my side. His eyes staring blankly as he waits for me in Valhalla.

"You were alway the romantic. Old and deaf," said the blonde, "so I don't hear death coming."

"How about split-roasted like a hog, next to a warm fire?" Malaya said to herself, not realizing she was looking back again.

"I don't get it," said the blonde.

Caitlin smiled and leaned in. "Do you know how the hog is hung over a fire? Penetrated from back to front."

"Oh," a devilish smile crossed her face. "Can I change my answer?"

"Darn," Malaya said, turning around. "I think he saw me."

"Aye, they are on the way."

Two of the men settled around the blonde, while one sat next to Malaya.

Caitlin cleared her throat. "Malaya, you already met my father and sister, Ava. Now, meet my brother Thorfinn."

"Malaya, what a unique name." His voice was deep and dark, like his dark gray eyes. He shared the same auburn hair, but his was more of a deeper hue that leaned brown. To her surprise, he was great at conversation, even grinning from time to time, but he kept his darker side a mystery. His hand grazed hers, prompting her to grab it. It was long and hard, with deep calluses on his palm.

"I'm a navigator. We tend to handle a lot of rope."

He leaned in, whispering how good he was at tying. Malaya can't help but gig like a girl. His warm breath tickled her ear, sending shivers down her body.

Cailtin squeezed in between them. When she left the bar, Malaya couldn't say. "I think you had enough fun, Thorfinn. He's some tea; it will clear your mind. But your mind's eye will be filled with fog in the morning."

"Do I need to murder you, sister? When will you mind what's not your business?" He gave Malaya a wink as he crossed his arms.

"It was her own request. You will see her in the morning. Now let her be."

The blonde and the other men were gone, and the inn was starting to quiet. *When did everyone leave?*

Caitlin continued. "And I will be in the room next to Malaya tonight. I have a meeting with her friends, the two brothers."

Even Caderyn is getting laid?

"The room is ready for you," said Caitlin. She pushed the tea into her hand, handing her over to another. Malaya looked at Thorfinn, who nodded with a defeated approval. She followed their version of a bellhop to her room.

By the time she made it up the stairs to her room, her mind had cleared up. It made her wonder how many recipes were lost throughout time. A tea that clears the mind of liquor this rapidly would make millions.

How much of the craft skills was lost, too, she thought, as she entered the uniquely carved door. Out of habit, she reached into the wool purse for a tip. She pulled out the gold coin Sigurd had given her.

"Sorry I can't give you this..." When she looked up, her guide was gone. She ran her fingers across the box Kat had given her, thoughts of everything that had happened since she left home running through her mind.

As Malaya ran her fingers across the box Kat had given her, her heart raced with nervous anticipation. *What secrets could it hold?* She swallowed hard, her mind buzzing with questions. The evening events' fading like a dream.

She sat on the soft bed holding the ancient, gold coin-shaped device, marveling at the intricate network of gears and wires beneath its surface.

Aigon tech, she thought, unable to shake the fact that this level of technology was lying around in ninth century Germany.

The realization hit Malaya like a bolt of lightning—they weren't the first time travelers. *Interesting, but what does it mean?*

She spent a few minutes analyzing the device, distracting herself from the box. Instead, she allowed her mind to race with possibilities. *A magnetic field... Sigurd did say this was some kind of communication device?*

It had to be. Sigrun mentioned she'd reach out to me, Malaya recalled. *This must be how.* Yet, as she examined it further, a sinking feeling settled in. *It looks like a one-way, onetime device. But what if... What if I can send her a message? A signal?*

The idea took root in her mind, blossoming with potential. *Yes, it could work, polarity could be reversed,* she mused, envisioning the mechanics of polarity and activation. *It's worth a shot. Who knows, it could help us out in a pinch.*

Pressing down on the central moon emblem, command prompt appeared directly in her field of vision, linking seamlessly to her neural translator. Intrigued by its advanced yet archaic design, she initiated a deep dive into its programming.

In just ten minutes, with skilled fingers and the intellect that made her who she was—she reconfigured the coin's internal coding. Her modifications transformed this mysterious artifact into a two-way communication device, bridging the gap between ancient lore and futuristic technology.

That should do it. I should be able to send her a message. She placed the coin in her purse and eyed the box

It's now or never.

As Malaya opened the box, a spider, surprisingly large and unnervingly quick, leaped out. Its size was enough to cover the palm of a hand, with legs that spanned wider, making it a terrifying sight.

She dropped the box in shock, her instinct to flee kicking in as she turned towards the door. But the spider was alarmingly fast, scuttling across the floor with a speed that contradicted its size.

Malaya's heart raced in her effort to escape, but the spider ascended her leg with frightening agility and bit her before she could reach safety.

It bit her.

A rush of chemicals flooded her brain, creating a state of panic, then a powerful euphoric sensation that made it hard to stand or keep her eyes open.

She woke, not feeling any effects from the bite, but she knew she was infected, recognizing she was standing in one of her parents' off-site laboratories. Her stomach sank seeing her father's old office at the top of the metal staircase.

The metal clanked as she walked toward her father's office. She stopped, seeing someone sitting in the chair.

"Kat," Malaya shouted, running to hug her friend.

"Sorry Malaya, but Katherine did not have time to refine my emotional subroutine," she said. Her face and body were motionless. "The spider infected you with a zepto-tech toxin that attached directly onto your brain, intercepting neuron signals. We call it *Black Venom*."

"A simple video would have sufficed," Malaya said, under her breath.

"The risks were too great. The discovery would cause a ripple in time, starting—"

"I know the consequences." Malaya rubbed her forehead. "Why am I here?"

"For the past few years, I have worked with Jose Castillo on a variety of clandestine missions," said Kat's avatar. "My primary mission was tracking United States Secretary of Defense Bradley Williams. My most notable discovery was your father's affiliation with General Williams and the Alpha Kings."

Malaya's chest sank. *My father and General Williams, the Alpha Kings?*

"Upon further investigation, I've learned that the head of the Alpha Kings wanted to kidnap Jordan, a debt owed to them by Jeff Grant and Lilith Castillo-Grant."

"What?" Malaya stood. "That can't be true. I have to get outta here. Please, let me out."

"Request denied. That's not part of my function."

Malaya slammed her hand on the desk. "How do I get out?"

"At the conclusion of the message."

"Continue."

"To protect Jordan, Lilith and Jeff, rid him of his identity and hid him in your grandmother's school, House of Angela. Once his identity was discovered, Jose Castillo decided it was best to hide Jordan in the past. For his actions, we were charged with treason. Message concluded. You have satisfied the requirements. Please stand by—connecting you to a predetermined date."

"Wait!"

Electricity scattered throughout the lab, causing small fires. A gust of wind blew Malaya's hair back as a small portal opened, just enough to allow her to see inside. It was the lab behind the wall, but she hadn't gotten on the elevator, yet here she was.

Kat appeared once again. Though she looked different, her hair was shorter, just above her neck. She still wore a leather jacket and boots. "Is it you for real this time?" she questioned.

"In the flesh. But we don't have much time."

"How am I-how are you here? Where is here?"

"It's complicated, but I opened a teeny-tiny worm-hole in your brain, and I'm sending my neurons back in time."

"Are you crazy?"

"It's your theory."

"I was twelve."

"Surprise, it works," said Kat. "Listen, this is important. You cannot return to SUV, no matter what. Come to old MEV." Her image fizzled, so did her words. "You are a wanted criminal, Achilles Teresi... *Seth* and General Williams teamed up."

Kat's image disappeared and the rest of the room burned, melted. She imagined this was what it felt like to be wrecked after taking a hallucinogenic. She closed her eyes. The smell of burning wood and her father's cologne forced them open.

A picture of her father sat on the small coffee table next to the cream couch by the fireplace — she was home. It was her favorite spot in the house, her first memory. The three of them would sit and she'd listen to her parents' talk and tell her stories. After everything, she realized they were telltale signs of what her mother and father were plotting.

"What is this?" Malaya said, looking down at her red poodle dress and a white mid-sleeve sweater.

"Have you ever asked yourself why we lived in such an average home?" The familiar voice caused Malaya to tremble.

She looked up, seeing her mom holding her father's picture—she was too shaken to respond.

"Your father," Lilith answered for her. "He wanted to stay grounded at home while ostentatious work took him, *us*, to new heights."

Lilith placed the picture on the table. "Do you remember how we used to dress alike, to prepare for your father's arrival?"

Malaya's breathing became shallow. How dare she pull on her heartstrings? She gritted her teeth as she was frozen in place despite the urge to approach her mother—she wanted to scream.

"I don't know what this is," Malaya finally said, "but you can cut the crap, and unless you're standing over my body while linking our brains with tech you carelessly brought to Scandinavia—this isn't real."

"It's very much real, and this is no tech. These are my favorite and most cherished memories. It's why my brain took us here when I intercepted your call."

"Okay, whatever... Black Venom is a freaking nightmare." Malaya turned around, tugging on the knob of the front door, but it didn't budge.

"Is that how we raised you, to give up, to quit?" Lilith said in Spanish. "Then again, you've changed, haven't you?"

"No, I haven't," Malaya said, trying the door again—she kicked it. "Ugh."

"I'm sorry about the lying to you about Jordan and Aaron—"

Malaya spun. She walked toward her mother. "Aaron? Was him screwing me part of the plan? What about people I had to watch die? Or the man I just—" She paused, unwilling to relive what she had done.

"Aaron's feelings were his own. He was there to protect you from the Alpha Kings. They are the reason we hid Jordan, but your grandfather took things into his own hands. Now we're here."

Malaya's hands trembled. Her breath caught in her throat as tears spilled down her cheeks, carrying the weight of betrayal and hurt, her heart pounding painfully in her chest. "You should've come to me," she cried, the pain in her voice barely a whisper against the chasm of her shattered trust.

"I did. You turned me down already. You're not built for this. You're too weak and it's our fault, *my* fault. I coddled you. Now, look at you. You still haven't realized your full potential. That's why you'll never catch me. Here I thought I needed you, but I realized I'm in full control, just steps away from Elvir, right under your noses and you're wallowing—it's disappointing."

Rage surged through Malaya. The house shook hard enough that pictures on the wall fell, her mother vanished, and she woke up on the floor inside the inn. She jumped up, feeling a little groggy, but otherwise motivated—Lilith underestimated her.

Rest was for the weary.

She rushed out. It was quiet. She heard Kasumi's voice in a room a few doors down. Bursting through the door, she paused as the scene before her added to her scars. This was one of those moments when her memory worked against her. Kasumi's feet were resting on Vasilis's shoulders, while beads of hot sweat dripped down his naked back.

Unfortunately, Malaya was too stunned to move before Vasilis turned around, disengaging from what Malaya perceived as her shattered insides.

It was as if her eyes were moving on their own. She wanted to look away, but it all happened in a breath. Her wide eyes followed his anatomy of perfection from chest to waist—a masterpiece of chiseled stone, lathered in sweat, his manhood, angry and imposing.

Malaya turned around, feeling the blood rush to her cheeks.

"Oh my god, I'm so sorry—I thought you were alone."

God, how did that... no, stop it. But she's so small.

"I'm sorry, I will go."

"Wait!" Kasumi called out. "It must be important."

Her mind replayed the scenario over and over.

Jesus, she was getting pounded. Malaya, stop it.

"Are you okay?"

Malaya dared not turn around. She wanted to bury her head in the sand. She wanted to be anywhere but here.

She sighed, turning to them, doing her best to avoid their gaze. But the situation continued to replay in her mind like a broken video until she felt the trickle of heat between her legs.

Vasilis stood up.

"Oh god," she turned away again. "What the hell, cover up!"

"Have you never seen a naked man?" Kasumi asked, her voice tinged with amusement.

"Perhaps not a man quite like me."

Malaya rolled her eyes. "Are you done?"

"You should join us. I'm not a jealous girl," Kasumi teased.

"We have something!" shouted Canderyn, bursting into the room with Ylorb.

"Guess this turned into a party," Malaya remarked.

"Luckily, we have plenty of room on the bed," Kasumi teased.

Ylorb and Canderyn had barely begun recounting their story when Inoichi arrived. His innate caution and protective instincts had long since earned Malaya's respect. The brothers presented an arrow they had discovered outside, marked unmistakably with Zoya's signature—a motif of her tribe.

Every time we take one step forward, we'd take two steps back, but not this time. She surveyed those around her, her friends who had become more like family. Not anymore. Lilth was trapped. *I'll play your fantasy game and beat you. No more holding back. Even if I sound crazy.*

Malaya took a deep breath before she explained what had happened back in the room as best as she could, given she wasn't even sure of the events herself. Her mother was reckless, and this was their chance to take advantage of her slip-up. She assured Vasilis it was not a dream or vision. She knew her mother was close, using a signal to connect to her translator. How else would she tap into her mind?

"Whatever is behind the thirteenth door must lead to Elvir," Malaya said. "There is no doubt they are there now."

"If Ylorb is correct about Canderyn being the Vessel, then we must leave him," said Inoichi.

Everyone agreed, though Canderyn protested, wanting to be there for Trahen. Ylorb wasn't much of a fighter, but they couldn't afford to hand Canderyn over to Lilith.

Kasumi sat up, holding sheets over her naked body. "Rest up, we will explore before first light," she said with a tone of finality, compelling everyone back to their rooms.

Unable to sleep, Malaya made her way back to the bar, which was empty except for the bottle of Inoichi's drink—a forest green ceramic bottle. She uncorked it and chugged some before returning to bed. As Malaya lay in her straw bed, the world seemed to spin. Not because of her mother, nor Ylorb's untimely arrival, but because of the mead.

As she tossed and turned, her mind and body had other plans. She placed the blanket over her head as the situation began replaying in her mind's eye again. God, what was in Inoichi's drink?

It didn't matter; just like her prying eyes, her fingers took matters into their own hands, allowing Malaya to slip into a deep sleep.

MALAYA

Iceland, 871

*Y*ou're not built for this. You're too weak. That's why you'll never catch me. Lilith's words replayed in Malaya's mind, which was still a bit fuzzy from whatever poison she had ingested, courtesy of Inoichi. As always, he was by her side, a true friend, a protector, a Champion—as was Vasilis.

Vasilis, she thought, but decided against dwelling on it, given the freak show she had walked in on, glad that he and Kasumi were more than a few paces behind.

Their voices echoed off the dimly lit cave walls, casting long shadows in the torchlight. For a moment, Malaya could have sworn she saw the shadows intertwine in a wild dance, mimicking the unrestrained passion she had glimpsed between Kasumi and Vasilis the night before.

"I'll never be the same again," she muttered to herself, quickening her pace, following Ylorb who led them down a narrow trail that grew darker with every few feet.

Plunging deeper into the cave, the surrounding darkness thickened into an almost tangible oppression. The torches in their hands sputtered and flickered, feeble lights struggling against the suffocating embrace of an all-consuming shadow.

Malaya's stomach sank, longing for the simplicity of heels and dresses, sipping virgin cocktails, watching a horror movie—now she was starring in one. What lay ahead was something she wasn't sure she wanted to face.

What if Elvir was real? What if there were things beyond the realm of science?

Doubt crept into her bones, as did the chill in the air. Leading them was Ylorb, a man who once saved her life, shot with an arrow, and kidnapped by her mother. Yet, she had to admit the direful aura around him.

No, Malaya, she silently vowed. *She wants you to doubt yourself.*

Malaya let out a deep breath, refusing to give into her mother's mind games. Whatever's on the other side doesn't matter. She had warriors fighting alongside her. She had the leg up on her mother. Canderyn was the Vessel and he was safe.

She had set them up for a trap, but now it would be Lilith falling into one. *I'm coming for you, Mom.*

They approached a glacier chute into a cave. Ylorb turned to them as if to ensure them that this was the way. He was the first down, and the others soon followed him.

Dark blue ice lined the walls in a place made more beautiful by a blue crystal ceiling and river that flowed into the mountain. Goosebumps covered Malaya as she analyzed the glowing petroglyph carved into the walls that depicted a life, a world before this one.

"This was an ancient civilization," Malaya said, continuing along the path. She stopped, her heart pounded, seeing markings made with chalk. "These are recent, handmade."

"Lilith perhaps," said Kasumi.

"Over here," Vasilis called their attention to the black ash on the floor. "Explosives."

"This door was sealed with a magical barrier," said Ylorb. "Force was and is not the answer."

"Yet, Lilith must have found a way in," said Inoichi.

Malaya found herself standing before the door, feeling a mystifying pull towards it. It wasn't a physical sensation but more like a subtle nudge, a vibration in the air calling out to her, reminiscent of an experience she once had in Germany.

Beside her, Kasumi stepped closer, their attention captured by the door. They exchanged glances.

"Sigrun's door?" they voiced in unison, their words hung between them more as a question than a declaration.

The door's rustic, deep brown metal bore a striking resemblance to the hatch that had led to the discovery of a girl in stasis—a phenomenon alleged to have spanned centuries.

Once, Malaya would have scoffed at such claims, and a part of her still harbored skepticism. Yet, as she stared at the door, she knew that this was the first step to catch her mother. A shiver ran through her, goosebumps spreading across her skin.

"Malaya," Inoichi's voice broke through her reverie, his tone laden with curiosity. "What does this have to do with the red-haired girl?"

"I am lost," admitted Vasilis,

"Of course you are," Malaya couldn't help but retort.

"No need for sharp tongues," Vasilis said. "Admittedly, my talents lie chiefly in wielding my two swords, and you've had the privilege of witnessing both."

A flush of embarrassment colored Malaya's cheeks. She gritted her teeth. She grunted, deeply wanting to punch Vasilis. Kasumi sensed it and stepped in front of her. "Can you open this door?"

Malaya nodded.

As Malaya neared the door, a quiet whisper of fate echoed in the vast space, pulling her towards it. The markings on the door glowed softly under her gaze, a luminescence visible the closer she got to it.

"Are you seeing this?" she murmured, more to herself than to her companions, her voice barely above a whisper.

The symbols before her seemed to dance, emanating an other-worldly glow that was both mesmerizing and difficult to put into words.

She thought of her mother. How had she gotten past this door? Was it tech? How much of the Aigon language or lore did she know?

Malaya shook away the thought, knowing this puzzle was hers to solve now. "What are you trying to tell me?" She whispered, passing her hands over the illuminating symbols.

The ancient symbols before her served as vital instructions, a cryptic guide to unlocking the secrets that lay beyond the formidable barrier. She took a measured step back, her gaze sweeping over the symbols with a renewed sense of purpose.

Turning to her friends, she shared her revelation, her voice steady despite the knots tightening in her stomach. "Light the wall lanterns," she instructed, outlining a specific pattern for them to follow.

This sequence, reminiscent of strategies from her favorite RPG game, now took on a significance far beyond the virtual trials she had once enjoyed. There was no celebratory sound to mark her success, no musical chime of achievement.

Instead, a gust of ancient air hissed, carrying with it the scent of moss and stone long untouched. The stone wall before them spiraled open, the grinding of stone on stone echoing like a distant memory. A yawning void awaited, its shadow stretching toward them like an unspoken challenge.

"Well," Vasilis started, his voice steady though his grip on the sack betrayed his tension, "if we are to venture into the unknown, we must prepare for a fight."

He crouched to retrieve their weapons, each piece a reflection of its bearer. Inoichi unsheathed his katana, its pommel wrapped in the black serpents that seemed to writhe under the flickering torchlight. To him, they were symbols of power, rebirth—and perhaps the inevitability of death.

Vasilis held his kopis, the Cerberus hilt glinting in the dim light. He tightened his grip, the three-headed guardian etched into the blade a silent reminder of his role: protector.

Kasumi secured her kunai, her fingers brushing the smooth curve of her fox mask. It had once saved Malaya's life, and now, as she slid it into place, it whispered a promise of cunning and resilience.

Each prepared in silence, their unspoken bond reinforced by the weight of what lay ahead.

Ylorb raised a brow. "Does that protect your face or neck?"

"No, the fox is my spirit guide, either to victory or to my ancestors." She slid it over her face. "Shall we?"

"Here we go," Malaya replied.

Warm air melted the cold from her face as they entered the area beyond the door. Weeds grew along the decrepit, stacked stone walls. They crept through the area like a carnival haunted house, anticipating Lilith or anyone to jump out at any moment—no one did. They continued down the lengthy, cracked stone path.

Inoichi lowered his katana. "This is ridiculous. This may as well be a maze. We can't cover this much ground."

"We just need to make it to the end," said Kasumi.

"If the walls don't come crashing down on us first," said Vasilis.

A massive stone arch gave way to a spacious area. Well-crafted wooden pillars aided the high ceiling. Two stone stairways sat on either side of the room that led to a rustic gold door with intertwined stacked metal circles.

What kind of metal is this? Malaya thought, rubbing her hand across the unusual surface, analyzing the markings and symbols. *Another puzzle.* She smiled even through all the uncertainty, potential danger, and disappointment.

"It has seven different dialects," Malaya said.

"This one I recognize from my father's box," said Inoichi. "It is of the Nara era in Japan. It translates to kami."

"Shinto on a Norse artifact," said Kasumi. "How?"

"Japan may foster one of the Seven," said Ylorb. "As do other nations."

"Shared history between nations is poetic," said Vasilis.

Malaya translated the symbols. "*Age of the Gods, the Viaen, Ngati, the protectors.* I can't see the rest. The language is—"

"Aigon," Ylorb said, with notable frustration. "Do you think you can solve it?"

"Yes," Malaya said bluntly.

"Look at this," Kasumi said, her eyes drifting above the door.

To lift the veil and see the light,
One must first endure love's darkest night.
Pious manacles break, unleashing the soul,
Within the depths of despair, one finds them whole.
Through suffering, our true strength is forged anew,
As pain transitions us on planes we never knew.
A light dims to let new powers rise,
From shadowed depths, awakened spirits fly.

"What do you think it means?" Vasilis questioned.

"A mystery for another time," Kasumi replied, turning her gaze to Malaya, a silent nod shared between them.

Malaya pieced together the markings and equations like a complex puzzle laid out before her. What she lacked in physical combat skills, she compensated for with her sharp intellect—this was her battleground, her weapon of choice. As she delved deeper into the task, clarity emerged amidst the chaos of lines and curves.

The symbols—a complex mix of Taino lore and familiar dreamlike patterns—whispered secrets from a distant past. Some matched those on another mystical door she had encountered. Realizing she was deciphering the Aigons' language, the fallen gods sent a shiver of awe through her.

Then, a new phrase appeared in the ancient script: *"The veil of time should forever blanket the Sages of death."*

This cryptic message, steeped in the lore of a lost civilization, unlocked the formidable powers Malaya was about to confront. The complex array of symbols—from Taino to Greek, Egyptian to Yoruba—raised more questions than answers, yet they felt ancient and eerily pertinent.

As she deciphered the message, a flood of emotions and uncertainties overwhelmed her. Was she on the cusp of uncovering a truth long obscured by the sands of time—a truth that could reshape her understanding and the world's balance?

These carvings seemed to form a mystical bridge to forgotten lore, echoing the grim tales of those who had once sealed away a great evil. Could there be any truth to these legends?

I can't think of the what-ifs, Malaya thought, pushing aside the creeping doubts. Her mother was on the other side, and she had a chance to catch her..

The symbols glowed. She dragged her fingers across each one. *Uxoria? Dawn of the awakening... Imperfect world. Cryptic yet symbolic. Nigredo...* She pushed in two odd symbols—two slots opened.

She asked Inoichi and Vasilis for their weapons and slid them into the slots. The sound of churning metal echoed as the metal plates spun in place—the door opened. An intense rush of heat and an illuminating red light hit their faces. Malaya stood motionless.

"Ready?" Inoichi asked Malaya.

"How is this possible?" Malaya whispered, stepping into the cavern, pausing as the breathtaking vista unfolded before them.

Massive yew trees with branches laden with astral purple leaves arched skyward, their intertwining limbs cradling fruits that ignited an unexplained hunger in Malaya—a blend of desire and apprehension.

Nearby, a creature with lush, black fur, part monkey and part something else, met her gaze with its large, silver eyes. Its piercing, almost human look seemed to delve into her soul, offering both an invitation and a warning.

The air buzzed with luminescent insects performing a delicate ballet, their eerie glow casting ghostly lights against the cavern's shadowy interior. Neon-blue birds flitted through the foliage, their brilliant colors and soft chirps enhancing the surreal beauty of the scene, amplifying Malaya's wonder and unease.

At the center of this fantastical flora lay an oasis, a vibrant jewel set against the surrounding volcanic barrenness. The sight, both breathtaking and otherworldly, momentarily eclipsed her fears with awe. The garden was terrifyingly beautiful, pulling at her curiosity while her instincts urged caution.

This place was more than an alien ecosystem; it was a fantasy come alive, a leap into a story once thought fictional. Now, Malaya navigated a reality not shaped by her choices but by the drastic actions of the Cabinet and the day her mother stole the QPC. Always a step behind, she was poised for change.

For too long, Malaya had placed her trust in those she thought wiser. She had served a government she respected, clung to hope that her mother would reform, and held faith in her father.

Now, as her fingers traced the runes on her necklace, a torrent of emotions—betrayal, sadness, appreciation—washed over her. Her father's legacy endured in love and deception, shielding her from beyond the grave even as he misled her.

Shaking off these thoughts, Malaya rejected the constraints of past rules, embracing a new freedom. Gone was the girl once cocooned in a world of deceit.

To them, she was just a lab scientist, ill-equipped for fieldwork. She had believed it too. But with support from many, Malaya had executed her plan flawlessly, leading her to this vast, otherworldly realm, closing in on her mother.

Sure, she had made some mistakes along the way, but she also made new friends—and Vasilis. Each misstep was a lesson, each new friendship a beacon guiding her out of isolation.

Taking a chance, she reminded herself, *was the catalyst for the creation of the greatest inventions.*

She wasn't sure if this immortal being truly existed, but she knew the vast powers of this realm were not her mother's to command—no more than Inoichi and Vasilis were mere weapons for governmental use. They were people, just as the countless lives her mother had taken over centuries, bending history and treating humans like malleable particles.

Today, it would all end.

The ground beneath their feet trembled, a subtle yet unmistakable sign of the cave's volatile heart.

"Let's go," Vasilis urged, breaking the spell. His voice, usually confident, carried an edge of urgency as they descended the rocky path into the heart of the cave.

As they made their treacherous descent, skillfully evading small boulders and carefully navigating around rivers of lava that defied gravity, they noticed a peculiar rise in temperature in the surrounding air.

Meeting them at the end of their rocky path was another surreal sight—a milky blue oasis. Its waters were calm and inviting against the backdrop of molten flows and rocky surroundings.

"Just what we need, a hot spring," Inoichi remarked dryly, dipping a finger into the water.

His attempt at humor, a brief reprieve from the tension, drew a smile from Kasumi. "Another joke," she said. "I'm impressed, little brother."

"The color of the water, it's unnatural," Malaya observed, captivated by the serene yet alien beauty of the lake.

"What does any of this mean?" Ylorb pondered aloud, echoing the question in everyone's minds.

Vasilis eyes darted across the unnatural, and all too surreal surroundings. "And. What exactly are we looking for? Is Elvir hanging around here?" his voice filled with sarcasm.

"We must remain diligent…" Kasumi's eyes followed a butterfly. She grabbed it and showed Malaya. "This is the only insect that doesn't glow."

"It's Lilith. She's watching us," Malaya said, looking around. "Okay, you can come out now—it's over!"

Malaya's command was abruptly interrupted by a series of thunderous thumps, drawing their attention and quickening their pulses.

"Did the cave symbols speak of Ngati?" Ylorb asked, his voice tinged with concern.

"Yes," Malaya answered, the realization dawning on her. "Ngati, the protectors of what lies hidden in the sanctum of consciousness."

As the thumps grew louder, the group braced themselves. The trees shuddered violently, sending a flock of birds into the sky in a panic. And then, they appeared—two monstrous beings, their presence formidable and their intent clear.

"What the…" Malaya trembled at the sight of the two monstrous twenty-foot-tall beings.

Their lean, muscular build resembled that of seasoned athletes. Each muscle rippled beneath their cool blue skin, which otherwise appeared flawless. Brown hide wrapped around their hips and wrists, adding a rugged, primal edge to their appearance. But what caught Malaya's attention most was the absence of hair on their heads and faces, their features contorted in anger.

As her gaze sharpened, she noticed something that sent a shock of surprise through her veins—a latch discreetly nestled amidst their features. It dawned on her with a sudden revelation—they were wearing masks.

These are warriors. The realization struck her with a jolt, adding an unsettling layer of danger to these already imposing figures. *Am I going to die here?*

"Spread out," Kasumi commanded, her voice steady yet tinged with an undercurrent of fear. Paralysis gripped Malaya and the others, awe and fear momentarily holding them in place.

An arrow thudded against the taller giant's head, a second one missing as the giants moved with unexpected agility. "Zoya!" Malaya called out, spotting Zoya and Taznit entering from the same path as the group.

Elias and Midas, clad in traditional bronze Spartan armor, followed closely, standing beside Viking warriors whose formidable statures matched Midas'.

Lilith emerged, capturing the cavern's attention. Her dark purple dress flowed and a gold circlet crowned her head. A ragged Trahen stood before her, bound, his face a mix of dirt, sadness and fear. Next to her, Canderyn was also bound , a sword at his throat. A sword held my Thorfinn. The realization dropped over her like boulders. Inoichi was correct. It was all a lie, Caitlin, the inn. *Lilith was probably in one of those twelve rooms. What a fool I am.*

Thorfinn gave her a slight shrug. *Why do I always fall for the bad-boys?* she thought,

But it was the next man that emerged that shook her to the core. The man in a black tunic and trousers, with deep brown locks tied back, who made Malaya's heart stop. "Aaron?" she gasped.

He met her gaze from the ledge, his expression one of regret and resignation. Silently, he mouthed, "I'm sorry."

A tidal wave of emotions overwhelmed her—shock, rage, and the piercing pain of betrayal, deeper than any blade. Part of her had fool-ishly hoped he would change sides for her. Yet there he was, Aaron, her lover, the man she had entrusted with her heart, now stood with the enemy, a traitor to everything they had built together.

Driven by a rising fury, Malaya moved toward him, stumbling over the rough terrain. With each ragged breath, her anger blended into a dull throb that echoed the shattering of their bond.

She stopped nearly fifty feet away. Tears blurred her vision and her hands trembled at her sides.

In the din of battle, all she could muster was a whisper, "How could you?" as the realization of his betrayal fully set in.

A mere flick from the giant sent her crashing back to the ground. The wind blasting out of her lungs. She struggled to her feet. Her body trembled as fear overcame her. Through blurred vision, Malaya saw an armed Kasumi scale a boulder heading for the giants.

"Kasumi, wait!" shouted Vasilis, running after her.

She leaped off the edge, letting her kunai fly. They didn't try to dodge it. Instead, they let it rebound and swatted her mid-air. Vasilis absorbed her, and they crashed to the ground.

"Subdue them," Lilith ordered, her men attacking the giants. "Bring me Vasilis and Inoichi!"

As Elias and Midas advanced toward Vasilis and Kasumi, their intentions clear in their swift, menacing strides, Inoichi found himself expertly handling the warriors that surrounded him, each swing of Divine Wind a testament to his skill.

Malaya, attempting to recover and join the fray, barely noticed the shadow looming over her—a figure detached from the main skirmish.

It was Zoya who saw an opportunity in her vulnerability. With a swift, calculated move, she delivered another powerful kick to Malaya's stomach. The impact was immediate and brutal, forcing the air from her lungs and sending her sprawling to the ground in agony.

"Liar," Zoya shouted, standing over Malaya.

Despite the enemy before her, Malaya couldn't tear her eyes away from the horrific chaos around her. The clash of metal and the cries of the wounded filled the cave, overwhelming her senses. The air was thick with the stench of blood and decay, a nightmarish scene pulled straight from a horror film.

Bodies lay scattered, brutally halved by the giant's axe. Some soldiers writhed, reaching for their severed limbs, while others' screams of despair were drowned out by the relentless clatter of combat.

This is war, this is death.

"Please, listen to me," Malaya said. Zoya attacked without a response. A wild kick. She dodged her next attempt, able to pick herself up. "Why are you doing this?"

Zoya's blade hissed as it cleared the scabbard—a menacing curved sword that gleamed with deadly intent. "Your mother says you are still too blind and weak," she snarled, lunging forward with a vicious swing.

To her own surprise, Malaya's sai flashed up instinctively, catching the blade between the prongs with a metallic clang. "You're wrong," Malaya gritted out, muscles straining as she held Zoya at bay. "She's wrong."

Desperation fueled Malaya's counterattack. She lashed out with a kick, her foot connecting with Zoya's thigh. But the blow seemed to glance off her opponent's iron resolve. Zoya pressed forward, a relentless force driven by deep-seated anger.

Malaya danced back, narrowly evading a powerful strike aimed at her head. The blade's keen edge whispered past her cheek, a hair's breadth from drawing blood. In that split second, an opportunity presented itself.

Dropping low, Malaya seized Zoya's arm and pivoted, using her opponent's momentum against her. With a deft twist of her hips, she executed a perfectly timed throw, sending Zoya crashing to the ground.

The impact reverberated through the earth, leaving both fighters momentarily stunned. Malaya stood over Zoya, chest heaving, a flicker of triumph in her eyes. But the reprieve was short-lived. The battle was far from over, and Zoya's fury was only just beginning to ignite.

Before Malaya could capitalize on this moment, she felt a sudden constriction around her neck. An arm, strong and unyielding, wrapped tightly, cutting off her air supply.

"You left me for dead," a familiar man's voice hissed in her ear, a whisper of betrayal and vengeance. "May you forever remember my name, Taz—"

The tense moment was shattered as the man's grip loosened. Malaya tumbled to the ground, gasping for air. She scrambled away, her eyes catching sight of Aaron. He was moving with deliberate intent toward Zoya, who was now standing protectively over her fallen husband.

"Do it now," Zoya shouted toward Aaron, accepting her fate.

"Stop," Malaya pleaded, stopping Aaron. "Show me you're not a monster. Don't do this."

"Watch out!" Aaron dashed toward her.

Malaya's eyes widened as the giant's foot plummeted towards them with fatal swiftness. Time slowed to a crawl, her heartbeat thundering in her ears. In a selfless act, Aaron pushed her aside and met the giant's stomp head-on. A deafening thud resounded through the cavern, and when the dust cleared, Aaron had disappeared—swallowed by the earth, leaving only eerie silence in his wake.

"Aaron, what just happened?" she said to herself.

"Mommy says it's time to come home," Elias's voice cut through the eerie quiet, latent with a mocking warmth.

Malaya recognized him immediately by the icy blue eyes that glinted with a cynical smile, a stark contrast to the chaos around them.

"Elias!" Vasilis shouted.

Relief surged through Malaya, seeing Vasilis.

"Face me like a man."

"You're still stuck in the past when you should be looking forward to the future," Elias said, extending his arm. A seven-foot titanium dory revealed itself from his brace.

Vasilis held up his forearm, a Spartan shield sprawled from his vambrace. "Fair enough," Elias smiled. "But you still have a dead man's sword."

Should I interject? I would only get in the way, she thought.

"Today your blood will satisfy the hunger of my father's sword," Vasilis said before attacking.

The dory was like an extension of Elias's arm; the way he attacked—inching close to Vasilis's limbs but ricocheting off his shield.

F, it. Malaya tried to help. If he was there to take her, this was her battle. She tried, but their speed and ferocity were second to none.

"Move, girl," Vasilis shouted, shoving her aside.

"You were once my brother," said Vasilis. "It is my duty to make sure you die with honor."

Vasilis allowed Elias's spear to hit his chest plate. He hacked at Elias's fingers, forcing him to release the spear. Elias smirked, unsheathing his sword. "Our fathers were like brothers," he said, a small shield extended from his vanguard.

"And like your father, you stabbed me in the back," Vasilis said.

Elias roared in anger, clashing the small shield against the larger one. Vasilis dodged the jabbing blows directed at his feet. Malaya tried to interfere, only to be beaten back to the ground by Elias's shield.

"Let us finish this," Elias smiled. He swung mightily toward Vasilis, so fast it was hard to keep up with, even for Vasilis, who couldn't stop the blade from piercing his shoulder. Vasilis groaned, but swung his blade with a force that severed Elias's arm.

Elias screamed in agony, but kept his grin as the red fountain poured from his wound. Both men fell to the ground as blood pooled around them. Malaya rushed to Vasilis. She put pressure on his shoulder.

"Fool, you gave up your arm but didn't hit my vein," Vasilis said. She helped him to one knee.

Elias opened a small sack from his waist, applying a black gel on the wound—ceasing the bleeding. "Who said I wanted a one-shot kill?" He laughed, removing a black device from his waistband, clicking it, freezing his severed arm. "That blade was spliced with the same poison Kara gave to Seth."

Malaya saw sweat pour from Vasilis's forehead. She could feel his heart racing. Lilith appeared out of nowhere, opening a vortex, shoving him in with a wave of her hand. *Was that how she saved Aaron?* Malaya thought. *A new device?*

"Bring him back!" Vasilis jumped up and charged at Lilith.

"That's far enough," Lilith said, extending her arm. The iris of her eyes changed red, with an odd black symbol circled inside of it.

Vasilis screamed in agony as his helmet crinkled on his skull. He dropped his sword and fell to his knees.

"Please stop!" Malaya shouted from her gaping mouth as she watched his sword levitate to her mother. *This can't be happening.* She watched her mother wave her arm—Inoichi froze in place. His sword floated from his hands and hovered toward Lilith.

With a flick of her wrist, she tossed Inoichi. "Watch out," Malaya shouted. Her mother slid Inoichi away from a falling giant axe.

Malaya left Vasilis to chase Lilith, who made it past the giants. Canderyn ran as gladiators chased him while Ylorb failed to fight off the Vikings and the enormous limbs from the giants. *We're going to die here.*

"We all have to fight together," Kasumi shouted, calling her attention as she and Midas tried to fend off the giant. They attacked with fury, to no avail.

Their skin is more like an exoskeleton, Malaya thought. Her eyes gleamed with hope, realizing they were attacking the giants the wrong way. "It's armor!" she shouted! "Aim for their soft spots!"

"Give me your weapon," Kasumi shouted at Midas. He tossed her his axe, and she wrapped it around her chain. She tossed it back, and he swung the chain at the giant's neck, leaving a deep gash.

The giant let off a roaring cry. *A woman*, Malaya thought. The ground rumpled as the other ran over, removing its mask, exposing his thick gray beard and tired skin.

"Wait," Malaya shouted. "We can reason with them. They're just protecting their land."

"Time to end this," Vasilis shouted, chucking the spear at Lilith.

Before Malaya could scream a warning to her mother, Lilith waved her hand and the spear veered off towards the giants. The scene was surreal—her mother's immense power commanded not just her followers but the very laws of physics, bending reality to her will.

I don't know if we can stop her, Malaya thought, feeling a heavy knot of doubt in her stomach. Tears welled up in her eyes as she fought the pain of her failures.

Yet Malaya knew they couldn't retreat. Her friends, the timeline—it all depended on her. *We have to stop her, for everyone's sake*, she vowed, despite the creeping despair, that it might already be too late.

The giants groaned, their bodies collapsing with a series of thunderous thumps that vibrated through the ground—signaling the end of the chaos. As silence enveloped the cave, Vasilis made one last attempt to approach Lilith. With a dismissive wave, she knocked him back, sending him sprawling onto the rocky floor.

Malaya stood frozen. Her mind raced, trying to piece together the unexplainable, watching her mother and her crew stand in front of a lake.

Lilith handed Trahen a rune in his hand. With Midas's sword at his back, Trahen placed the purple stone in a concrete slot. The lake drained, revealing stairs.

"Bring the Vessel," Lilith commanded.

Aaron appeared from gray smoke. The gladiator pressed a blade to Canderyn's throat.

Malaya's stomach sank. A combination of anger, sadness, and the impossibility of everything twisted within.

"Take their weapons," Lilith said. She squeezed her fist. Inoichi and Vasilis groaned. "Please stop fighting. No one has to die, especially not for Bradley Williams or any other order. Your lives are too important."

Malaya clung to Kasumi as two towering Vikings approached, their long shadows converging on the ground like dark streams merging into a river. She recognized them from the inn—the dark-haired one and the blond who had left with a third companion.

As they drew closer, the realization dawned on Malaya; she was not the cat in this game, but the mouse, and her pursuit of her mother had been the cheese in a trap.

A rugged, auburn-haired man trailed behind the Vikings. Malaya's breath caught. "Finn?" she called, her voice tight with anger and betrayal. It had all been a setup.

They moved with swift, unyielding precision, snatching weapons, disarming both Malaya and Kasumi. As Finn reached out for her prized coin, Malaya's grip tightened instinctively.

"You're not stealing from me again, are you, Mom?" Malaya spat defiantly, her words laced with both defiance and sorrow.

Finn paused and glanced back at Lilith, who gave a subtle nod. With a reluctant grunt, he backed off, leaving the tension thick in the air.

A piercing voice echoed from the entrance of the cave, "I hope I'm not too late."

Malaya whipped around to see a man poised at the top of the cave. He was dressed simply in a loincloth. His helmet bore a crest, signaling his prowess, and manica arm guards paired with a greave on his left leg, all made of shimmering metal that caught the natural light cascading from the cave walls. It was the man who had kidnapped Hilda; a warrior—a Champion.

"Quintus," Vasilis growled.

LILITH

Iceland, 871

Lilith gracefully descended the wet stone steps into the remnants of what was once a lake, leading the way into a vast, shadowy dungeon. The only sources of light were the fire-breathing gargoyles lining the walls, their flames casting eerie, dancing shadows and bathing the space in a sinister glow.

In the heart of the dungeon stood a towering one-hundred-foot statue, flanked by six warrior statues, each uniquely armed and armored. Time had nearly erased their features, leaving them almost unrecognizable, but two stood out sharply—one clad in ancient samurai armor and another in traditional Greek war attire—the lambda V on its shield.

These figures stirred something in Lilith, a reminder of the secrets she kept, which Lilith pondered might be an omen or a warning. Yet, she could not afford to dwell on these thoughts now.

One problem at a time, she reminded herself.

As they ventured deeper into the dungeon, her thoughts briefly turned to the mystical fires emanating from the stone gargoyles. How long had they been burning? Who had lit them? The heat wrapped around her, echoing the serene calm that settled over her spirit. A comforting reminder that she was going to win.

This calm quelled the urge within her to choose a nobler path—an urge mirrored in the fierce gazes of Vasilis and Inoichi, and in Kasumi's eyes, which blazed with a silent, protective will Lilith could not find within herself. She could not be Malaya's life vest, as Kasumi was; instead, she was the torrential rain destined to wash away the looming evil.

Yet, in her storm, she vowed to send a raft—to offer a means for them to navigate the flood of her wrath, in her quest to save the Darviants and support the warriors by her side.

The sting of betrayal was sharp, each harsh word to Malaya searing Lilith's throat. She had called her daughter weak, yet Malaya had shown her strength, not just weathering the storm but thriving amidst it.

If not for Malaya's resilience, the door needed to unleash Elvir would still be locked. Now, Lilith held the Vessel, Canderyn, captive along with his Darviant brother, Trahen, who could forge weapons for Elvir's army.

Her plan had taken shape perfectly. Quintus had shown up, late as always, but at least she could breathe, knowing she had yet another Champion on her side. She was just steps away from waking Elvir and bringing the war to Japan.

She wanted to secure Vasilis and Inoichi's allegiance to truly unite against Elvir. Once done, Malaya could return to the present, and Kasumi to her realm, sparing their mothers the grief of losing another child.

You will understand soon, Malaya, once the world has changed for the better. She watched closely as her men carefully positioned Canderyn on the ceremonial smooth stone table at the apex of the area.

It was a necessary step in the ritual, one that would ultimately secure humanity's safety and pave the way for a better future.

All the research Lilith had invested in unraveling the details of this sacrifice was coming to fruition. She knew everything—the necessary blood of the Vessel of the Sage, the exact ritual that needed to coincide with the eclipse. In just a few moments, she would secure the final piece of the puzzle.

"You can't do this!" Trahen said as they lay his brother, Canderyn, on the table.

"He is innocent." Ylorb exclaimed.

"You can't do this!" Trahen's desperate plea reverberated through the chamber as they tenderly placed his brother, Canderyn, on the stone table.

"He is innocent," Ylorb's anguished cry pierced Lilith's heart like jagged shards, a painful reminder of the cruelty of their gods' demands.

And yet, she knew her own God, in his infinite judgment, would exact an even greater toll. She clasped the cross around her neck, offering a silent prayer for forgiveness, grappling with the enormity of her transgressions.

What is the repentance for the disruption of a timeline? For allowing one soul to be sacrificed so others could intrude upon its place?

The thought sent shivers down her spine, and she fought to suppress the rising tide of anguish, seeking solace in the grim certainty of the blood-stained future that awaited if she failed to act.

"It's okay, brother. I will die in peace," Canderyn said calmly as they secured his wrists and ankles. "Soon, I will lay my head on the breast of she who welcomes me to the Land of the Young."

"Give him his weapon!" Trahen demanded, his voice echoing through the chamber.

Lilith gave a slight nod to one of her followers, a Northman clad in battle armor. He pulled a dagger from his belt and handed it to Canderyn with a solemn gesture.

"Thank you," Canderyn murmured, grasping the weapon that would ensure his passage to Valhalla.

No matter how fierce the others were for battle, they were all disciplined and obedient, thanks to promises unfulfilled. *Soon*, Lilith vowed silently as Canderyn awaited eternal peace.

Quintus, Midas, and Aaron stood by her side. Even if they had not questioned out loud, they wondered whether this was right.

Here they were facing people they loved or admired, ready to take the life of a man who, like them, had a family. There were times she questioned this as well, but the life of one could save billions.

It wasn't easy watching Trahen and Ylorb helplessly beg for their brother's life. She imagined the pain she'd feel if this was her loved one on the table. But this wasn't supposed to be easy. Sacrifices had to be made, and they all made them—none greater than Canderyn's.

"Midas, bring the war hammer," Lilith instructed.

The screeching sound of the metal rubbing against the concrete echoed throughout the room. Midas dragged and placed it into the port next to the table—purple fire ignited on all four sides.

After Midas and Quintus removed the blades from Inoichi and Vasilis' hilts, they handed them to Lilith. Anxiousness turned her stomach as she stood in front of two aged, hilt-less long swords impaled into the ground in front of Elvir's statue.

She was so close. Everything she prophesied, the nightmares will cease to exist, as Elvir will help win the Great War. Her stomach sank as she placed the warrior's hilt on the stoned swords.

Light exploded from the symbols underneath Canderyn. Despite the odd shapes, the old blades and hilts boned together. The foundation rumbled. It wouldn't have been a surprise if the ceiling came crashing down. Part of her wondered if she'd done something wrong, but she had no reason to worry.

She followed the instructions perfectly. It was all coming together. Still, too much was on the line, a world war, Darviants. She needed insurance, even for Elvir. Having four Champions was better than two.

"Understand, I am not your enemy," Lilith shouted over the rumble. "They lied and manipulated you. I'm asking for your loyalty, for your help."

Inoichi stepped next to Kasumi. "I will not bend the knee. I will not be manipulated, I am the heir to the shogunate."

"What's an emperor, a ruler, to a god?" Midas said. "This is not about your title. Your faith lies with us, with her. In case you have forgotten, you are dead."

The rumbling grew as the jaw of the giant statue opened. She felt his power erupting. Years of studying didn't prepare her for this, despite everything she experienced. She tried to contain what fought to come out, needing to convince Inoichi and Vasilis one last time. Lilith extended her arms. Everyone froze in place, except for Vasilis and Inoichi.

"What is this?" said Inoichi.

"I slowed everyone's brain and neuronal synapses and but accelerated yours, altering your perception," Lilith explained, her arms trembling uncontrollably. This technique, though familiar, like a hangover after a night of binge drinking, but she wanted them on her side.

"I need you both to help control Elvir," she said. "Help me save the world from a greater evil, be the heroes you were meant to be. The swords you see before you can reseal the Sage. Only those with the blood of a Champion and a bond can wield them to seal Elvir.

"Quintus and Midas don't have a relationship. Nor do they have a strong enough bond to put the monster back—you have that bond."

"We are not puppets," Vasilis said. "Both you and General Williams are using us to fulfill your own agendas. At least he was honest with us from the start. You have done nothing but lie and manipulate."

Lilith's eyes lowered. "I wish I could have been honest with you from the start. I honestly wish I could tell you more. Bradley, he is destined to be a monster. He doesn't know that he's the torch that scorches the earth. Together, we can prevent that."

"I do not care," said Inoichi. "My family... I am dead because of you, because of the Spartan you sent, and what? Now you wake an immortal being you cannot control. I will not bend the knee to you."

"Seth was under orders not to murder Ieyasu, and he would have killed you," said Lilith. "You survived that battle because of me. Both your family's lives are better, and for that, I bore the burden of the bad guy. You want to stop me? Do it after you fulfill your destiny. After you save the world. I am not asking you to bend the knee, I'm no queen or monarch."

"No," Inoichi replied.

"Not even for your love?" Lilith said. "It's a tragedy because Mizunami will do anything for you—and she has. I gave her everything you couldn't, true power, and a legacy her family didn't have, a legacy once destroyed by your family. Yet, her truest desire is to be reunited with you, and you won't let go of your pride for her."

"Don't let her manipulate you," Vasilis. "If that were true, she wouldn't have needed Elvir to win the war. The Tokugawa clan will regain power."

The eye of the statue opened a bit. Lilith struggled to keep them closed. "I don't control Mizunami, but I'm willing to bet she will choose to assist in my endeavors. Why not assist her? What is power without someone to share it with? Vasilis, your father, had your mother, and your *mother* has Agis. I had Jeff and Ino... you have Mizunami. Without it, we end up like your father, Inoichi."

"You don't get to speak of my wife or my family," Inoichi said.

Lilith felt herself losing control. "And Vasilis, I felt your power even as a child—it's why I chose you. I'll make the impossible possible, granting your deepest desire. I will reunite you with your mother. It's that simple."

Somehow, Malaya broke free with a force too powerful to contain. The rune around Malaya's neck shone brightly, a symbol of protection, a shield against the physical wounds inflicted by the battle across time. It was a gift from Jeff, Lilith's true love, reaching out from beyond the grave to protect their child. And Lilith was the blade threatening to pierce that armor.

She felt a pang of longing for the days past where she spent Saturday mornings cleaning the house, with Jeff and Malaya watching cartoons together—when they vacationed together, fought over the last slice of pizza.

Now, here they were, fighting one another, and there was nothing protecting Malaya from the daggers Lilith used to pierce her heart.

She looked into her daughter's eyes, seeing the wounds of her treachery reflected in them—betrayal, pain, and scars that nothing could heal. A knot formed in her throat. She deeply wished there was a way to shield Malaya's heart and soul, to wash away the blood staining her hands, but she knew she couldn't.

Despite the pain she caused Malaya, Lilith knew she couldn't let her emotions interfere with the greater threat looming over the world. *You have to walk across the desert. I will wait for you on the other side to wash your calloused feet. Then, together, we will burn everything down.*

"It's always a simple task with you," Malaya said.

She eyed Malaya's hand, fidgeting with the gold coin. "You've grown so much, Malaya."

"Yet, here you are trying to control me, to control us. You destroyed our family and the lives of so many—"

"You still believe you have everything figured out," Lilith interrupted. "True wisdom is in knowing you know nothing. If you did, you'd understand you should be here by my side..." Lilith's words trailed, feeling the force from Elvir's magic pushing against her. She dropped her arms and fell to a knee in exhaustion.

Rumbling shook the room, Elvir's eyes opened—everyone looked up at the statue.

"Can't be..." said Kasumi, removing her fox mask.

Purple smoke flowed from the monstrous statue's mouth. The haze bypassed the stone table with the unconscious Canderyn. The haze seemed to have a mind of its own.

"Brother, watch out!" screamed Trahen.

Ylorb shoved Trahen to the ground. "It's my turn to protect you." He turned to Inoichi and stabbed him. "You were right. I am a traitor."

Inoichi punched him in the mouth, then fell to his knees. "I knew it…I'm going to kill you." Kasumi fell to Inoichi's side, putting pressure on his wound.

"Inoichi," Vasilis shouted, running toward them.

He can't stop the transformation, she thought.

Lilith held Vasilis in place.

"Sorry, brother. This is for the best," Ylorb said, looking at Trahen. "Lilith offers what no one can. A chance for me to be something other than useless."

Smoke swirled around Ylorb's boots. His eyes filled with fear and regret. "Help me," he cried. The haze rose, crashing into his mouth, eyes, and ears, lifting his body with it—he cried out in pain.

An intense bright green aura and robust laugh soon replaced the horrid screams.

She looked at Trahen and his brother—everything made sense. *Ylorb knew Canderyn was never in any real danger. It wasn't Canderyn—it was Ylorb.*

"I-I can't believe it," Lilith stammered, seeing a pronounced physique of a man who stood at least nine feet with eyes deprived of any resemblance to the man whose body he took over. No one made any sudden moves.

"Ylorb?" Lilith questioned.

"Who you knew as Ylorb barely exists," he said, stretching like he awoke from a deep slumber. "For I am no mortal but a god, and you will kneel before me."

"Elvir, I have freed you."

Elvir smiled, then kicked Inoichi into his sister. He dashed toward the hammer with a speed so fast it was difficult to see. He removed it from the ground.

"I always test my weapon and my power," Elvir said before slamming his hammer into a Viking, sending him flying into the air.

"Stop!" Lilith said, doing what she could to prevent Vasilis from attacking.

Ten Vikings fell to their knees. "We are here to serve you. We helped her to awaken the one blessed by Odin," one said.

"Odin," Elvir laughed. He raised a brow as if he did not believe them. "Loyal ones. Show them what you will do for your god."

They rose, readying themselves to attack on his orders.

"Protect Lilith!" Quintus ordered.

An armed Aaron and Midas appeared. And then so did Zoya, with fire back in her eyes. *Taznit must have lived.*

The Vikings who opposed Elvir stood in front of her warriors as the first line, ready to face those who betrayed them. An all-out battle wouldn't help her plans—she needed them for Japan. Her body trembled, trying to keep the raging Vasilis in place.

"Don't attack," Lilith commanded.

Elvir held his men in place. "I have a question. If you freed me, then the Aigon is here. Where is he, the blacksmith?"

"I have him," Lilith directed her eyes at Trahen, unsure if that statement was true.

"A child," Elvir laughed. "This will be too easy." He smashed a Viking protecting Lilith before sending his warriors after everyone.

"Protect Trahen," Lilith said.

A red blur rushed Elvir. Lilith slowed her perception, allowing her to see the action unfold. To her amazement, fox ears sprouted from Kasumi's hair, and her pupils transformed into vertical slits. The colors of her eyes were equally breathtaking: one a cool ice blue, the other a bright amber. She lunged at the Vikings, slashing their throats with her bare hands before hurling a shuriken at Elvir and another at Lilith.

She smashed into the Viking, slashing their necks with her bare hands before throwing her shuriken at Elvir and another at Lilith.

She let Vasilis go and stopped the shuriken. *Shit.*

"This is your fault!" shouted Trahen, rushing toward her.

A Viking tried to stop him, but a dagger met his neck. Quintus quickly attacked Trahen and knocked him out with a punch. She struggled to stand, feeling the results of using too much power.

Lilith saw Malaya in shock as Elvir tore through the Vikings. *Don't just stand there.*

Vasilis pulled the stone sword from the ground and rushed to Malaya's aid. "Move!" he shouted, snapping her from her daze.

Lilith sighed in relief.

Vasilis kicked Inoichi. "Did you die from a scratch?"

"I'm fine."

Indeed, he was. Inoichi snapped the other sword from the ground.

Lilith watched them run through Elvir's warriors as if they were never injured, arguing over who'd fight Elvir. *The ghost radiation must have helped accelerate their healing, too.*

"I will drink your blood, Spartan," Elvir said, dropping his hammer.

"You're going to regret that," Vasilis said, swinging the great sword.

"Too slow." Elvir kicked his hammer up, catching, then slamming it into Vasilis—sending him through the air.

Elvir caught Vasilis's chest plate mid-flight, ripping it off his body, sending him in the opposite direction.

"Fool," Inoichi grunted, staring at a fallen Vasilis. "It was my turn, anyway."

Inoichi rushed Elvir, who swung at him. Inoichi ducked, then stabbed him in the abdomen — to no effect. Elvir grabbed Inoichi's head, slamming it into the ground, shattering his helmet.

A shuriken hit his neck with no effect—further angering him. Kasumi stood on the other end. She picked up a Viking shield. Elvir ran at her, kicking in the shield, launching her through the air. She landed on her feet—five glowing tails sprouted from her.

Amazing.

Elvir was fast, but so was she. Still, no matter what Kasumi tried, Elvir had a counter for it. He grabbed her neck—the aura faded.

"Kasumi!" Malaya shouted, grabbing her axe.

Midas duplicated himself, sending the clone to put Elvir in a chokehold—Midas hammered away at his stomach.

Elvir tossed Kasumi and rammed Midas against a wall. "Die, girl!" Elvir swung his hammer at Malaya.

Midas's duplicate stepped in the way, absorbing the blow.

"You will not hurt her!" Lilith shouted, finding the strength to hold Elvir in place.

Midas grabbed one sword and Quintus the other, and pointed them at Elvir.

"Champions," Elvir said. His eyes dropped suddenly.

Lilith smirked. "You are under my control," she panted. "As long as I hold the Champion's weapon and the blacksmith who can bless them, you will do as I say."

Elvir groaned. Lilith felt him slowly surrender. Relief set in as she let him go—he kneeled. "I am at your command."

"To the golden doors behind the statue," said Lilith.

Trahen tried to run, but Zoya and Quintus grabbed him. "Please, let me help my brother," he cried as they dragged him away.

The doors opened, and water poured from the mouths of the gargoyles. "Are you going to leave him, us, to die?" Malaya said, frantically trying to free Canderyn.

"I'm sorry," Lilith said, locking eyes with Malaya. "You will live. I have seen it."

Lilith's eyes watered as the gold gates closed, trapping them inside.

KASUMI

Iceland, 871

Regaining consciousness with Vasilis's help, Kasumi immediately sensed the urgency reflected in his panicked expression, mirroring the dirt and blood that marred her own face. Her mind raced with the realization that they were trapped, with no apparent way out.

There has to be a way out, she thought, her heart pounding as her eyes darted across from one end of the chamber to the other.

Frigid water roared as it poured from the oasis entrance. The animals had long fled. Clouds of smoke and steam fogged the area. The once-tranquil oasis had transformed into a cauldron of chaos, the relentless deluge eroding their footing with each passing second.

Kasumi knew their time was running out. They had to act fast or risk being consumed by the very forces unleashed.

With a deep breath, Kasumi steadied herself, drawing upon the ancient wisdom of her clan. She met Vasilis's gaze, a silent understanding passing between them. She urged Vasilis to help Canderyn while she searched for her brother.

"There is no exit," Inoichi shouted.

Relief calmed Kasumi, grateful her brother was alive, but it was short-lived. She searched the foggy area. "Where's Malaya?"

Inoichi pointed at her, kneeling. Tears of defeat and disbelief soaked her face, but she was alive. Kasumi looked back over her shoulder at Inoichi. He shook his head, confirming what she already knew.

A pang of helplessness burned within her,, but Kasumi smothered it without hesitation as the realization set in. This wasn't a battle for a shinobi, a ninja, a samurai, or a Tenge.

For the first time, Kasumi was neither sword nor shield—she was the compass, guiding Malaya and the others. Her journey of self-discovery was the pursuit of the elusive Ninth Tail, her true purpose. She had once wielded sword and shield to protect the world from doom, but that was not her role. Inari had created the Tenge to stand with the Champions against the immortal.

Become the queen to the king. Azmani's words echoed in her mind.

Kasumi was meant to serve alongside the others, while the true warriors—the Champions—were the ones destined to face sealing the Sages directly. Though Kasumi had willingly chosen to accompany Malaya on her journey, the others were compelled by fate to traverse through the realms of time, their destinies intertwined with Malaya's.

Initially, Kasumi hadn't fully recognized Malaya's strength—a resilience that matched that of any seasoned warrior. Yet Malaya remained untapped, her potential brimming with enchanted gifts, waiting for her to seize control.

"This is not my journey to lead," Kasumi whispered to herself, as she looked upon her companions.

In that fleeting moment, she released the burden weighing not just on her shoulders, but on everyone else's. It was time to relinquish control and trust her friends.

With the water now reaching her thigh, and the cold reaching her bones, she turned to Malaya. "Look at me," Kasumi urged, lifting Malaya's face by her chin—wiping her tears. "I understand how difficult this is for you. But you're the only one that can help us. We'll drown if we don't move fast."

"I-I can't," Malaya said, looking down at the water covering her ankles. "I'm sorry."

Who can blame her? She was defeated in every aspect of the word. But there isn't any time to dwell, Kasumi thought, unwilling to look back at her own failures.

"Why must you doubt yourself? You are gifted in ways we could only imagine. This feat where we are now is greater than any we've faced thus far, but also plays to your strengths. You must rise above it. Do what you do best, solve this puzzle, and lift us from this dreadful place. If not, we will die."

"Logic, Kasumi," Malaya stammered. "I deal with logic, and science. This is not science or logic. Giants, evil spirits, magic?" She threw her arms up in defeat.

We weren't supposed to be here. This was not our world—so maybe this is it, Kasumi thought, daring not to speak it out loud, seeing what this had done to everyone.

Canderyn mumbled to himself, which didn't help Vasilis temperament, who lacked the confident charm in his demeanor. He wasn't alone. They were on edge as they stood atop the pier where Lilith awakened Elvir.

"Why am I here? I was not supposed to be here. I did everything right," Canderyn mumbled, sparking an idea in Malaya's mind.

"We won't die here," said Malaya. She wiped her tears, looking at Canderyn. "You can help us. It all makes sense now."

Canderyn shook his head, his hair waved on his face. "I do not possess the knowledge."

"Don't think about *this* life but the one before it," said Malaya.

The words seemed to take a lot out of her. She swallowed her pride as it all came into focus. Was this Malaya displaying the acceptance of the world she was in and why she didn't need to fight it?

Kasumi felt a sense of pride, seeing Malaya embrace the possibility of a world beyond science. Were they just words? *Did she truly believe? Had she truly accepted the unknown tapestry of magic?*

"My life before this one..." Canderyn trailed off.

For a brief moment, he froze, his golden eyes scanning the expanse of the cave as if searching for something—maybe his old voice, or perhaps a new one. Kasumi understood that feeling all too well, the sensation of being both oneself and someone else, or even something else entirely.

"We need to get to higher ground now," Inoichi said.

"No, I'm okay... I think," said Malaya. "Canderyn, listen to me. Ylorb told me you taught him Aigon, that means you can help us because—you're one of them." Malaya's words pulsated with an aura of shock and confusion.

"I'm not evil," cried Canderyn.

"No, but you are an Aigon," Malaya said, lifting Canderyn's head. His tears glimmered, streaming down his beard as if to wash away the green in his eyes that were now a shimmering gold. "He passed out not long after Ylorb changed. That wasn't a coincidence. It was by design."

"That's great, but the pressure is increasing," said Vasilis. "We're running out of time."

"So, who are you? Why are you here?" Inoichi said.

"I can't remember," Canderyn closed his eyes, searching for answers. He rubbed his head vigorously. "Water... animals... my energy."

"They've both lost it," said Inoichi. "They hit their heads too hard. If he doesn't get his mind together quickly, we will not survive this."

Canderyn stuttered, pointing at the ceiling. "There is an exit!"

"Where?" questioned Vasilis.

"High ground, the water, the animals, his energy." Malaya looked up, lost in thought.

"We have very little time." Vasilis stated the obvious.

"Shut up brute," Malaya snapped. "The water, this room, it's all enchanted. It was designed to trap anyone who broke the seal but look around. All the insects are gone. There is a way out, an exit."

"It's part of the balance that exists," said Kasumi. "There always has to be a balance, like yin and yang."

"Yes, even in magic, and like science, there's a power of law. Canderyn bloodline is the key," she said, pointing to the ceiling.

Before anyone could respond, cold water raged from the mouths of the concrete creatures, filling the room quicker than before. "Grab the wood!" exclaimed Inoichi.

"This is it, now or never," said Vasilis.

Kasumi glanced at everyone as they were inches from the ceiling. "If this is our end, it was an honor to have fought and died alongside you all," she forced the words out, feeling the guilt of not being able to save them. *It can't end like this.*

"We're not dying today," Malaya said, determined more than ever. "Canderyn, you can produce some type of energy. The stories my mother told of the gods, the powers you hold, are in your hands, literally. Touch the ceiling!"

Everyone held hands and inhaled before they were submerged. Kasumi couldn't see past the murky, frigid water, nor could she see death. There was no fear or panic, only shame. She let them all down, leaving their fate in the hands of a forgotten god.

It should have been me. They have suffered enough; they are my heart.

As the ceiling parted, a cascade of bright blue light descended, enveloping Kasumi in its ethereal glow. Rays of illumination reached down, touching her soul, immersing her in a profound sense of clarity. This wasn't merely light; it was a celestial baptism, cleansing her very essence, washing away the grime of mortal worries and fears.

In that transcendent moment, Kasumi felt enveloped by the pure essence of the universe. A sense of completeness and fulfillment suffused her being, as if all the fragmented parts of her soul were coalescing back into wholeness. The world around her melted into a blur of radiant light and vibrant sensation, bathing her in the core of existence itself.

The surrounding air crackled with energy, each breath she took imbued with peace that was both invigorating and serene. She was lifted from the mundane, her spirit soaring into the sublime.

Her heartbeat resonated like a single drop of water echoing in the vast chasm of the cosmos, in perfect sync with the universal pulse that seemed to open its arms wide, welcoming her into its embrace, a cosmic recognition of her journey towards enlightenment.

In this moment, Kasumi reached a state of perfect harmony with the kitsune, a sublime existence where every question found its answer and every doubt dissolved into the cosmic expanse. The natural waves of the small oceans carried them to shore. A bay, untouched by man, greeted them, and so did a deep cave with vegetation. The neon animals lit the inside.

"Nirvana," the word felt as refreshing as cold water on her tongue after days in the summer's heat.

She had attained the ultimate union with the divine essence of the universe—a profound peace that transcended the physical, bathing her in the infinite glow of enlightenment.

Kasumi laughed. The others followed in unspoken disbelief that they survived.

KASUMI

Iceland, 871

This is unbelievable, Kasumi thought, unable to take her eyes off Canderyn and the cyan flames engulfing his hands. "Look," she called the others' attention.

Vasilis and Inoichi prepared themselves, anticipating a fight. "No subtle movements, friend."

"Relax," said Malaya.

"Quiet, ugly," Vasilis shouted.

"Screw you, Neanderthal."

"You two need to stop it. Now," Kasumi said.

"Fear is unnecessary. I am not the enemy," Canderyn's voice bellowed with the clarity that existed in his eyes.

No longer did he have the confused look. He was complete. "I know who I am, and I am still he who exists in the flesh, but I remember my life as the Aigon god, the forger, Cykius."

From the fire surrounding his hands, he summoned two weapons, a large cyan shield and a battle-axe. The weapons glowed, though they appeared solid as steel.

"Was this your plan?" said Inoichi, still ready for a fight. "To awaken your powers?"

"I am a god no more. None of us are," he said, disappearing the weapons. "I was sworn to guild the Champions, special warriors, born with the power to defeat the Seven. Lilith thought you two were Champions. You have their blood," he said, suggesting Inoichi and Vasilis with his eyes. "But you are no match for Elvir."

They frowned at the notion. Kasumi smirked at their disappointment. She recalled what Lilith said about them being in sync. If they were going to stop Elvir, they needed to work as a team. "Perhaps Malaya and I could do the job for you."

"Do not mock me," Inoichi grunted. "I am still—"

"Your *shogun*," Vasilis interrupted.

"I guess there's hope for them," Malaya said.

"It will take time, training, and hardship to bring you two together," said Canderyn. "As long as Elvir walks the earth, I will assist you in your endeavors."

"What about your brother?" said Kasumi. "If you are the one who forges the weapons to seal Elvir, then he is useless to them."

"And the weapons," added Vasilis. "Lilith thinks she can control him. They could be in Japan for all we know."

Inoichi frowned as Canderyn placed a hand on his shoulder. "They are still here."

"Lilith used a lot of energy," said Malaya. "She looked faint and her medallion barely had a charge."

"We can attack now. They won't expect it," Inoichi said.

"No," Kasumi said.

"Why not?" questioned Malaya.

"We must rest, plan, eat, heal, and attack at full strength. They have Elvir—we saw what he could do."

Everyone agreed.

A beach within a mountain, I have seen it all. The sand beneath their feet displayed a striking blend of black and tan hues, adding another layer to the intricate world within the world. In the distance sat caves and small forests, their allure heightened by the presence of colorful glowing insects and lush vegetation.

Kasumi, and the others, ever resourceful, thanks to time spent in the wild, hunting in foreign lands, had fashioned makeshift fishing rods from string and hooks they held within their grasp.

They discovered a rock formation resembling a spear, a perfect spot to cast their rods into the water. Seated side by side in companionable silence, drinking in what transpired. Before long, the four of them reflected on the events that had unfolded, their spirits somewhat broken by their recent defeat.

The fish came fast enough, and it cheered their mood with every catch. Vasilis and Inoichi eventually made it a competition, and Canderyn, always the steward, cooked the abundance of fish, and they ate over a fire, the savory aroma mingling with their conversation as they discussed their next strategic moves.

Kasumi, however, remained silent, her thoughts turning inward like leaves caught in a gentle current. At times, her gaze flickered to Vasilis, a quiet reminder of the love that still burned within her.

Yet, alongside these tender embers, another fire stirred—a flame of contemplation.

Her thoughts lingered on Nirvana, the elusive Ninth Tail, its essence brushing the edges of her consciousness. Through her trust in Malaya, Kasumi had shattered the cycle of rebirth, freeing herself from the world's bindings and unlocking a hidden power. As her eyes fixed on the crackling fire before her, she slipped further into a trance, her senses sharpening with every breath. She did not merely understand the kitsune's intent; she felt her presence thrumming in the air, a fierce and unrelenting drive to destroy the Sages.

As the fire crackled, Kasumi's sense of self began to waver, making her feel as though she was both beside the fire and within it.

She watched, almost as an outsider, as her form by the fire reached out, walking towards what seemed to be a shadowy enclosure—a cage crafted by her own doubts and fears, the cage of the fox.

Tentatively, Kasumi extended her hand toward the vague silhouette of the cage. In response, a clawed hand—a reflection of her inner spirit, graceful and fox-like—emerged from the shadows into the flickering light of the fire. It was a beautiful, yet fearsome hand; it was unmistakably her own.

The hands met, fingertips touching in a moment of profound understanding. They stared at each other, two parts of a whole, recognizing and accepting their shared flaws and strengths in a silent communion that bridged the gap between the physical and the spiritual.

Yet, darkness lingered still—there is always darkness. In the shadows of her mind, Kasumi felt the subtle call of Inari's will, a beckoning that stirred her spirit and ignited a sense of purpose within her.

Flashes of the hidden message in the cave flickered through her thoughts as she felt her hand brushing over the cold stone. *As pain transitions us on planes we never knew. A light dims to let new powers rise. From shadowed depths, awakened spirits fly.*

No. She would not allow herself to succumb to the will of a god, not until she saved Canderyn's brother. That was *her* will. The fox was a slave to Inari, but she would not. She silenced the whisper of what lay in the pit of the nine tails's true power.

Without a word, he extended his hand, and she accepted it, allowing him to lead her away from the others.

Together, they sought refuge in a secluded cave illuminated by the natural blue light emanating from its walls. Kasumi could see the intensity of Vasilis's gaze, his concern palpable.

"You've been quiet the entire time," Vasilis said. "Distant even."

As she spoke, Kasumi felt the weight of her newfound understanding pressing upon her. She yearned to share the euphoric sensation of awakening the power of the Nine Tails, yet beneath the surface, questions lingered like shadows in her mind.

How could she be certain of her destiny, of the path that lay ahead? She longed to believe that ascension awaited her once her mission was complete, but when she could not say.

She hesitated, the words caught in her throat, unwilling to burden the man who had been pained by betrayal and loss.

No, she was to do as she had learned from the years of uncertainty and a tomorrow that may never come. She had, as the monk said, found both Nirvana and love—she did not have to die to get it.

"I was simply contemplating our life together," she lied, her voice steady despite the turmoil within. "And how I want to cherish every moment with you."

Without allowing him a chance to respond, she leaned in and pressed her lips against his, tasting the solace on her tongue against his.

Vasilis paused, his gaze locking with hers, a question still burning within his eyes. Yet, amidst the unspoken inquiry, another type of heat enveloped Kasumi—a warmth that stirred a longing deep within her core, igniting a fire she could hardly contain. It was a blaze fueled by unspoken desires and suppressed emotions, yearning to be unleashed.

Vasilis held the power to quench the flames, but she knew that the true longing in her heart could only be satisfied when he found the courage to ask the question that lingered between them.

"You can ask me, you know," Kasumi said.

Vasilis smiled. "A fox, is it? What is the tale behind your transformation?"

"It's a *kitsune*, I'm Tenge." She kissed him again.

"Why two different colored eyes?"

"It's a long and uninteresting story. But in short, there are nine tails of knowledge, each with different abilities. I've reached the Ninth Tail of Enlightenment."

"So you have nine abilities?"

She smiled. "Yes, not counting my base abilities upon transformations—speed, strength..." she trailed off, leaning in to kiss him.

"Blah?" Vasilis smiled. "You've been around Malaya too long. I truly want to know."

Where would she start? Like the circle, there was no beginning or end, just a continuous journey. This was part of her for so long. She could hardly remember life without it.

Battling Elvir, seeing Canderyn, and even the werewolf they met called Rafik. It all made sense. This journey, the gods, the life after her true purpose. No matter how fierce she fought it, as kyuubi, serving Inari, was calling her—Mei helped her realize that. And now, a new moon shone on a dark trail. Vasilis's engagement warmed her, though it was surprising—her facial expression gave that away.

"What color is it usually?" Vasilis asked. "Is it the whitish-blue?"

"No. When a kitsune matures, she turns into a kyuubi, which translates—"

"Nine tails." Vasilis smiled. "I picked up a few things."

"I'm impressed, and yes, nine-tails. It's an ascension into an enlightened state."

"It's an evolution," Vasilis added. "And what does this mean for you? Have you evolved?"

She turned away from him, standing at an edge that overlooked a colorful cave. "I do not know. I think so. I cannot shake Elvir or Canderyn from my head. I am armed with more knowledge, yet I have more questions than ever before. Like, where does fantasy and reality intertwine?"

"I'm sure you will find the answer you seek. This world has shaken all of us to our very core," Vasilis replied. She felt his arms slide around her waist. His breath sent chills up her spine as he spoke. "But it's not the first time. It happened to me, and each time we travel, I grow stronger and wiser. For you, it's no different. Perhaps your kitsune yearns to ascend past this mortal world. You may have to allow her to go and not fear the change."

Ascend past this mortal world. The monk came to mind. Then, so did Jesus, for some reason.

"It's my family that troubles me," she said. "They paid the ultimate price, and I was not there to help them. I was not there to die in their place.

"It's not your fault, nor are you some mere mortal."

"Both attacks on my family. I was off playing fantasy. Doing what my heart desired without looking at the conduces. I was selfish. I did not give myself the opportunity to save them."

"Yet you were here to save us all. And you continue to do so every day." He kissed her neck.

"Yet I almost failed you all."

I have extinguished my three fires. They need more time here. Their purpose is not fulfilled. She thought. *I finally have the opportunity to save this new family. Malaya, Ino and Vasilis have suffered enough. I have to try. Jordan, Trahen, Canderyn, and Ylorb deserve more.*

"You're right," she said. "Somehow, I will liberate all of my family."

"Yes, you will," Vasilis said. He picked her up. "I thank you for liberating me."

She wrapped her legs around his waist, only now realizing one of her tails was sprouted. They intertwined on the grass, with a fury only a Champion and a Tenge could. There were no wasted moments or motions in their time passion. It was unlike any before it. Vasilis's arms kept her warm. His beating heart was music to her.

Despite the horrors they faced, this moment was perfect. Still, she could not shake her feelings. He knew that.

"You're still troubled?" Vasilis asked, breaking the silence as they laid.

"I'm worried about Malaya."

Vasilis scoffed.

She sat up. "You need to give her a chance. She needs you. We all must band together. For you two, it's about something more. Your lives, your fates, more than any of ours, are intertwined. Show her the real Vasilis, and she'll come around."

"I admit, I have not been fair to her or your brother. They don't make it easy."

"Neither do you," she said, placing her head on his chest. "I love you, Vasilis. You changed my life in ways I could never imagine. You made me feel things I thought I couldn't again."

"I love you too. And I will continue to help elevate your happiness as we live out our days in Japan."

"No, Japan is *your* dream, not mine. I want to see the future."

"You will. Japan still exists there, though it is vastly different."

"You must become the leader you were meant to be. Malaya needs you. We need you."

She could hear his frustration in his breathing. He unwrapped his arm. She stood up. "Maybe you should take this time to think about what is at stake," she said, putting her kimono back on and grabbing the sack. Vasilis stood up and grabbed her wrist.

"What do you want from me?"

"To grow up. This hate you have for the world, replace it with love. This distrust for you comrades. As I've learned. In the end, only three things matter: how much you loved, how gently you lived, and how gracefully you let go of things not meant for you."

Kasumi hugged Vasilis, her forehead on his chest. "Promise me you will let go and love always."

"I promise."

After Vasilis had succumbed to sleep, Kasumi donned her dark blue garment and armed herself. She knelt, her eyes closed, seeking to still her mind and spirit.

This mission sought the favor of the kami, for her actions tonight could shift the balance of power. Behind the darkness of her closed eyelids, the faces of her adversaries surfaced. She made it a ritual to envision them, offering prayers for their souls before she claimed their lives.

Tonight, she was poised to repeat what had become a familiar act of salvation—protecting those unable to defend themselves. There was no reason to expose the others to danger.

This task was meant for a master of the shadows, one who could weave through darkness as if it were a cloak, guiding her towards a being whose power saturated the air with its intensity, making it almost palpable.

Lilith came to mind, the woman who made this possible. Her vision came at the cost of endangering mankind, yet she bore the cross between her breasts, a symbol of the God she worshiped. In her mind, her actions were right. Extreme measures needed to be taken to ensure the safety of Darviants. She respects her for that.

Kasumi knew all too well what it meant to sacrifice. She knew what lengths she'd go to in order to insure the meek did not succumb to those who abused their power.

With her prayers whispered into the ether to the ears of God. Kasumi turned to her journal, the stream of her thoughts, her fears, and her hopes mirrored onto the pages. She sought to immortalize her spirit, a reflection of a life lived in the service of a cause greater than oneself. Or at least, she hoped.

The ink materialized on the page, each word slithering across the paper like an echo of her past, participants in a delicate dance in time she moved through with grace and resolve.

With every stroke of her pen, Kasumi traced the contours of her journey, her thoughts blending into a narrative that transcended the here and now. One passage stood out for her.

In the path to Nirvana, enlightenment is marked by compassion and the desire to ease suffering. In this light, even Jesus' sacrifice, despite betrayal, reflects these values—taking on the pain of others for the greater good.

Her journal was then placed in her sack. The small scroll never left her side, but she didn't want to risk the damage. She knew she was up against.

Since I have reached Nirvana, then I must demonstrate the transformative power of love and compassion, she thought.

Yet, deep within, the kitsune stirred, its growls echoing the battle cries for a destiny not yet embraced—a hunger unquenched, yearning for the fate the gods had woven.

The cold stone of the cave held no warmth, but it could not rival the chilling surge of divine power coursing through her—a feeling like winter's first kiss on skin still warm from a hot spring.

Tonight was not the time for the kitsune's bloodlust. That hunger would have its moment, but not now. With kunai in hand and the weight of untapped possibilities, she steeled herself, her heart pounding like a warrior's drumbeat.

In the distance, she saw it: a fox glowing with an ethereal light, its aura dancing like fireflies in the dark. Her breath caught. This was the third time she had seen the fox, but never like this—not since she had reached Nirvana.

Perhaps it would be the last. She would not surrender to the nine tails' power, nor yield to Inari's will. Her resolve, forged through the teachings of Sigurd and Mei, was unshakable.

Yet, as she met the fox's gaze, she felt its infinite wisdom and purpose—like whispers of ancient spirits pressing a divine truth into her soul: We are the protectors of these Sages.

She remembered the fear in Mei's eyes at the tales of immortal beings who had slain her ancestors, cursed to roam the earth like shadows. Kasumi, too, had seen it with her own eyes: the sacrifice Inari made, placing part of herself within the Tenge to defeat the Sages.

Perhaps Kasumi needed to reconsider her approach. Yes, she would rescue Trahen, and regardless of whether Elvir awoke, she was resolved to slay him. However, eliminating Ylorb in his sleep would simplify matters—a silent death for a man who harbored a monster within.

One death to save a realm, she reminded herself. Whether innocent or not, Ylorb's existence posed too great a risk.

This was the shadowy path of the shinobi, marked not by honor but by necessity—doing what must be done, decisively, without hesitation. Her resolve kindled anew, an unwavering flame within her. She steeled herself, took a deep breath, and moved decisively toward her guide—

"Where are you going?" a familiar voice broke through the silence of the cave, startling her.

She knew who it was long before he emerged from the shadows, his presence a reminder of the journey ahead, like a beacon guiding her through the darkness. Inoichi, she looked back at her brother.

"Do you see it?" Kasumi asked.

"See what?"

Kasumi turned her gaze back to where the kitsune was. Of course it was gone.

Inoichi's voice cut through the thick air of the cave. "I am not a child. Do not try to distract me," he growled, calling her attention. "I know what you are doing, big sister." He shook his head. Torchlight flickered across his angry face. "Rest food. That was bullshit. You had to be the hero. You must always be the hero."

A wave of guilt washed over her, yet she did not waver. "Why risk all of our lives when I can do it alone?" she contoured. "I have infiltrated the enemy line many times, scaled impregnable castles with high walls of stone. Yet, and always, my mission was successful. I will free Trahen and steal the hilts. This is not a task for any of you, this is a task for a shinobi, and that is who I am."

"A shinobi," Inoichi's words, a venomous tone echoing a harshness they both knew from their father, "you are also a samurai. Bound to protect your Shogun. Is that not the oath you take as a great guard? Am I not your shogun?"

Kasumi's eyes softened, betraying her inner turmoil. "You are the rightful shogun, but you are my *little* brother. This is me protecting you, my lord. And I refuse to fail like I have failed father and Fukumatsumaru..."

At the mention of his name, Inoichi turned away, his body tense, the pain palpable between them. "That... that is on me," his voice strained through gritted teeth. "Before this, you had proper preparation, planning, and use of essential tools. I saw. We all saw that you can destroy thousands of enemies. I believe that, but you are not prepared."

"But I am, brother. Kyuubi has awakened, and you can be *messy*," she said, attempting to walk past him—he stepped in front of her.

"Tokuhime. Please," he said, knowing how to tug on her heartstring, and using her youth name was one of them.

For a moment, it took her back to before all this, how Fukumatsumaru and Hidetada would beg her to teach them how to jump the trees. For a moment she could hear them laughing as they raced, hopping from tree to tree.

To them, it was fun. Little did they know it was their ability to control chakra. It was just fun for them back then; they were just children. Here Inoichi stood, stronger than he knew, but not strong enough to change her mind—he knew that.

"Nobuyasu." Kasumi smiled. "You were always so cute when you were angry. Please have faith in my abilities, who I've become, much like I have faith in yours."

"I would never dishonor your skills. You just deserve better than being a sword."

"I'm not fit to rule. I am who I am, a warrior," she said. "So let me be that, little brother."

Inoichi gave her a slight smile. "You're too precious. I will forever be by your side."

Guilt overtook the moment. What she was about to do next would be hard for Inoichi to forgive. *I'm sorry, brother.*

She grabbed him by the neck and pressed her forehead against his. With a swift motion, she drove a dart into the back of his neck. The paralyzing agent took effect immediately, particularly potent in that vulnerable spot.

As he opened his eyes in horror, she glimpsed the vibrant flames of the kitsune reflected in their brown depths, its cool powers creating a mosaic sense of acceptance and pertinence. Her brother's lips parted as if to say something.

Had he seen it too? She wondered, but no words emerged. Nor would they. The poison had worked even on someone as strong as Inoichi.

His body slumped in her arms and she laid him down gently, choosing at least for the moment to ignore the divine guide at her back, serving as a silent witness to the consequences of her actions.

As she buried her face into his chest, her tears flowed freely, like dark ink spilling over a blank canvas, marking him with her guilt. She stood motionless in that spot, her grief flowing untouched until it had all bled out, leaving the canvas soaked but intact.

When she lifted her face, the ink had dried, her emotions sealed beneath the veil of composure.

"Yes, brother," Kasumi finally spoke. "We shall always be side by side. But I will not risk you. I am alone. I am the shadow."

MALAYA

Iceland, 871

Malaya crept past the sleeping Canderyn, hoping her dark shinobi garments concealed her escape. Invisibility was critical to her mission. No longer will she stand idle and allow anyone else to right the wrongs of her mother to save her world. Her mother needed to be stopped, and she had to be the one to do it.

Kasumi taught her better than that. Lady Azmani taught her to stay close to the shadows, which allowed her to slip past Inoichi, who kept watch.

An odd feeling carried her down the cavernous cave where her mother turned enemy was just a few yards away. The double gold door led into the dungeon. She pressed her back against it, taking a deep breath.

I just need to get Trahen, and I'm gone. In and out, she thought.

"Why do you hesitate?" said Kasumi, appearing from the shadows.

"God, you scared the crap out of me," whispered Malaya. "What are you doing here?"

"Same as you, apparently. You must return to camp; this is no mission for a pup."

"*Pup?*" Malaya scoffed. "I've trained just like you. I have faith in myself, and I *need* to help."

"And you have. We're alive. Now, it is up to me to retrieve the two hilts and the hostage."

"My mind is made up."

Kasumi smiled. "You remind me of myself. You will need more than a dagger," she said, handing her a shuriken.

They walked down the long stairway until they reached a rustic wooden door that opened into the dungeon. All Malaya could do was assist by covering Viking's mouth while Kasumi incapacitated the guards.

Questions still burned within Malaya about the complexity of a warrior's life. She had killed a man.

How was she any different from a murderer?

Within the darkness, Malaya watched Kasumi preserve life with the harsh delicacy as dwindling fire. She chose not to kill as did Inoichi, yet they would forever bear the burns of the lives they had taken.

Lost in her thoughts, Malaya couldn't help but draw parallels between her own situation and the story of Moses, a man chosen by God despite his imperfections.

A laugh escaped her, one tinged with irony, considering who she was when this all began. Now she was drawing parallels between biblical narratives and the words of Augustine.

True justice seeks not suffering, but the restoration of righteousness and order.

In the shadowed corners of her mind, Malaya wrestled with the haunting truth—her actions aligned her, in some dark way, with murderers. Yet, this grim acknowledgement came with an understanding that her choices transcended mere violence. They were, instead, a necessary thread in the complex pursuit of the greater good, where moral fibers were intricately woven by a higher order.

This understanding, a bitter pill swallowed in the silence of her own mind, didn't lighten the burden of her choices. Instead, it painted her actions with shades of a tragic heroism, a painful reminder of the complex web of morality she navigated—a labyrinth where right and wrong blurred into shades of necessity and survival.

Blood will forever stain her hands, as the actions of her mother would pain her soul, yet she found solace in the company of those who navigated the warrior's path without losing their inner light.

Among them was her friend, Kasumi, who was more than a woman, more than a warrior—she was something else. As the shocking truth unraveled within, her stomach churned with the realization that her friend was—a Darviant.

"Why didn't you tell me about the kitsune?" Malaya whispered.

"This is not the time. Besides, would you have believed me?"

"If you transformed, um, I would like to believe so."

"To have you believe in the form of an act was not my desire. You are not as shallow as you think you are," said Kasumi. "Now, please, focus."

They crept underneath a large arch into a cave-like space. A small bridge hung by rope over a pond, where dozens of luminous fish lived. The colorful glow from their backs cast a caustic light throughout, reflecting on the stonewall they used to conceal themselves.

On the opposite side of the bridge, steps led to a large wooden door that centered on the dome-shaped area. Midas slept on one end, while Trahen slept in a cell on the other. With their backs against the wall, they tread carefully to ward Trahen, trying not to fall into the water.

Malaya attempted to pick the cell door's lock until Kasumi took over. All she could do was watch as the door unhinged. They looked over at Midas, who was still fast asleep—so was Trahen.

"Trahen," whispered Malaya. She placed her finger on her covered face before slowly opening the steel bar door.

"Wait," Kasumi said, holding some type of oil.

It was too late. The door screeched loud enough to wake the dead. Midas jumped to his feet, confused but ready for battle. Kasumi and Malaya locked eyes for a moment.

"I'm sorry," Kasumi said, shoving Malaya into the cell, locking her in. "I love you too much to risk your life. This is my fight."

"No! Kasumi," pleaded Malaya, a fruitless effort.

Kasumi gripped the ball end, twirling her kunai. Sparks flew, the metal scrapped the ground—Midas shrugged her off. "You must have a death wish," he said, washing the sleep from his face with the water.

"Bathe, but the blood of the innocent will forever stain your hands," Kasumi said. "Where are the weapons?"

Midas' eyes gave away the long sword wrapped in cloth hiding behind his chair. Malaya searched her pockets for a solution, a way to get out. She only had her dagger and a shuriken. *Here goes nothing*.

Malaya turned to Trahen. "Rumor is, you have... abilities." She held out the shuriken. "Can you change this into something to pick the lock?"

"I can," he said, grabbing the metal.

"A way out," Malaya said before describing the tool down to the very tip. If he was what they said, her impeccable memory with his gift would give them a way out.

After a few tries, Trahen created the tool she needed. Her jaw dropped, but there wasn't time to marvel at the impossible feat. Then again, the impossible was all Iceland exuded. Malaya rushed to the door, frantically picking the lock. Luckily, Midas and Kasumi were settling old debts.

"Your death is a debt owed to my family," said Kasumi.

"In Japan, I did what was necessary, what Lilith asked of me," Midas said, trying to keep his voice down. "You saw her power."

"Is that all you do? Follow orders."

"I am but a soldier. Perhaps I deserve to die for what I did, but this is not the time to determine whether you'll deliver that sentence. Put your weapon away before you wake the others."

"No."

Malaya looked up to see Kasumi's eyes glowing a bright amber. Long, sharp nails protruded from her fingers.

Midas unsheathed his sword, but she was too fast. Her chains wrapped around his sword, disarming him. She continued her onslaught, bringing the chain around for another turn. This time, it wrapped around his forearm.

"You are mine," Midas said, yanking her.

Kasumi clawed at his abdomen, ripping his armor. Midas dropped to a knee, and she jumped on his neck—squeezing his neck with her thighs.

Focus, Malaya continued to pick the lock, desperately wanting to help free Trahen. Countless scenarios raced through her mind as she struggled for freedom.

Loud thumping made things difficult—she realized it was the sound of her heart—dizziness made it hard to stand, let alone remember what Azmani taught her.

My meds, she thought, but realized she hadn't taken them, nor did she need them. She closed her eyes, recalling her lessons.

Not knowing is Buddha, Kasumi told her. *You can keep your mind at peace. If you don't know or expose yourself to anything negative.*

The lock started to open, but not fast enough. Though it didn't appear Midas wasn't going anywhere.

"You're strong," Midas said, struggling to break free. "I can see why he loves you."

Midas cloned himself. Malaya couldn't believe her eyes. She wondered if she was still feeling the effects of the spider bite. His clone grabbed Kasumi, tossing her toward the water.

"Kasumi!" she shouted.

The clone dissipated, and the real Midas mounted her fallen form. "Don't worry, Malaya," Midas said, struggling to push her head underwater. "I will not drown her. She just needs to sleep!"

"Then you will die an honorable death," Kasumi said.

"No one has to die," he replied.

"At least I'll look in your eyes before I take your life. A courtesy you did not afford Vasilis."

"You speak of what you do not know," Midas said, forcing the side of her face into the water.

"Kasumi, please fight... change!"

"Perhaps you should concentrate on the lock before your friend dies," said Trahen.

"Maybe you should stop talking so that I can concentrate," snapped Malaya, unable to take her eyes off the battle.

***

Kasumi dug deep within herself and forced her head above water, gasping for air as she used the last of her strength.

"I know enough," Kasumi mustered. "No, you didn't kill Vasilis, but you did nothing to stop it. A mindless puppet you are, but not soulless. So why do you always fight for the wrong side?"

Midas responded by driving Kasumi's head underwater again. The cold, murky depths drowned out Malaya's voice.

Change... the thought echoed deep in her mind.

Kasumi had already changed more than she originally intended. Two tails were usually more than enough for most foes, but this opponent was a Champion. She would not disrespect him with anything less. However, she didn't know how much control she had left, and she couldn't risk Malaya's safety.

Compelled by necessity, Kasumi invoked the power of the fifth tail. Its capabilities far surpassed the subtle manipulations of the fourth tail's dreamscape abilities, offering a more direct form of strength needed for this confrontation.

Yet, embracing this power was not without its consequences. Her body writhed in agony as joints twisted and bones reformed, reinforcing her physical form to withstand and administer greater force.

A raspy voice broke through, "That's enough, brother," Elias said.

She felt the grip around her neck and head loosen. Kasumi's head emerged from the water—the surrounding water illuminated by the glow of her amber eyes. She broke free from Midas's grasp and slashed his face. Her reactions were so quick, she could feel his skin tearing beneath her fingernails. He roared in pain, clutching his face.

The cage was open, and there was no going back now.

***

Malaya's stomach churned and her hands trembled as she witnessed the transformation before her, viewing it through the distorted prisms of a cell door. Five majestic tails unfurled from Kasumi's form, each moving with a life of its own. Her eyes glowed a deep, luminous amber, capturing the primal essence of the wild.

Kasumi's face and body had undergone a startling metamorphosis; her features were now those of a fierce, fox-like creature. Long, sharp teeth gleamed from within a snout that had replaced her nose and mouth, and thick fur bristled where smooth skin once was.

When she growled, it was a powerful, resonant sound that vibrated with the timbre of her human voice, intertwining the familiar with the surreal.

"Don't underestimate me," Kasumi said.

Next to her, Elias stood, radiating confusion and the sheer impossibility of the situation that overwhelmed Malaya like a deluge of unanswered questions. She had been certain Elias was gone, transported back to the future, yet there he was, standing unharmed next to Kasumi—unarmed and as if he had never lost an arm in battle.

Malaya's breath hitched in her throat, her instinct to yell stifled by shock.

Then she noticed something even more bizarre: Elias s mouth moved in perfect unison with Kasumi's. Synchronized with her actions, he lunged at Midas, aiding this transformed version of Kasumi.

Together, they overwhelmed Midas, slamming him to the ground with a coordinated assault before Kasumi mounted him.

Malaya looked desperately at Elias for a sign of his intentions, but in a blink, he vanished into thin air. It was then clear to her; the figure she saw wasn't Elias at all. It was an illusion crafted by Kasumi, a spectral deception woven into the fabric of the fight.

Malaya whispered under her breath, "A fox's trick," just as the dungeon entrance swung open. Her eyes darted up to see Zoya and Taznit bursting through the door, flanked by ten other warriors. At that moment, the second lock of the cage door clanked open.

"Okay, Trahen," Malaya instructed quickly, "as soon as this gate opens, run past the bridge and don't stop until you reach our camp. Go get help."

"I can fight, my lady," Trahen protested.

"I know," Malaya responded, her voice firm yet reassuring. "My mother wouldn't want me dead. We need you to bring reinforcements." She swung the cell door wide open. "Run now!"

Taznit sprinted after Trahen, determined to recapture the blacksmith. Malaya could only hope Trahen was fast enough to escape as he dashed toward safety. She quickly turned her attention back to the fray.

Eyeing the greatswords that Midas was guarding, she decided instead to aid Kasumi. However, before she could reach her, Zoya tackled her mid-stride, sending them both crashing into the pond. A sharp punch to Malaya's face from Zoya sent bright lights exploding across her field of vision.

As Malaya sank into the pond, the sounds of the fray muffled by water, she felt blood ooze from her nose.

Surfacing for air, she was met immediately with another fist to her face. She blocked the punch and retaliated with a headbutt followed by an elbow strike to Zoya's jaw, sending him sprawling half out of the water, struggling to her feet.

Malaya paused momentarily, taking in the sight of her handiwork, before her concern snapped back to Kasumi.

The dungeon's air abruptly chilled, a piercing cold that seeped into her bones. A spectral, icy blue mist swirled around Malaya, entrapping her like a leaf caught in a whirlwind. She tried to move but found herself frozen in place, her limbs unresponsive, held by what might as well have been the devil himself—Elvir.

He loomed at the top of the stone stairway, his presence commanding the freezing mist that rendered her motionless. Malaya's heart pounded fiercely, her breaths visible in the frigid air.

Then the low, rumbling growl of a beast echoed through the dungeon, sending a wave of dread through Malaya. She saw the beast—once her friend Kasumi—approaching with bared fangs, her eyes wild and unrecognizing.

"Kasumi... it's me!" Malaya cried out, her voice cracking as despair gripped her. She braced herself for the end, closing her eyes tightly.

Zoya's voice pierced the cold air. "Kasumi!" She pushed Malaya out of the way and charged at the transformed Kasumi, chain in hand, shouting, "Let the chains of peace guide you!" Despite the beast's fearsome appearance, Zoya looped the iron ball around Kasumi's leg.

The links of the chain glowed a soft green, and Kasumi's monstrous advance halted. Zoya's intervention had saved Malaya just in time.

The freezing mist dissipated slightly, allowing Malaya a moment of respite as she watched, heart still racing, the standoff between her friend now paused by the chains of peace. The eerie glow from the chain seemed to calm the savage beast, bringing a momentary peace to the chaos that had unfolded.

***

Kasumi gasped as she regained control of her body, but she could feel it was only temporary. A sense of dread settled over her as she surveyed the horrific scene. Vikings lay dead, torn apart. Elvir stood at the top of the stairs, his hand outstretched, yet he was not moving. In fact, no one was.

Malaya stood frozen as time seemed to halt. The dungeon darkened as if a veil had been draped over it. A tall figure loomed in the shadows, adorned in an oversized white cloak, her thick black hair draped over a white kimono decorated with red flowers. Her skin was as white as snow, and several glowing foxes stalked, circling their master.

Kasumi gasped, "Inari."

"Why are you here?" she managed to ask, her voice a distant whisper.

"What have you done? Free me! I don't have time for riddles. It's time to retreat and regroup," Kasumi demanded.

She attempted to move closer, but her legs did not respond. She found herself growling at the foxes.

"If you retreat, you will lose, and all will be lost," Inari responded calmly.

"I have two Champions and an Aigon; we shall win," Kasumi asserted.

She turned her head, her frustration apparent. "How did the last fight go? Did the boys grow into men overnight? Will they win without weapons?"

Kasumi shook her head. "We are Nine Tails now; we will find a way. If not, we will fall back and prepare."

"You don't have the means to leave, only Lilith does. And your knee is too stiff to bend," Inari pointed out.

A growl escaped Kasumi's lips. "What would you have me do, then? We both know the Sage is immortal. It can only be sealed."

"You know what you must do. You have ascended. Your true nature washed away. You are a powerful queen. What will you do for the king of this game?" Inari challenged her.

To lift the veil and see the light, one must first endure love's darkest night, Kasumi mused silently, her gaze sweeping over Malaya, frozen still, before resting on Elvir. *Pious manacles break, unleashing the soul. Within the depths of despair, one finds them whole...*

This reflection brought a calm resolve to Kasumi. With determination etching her features, she affirmed, "I'll do what must be done." Her eyes, now fixed on the task ahead, radiated a quiet intensity, ready to face whatever lay before her with unwavering resolve.

Inari nodded with a devilish grin. One by one, the foxes disappeared into the shadows, followed by the goddess.

"God lend me courage," Kasumi whispered.

The veil lifted, and Kasumi leapt into the air, her claws digging deep into Elvir's giant hands, gashing him and freeing Malaya. She could feel the burning ice of Ki igniting her glowing eyes.

Through the reflection of a shocked Elvir, her eyes burned an ice blue. Nine tails, clad in a white coat, sprouted from her, the light blue vulpine aura searing Elvir. He tossed her aside, but she landed gracefully on all fours. Kasumi opened her mouth, and blue flames burst forth. Elvir dodged the attack nimbly.

He opened his hand, and his war hammer materialized out of a shimmer. Elvir lunged at her with a backhanded swing.

"Your mind is mine!" Kasumi declared, her voice resonating with confidence as she attempted to bend Elvir's will. Although she knew fully subduing him was beyond her—given his immense power—she only needed a brief moment of control.

Elvir, a behemoth frozen in place, was temporarily subdued under Kasumi's influence. But as quickly as she had seized his mind, he shattered her psychic hold, regaining his freedom. That fleeting moment of stillness, however, was all Kasumi required.

In that critical instant, she focused her energy, condensing a sphere of blazing Ki around her fist. The glowing orb pulsated with intense heat and raw power before she thrust it forward, launching it directly at Elvir's chest. The impact erupted in a brilliant explosion, staggering the giant and creating the vital distance she needed between them.

A vibrant divine fox aura, similar to Canderyn's Ki axes, appeared, its bite as fearsome as its form. The fox attacked Elvir while Kasumi closed her eyes and summoned her inner Ki. She knew there was no turning back; soon, she would lose herself, and the kitsune would take full control.

"Vasilis, hurry," she thought desperately.

She glanced at Midas, who had recovered. Understanding her intent, he nodded. She pointed her tails to a central point, and energy began to coalesce.

Black lightning cracked and sparked as a blue fireball erupted into a perfect sphere.

"Look out!" shouted Midas before tackling Malaya into the water.

The heat from the flame scorched the surface above them. When they emerged, Zoya was unconscious. Elvir, however, protected himself with an ice shield that likely dispersed the blast. Kasumi had fully transformed—it was palpable.

***

Kasumi, now a being of folklore, smiled and opened her other hand this time. Kasumi passed her opposite hand over it as if she was creating an invisible sphere. This time, lighting appeared. She ran towards Elvir with the electric ball behind her, like a bowler, raising the ball before the perfect release.

Before she could throw it, the ball disappeared. It was as if her cord was pulled and her energy with it. Kasumi looked back at her hand while still running. Her eyes flickered back to amber.

"Kasumi!" Vasilis's voice echoed far behind Malaya.

Suddenly, her legs woke up. She tried to run, but she was yanked back by Midas. "You'll get yourself killed," he said, wrapping her in his arms and lifting her off the ground.

Malaya could only shout, but her eyes were locked onto Kasumi as Elvir's hammer met the side of her head, slamming her into the wall.

"No!" Malaya shouted.

Kasumi struggled to get up, her face covered in blood. For a moment, Malaya thought she had time. Any second now, Vasilis would leap into the air and attack Elvir just in the nick of time. But unlike a movie villain, there was no monologue or toying with his prey. Instead, Elvir ran after her, ripped a chain from her hand, and choked her with it.

"Elvir, release her!" Midas exclaimed, but Kasumi

Malaya fought, but Midas' grip was absolute, and so was Elvir's. Kasumi fought for freedom and air. Malaya reached for her dagger and stabbed Midas—shattering his collarbone. She rushed Elvir.

There was no fear, no hesitation, no one to stop her, only conviction. She stabbed Elvir's armpit. He swatted Malaya off like a fly—she smacked into a wall, hearing something crack. The wind got knocked out of her. She gasped and then tried to stand, but her body refused.

Blood dripped from Kasumi's nose, spilling onto Elvir's hand as he tightened the chained kunai around her neck.

"No!" Vasilis shouted, his voice filled with pain and rage as he sprinted and shouted.

Vikings stormed the dungeon, rushing the narrow wooden bridge, failing to land a blow on Vasilis. Her vision blurred, but she could see Elvir holding Kasumi's limp body with one hand. He cut the ropes to the bridge with the other.

Vasilis's relentless rage drove him through the pond and the Vikings with ease. His war cries unsettled even the battle-tested Vikings. Even with a makeshift spear, he was unstoppable.

"Hold on, he's coming for you," Malaya's voice barely whispered.

More Vikings attacked Vasilis, but his fury was too much. He was like an angel fighting mortals. Inoichi and the others soon appeared. Vikings attacked him and Canderyn, but Aaron forced them back only to hold the captive with a dagger to his throat.

Lilith appeared with Quintus. In a blink, Aaron disappeared, then reappeared in front of Elvir, tossing Quintus the glowing greatsword.

"Yield, you've done enough damage," Quintus said, forcing Elvir to drop Kasumi. Midas stood with the two swords. "Elvir, obey, or your soul will be returned to slumber," Lilith commanded, revealing a dagger.

Elvir raised his arm in surrender, yet he bore a satisfied grin on his face.

"We need to go now," Lilith said. The gold dagger shone a luminous yellow light before a vortex opened.

Unlike the usual wormhole, this one swirled in place. Quintus handed Midas the twin European swords, then proceeded to gather his personal items. All the warriors stopped attacking, returning to Lilith's side.

Finn locked eyes with Malaya, his gaze filled with an almost apologetic expression, but it didn't matter. The weight of responsibility for the horror they all faced rested on his shoulders as much as anyone's.

She looked away and hobbled to Kasumi. A single tear ran down Kasumi's face. Her eyes traveled from Malaya to Vasilis, then Inoichi, as they kneeled next to one another, but she couldn't speak—her breaths were slow and shallow.

Kasumi's eyes stopped moving. The amber was gone, and her eyelids closed softly. "Kasumi!" cried Zoya, crawling to her side.

"Malaya, please give her the medicine," Vasilis said.

"I-I," Malaya stuttered before looking at Lilith.

"I'm sorry, baby. Neither of us can save her."

Zoya stood up and walked away. Malaya sobbed as she cradled her friend—Vasilis sat motionlessly. Inoichi wiped a tear from his face and bowed his head. Trahen and Canderyn kept their eyes on Elvir's sadistic smile.

"I didn't mean for any of this to happen," Lilith said. Her tone was soft and concerning, yet meaningless. "I'll leave you all to do what you have to for your friend."

Midas glanced at Quintus as the fellow Champion disappeared through the portal. Lilith signaled to Zoya. They also left through a wormhole. A bloody Midas and Aaron stood at Lilith's side.

Vasilis marched toward Midas. "I'll kill you first, coward! You could have saved her!"

"Vasilis, please!" Malaya shouted. "Don't, not now. I promise we'll get justice for her. "

Malaya's eyes pierced Lilith, who looked as if she wanted to say something. Aaron too, but neither said anything.

"You have what you want, Lilith. Now go!" Malaya shouted, and her mother, along with everyone except Aaron and Midas, disappeared.

"A woman so strong she'd die for strangers is a sight like no other," said Midas. "Apologies would bear no weight, but I am sorrowful."

He planted his great swords in the ground. "Trahen, please replicate them."

Aaron looked at Midas. "I understand why you have to do this, but I hope you know what this means."

Midas nodded. He stepped back, allowing Vasilis and Inoichi to grab their weapons.

"Wait," Trahen said. "If Elvir or Lilith know you can't control him, everything you worked for will have been for nothing."

"It's more than that," added Canderyn. "Elvir lives for chaos, war, destruction. And he may free the others."

"Lilith made him a promise that is sure to keep him at bay," said Midas. "We will be fine, but I will see to it that Kasumi's death was not in vain. Once our mission is completed and *our* world is saved, I will slay the *god*. If either of you try anything before then, Lilith will kill you." He looked at Vasilis and Inoichi. "You can still join the fight if you choose."

Vasilis and Inoichi said nothing; both had death in their eyes.

Trahen lined up the two old swords and kneeled before them. His hands hovered over them, a luminous blue light derived from his palms, transforming the weapons into a copy of the two swords.

"These weapons are powerless," Trahen warned.

"Understood," Midas said, picking them up.

"For what it's worth, I'm sorry," Aaron said.

"It's worth nothing," Malaya hissed.

She turned her back, hearing the electric crack of the wormhole open and then close. Tears stream from her face. Aaron was another loss in a never-ending cycle of death and betrayal.

With Lilith gone, Canderyn handed the swords to Inoichi and Vasilis.

MALAYA

Iceland, 871

Malaya sat hunched on a cold, jagged step in the vastness of the cave, its emptiness amplifying the weight of her grief. Warm tears cascaded down her cheeks like raindrops in a storm, the aftermath of her misguided actions.

Each sob wracked her body, the pain more agonizing than the physical blows she endured from Elvir. Raw emotion intensified, the burden pressing upon her like a suffocating weight.

I led them into a trap, Malaya scolded herself. Her friend was dead, and she had no way home. *It's all my fault. I wasn't smart enough. I was so blind. If I had...*

In the midst of her despair, a gentle hand came to rest on her shoulder, offering a warm touch against the coldness clutching her heart. She lifted her head to meet the hardened eyes of the man she had let down, the one she considered as close as a brother.

"I understand how you feel," Inoichi said, his face as gentle as his tone. "But we need you."

"Me?" Malaya replied, tears streaming down her face. "Who am I? I'm nothing but a scientist who was in over her head who got her friend killed."

"My sister's death is not your burden. It is my own ignorance, and stubbornness. I should have stopped her, but—"

"So it's your fault," Vasilis's voice thundered across the vast cave as he made his way to them.

Inoichi snapped his head around, taking a defensive stance.

"Please, do not do this?" Canderyn said, stepping in front of Vasilis. "You must focus. Work on becoming one, or you will not stop Elvir."

"Who are you but a useless, disgraced *god?* You don't know shit!" Vasilis said, shoving him aside.

"You dishonor my sister with such savage behavior," said Inoichi.

"No, she is dead," Vasilis said, raising his weapon.

Inoichi stepped in front of Malaya, easing her aside, Divine Wind at the ready.

Vasilis charged like a bitter enemy, his speed nearly blinding, but Inoichi swiftly sidestepped, evading him with ease.

"You must not!" Canderyn warned.

"Quiet!" Inoichi and Vasilis said simultaneously.

Vasilis took another swing and missed again, allowing Inoichi to knee him in the stomach. "I do not wish to hurt you," Inoichi said.

Undeterred, Vasilis attacked again with fury. "Vasilis, stop!" Malaya shouted, barely able to follow their movements.

Their swords clashed, a blinding light engulfed the cave, and a shockwave sent them flying. Malaya opened her eyes. Both swords were shattered like glass, and the metal dissipated.

"Idiots!" Canderyn shouted, stretching out both his arms, one to Inoichi and the other to Vasilis.

A radiant aura enveloped his hands, unleashing a whip-like surge of light that coiled around their necks with swift precision. With a casual gesture, he drew the warriors toward him, effortlessly lifting them off the ground as if they were weightless.

His voice reverberated with seething anger. "You fail to comprehend the gravity of your actions. Champions are meant to unite, not divide. Champions must work together. Midas and Aaron made a mistake in giving you those blades. Now, look at them? They were meant to defeat a great evil, not one another."

As Malaya's gaze shifted between Vasilis and Inoichi, she noted the unmistakable blend of awe and shame on their faces, a reflection of her own emotions.

Amidst the unfolding magic, she found herself reflecting on her previous blindness. Her once comforting reliance on medicine had become a symbol of this blindness, a result of her mother's deceit. Her mother's actions had skewed Malaya's perception, trapping her in a narrow reality while concealing the enchantments around her.

It was like a veil had been draped over her senses, hiding the mysteries of the world and leaving her oblivious to the magic that had always surrounded her. How could she have been so blind? She pondered the wonders she had missed, ensnared in her constrained view of the world.

Now, as the words echoed in her mind, Malaya realized she had been blind to magic. But with this newfound clarity, she found herself on the brink of a revelation. Was she truly ready to embrace what was to come?

"My apologies," Vasilis uttered, grabbing Malaya's attention to the Aigon trapping Vasilis and INoichi in his power. "Once her mind was made up, Kasumi was an unstoppable force. It is not your burden, brother. That belongs to Midas."

Inoichi grunted. "You are forgiven."

Canderyn released his hold. Vasilis and Inoichi massaged their necks.

Vasilis looked at Canderyn. "What of the weapons?"

Canderyn sighed as he picked up the hilts. "My power is limited. I can craft and enchant your weapon. As for the other, I must find someone who can—one with great power, gifted by the gods."

Malaya looked at Trahen. "What about you?"

"I can only create what I have mastered. I would need to train, as does Canderyn, to capture the essence of the weapon. Axes and swords are easy, but Inoichi's blade was specially crafted."

"We can find your blacksmith soon enough, but my sister..." his voice trailed. "We must bind her in cloth. I must take her home, but I cannot do that without you getting us out of here." He looked at Malaya.

"I don't know if I can."

"Allow faith to guide you," Canderyn said, handing Malaya Kasumi's mask and chained kunai.

I don't know if I can.

Malaya helped Trahen gather the cloth to wrap Kasumi. Inoichi carried her as silence guided them to their camp. It was then she came across her sack. She stared at it for a moment, not sure what to do. She knelt, then opened it. There was a scroll in it.

It's a journal.

Malaya's Japanese was top-notch, but she used an older dialect, which made it more difficult. She was sure if it was correct to read it, perhaps it was best for her family to possess it. But she had to know why. Why did Kasumi take that risk on her own?

The level of education shocked her. *I had no idea she had a passion for philosophy and theology.*

Her fight was breathtaking. An epic inner battle side of her. A fight between demons that Malaya never realized. A mask that hid her deep pain. The struggle of the realization of Nirvana and the interest of Jesus Christ's sacrifice.

Her words turned Malaya's stomach and knotted her throat. There was an uncanny expression of compassion, empathy, and love, with a deep sense of selflessness. *I have to study this.*

The water sparkled more than before, luminous birds sang, and Malaya rested against a tree. Kasumi's words echoed in her mind. *If I'm going to win, I must sacrifice and help stop the suffering of others... for the greater good.* She closed her eyes, not realizing how tired she was, she drifted off. But she awoke on the black sanded beach.

Kasumi's body lay in a boat. Canderyn handed Inoichi the torch. He and Trahen sang in Norse. Malaya understood every word about a world beyond the flesh where souls lay to rest for eternal happiness and peace. They all watched the boat ride the waves.

Chills ran through her body, forcing her head up. *It can't be*, she thought, staring into the eyes of the nine-tailed kitsune. It winked as it ascended into a blinding light.

"We meet again," a voice echoed.

Malaya's gaze met the familiar face clad in rustic, smokey silver armor that absorbed the flames. Her fiery red hair that flowed like a blazing river framing a young face. Her bright gray eyes offered some solace in the darkest of times.

"Sigrunn... How..." Malaya's voice trembled in the dimly lit cave as her eyes swept over the familiar faces gathered around the flickering flames. "How did you get here?"

"We received your signal," Sigrunn replied softly, her tone weighed down by sorrow. She gestured towards Gier, silently acknowledging Malaya as he conversed with the others.

Malaya's fingers brushed against the coin in her pocket, its faint glow a tangible reminder of their connection, and proof of how much of the world, past or present, that she truly did not understand. "It worked," she murmured almost to herself, the realization sinking in. "It actually worked."

"It did," Sigrunn agreed softly, settling beside Malaya. Her gaze drifted towards Kasumi's motionless form, hidden behind her mask, as she and Malaya clasped hands. "I regret not arriving sooner—"

"Don't," Malaya interjected, her grip tightening around Sigrunn's hand. Tears threatened to overflow like a dam struggling against a relentless tide. "None of this is on you, and you're here now, so thank you."

"No need," Sigrunn said, her voice filled with gratitude. "After all you've done, what you've overcome... I'll be thanking you for a lifetime." She stood up and extended a helping hand to Malaya.

Malaya accepted the gesture, no longer feeling any effects from Elvir. The only remaining pain was a heart crushed underneath the weight of guilt that she dragged Kasumi into this.

As Sigrunn led her towards the others, Malaya's eyes scanned the vast expanse around them. It was a stark contrast to the darkness of their recent ordeal, a bright and beautiful landscape stretching out before them.

"You are not stuck here," Sigrunn's voice broke through Malaya's thoughts.

Malaya scoffed. Her mind drifted to thoughts of her mother, a surge of nausea accompanying the realization of her role in their current plight. *This was all her fault.*

Her mother had unleashed an immortal being, a force capable of reshaping the very fabric of time itself, leaving them stranded and powerless. Yet, she had the ability.

How? What kind of power could grant such abilities?

The question lingered in her mind, drawing her back to memories of her encounters with Mei and the mysterious Aigon technology.

Could it be technology or was it something more mystical? The thought sent shivers down Malaya's spine.

Despite her instinct to dismiss the notion as implausible, the events she had witnessed left her questioning the boundaries of possibility. She looked at Sigrunn, who offered up a flicker of hope, a solution that she wasn't sure was possible.

"There's no way home, Sig," Malaya said. "There's no way back to Japan. Before you came, there was no way out of this cave. My mother made sure of it."

Anger rose inside of her as the words left her lips. She was always two steps behind her mother. *Even if I could reactivate the medallions, she may have made it so that we'll end up wherever or wherever she wanted us to be.*

Sigrunn's offer interrupted her tumultuous thoughts. Extending a partially bloomed flower to Malaya, its vibrant colors captivated her senses, swirling like a kaleidoscope in motion.

Leaning in for a closer look, Malaya discovered that the mesmerizing magic of the bloom was not merely botanical, but a fantastical feat of mechanical artistry.

Its intricate mechanism pulsed within its core, dancing and weaving like a living entity, emitting a mystical aura that left Malaya hypnotized.

"What is this?" Malaya asked, her eyes locked on the marvel in front of her.

"It is Aigon technology, from my family. We come from the lineage of Time Gods. Once it blooms, it will send you home."

"And the power source?"

"Magic..." Sigrunn replied with a smile, a hint of mystery lingering in her gaze.

Malaya lifted her gaze. Before she could ask more questions, Gier walked over.

"We do not have enough power to get everyone home," said Gier. "Five at the most. Given the dense nature of the mortal body. The others must wait for the flower to blossom."

"Cykius," Sigrunn said. Her eyes looked at Canderyn. "Inoichi's world has the smithing god you need. I am sure of it, though I do not know how I know, but I do."

"You are still discovering the depths of your abilities," Canderyn said. "So, who among us will stay?"

Malaya turned to Inoichi. "You should probably go home and give Kasumi a proper goodbye. Canderyn has to forge the weapons, and Vasilis, you are a Champion, as is Ino. My mom wouldn't have left me here if she thought I was in danger. It's only logical that I stay."

Sigrunn touched Inoichi's medallion. The surrounding lights flashed brighter than ever before, and Malaya's eyes widened. "How... What did you do?"

"Gave you more time," replied Sigrunn.

"Why?"

"It's not time for you to know why."

"What am I supposed to do?" Vasilis fumed. "Kasumi, she was my love, and Malaya I—I can't just leave you here."

Malaya could see the look he and Inoichi gave one another. "Both of you can go. I don't need a bodyguard."

"We know you can take care of yourself," Vasilis said, "but funerals are not for me. If I am being honest, I have grieved and made peace. My last conversation with Kasumi was about unity and friendship. Perhaps it starts now. If you will have me."

Malaya's eyebrows raised. "Uh, of course."

Inoichi placed his hand on Vasilis's shoulder—they nodded at one another. "'Til we meet again."

Inoichi grabbed his sack and quickly stuffed the hilts of Divine Wind and Forsaken inside. He then pulled out the extra medallions that Kat had given them and handed one each to Trahen and Canderyn.

Trahen walked toward Malaya. "Thank you, my lady."

Inoichi lifted Kasumi over his shoulder and vanished through time.

Malaya thanked Sigrunn and Gier, who vanished as quickly as they came. She programmed her and Vasilis's destination into the flower.

"Are you ready?" Malaya asked Vasilis. He nodded.

Vasilis looked into her eyes. "I promise you, we will save the world."

The End

Glossary of Terms and Acronyms

A

Aphaeleon Orbs – Ancient relics infused with divine power, each tied to a Sage and representing a distinct color and energy. They are vital to maintaining balance and controlling the power of eternal entities.

Attobots – Microscopic technology used to create the **Cowan Shield** and other advanced devices, playing a significant role in memory protection and manipulation.

C

CCT (Cognitive Corteotransmitter) – A device that allows information to be transmitted between hosts, enabling direct sharing of thoughts or memories.

Cowan Shield – A memory-protection chip that isolates consciousness from space-time disruptions, preserving memories during paradigm shifts.

D

Darviants – A term derived from Darwin's evolutionary theories, describing humans with supernatural abilities such as telepathy, technopathy, and elemental control.

E

Elite Eight – A covert group of highly skilled operatives deployed for missions beyond the scope of traditional black ops.

G

Ghost Jump – A quantum-based method of transportation that renders the jumper semi-transparent and untouchable while navigating the quantum plane.

I

I.C.E. (Infusion of Cybernetic Encryption) – Advanced cybersecurity technology used for creating the impenetrable **ICE Wall**, a key defensive system in the series.

Intrepid – A space station used as headquarters and a key base for time travel operations led by **Lilith** and the **MAD** group.

J

Jet – A volatile, highly addictive substance used to enhance the **Zeta-verse** experience, allowing users to merge their consciousness with an alternate reality.

L

Lucy – An AI system capable of monitoring time travelers, detecting anomalies, and generating historical maps for navigation.

M

MAD (Militant Anti-Destruction) – A faction dedicated to preventing catastrophic events and maintaining temporal stability.

Medallion – A Mayan calendar-inspired time-travel device used to navigate different eras, equipped with dials and charge indicators.

N

Nanotech – A general term for advanced nanotechnology used for healing, enhancement, and other transformative purposes.

Q

Quantum Power Cell (QPC) – A scientific marvel harnessing anti-matter and negative radiation to stabilize wormholes and enable time travel.

QuantumPod – A particle accelerator functioning as a portal, stabilizing matter for safe time travel.

Quantum Room – The primary location of the time-traveling **Ring**, equipped with supercomputers and an advanced navigation interface.

R

Red Alert – A rogue group led by **Jin, Lily, and Luke**, responsible for distributing **Jet** and disrupting temporal order.

Royal Kama – An elite private military force aligned with key power players in the series.

S

Sages – Immortal beings tied to the **Orbs of Aphaeleon**, each representing specific regions, powers, and colors.

Sun Dagger – A mystical artifact connected to the **Time Rune**, last wielded by **Lilith** in the second book.

T

Time Runes – Mystical artifacts representing **health, soul, intelligence, and time**, each granting unique powers to their bearers.

Tizona – A majestic **Rhomphaia** sword with griffin motifs, wielded by **Quintus** and symbolizing ancient heroism.

U

United Nations of Asia (UNA) – A geopolitical alliance consisting of major **Asian nations**, formed for economic and military cooperation in the evolving global order. The UNA plays a critical role in the balance of power in *A Dance in Time*, wielding significant technological and strategic influence.

Z

Zeta Verse – A revolutionary virtual reality program interfacing directly with the user's **central nervous system**, blurring the lines between reality and digital escape.

Zeta-Pods – Specialized devices enhancing the **Zeta-verse** experience by improving throughput and reducing latency.

ACKNOWLEDGEMENTS

J.C. Hidalgo

Twelve years ago, a 26-year-old Jay—a bored office worker—started writing a story on yellow sticky notes. A story about a Spartan. That night, I went home and told my wife (then my girlfriend) about it, along with my nephew Carlos—only to be sent back to the drawing board. So, instead of doing my job, I refined the story.

Later that week, I told the story to my BFF, Mike. He claimed he once took a writing class and offered to help me edit. To this day I'm not sure if he actually did.

Twelve years, three major edits, a book split, a title change, and countless revisions later... we arrive at this book. And of course, the number of people who helped us along the way is countless.

I'll start with the first two that started the journey:

My wife, Vashty—whom I dedicated this book to. She put up with a daydreamer writing late into the night, spending way too much time on this book, and, like everyone on this list, stuck by us and wholeheartedly believed in us.

Carlos—who helped us create characters, bios for fictional people, and was always open to a beta read.

My kids:

Jayden—who always gave me ideas and knew I would write "peak fiction." He always told his friends his father would be an author. Well... I am one now!

Emma—who, at nine years old, has only ever known me as a writer. She's been the bright ray of light that lifted me in my darkest hours.

My mother—who never stopped believing in her son's dream, even when many family and friends didn't.

All my siblings—always looking for ways to support me.

And to Mike—who, for some reason, puts up with my craziness.

Our beta readers: Oskar, Maddy, and Nadene who helped craft this truly unique series.

ACKNOWLEDGEMENTS

Michael M. Johnson

I'll keep this simple and sweet.

To my beta readers—Oskar, Maddy, and Nadene—thank you for your time, insights, and patience. MVP's

To my family and extended family: each of you played a role in making this possible, whether directly or in spirit. My mom, Michelle, the OG of the family, my babies Alyiah, Alice, and Arya.

To the love of my life, Cruz Antonia Reyes—thank you for your support, your honesty, and for always being my sounding board.

Trevon and Carlos—your support has been insane in the best way possible. I can't thank you enough.

To Vashty, the wife of the man without whom none of this would've happened—Juan Hidalgo, my brother from another mother (and father, and entire family tree). What started as a simple idea about a Spartan searching for his mother—and me wanting to be his "editor"—turned into us wheezing our way through creation until we gave birth to this greatness.

Thank you.

ABOUT THE AUTHORS

J.C. Hidalgo is the co-author of the captivating fantasy series *God of Times Series*. With a passion for blending history, science fiction, and fantasy, Hidalgo crafts immersive tales that transport readers to new worlds.

When not weaving epic stories, Hidalgo embraces his inner child through a love of all things geeky, from anime and video games to cars. He is also an avid reader, always eager to explore new realms of imagination.

Family is the center of Hidalgo's world. He is married to his high school sweetheart and together they have built a life filled with love, laughter, and unforgettable adventures. As a father, Hidalgo cherishes the opportunity to create lasting memories with his family, whether it's through their shared passion for travel or cheering on their favorite sports teams.

With a heart full of wonder and a mind brimming with creativity, J.C. Hidalgo invites you to join him on a journey through the pages of his enchanting novels.

Michael M. Johnson is one half of the creative force behind the fantasy, science fiction, and historical fiction chapters of the *Gods of Time Series* bringing gods and legends to life with a flair that's all his own. When he's not building worlds or dreaming up characters, Michael is just a regular guy who loves spending time with his family, indulging in his love for food, and getting way too invested in American Football.

Though he might joke about traveling as much as a sloth—slow and not very far—Michael has a deep and abiding love for exploring new cultures, religions, and cuisines through his research. He's determined to visit the places that he brings to life in his books someday.

Off the page, Michael might seem like he prefers the quiet life, watching movies or catching up on his favorite shows, but don't let that fool you. He's always plotting his next story, diving deep into the lore that fuels his series, or disappearing into his latest book addiction. Writing isn't just what he does—it's who he is, and he wouldn't have it any other way.

@J_C_Hidalgo

https://twitter.com/j_c_hidalgo

@mikemjohnson

https://mobile.twitter.com/mikemjohnson

You can sign up to be notified of new releases, giveaways and pre-release specials.

Diamondwolfpress.com

If you loved this book and have a moment to spare, we would love a brief review. Your reviews will help us become better writers for you.

FREE Bonus Story

A Whisper in Time – the prequel novella to A Dance in Time

Available free when you join the reader list at DiamondWolfPress.com

Coming Soon

Gods Time Book II

In the second installment of The Gods of Time, the fractured bond between Malaya and Lilith spirals into chaos.

As mother and daughter wage an ever-deadlier war across time, old allies and new enemies emerge. Malaya and Vasilis must navigate shifting landscapes, divine agendas, and unraveling timelines. With humanity's future hanging by a thread, the past and present collide in a war neither side can afford to lose.

Discover the Untold Origin of Kasumi in Echoes of a Kitsune

Before she was the blade in the shadows, before she crossed time to stand beside Malaya and Vasilis in the war to save humanity—

she was Furihime Tokugawa.

Born into nobility during feudal Japan's most volatile era, Furihime's life was meant to follow the quiet path of tradition. But fate had other plans. Betrayed, hunted, and stripped of everything, she finds salvation in the form of ancient fox spirits—the **Kitsune**—and embraces a destiny steeped in myth and vengeance.

Transformed into the warrior known as **Kasumi**, she rises from the ashes of loss to protect the innocent and fight back against oppression with the fury of a goddess.

Echoes of a Kitsune is the gripping prequel to *A Dance in Time*, weaving historical fantasy and rich Japanese folklore into the unforgettable origin story of one of the series' most iconic warriors.

Step back in time. Witness the rise of the Kitsune. And uncover the legend behind the mask.

Thank you very much!